BOUNTY OF A STOLEN EMPIRE

MARTIN COHEN

I_AM SELF-PUBLISHING

@iamselfpub
www.iamselfpublishing.com

To Diana, Claire and Nadia with all my Love

Author's Note

Having spent three years researching the abundant records of the life of the Countess of Blessington I discovered too many contradictions, omissions and unsubstantiated statements to enable me to complete a comprehensive or coherent biography of this remarkable woman. This story therefore offers plausible, if not necessarily the most probable explanations to the many unanswered questions posed by the available sources and should be read only as a fantasia based on the lives of its protagonists.

All the named individuals were real people. Others who evidently or possibly existed but whose names are unrecorded are, I trust, readily identifiable by improbable aliases vaguely indicative of character. Brief guides to some of the less well-known figures are included in the Historical Notes in Appendix A.

Unless otherwise cited, all the quotations shown in italics are the countess's own words - the majority from her *Desultory Thoughts and Reflections*. The entries in her lost Night Thought Book are entirely fictitious.

No attempt has been made to overcome the complexities of comparing the value of money in the Countess's lifetime with the present day, but as a general guide multiply by 500 - e.g. £1,000 = c£500,000.

MC

I have seen no other so striking instance of the inferiority of art to nature as in this celebrated portrait of Lady Blessington. As the original stood before it, she fairly killed the copy, and this no less in the individual detail than in the general effect.

P. G. Patmore, on the unveiling of *The Countess of Blessington* by Sir Thomas Lawrence at the Royal Academy, 1822

'Was she a real person?'

Was I a real person? I can scarcely believe my ears. The man standing six feet from me is one of the best-known historians in the country. He is an authority on the Regency and Victorian era and has never heard of me. Perhaps I should not be surprised. I must face reality. For all the world, the gaudy masterpiece fascinating the professor is the last remnant of my existence. Even if he does not know who I am, he surely knows that Sir Thomas Lawrence was the most acclaimed portrait painter of his day. Why would Sir Thomas waste his time painting a fictitious *Countess of Blessington* with half the nobility of the civilised world impatiently waiting for him to finish their portraits?

I am sitting on a four-sided divan, the centrepiece of the front state salon of Hertford House, home to the Wallace Collection in Manchester Square. Manchester Square was once my home and I am thrilled to find so many of its magnificent Georgian facades meticulously preserved with the original features that were never there in my time. Urban grandeur possessed my mind like a narcotic drug. The abundance of the great city inspired my every word and deed and I do not complain that the architects of the present romanticise the past or that they lie, just as I lied.

Unlike so many of my late Georgian and early Victorian contemporaries, I was not oblivious to the simultaneous destruction of poverty and wealth. I debated its cause and effect with the most erudite and influential figures in the land; poets, politicians, peers and prime ministers: Peel, Wellington, Russell, Grey, Disraeli. I counselled the greatest writers of my time, of all time: Byron, Dickens, Landor, Bulwer-Lytton, Marryat, Thackeray. In France and Italy, I befriended royalty and the noblest of the noble. Did I influence them? I want to believe so. It is a vain belief but I see nothing wrong in vanity. I excel at vanity. Why should I not take credit for disdaining injustice and corruption while the self-styled quality gorged itself on the bounty of a stolen Empire?

No one was more cynical than me yet I could never exorcise my guilt. I was as culpable as those I castigated with my tongue while simultaneously permitting my pen to be a slave to inhibition. Convention distorted my writing like a government health warning: 'plain speech causes death'. I was the best-read woman in the land and the highest-paid author – for a while – yet all I did was fill the hollow heads of my readers with worthless delights. What harm would down-to-earth reality have done them?

'Wit is the lightning of the mind, reason the sunshine, and reflection the moonlight; for all as the bright orb of the night owes its lustre to the sun, so does reflection owe its existence to reason.'

The absurdly confident historian, who also interprets art to evidently blind television audiences, is boring a small group of research students with an impromptu lecture on Lawrence's subtle capture of the mocking smile. I never really liked my portrait. Sir Thomas was only too well aware of all the scandal, prejudice and envy I had to endure. Surely he could have produced something more modest. The Royal Academy still has my husband's letter telling him that he exposed *'too much of my bust'*. And what did he do? He added that tiny posy above the dress. Every man who comes into this gallery leers at the picture as if there isn't enough female flesh on display in the twenty-first century. Even the eminent academic is adding a few ill-informed niceties to prolong his pathetic pleasure.

'Forgive me for interrupting you, sir, but I can assure you that the Countess of Blessington was a real person. In fact, she lived one of the most remarkable lives in history. Doubtless you spent many years in study and research to qualify as a television personality but dare I suggest you go back and take another look at your books and sources? You might be surprised at how many times you missed the countess's name.'

My scepticism is lost on the great man.

'Thank you, madam, I shall do that. She might make an interesting subject for a future series.'

He smiles indulgently and turns to one of his students. 'See what you can find out about the Countess of Blessington.'

The obsequious youth taps out an electronic note, glances at it for the last time, and the little group moves on leaving me to contemplate my own image two centuries ago.

A man in his seventies walks slowly into the gallery. He is bald, lined and his face betrays an eventful life. He examines my portrait, glances at me for a moment, again at the picture, and sits down by my side.

'If you don't mind me saying so, madam, you bear a striking resemblance to this lady. Did you know she was once considered one of the most beautiful women in the country?'

'Thank you for the compliment.'

I have been here for an hour and this is the first person to have noticed any similarity. Perhaps my smart modern clothes and hairstyle make me unrecognisable.

'The Countess of Blessington is said to have taken great pride in her appearance. She believed pride in appearance mattered and will always matter. I think she was right, it still matters, even if the idea is somewhat dated.'

'In her day pride in appearance was everything', I reply. 'It was paramount for a person like the countess to be among the *visited*, and for that, not only she but her homes and possessions had to look the part. All the houses, châteaux and palaces in which she lived were as imposing and opulent as this historic gallery.'

'Yes, I've read she was an extraordinary individual: an intense intellectual yet a capricious pleasure seeker. She changed her name from Margaret to Marguerite. I suppose she thought it sounded more distinguished though she must have known that all it means is daisy. French was just one of the half a dozen languages she spoke fluently.'

'You apparently know a lot about the countess? No one else here seems to have heard of her.'

'I have been studying her life. I'm trying to write her biography.'

'That's a strange ambition for a man. Since feminine emancipation it seems that only women write about women. It used to be thought that women lacked the intellect to appreciate the male mindset. Now it's the other way round.'

'The three major biographies of the Countess of Blessington were written by men and all quote Samuel Parr's observation of her *"shrewd and masculine mind"*.'

'Is that why you are interested in her?'

'In a way, it is. I once wrote a thesis on personal finance. That's when I first came across Lady Blessington. Personal finance, like pride in appearance, is a matter we think about all the time but seldom say what we think. Both were predominant in the countess's life. Did you know that she was the first person to commend hire-purchase credit to this country?'

'And the first to call it the new Aladdin's lamp. She aroused its genie a hundred years before it granted the wishes of the twentieth-century masses. Like the Countess of Blessington herself, her lamp always had a bad press but in reality hire purchase caused far more happiness than misery and the countess did far more good than harm. Today she would prefer to be thought of as a businesswoman rather than an author.'

'That had not occurred to me.'

'Yes, she possessed a remarkable ability to exploit her multifarious gifts when in need of money. She was adept at exploiting her femininity and the cultivation of influential people. Today a woman like her might flaunt her business skills; in the nineteenth century she was expected to keep them to herself.'

'I take it, madam, that you are familiar with Madden's *The Literary Life of the Countess of Blessington*? I've ploughed through his three great tomes searching for clues about her younger days, but the chaotic collection of correspondence he uses to pad them out all dates from about the last twenty years of her life. By then she was a practised fiction writer and had learnt to sidestep the unpleasantries of her past. Two thirds of her life remain a mystery.'

'Lady Blessington had to be careful of what she put in writing. She was like today's celebrities; scandalmongers and blackmailers pounced on her every word and deed but she was also much loved, even by some women.'

'Her contemporaries say she was rude and sarcastic.'

'Yes, she sometimes resorted to polite cynicism and satire which, as she said *"like conscience, reminds us of what we often wish to forget"*. As she encountered more scroungers, spongers and sycophants, the countess's wit inevitably became more sardonic. The horrible experiences she endured as a young woman made her wary, especially of the shallow superior socialites lacking the wit to ascend the brilliance of a low-born Irish arriviste. I, that is she, despised those who took their unmerited privileges for granted.'

Speaking in the third person is becoming increasingly difficult.

'You must admit that Lady Blessington's relationship with the Comte D'Orsay was, to say the least, a paradox. No one took their unmerited privileges for granted more than D'Orsay.'

'Alfred's biographers portray him as a man who lived only for his mirror but the countess saw in that mirror the reflection of the man he was.'

'What sort of man do you think D'Orsay was? Was he in love with you? I'm terribly sorry; was he in love with the Countess of Blessington?'

Like me, the old author is finding it hard to maintain the charade.

'I think he was a man who took pride in his appearance.'

'I was referring to his sexual propensities. Surely he was more than a casual acquaintance to all those Regency dandies who fawned over his masculine beauty? Do you think he was homosexual, bisexual, or could he have just been heterosexual? And what about the Earl and Countess of Blessington themselves, what were they?'

I refrain from laughing. 'These are among the questions I shall let you answer for yourself.'

'It seems I have no choice, but I must go now and complete your biography. Goodbye, thank you for talking to me, Lady Blessington.'

'You won't weave in too much fiction, will you?'

--

My future biographer leaves me and a past one appears. His face is pale, his hair thin and his complexion sullen. Excess work and worry over matters none of his concern have maimed the zest of his youth. His lacklustre eyes look anxious. He is in a hurry to finish something unimportant. R R Madden is always in a hurry to finish something unimportant.

'How good of you to come, Dr Madden; I'm surprised at your audacity. Do you realise there are people here who don't even know that I was a real person? You were supposed to be my official biographer. I gave you my papers and told you all about my life, and what did you do?'

'I fear, Lady Blessington, I did not do very well. I was so deeply engaged in works on the abolition of the slave trade and reform of the colonies that I didn't get round to writing about you until you'd been dead for five years. By then I had muddled up your correspondence and lost half my notes. I simply put down everything as I found it.'

'Yes, and look at the result. Sixteen hundred pages of incomprehensible nonsense, glaring errors and long unexplained gaps. Who did you imagine could complete a picture from your ill-fitting multi-piece jigsaw? Let me tell you what Michael Sadleir said about it.'

'Unfortunately, the discretion necessary at the time he wrote and, even more disastrously, his own genius for disarrangement and prolixity turned what should have been a treasure house of original material into a heart-breaking jumble of repetitions, irrelevancies, inaccuracies and self- contradictions.'

'Frankly, I think Mr Sadleir was extremely restrained.'

'If it is not too late, will you accept my apology, your ladyship.'

'It is too late, and I will not accept your apology, Dr Madden. Stay here and let me remind you of what I told you to write. And do try to concentrate.'

2

And so to the truth, the whole truth and more of the truth than is strictly necessary. Believe only what I am about to relate. This and this alone is the complete and unvarnished story of my life. I shall avoid the imperious prose convention demanded of my literary work and correspondence and use only the plain speech of everyday conversation, but please do expect the foul-mouthed expression and ribald humour attributed to me by my ignorant contemporaries. Yes, occasionally I amused my friends in private with a few sharp words of retort. 'Vulgar woman', 'mindless harridan', 'morals of the gutter', 'whore', 'venomous slanderer', 'liar', 'cheat', 'swindler', were all said of me.

According to the old song, it's a long way to Tipperary; from practically anywhere. Who knows or would want to know more? I am searching a digital map for the remnant of Knockbrit. Ah, here it is, swallowed by time in a still sparsely populated southern corner of the Irish county. There was never much there. The aerial scan shows that clean-lined houses with neat gardens have replaced the old unkempt smallholdings but I can see no shop, cafe, petrol station, public house or even a church – no soul. Knockbrit has little more to commend it now than on that inauspicious day in 1789 when it welcomed me to the world.

The late summer sunshine of the first of September failed to ease my mother's pain; less in her body than her mind. Her first child, my sister Anne, was not expected to reach maturity and predictions for my elder brothers Edmond and Michael were no better. Morbid reflection on the pale green pallor of her new born baby reduced her to tears. Normally she never cried. She possessed the gift of mentally obliterating misfortune. This gift, or perhaps I should say failing, had entered my genes. How many times would I escape within myself to a fool's paradise? How many times would I put my faith in a false omen? And how many times would I regret my arrogance?

But every birth is an occasion for celebration. My hot and sweating father, mud splattered from his morning ride, burst into the bedroom to inspect the latest addition to his neglected financial burdens. His hopes of a strong son to compete with him at the blood sports in which he reigned supreme, or thought he did, had been dashed for a fourth time. He made the necessary effort to smile.

'Good luck, girl. You'll need all the luck you can get,' were his last words to me before giving me my first riding lesson six years later.

My mother did not wish me good luck. She prayed for a change in her own. And her prayer was answered. She had given birth to the first of three, yes three, future countesses. My father never said a prayer in his life but his most ardent wishes were also to be granted. Two of his sons would serve as officers in the British army and future generations would be added to his insignificant dynasty. I too never said a prayer in my life. If I had, I would have thanked the

Lord for not permitting my parents to discover the utter absurdity and futility of their lofty hopes and aspirations.

Father was a slave to vanity and misfortune and Mother to a vision of the past. Her name was Ellen, known to everyone as Nell. When I was born she was still in her early twenties but the beauty she bequeathed to her daughters was already shattered by suppressed anxiety and submission to her husband's headstrong demands. Her few friends saw her as repressed and subdued. They were wrong. She was a woman of elusive ambition, capable of exerting herself in desperation; her strength drawn from uncompromising religious faith and a half-mythical family history.

My parents were snobs, gullible dreamers, but I have too much of them in me to write them off as malicious or uncaring. A cancerous claw encompassed them, clamping their every thought and action, gripping them by a single obsession, the fraying thread on which their marriage hung, the raison d'être that once drew them together – the social ladder and its ascent. Every foot they raised severed another rung. The nearest they came to success in life was in the nurture of their children. And that certainly left a great deal to be desired.

'Thanks to you, Dr Madden, all my subsequent biographers and so-called historians have gloated over my father, Edmond Power's misfortunes and exaggerated them out of all proportion.'

'Possibly that is true, Lady Blessington. I never met your father but I heard no good of him.'

I will not deny that Father was coarse and ill-tempered but neither will I accept that he was a mindless monster given to constant violence. Like every flawed human being he had redeeming features. Time and again he strove for recognition. Time and again it eluded him. Today he would simply be called a loser. He was grossly extravagant, and who am I to condemn him for that? He was unfaithful on occasion, and who am I to condemn him for that? He put his trust in princes and, least of all, can I condemn him for that. He believed himself a gentleman born and craved to be the best of that spurious breed. Tall, well-built, handsome and always immaculate, he took infinite pride in his appearance and relished being known as 'Beau' Power, though to most people he was simply Ned. What he did not spend on personal affectation he squandered on drunken carousal and losing at the card table to his supposed peers. He lavished money on horses, carriages, hunting dogs, guns and all the paraphernalia of the country sports that gave vent to his boundless energy and the frustrations of passive pursuit of unwarranted wealth and honour.

'A gentleman isn't a bloody trader. He's got better things to think about than money', justified all extravagance.

'Pride and poverty are the most ill-assorted companions that can meet. They live in a state of continual warfare and the sacrifices they extract from each other, like those claimed by enemies to establish a hollow peace, only serve to increase their discord.'

Like most minor Irish squires of his time, Edmond 'Beau' Power was a drunkard. When crossed he made his displeasure manifestly plain, yet compassion lay beneath his assumed persona. For all my sins he never intentionally punished me or barred me from his door. Those who knew him in old age told me I was his proudest boast. Or was it one of my sisters?

My mother admired and possibly loved her fine-looking husband, a man befitting her illusionary social status. She would not hear a word against him until the day she predeceased him. Hindsight – I excelled at hindsight– it taught me that I owe my imagination to my mother. Had she written fiction it would have been far more romantic than mine.

We lived well, that is for late eighteenth-century provincial Ireland. The food on our occasionally scrubbed table was boring but adequate; potatoes and more potatoes. Mother, helped by the gloomy emaciated local girls she referred to as her maids, made our simple tasteless clothes, while Father's country attire was exquisitely crafted by a master tailor. He wished to be seen as a sportsman and a gentleman. He also wished to be seen as a dutiful parent, so he sent his children to a private infants' school. He thought it a waste of money. He was right.

Edmond Power, only son, orphaned at the age of sixteen, inherited his father's house and stables at Knockbrit, as well as the land at Curragheen in County Waterford that he grandly referred to as his family estate. He boasted that it yielded fifteen-hundred pounds per annum. It was nowhere near so much. He once testified in court to an income of four hundred pounds, which I suppose might have been true in the best of years.

Whatever it was, it was enough to aspire to gentility. There was no income tax and labour was cheap. He boarded grooms and stable lads in outhouse lofts and if they did a job well he might toss them a few coins. For a similar pittance Mother's maids did her domestic chores badly. She despaired of housework; a fruitless task, constantly growing with her family and the number of men who came to drink at Father's expense in the evenings. Squires, farmers, traders, dignitaries and bored locally-billeted officers all had invaluable roles to play in the ambiguous aspirations of the over-generous Edmond 'Beau' Power.

My early memories reek of staleness: decayed poteen, ale, wine, tobacco, excrement, urine and vomit, courtesy of Father's so-called friends and their horses and dogs that supplied our peasant tenants with fertiliser. Staleness soaked indelibly into the floors, rafters, furniture, bedding and clothing but not into me. I was protected by a world of make-believe. I was a noblewoman descended from the knights of chivalry who loomed large in my dreams of a glorious future and in the stories I invented for my ailing and infant siblings – the fictional fame of their fearless forebears and of course their ladies; ladies they defended and ladies who defended them. Like most small girls, I was captivated by the magical ascent of Cinderella but unlike the others I was not destined to be disillusioned. I had a head start. I was a wretched unwanted child.

'A handsome prince will find me wherever I am. He will be rich beyond the dreams of avarice. He will marry me, take me to his realm of the brilliant and the bounteous and we will dwell in glorious palaces forever. I shall be an exemplary princess, admired by all for my beauty and wisdom. The air in my palaces will be perfumed with orange blossom and I will touch nothing unless cleansed beyond blemish by my faithful servants,' I wrote in my long-lost secret Night Thought Book and I believed it.

The faithful servants of my childhood were contaminated air and bad ventilation. They immunised me against the onslaughts of disease endemic to a squalid Irish farmhouse. Mother was immunised too. There was no contamination on the spiritual planet that revolved in perpetuity around the sun shining from the haloes of her sainted ancestors – the Desmonds and the Sheehys. Her maiden name was Sheehy. Thus, by her lights, beyond a shadow of doubt she was a direct descendent of Maurice Fitzgerald, first Earl of Desmond, founder of one of the most powerful dynasties in Irish history, who died in 1356. That his line survived only until 1607 when the sixteenth earl was executed for treason in the Tower of London, leaving no issue, did not concern my mother.

'You're an intelligent man, Dr Madden. Did you seriously believe there was any truth in that ridiculous *pedigree* you reproduced at the start of my *Literary Life*? By what stretch of the imagination does it demonstrate a link between the Earls of Desmond and Mother's family? Yes, it shows men called Sheehy marrying supposed descendants of Fitzgerald but my grandfather, Edmond Sheehy, was born a century and a half after the death of the last survivor. Thank you, at least, for stopping short of attributing the document to me. I can assure you that if I had intended to invent evidence of noble blood, as I was tempted to do so many times, don't you think I would have produced something at least marginally credible, not a patchwork of genetic gibberish?'

'But I've seen the manuscript. Some of it is in your handwriting, Lady Blessington.'

'I simply added a few fictitious names to please my mother. To her, it was a sacred icon. I never discovered how she came by it or who in their right mind spent their precious time poring over church annals and scraping moss from ancient tombstones for such a thankless purpose. You must have observed how the confused and broken line is desecrated by a dearth of dates and detail. It spanned five centuries and named sixty or more individuals, but to my mother every name was sacrosanct and absolute proof of her, and therefore my, noble origins.'

'Did you try telling her that Sheehy is a common Irish name?'

'"There's nothing common about this family," was always her reply. But, Dr Madden, your horrific forty-page account of *"The Fate of the Sheehys"* is too bad to be true. My grandfather and his cohorts executed with him might not have been entirely innocent martyrs but I cannot dispute that they were convicted for no other reason than their Catholic faith.'

'On four occasions you yourself witnessed the inequitable mindset of the Irish courts. The facts are well-documented, Lady Blessington. In 1766 the Reverend Nicholas Sheehy, his second cousin Edmond, your grandfather, and six others were found guilty in separate trials of *"compassing rebellion and traitorously preparing, ordaining, and levying war against the king"* and a string of similarly preposterous charges. Still extant supplications from irreproachable supporters and irrefutable pleas written from condemned cells were dismissed out of hand, and all the defendants were hung, drawn and quartered in the interests of greed and prejudice.'

'And that, Dr Madden, was just one of many reasons I came to abhor Ireland and the Irish. As a child I witnessed the poverty and distress caused by the religious roots of injustice. As a young woman, I studied the hallowed bigotry that annulled the allegiance of generation after generation of emigrants. And now, in the twenty-first century, I find their descendants around the world glorying in their Irish blood and extolling their one-week golfing holiday at a resort the name of which they cannot pronounce.'

Mother was the eldest of the four children Edmond Sheehy kissed goodbye before being dragged to the scaffold. She was five years old. Every time she told the story of the medieval execution, she was more traumatised by the blood, gore and screams she neither saw nor heard. No mother would permit her children to watch their father being cut alive from the noose, disembowelled and butchered into four. I doubt Mother remembered her father at all. She claimed he was a fine looking man, respected by Catholics and Protestants alike, a gentleman and an accomplished sportsman; a romanticised picture of the young Edmond Power, who must have married her for reasons of lust, since her father's money and possessions were all of course confiscated.

She said that Father also came from a fine Catholic family. I was never convinced. His history was of even more dubious provenance than Mother's. It could not have been much to be proud of or he would have told us and everyone else, but I never heard him mention his parents or childhood. I would not be surprised if he adopted Power as his family name to match his affected persona. All I know is that his father was called Michael.

'Pride prevents not the commission of unworthy actions, though it forbids the avowal of them.'

When I was eight years old and Father just turned thirty, he announced that he had sold our house in Knockbrit and bought a larger one nearer to his land at Curragheen more befitting to his status. We were to move to Clonmel, the county town of Southern Tipperary.

'We shall live in the splendour of a golden city of abundance', I wrote.

The ancient garrison town of Clonmel was no golden city of abundance but there were a few retail shops – novel phenomena in provincial Ireland – and lively markets. I looked forward to parties, plays, fairs and above all attending a real school. I was not sad to leave the homespun school at Knockbrit nor its one teacher who taught me nothing. I was sad to leave Miss Dwyer who taught me everything.

Miss Dwyer, a spinster of indeterminate years, lived alone about half a mile from our house in Knockbrit. On the first and only day Mother accompanied me to the infant school, she introduced this improbable acquaintance as we passed her door. I had just turned five. Even at that age I recognised a kindred spirit. Every day I stopped at Miss Dwyer's isolated cottage to delay returning home and, whenever possible, went back at the weekends. In contrast to ours, her home was clean, comfortable and quiet. She gave me hot milk and home-made cakes but these were not the attraction. Crammed bookshelves covered her every wall from floor to ceiling and new volumes regularly arrived from Dublin or London. How could there be so many books in the world and so many authors? At first I could barely read the titles but was fascinated by them all, unlike *Alice*, even those without pictures or conversation.

Miss Dwyer recited poems. I wanted to be a poet. Miss Dwyer read stories. I wanted to write stories. I astonished her by anticipating the plots of Shakespeare's comedies by the second act. They were all so much the same that I wondered why the bard was so revered. Miss Dwyer explained the merit was not in the story but in the poetry of language. She did not know that one day I would make a career of failing to emulate it.

'I shall dwell among the nobles of the utopian Italian cites of Shakespeare's dreams', I promised my notebook with inspired foresight.

Miss Dwyer recited the legend of King Arthur and, at bedtime, I recreated the tales of the Round Table for my brothers and sisters. Spenser's *Faerie Queene* had an especially prophetic ring:

> *And to him she said: Fie, fie, faint-hearted Knight*
> *What meanest thou this reproachful Strife?*
> *Is this the Battle which though vauntest to fight*
> *With that fire-mouthed Dragon, horrible and bright?*

> *Come, come away, frail, feeble, fleshly Wight,*
> *Ne let vain words bewitch thy manly heart,*
> *Ne devilish thoughts dismay thy constant spright:*
> *In heavenly Mercies has though not a part?*
> *Why should'st thou then despair, that chosen art?*

The real-life knights I had yet to encounter were certainly frail, feeble, fleshy Wights, but I was not Spenser's *Una*. My most barbed repartee never shamed one real-life knight into the gallantry of a St George. My knights expected me to slay their fire-mouthed dragons for them. And I did. I had a fire mouth of my own.

Miss Dwyer corrected my childish scribbles and told me I had the gift of poetry. She read a new poem that she said I would love. The enchanted allegory and the humour were not wasted on me, but I did not love *The Deserted Village*. Oliver Goldsmith was Irish. His village was Irish. It was Knockbrit with its decaying little farms, derelict dwellings and despondent peasants. Knockbrit was anything but an exaltation of times past. All Irish villages were deserted and for all my misadventures, I had no qualms about joining their deserters.

I never found virtue in glorifying nature for its own sake. I extolled only the sophistication, gaiety and society of the great city: London, Paris, Florence,

Rome, Naples. In *The Magic Lantern,* my first published work, I describe a summer day in Hyde Park. In my park there are no trees, shrubs, flowers or birdsong. There is not a blade of grass, yet the scene encompasses all that for me abounded with romance and vitality: the coaches and carriages, the horses and gleaming harnesses, the fashions and the fantasy of *le beau monde.*

Our new larger, seemingly splendid, featureless house stood alone on Súir Island, an elongated triangle of land on the River Súir, the time-honoured boundary which divides County Tipperary from County Waterford. Today, a sign near the weir by the southern bridge reads *Lady Blessington's Bath.* What madman imagined me going out to bathe in that cold muddy water? It's foul enough now. I scarcely need say what it was like two centuries ago!

I learnt but never stooped to speak the Gaelic tongue with which I coloured the lower-class Irish characters in my novels. Clonmel, *Cluain Maela,* means honey meadow. How nice: an idyll of bees buzzing over a carpet of green, mottled with golden buttercups – a land flowing with milk and honey. Clonmel was a land flowing with hard-headed merchants, manufacturers, brewers and mill owners thriving on the backs of impoverished labourers; peasant workers, male and female, eking out an excuse for a living, toiling in fallow fields and filthy factories, and on Sundays flocking to impotent churches to pray for more work and more money.

'In the cities of my prince's realm there will be no dirt, dereliction, deprivation, dejection, disease nor desperation. Workers will not poison their bodies with alcohol, nor clergy their minds with false hope.' Not all my childhood predictions came true.

I did not lack compassion but neither did I come to terms with the paucity of ambition where there was no expectancy from God, man or state. Detached employers, accumulating the fat of their boundless lands were loved and respected rather than challenged by their oppressed labourers. Through my eponymous heroine *Grace Cassidy,* I was to demonstrate that oppression can be conquered by self-belief and perseverance. How ridiculous! There was nobody like Grace in Ireland. In any case, the working classes were generally illiterate, and those who could read could scarcely afford my novels, let alone benefit from their message.

When we first arrived in Clonmel I was too young to concern myself with such weighty matters. I was full of excitement and anticipation. My parents too looked forward to a prosperous future. Even Mother was more animated than usual.

'Imagine, your father's going to be a businessman'.

'Will we be rich?'

'I dare hope so, Margaret.'

Stupid woman!

Hunt & O'Brien, a small firm of corn and butter merchants, had persuaded father to invest in a partnership. He had no experience of the trade or of any trade. He saw no reason to inspect the books of account. A gentleman did not concern himself with plebeian trivia. Edmond 'Beau' Power inspected a creaking warehouse crammed with crates, sacks and barrels: a cache to be turned to cash he let himself believe. He did not ask why so much stock was carried, if it was paid for or if it could be sold before it rotted. He made no enquiries about the state of the market or the conduct of the business.

Instead, at his own expense, he built a new warehouse behind our house on Súir Island. When it was finished Mr Hunt and Mr O'Brien informed their young partner that the firm was running at a loss and could not afford to rent a larger building.

'We'll be frank with you, Ned, our need is as great as yours, but none of us can draw a brass farthing, until we pull in some new business.'

Edmond Power, gentleman and businessman, eventually ceased cursing, ranting, raving and threatening and, for once, sensibly refused to invest more money. A man of his stature would not sully his hands with the practicalities of base trade. There was just one sphere in which he would demean himself to make a contribution. The term public relations of course meant nothing to him – it was not coined until the late twentieth century – but, with good reason, he believed himself a master of the honourable science of goodwill creation.

Staleness again permeated our floors and rafters. Now merchants and farmers joined the mêlée of aspiring gentlemen the ever-convivial 'Beau' Power welcomed with open bottles.

Father prohibited his children from these entertainments and we happily obeyed. His influential revellers were as dreary as they were drunk. But one summer evening, a splendid soldier came riding across the north bridge on a horse of virgin white. The soldier's uniform was as pretentious as those I invented for the princes of my fairytales. His royal-blue tunic dripped with medals and insignia surrounding a diamond-encrusted golden sunburst star. His buttons and buckles were a hoard of pure silver. Four-inch fringes hung from his gilded epaulets. A glorious white plume rose from the tall helmet which he removed to acknowledge Father's grovelling bow, exposing a head of incongruously unruly red hair.

I could not see the man's face clearly from my attic bedroom window but knew instinctively that he was King George or one of the English princes. My younger sister Ellen and I tiptoed downstairs and peeped through the drawing-room door. Father and his cronies were crowded round the newcomer and we could see only the polished leather of his riding boots reflecting the room like a mirror. I felt a slap on my ear and Mother quickly ushered us away.

The soldier looked round and for a moment I thought he smiled at me. He was the handsomest man I had ever seen.

'We only wanted to look at the king.'

'He's not the king. And he shouldn't be here anymore than you should be downstairs. He's not old enough to be drinking with your father and those men'.

'If he's not the king, then who is he? He looks very important.'

'All I know is his name's Lord Mountjoy. They've just made him Lieutenant-Colonel of the Tyrone Militia, or something like that. I don't understand why, he's just a boy. But your father's very proud. He's never had such a high-ranking officer to the house.'

'Will he come again?'

'I doubt he'll stay long in Clonmel. Who would there be to interest him here?'

I became obsessed by the first knight of chivalry encountered in the flesh. He became the hero of my childish fantasies; Saint George, King Arthur, Sir Lancelot and Cinderella's prince destined to return and carry me off to his realm of beauty and happiness.

And Lord Mountjoy did come back; once, I think, but I did not see him then.

Father's strategy worked. His gratuitous hospitality impressed a widening circle of invaluable parasites and the now Hunt, O'Brien and Power began to show deceptive signs of recovery. Certain that his pains would be richly rewarded, Father redoubled his efforts to pursue the life of a gentleman and as a result neglected not only his partnership but the estate that provided his one reliable source of income. Fortunately, among his regular guests was an amiable banker called Solomon Watson, always happy to oblige his old friend, Ned Power, with a loan at what he termed a fair rate of interest.

One morning, about a year after Lord Mountjoy's visit, Father returned from the hunt earlier than usual in an extraordinary state of excitement. I heard him shouting above the clatter of his horse's hooves. I heard him fling open the front door. I heard his fuming and expletives and the crash of his boots splattering mud as he threw them across the living-room floor.

'This house smells like a pigsty, and it's just as filthy. It's disgusting. Get it cleaned up. I want every inch of the place shining like new. Come on all of you, sweep, scrub, polish! Nell, get the finest bloody joint and see it's roasted properly. Tonight, we're having a feast fit for a king.'

I was accustomed to Father's volatile moods but this was quite a novelty. Housework was so far beneath his dignity that I was surprised he knew of its existence. He had never before shown the slightest interest in his visitors' opinion of the house or what they ate.

'Men come here to drink in my company, not to inspect the bloody premises', he would explain.

'Are we expecting some important people, Ned?'

'No, there'll be just one but he is important. Now will you get on with it, Nell? You've no time to waste!'

Mother bought, borrowed and panicked. For hours she, her maids and children worked like incompetent Trojans. We drew water from the river, washed, polished and repaired. We rearranged the furniture. We gathered wood to build a roaring fire. Edmond 'Beau' Power, gentleman, sat, lambasted, complained and drank. Never before or again was his house so clean and tidy or his table better set. The important visitor would surely be Lord Mountjoy returned to win my ten-year-old heart.

My second real-life knight turned out to be an unprepossessing middle-aged bachelor with a fixed smile exuding a hail-fellow-well-met conviviality that made my flesh creep. I did not like the look of him. Mother liked the look of him. It was not often that her hand was kissed by a Protestant viscount endorsing Catholic emancipation as if his life depended on it.

Richard Hely-Hutchinson, First Viscount Donoughmore of Knocklofty, had been a front-bench spokesman in the recently dissolved Irish House of Commons. Now he was among the twenty-six Irish Representative Peers honoured with a seat in the House of Lords at Westminster. He was also one of the richest men in Tipperary, a County Governor and – fitness not being a prerequisite of the nineteenth-century soldier – a general of the militia. I had heard Father's constant complaints about the business of Hunt, O'Brien & Power and I was old enough to understand that such an influential figure might help make it prosper.

It was not the corn and butter trade that brought Viscount Donoughmore to Súir Island.

'So you're the 'Beau' Power I've heard so much about. A pleasure to meet you, sir; it's a great honour to be in your house.'

The first was true. The viscount had heard that Father was the sort of gullible ruffian he was looking for to impose the rule of law in Tipperary and Waterford. In next to no time they were an ill-matched pair of old comrades, two denizens of Ireland, men of the world engaged in conducive debate in which Father's role was to confirm that he and his noble guest were of one mind.

'As you and I know this whole area's infested with rebels, Beau. There are more of them than you think, and I have to tell you those boys are dangerous. They'll kill and rob anybody who stands in their way. I need men of authority to make sure they behave themselves. I need brave men, real men like you.'

Father did not understand where his distinguished visitor's argument was leading but at the end of each sentence dutifully nodded in deferential concurrence.

'In short, Beau, I've come to ask permission to put your name forward as a Justice of the Peace. Are you up for the job? Of course you are. Here's to your success.'

Father could not believe his good fortune. He opened his mouth to thank his unsolicited sponsor, but no words came and again Viscount Donoughmore answered his own question.

'So you accept. That's the spirit. There's just one small snag. It's nothing serious, Beau, but it could, shall we say, cause you a little embarrassment if you're seen arresting Catholics when you're one yourself. But don't worry, that can be put right soon enough. You don't mind, do you? Of course you don't. Count on me. I'll see you're not sorry.'

Three weeks later, Edmond Power, prospective guardian of the law, at a private service in the chapel of the Donoughmore country seat at Knocklofty House, three miles west of Clonmel, was baptised and confirmed in the Established Church of Ireland. In homage to her pure Catholic pedigree, Mother rapidly revised her opinion of her husband's godfather and attended neither the mock ceremony nor the celebration in its wake. Instead she eased her conscience in the rain-drenched churchyard; confessing by the probably empty grave of her martyred father, the descendants of whose persecutors her husband was about to join.

Edmond Power, qualified magistrate, was carried home the following morning, the loser by some margin in a drinking match with the guardian of his new creed. A few weeks later he was sworn in and given access to a small troop of dragoons who the militia fed, boarded, supplied with horses, weapons and uniforms and even paid a small bounty. In accord with British military tradition their commander was expected to give his services and supply his own equipment for the honour of the nation. Edmond Power JP was only an arresting magistrate, entitled to neither a seat on the bench nor any form of stipend.

Viscount Donoughmore hastened to offer his congratulations. 'You will never regret this day, Beau. Bring those rebels to justice and I'll personally see to it that every door in the land is open to you. Did you know half the House of Lords started out as magistrates? I don't mind telling you their pensions are a king's ransom. Who knows what's within your grasp?'

The noble lord knew.

Father was a changed man. He was Lord Power of Curragheen already and,for the first and last time in his life happy while sober. His elevated position offered endless opportunities to show his bravery and athletic prowess to the lesser citizens of Clonmel. Night after night Magistrate Power and his band of feckless mercenaries, fortified by liquor and obscene language, loaded their guns and rode forth into the unknown: their mission to seek out and destroy terrorists, real and imagined, at the behest of the British government.

Today it is of course unthinkable that a British government would condone such militancy abroad.

The majority of dangerous insurgents had perished in the barbaric massacres of the Irish Rebellion of 1798 and by the time of Father's appointment the number of their survivors had largely diminished. Now only small resistance groups mushroomed from time to time around the country, but the pending redundancy of his office presented no barrier to the ambitions of Edmond Power JP.

Like every good soldier, Father questioned neither his orders nor the cause for which he was fighting. Any Catholic wandering abroad and unable to state his legitimate business faced the new magistrate's merciless zeal. I dread to think how many innocents he apprehended or how many prosecutions, prison sentences and even executions resulted from his fearless defence of British rule in Ireland.

With every arrest, Lord Donoughmore applauded from the sidelines and showered his recruit in praise. He even invited him to Dublin Castle to be commended for bravery by the Secretary for Ireland in person. Wealth and honour loomed ever larger. Edmund 'Beau' Power, resplendent in elaborate shirts and foppish white cravats, swaggered through the streets of Clonmel practising the assertive air of a nobleman. 'Watch out, here comes old Shiver-the-Frills,' shouted the children and ran away. Father delighted in their complimentary mockery. He was a proud protector of the peace and presumed that all Clonmel deferred to him in gratitude.

Such arrogance from a convert could not go unpunished. Just men of the town met and resolved to teach their jumped-up guardian a lesson. Late at night they formed a torchlight procession and marched on to Súir Island. Courageous and determined, they slaughtered the four innocent cows that supplied our little dairy, flung their torches at Father's stables and warehouse and scampered off to toast their triumph in a tavern on the far side of the town.

The cracks and snaps of blazing timber were deafening. Pillars of black smoke rose from splattering red flames. Horses whinnied like a chorus of sopranos and a sickening smell of burnt leather emanated from the tack room. With all the focused determination of a sportsman in training, Father sobered himself up and fearlessly plunged into the burning stables and freed his beloved horses. Then, swinging a tooled saddlebag as an improvised flail, climbed into the loft and ordered his three grooms to extinguish the fire. The terrified boys might have fled for their lives leaving the stable block to burn had not their brave employer politely pointed out that they were on an island entirely surrounded by water. They grabbed every bucket, can, urn and empty wine bottle they could find and, scurrying to and fro, spilled enough water to prevent the spreading flames from devouring the house. They salvaged the warehouse too but not before the melting butter burst its barrels and congealed into a foul-smelling oily yellow stream that took them a fortnight to scrape away. Mother allowed the heroic grooms to sleep on the stone floor of the scullery until the stables were repaired. They were delighted with their reward.

Edmond Power raged and cursed. Whatever it took, he would find the culprits and make them pay. It took a great deal of time, effort and money but, needless to say, the Catholic avengers vanished into the ether together with another tranche of his capital.

Early in 1802 Father was honoured for his services to the suppression of Irish terrorism. He did not receive his coveted peerage, a knighthood or even so much as a citation. Representative Peer Viscount Donoughmore chose to recognise his protégée's achievements in more practical fashion. He hung the proprietorship of the *Clonmel Gazette and Munster Mercury* around Father's neck; an order he obeyed with grateful reluctance.

'A newspaper's just another bloody trade, no better than the corn and bloody butter business.'

I was still too young to foresee danger in Lord Donoughmore's largesse. Owning the local newspaper sounded exciting. It would make Father rich and important. Perhaps he really would receive the peerage about which he was constantly boasting. The future Lord Power was unaware that to win his spurs every knight of chivalry had to demonstrate his financial strength, measured in horses, as well as his physical strength. The legends of old overlook such practicalities. They take away so much of the romance.

'As you and I both know, Beau, there's not a newspaper in the whole of Tipperary worthy of the name. It's high time somebody told the truth about what's happening in this country, and who better than you to tell it. Who is there around here to question what you say? Your name's Power, now you have power.' Viscount Donoughmore, politician and puppet master, laughed aloud and alone at his own weak joke. 'What's more it'll bring you prestige, Beau. It'll make you rich too and look good when you're up for the peerage. I know you don't have any experience of this sort of thing, but don't give it another thought. I'll always be there to help you out', said the bountiful aristocrat.

The *Gazette's* previous proprietor had spent the last seven years in the debtors' prison, bankrupted by Donoughmore himself.

His lordship slapped the fledgling journalist on the back; a meaningless gesture that achieved its precise object.

'Lord Donoughmore knows what he's doing, Nell. He said it'll help speed things up with the Lords.'

Mother did not reply. She now had nothing but contempt for the man who lured her husband from the one true faith.

Viscount Donoughmore had accepted the dilapidated press and premises of the long defunct bi-weekly partly in lieu of debt, and after having failed in numerous attempts to sell it, was inspired to revive the newspaper as a political platform. But as a County Governor he could not be seen to blatantly influence voters and thus required an innocent minion to ensure anonymity, and who could be a more innocent minion than Edmond Power JP?

Since his appointment Father had taken an uncomprehending interest in politics. As a prospective member of the House of Lords he held no particular political convictions but fraternising with adherents of the so-called *Castle* party, diehard supporters of British rule in Ireland, brought him into contact with the most influential of the local worthies. Among these was the Right Honourable Member of Parliament for Clonmel, Colonel John Bagwell, man of principle, man of the people and as rich and devious as his neighbour and nemesis Donoughmore.

In order to leave no doubt about its legal proprietor's responsibility for the content of the new *Clonmel Gazette and Munster Mercury*, the de facto proprietor required Father to prefix its title with the word *Power's*. Every edition would also carry an endnote: '*Printed by Edm. Power*'. Edm. Power was no printer, and nor was Lord Donoughmore. He had no need to be. The press functioned admirably from the comfort of his study at Knocklofty House.

Irish politics, as always, were dominated by religion. Edmond Power, proselyte, held no particular religious convictions. Lord Donoughmore also held no particular religious convictions. His vehement advocacy of Catholic emancipation shadowed his father, John Hely-Hutchinson, statesman and Provost of Trinity College Dublin, a position banned to Catholics. Lord Donoughmore had voted in favour of every pro-emancipation bill defeated in both British Houses of Parliament.

John Bagwell MP's faith, like Viscount Donoughmore's, was entirely political. Regardless of the nature of the bill the member for Clonmel voted with his sights set on an appointment to the Privy Council. He wholeheartedly supported every prime minister, Whig and Tory, but to their regret no vacancies arose while he sat in the Commons.

Without consulting its proprietor, Lord Donoughmore appointed a highly-experienced journalist called Bernard Wright as the first - and last - editor of *Power's Clonmel Gazette*. Wright, a Catholic convert, had for many years lived in France where he had edited a prestigious Parisian journal and written prolifically in support of the French monarchy. The Revolution, however, respected neither patriotism nor piety, while in the freedom of Napoleonic France the monarchist proselyte had been arrested, imprisoned, flogged, starved and extradited. In London Wright found journalism a closed shop to Catholics and so moved to Ireland to support emancipation, but there too could find no appropriate outlet for his talents. As a final resort he accepted Donoughmore's miserly offer.

Father too was a monarchist who had converted *from* Catholicism. Wright was small, nondescript, a writer, a thinker and a poet, while his puppet employer was tall, handsome, brash and proud of his success in arresting and imprisoning Catholics. This unholy alliance might have been a recipe for beneficial failure in three weeks were it not for Lord Donoughmore's discreet intervention, which proved a recipe for disastrous failure in three years.

'Let's leave the publishing to the professionals, Beau? Is the rough and tumble of a newspaper office for gentlemen like you and I? Of course it isn't. There's important work to be done. Far too many of those rebels are still at large.'

Father was greatly relieved by this excuse to absent himself from his own press office, where in any case there was nothing for him to do.

Nineteenth-century provincial newspapers kept their isolated readership abreast of national and international affairs, at least a month in arrears. Bernard Wright was especially adept at dramatising the illustrious abominations of the Napoleonic age in prejudiced translation from French journals and also at plagiarising the Dublin and London press. Under his scholarly pen *Power's Clonmel Gazette* brought wisdom and enlightenment to Tipperary, despite which the circulation steadily increased.

Like all rural newspapers, the *Gazette* was mainly bought for the enthralling agricultural market prices prominently displayed on its front page. When, as was usually the case, there was no other local news, Wright filled his space with innocuous letters to the editor that he wrote himself, or copied transcripts of court cases and repeated them time and again. Adverting was artless and factual – a reward for apprehending a criminal, for recovery of stolen goods, a house for sale, a farm, a plot of land, a horse, a quantity of timber, a selection of guns and pistols, a livestock auction. All appeared banal and apolitical.

Bernard's attempts to enliven the paper with an occasional stab at humour, taught me that it was a genre best avoided in writing.

'A German literatus has discovered that the word in Hebrew which is commonly translated as rib, more probably signifies a tongue and consequently that Eve was taken out of part of Adam's tongue. This is extremely probable.'

'Lord Nelson was made a Doctor of Civil Laws on his visit to Oxford. It was expected from his knowledge of the canon law he would also have been made a Doctor of Divinity.'

At the age of thirteen I made my first venture into nepotism. I went to the press office and boldly asked the editor to publish my simple poems and essays. I found Mr Wright not the religious fanatic and counter-revolutionary Father described but a rational and enlightened gentleman, since he immediately recognised my literary talent. Speaking in French, we formed a guarded friendship and he happily printed my first attempts at the sort of sombre sentimentality which, in later life, I would simultaneously scorn and exploit financially.

The literate ladies of Clonmel were always elated by gloom and misery:

> *Farewell, Oh farewell to the Day,*
> *That smiling with happiness few!*
> *Ye Verdunes and Blushes of May,*
> *Ye songs of the linnet, adieu!*
>
> *In tears from the Vale I depart,*
> *In anguish I move from the Fair;*
> *For what are those scenes to the heart,*
> *Which Fortune has doom'd to Despair?*

Bernard Wright included so many similarly dismal anonymous poems that I am uncertain if this was one of mine, but my contributions undoubtedly were a factor in the unlikely success of *Power's Clonmel Gazette*. With the growth of circulation Edmond Power began to take an increasing interest in the newspaper's production and for the first and last time in his life became gainfully employed, when sober and in the right mood. Maintaining a diplomatic distance from his levelheaded editor, Father rolled up his gentlemanly sleeves and condescended to take tuition from his questionably skilled printer, James Reynolds. Reynolds guided him through the labyrinth of levers, spindles, rollers and plates that comprised the primitive press, which under the ink-stained hands of the novice operator collapsed and fell to pieces. Reynolds pronounced the old machine inoperable. Unless it was replaced immediately, he said, the *Gazette* would have to close down. As always, when money was required in Clonmel, heavy commitments detained Lord Donoughmore in Westminster. Edm. Power, respected printer and magistrate, however would not be seen to abort the newspaper he neither loved nor read.

Reynolds advised him of the latest advances in printing technology and the ever-accommodating Solomon Watson advised him of his latest interest rates.

On Saturday 11th December 1802 *Power's Clonmel Gazette* shed its dated mantle and emerged as the most modern provincial newspaper in Ireland. Its title appeared in bold block capitals, its print in a sharp new format and the cipher ʃ denoting the letter s had vanished before its time. So much space separated the printed lines that the more discerning reader could write in his own news and improve on the original. In celebration of this great occasion Bernard Wright wrote a special editorial:

> *'It does not often become the duty of a provincial editor — neither perhaps is it in his best interests — to indulge in political observation and commit himself to the opinions of party. To give a copious and well selected display of foreign and domestic news in general and to leave his readers to form their own conclusions from impartial relations — is more immediately his office. ... [But] we cannot totally exclude ourselves from taking an active interest in public affairs. What we think greatly meritorious we will applaud; what injurious we will condemn.'*

The word *we*, repeated four times in the last two sentences, meant the ever-absent Viscount Donoughmore of Knocklofty.

3

A severely dressed woman looking about twenty though is probably in her forties walks purposefully into the gallery. In one hand she holds an over-priced designer-logoed handbag and in the other a six-year old boy in a discreetly stained school uniform.

'You said there'd be suits of armour like knights used to wear, Mum.'

'They're in another room. We'll go there in a minute. First let's look at some of these lovely pictures by famous artists.'

'Why are they all so black?'

'They're not all black. This one's quite colourful.'

'Who is she?'

'Read what it says.'

'The Count-ess of Bless-ing-ton. What's a countess?'

'A countess was a lady married to a count or an earl.'

'What does married mean?'

'You know what it means. Hasn't your teacher explained at the after-school comparative religion club? It's when people go through a ceremony to show they love each other. Oh all right, go on then, go and look at the armour. I'll be with you in a minute.'

The woman turns towards me with an exasperated gesture intended to solicit sympathy.

'He's six years old. He's at the most expensive primary school in London. I pay for two private tutors and he says he doesn't know what marriage is.'

'Dare I ask if you are married?'

'Good heavens no; I haven't got time for that sort of nonsense. I have a partner. Don't ask me where he is. The last I heard he was playing the bagpipes in Venezuela.'

I want to laugh but the woman clearly has no sense of humour.

'And when he's not playing the bagpipes, does your partner play a part in his son's upbringing?'

The woman's incredulity tells me that my question is futile.

'What he chooses to do is not my business. I've put the boy's name down for eight public schools. Just that cost me more than his father earns in a year.'

'So you are bringing up your son alone. Do you not find it difficult?'

'No, why should I? I'm the financial director of an international IT company. If I can do that then I can bring up a child. Normally I do seventy hours a week but I take my ten week's holiday to coincide with the school. That gives me adequate time to instil the elements of culture into the boy's head. He'll have no chance of a place otherwise. And I will not have him let me down.'

The vision of ten weeks' hard labour endured by both mother and son makes me appreciate why paid holidays were unthinkable until a century after my death. Were they really a healthy innovation, I wonder?

'Do you not believe your partner is under a moral obligation to assist you and his son financially?'

'I have no idea. If you expect a man to be a good provider, or whatever the trite cliché used to be, you're living two hundred years in the past.'

I point to my portrait.

'The Countess of Blessington lived two hundred years in the past. I imagine her husband would have been a good provider. She is well dressed and has elegant jewellery but you will notice that her hands are posed to obscure her wedding ring. Do you think she was trying to demonstrate that she was an independent woman like you, or was Sir Thomas Lawrence just a little careless?'

The woman has no time to answer my question before the small boy comes running back.

'Come on, Mum, they've got awesome suits of armour and cool helmets, shields and swords and stuff. Was a knight like a superhero?'

The unmarried mother makes a superheroic effort to return my smile before being dragged off to deal with this and similar cultural questions prerequisite to a candidate for a public school education.

--

Father's land and the corn and butter trade yielded less and less income while *Power's Clonmel Gazette*, though apparently successful, showed few signs of returning the investment Lord Donoughmore required him to inject into his award for bravery. The more Father's capital depleted, the more he spent on entertaining in the interests of his passionate pursuit of a profitless peerage. Insolvency was no deterrent to a man of his aspirations.

Edmond Power, gentleman, enrolled six of his seven children - Mary Ann was just two years old - into Clonmel's most reputable school: a private establishment where profit subjugated education. Towards the end of 1803 the proprietor-headmaster read out a list of names at morning assembly. 'The following shall be excluded from all further lessons until last term's tuition fees are settled.' The list included Anne, Edmond, Michael, Margaret, Ellen and Robert Power. My three older siblings had from birth been tormented by something the doctor called consumption, for which there was no known cure, and were often too sick to attend school. Father thus withdrew them and employed a tutor who proved more costly.

Miss Dwyer had taught me well and instilled the love of knowledge. I effortlessly outshone the other children in the overcrowded classrooms where undertrained and overworked teachers had neither the time nor wit to observe my talents let alone encourage their development. Bored, disillusioned and to save Father's money – no, he never thanked me – I asked the school to remove my name from the register. In the mornings, I accompanied my younger sister and brother to a side door where a sympathetic teacher let them slip into her classroom while I slipped away.

Sometimes I visited a friendly widow who, by Clonmel's standards, was cultured and well-read but I soon tired of her exuberant enthusiasm. She was not Miss Dwyer. Nothing could fire my imagination like Miss Dwyer's inspirational teaching - until the early onset of puberty.

Since I was a small child, my siblings had taunted me for my plain and sickly looks. They called me Sally; the scarecrow 'Aunt Sally' at which they threw stones. Then without warning or the aid of a fairy godmother, from an ugly sister I became Cinderella transformed. My face, hair, eyes, body, legs and breasts evolved into magnets to the opposite sex. I revelled in admiration and discouraged no one.

'A handsome prince will find me and take me to an enchanted world of eternal happiness,' I wrote in my Night Thought Book.

I blotted out the staleness of Súir Island, Father's acerbity, Mother's delusions and my conscience-driven obligations to my sick and troubled family. Clonmel was full of young people – I should say young men – who I met at the social evenings they called 'coteries'. For a few pence we enjoyed hours of fun and laughter in a shabby community hall where a loud and lively fiddler played traditional Irish dances; the céili, the jig and the quadrille. Sometimes he treated his captive audience to a waltz: a dance for individual couples. One boy holding one girl – early nineteenth-century sex education!

I am joined by a tall serious-looking man in a pin-striped wide-lapelled double-breasted suit. He has thick silver-grey hair and sharp eyes: a quintessential Englishman of the interwar years. He could be an accountant, a bank manager, a solicitor or any other unimaginative professional.

'May I take it that you are Lady Blessington? Allow me to introduce myself. My name is Michael Sadleir.'

'I am delighted to have the opportunity to offer you my sincere thanks, Mr Sadleir. Not many women, or men for that matter, have been honoured with two biographies in the same year by the same author. Your painstaking attempts to make them different are most impressive. But whatever possessed you?'

'In those days, your ladyship, I was a popular historian, I suppose rather like the celebrities they now have on television, except I earned a lot less. My publishers said *The Strange Life of Lady Blessington* was too serious for their readership and asked for a lighter version, but their readers were no more interested in *Blessington D'Orsay: A Masquerade* than my first attempt. *Fanny by Gaslight* was my only bestseller but that contained more sexual inference.'

'When I became a writer, Mr Sadleir, there was no choice but to avoid sexual inference – I excelled at avoiding sexual inference – but surely by 1933 there should have been no reason for you to be so circumspect. What exactly did you mean by: "*In maturity* [I] *was not all of a woman. On no other basis can* [my] *life and character be interpreted*"? Let me assure you, Mr Sadleir, I was all of a woman. Take a long hard look at Lawrence's portrait. Not all of a woman? Sexual inference oozes from every brushstroke. I defy you to find a more explicit example of femininity in this entire gallery? There is certainly another basis on which my life and character can be interpreted. Sit down next to Dr Madden and let me be your interpreter.'

While my parents thought I was at school, I proved that I was all of a woman. I was found by a handsome prince who took me to an enchanted world of eternal happiness – well, temporary happiness – a wondrous experience I yearned to repeat. Clonmel was suddenly filled with handsome princes waiting to take me to temporarily enchanted worlds. And I loved them all - well, more than one. I flaunted my new-found charms at the coteries, the amateur theatre, at parties, at market fairs, even in the street. Who was there to restrain me? Mother was only too pleased to have a self-willed fourteen-year-old out of her house.

'It is a blessing from the mother of God that Margaret is keeping away from Ned's drunken friends,' she told a churchgoing acquaintance.

'That's right, Mrs Power, Clonmel is a good Christian town. There's not a safer place in all Ireland.'

Who cared what happened to the daughter of a religious turncoat?

The archaic forms of contraception then known were shameful secrets divulged only on marriage and not always then. Now, in the twenty-first century, schoolgirls are taught to understand the consequences of sexual intercourse and women have constant access to professional advice through their child-bearing years. Yet there are those who still deprecate these priceless privileges, forgetting how, over many centuries, thousands like me suffered for our ignorance.

I did not understand the changes taking place in my body. The only person in whom I could confide was my sister, Ellen. She was just eleven months younger than me and similarly mature for her age but menstruation meant no more to her than to me. Whispering like criminal conspirators in our shared attic bedroom, we worked out what was happening but not who the father was. The boy to whom I lost my virginity or one of the others?

I brought Mother back from the sainted realm of the Desmonds and Sheehys. She screamed so loud that Father heard her out in his stables, tore himself from pampering his horses and ran into the house. Mother's hysteria and my shamefaced tears could mean just one thing. I braced myself for the sting of his whip. A miracle occurred. He turned to stone. His petrified eyes gazed at me with unprecedented intensity. First he looked surprised, then perplexed, as if I had suddenly appeared from out of a cloud. He had seen something, something new, something valuable. Under no circumstances would the daughter of Edmond Power, magistrate and gentleman, be permitted to ruin his noble prospects by bringing an illegitimate child into the world. Its father would marry me, at gunpoint if necessary, and pay for his misdeed.

'Alright, who is he?'

'I don't know: one of the boys I met at a coterie. I can't remember his name,' I said almost truthfully.

I muttered a barely audible apology but Father was not listening. Other matters were playing on his mind – debt, serious debt – the unrelenting incoming tide of financial ruin. He was being assailed by creditors. The bank was demanding interest. The affairs of Hunt, O'Brien & Power were moving rapidly from uncertain to irredeemable. *Power's Clonmel Gazette* was bad news and disgruntled tenants were withholding rents. Tutors, doctors and medicines compounded his burdens while something in his intermittent conscience compelled him to fight, regardless of cost, to prolong the futureless lives of his sick children until the last embers of hope were extinguished.

'Listen, I know every lad within ten miles of Clonmel. I know their families too. There's not a shilling of honest money between the lot of them. What the hell am I supposed to do?'

'Difficulties vanquish the weak but are vanquished by the strong.'

My instincts told me what the hell Father was supposed to do. He was supposed to turn adversity to advantage, as I would soon have to for the first of many times. Shivering and sweating, I tried to find a way to explain the foreign concept of strategy. Then, a second miracle occurred. A flash of inspiration ordained by the devil himself penetrated Edmond Power's pretentious skull. He knew a young officer, a man given to recklessness, a man boasting physical and sexual prowess, an unmarried man from a rich and prosperous family, a man so naïve that even he could outwit him. Regardless of consequence, the grandchild of Edmond Power JP, public servant and aspirant peer, would be born in wedlock. My hand was to be offered for sale.

'There are no persons capable of stooping so low as those who desire to rise in the world.'

I uncovered my eyes. Father had vanished leaving my flesh unblemished. Damaged goods fetch poor prices. Mother neither showed emotion nor uttered a word of compassion. As always, she let her troubles slide into oblivion through the unctuous serenity of the Desmonds and Sheehys.

That evening I entered the forbidden drawing room. Perhaps I was hoping to find another Lord Mountjoy or even Lord Mountjoy himself but there were only the usual middle-aged squires, officers and supposed gentlemen grinding their teeth to laugh at humourless jokes. Bored young subalterns, conscripted into fruitless service by prestigious families, glared at me vacuously, making the illiterate farm boys who flocked into Clonmel on market days indeed seem like princes. Somewhere among this shifting cluster of colourless uniforms – civilian and military – was the man with whom I was to spend the rest of my days.

I did not complain nor become distraught. In fact, I thought the idea of being purchased in matrimony by a mysterious stranger was romantic and intriguing. I was ready to do anything, go anywhere, with anyone to be free of my parents' house of staleness, sickness and showmanship.

The dinner staged for my sale was less elaborate than for the visit of Viscount Donoughmore. This time I was the only table decoration. And this was the only time Father ever threatened me or any of his daughters with violence. If I so much as a hinted at my pregnancy, he would whip me as he never whipped his horses. How I wish I had given him the opportunity.

I did as I was told and tried to look virginal. Normally before an auction the potential bidder appraises his lot. Before this one his lot appraised the potential bidder. I wondered if the young officer sitting across the table could see me at all, let alone appraise me through the drunken haze evidently blurring his dull eyes. His vacant stare betrayed no evidence of lust. That would have been better than nothing but he hardly glanced at the low-cut dress I had chosen to divert attention from the as yet invisible signs of my condition.

Father introduced the Honourable Captain Maurice St Leger Farmer of the 47th Regiment of Foot, below average height, slightly built, with oiled sandy hair and a military moustache. His uniform was clean and well pressed and his accoutrements polished by his assigned batman. I did not find his drunkenness offensive. A sober officer in our house was rarer than romantic love in Clonmel. Nonetheless, having come to meet his bride, Captain Farmer might have attempted some gesture of courtship, a few flowers perhaps. I tried light conversation. My would-be fiancé responded only with inane smirks, yet laughed uproariously at Father's vulgar jokes. At the end of the evening, he staggered away without a word. I knew no more about him than when he arrived, and he knew no more about me.

Captain Farmer was not the only bidder for my hand. Captain James Murray indulged me in intelligent conversation and brought a gift; four small volumes of Choderlos de Laclos's *Les Liaisons Dangereuses* bound with a white ribbon. I had read Miss Dwyer's copy in the original French but for the rest of my days treasured my suitor's intuitive offering, once described as *'the most cynical fiction ever penned'*; not that I ever needed a manual on cynicism. After dinner Captain Murray discreetly wrote his bid on a scrap of paper. Father showed it to Captain Farmer who immediately slurred aloud his counter offer of three-hundred pounds. Captain Murray rose, politely thanked Father and his successful competitor, wished me good luck and took his leave. I presumed I would not hear of him again. I was wrong, though I never discovered how much he had offered. Either the proceedings were too distasteful or he was not rich. I thought three hundred pounds more than the content of a banker's strongbox and presumed my intended husband to be rich indeed. Then I knew no more about money than marriage but was soon to learn a great deal about both.

I remained fascinated by this curious young man so keen to buy me as his bride. Father congratulated me on my good fortune. My fiancé was the eldest son of a knight of the realm and heir to a baronetcy. It no longer mattered to me that the Honourable Maurice St Leger Farmer was the antithesis of the knights of chivalry of my shattered dreams. It mattered to me that he was English and that one day I would be the lady of an English knight, liberated forever from the claustrophobia of Ireland.

On 7th March 1804, at the age of fourteen years and six months, I was married before paid witnesses at the old St Mary's Church, Clonmel. The Reverend William Stephenson's brief ceremony, as meaningless to me as to my bridegroom, was another non-Catholic service Mother declined to attend. She did not approve of the Established Church of Ireland, affiliated to the Church of England since 1801. To me the niceties of denomination were as irrelevant as they were indistinguishable. I had rejected faith from the first dawn of reason and in England it would be quite inappropriate for the future Lady Margaret St Leger Farmer to be a Catholic. The future Sir Maurice was an enigma, but whatever he turned out to be, I was determined that my marriage would be happy and enduring.

We left the church in my husband's carriage. Father waited by the gate, waved us off, hesitated for a moment, turned and walked away. I detected no contentment in his face but believed that he was satisfied with his bargain and felt exonerated for my folly. My reassurance did not last long. We had barely reached the outskirts of the town when Captain Farmer fell upon me like a wild animal, groping my body, gripping my breasts, lifting my skirts, grappling with my petticoats. The more I implored him to be gentle, the rougher he became. I sealed my lips so as not cry out. My husband too made no sound as he tore off his uniform and launched himself into some sort of feral act, while his coachman and groom remained unconcerned by the vehicle rocking precariously behind them. Their job was to watch the road ahead.

Maurice St Leger Farmer had paid for his conjugal rights and intended to exercise them there and then. It was my duty to concede, and why not? Momentarily the prospect seemed exciting. I had savoured the act before and there was no reason why I should not savour it again – and the sooner the better. My lawfully wedded husband would be convinced that he had fathered my child. I prepared myself to submit. Nothing happened.

Maurice's head dropped onto my dishevelled shoulder. He floundered and struggled but soon his strength drained. Did he know where he was, who I was or what he was doing? His eyes were wide open, yet he was losing consciousness. Surely he could not be drunk. I could smell no alcohol on his breath. I had lived with drunkenness all my life and seen the worst of its repercussions but Maurice had celebrated his wedding with just one glass of red wine. When I pushed him away he did not resist. For the remainder of the journey he sat motionless and silent, his eyes open but expressionless. Was he asleep or in some sort of coma?

The coachman at last opened the small communication hatch and observed my distress – how astute! 'It's alright, Mrs Farmer, he'll be fine when he gets home'.

It was late afternoon when we reached Poplar Hall, an isolated decaying stone mansion blackened by aeons of smoke set in desolate countryside near the village of Ballitore in County Kildare. Our carriage drew up in front of its splitting timbered porch. This then was Maurice's home: grim, characterless and curiously mysterious like its owner. Maurice was not its owner. The house, everything in it and the estate in which it stood all belonged to his father. Sir Fystite St Leger Farmer had moved to England after the death of his Irish wife, leaving Maurice and his brother Walter in charge of his property. My knighted English father-in-law, who I never met, was probably as mad as his sons.

A rich man is never mad, he is simply eccentric. Sir Fystite was so eccentric that it had never entered his head to provide his heirs with any form of financial support. Neither Walter, who I also never met, nor Maurice had any income apart from their officers' pay, which in Maurice's case had been permanently halved for insubordination.

His groom opened the carriage door, lowered the steps and helped me down.

'Don't worry, Mrs Farmer, he's often like this. 'He'll wake up presently. You go in. Mrs Ardboyle'll look after you.'

The young groom nervously carried my bag to the porch, dropped it on the doorstep and ran off to assist his colleague uncouple the coach still occupied by my mute bridegroom. Sir Fystite's aging retainer opened the door, muttered a word or two of welcome, carried my bag up to a mahogany-panelled bedroom and left me alone. I sat down on a creaking four-poster and attempted to take in my surroundings. It was almost dark and there was no lamp. After seemingly forever, the sombrely clad housekeeper brought my wedding breakfast – a cup of tepid milk with a dry piece of bread – and a used candle.

'If I were you, Mrs Farmer, I'd keep the door locked for a while.'

'Why should I do that? I cannot lock my husband out of his own bedroom.'

'Please yourself, but it's usually best to wait until he calms down a bit.'

'He seemed quite calm to me. I think he was asleep when I left him.'

'He is not asleep, he's drunk,' she said.

The candle burnt itself out and in the darkness I heard Mrs Ardboyle slam the kitchen door and slide its iron bolt. Half an hour later I heard Maurice let himself in and walk across the front vestibule, apparently sane and sober. I heard his footsteps on the wide oak staircase and heard him open the bedroom door I had stubbornly refused to lock. I felt him slapping my face, pushing, pulling, wrestling, trying to force me into submission. This time I cried out. I shouted again and again: 'Stop hitting me and I'll submit.' Maurice did not stop, yet a defect in a deep recess of my brain made me want to love this deranged man. Again nothing happened. Nothing ever happened. Within minutes my husband was lying half naked by my side, panting with exhaustion. Again he appeared to lose consciousness. Again his body was lifeless, his face expressionless, his eyes wide open. He had not addressed a single word to me in the eight hours since we were pronounced man and wife.

Throughout my time at Poplar Hall, Captain Walter St Leger Farmer was serving as a sentinel at the penal colony of Australia. I heard that he was as studiously barbarous as Maurice and an equally monstrous liar. Many years later, in response to an article written by my niece, Walter sent a long and preposterous letter to the *Dublin Evening Packet* alleging that Captain James Murray had violently attacked Maurice in a fit of jealousy after I accepted his proposal. If only it had been true. According to my brother-in-law: '[It was] *an undoubted fact* [that our marriage] *was in every sense a love match – Captain Farmer* [by then deceased] *has not shown the slightest sign of insanity at any time in his life.'*

'Even you, Dr Madden, managed to discern that "*several statements* [in Walter's letter] *are entirely at variance with* [your] *impression of facts.*"'

'Indeed, Lady Blessington, I discovered that Farmer was twice certified insane while in the army.'

35

The house of which I was now mistress had just one redeeming feature. It lacked the staleness of Father's debauched revelry. Soon I was yearning even for that. Our only visitors were officers detailed to escort Maurice from the regimental camp when he was relieved of duty. Invariably they declined my offers of refreshment and left quickly. They knew their captain. A drop of poteen, a half pint of porter, a few sips of wine and they would have to fight to restrain him.

Hard as I tried to seduce my husband, he never managed to consummate our marriage. He accused and, without evidence, convicted me of causing his impotence and frustration. With unprovoked tirades and ferocity, he sentenced me to what now would be called house arrest, punctiliously locking and bolting the front door every time he went out. The servants' entrance was however always unlocked. I could have left if I had wished. I did not wish to leave. My body ached and my energy was drained. I wished only to rest and not be seen battered, bruised and bedraggled. And where was there for me to go in that lost corner of County Kildare?

I tried to talk to Maurice about his problems but could find no common ground to elevate him even to the intellect of a fourteen-year-old girl. Our brief agonised conversations invariably ended with us sitting silently opposite one another like a pair of stone gateposts. The only person in the house with whom I could communicate at all was Mrs Ardboyle.

'Why does Captain Farmer act so strangely? Does he suffer from some form of insanity?'

'I have heard that said often enough. It's not true. He was always perfectly normal and still can be sometimes. The Farmers are a little eccentric but they're a grand family. They never say a bad word about anybody.'

I was old enough to be sceptical of this overused shibboleth in praise of those, usually deceased, with nothing better to commend them. Why was there no one from this grand family to say a word, bad or good, at my wedding?

'How long has he been like this?'

'I'm not sure. He was such a quiet kind boy when Sir Fystite first brought him here. It was before the drink got him. He seems to have got worse lately. I think there's been trouble at the camp.'

'Perhaps he is ill. Should I send for a doctor?'

Psychiatry was a science of the future but I had read that, while there was no remedy for sicknesses of the mind, certain recognised diseases causing abnormal behaviour could be treated. Alcoholism was not a recognised disease.

'You'd be wasting your money, Mrs Farmer. I've seen it all before. There's nothing they can do about the drink.'

'I don't understand. Captain Farmer drinks so very little?'

'You should have been here a year or two ago. Every night, with or without company, he'd drink till he was paralytic. Now just a drop and he's gone. You never know when the rage will start. It can be straight away or in an hour. It doesn't usually last long. He'll always get over it. Sometimes he falls down and hurts himself. I do hope he hasn't hurt you, Mrs Farmer.'

I did not answer. My injuries were plain enough for her to see. Father and his influential friends had made me impervious to the obscenities that accompanied Maurice's frenetic tantrums, but could not protect me from the physical onslaughts that followed his failures at what might now be called marital rape. Still I remained confident that I could overcome the whims of his insanity – until the night Mrs Ardboyle noticed. She could not take her eyes from my swelling waist. Her jaw dropped and I read her mind. 'Was Captain Farmer really capable?' She hugged and kissed me. For a moment, I thought she smiled. It was probably a delusion.

'Does Captain Farmer know?'

Nothing I could do or say would prevent the jubilant family servant from grabbing my arm and dragging me down the great staircase to convey the good news certain to cure her employer's madness.

Oh yes, Maurice was mad, but not so mad he was unaware that his marriage was unconsummated. First he directed his rancour at Father: 'filthy liar, bastard, fraud, swindler, cheat, thief!' And then at me: curse after curse, blow after blow, kick after kick, torture after torture. He drew blood from my head, my body, my arms, my legs. I fell to the floor and, over and over again, screamed for him to stop. The Honourable Captain Maurice St Leger Farmer did not stop. In those few minutes – few hours – he lost not only his senses but his one and only chance of fathering an heir to his family title.

'And who was there to say the child was not yours, Maurice? Not me.'

And in those same few minutes I lost my one and only chance of becoming a mother. My unborn baby and my fertility had been simultaneously murdered.

The rampage at last abated.

'Get out of my sight. I never wish to see you again.'

It was a wish that I would have gladly granted had I even the strength to get up and walk.

Maurice shouted at Mrs Ardboyle.

'Get rid of it!'

The superfluous order contravened the Catholic creed, but Mrs Ardboyle was more faithful to the house of St Leger Farmer than to God. Ignoring my screams and wounds she pushed me with her legs across the cold flagstone floor into a storeroom at the back of the staircase, furnished with nothing but half-empty shelves beyond my reach.

I never again experienced such pain. I never again saw my mockery of a marital bed. And I never again saw my husband. I had been married for just twelve weeks.

I promised to relate the whole and unvarnished truth but now that I reach its lowest ebb mere words are scarcely adequate to describe the grotesque miscarriage that left me permanently sterile. For two days I lay immobile on the stone floor of the icy closet: two terrible days of bodily torment that endowed me with the mental fortitude to sustain me through the worst and best of times future.

Only now can I relate exactly what occurred on and in consequence of that fateful evening.

Mrs Ardboyle had grabbed me by the wrist and, pulling and pushing, led me down to the front vestibule. It was past ten. At that hour the house was normally dark and deserted. I had not been told to expect visitors yet lamps were alight on the table and on the mantelpiece above the stone fireplace. Maurice was in his captain's uniform and the flickering flames reflected in the silver of his buckles and badges. I thought complimenting his smart appearance might help absorb the shock he was about to receive but changed my mind. Nothing would have helped.

The front door was open. Outside on the forecourt solders in similar uniforms were waiting decorously by their horses. These gallant officers were not under orders to intervene in domestic violence or to come to the aid of an apparently unfaithful wife. They were under orders to arrest Captain St Leger Farmer, escort him back to their regimental camp at the Curragh of Kildare and guard him through the night.

As the housekeeper pushed my bloody body out of the back of the vestibule the men of the 47th Regiment of Foot pushed my husband out of his own front door. The following morning, Captain St Leger Farmer appeared before the preliminary hearing of a court-martial, charged with drawing his sword in anger against a superior officer, Lord Caledon, his regimental colonel, no less – a capital offence - and was confined to the camp prison pending formal proceedings.

Though the crime was characteristic I was never certain of the extent of my husband's guilt. Court-martials were the most inequitable of trials. Would any officer risk promotion by appearing as a witness for the defence? Is it different today? Captain Farmer's assigned military lawyer, with practised panache, apologised for the atrocious indignity inflicted upon the unscathed regimental colonel, ploughed through a plethora of platitudes, before triumphantly producing two certificates of insanity and saving his client from the firing squad.

Captain St Leger Farmer was pronounced guilty of an unbalanced mind, discharged and barred for life from military service. On appeal, he was granted permission to sell the commission his father had purchased to ensure that he never returned from boarding school. Sir Fystite made a brief visit to Ireland, arranged the sale and disbursed the proceeds on the customary bribes to secure a position with the East India Company and the purchase of a one-way sea passage. The eccentric Sir Fystite was of course unaware that his son was married.

We were both fortunate. If Maurice had not been arrested on the very night when Mrs Ardboyle revealed my pregnancy, he would certainly have murdered me and no plea of insanity would have exonerated him from execution in a civil court. With this macabre consolation, I nurtured no animosity towards my first husband or anyone else. I believed in forgiveness not vengeance.

'Forgiveness is a slave for the wounds inflicted by unkindness; while rancour serves to keep them unhealed.'

I recovered consciousness on the morning after my second night on the stone floor of the cold claustrophobic closet. Mrs Ardboyle had made no attempt to clean away the repulsive detritus still emanating from my body. She had brought me nothing to eat or drink. She had not even looked in to see if I was dead or alive. And she had been the one person in the house I believed I could trust. In excruciating pain, I forced myself to my feet and staggered three steps to the door a mile away. I needed water. Supporting myself against the rough wall I tried to reach the kitchen but managed only ten more feet before I fell on the flagstones behind the staircase where I had been thrown two days before. I lay paralysed for half an hour or longer. Mrs Ardboyle and other servants a room away were deaf and blind to my emergence from my condemned cell.

Suddenly there were horses. They had brought Maurice back. Now he would kill me. There was nowhere to hide even had I the strength to move. The sound of hooves on gravel grew louder. The voice of a rider became clearer: a familiar voice, a loud and angry voice, a voice I would never again have cause to fear.

The butt of a rifle hammered on the heavy door – bang, bang, bang.

'Farmer, come out here. Show yourself, man!'

A brave messenger, Maurice's coachman perhaps, had galloped to Clonmel with news of my plight and the bold Lord Power of Curragheen, latter-day knight of chivalry, had donned his shining armour and ridden to liberate his daughter in distress. There was honour in Ireland, after all.

No messenger had been to Clonmel. Father's mission was no knightly crusade, and if there was honour in Ireland he was far from its exemplar.

Maurice's coachman and groom scurried into the stable and barred the doors. Mrs Ardboyle and the other servants ran to the kitchen and slid the bolts. The banging and shouting grew louder. Then silence. Father roared: 'Break it down, lads.' For five minutes – an eternity – his dragoons battered at the heavy timber with axes, spades and rusty implements found around the neglected farmyard but their cacophonous hammering made no more impact than the butt of Father's rifle.

'OK, that's enough, lads. Stand back.'

A deafening explosion. The lock gave way. Father pushed down the door with his shoulder and jumped over it into the vestibule, his rifle still smoking.

'Farmer, Farmer, Farmer. Where are you? Come out, you bastard. I know you're in there somewhere.'

I was never so happy to see that ridiculous frilly shirt or to hear the foul expletives expostulating from the mouth of its gentrified wearer. In this mood no force on Earth could stop a man like Edmond Power. He stopped, stunned and silenced. A half-dead tribute to man's inhumanity, soaked with blood, pus, urine and excrement was trying to crawl towards him.

'A profound knowledge of life is the least enviable of all species of knowledge because it can only be acquired by trials that make us regret the loss of our ignorance.'

'You must be Lady Blessington. To be sure, you couldn't be anybody else.'

A short plump middle-aged man removes his brown bowler hat and attempts to bow. A gold watch chain hangs from his high-buttoned waistcoat.

'And you are?'

'My name is Joseph Fitzgerald Molloy. I'm your greatest admirer. Was it not me who wrote your most elegant biography?'

'Oh yes, *The Most Gorgeous Lady Blessington*; I've read both thin volumes; the most succinct and least informative of my biographies. You are Irish, Mr Molloy. As I recall the Irish are renowned for what has become known as the gift of the blarney. Could you not have used a little more imagination?'

'I did my best, your ladyship, but all I had to go on was Dr Madden's conundrum and I gave up trying to solve it. It was all too complicated, so I wrote only what I believed to be true. At first I called it simply *Lady Blessington* but changed the title to make it sound more seductive, if you see what I mean?'

'I trust no one expected it to contain anything erotic. They would have indeed been sadly disappointed, Mr Molloy.'

'I thought you were the perfect lady. I've been listening to what you were just saying and now I think so more than ever. Few women could have overcome an experience like that and gone on to achieve as much as you.'

'And do you still think of me as *The Most Gorgeous*?'

'Nobody will ever deserve that accolade more than you, Lady Blessington.'

'Sit down with Dr Madden and Mr Sadleir and listen to the rest of my story. But be warned, you might well change your mind.'

Father laid his gun on the vestibule table and ran to where I lay. He had brought four of his dragoons and, incredibly, my brother Michael.

'What the hell's this?'

It was an unnecessary question. He crouched down and lifted me from the floor. I weighed nothing in his arms. Michael removed the gun, took off his jacket and folded it into a headrest. A dragoon spread his scarlet tunic and Father laid me on the makeshift bed. I would like to say he did so gently. He did nothing gently. Michael covered me with another man's tunic. He did it gently. Michael did everything gently. The rough cloth was a down mattress. I wanted to thank my rescuers but speech was another casualty of my ordeal. I pointed a trembling finger at the kitchen door.

'He's in there. Come on, lads, let's get him.'

The bolt succumbed and seconds later Father dragged Mrs Ardboyle out as roughly as she had dragged me.

'Where's Farmer? What has he done to my daughter? Tell me or I'll murder you like I'm going to murder him.' Father slapped the housekeeper hard across the face. She barely flinched.

'Captain Farmer's gone. They took him away.' Insolent and defiant, Mrs Ardboyle kept her composure.

'Who took him away?'

'The soldiers, the ones who came for him.'

'When will he be back?'

'I don't know, maybe never. He's got trouble with the regiment.'

'I am the Magistrate Edmond Power. Did he leave me my money?'

So this was what bought Father to Poplar Hall. On his wedding day Maurice paid just ten per cent of his bid for one used child bride, beautiful and self-willed, and promised to settle the balance by monthly instalments. From his army pay?

'I know who you are, and if it's money you're after you've come to the wrong place. Captain Farmer owes me more than he owes you. And don't think I don't know all about your little deal. You should be ashamed of yourself.'

'I'm her father. What have you done to her?'

'I've done nothing. What did you expect, marrying her to a man like Captain Farmer and in her condition? And don't tell me you didn't know.'

Two of the dragoons grasped their commander's arms from behind. It was all they could do to prevent him strangling the housekeeper with his bare hands.

My hitherto sick brother Michael raised his voice in anger as he would never do again. 'She's had nothing to eat or drink, woman. Bring some food and water, and now.'

Avoiding Father, now restrained by all four dragoons and still roaring murderous threats Michael followed Mrs Ardboyle to the kitchen, brought out a cup of tepid water and gently held it to my lips. I took a sip or two. Minutes later Mrs Ardboyle reappeared with a half a loaf of bread and some sweating cheese. I ate too quickly and felt sick.

'She's filthy. Get her washed, bring some clean clothes and burn everything she's wearing.'

Was this really my gentle brother?

Mrs Ardboyle shrugged, went back to the kitchen and returned with a maid floundering under the weight of a bucket of the same tepid water. Showing little concern for my modesty or pain, they removed my clothes, washed away most of the blood and gore and covered me in an old dress that once belonged to Maurice's late mother. She must have been the size of an elephant.

'Experience has taught us little if it has not instructed us to pity the errors of others and to amend our own.'

Outside on the coarse gravelled courtyard, Edmond Power, officer of the law, at last took control of his senses. He looked round, first at the house, then at the estate and began to think irrationally. 'This is a big property. It's worth good money. Farmer should be able to pay his dues. But that bitch of a housekeeper said he owes her more than he owes me. That can mean only one thing: he's bankrupt. And if that's the case, it makes sense to take what he owes me before the bailiffs turn up. It's perfectly legal to take goods in lieu of debt. The woman said Farmer won't be back for a long time; maybe never, she said. I can't leave the girl in this house. I'll have to take her home and pay another bloody doctor. I'll have another bloody invalid on my hands for God knows how long. How the hell am I going to get her home? She'll die for sure if one of the lads ties her on the back of his horse.'

Aloud he said, 'OK, let's see if the good Captain Farmer has a decent carriage to his name. Come on, lads!'

The dragoons again set to work with their implements. The rotting beam securing the inside of the stable door yielded to half-a-dozen strokes. The coachman and groom emerged, dishevelled, trembling, their hands above their heads – the surrendering remnant of a vanquished army in a bad painting.

'What horses do you have in there?'

'Just the six, sir. They're very good horses, sir.'

'Carriages?'

'Two, sir. They're very good carriages, sir. One open, one closed, both for two horses, sir.'

'Harness them and saddle up the others. And be quick about it.'

Father slowly moved his hand an inch closer to his discharged rifle. The men ran back into the stable like a pair of frightened mice. Five minutes later they led two harnessed carriages and two saddled horses out into the courtyard. As the coachman said, they were all very good.

'We can load a fair bit onto those wagons, lads. Come on, let's see what's in the house.'

Yet again Michael astonished me. He spoke firmly but gently. 'Father, the reason I came here with you today was to stop you doing anything foolish. You know this house does not belong to Captain Farmer and these horses and carriages aren't his. He has no money to pay you, and you know that too. They say he's insane and a criminal but if you take away a single thing you will be no better than he is. All we need is a carriage to get Margaret home but we'll borrow it, not steal it.'

Once again my unstoppable father stopped, overtaken by a better nature that seldom surfaced. He was a magistrate, an officer of the court, a Justice of the Peace. Time and again he had been commended for bravery. Magistrate Power, soon to be Lord Power, could no more afford to be denounced as a common thief than he could afford anything else. Sir Fystite Farmer's brand of eccentricity involved neither money nor mercy.

Michael ordered the groom to return the open chaise to the stables and Mrs Ardboyle to fetch blankets. My brother carried me out to the closed carriage, gently laid me on the padded seat and made me as comfortable as he could.

I was brought home in the same vehicle, drawn by the same horses and driven by the same coachman and groom who drove me from my wedding. Father rode to the right and Michael to the left. The four dragoons followed behind in convoy. I imagined passers-by on that deserted Irish road mistaking me for a rich and idle countess travelling with an entourage of eight servants, but fell unconscious before I could luxuriate in this or any other fantasy.

'When I am a princess I shall travel abroad admired by all in a coach of white, green and crimson, built to my own desire, drawn by my own exquisite horses, driven and attended by my coachmen and footmen, immaculate in my own livery', I had written five years earlier.

4

A disorientated couple in their fifties glance tentatively around the front salon. He is tightly buttoned into his rarely worn Sunday best. His wife is small, shapeless and colourless. She has gone to a great deal of trouble to select her most uncomfortable finery to appear as inconspicuous as possible. They are in London for the first time on a cheap coach excursion. An exciting adventure, but they should have read the travel agent's advertisement more carefully: 'Special offer includes free conducted tour of the Wallace Collection, London's most beautiful museum.' The beauty of London is in its shops not its culture.

'Nice to see one that's a bit pretty for a change', he says. 'The Countess of Blessington, I wonder who she were? Where's Blessington any road, somewhere posh down south, like Brighton?'

'You don't think she lived in Rochdale, do you?' she says. 'You had to be rich in them days to get your picture painted. It were before they invented cameras.'

'That's right, it were a big deal, like driving round in a Mercedes to show you've got more brass than everybody else. Let's see, by Sir Thomas Lawrence. Bet he were top-notch. If you had him it'd be like having a Rolls. Her old man had to be a count or something. He'd be loaded.'

Unwisely I feel compelled to comment. 'Do you really think people are impressed by such things these days? Nobody looks twice at an expensive motor car.'

The couple are surprised, but not by my question. For a middle-class stranger to speak to them unbidden and as equals is as improbable today as it was two centuries ago.

'It's OK to say that in London, miss. Everybody 'ere's got a job. It's a different story where we come from. It's not so easy to make money up north,' she says.

'I am told there are many successful people in the North of England.'

'Not that many. Soon as they make a few bob, first thing they do is get themselves a private jet and bugger off to Majorca or Marbella so they don't pay income tax,' he says.

I warm to this couple. They are proud to be working class and see no reason to pursue any other lifestyle. They do not ask for sympathy but I feel sorry for them. Their aspirations, if they have any, are sucked dry by anachronistic convention. It is fruitless, I know, but I continue to argue.

'Contrary to the impression you might have gained from the media the overwhelming majority of successful businesspeople, wherever located, work hard, create jobs and provide people like you with affordable goods and services. True, the press love to report cases of fraud and tax evasion but in reality the economy and good causes like this gallery are dependent on ethical enterprise. Would it surprise you to learn the lady in that picture was a hard-working businesswoman?'

They stare at me as if I am raving mad.

'It would more than surprise me,' she says. 'Look at her. Are those the hands of a working woman? How many times did she do a full day and come home to a family to be looked after?'

'Far more times than you might think,' I say.

'Don't give me all that, miss. It were the same then as it is now. Her class never did a stroke. All they did was spend their brass on all this useless stuff they've got in here and go on holidays to posh places with the other lazy crooks,' he says.

I respect these people's simple tenets. They are incensed by unfair distribution of wealth and proud of their stagnant achievements. They detect no hint of strife in the paint on my portrait or the flesh on my face, and, best of all, do not connect me with Ireland.

Their tour guide beckons to them to rejoin her group but my friends avoid eye contact and demonstrate a new found independence. They hurry away to Oxford Street to purchase bargains to be envied by their equally unfortunate friends at home. I have won my argument.

--

Our dismal cavalcade reached Súir Island in the warm twilight of a late spring evening. Michael gently carried my emaciated body up to my attic bedroom. He ordered the coachman and groom to return the carriage, gave them small gratuities and promised to send back the borrowed clothes washed clean of my blood and vomit. And he did.

When I regained consciousness I was still bleeding and in pain. Mother showed no compassion. My homecoming meant extra work, another mouth to feed and another invalid to be cared for from her over-stretched budget. 'You'd better get well soon, Margaret,' she said more as a demand than an encouragement and, muttering about the house turning into a hospital, went downstairs leaving me to sleep.

Father prevailed upon the generosity of our long-suffering family physician of limited skill. His diagnosis was obvious and to say the least, pessimistic. 'Your daughter's been badly hurt, Mr Power. She's lucky to be alive. She might have a chance if she stays in bed.'

'For how long, doctor?'

'It could be months. I'll mix up some medicine and bring it next week.'

The impoverished doctor, who no longer bothered with bills, gathered up the few coins Father left for him on the table.

There had been changes in my absence. Anne and Edmond had grown weaker and were bedridden more often. Ellen had been sent to work for Hunt, O'Brien & Power. She sat for twelve hours a day in an ill-lit office copying incomprehensible ciphers into unwieldy ledgers. There were no toilet facilities, no breaks for refreshment, no holidays apart from Sundays and for every error a deduction was made from her pitiful wage. Years later I described her conditions to my friend Charles Dickens. He was not at all sympathetic. He said my sister should have considered herself lucky that she did not work for a lawyer.

Father had despaired of the corn and butter trade. There had been long, loud and angry arguments with Mr Hunt and Mr O'Brien. They accused him, with good reason, of failing to pull his weight and with equally good reason he accused them of lack of initiative. I agreed with both. What had they to show for decades of mindless compliance with the archaic traditions of their trade? And what had Edmond Power, aspirant gentleman, to show for ranting about the vulgarity of trade in general?

'Why have those two bastards never got a ha'penny in the bank? Where's the salary I'm supposed to get? How long do they expect me to go on promoting their squalid little business? When are they going to reimburse all the money I've laid out? When am I going see a return on the capital they said they'd put to work for me? It cost me enough to rebuild their bloody burnt-out warehouse, and where's my rent?' These were not unreasonable questions. It was unreasonable to address them to my thirteen-year-old sister. Ellen was female and therefore lacked the mental capacity to understand even the simplest precept of business – as the world of commerce vehemently maintained until the latter half of the twentieth century.

Edmond Power, male, lacked the mental capacity to understand even the simplest precept of land management. He wantonly neglected his tenants, who in appreciation tugged their forelocks, grovelled and paid such rent their meagre production afforded. The more Father cursed, threatened and evicted, the more deferential the poverty-stricken peasants became. They despised Edmond Power and the class to which he aspired but never complained loudly enough to drown even the sound of broken fences, unhinged gates, dilapidated barns and derelict dwellings silently crying out for their share of his squandered inheritance.

While weeds and wildlife flourished in the vacant fields of Curragheen, each morning Father adorned himself in his coat of scarlet pink, white breeches, ruffled shirt and cravat and galloped off on his immaculate chestnut charger; the most distinguished huntsman in County Tipperary. The local squires with whom he competed and fraternised did not dress up for everyday hunting and Edmond 'Beau' Power never discovered that his appearance was the butt of their cruellest jokes.

As soon as he left the house Mother began her morbid intonation: 'What would the Earl of Desmond think? Can the blessed Father Nicholas Sheehy believe it has come to this? What will I say to my sainted father on Sunday?'

She would say the same nonsense as she had said every Sunday for twenty years. And what good had it done?

Mother had become a slave to domestic economy. Down to one part-time maid, she muddled through the cookery, nursed her sick children and prepared for Father's guests to desecrate her efforts in the evenings. In the three months of my absence she had aged visibly. Lines marred her once-beautiful face and the jet black hair I inherited had turned almost grey. She was in her mid-thirties. I was consumed by guilt. By what right did I mock Mother's bizarre beliefs when

46

my own life was dedicated to fantasy? Why did I never recognise the virtue of her mindless devotion to her husband and stale house of ailing children?

Edmond Power, magistrate and gentleman, was still undaunted by his dwindling income. The blinding brilliance of the peerage still eclipsed the advancing spectre of the debtors' prison. There was no such thing as a financial problem in the House of Lords.

Michael's recovery was the one change for the better, or should have been. His ambition was to make Father proud by enrolling in the army. What more befitting complement could there be to Edmond Power in the ermine of a peer than his son in the uniform of a British officer? Yet Father adamantly refused to assist Michael to buy a commission. Not of course for reasons of economy, but because he was now certain to outlive his older brother and become the natural successor to the phantom Power baronetcy. Worse still, Michael insisted that he would never accept an unmerited title. To Father this was not simply an insult, it was tantamount to lunacy; a view with which I would have agreed had there been the remotest chance of a title to accept. Whether or not an honour, rank or title is merited has no bearing on its social value.

'You're strong enough now. You want a commission, boy, earn it like a gentleman.'

Michael was not a gentleman. He was a gentle man, the antithesis of a noble savage. But lucrative employment for a gentle man, or any man, was alien to rural Ireland. My brother would probably be too old to serve in the army by the time he had saved enough to buy a commission.

Nonetheless, Michael pursued his ambition. If he could not make enough money to allow him to defend his nation, at least he could defend his family from the onslaughts of starvation. In all weathers he walked to Curragheen, single-handedly repaired fences and gates, laid hedges, constructed paths and earned the tenants' gratitude and respect for Father. Overtaxing his reviving strength, he ploughed abandoned fields, cultivated fruit and vegetables, harvested corn and reared pigs, sheep and cattle. He hewed logs for fuel and fished the River Súir but only for food. To Michael angling for pleasure was as abhorrent as any blood sport. I despaired of his tender-hearted principles.

In his inimitable style, Father echoed my sentiments. 'What the hell are you doing milking a cow? You're a not a bloody farm hand, you're the son of a gentleman. Try behaving like one.'

When frustration erupted into violence, Ellen and I dressed Michael's wounds and tried to explain how much Father would appreciate retaliation. Michael never retaliated. He adhered to the biblical adage of honouring thy father and mother, right or wrong. His one lapse at Ballitore haunted him for the rest of his days. Father no more appreciated being honoured by his ungrateful son than being supported by him. Michael never complained, gambled, drank, womanised or propounded extreme opinions. What chance did the poor boy have of success in life?

The heroes and heroines of my novels would embody all the human weaknesses I encountered - brutality, adultery, vice, cruelty, laziness, vulgarity, crime and, worst of all, ambition - but I always balanced them with gentle deficient characters crafted with Michael in mind. Like every good Victorian novelist, I told my readers that there is inherent righteousness in the world. Possibly some believed it.

After a week the doctor returned with a bottle of improvised medicine and repeated that months of bed rest were my only chance of survival. Today in Britain, every patient has free access to general practitioners, specialist physicians, hospitals, subsidised medicines, convalescence and even financial support. In 1804 these were luxuries beyond the bounds of cerebral conception. Two options were open to those without the means to pay – recover quickly or die.

Mother was right. I was almost fifteen and old enough to earn my keep. I could not lie in bed while my younger sister was put out to near slave labour. Three weeks after my return, Ellen woke me at six on a wet Monday morning, helped me dress and held me vertical while I limped across the south bridge into County Waterford.

In half an hour we reached our destination, perhaps three or four hundred yards from home. A weather-beaten sign swinging in front of a shabby one-story premises read *Hunt & O'Brien*. 'Power' had yet to be added. Ellen let us in. Why was she was entrusted with a key? Once inside she relocked the door and opened a pair of peeling shutters to admit as much of the dawn light as the grimy window would permit. The single room that passed for an office was furnished with two antique partners' desks, one covered with papers and the other with dust. Against the windowless back wall stood a long high wooden bench at which Ellen worked. She climbed onto an unsteady stool and began writing, while I sat down to rest on the less dusty of the partners' chairs.

'Will Mr Hunt and Mr O'Brien be here soon?'

'I doubt it, Margaret. Mr Hunt only looks in about once a week. I don't know why. He's getting old and he's not well. He should have retired a long time ago but he says he can't afford it. I don't think that's true. And I never know when Mr O'Brien will turn up. He goes out a lot.'

'Where does he go?'

'Apart from on market days, he goes to see customers.'

'To sell them corn and butter?'

'No, to try to get them to pay their bills.'

Ellen pointed to the pile of papers on the desk in front of me and raised her eyes to the ceiling.

'They're reminders waiting to be sent out. Most of them are months overdue.'

'Does nobody come here?'

'Not often. They think Father might be around. They're terrified of him, but he doesn't come here anymore. Mr O'Brien does all the buying and selling himself.'

Presuming that I was also to be employed as a bookkeeper, I heaved my aching body onto the stool next to Ellen and tried to follow the figures she was laboriously copying out in immaculate copperplate. They were meaningless to me, but it was clear enough that Ellen was piercing many more papers onto the metal spike marked 'purchases' than onto the one marked 'sales'.

'Does no one else work here?'

'I've heard that there used to be one or two clerks before I started but they've been sacked. I am not sure why. Mr O'Brien says there isn't enough work. That's not true. Look how many bills there are. I have to do all the office work myself. It gets very lonely. I cannot tell you how happy I am to have you here, Margaret.'

'Are you saying Mr O'Brien leaves you here alone all day? Doesn't he realise you could be in grave danger?'

Ellen shrugged. 'I've only been here a few weeks. I think a couple of boys and a clerk work at the warehouse back on the island. They never come here. The only people I see want money but I don't have any to give them so I keep the door locked. Sometimes they get angry and shout at me from outside, though they know it's not my fault.'

'Perhaps I should try to tidy up a little while I am waiting for Mr O'Brien.'

'Mr Hunt won't be pleased. He says if we look too prosperous people will think we can afford to pay them. Then they'll sue us, and goodness knows what else.'

Instinctively I knew that this was a false premise, and scribbled the paradoxical maxim that would sustain me for the rest of my life:

'When you are poor, you cannot afford to look poor.'

Disregarding Ellen's caution and my persistent pain, I did what little I could to make the room look more welcoming. When I could no longer stand I again sat down at Mr O'Brien's time-worn captain's chair and tried to order the letters strewn on his desk – demands, more demands – some crude, some threatening, others from lawyers. 'Dear Sirs, Unless….'

After about two hours, we heard someone shouting outside. More out of curiosity than bravado I motioned for Ellen to open the door. The angry heavily-built farmer was startled to find himself welcomed by two young girls and made a concerted effort to modify his language.

'O'Brien's hiding himself as usual, I suppose. Well, tell him from me, miss, it's ten pounds, nine shillings and four pence ha'penny he owes me. It's four months now and if I don't see it this week, I'll find him wherever he is, and I'll do to him whatever I have to do to get it out of him. And tell him not to think his High and Mighty Mr Shiver-the-Frills Power is going to frighten me.'

This was another moment of discovery. My innate business acumen suddenly pierced its naïve surface. Fighting to hold myself upright behind the large once-imposing partner's desk, I nervously assumed an air of instinctive authority and assured the irate creditor that with Hunt, O'Brien and Power his money was as good as in the bank.

Ellen turned on her stool and smiled enticingly.

'How nice to see you again, Mr O'Sadcrop. I always think of you as our best-looking and obliging supplier. Come back at the end of the month and I promise I'll be here with something for you.'

The man's hostility melted like ice in hot water. Discoloured teeth appeared through his rough beard as he struggled to respond to the unfamiliar courtesy. I had learnt my first lesson in the illustrious science of credit control.

'Praise, however insincere, is the only gift for which the recipient is always genuinely grateful.'

When the farmer returned at the end of the month he received exactly what he was promised. Ellen fearlessly opened the door, smiled seductively, permitted him to enjoy her company for five minutes and sent him away armed with the confidence that his account would be settled on that most unspecified of dates - as soon as possible.

Mr O'Brien arrived at three in the afternoon and, ignoring me, immediately dropped a handful of coins onto Ellen's desk. 'Credit this to Grudge, Miss Power, and get it round to Sol Watson's bank before closing time. We can't have him dishonouring any more drafts.'

Ellen completed a form in triplicate, put on her bonnet and hurried off. Why, I wondered, had it taken most of the day to collect such a small sum from just one customer?

Mr O'Brien was a tall, gaunt, balding nervous wreck. Every few minutes he slapped down his left hand with his right to stop it shaking, mostly with little success. Showing no awareness of the pains I had literally taken to tidy his desk, he skimmed through his papers, jotting down figures, scribbling notes and wrestling with a dozen urgent problems simultaneously. When at last he returned his desk to the disorder in which I found it, he finally acknowledged my presence.

'The name's O'Brien. I've told Mr Power we can't pay the going rate. Trade is very slow at the moment. There's not enough work here in the office. When Miss Power gets back I'll take you round to the stores and show you what you have to do. You can start in the morning.'

Mr O'Brien, oblivious to my frailty, returned to shuffling his papers and said nothing more until Ellen returned and we set off back to Súir Island. Defying my agony compounded by the heat of the afternoon I forced myself to keep pace with my employer's long purposeless strides. It was the first time I had been inside the restored but still charred warehouse. A putrid smell made me feel nauseous. Perspiring, exhausted and fearing that I might vomit, I sat down on a leaking grain barrel and tried to take in my surroundings. Two dust-covered boys of about my own age were unloading a supplier's wagon and dragging in sacks and crates. Where there was space they heaved them up onto creaking wooden racks, and where there was not, dropped them at random on the earthen floor.

Mr O'Brien led me into a small partitioned area he called the stock office. It was as disordered as the similarly misnamed sales office where we had left Ellen alone, but dirtier and dustier. My job, he said, was to enter details of every stock movement into two large scuffed leather-bound ledgers marked 'Goods In' and 'Goods Out'. Some blunt quills protruded from a dry inkwell - the tools of my new trade.

'There's a ha'penny off for every mistake. You start at six-thirty in the morning. The boys will show you around. Just let me know if they come on strong.'

Comforting as I found Mr O'Brien's fatherly concern, I could not help wondering what he would do if the boys did 'come on strong'.

It was almost six in the evening. The indecisive Mr O'Brien decisively permitted me to leave early. I staggered the last hundred yards back to the house, crawled up to the attic and fell on my bed, too drained to think for long about my first day at work. I had learnt only that Hunt, O'Brien & Power was sick and, like me, had either to recover quickly or die.

The following morning, I was again greeted at the warehouse by the putrid aroma.

'Where does the nasty smell come from?' I asked the taller of the dusty storemen.

'It's only the butter, miss. It soon goes off this time of year. Don't you worry, we'll throw it out. The farmer takes it and feeds it to the pigs. They don't mind the stink.'

The boy thought this an hilarious joke.

'Does the farmer pay for what he takes? Butter is expensive, isn't it? Should I make an entry in the 'Goods Out' book? '

Both boys thought this an even more hilarious joke, and I took their inane laughter to mean that I would be wasting my time.

In a corner of the tiny stores office I found an incongruous luxury; an old besom with half its birch twigs intact. Slowly persevering, I made some inroad into the accumulated filth and the little room became almost fit for purpose. My besom also proved a deterrent in case the boys came on strong. The boys never came on strong. My unhealed scars and my broomstick probably made them believe that I was a witch. Only a witch's spell could have turned that scorched and stinking warehouse into a one-student school of business studies.

The modern student of business has access to a plethora of academic and practical training, data and literature. Yet none explain how the reflexes of those abnormal beings gifted with true acumen intuitively perceive and react to the perpetual motion of supply and demand. The time-honoured stigma of trade has faded to a shadow. Business is an honourable profession. Even the so-called glass ceiling of male prejudice is cracking under female persistence. In my time the ceiling of male prejudice was penetrable only by femininity itself – within the bounds of virtue, of course.

'Mr O'Brien says trade is very slow at the moment,' I said to the shorter of the dusty storemen.

'Well, does he, now? What's he talking about? It's August. It's the harvest season. You tell him from us, miss, there's no way we can cope with all the deliveries coming in. You can see for yourself, the place is bursting at the seams. And O'Brien expects us to do the paperwork too. That's not our job, miss. The old boy who used to come and write up the books is off sick. We've not seen him for months. I don't suppose we'll see him again. Who'd want to work in this dump?'

The boys were barely literate. I laboured long and hard to interpret their rough notes scrawled on scraps of paper and taught myself to write at speed – the invaluable skill destined to destroy my novels. Still it was weeks before the records were up to date. I might have completed the task more quickly had I not been mesmerised by the animated theatre of goods in and goods out framed by the small internal window of my crude office. I watched frenetic activity mutate into stagnation and tried to interpret its causes and effects. I set myself a conundrum. Change chaos into solvency in the least number of moves? I noted obstacle after obstacle and listed simple methods by which they could be surmounted.

'Common sense is the most uncommon of all senses.'

Not all of my *Desultory Thoughts and Reflections* were entirely original.

Common sense taught me that to my employers I was just a child and a female child at that. I feared derision more than censure. My solutions would be as meaningless to the anxious Mr O'Brien as to the anachronistic Mr Hunt, while Father would fly into a rage at the mere mention of the corn and butter trade.

By 1st September 1804, my fifteenth birthday, my health was almost restored and my mind closed to the trauma of my non-marriage. Work is the most proficient of medicines. Denying myself the luxury of nursing old wounds I drove my quills through the inexorable stifling dust in a coma of enthusiasm. The days grew shorter and my hours longer. Winter came. With no stove or insulation against the constant draughts, bundled into blankets, I toiled by candlelight turning the monotonous chores of a lowly clerk into intricate intellectual exercises. The more they challenged me the more confident I became that I, and I alone, could recover Father's foolhardy investment and with it, my own self-esteem. But without his trust I was impotent. I would have to apologise and, as humbly as my nature permitted, beg him to believe that I thought well of all his endeavours. I was still angry with Father and thought that it was he who should have apologised to me.

Now, reflecting on a lifetime of my own errors and misjudgements, I know that I was wrong but it is too late to atone for my severe censure.

'Some people seem to consider the severity of their censures on the error of others as an atonement for their own.'

It was one of the rare evenings when Father was neither expecting guests nor planning an escapade in the name of the law. He had had a good day at the hunt and I caught him before he drowned his exhilaration in poteen.

'I know that I disappointed you, Father. You were trying to do your best for us all. You are not to blame for Captain Farmer's madness. May I give you my solemn promise that I will never be a burden to you and will soon make you proud of me?'

I could scarcely envisage fulfilling either my promise or my prophecy yet my rehearsed improvisation touched the appropriate nerve. Father waved his free hand in an expressionless gesture of approval.

'Margaret, I have to tell you I'm at the end of my tether. There's no money left. Everything's pledged to Sol Watson's bloody bank.'

I was unmoved by Father's confession of what I knew only too well. I was moved by hearing my name from his lips. It was the first time he had addressed me as Margaret, or by any other name. He was speaking to me as an adult – a married woman. I seized my opportunity.

'If you will permit me, I can help you repay your debts, Father.'

'If only you could, Margaret.'

'I think I can, Father. Will you come with me tomorrow and talk to Mr Hunt and Mr O'Brien? You know they have the greatest respect for you. Exert your authority and make them listen. Let me tell you what to say? I am sure that it will be to your advantage.'

What I intended to tell Father to say was to my own advantage. My only fear was that his idea of exerting his authority would be to no one's advantage.

'Those two useless bastards; there's only one thing I have to say to them and that's get out.'

Father drained and refilled his glass. His congeniality had begun to abate. Time was precious.

'You are quite right, Father, as you always are. Mr Hunt and Mr O'Brien are useless, as you say. It's time for Mr Hunt to go, but only you can make him do the right thing.'

'If I had my way, I'd kick the bastard straight out of the door. But he says it's legally his firm.'

'It is not his firm, it's yours, Father. You invested your money. You built and restored the warehouse. You bring the customers. What does Mr Hunt do? '

Father did not answer. A gentleman does not concern himself with practicalities.

'Maybe it is my bloody firm, but what am I to do? I've told you, Margaret, I've no money to buy Hunt out.'

'Father, it's not a question of money. Mr Hunt has more than he will ever spend. He never draws his salary. He's a widower with no children. All he lives for is to waste my time at the warehouse reminiscing about how things were done forty years ago. Why not tell him that if he retires he can still come in when he feels like it? Just say that you value his experience.'

'He'll still want to be paid off.'

'You are right, as always, Father. He'll ask for a pension to save face. He doesn't need it, so offer him say three shillings a week and more when the firm can afford it.'

'That lousy firm hasn't got three shillings, Margaret!'

'I promise you it will soon have that and a lot more. Hunt, O'Brien & Power is perfectly capable of providing you with an income befitting a man of your standing.'

'Listen, Margaret, nobody's going to get a penny while O'Brien's running the show. He's a bloody thief. I ought to arrest him and throw him in gaol with the rebels. They'd tear him to shreds in a week.'

Mr O'Brien had neither the wit nor the courage to be a thief. In any case, all the money that came in was snatched away faster than he could count it, let alone steal it.

'Yes, Father, I agree with you wholeheartedly. He is a thief. I will watch him for you. As soon as I have the evidence, you must arrest him. Meanwhile, with your blessing, I can ensure that he manages your firm honestly.'

'Are you trying to tell me you want to run the show yourself? No, Margaret, the market is no place for the daughter of a gentleman. The atmosphere's hostile. The only reason I'd go there myself is to arrest one of them. The whole bloody lot should be in gaol. They're all bloody thieves.'

The level of liquid in the poteen bottle was descending fast. I had to be quick.

'Of course, Father, I would never disgrace you by going to the market myself but I can teach Mr O'Brien how to make money for you there. As you've often said so rightly, he's weak and gullible and lets the traders cheat you. That's as bad as being a thief, isn't it? So please, let me implore you again, come with me tomorrow and stop him. Mr Hunt and Mr O'Brien will listen to you. They may not say so but they have love for you in their hearts.'

Father's partners had no love for him in their hearts nor anywhere else, but I knew he would not resist the chance to express his heartfelt opinion of them. He despatched unfriendly messages to their homes.

'Be in the office at eight tomorrow morning, I have important things to say. Power'.

I handed Father a copy of the speech I had drafted in unfounded optimism and we rehearsed together for five minutes. Then he fell asleep.

Edmond Power's address to his partners on that windy November morning in 1804 contained few of my original words yet somehow produced the desired result. I recoiled at his forthright irrationality.

'From now on my daughters, Margaret and Ellen will represent my interests here. You'll listen to what they say or you'll listen to me and you won't like what you hear. Do you understand? The old partnership's dead. Now it's me and you, O'Brien – sixty per cent me, forty per cent you, and don't ask for more because that's a lot more than you ever earned.'

After each sentence Mr O'Brien slapped his left hand down with such force that only the pile of unmet demands prevented him breaking through the cracked surface of his old desk. Mr Hunt, short, grey, pot-bellied and baselessly self-assured stiffened to appear businesslike, took illegible notes and spilt ink. The normally dispassionate Ellen froze on her stool. Even I felt momentarily apprehensive.

'And you, Hunt, you've been getting away with murder far too bloody long. It's time to go. You don't do a stroke anyway. But listen, I'm a fair man, my daughters will work out what you're owed and you'll get it when the firm's got it, and not a minute before. Till then you get three shillings a week and consider yourself lucky. You can come in if you like, as long as you don't interfere.'

Edmond Power's message resounded for a hundred yards around, while his trembling partners reacted precisely as I predicted.

As the redoubtable teacher, Dr Parr, taught the world, I had a *'shrewd and masculine mind.'* Today I might be thought a feminist pioneer undaunted by a male environment. I was no such thing. I was simply more mature than most girls of fifteen, more desperate and infinitely more ambitious.

No one said a word. The decree of Edmond Power, sleeping partner, was set in stone. With a final snarl of defiance, he pulled himself up to his full six-foot-three-inches, straightened his tailored coat and strode out of the door. He had business in Waterford. No one questioned its nature.

Mr Hunt blotted his notes, wiped the ink from his hands, shirt and trousers, and boldly followed his former partner at a safe distance. At his favourite tavern he re-enacted the melodrama for the benefit of the disinterested landlord.

'So that was my reward for a lifetime of work and dedication. I shall never again darken the doorstep of Hunt & Company.'

Mr Hunt always used his firm's name from the days when '& Company' meant nobody. Now he had no company at all. He was soon back bearing a pipe of peace smoking with worthless experience.

Mr O'Brien, the nails of his right hand pressing into his left like a lobster's claws, proceeded with the utmost caution. Mr O'Brien always proceeded with the utmost caution. Proceeding with the utmost caution caused all his most expensive mistakes. He would have to learn the abstract art of calculated risk.

Father was now the absent self-crowned king of this desert domain and I his chamberlain. My words were his words and my deeds his deeds. He would take credit and I would take blame. Mr O'Brien's decisions would be my decisions. I proceeded with the utmost caution, like an uncoiled spring.

I slid down from my stool and sat at Mr Hunt's desk.

A long pause.

Mr O'Brien released his left hand. 'What do you want me to do, Miss Margaret?'

Ellen answered for me. 'Take no notice of Mr Power. This was always your firm and it still is, Mr O'Brien. It's not for us to tell you what to do. We are just young girls. We know nothing about the corn and butter trade. No one understands it better than you. We want only to help you, don't we Margaret?'

Ellen's reply was untrue in law, fact or intent.

'How can you help me without poor, Mr Hunt? I know I don't have the right to say so but it was very wrong of Mr Power to dismiss him. He was the finest partner a man ever had.'

Mr O'Brien hated Mr Hunt.

Another pause.

'Don't be upset, Mr O'Brien. You are free to make your own decisions now. Think of all you will be able do,' I said unsympathetically.

'What do you mean?'

'For example, you said Mr Hunt only insisted on keeping open late because it was normal when he started the firm. But now we never see a soul after seven o'clock.'

'Do you really think we should close at seven, Miss Margaret?'

Ellen again replied for me. 'No, I think we should close at five but if you are really busy, Mr O'Brien, of course Margaret and I will stay late. Won't we Margaret? You have often said that you would like to spend more time with your lovely wife and dear little boys. And now you can. Mrs O'Brien will be so pleased.'

Ellen had never met Mr O'Brien's wife or children.

The false science now taught as assertiveness came as second nature to me. I shamed Mr O' Brien into cooperation and, one by one, allowed him to slaughter Mr Hunt's herd of sacred cows which for years had trampled over his ineffectual attempts to alter the status quo.

'I've been trying for years to explain to Mr Hunt that shorter working hours can be more productive,' lied Mr O'Brien.

The next day we arrived an hour later than usual and left two hours earlier, or was it three?

I ticked the first item on my list.

Next, I reminded Mr O'Brien of his legal obligation to inform the customers that Magistrate Power was now the senior partner. Within weeks all the bills were being paid on time, and Mr O'Brien was visiting only creditworthy buyers— to sell them corn and butter.

Another tick.

Entirely on his own initiative, he came to inspect the warehouse.

'Now that you mention it, Miss Margaret, there is an unpleasant stench in here. How many times did I tell Hunt that butter can't be stored for more than a couple of days in the summer? His farmer friend will just have to find another way to fatten his pigs.'

One more tick.

Every week Mr Hunt came as predicted, drew his unneeded three shillings and offered the benefit of his disapproval.

Mr Hunt hated Mr O'Brien.

'How do you expect to do business working half a day, O'Brien? You can't refuse credit because an honest man's a few months in arrears. It's not done in this trade. And why have we stopped buying from Seamus O'Cozener? He's never let me down since his father was best man at my wedding.'

O'Cozener was not the only one of Mr Hunt's devoted suppliers who for years had taken his loyalty for granted and overcharged unmercifully. These affable hard-headed dealers, however, were grateful enough to accept my, that is Mr O'Brien's generous offer of thirty per cent in full and final settlement of their outstanding accounts.

'What a clever idea, Mr O'Brien. I would never have thought of warning them that if we were made bankrupt, they would receive nothing at all.'

Tick.

'Experience enables us to detect the errors of the past, but seldom guards against of those of the future.'

One morning Mr O'Brien found a copy of *Power's Clonmel Gazette* on his desk opened at a competitor's advertisement displaying his delivery tariff. The experienced Mr Hunt always considered that offering such services pandered to idleness and could never be profitable. Within a year Mr O'Brien had five new wagons with *Power & O'Brien* painted on both sides and was profitably relieving our idle customers of the inconvenience of using their own transport to collect more goods than they paid for.

More ticks.

As the firm's fortunes improved, I, that is Mr O'Brien purchased new office furniture and had the premises cleaned and decorated. He had never been able to convince Mr Hunt that the appearance of prosperity creates confidence.

When you are poor you cannot afford to look poor.

I was determined to see the corn and butter market at work with my own eyes and, regardless of his mature anxiety, eventually persuaded Mr O'Brien to take me with him. Father had called the atmosphere hostile, a rare understatement indeed. Traders and farmers shoved, jostled, shouted and cursed in gladiatorial contest. The prize was profit and the contest had no rules.

I was not the only woman at the market but the youngest and most conspicuous. Soon I became a familiar figure in this male-dominated frenzied inferno but feared no abuse. After the enlightening experience of my marriage I had lost interest in the opposite sex, temporarily. I repelled the persistent as easily as I distracted Mr O'Brien's opponents, who in appreciation endowed me with poetic sobriquets which proved of little use when I became a poet.

Bargaining demands quick thinking. I excelled at quick thinking. I thought on and with my feet: one kick meant bid; two meant stop. I hurt Mr O'Brien but not as much as he hurt the sharp dealers who thought they could outwit me – I mean him.

Red ink melted into black. Solomon Watson raised his hat to us as he passed in the mornings. I tore up my list and congratulated the junior partner.

'If only Mr Hunt had listened to you before, Mr O'Brien,' I said.

I must not give the impression that the revival of Power & O'Brien was a quick or easy process. Every day new demons sprang up and threw obstructions in my path. I surmounted them all except the temptation of social ascendancy.

·

5

Sir Thomas Lawrence, tall, aloof and too well dressed for an artist is examining the invisible flaws in my portrait. He wishes that he could take a sharp knife, slash the canvas to shreds and start again.

'Do you not think it is my finest work, Lady Blessington?'

'No I don't, Sir Thomas. How could it be? You surely remember when Lord Blessington brought me to your studio soon after we were married and all the hours he spent telling you precisely how he wanted you to paint my portrait, and how he repeatedly changed his mind. I am surprised that you did not hand him your brush and tell him to paint it himself.'

'I could not afford to do that, your ladyship. Lord Blessington was my most generous client. He commissioned a great many portraits, including great actors of the day in their most celebrated roles. You will have seen my monumental image of John Philip Kemble as Cato, in the National Portrait Gallery. I don't remember how much his lordship paid me for it.'

'But you do remember that dreadful necklace he bought especially for my portrait. It cost him a small fortune and he didn't even notice that you reduced it to a bracelet. I never wore bracelets.'

'Lord Blessington was passionate about your portrait. He wanted it to hang opposite his front door so that his visitors saw it before they saw you. He apparently enjoyed watching them gasp at how much more beautiful you were when they met you in person. He expected me to flatter you and not flatter you at the same time. I worked on it for almost four years and still did not produce a masterpiece.'

'In which case, Sir Thomas, permit me to offer you another chance to produce one.'

'I take it that, like us, Lady Blessington, my subject is dead. How can I be expected to know what he or she looked like?'

'Regrettably, Sir Thomas, no image survives but I can describe him perfectly adequately. He was six-foot three inches tall, handsome, a fine figure of a man but his physical features are unimportant. Capture his contradictory depths as you as did when you painted me and you will have a true masterpiece.'

'Please, go on, your ladyship.'

'I want you to depict, Edmond 'Beau' Power as a sportsman, a genial host, an aspirant nobleman fading into the shadow of his own delusions of grandeur.'

'Indeed, Lady Blessington, this is an interesting challenge. But why do you need a portrait of your father when you recall him so vividly?'

'In order, Sir Lawrence, to show the world that my husbands, lovers and intimate male friends - not including Captain Farmer - were all my father in different guises.'

--

The history of modern Ireland is dominated by its 'time of troubles', the on-going cycle of conflict, tragedy and death terminated by the agreement signed on Good Friday 1998. The document ended the troubles but did not heal their wounds. Perhaps they will never heal. Two centuries ago in Ireland, Edmond Power endured a private time of troubles: another on-going cycle of conflict, tragedy and death, terminated on a given day with wounds that never healed.

One morning early in 1803 Viscount Donoughmore of Knocklofty made an impromptu visit to the office of *Power's Clonmel Gazette*. The de facto proprietor politely ignored the fawning welcome of the legal proprietor and proceeded to rudely interrupt the concentration of his underpaid editor.

'Bernard, how are you? You're looking well. I just called in to congratulate you on the circulation; up almost ten per cent. Well done, my boy. You don't mind if I take a glance at next Saturday's edition? Of course you don't.'

The Irish Representative Peer took the half-finished copy from the editor's desk and scrutinised it intently for almost a minute.

'You're the editor, Bernard, and you can write whatever you like but put in more about England. Do people over here know what is going on in Westminster or the king's views on Ireland? Of course they don't.'

'I'm told that George the Third is opposed to Catholic emancipation, sir.'

'That's because a lot of lackeys tell him it'll weaken his sovereignty. Remember the king of England is also the king of Ireland and always will be. Make the Irish people proud of him, Bernard.' Lord Donoughmore again glanced at the manuscript. 'There's nothing here about the Right Honourable Member for Clonmel's speech in the House.'

'Has Colonel Bagwell made any speeches recently, sir?'

'Oh yes, he has made a quite few. One minute he objects to taxes on essentials being levied on the Irish poor, then one word from Addington and the next minute he's backed down. Bagwell votes with his pocket. Off the record, Bernard, I can tell you for a fact that on two occasions he took hefty bribes to change his vote on the Act of Union, and then had the presumption to up the ante for a third. As I said, it's not for me to tell you your job but people over here have a right to know what is happening in London. Some of them think Pitt's still prime minister. I wish he were. Bagwell would be out by the scruff of his neck.'

'I agree, sir. If anybody could get emancipation through parliament, it would be Pitt.'

'Don't worry, Bernard, Addison won't last long. He wants to introduce income tax. Who's going to vote for that nonsense? Pitt will be back and that's the last we hear of it. Do we agree? Of course we do, so let's come out and support him. Bagwell is a turncoat and we will have no truck with turncoats, will we? No, we will not.'

Edmond Power, once a Catholic, nodded in concurrence.

Donoughmore sat down at a free desk and made the necessary incomprehensible clarifications to the editorial. When he had finished his professional editor scanned the result.

'Are you sure this is what you want, sir?'

'It's not half the story, Bernard, but it will do for now.'

'Then this is how it shall appear on Saturday, sir.'

'Go ahead, Bernard, do as his lordship tells you. I will have only the truth in my paper,' said Father, who read neither the original nor the revised editorial. The anonymous word of the patriotic peer was sacrosanct.

The day Father had irresponsibly assigned the renamed *Power & O'Brien* to my and Ellen's feminine care marked the start of our slow metamorphosis from simple Irish girls into grand English countesses.

'You're right, Margaret, it's bad enough that you and Ellen have to work in trade but I'll permit no daughter of mine to walk the streets with the common herd of this godforsaken town. From now on you will ride like ladies or use a carriage if you need to.'

At last I was free of the mortgaged staleness of Súir Island. At the first opportunity I rode back to Knockbrit. It was eight years since I had seen Miss Dwyer and her book-bound cottage. It might have been eight days. Nothing had changed. My ageless teacher was surprised, delighted and perplexed by the mature fifteen-year-old woman smiling on her doorstep. The few letters I had sent when messengers were available were assiduously purged of my private pains and problems.

'Shall I call you Miss Power, now?'

'Certainly not, you know my name is Margaret.'

'Then you must call me Anne.'

I could not, then or ever, bring myself to address Miss Dwyer by her first name. Nor could I bring myself to reveal that I was no longer Miss Power or the ugly catalysts that accelerated my maturity. I did not even confess my involvement in trade. In Miss Dwyer's scholarly domain, the very word would have thrown up the unsavoury connotations it retained until well into the last century. Still today, there are people unable to accept that business administration involves the intellect and inspiration of a learned profession or an academic discipline.

With transport at my disposal, every evening, as soon as I finished work, I galloped from the dark world of Power & O'Brien into the enlightenment of Miss Dwyer's cottage. I did not rest, eat, drink, wash or change my clothes. Often I stayed late into the night, sometimes all night. I neither feared nor encountered danger on the road. My quest for knowledge permitted no time to ponder such perils.

As a small child I had thought of Miss Dwyer simply as an interesting and amusing friend. Now she revealed her vocation like a garden in perpetual bloom. She taught me Latin, Greek, French, Spanish and Italian. She knew mathematics, history, physics and philosophy. She could unravel the ancient art of rhetoric and the modern science of economics. Together we analysed Adam Smith's newly published *Enquiry into the Nature and Causes of the Wealth of Nations*. Why in the twenty-first century is economics, the most theoretical of the arts, pre-eminent when rhetoric, the most pragmatic, is all but discarded?

No art or science was pre-eminent or discarded at Miss Dwyer's college. She transformed the incomprehensible into the fascinating. She made studious sagacity smoulder with sensation. She taught me the motto of Chaucer's Prioress: *Amor vincit omnia;* Love conquers all. Trade taught me *Aurum vincit omnia.* Gold, the eternal euphemism for money, conquers all. Stripped of sentiment, this shameful precept is honourable and indisputable. I stripped myself of sentiment and mined both love and money.

Having employed a competent clerk to control the warehouse, I now worked on the newly polished leather of my - formerly Mr Hunt's - antique desk and initiated myself into the esoteric art of business correspondence; deferentially dominant and diplomatically decisive. 'May we respectfully remind you of our invariable terms of business…'. I always took my letters to the post office myself because I needed fresh air, exercise and a break in the day. I lied. I went there to meet a young man who came to despatch letters and parcels to his family in Italy which I doubt they received. My Italian was a little better than his English and we soon became close friends, together practising our languages and other arts.

With the exception of Miss Dwyer, Carlos Bianconi possessed the clearest mind I had yet to encounter. He embodied that rarest of unions: a true romantic artist possessed by the spirit of enterprise. Carlos had fled Napoleon's invasion of North Italy and for many months endured atrocious experiences, worked his way across Europe until finally he reached the house of a distant relative at Carrick-on-Súir. With no English or prospect of employment, Carlos began making exquisite engravings of the Irish landscape and peddling them on foot from town to town. His work proved so popular that within a year he had rented a small corner shop near his uncle's house and set up as a fine-art printer and framer. Despite the improbable location Carlos soon found himself with as much work as he could handle, but also with a practical problem. Clonmel, ten miles from Carrick-on-Súir, was the nearest place where suitable materials were sold and the only unencumbered route was the river. Rowing an open boat back and forth in all weathers was an uneconomical time-consuming drudge the young artist did not enjoy.

'There must be a better way, Margaret. The man who will provide Ireland with proper roads and a public transport system will become very rich', he predicted in bad English.

'Then that man will have to be you, Carlos. You don't expect an Irishman to take that sort of initiative, do you? Instead of drawing pictures, draw up some plans,' I suggested in excellent Italian.

And Carlos did draw up some plans; elegant, ingenious, imaginative and impractical. Each time we met, he produced another utopian inspiration for me to correct. His ideas were so clever that I was convinced that they would one day revolutionise the nation's entire transport system and that he would become the most respected man in Ireland.

When I left the country three years later Carlos was still running the corner shop and rowing his boat.

Prosperity returned to Súir Island. Father drew more than his share of the precarious profits of Power & O'Brien and Ellen and I contributed some of our enhanced wages. Michael sold his excess production and fulfilled his deluded obligation to give Father the entire proceeds together with the rents collected from his deferential tenants. And *Power's Clonmel Gazette* remained tentatively profitable.

Father paid the doctor in full for his medicines and hopeless attendances on Edmond and Anne and settled the outstanding school fees for Robert and now Mary-Ann, while Mother employed new maids, who cooked, cleaned, laundered and sewed as badly as their predecessors. As befitted our positions at Power & O'Brien, Ellen and I had new bonnets, dresses and riding habits made by a professional dressmaker. Father extended his wardrobe and rebuilt his stables. He purchased horses and new livery for his grooms and even paid them wages when he remembered. The winners at his card table too received their dishonest share of his children's earnings. I believed this made him happy. I sincerely hope so, because he was about to be unhappy for a very long time.

That evening I returned early from Knockbrit. Approaching the house, I was unnerved by an ominous silence and a dearth of lighted lamps. No horses? No visitors? No singing or shouting?

In our still shared attic room I found Ellen in tears. Ellen never cried. Normally she was the soul of restraint and took all adversity in her stride.

'Whatever is the matter? Where's Father?'

'Downstairs in the wine cellar – where do you think?'

Ellen's contemptuous upward glance expressed her plight in a thousand words.

'Has something happened to Edmond? Is he …?

'They don't expect it to be long. The doctor gave him a potion to put him to sleep.'

Our eldest brother had contracted scarlet fever which compounded his tubercular condition.

'Anne?'

'The doctor said she's showing no sign of the fever at present but it is, or can be, contagious. She looks as white as a ghost.'

Ellen's tears were more of despair than sorrow. I moved closer to embrace her and saw that they were not only for our brother and sister.

'There is something else?'

'I think so. Two men came. Father is in a worse mood than I've seen him for a long time. He keeps saying he's ruined.'

'Who were these men? What did they want?'

'I don't know, men in black suits. I think they've been before. There was a lot of shouting. They left papers. I heard one say five-thousand pounds. They kept using the word libel. I don't know what that means. Telling lies?'

'It's something like that, but I am sure it will turn out a mistake. I'll speak to Father in the morning.' I tried and failed to sound reassuring.

In the morning I did not speak to Father. I spoke to Mother and again tried and failed to sound reassuring. Edmond had not woken from his induced sleep. There was no drama. Mother did not scream out loud as she did when she learnt of my illegitimate conception. She was a devout Catholic. Death, she believed, is ordained by God and therefore brings no disgrace. God ordained just one illegitimate conception and decreed that all others shall bring disgrace. Religion is always rational.

Edmond had not been named after his father but his martyred grandfather and was thus entitled to a funeral befitting a first-born descendant of the noble Earls of Desmond. This was what mattered to Mother. Ancestral pride absorbed her sorrow. All the Desmonds and Sheehys in her hallowed pedigree would be overwhelmed with grief and, from Heaven, join the congregation and mourn with her.

Uncertain if this was within the gift of the dead but mindful of Father's pending ruin, I dispatched Michael to the church to make the most economical arrangements possible. The parish priest managed to say that Edmond's death was a blessed relief. I doubt if it was blessed but it was certainly a relief to all except Father, who had lost the rightful heir to his ever-elusive peerage. He remained grief-stricken until a dawning of sobriety permitted me to make a discreet enquiry about the men in black. Father was in no mood for discretion.

'He's suing *me* for bloody libel. That's what he's doing. What the hell does he think I've got to do with it? He knows I never wrote a bloody word in that stinking, lousy paper and now the bastard has the bloody impertinence to tell me he wants five thousand pounds.'

'Is someone intending to sue you in the court, Father? Who is it? What is he accusing you of?'

'That bastard Bagwell; you know Bagwell, local bigwig, used to be mayor, owns the whole bloody town and half the militia. He calls himself the Right Honourable Member for Clonmel. He never got a vote he didn't pay for. He's got more bloody money than God, but did he pay me when I voted for him? No, he went round telling everybody I was his best friend. What chance do I stand against a pig like that?'

'Surely Colonel Bagwell cannot be claiming that he has been harmed by something you wrote in the *Gazette*?'

I sometimes wondered if Father could write his own name.

'I don't even read that lousy paper, let alone write it'.

'Of course not, Father. Mr Wright is the editor. He decides what goes in the paper and must accept the responsibility. He writes almost everything himself.'

'Wright! Wright? The bastard cleared out weeks ago. I don't know where the hell he is. Maybe he's gone back to France or somewhere they've never heard of Ireland. We've seen the last of him and good riddance, Margaret.'

'How do you keep the paper going without an editor?'

'Lord Donoughmore sends clerks over from Knocklofty. They're useless. Half the editions don't get finished in time to go to print. If Bagwell wins we'll have to close down. I suppose that's what the bastard wants.'

I had been too heavily committed to be concerned at not receiving my complimentary copies in recent weeks. I relied on the more accurate and informative market reports in the *Dublin Freeman's Journal*.

'I do not follow, Father. Who wrote what and why was it in the paper? I'm sure it can't have been serious. Nobody takes any notice of anything in the *Gazette*. There's nothing in it which would upset a kitten.'

'I don't know what happened. It was last December. There were a lot of bloody letters to the editor. How should I know who wrote them? They all came from cowards who signed silly names to make it look like they knew what they were talking about. Bastards! Names like *'Cives'* and *'An Inhabitant'*. Oh yes, one I remember was *'Hibernicus'*. Wright said that's Latin for Irishman.'

'But where did these letters come from?'

'How can I remember where they came from, Margaret? You know Sol Watson, the banker, he sometimes brought things for the paper. There was an article by some pig calling himself *'The Contraster'*. That's the one that upset Bagwell the most. Bastard!'

It occurred to me that this type of incoherent tirade might not be entirely appreciated in a court of law.

'Have you spoken to a lawyer? Mr Grady has been your friend for a long time.'

'Sure I spoke to Henry Grady. He said who wrote what doesn't matter. That's what bastard lawyers always say – it doesn't matter – it's irrelevant. Everything's bloody irrelevant. According to him, it's my paper and I have to pay up. Where does he think I'm going to find that sort of money?'

'What about Lord Donoughmore? You told me he said that he would always be there when you needed him? I am sure he'll help you?'

Lord Donoughmore never helped anyone other than himself.

'The last I heard his lordship was in London. His clerk said he had heavy commitments at the House of Lords. Anyway, if Bagwell hears Viscount Donoughmore's behind me he won't want five thousand, he'll want ten or maybe twenty. Everybody knows Bagwell hates him because he's the better man. The bastard doesn't care about all his lordship does for this country. Bagwell should have been a lawyer. He thinks it's irrelevant; it doesn't bloody matter. All that bloody matters to him is getting himself elevated to the peerage. What sort of man is that? Bastard!'

The summons, like all well-drafted legal documents, was a mass of minutiae, padded out with essential irrelevancies and obscured clarifications.

Henry Deane Grady, a highly reputed Dublin advocate, had a country house near Clonmel and sometimes accepted Father's invitations for what would now be called networking. Father, reluctantly accepting my advice, visited his old friend.

'You and I, Ned, go back a long way. Believe me I am sincerely saddened to find you in trouble. It will be an honour to represent you and, rest assured, I will if I can. When I get back to chambers I'll have my clerk check the niceties of conflict of interest and let you know as soon as possible.'

In lawyer speak this meant Mr Grady was hoping to be instructed by Colonel Bagwell, who he knew could afford a higher fee.

Theology was the one subject Miss Dwyer refused to teach. She had explored the depths of the world's diverse faiths and found solace in none. Religion, she said, had served mankind only as the inspiration for architecture, art, music and literature.

'There is not a scrap of evidence that a so-called god influences the course of life on Earth, and if a god is omnipotent how can it be influenced by human supplication? There is more in the natural world than our minds can absorb without wasting valuable time trying to understand supernatural worlds invented by men to answer the unanswerable.'

I was among the rare creatures born with the strength of mind to combat indoctrination and Miss Dwyer's arguments endorsed my atheism. My parents of course disapproved. God created the aristocracy in His own image and no mortal had the right to repudiate His wisdom. Nonetheless it was appropriate to respect religion in public and, since Father was a convert, I felt free to select any form of Christianity appropriate to the occasion.

I sat in the Catholic church stern-faced, prayer book in hand, a picture of innocent piety, my mind on serious worldly matters. Edmond bequeathed his fever to Anne and brought her suffering to a painful end in just six weeks. My parents, my four surviving siblings and I sat for a second time amidst sacred opulence, stern-faced, prayer books in hand, pictures of innocent piety, our minds on serious worldly matters. Only Mother's mind was not on worldly matters, serious or otherwise. The heavenly host of Desmonds and Sheehys had again come to mourn with her and welcome another departed soul for her to commune with on wet Sunday mornings. The non-Catholic Edmond Power JP, scourge of Clonmel, shed pitiful tears. I tried to comfort him with the heretic prophecy that he would never see the inside of a court of bankruptcy. If that counted as a prayer, it was to be answered. He was not destined to that dreaded fate but to far worse.

'Courage is often the effect of despair for we cease to fear when we have ceased to hope.'

I permitted Father just one night of inebriated grief.

'Whatever it costs you must get Mr Grady or another advocate, Father.'

'And am I to find the money out of thin air, Margaret?'

'Yes, Father, you are and you will. You cannot afford to let a man like Colonel Bagwell see that you are in no position to defend yourself. He must see that you intend to fight and to win. I beg you, go back to Mr Grady and say you will pay whatever he asks.'

'I don't need Henry Grady. No bastard lawyer's worth a smell of anybody's money.'

'You are right as always, Father, lawyers' charges are out of all proportion to their work. But Colonel Bagwell is desperate to preserve his reputation and win the next election. He can afford the cleverest attorneys. If you try to represent yourself, they'll tear you apart like your hounds on a fox. Think of your friend *Viscount* Donoughmore. He is also a politician and used to be an advocate. Wouldn't he move a mountain to defeat an upstart like *Mr* Bagwell?'

My sharp emphases rammed the centre of their target like the arrows of a master bowman. John Bagwell, Right Honourable Member of Parliament, retired Colonel of the Tipperary Militia, millionaire, industrialist, landowner, cohort of the Prime Minister and the Prince of Wales could not procure a seat for himself in the House of Lords. He insisted on being called 'Colonel' Bagwell for want of a better handle to his name.

'Sure Donoughmore can afford lawyers. He said he would be there when I needed him, Margaret. Well, I need him now and where is he?'

I was shocked and relieved. Father had never before omitted his patron's title. I neither knew nor cared where Donoughmore was when he was needed. Miss Dwyer's lessons in rhetoric were there when I needed them.

'Again you are right. Father. Lord Donoughmore is rich but does he pay you for your responsibility to his newspaper? Lord Donoughmore is rich but does he reward you for risking your life him? Lord Donoughmore is rich but will he defend you against his most bitter adversary? Will he pay for your lawyers? Will he testify in your defence? Will he lift a finger to help you? Will he commend you for the peerage?'

I could hardly refrain from shouting 'no' after each of my vitally superfluous questions.

'You're telling me Donoughmore's as big a bastard as Bagwell, Margaret? I'd not thought about it too much, but I suppose you're right.'

'Does it matter, Father? You are worth more than Donoughmore and Bagwell put together. You are more of a man than this whinging Colonel sobbing over a few true words in the paper. He has not lost five thousand pounds; he has lost nothing. Even if he has a case according to the letter of the law, he still has to gamble on the spirit of the law and the sympathy of the jury.'

I believed little of what I had said. I spent the rest of the day forging a petition and discovering that, however arbitrary the process of law might seem, the uninitiated are unwise to intervene.

At the tenth attempt I produced a passible impersonation of a defendant at the 1804 Clonmel Summer Assizes:

'I, Edmond Power, Justice of the Peace, irrevocably deny that *Power's Clonmel Gazette and Munster Mercury* under my proprietorship published letters, articles or statements which can be construed by any interpretation as detrimental to the said Colonel John Bagwell MP.

It is my intention to plead that I have no case to answer. But should the Court be unable to concur, please inform the plaintive that any charge he pursues against me shall be vigorously defended.

The plaintiff's allegations are not only false but deliberately overstated and far-reaching. I therefore humbly request the Court to grant an adjournment until the Winter Assizes which will provide adequate time for me to prepare my evidence and assemble the substantial number of witnesses who will irrefutably establish my innocence.

Signed: Edmond Power, Magistrate, County Tipperary.

Father glanced at my amateurish composition and signed it without comment. I made two additional copies in the hope that one would reach Colonel Bagwell and delivered them to the newly-built Clonmel Court House. The clerk glanced at the fruit of my pains, shrugged and tossed it onto a heap of more important looking documents.

'Advise Mr Power not to expect a quick reply, miss. The judges are all heavily committed at present.'

Having assured the clerk of Father's boundless patience, I returned home thankful that no judge in history has ever been other than heavily committed.

The following morning a messenger appeared bearing a formal communication under the seal of His Britannic Majesty's Courts of Justice:

'The Court has reviewed the petition of Edmond Power JP and finds no reasonable cause to reschedule the case of Bagwell versus Power listed for hearing before Lord Norbury and a special jury on 11th August 1804. The necessary statutory notices advising the Assize agenda were properly served on the due dates, and the time allocated for the preparation of the defence is adequate in accord with precedent.

Counsel for the Plaintiff estimate the proceedings will occupy no more than three days of the court's time.

I beg to remain your obedient servant, etc. etc. …. Clerk to the Court'

It did not surprise me that the judges had been neither heavily committed nor helpful. It surprised me to learn that I had been callously misled. Just three weeks remained to prepare a defence. Father did not seem to care. He said he 'couldn't wait to get the whole stinking business over with', yet he had neglected the whole stinking business for six months. My only hope was that Colonel Bagwell's proposal of a short trial implied that he was unprepared to risk losing a weak case. It implied nothing of the kind. Colonel Bagwell's unenviable reputation and improbable peerage were at stake. Father's unenviable reputation and improbable peerage were also at stake. He returned to his wine cellar and I returned to my writing table. This time I impersonated Mother.

Mother had often spoken of the 'lovely Mrs Mary Bagwell' as if she were a close friend. Before each election this lovely lady made bounteous visits to those women in her husband's constituency less privileged than herself. Every woman in her husband's constituency was less privileged than Mrs Bagwell and was delighted with the little gifts and political tracts she distributed with no intention of influencing their own husbands' votes. Mrs Bagwell never failed to remind them that she was a loving wife and caring mother herself and fully empathised with all their problems. She would surely be sympathetic to a woman who had lost two children. And indeed, the lovely lady sent a favourable reply to my forged request for an audience.

Marlfield House stands high on a hill overlooking the ancient walls of Clonmel. In the early nineteenth century it was the epicentre of the accumulated estates of Colonel John Bagwell MP, a self-made man whose millions were derived from his flour mills and I was not the first to observe the aptness of his name, though my plays on 'bagging well' were more ladylike than most.

Mother seemed more anxious to speak to Mrs Bagwell than I had expected. I agreed to accompany her and, surprisingly, Ellen asked to join us. She said that something had stirred in her memory.

A pair of liveried sentinels threw open the high baroque gates of Marlfield House, admitted our smallest carriage decorated with black ribbons left over from my siblings' funerals, and immediately slammed them shut. The three of us dressed in deep mourning, our faces covered with long black veils, drove on through half a mile of arable wealth and alighted on the golden forecourt of the majestic mansion.

The lovely Mrs Mary Bagwell, disinherited sister of Baron Ennismore, first Earl of Listowel, warmly welcomed everyone to Marlfield House provided they could further the ambitions of her husband and sons. We did not fall within that exclusive category.

'Colonel Bagwell and I were devastated to hear of your tragic losses, Mrs Power. Ah, such a waste of young lives. I trust our wreaths were delivered.'

Mrs Bagwell dabbed the corner of one eye with a tiny lace handkerchief. I did not remember any wreaths being delivered.

'But how might I assist you today?'

Mother floundered through the spontaneous plea for compassion I had taught her. It was a futile exercise. Mrs Bagwell was fully conversant with her husband's affairs.

'I do appreciate your anxiety, Mrs Power. But why, oh why, did Mr Power publish all those horrid lies about my beloved John? You cannot begin to imagine the distress caused to my family. I can hardly bear to think about it.'

Mrs Bagwell now dabbed the corners of both eyes, before delicately tugging at a silken bell cord. A butler appeared with a jug of cold water and one cut-glass tumbler. Marlfield House was renowned for its hospitality. Mrs Bagwell's cooled composure emboldened Mother, who, despite the heat of the summer day, spoke more coherently than I had ever heard her before.

'Mrs Bagwell, we've come to assure you that Mr Power has only the greatest of respect for your husband. Ask anybody in Clonmel. Edmond has always been proud to call Colonel Bagwell his friend. Surely you haven't forgotten how he bought drinks for your supporters at the elections? Edmond would never say a word against his Member of Parliament, let alone print one in the paper. You must have known Mr Wright, the editor. He decided everything that went into the *Gazette*.'

Mrs Bagwell posed with impertinent patience while Mother perspired and persevered.

'I tried to read the letters that upset Colonel Bagwell. I didn't understand a word of them. I couldn't find anything offensive, any insults or even the Colonel's name. Surely everybody's forgotten what was in the paper last Christmas.'

Mrs Bagwell brushed aside Mother's momentary triumph like a crumb on the velvet of her Queen Anne chair.

'Mrs Power, every edition of *Power's Clonmel Gazette* proclaims your husband to be its sole proprietor. He therefore accepts full responsibility for its content. His allegations imply that poor John misappropriated the taxes of the good citizens of Clonmel, the very people he thanked through the *Gazette's* own columns for electing him to Parliament for a third time. Yet Mr Power went so far as to permit his correspondents to accuse my honest husband of stealing from the brave men of the regiment to which he has devoted his life. It is an outrage, Mrs Power!'

Mrs Bagwell again gently tugged her bell cord and her butler replenished her supply of cold water and lace handkerchiefs.

'I don't know where it said all that, Mrs Bagwell but who would believe such nonsense about the Colonel? Everybody in Clonmel loves him and we all love you too. We know how much you both do for the town. *The Gazette* has nothing but praise for you.'

Mother's spontaneous fluency continued to surprise me. Not only was I unaware that she ever read the *Gazette* I had no recollection of anything Colonel Bagwell had done for the town, nor did I know anybody in Clonmel who loved him. The more polite referred to him as the Useless Old Money Bag.

Flattery made no impression on Mrs Bagwell. Sycophants were an inconvenience of her birthright. Her husband was the only untitled member of her family and her first duty was to defend his noble aspirations.

Mother's similar duty accounted for her next agitated outburst of oratory.

'Like yourself, Mrs Bagwell, I am descended from a noble family. You will have heard of the Earls of Desmond. If my father were alive today he would be Lord Edmond Sheehy. He was a great man; a champion of the people, a public servant like Colonel Bagwell. He was a saint like the martyred Father Nicholas, executed with him for no reason at all. My mother was left penniless and alone to bring up her children but Edmond rescued me from a life of poverty and shame. He is a good man, Mrs Bagwell, and you are a good wife and mother. I beg you not to let my family be ruined again.'

Mrs Bagwell rose from her chair and looked down at Mother with benevolent contempt.

'Oh, your father was *that* Sheehy, was he? Well, you are deceiving yourself if you think he and his cousin were saints. They were nothing but a pair of rabble-rousers and wanton murderers. John has told me all about those two – and he should know. His father, William Bagwell, was one of the innocent people they slandered at their disgusting protest meetings. The Sheehys were cowards. Like Mr Power, they used unmistakeable insinuations for fear of naming honest men. And as I recall, they accused their betters of stealing their taxes without evidence, just as your husband is now accusing my dear John. I am sorry to disillusion you, Mrs Power, but your father, his cousin, and all their fellow conspirators were proven guilty beyond reasonable doubt. My father-in-law himself swore in the witnesses and sat as a member of the special jury. No fairer trial was ever held in Ireland.'

Mrs Bagwell paused for breath. I remembered that Father's trial was also to be heard before a special jury.

'I regret I cannot help you, Mrs Power. I bid you good morning.'

The emotion of her long speech made Mrs Bagwell feel quite faint. She tugged the bell cord again and sank into the overstuffed cushions of an ornate settee. Her butler, without water or handkerchiefs, directed us to the door.

Mother and Ellen ran from the room while I lingered to admire the gleaming gilt, pious paintings and clusters of crystal chandeliers that decorated this glorious temple to Mammon; the first of the many in which I would worship.

I tried an approach nearer to its owners' hearts.

'If you will permit me, Mrs Bagwell, your husband is claiming five thousand pounds in damages, yet he has suffered no damage and lost nothing. Perhaps you be good enough to ask him to consider a printed apology and the sum of one thousand pounds? He must surely be aware that that is more than the court will award.'

Mrs Bagwell's patience and her graciously allocated fifteen minutes were exhausted.

That evening a message was delivered to Súir Island.

'My Dear Power,
    The derisory offer conveyed by your family is an additional insult and thus declined.

Bagwell'

6

It is lunchtime. People are coming in to dine in the Wallace Collection's exquisite restaurant beneath the glass roof which now covers the once open quadrangle of Hertford House. Before joining the pressured professionals amplifying their vocal cords to be heard above the music of the unheeded pianist, two solicitors pause to discuss grave matters of law.

'Bricks and mortar, bricks and mortar every time, you can't go wrong,' says the lady solicitor.

'Conveyancing is like watching paint dry. Divorce; that's where the money is. What you want is a husband who doesn't use the loo brush or a sister-in-law who walks out with the heirloom wardrobe under her arm. Five thousand up front, five hundred an hour and tell him he's got off cheap when he has shelled out millions,' says the gentleman solicitor.

'No more whinging matrimonials'.

'The man who doesn't get there is the man who gives up'.

'I've done criminal, it's immoral'.

'Thank God, we don't have courts of morality in this country'.

'But still there are too many miscarriages of justice'.

'There's no such thing as a miscarriage of justice. In the courtroom a lawyer is a bludgeon. You can't do it if you know the facts. Never forget that there are far more guilty people out there walking the streets than innocent ones rotting in gaol.'

'Prison is a soft option for the convicted. It's their families that go through the pain.'

'You'll never win a case if you start worrying about the defendant's wife and kids. No patient would ever get out of the theatre alive if the surgeon gave a damn about the poor sod he's chopping up.'

'I'm thinking of becoming a barrister. A QC charges at least two thousand for a one page opinion.'

'Yes, and what does it tell you? Don't come back here if the judge disagrees. It is not my function to predict your chances. I'm a barrister not a bookmaker. Oh, and my favourite: I am not instructed to provide original ideas'.

'A barrister I once knew successfully defended an Australian pornographer by likening his filthy magazines to the pin-ups they sent out to distract the forces in the Second World War. The innocent publisher prefaced his next edition by naming his learned counsel over a picture of the rear of a naked blonde, and expressing his thanks for "getting me out of the stinky-poos".'

'That, I take it, was before pin-ups demeaned women and the Internet brought the benefits of free pornography to all,' says the gentleman lawyer.

'It was a long time before that. But look at this picture, if this does not demean women I don't know what does. If Sir Thomas Lawrence was alive

This dialogue, with the exception of the last two speeches, is constructed from statements and phrases said by barristers and solicitors to or in the presence of the author.

today, I wouldn't hesitate to prosecute him if I was instructed by a cranky women's libber - and I'd win,' says the lady lawyer.

When compelled by circumstances, I studied the chaotic twists and turns of the learned verbosity of the law. I thought advocacy was my true vocation and felt incensed at being prohibited from the profession by my gender. But overhearing this conversation today makes me realise that I would have made a very poor lawyer. I could never have been so cynical.

--

Broad shouldered and heavy bearded, Henry Dean Grady cut a formidable figure framed by the bay window of his first floor Dublin chambers, his massive oak desk piled high with the dusty briefs of cases long-since forgotten. He was furious. He had not heard from Colonel Bagwell's legal agent and would have to squeeze his old friend's defence into his sparse schedule.

'Ned, I will be honest with you, you have a perfectly winnable case, but it's not going to be easy. It seems Bagwell has briefed Burrowes. I know Peter Burrowes of old. He gives no quarter, and with a rich client like Bagwell he'll have a dozen top attorneys buzzing around him like wasps with stings at the ready. A team to match will not come cheap. It will be a hundred guineas but I will get Curren for you. Nobody in Ireland handles a case like this better than John Philpot Curren.

But I have to warn you, you can never be certain which way it will go in court. I am sorry to have to ask you, Ned, but I dare not represent you without a banker's indemnity.'

This was lawyer speak for lack of confidence in the case and his client's ability to pay. Henry Dean Grady smiled benignly, a picture of self-assurance.

'Listen, Henry, whatever it costs, you're going beat this bastard. Every word in those articles and letters is the absolute truth, and you're going to prove it. Don't worry I'll get you your indemnity. Bagwell's a bigger crook than all you lawyers put together.'

Henry Dean Grady thoroughly enjoyed Father's tasteless joke. His exemplary reputation depended upon overcharging.

Solomon Watson was among the most respected figures in Clonmel. He had been a pillar of the Established Church of Ireland since forsaking the Quaker tradition of his birth in order to receive the Lord's blessing upon the deadly firearms essential to the defence of his customers' money. Mr Watson, like Mr Grady, cut a formidable figure: sombre and aloof, unhealthily thin, close-shaved with the meticulously combed silver hair of a man of integrity and an astute businessman in his own right. He was Power & O'Brien's banker and I thought I knew him well, but the congenial individual who welcomed us into his private office was a complete stranger.

'My dear Ned, how long have we been friends, fourteen, fifteen years, is it? Good God, what sort of people are we if we can't help one another at times like this? You need an indemnity and you shall have one. Don't even think about security: neither of us is going to lose one brass farthing. I know you for an honest man and I will tell you, in confidence and from a lot of experience, Colonel John Bagwell is not that. Everything you published was the truth. The people of this town have the right to know how their so-called parliamentary representative robs them of their taxes.'

I was unnerved. Why was Mr Watson suddenly so supportive and amenable when everything Father owned was already mortgaged to the bank? What made him so confident when Mr Grady expressed reservations?

In the bat of an eyelid it was the eleventh of August 1804. I sat in the public gallery watching the imperious Peter Burrowes stride into the courtroom to open the Clonmel Assizes. With him were twelve feral attorneys in grey wigs; pagan warriors exposing mottled replicas of their brains to intimidate guilty and innocent alike. Burrowes unleashed his case, as the *Freeman's Journal* put it, *'with great force, accuracy and animation'*. His opening speech proved beyond doubt that all gods were redundant while a being as pure and virtuous as John Bagwell MP trod the Earth.

For the first of a hundred times the plaintiff's advocate thundered *The Contraster's* criminally outrageous statement:

> *'What says the patriot and the soldier? That a person honoured by a Commission long-sought from the most gracious and glorious sovereign in the world seeks to weaken the loyalty of those under his command by withholding that sovereign's bounty.'*

Perplexed by the jargon, Father left the court. The bigotry had already made him ill and he went home to take a cure from his cellar. I felt as sick as Father but, come what may, I was determined to hear out the proceedings. Colonel Bagwell was blindingly conspicuous by his absence.

Peter Burrowes cited extract after extract from what he termed *'the essays'*. All were deliberately ambiguous, yet he asserted the unquestionable clarity of their inference. They were monstrous libels against the person of John Bagwell of Marlfield, Member of Parliament for South Tipperary, Colonel of the Tipperary Militia and benefactor of the town of Clonmel. Burrowes shouted contemptuously at the jury the indubitable fact that Edmond Power, an up-start newspaper proprietor, had deliberately set out to destroy his client's reputation and to annihilate his lifetime of unstinting public service.

I thought of Father's ever-absent mentor. Who had given a lifetime of the most unstinting public service, Bagwell or Donoughmore, and who served the public least?

Among Bagwell's unstinting public services was the *'control and direction over the tolls and customs of the town of Clonmel'*. Peter Burrowes would present indisputable evidence that these revenues were without exception legitimately employed for their democratically authorised purposes, and in no other way. He would demonstrate beyond reasonable doubt that his client distributed every last penny of the *'bounties entrusted to him by the Crown'* according to the letter of the law.

The correspondent *'Civis'* had described *'our streets covered with filth, stagnant water and rubbish of every description'*, and the special jury was selected from citizens of Clonmel who endured these conditions every day. Surely they harboured doubts about the deployment of their taxes.

Henry Deane Grady harboured no doubts. He sprang to his feet and entered not one plea, but two: *'Not Guilty'* and *'Justification'*.

The *Freeman's Journal* balanced its report. '[Mr Grady delivered his defence] *in the best manner we ever observed in him.'*

Edmond Power had committed no libel whatsoever. *Power's Clonmel Gazette and Munster Mercury* printed the truth and nothing but the truth. The dissemination of the *'essays'* in question was wholly justified in the public interest. *'The plaintiff's character has not been deprecated: his reputation has not been compromised socially, politically, militarily, financially or in any other way. Yet Colonel John Bagwell dares claim damages of five thousand pounds. Mr Bagwell is not entitled to recover any damages because he has not suffered any injury by the publications in question.'*

The witnesses' names were called: twenty-two for the plaintiff, Bagwell; four for the defendant, Power. Thomas Quin JP, an older and wiser magistrate, appeared for the plaintiff. Mr Quin was the most credible witness in court. His evidence was totally unbiased and thus of no assistance to Bagwell's case:

> *'I believe Mr Power to be a very honest, industrious man of a respectable family… I do believe he is not a malicious man. I have never heard any person declare he was… From my knowledge of him for many years, I believe him to be a man of too much integrity to set forth anything in his paper that he did not believe to be truth.'*

Mr Quin had heard, before and since publication of the alleged libels, that *'men* [under Colonel Bagwell's command] *were defrauded of their bounty'*.

Another plaintiff witness of indeterminate allegiance, a brewer called John Malcomson did not take the oath but affirmed as a Quaker. Malcomson was a popular figure in Clonmel, intelligent and well versed in local gossip. He too had known Edmond Power for many years and considered him *'free from any malignity or malice'*. Cross-examined by Grady's colleague, Mr O'Driscoll, Malcomson claimed to be aware, that about two years ago, Colonel Bagwell had been called before a military court of enquiry into the withholding of soldiers' bounty. The abstemious brewer had heard that this enquiry was presided over by Bagwell's son but could not say how many, if any, of the soldiers' complaints were redressed.

O'Driscoll persisted. Malcomson claimed that Bagwell had *'told him that he would pursue the suit against the defendant for publishing the libel and make him smart for it'*. Then he added a curious statement: *'I told him* [Bagwell] *that Ned Power told me, let the law suit determine as it might, the loss would not fall on himself but upon others.'*

Neither I nor the jury understood the vital implications of this information.

Three spineless demobilised soldiers formed the backbone of the case for the defence. With nothing more to fear from their former commander, Thomas

Hogan, Michael Nagle and James Murphy had gratuitously agreed to confirm that, as implied by the alleged libels, Colonel Bagwell had withheld their rightful service pay.

Mr O'Driscoll knew that the trio had been propositioned and bribed by Bagwell's agent and so pursued Malcomson, who knew this too.

> *'Did they go to Marlfield House some days before this Assizes?*
> *'I have heard they went to play billiards with Colonel Bagwell.'*
> *'And can you tell me if it was then they got their cue and if there was any pocketing in the game?'*

Only lawyers appreciate this type of humour. The judge, Lord Norbury, feigned incredulity and the joke had to be explained to him. No one, he asserted, ever tampered with evidence in his court. This was a better joke but there was no laughter or explanation.

Suddenly Malcomson, called by the plaintiff, mustered the courage to speak positively for the defence. He admitted to having seen the three soldiers - defence witnesses - sign testimonies written by Bagwell's law agent. I felt sorry for the brewer. His courage would ensure that he received no further orders from the hospitable Marlfield House.

None of gentlemanly officers who regularly drank Malcomson's best ale at Súir Island had been prepared to take the stand in support of their host. They had no knowledge of misappropriations, soldiers' complaints or sham tribunals adjudicated by the Colonel's son. Just one man dared to speak out. Recruitment officer, Lieutenant John Garratt, testified that Colonel Bagwell had ordered him to pay the soldiers less than their legal entitlement. Bagwell had ordered him to recruit '*low* [small or weak] *men as cheaply as possible*' and then refused to reimburse his expenses. The Colonel would not disclose what happened to significant '*surplus funds*', such as pay due to deserters. I suspected that the recruitment officer was not as bold as he seemed. I was right. I later discovered that he was Solomon Watson's nephew and had been paid for his evidence by Father's agent.

Sergeant Thomas Hogan, his bribe from Bagwell squandered on liquor, appeared in his shabby old uniform unworn for years. He staggered onto the stand and stammered through the evidence scripted by the plaintiff's lawyers. It was riddled with incoherent lies that failed to contradict Malcomson's sober testimony. Hogan stated that he neither met Bagwell at Marlfield House, nor played billiards there. The plaintiff's agent, he claimed, advised him to say only that he '*told Mr Power he never applied for bounty money… I did not think I was entitled to it*'. Sergeant Hogan's evidence was worthless to both sides.

Corporal Michael Nagle had drunk even more than Hogan and completely forgotten what he had been told to say. Instead he employed his fortified courage to air some long-nursed grievances. Colonel Bagwell had denied him his clothing allowance and made him pay for his uniform from his own pocket. When Nagle asked the Colonel for his "marching guinea", '*he told me not to bother him'*. Unwittingly, Corporal Nagle proved the most helpful of Father's pathetic show of witness.

Sergeant James Murphy did not appear. He was too confused about which side he was supposed to be on. All seemed to be going well for the defence.

Bagwell's counsel called a string of impeccable witnesses: high-ranking officers, magistrates, parliamentarians, gentlemen squires and officials of the Auditor General's office, all composed, coherent, coached and compensated. Pay officers cited a jumble of figures which, they said, showed the honest distribution of all moneys entrusted to their regimental colonel. But the complexity of their evidence posed more questions than it answered. The officers closed ranks so tightly that their sleeves began to fray. Not one of them could recall any complaints against Colonel Bagwell or even a court of enquiry. I discerned stifled laughter.

Opposing counsel massaged and manipulated the evidence, inconsistently repeating incomprehensible phraseology, deliberately boring and confusing the jury. At last John Philpot Curren rose to sum up for the defence and earned his hundred guineas with a speech of Shakespearian stature seldom surpassed in the courts of Ireland.

The twenty-first century inquiries which have done so much to muzzle the British press might have done well to have heeded Mr Curren's plaintive cry for the defence of uncensored expression. Allow me to cite an extract from his speech, as recorded in the '*Accurate and Faithful Report ... of a Trial for Libel... taken in shorthand by Mr Angell of Dublin.*'

> '[I am] *oppressed and heart-stricken by the spirit of departed liberty, before the few remaining privileges of a free country – those of a free press – were consigned to the grave and extinguished forever. This is the action of a rich man against a poor one, in whose person the liberty of the press was to be punished and put down. Would the jury wish to see its annihilation? Would they walk in procession to the grave of its freedom at the command of Colonel Bagwell, and having buried it then bemoan its non-existence? Was it the wish of the plaintiff to extinguish in Ireland the race of printers? He had seized on one of them – caught him; but having entrapped, he would not at once destroy him like a rat but would only burn him in part, singe him on the back, and then send him slinking away among the other terrified creatures of the press to warn them against publishing in future any similar productions. If the plaintiff's views against the press were to be carried out there would be an end to all security against wrongs, all disclosure of abuses. Mr Angell, the reporter then in court, might cease to take notes and at once take his flight to heaven.*'

For two hours John Philpot Curren entranced the jury with poignant chronicles of fraud, deceit, vengeance, venom, nepotism and abuse of office. No honest juror could fail to find for Father.

Mr Curren resumed his seat. It was almost ten in the evening of the third and last day of the trial. Not Peter Burrowes but Bagwell's colleague, the Attorney

General, rose to close for the plaintiff. He commenced with elaborate praise for his learned friend, who had '[lain before the jury] *in every point of view, the object of this action'*. When he had finished pouring burning coals upon Curren's head the Attorney continued:

'I shall not think it necessary to go much at length into a discussion of this case at this late hour of the night... I shall be as concise as possible in the few observations which I have to make.'

He then covered the same ground as his adversary, slowly and systematically failing one by one to demolish his arguments. Unable to match Curren's eloquence he padded and prolonged his few observations in an unending monotone, taking advantage of the jury's and even the judge's lagging concentration in the small hours. From time to time brief flashes of inspiration disturbed their slumbers.

'My client has not brought forward this action on motives of vengeance or to seek vindictive damages. ... He ought not to be any longer a representative for this county but to be driven from the society of gentlemen if he really was guilty of the acts imputed to him. ...

The Attorney General droned on, trivialising the highly damaging assertion that there is *'some impropriety in the conduct of his client and his attorney'*. Hogan and Nagle *'did not say in court anything different from what they declared to be the truth'*. The Attorney General avoided words like bribes, incentives or threats but one fragment of his oratory is worthy of note.

'I know not Mr Power, the defendant: I have heard much of his poverty. I know not but he is as well able to sustain damages as my client: but this I know, gentlemen, that no man should come forward with a dagger in one hand and his rags in the other.'

The judge was as relieved as everyone present when at last learned counsel ended his closing speech. Lord Norbury's instruction to the exhausted jury was brief and succinct. Colonel Bagwell's action was *'good in law'*, and should be sustained.

'I shall leave the whole of this case to you, as to the quantum of damages you may think proper to give.'

It was almost three o'clock on Sunday morning. Colonel Bagwell arrived and took a seat near to me in the public gallery. Peter Burrowes nodded to him affirmatively. Father had lost.

The jury retired for less than ten minutes, found for the plaintiff and awarded him four hundred pounds – with sixpence costs.

At first I was unable to absorb the verdict. Then it all became clear. The judge had awarded no public apology or denial. Four hundred pounds was just eight per cent of the five thousand claimed and less than half of the one thousand I had offered. Sixpence costs was a deliberate affront. Bagwell's expenses would run to many hundreds of pounds. Father had won.

Outside the courtroom I hugged and kissed Mr Grady and Mr Curren. They were horrified. There was no place for demonstrative feminine gratitude in the judicial code.

Colonel Bagwell did not speak to his attorneys. He had not paid them for a pyrrhic victory. Before leaving he turned to me. 'Miss Power, be good enough to tell your father that he can expect to see me again in court.'

The proven patriot and soldier neither appealed against his award nor brought another action, but he and Father were indeed destined to face one another across the hard wooden benches of the Clonmel courtroom.

A week later the legal proprietor of *Power's Clonmel Gazette* in an ink-stained leather apron proffered a cool welcome to an expected visitor. Viscount Donoughmore paid no heed to the appearance of his normally over-dressed minion.

'No doubt your lordship heard the news when you were over in England. You were sorely missed in court, sir.'

His lordship offered an affable apology, as if he had been a minute or two late for an insignificant appointment.

'Unavoidable, Beau; you know I would have moved heaven and earth to have been there, but heavy commitments - the call of British Government. Did you need me? Of course you didn't. Well done, my boy, there could not have been a better result all round. The important thing is that you and the paper were cleared of wrongdoing. Bagwell won't bother you again. He's got what he wants. Now he can go round saying his good name has been upheld in a court of law. Nobody will listen of course but nor will they sue him for stealing their taxes. It's a shame, but come on, Beau, let's forget Bagwell and get the paper out.'

'That, as you can see, your lordship, is what I am trying to do. I'm down to printing it myself. Reynolds has gone. There was a big row after Wright wanted to stop him printing the letters and articles about Bagwell. They both knew who wrote them and one of them must have destroyed the originals in case the handwriting gave the culprit away. Somebody must have paid a lot of money to keep them quiet.'

Viscount Donoughmore showed no indication of understanding Father's inference.

'Don't worry, Beau, the world out there's full of editors and printers. I'll send over a couple more boys from Knocklofty until you find replacements. Meanwhile, I have some news but it's not for the paper just yet. There have been new gangs of rebels spotted in the region. You'd prefer to do some real work, wouldn't you? Of course you would.'

Lord Donoughmore's clerks knew no more about editing a newspaper than Father. The *Gazette* became a ghost of its short-lived glory. Circulation dropped. Advertisers withdrew. Recruitment proved impossible. Who would join a newspaper en route to the graveyard? A front-page appeal to '*the astonishing number of persons who are indebted to this paper for advertising and by subscription*' yielded nothing. And at the end of 1804 *Power's Clonmel Gazette and Munster Mercury* silenced its depreciated modern press forever and Edmond Power washed the printers' ink from his hands for the last time.

Colonel Bagwell proved that rarest breed of litigant genuinely more concerned with principle than money. He did not even pursue Father for his derisory award. As Donoughmore predicted the honourable Member of Parliament spent more on publicising his exoneration than on the case itself.

In accord with the time-honoured convention of the bar, the clerk to chambers permitted a respectable interval to elapse before submitting:

'Henry Deane Grady, of counsel, presents his compliments to Edmond Power Esquire, Justice of the Peace in the counties of Tipperary and Waterford, and begs to inform him that the cost of his defence in the matter of Bagwell versus Power amounts to six hundred and thirty-two pounds, inclusive of expenses.'

The included expenses were not itemised. It was unthinkable that an honourable barrister's charges might be disputed. Indeed, Solomon Watson asked no questions before honouring his indemnity - in a curious fashion.

'I'll be perfectly honest with you, Ned. Don't let this go any further but I can tell you Colonel Bagwell is an important customer. He deposits a lot of money with my bank and I cannot afford to upset him.'

This was hardly a betrayal of confidence. Even Father could appreciate that if Bagwell discovered how the defence was financed it might be highly embarrassing for Mr Watson.

'But you've no need to concern yourself, Ned. There is a simple enough solution. I have had a word with another customer, Charles MacCarthy. You remember Charles? I introduced him a few weeks back: charming man, very rich? Well, he has agreed to pay your indemnity from his account here, after which I'll reimburse him and nobody will be any the wiser. Charles will be staying at the Great Globe on Wednesday. Meet him there for a drink and he'll sort everything out.'

This arrangement sounded inexplicably devious to me but Father was in no position to argue. Mr Watson was fully aware that Father was unable repay his loans from the bank and had every right to withhold the unsecured indemnity, yet he proved as good as his word. Mr MacCarthy gave Father a draft, and Mr Grady's clerk gave him a properly stamped receipt. In drunken celebration of the demise of *Power's Clonmel Gazette*, Father lambasted Bernard Wright, James Reynolds and everyone connected with the paper. Only Viscount Donoughmore, guardian of his future peerage, escaped his wrath. Again and again, he slurred the same old incantation.

'Newspapers, they're another stinking trade, that's what they are, a bloody mess. All trades are a stinking bloody mess. I'll have no more to do with trade. No trade will ever be good enough for a gentleman.'

Trade had to be good enough for the daughters of a gentleman. Ellen and I were left to clear up the stinking bloody mess: an unpleasant, time-consuming and expensive business. Mr O'Brien charitably donated the firm's stretched resources. If his partner were declared bankrupt, then he would be too.

Lord Donoughmore donated nothing. Why should he? He never had any connection with *Power's Clonmel Gazette*.

'My dear Beau, in twenty-four hours that paper and everything in it will wash away with the tide and all will be forgotten. Of course it will.'

Injustice is never forgotten in a day.

Father did not forget the case he had lost and won. Soon he was back in full frilly harness boasting of the testimonies to his honest and upright character. He lost no opportunity to tell the disenfranchised of Clonmel how, in court, *he* had vanquished their despised Member of Parliament. Simultaneously, their despised Member of Parliament lost no opportunity to tell the enfranchised, how, in court, *he* had vanquished their despised newspaper proprietor. Both had been absent throughout the trial.

For two more years Michael, Ellen and I continued to support Father's folly. He ignored all our appeals to attend to his financial affairs, and resumed his unaffordable entertaining and hunting with the faithful friends who had vanished when he required their aid.

'Those who would preserve a faith in friendship should never require its aid.'

We did not ask how Father spent his days or the nights when he did not return home. We closed our ears to the ubiquitous gossip. Ned Power, magistrate, sportsman and gentleman, indulged in everything from violence, theft and fraud to employing prostitutes and attending orgies. The most disturbing of these whispers persists in Clonmel to the present day. My birth mother, say the knowing, was a mistress of Lord Donoughmore who paid Father to take me off his hands.

Do the purveyors of this nonsense really think that if it were true I would not have exploited my noble origin to the hilt? There is not a scrap of evidence that Donoughmore had a mistress let alone a child. He was never married, and like all rich lifelong bachelors was rumoured to be homosexual. I have no evidence of that either.

The months passed uneventfully. Michael, hampered by dwindling resources, continued to provide our food and maintain Father's land without assistance. Power & O'Brien, operating from larger offices and employing a full complement of staff all working a twelve-hour day, struggled but remained profitable. By my seventeenth birthday, I had mastered the self-fulfilling art of delegation and coached Mr O'Brien so thoroughly that I had rendered myself redundant. I could hardly wait to leave and seek new challenges, and Mr O'Brien could hardly wait for me to find them.

Still I went to Knockbrit; to the exclusive school where Miss Dwyer taught me how to consume and draw nourishment from the great minds of the past, and predicted that I would one day be among them. I would be a luminary and walk with kings but first had to lose the common touch. I rehearsed like a Shakespearian actor, mimicked the sounds of an entire menagerie, blew bubbles in water and breathed and panted like an exhausted athlete but my Irish lilt, which everybody but me found so delightful, stubbornly persisted.

Ellen was equally ambitious – in many ways more ambitious – and although she sometimes came with me to take advantage of Miss Dwyer's free education, she did not share my passion for learning. She chose a different kind of tuition which was far from free. Sometimes I went with Ellen to her tutor who charged by the hour, sixty minutes precisely, for lessons in the attainments of the lady of fashion. The lady of fashion does not concern herself with money. Her husband provides for her needs and pays a hierarchy of servants for her to supervise in accordance with a strict code of rules. The children of a lady of fashion are brought up and educated as dictated by inflexible convention and without the intervention of parental love. The lady of fashion occupies herself with more edifying matters: elegant entertaining, etiquette, personal adornment, music, embroidery, dancing, deportment and, most important of all, elocution.

I must not convey the impression my last two years in Clonmel involved no pleasure. Quite the contrary, memoirs of local contemporaries abound with anecdotes involving two exceptionally beautiful young sisters enlivening the town. Ellen and I loved the amateur theatre and often performed ourselves. Well-off parents of eligible sons regularly invited us to balls and parties. Since I was married, I very properly discouraged serious suitors and mindful of my misadventures, Ellen too sidestepped her many admirers, or so she told me.

Michael showed no further signs of the sickness that had marred his childhood. He grew as tall and handsome as Father and from unrelenting labour developed a muscular physique but remained cursed by his gentle self-deprecating nature, and thus did not attract the opposite sex. I myself had little patience with unassertive men. He was still only nineteen and time was on his side, or so I thought. Meanwhile he still showed no more interest in continuing Father's ethereal noble line than Father showed in his heir's practical husbandry.

'What are you doing wasting your time digging potatoes? Get on your horse and do some man's work. What are you scared of - a few no-good rebels?'

Michael did not get on his horse but was indeed wasting his time. Digging potatoes would never earn him enough to buy a commission in the British army. And even had wealth and honour been realistic rewards for pursuing insurgents by 1806 few remained to pursue. But as their numbers grew less, Magistrate Power's zeal grew more. Still he took his prisoners, regardless of guilt.

The Court of his Britannic Majesty, not arresting magistrates, administered justice in Ireland.

I have to confess there was one suitor that I made no effort to repel. He was not my first or my last extra-marital lover, but the only one I loved in the true sense of the word. He was the only one undeterred by my intellect, my involvement in trade or my marriage. And he was the only one I was foolish enough never to deceive.

'Dr Madden, Mr Sadleir, Mr Molloy, you all know who I am talking about but before I say more, let me correct your misconceived versions of our meeting. Father did not introduce him to me, as you seem to think. Edmond Power seldom learned from his mistakes but after the debacle of my marriage he never again attempted to influence his daughters. And Captain Thomas Jenkins was not a man to carouse with the vulgar bourgeoisie. He never set foot on Súir Island or met Edmond Power.'

In the summer of 1806, Ellen and I received an improbable invitation. "Miss Anne Dwyer requests the pleasure of your company ...". Could Miss Dwyer really be holding a dinner party? I had never seen so much as a casual visitor at her cottage. 'I would like to introduce you to some relatives, my cousin's children,' was all she would say. We accepted more out of curiosity than the expectancy of a pleasurable evening. Did a solitary soul like Miss Dwyer know how to entertain? An unnecessary question. My omnipotent teacher was an accomplished hostess. Her bookshelves were dusted, her table decorated with wild flowers and French wine had been delivered from Dublin.

We arrived before Miss Dwyer's relatives, who we assumed to be female and middle-aged, and were thus pleasantly surprised when two young officers in dress uniforms dismounted outside. Thomas was twenty-seven and his brother, Stadfast, a year younger. They were tall, upright, fine-featured, and exuded the breeding of true gentlemen. It was my first encounter with that supreme breed of mankind which naturally spoke the King's English with a flawless accent. Educated at Eton and Oxford, they had completed grand tours of all the civilised lands of Europe and Asia. They drank without drunkenness, ate without gluttony, laughed without vulgarity and conversed without trivia. This dinner party would be the paradigm I would fail a thousand times to replicate as a society hostess.

Miss Dwyer had never spoken about her background but now revealed that she was born in England, the only child of an Irish father and an English mother descended from a long-dispersed noble family. Miss Dwyer's parents had lived and prospered in Ireland but had both died young leaving her their sole heir. She was not a spinster by choice. She had buried three fiancés. But Miss Dwyer's past did not interest us as much as Thomas and Stadfast's future.

In the weeks that followed I was too heavily committed to my own affairs – should I say affair – to think about Father's. In fact, by then I seldom gave him any thought at all, until the morning I discovered him in the dining room pouring over sheaves of legal papers spread across the dining-room table. A more uncharacteristic pose was hard to imagine. He had been subpoenaed to present an onerous testimony in court, yet he declined my offer to write or edit it for him.

I was in love and had no desire to waste irredeemable time following the minutiae of another indecipherable legal battle. But I did. Edmond Power, magistrate and gentleman, was embroiled in a civil action so absurdly monstrous in its complexity that *Bagwell v Power* was a pantomime by comparison.

Again on a hot summer day I climbed the stairs to the public gallery of the unventilated Clonmel courthouse. It was 14th August 1806, precisely two years after his last court appearance, Edmond Power JP stood tall before a judge and jury at the Clonmel Summer Assizes. He was neither plaintiff nor defendant but the principal witness in the matter of *MacCarthy versus Watson.*

The issue was straightforward enough. Charles MacCarthy asserted that Solomon Watson had failed to reimburse him for the indemnity he had paid Edmond Power at the Great Globe. There was more to it than that of course. Unknown to me, the case had been summarily heard at the Waterford Spring Assizes, where no verdict had been reached, and Watson, as defendant, had called for a retrial. This was extraordinary. Solomon Watson was a wealthy man and could comfortably afford six hundred and thirty-two pounds. More extraordinary still, Mother and Ellen were listed to appear for the plaintiff. Neither had met Charles MacCarthy and refused to tell me why they had agreed to support him.

I observed some familiar faces in court. Watson had briefed Peter Burrowes and a defence team including Henry Deane Grady. Mr O'Driscoll, who appeared for Father in *Bagwell v Power,* led MacCarthy's ten senior attorneys. The legal costs on both sides would far exceed the sum at stake.

The court clerk read out the correspondence between the parties. MacCarthy demands six hundred and thirty-two pounds. Watson *'does not perfectly understand'.* MacCarthy threatens legal action and adverse publicity. Watson simply acknowledges receipt of the letter. I was confused.

The first witness, a curiously named magistrate, Lorenzo Hickey Jephson confirmed that '[he had known Mr Power] *a number of years'* and that he was *'a man deserving credit on his oath.'*

The creditworthy Mr Power spent an entire day in the witness box, but subjected to barbarous cross-examination he answered all the attorneys' questions clearly and fluently. I felt proud of him though I guessed that he had been coached and bribed. Suddenly there was a revelation.

> *'Were you ever tried in a criminal business?'*
> *'Never.'*
> *'Do you count a trial for assault and battery a criminal business?'*
> *'No, indeed I do not.'*
> *'Were you ever tried for an assault?'*
> *'I was once tried for an assault and wrongfully found guilty.'*

I was prepared to believe him. It was probably a minor incident long ago. Father never resorted to unprovoked violence; but I was not prepared to believe that he lied to me about his dealings with Mr Watson.

MacCarthy's counsel alleged that Watson brought the libellous letters to our house and secretly dictated the *'essays'* for publication. Father replied that he was *'confident'* that Watson was their author and immediately contradicted himself. *'Watson was not capable of writing so severely'*. Yes, Watson's bank had lent him the hundred guineas to pay John Philpot Curren aside from the indemnity. Responding to Mr O'Driscoll, he revealed that Viscount Donoughmore had recommended him to approach the bank to fund his defence. This was a surprise but I was relieved that Father had at last openly associated Donoughmore with the *Gazette*.

There were more surprises to come. Mother testified that she was afraid to come forward at Waterford but now said that Mr Watson was in the habit of coming to our house during the day and bringing papers for Father. From snippets of overheard conversation, she was convinced they were the libellous articles and letters and was sure that Watson had written them. She had never trusted Solomon Watson and *'received him coldly'* believing that he would get her husband into trouble. Ellen then testified that when she was twelve or thirteen she too saw Watson and the printer James Reynolds at our house a number of times. *'They would call for pen, ink and paper which I brought and always left the room'*. She recalled Watson saying, *'we have the best thing of all, about the patriot and the soldier; it is the severest thing against the Colonel.'*

So this was what stirred in Ellen's memory when she asked to come to Marlfield House to appeal to Mrs Bagwell's better nature. Still I could not believe that the shrewd and prudent Solomon Watson could have written the alleged libels. I was not called to give evidence. I knew nothing to the detriment of our banker and would not have testified against him if I did. Power & O'Brien was dependent on his goodwill and I was not present at the clandestine meetings at our house, which I suppose took place while I was preoccupied in Clonmel prior to my marriage.

The proceedings dragged on. I listened patiently to the interminable repetition of witness after witness and the incomprehensible explanation of counsel after counsel. *Bagwell v Power* was contested all over again. Hairs were split over the authorship of the so-called libels. But this was a side issue. What mattered was who paid who? Who did not pay? And why?

Lengthy testimonies overflowing with irrelevancies, true and false, degenerated into an intricate labyrinth from which the judge himself could find no exit. I watched the Right Honourable Mr Justice Daly taking meticulous notes, apparently losing the thread of both arguments and ineffectually scratching his wig. Eventually he concluded:

'In every view of this mysterious case there were difficulties to be met with... which involved the guilt and baseness of one or other of the parties to this suit'.

This is as close as a judge ever comes to admitting defeat. He directed the jury to order Watson to pay MacCarthy three-hundred-and-sixteen pounds: precisely half the sum claimed – the Judgment of Solomon.

The reputation of Watson's bank was more enhanced than damaged by the exaggerated press reports in the aftermath of these bizarre proceedings. Father's reputation was enhanced too, or so he thought. He could, and of course did, boast that in open court he had been proclaimed a man of honour who paid his debts. Colonel Bagwell's reputation was not enhanced. Again, enraged by the verdict, he swore that he would 'see Edmond Power smart in court'. This would transpire to be one of the few promises the Honourable Member for Clonmel kept through his long and undistinguished political career.

Determined to learn the truth, I obtained a copy of the trial transcript and spent a day ploughing through a hundred speeches and testimonies, dissecting, destroying and misinterpreting until a grotesque canvas emerged. The obvious solution obliterated by pretentious phraseology had defeated the learned judge and it defeated me – until the next time I saw Solomon Watson outside his bank. As always, or at least since Power & O'Brien became solvent, he raised his hat and greeted me with cultivated pleasure. I had only to glance once at the cold, affable integrity radiating from our banker's undernourished face to solve the mystery of *MacCarthy v Watson*.

Solomon Watson was the most respected banker in Tipperary and a senior member of the Clonmel council. He had been impaled by the horns of a terrible dilemma. He held irrefutable evidence that Colonel Bagwell had defrauded the town council and misappropriated substantial sums intended for the men of the militia. But Mr Watson was a man of honour who rigidly held to the highest principles of his profession. He could never breach confidentiality, even in court under oath, though he felt it his public duty to expose the crimes of his richest and most powerful customer.

He had thus been relieved when another customer, Charles MacCarthy, no friend of Colonel Bagwell, offered to finance the publication of the truth and to cover the costs should the politician sue. MacCarthy gave Watson the letters and articles and money to pay Father to print them. Watson then brought them to our house where he met James Reynolds who he also paid to make copies for typesetting. Watson then returned the documents to MacCarthy.

When Father lost his case against Bagwell, MacCarthy insisted on paying Father's indemnity himself at the Great Globe, or anywhere other than at the bank. This had made Watson suspicious. He inspected MacCarthy's account and discovered funds deposited by Lord Donoughmore, another customer. Realising that he had been deceived, Watson refused to reimburse MacCarthy because his lordship had already paid him the six hundred and thirty-two pounds. Not only that, but Donoughmore had deposited more money in MacCarthy's account than he had given to Watson to pass on to Father and Reynolds. Donoughmore had also funded Mr Curren's hundred guineas.

MacCarthy remained unaware that Watson knew about the Donoughmore deposits and boldly took legal action, supported by Father who was also unaware of the truth.

Bernard Wright resigned immediately upon discovering that Reynolds had printed the offending documents against his expressed wish, whereupon Reynolds immediately destroyed his copies and disappeared.

Neither Watson nor MacCarthy was the author of the alleged libels. Only a mind as devious as that of Viscount Donoughmore could have composed such vicious attacks on his nemesis Bagwell and devised such an intricate plot to distance himself from them. On discovering the deposits Solomon Watson guessed that Donoughmore was the author of the letters and articles, but again his moral principles prohibited him from favouring one customer over another.

The judge too might have guessed the truth but could not believe that there is such a thing as an honest banker.

'The really good and high-minded are seldom provoked by the discovery of deception; though the cunning and artful resent it as a humiliating triumph obtained over them in their own vocations.'

If I could find a path through this chequered maze which defeated a distinguished judge and learned counsel, I could face the future with self-assurance and determination. I was ready to leave Clonmel forever.

The gallant Captain Jenkins reciprocated my love. Together we celebrated the warm summer evening of my seventeenth birthday by taking a picnic into the hills above the medieval town of Clonmel which frame a picturesque panorama when it is not raining. Against the backdrop of a scarlet harvest moon Thomas fell to one knee and in the finest English tradition asked for my hand. This was predictable enough but I was unprepared. I blurted out that I was already married and presumed that I had ended another ill-fated romance.

Thomas showed no hint of surprise, disappointment or anger. Why should he? He was English. In fact, he said nothing at all. He simply motioned for me sit beside him on the grass and listened while I explained the inexplicable. He listened for an hour, two hours, more perhaps. Thomas was a good listener. I needed a good listener to explain the passions competing in my mind. My tears flowed. Thomas remained silent. He could think of nothing to say. To a captain of the Eleventh Light Dragoons, I probably sounded like a general on the eve of battle ordering him to plan a campaign. At last he spoke.

'Yes, I know all about St Leger Farmer. Everyone knew he was raving mad. He was certified insane, twice I was told. Usually the army hushes up rows between officers but Farmer was so deranged they were afraid he would do some serious damage. The court-martial was a sham to get rid of him. Do you know where he is now?'

'His father found him a job with the East India Company.'

'The East India Company! Sane men often can't take the life in India for more than a few weeks. A man like Farmer wouldn't last five minutes. He'll be back by now.'

'My sword of Damocles.'

'I'll make enquiries through the army, Margaret. When I find him, I will get him to grant you a divorce or have your marriage annulled.'

'Maurice will never listen to you but he's bound to be in need of money.'

'We will soon find out. Meanwhile, Margaret, I cannot permit you to return home. Your father can manage without you. From what you tell me, it might bring him to his senses. Look, I have a house in Dublin. You can live there until the end of my assignment. Then we will be free to go anywhere you wish, London, Paris, Rome.'

'What about your family, Thomas?'

'My father died four years ago and Stadfast will support whatever I do. Then there is only my mother and she's out of the same mould as Aunt Anne. There will be no point in trying to keep anything from her. You can rest assured of her discretion. As soon as I possibly can, I will take you to meet her at my family estate in Hampshire. You will love her, Margaret.'

'But what will they think in Dublin when they learn that you have a young woman living in your house?'

'We shall tell them that we are married. Listen, I Thomas take you Margaret to be my unlawful wedded wife. There you are, it is true, we are married. You are Mrs Thomas Jenkins and tomorrow morning you shall have a wedding ring.'

I doubt that either Thomas Jenkins or Maurice St Leger Farmer adhered to any form of Christian faith but I thought it reasonable to presume that, since I was now married to two non-Catholics, Catholicism could lay no further claim to my heretic soul. I stopped crying and began laughing. My fairy-tale fantasies, my only faith, had come true.

We are not told how Cinderella coped with the practicalities of living happily ever after, nor do we know why it never occurred to her to check that her prince was all that he appeared to be.

7

I have been sitting too long. I stand up, stretch my legs and step for a moment into the adjoining gallery. A tall mirror with elaborate gilded carvings reflects my present image and, through the open doorway, my past portrait. The over-simplistic affectation of modern fashion suits me better than the chaste romance of the equally uncomfortable satin gown in which Lawrence portrayed me.

An egocentric looking student, long dark hair falling over one eye, is scanning my portrait as if he is a connoisseur. He knows all about me. He knows all about everything and everybody except the girl with him, another student, the more intelligent of the two. Keeping my back turned, I watch them in the mirror and listen unobserved.

'Fancy her do you? Should I be jealous?'

'No, it's not that. When we came in earlier, I'd swear there was a woman sitting here on the divan who looked exactly like this Countess of Blessington. Didn't you see her, very smart, heels, designer handbag? It wasn't so much the resemblance, the raven hair and so on; there was something unnatural about her.'

'I suspect she was another boring art lover, like you.'

'Maybe, but she had the same condescending expression. Look at that face in the picture and you'll see what I mean. Doesn't she remind you of Margaret Thatcher in those old interviews: "I am right and you are wrong but I shall patiently explain"? What a pity old Lawrence couldn't paint an exasperated sigh.'

'Do you think that's how she was: too clever and presumptuous to bother with mere mortals? Some men go for women like that. You do fancy her, don't you?'

'I've read about her. She had a split personality. On the one hand she was a big-time intellectual, a writer, and on the other a good-time girl who blew her husband's money on affairs with blokes half her age. Maybe I do fancy her. I'll go and see if I can find her lookalike, shall I? '

The girl nudges his ribs and laughs. She does not find his joke at all funny. Of course he fancies me, bright young men always did. I had better stay where I am. I rather fancy him.

'She looks like an old tart to me. What was she, a rags-to-riches case?'

'Not entirely. Her father was a small landowner who ran the local newspaper in some Irish backwater. Got himself into all kinds of scrapes and ended up doing a murder. I must look them up again when I get back. I like a good murder.'

'Aren't there enough murders for you on television? '

'You mean those tuppenny-ha'penny American Sherlock Holmes re-hashes, where a criminal mastermind plans a murder to the nth degree and leaves a million clues for an idiot detective to find. They're all nonsense. Premeditated murder is virtually an unknown crime. I've seen the statistics. There were about three in England last year. If you have enough time to think about killing somebody, then obviously you're going to change your mind.'

'Did your sexy countess kill anybody?'

'Not as far as I know. She probably wanted to but, as I said, she was a writer. I suppose she put a murder or two in her novels, otherwise they wouldn't have been so popular.'

'Precocious wisdom is almost as much to be deprecated for youth as the premature maladies of age. Neither should arrive before the proper season as their presence indicates constitutional debility.'

I would like to correct the misconceptions of the precocious wisdom of this clever young man, but the girl wisely pulls him from my portrait and allows me to return to my biographers, anxious to learn more of what they omitted from their works.

--

The impractical enchantment of an elopement had worn off by the morning after my marriage of convenience. I had been rescued by a virtuous prince but I was nobody's idea of a maiden in distress. A thousand objections gyrated in my mind. How could I abandon my unappreciated achievements and delegated responsibilities? How could my parents and siblings survive without me? Were there yet more troubles in store for Father? Could I tear myself from Miss Dwyer? What sort of life awaited me in Dublin? Overestimating myself and underestimating everyone else – a practice I would invariably commend – I dutifully and methodically prepared myself to forget Clonmel forever.

'By relying on our own resources, we acquire mental strength but when we lean on others for support, we are like an invalid who having accustomed himself to a crutch, finds it difficult to walk.'

Following Father's trail, my brave English lover took a small detachment of dragoons and in the true spirit of St George rode forth unto Ballitore to seek out the heinous dragon and wrench my future from its evil fangs. At Poplar Hall, Thomas discovered, not a desolate house of horror but a thriving estate inhabited by an amiable squire and his young family.

'That's right, sir, this is Sir Fystite Farmer's old place. It's a year now since I bought it. You cannot imagine the state it was in. We had to perform miracles to get it back into shape.'

'Did you meet, Sir Fystite?'

'I'm glad to say I never had that pleasure, sir, but his agent told me all about his mad son and the child bride. Not that he needed to; even now it's all they talk about around here. They say young Farmer disappeared, and she went home and started calling herself by her single name, Powes or something. Sorry business!'

Thomas dismissed his men and continued on to Dublin to confront my father-in-law's agent.

'I've not heard from St Leger Farmer or his family since the sale. And frankly, if I never hear from them again it won't be too soon. Knowing Sir Fystite I don't expect he would have had anything more to do with his son after he packed him off to India. Walter Farmer? He's as mad as Maurice. He's gone to live in England.'

'There was a housekeeper, a Mrs Ardboyle. Do you know where I can find her?'

'I wish I did, sir. She and the coachman took six horses and two carriages, loaded them with everything they could lay their hands on and that was the last anybody saw of them. I reported the theft to the local magistrate but he did nothing. I wouldn't be surprised if he was in with them.'

For three weeks, Thomas persevered. He spoke to every man who had served or had any dealings with Captain Farmer. None could offer a clue to his whereabouts. All Thomas ascertained was that knowledge of my misadventure was far more widespread than either of us had imagined. Intuitively, I knew that Maurice was still in India but Thomas was more optimistic. He thought it most probable my husband had fallen victim to an oriental disease or, more conveniently, had died or been killed.

I set about making impractical arrangements for my departure. I tried to behave normally and behaved abnormally. The illusion of an English paradise overshadowed my every waking act. Thomas agreed that it would be unseemly for us to go to Dublin immediately. Meanwhile we would meet only in places where no one knew me and where we would be free from prying eyes. Prying eyes observed us in Tullow, in Fethard, in Waterford, in Cahir and as far away as Dungarvan by the coast. As the reports of our overt trysts became more lurid, Mother became more realistic.

'You and your clever carryings on, haven't you brought enough disgrace on this family? It's always you that gets your father into trouble, and after all he's done for you. He's too soft; that's his problem. When the new king honours his bravery, you can put your high-flown education to good use for once. You can write my name among the descendants of the Earls of Desmond: Lady Ellen Power, daughter of Edmond Sheehy, wife of Lord Edmond Power of Curragheen, imagine that.'

I was neither capable of imagining that nor being so cruel as to question Mother's reasoning. It was her way of telling me that she would be the happiest woman in Clonmel if I left.

Thanks to my ceaseless accolades, Miss Dwyer had become inundated with offers of new students and would probably be delighted to hear that I was going to put her tuition to good use. Before saying goodbye, I blurted it all out – well, most of it – but for all her scholarly dispassion Miss Dwyer was fully aware of my history. She said there was nothing shameful about my living with Thomas as his wife and gave me some books by advocates of free love. Their arguments were unconvincing.

Miss Dwyer could not speak highly enough of Thomas's family. She looked forward to coming to Hampshire to celebrate our legitimate wedding, to teaching our children, to delighting in our fame and fortune and reading my published works. She would do none of these.

Robert had left school and was helping Michael work the land. They were similar characters, modest, industrious, handsome and unattractive to women. Robert took pride in his Irish heritage and saw no virtue in serving in the British army. He saw virtue in serving the land and was soon demonstrating innate skills as his less talented elder brother's unbound apprentice. Michael never complained but they really did not like one another. Robert devised economic improvements for the estate, increased Michael's production and won the tenants' respect for *himself*. There even came a time – a very short time – when Father's small estate yielded an income befitting the lifestyle of a future peer of the realm.

'When I am a princess, my brother Robert shall maintain my prince's boundless lands in an English Garden of Eden and they will flourish forever', so read the last entry in my Night Thought Book before I burnt the fantasies of my childhood and from their embers kindled the fantasies of my adult life.

Drawing money that Power and O'Brien might well have owed me, I paid the school for Mary Ann to complete her education. My sister was now almost seven years old, healthy, kind and painfully shy, but already displaying too many attractive imperfections for me to believe that she would grow to be beautiful. She would need my help, but not just yet.

Mr O'Brien was so distraught to hear of my pending departure that he forgot to thank me for assisting him to make the firm profitable. It was the only time I ever saw him laugh. I diligently observed a period of notice, returning to the office at least three times to instruct Ellen to assume my duties. I was wasting my time. Ellen was not interested in the dishonorable labour of the corn and butter trade. Her trade was her feminine wiles, and like me, intended to move on to a more respectable occupation.

Ellen's future was the least of my concerns. She alone surpassed me in delicacy of feature, perfection of figure, elegance of movement, scepticism and acerbity. She thought only of becoming a lady of English society and rejected every suitor with a drop of Irish blood in his veins. Stadfast Jenkins was the perfection of an English gentleman and surely an ideal match, yet Ellen expressed intuitive doubts about his family and spurned his advances. She was excessively vain.

> '*Half the errors attributed to love have their source in vanity: and many a person has made sacrifices to this unworthy passion, who would have successfully resisted the pleadings of affection.*'

The unhelpful hand of providence intervened. The Napoleonic wars auspiciously intensified and Lieutenant Jenkins was ordered to re-join his regiment in Spain. Ellen was devastated at having missed the chance to turn down his proposal.

The most persistent of Ellen's admirers was the fabulously wealthy Colonel William Stewart, who claimed royal blood, though I was unconvinced of his relationship to the royal house more commonly spelled Stuart. Stewart's home was the magnificent Killymoon Castle, his family seat since 1671, rebuilt for him by Nash after being destroyed by fire. The estate is still claimed to be the most picturesque in Ireland. Yet for all his wealth and position, Stewart was Irish and therefore did not meet Ellen's exacting demands, or so she told me.

Father would certainly not miss me. After I confronted him with the true solution to the *MacCarthy v Watson* affair our relationship fell to its nadir. Now we avoided one another. I knew, but refused to admit, that in his crude manner, he loved me as a father. Forcing me into marriage remained on his conscience for the remainder of his sober days.

I felt no animosity. I was ashamed of despising our opposing similarities instead of moulding them to mutual advantage. His brushes with the law had subdued his demeanour. Still impetuous, but a little more cautious, he went to court only to provide evidence as an arresting magistrate. He chose his guests more discriminately, gambled and womanised less often and even thought about reducing his consumption of alcohol.

In commitment to my family, if nothing else, I met my maker with a clear conscience.

In the mortal world, having completed my preparations for my idyllic English adventure, years of illusion were shattered in a single day. I did not meet Thomas or visit Miss Dwyer on the evening of 21st April 1807. I chose to spend it quietly reading in my bedroom. Ellen was not at home. I never asked where she went.

It was about eight, almost dark. Suddenly there was a commotion outside. It all happened too quickly. What did I see? How did I react? Did I take my lamp to the window or run down to the front door? My memory is obscured – obscured by blood, the blood of a young man. A young man bound by a rope to a horseman – blood on his face, on his hands, on his clothes, on a rider and his horse. Men I could not recognise were loosening the rope, trying to lift the boy down. Blood-soaked neckerchiefs and a once white frilly shirt covered the young man's wounds. How was he injured? Was he still alive?

Mother stood by the door, cold, weak, confused. Then I saw Father, dishevelled, uncommonly pale, panic stricken; the immaculate and fearless Edmond 'Beau' Power! There were shouts: 'clean him up'; 'we've no time'; 'quick'; 'doctor'; 'hospital', 'gaol'; 'we can't let him die here'. I saw Michael bring a carriage from the stables and carry the injured boy to the vehicle. Quickly he climbed onto the driver's box and clattered away with the exhausted men following like distracted bodyguards.

It was all over.

Mother, hysterical, dismissed my questions. She saw no more than me. Our grooms and maids appeared when they were no longer needed. Servants, I was to learn, see and hear only what they should not see or hear.

Neither Father nor Michael came home that night.

The unmitigated slaughter of Catholics in the Irish Rebellion and its consequential atrocities brought vicious demands for retribution. The Act of Union of 1800 more aggravated than relieved the discontent. For years, gangs of surviving malefactors had roamed the country bent on liberation from British rule but by 1807 few remained. Lord Donoughmore was however right, there were still some who posed a severe threat.

There was no police force in those days. The Irish, then the British government left matters of law and order to the militia and untrained magistrates like Father. Edmond Power had to be constantly vigilant. He never left the house unarmed. Like every sane man who has ever possessed a firearm, he carried it only as a weapon of defence. In the ten years in which he over-zealously pursued his unpaid office, Edmond Power was never given cause to fire his rifle at an unarmed man. Such a suicidal act would have defied the one ethic he held sacred.

And on the fatal April evening in 1807 he made no exception to his rule.

'Dr Madden, you were right to question the account I gave you of the events that led to the grotesque scene I have just described. As you imply I was simply trying to exonerate myself and my family – well, mostly myself. What would you have done if your father was accused of murder while you were living in his house? I was not there. I witnessed no crime. I gleaned what I told you from the newspapers and from Father's biased reports.'

'I simply pointed out that it was in your interest to conceal the truth, your ladyship.'

'Yes, but then with your inimitable sense of confusion you went on to cite a series of more distorted and improbable versions. You have my sympathy, Mr Sadleir and Mr Molloy. I don't envy you the task of making sense of this man's agonised accounts. Listen carefully, gentlemen, and I will now tell you precisely what occurred.'

After a long afternoon of presenting mandatory evidence at the Clonmel court the ever-congenial Edmond Power invited four of his fellow magistrates to dine with him at a nearby tavern. They enjoyed a drink or two and were about to start their meal when a breathless messenger rushed into the dining room. The brothers Joseph and Patrick Lonergan, James Butler and a gang of wanted insurgents had been sighted a few miles south of the town.

'Good! I've waited a long time to get my hands on the Lonergans and their fine friends. They've done a lot of damage around here, and they've a murder or two to answer for. They're a slippery bunch, but this time they're not going to get away.' A. H. Hutchinson was the most senior of the present company and a relative of Lord Donoughmore.

'Oh yes, I know those boys alright, and nobody wants to see them hanged more than me. You all know that the Lord Lieutenant authorised me to offer a hundred-pound reward for the apprehension of any one of them.' This was the same Lorenzo Hickey Jephson who testified to Father's exemplary character at the *MacCarthy v Watson* trial.

'Then we had better claim those rewards, had we not? If we catch them in one go, we'll all do very nicely. I'll round up my dragoons and I'll get my son. It's about time he did some work.'

Edmond Power, defender of the Law, was less excited by the scent of reward than the scent of adventure and his first chance for many months to impress Lord Donoughmore.

'Sorry Ned, we don't have time. If we are not there before dark, they'll have vanished into the clouds.'

'You're right. The five of us will be enough. What are we waiting for? Come on, let's go.'

Father paid the innkeeper while the other magistrates, a little the worse for drinking on empty stomachs, drained their glasses, hurried out and mounted their horses, too heavily committed to the task in hand to thank their colleague or offer a contribution to his generosity.

Following the messenger's unclear directions, the five emboldened magistrates galloped onto Súir Island, past our house and on across the south bridge into County Waterford. After two miles, they turned into an unfamiliar byway, a potholed dirt track, thick with mud from recent storms. Two more miles of faltering over exposed stones and fallen branches brought them to a small group of ramshackle huts. The law enforcers stopped, dismounted and surveyed their surroundings. They had literally stumbled onto a remote corner of the vast estates of Colonel John Bagwell MP, and the men they sought were his tenants.

All was quiet and deserted. Then one of the magistrates spotted a young man working with a pitchfork in a walled kitchen garden, preparing the ground for the coming spring.

'That's him: that's Joe Lonergan, I'd know him a mile off.'

Father also recognised the youth. Without a word he leapt back onto his horse and raced towards the enclosure.

'Lonergan stop, stop where you are! Joe, I want to talk to you'.

Alarmed by the familiar voice, Lonergan spun round to find himself confronted by a horse and rider bounding the five-foot wall surrounding the rectangular paddock. Instinctively Lonergan hurled his pitchfork, crashing it into the stone wall and severing its prongs. Again he turned and ran with Magistrate Power galloping in pursuit.

'Joe, stop; stop.' Father raised his rifle and fired a shot into the air.

Lonergan did not stop. He reached the far wall and tried to clamber across the loose stones. Father reloaded his rifle and reined in his horse a few feet from the fugitive.

'Come on Joe, don't be a fool, you can't get away. I've got four men outside.'

Magistrate Power again lifted his weapon in a brief threatening gesture. Lonergan instantly snatched a heavy flint from the top of the wall, pivoted and flung a second missile. His aim was better. He brushed his target and the stone rebounded from Father's left arm to his right hand. Another blast shattered the silence of the early evening as the gun discharged its bullet into the young man's side below his chest. Joseph Lonergan let out a single terrifying cry, lost his grip, fell and lay motionless in the muddy paddock. It all happened in seconds.

In those seconds the other magistrates remounted intending to follow their colleague. None of them could boast the horsemanship of Edmond Power, sportsman, or had the courage to assault the wall. They galloped round the periphery and found the only opening, too narrow to admit a horse and rider. The four men all heard the second shot resound, dismounted, unsheathed their rifles and ran into the enclosure.

None of them had seen what happened. Yet, like every eyewitness in the history of jurisprudence, they instantly convinced themselves to the contrary. One thought entered four minds: His Britannic Majesty's Court of Justice will demand evidence.

The magistrates staggered across the muddy field to where Father was crouching over his bleeding victim. Their normally bombastic colleague was silent, shocked, dejected, repentant. His cherished rifle lay in a dirty puddle beside him.

'Don't worry, Ned, he's breathing, he'll live. He'll be fine. There'll be a doctor on call at the gaol.'

The magistrates lifted up the injured youth, awkwardly supporting his legs and shoulders. Blood seeped through his shirt. One man ran ahead and mounted his horse while the others, slipping and stumbling, carried their barely conscious prisoner out through the opening, where they heaved him up and secured him in front of the horseman as best they could with a tether rope.

Father told his colleagues to start back while he returned to the enclosure. His horse stood motionless. Lonergan's flint lay by its hoof. Father picked it up. It weighed about two pounds in his hand and showed traces of his own blood – invaluable evidence. He put the stone in his saddlebag, recovered his damaged rifle, remounted and again effortlessly cleared the wall. A few minutes later he caught up with the others lumbering back along the rugged trail encumbered by their unstable prisoner.

None of the five noticed the small gathering of onlookers drawn from nowhere by the gunfire and screams. Less preoccupied with their blundered mission, the terrified and distracted magistrates might have observed some familiar faces, the other suspects they had come to arrest. As soon as the enemy was out of sight, Joe Lonergan's brother, Patrick, James Butler and a notorious rebel called John Everard rode as fast as their horses would carry them with news of the dastardly crime none of them had witnessed.

Colonel John Bagwell MP, sympathetic landlord and champion of the oppressed, took careful note of their report.

Meanwhile the five magistrates retraced their footsteps to Clonmel. Roped to the front rider, Lonergan weakened and lost consciousness forcing the bedraggled party to move slowly and cautiously. They dared not accelerate even when, in the gathering twilight, they at last found the familiar road to Súir Island.

'We have to get that rope off him.'

'If your horse stumbles one more time, he'll be dead for sure.'

'Hold tight. Not far now, half a mile. We'll stop at my place there for a bit. We'll have a drink and a wash before we take him in.'

Father's invitation was issued from force of habit. He did not know what he was saying.

Michael opened the front door and instantly grasped the situation. The youth had lost a great deal of blood and he feared for his life. Unaided, Michael brought out a carriage, harnessed horses, lit lanterns, spread blankets and gently laid Joe Lonergan on the back seat - just as he had done for me three years before.

Ignoring the blood seeping onto his hands and clothes, Michael took the reins and, as gently as the road would permit, drove the prisoner from Súir Island to the old gaol by the Clonmel wall. It was less than a mile, a continent away.

Fortified by the adrenalin of fear and a stealthy brandy, Magistrate Power galloped ahead to summon a doctor. The other magistrates, carrying torches Michael had thoughtfully ignited for them, trotted behind. In the town centre the outriders concluded that they had no further part to play in this tragedy. Respectable magistrates could not be seen blood-stained and dishevelled at a prison. They thanked Michael, complimented his father's bravery, pledged their unfailing support and lit their way home. No, of course they never returned the torches.

Dr John Phillips, Clonmel's most competent surgeon, cleaned Joseph Lonergan's wounds and pronounced his diagnosis.

'I very much regret to tell you, Mr Power, the bullet is too deeply embedded to be removed. The boy is weak and still losing blood. He might recover consciousness but I will be surprised if he survives the night. There is nothing more I can do for him.'

'I understand, doctor.'

'You don't look well yourself, Mr Power. Allow me to dress that wound on your hand. Flint splinters can turn gangrenous.'

Before yielding to medical care, Edmond Power, drained and humbled athlete, handed a coin to the gaoler's wife, Mrs Jane Hayden, and asked her to get food and drink for his prisoner. He thanked and paid Dr Phillips and sat down on the stone floor. There were no chairs at the gaol. Late into the night, Father and Michael went to wake a priest from his bed. When they returned it was too late. Mrs Hayden, herself heard Joseph Lonergan's final confession: a confession to save his soul in the next world and my father's life in this.

The following morning Dr Phillips signed the requisite certificate – eighteen-year-old man – cause of death, gunshot wound.

On 23rd April 1807, Michael, Ellen and I were again observers at the Clonmel courthouse. It was the last time I would see the inside of that building but not the last time that I was to be an observer to the process of Irish justice.

Irish justice was as usual inequitable, though remarkably swift and decisive, in no way induced by the personal interests of a rich and powerful Member of

Parliament. In less than forty-eight hours from Dr Phillips's estimated time of death the coroner's court was convened and in session – *To try and enquire in what manner Joseph Lonergan, now lying dead in the gaol in Clonmel, was killed.'*

The function of the coroner's court is to establish the manner of death. *Killed* was a foregone conclusion.

On the bench I recognised Richard Needham and Edward Armstrong of the Clonmel council, political allies of Colonel Bagwell. An over-hastily selected jury solemnly filed in and took their seats. All were Catholics with no love for my turncoat father. Among them, I was surprised to see a rapidly aging Bernard Wright.

Peasant women and farm workers, old and young, coherent and incoherent were brought in and paid. Their collective memory of the events of just two days before was, to say the least, unhelpful. Shots were fired by a man on horseback and not on horseback. The man was and was not Edmond Power. He was accompanied and was not accompanied by other men. Joe Lonergan threw a stone and did not throw a stone. Michael Power was there and not there.

John Everard swaggered to the witness box.

'State your occupation.'

'Farmer, sir.'

'Did you see the incident?'

'Yes, sir, and Mr Power told me afterwards it was his intention to shoot *me* in the back.'

The gentlemen of the jury might not have liked Father but they knew his character. They would not believe that the proud Edmond Power JP would make such a cowardly admission to a known criminal.

Most outrageous of all was the *information* dictated by the illiterate Patrick Lonergan, too distressed by his brother's death to appear in person.

> *'Edmond Power of Clonmel came on horseback, and on seeing the said Joseph Lonergan deceased, at a distance from him of about one hundred and thirty-three yards did instantly, wilfully and feloniously present a gun ... and discharged the contents with design to kill the said Joseph Lonergan.'*

One hundred and thirty-three yards? Previously it was one hundred and fifty. No gun yet invented could fire that distance and certainly not with the extraordinary accuracy of Patrick Lonergan's eyes, evidently with the power to see through a stone wall.

Magistrates Jephson and Hutchinson read statements, convincingly worded in their own interests. The coroner summed up with ambiguous legal clarity:

> *'Joseph Lonergan might have been shot by Edmond Power, as magistrate of this county, in his own defence, and in the execution of his office.'*

He did not use the words kill or murder but how was I to interpret *'might have been'*? I was confused and charitable. Colonel Bagwell and his friends were confused and uncharitable.

Outside the court other magistrates gathered round and applauded Father, jubilant because they were not implicated. I was prepared to believe that they held him in high regard.

'It's all over, Ned. Let's forget about it.'

'It's all part of the game. You'll hear no more.'

'Joe Lonergan's dead in every sense of the word and good riddance to him.'

'Listen, we now know where Everard, Butler and the rest hide themselves. We'll have to teach them that it's bad manners to interrupt our dinner.'

The magistrates were so elated that they even offered to buy Father a drink. They toasted a quick and just verdict and the end of an ominous episode. The alcohol cleared Father's head sufficiently for him appreciate that neither he nor his friends had anything to celebrate, and to remember that his Member of Parliament, would certainly not be celebrating.

Edmond Power did not intentionally shoot at the unarmed Joseph Lonergan. Even at his most irrational – he excelled at irrationality – he was always aware that his gun was a deterrent and nothing more. But I too was irrational. I should have supported Father, not suspected him and been ashamed of his shortcomings. I chose to forget that in the eight years he served as the least appropriate of magistrates, not even his most ignorant critics accused him of improper use of his gun. I chose to forget that he did not fire on the hooligans who slaughtered his cattle and torched his stables and warehouse on Súir Island. I chose to forget that he had taken all his prisoners scathed by nothing other than vulgar language, and that some were indeed armed and dangerous. I chose to forget how often other magistrates took credit for their passive roles, basked in the reflections of his commendations and accepted his unstinting hospitality.

All that mattered to me was that the coroner's verdict left no stain on my character and that it would not deter Thomas from taking me to England, where honour and justice always prevail.

After the hearing, I thanked Bernard Wright, who I believed bore Father no ill will. I was wrong. He told me that he blamed him, not only for forsaking his religion but for permitting the publication of letters and articles libelling Colonel Bagwell. He was convinced of the honourable politician's innocence and, at his request, had returned to Ireland to publicise his good name and support for the Catholic community. I told Bernard the whole sorry truth. The high principled intellectual was shocked and I was greatly saddened when soon afterwards I learned that he had ended a life of self-imposed suffering by slashing his wrists. I think he was in love with me.

Thomas now regarded Father as a hero. He begged me to introduce him.

'It is simply good manners for me to assure your parents of my good intent, Margaret. I am sure that I will find your mother as beautiful as her daughters and your father an honourable Irish gentleman.'

I was horrified by the prospect of exposing Thomas to Father's snobbery and Mother's asinine delusions. As a compromise, I introduced him to Michael with whom I thought he might have much in common. They both spurned hypocrisy, never censured a word or deed and were always ready to concede the benefit of a doubt – charming fools.

We dined with Thomas at a remote country inn.

'Do you think it could have been possible that Mr Power was to blame for Joe Lonergan's death?' he asked Michael.

'I know my father better than anyone. He's making a show of being exonerated by the coroner but inwardly he has a soft heart and is greatly troubled. I saw him pay for Joe's doctor who couldn't help, and for food he didn't eat and for the last rights that were never administered.'

'Why would he do all that, if he had no feelings of guilt, Michael?'

'He did it out of humanity. That night I saw my father at his most compassionate. Mr Jephson and the others all testified that Joe's death was an accident. I am sure they spoke the truth.'

'I agree', said Thomas 'but the verdict was inconclusive. It might not quell allegations of manslaughter or, heaven forbid, murder. It will be a gift for the press. They will not miss the chance to castigate a former newspaper proprietor.'

'He's afraid of that too, said Michael. 'I take no pleasure from seeing him cowed.'

'Yes, we all saw Bagwell's spies at the inquest. I don't think they looked happy with the verdict. Bagwell depends on the Catholic vote. He'll want to be seen to support the Lonergans and he'll probably be saying that your father converted deliberately to persecute Catholics.'

'Do you really think Colonel Bagwell will pursue the matter?'

Thomas's thoughtless observations had put this question into Michael's mouth and we all knew the answer.

'As I said, Michael, I sincerely hope not, but I've heard that Bagwell went in person to comfort Joe Lonergan's mother. They say he took flowers and spent over two hours with her and Patrick.'

Michael, outwardly calm as always, was sharing my festering anxiety. 'Perhaps you are misjudging Colonel Bagwell, Thomas. A good landlord would naturally sympathise with his tenants' misfortunes.'

'Margaret has told me about your and your brother's work on your father's estate and I'm full of admiration, but not many landlords are like you, Michael. A man like Bagwell is not interested in his tenants' welfare. All he wants is revenge. He has probably offered to finance Lonergan's family to press charges against Mr Power. You have seen for yourself, Michael, how wily advocates forge a case out of the flimsiest evidence. And nothing could make their task easier than a bereaved mother sobbing for the jury's mercy.'

Thomas was thinking aloud, unaware of my distress. Ellen's tutor taught me that happiness is the only emotion an English lady displays in public. I should have attended more of her lessons. I discharged my anger with all the passion in the remnant of my Irish blood. I broke down in tears, irrational tears, vulnerable tears, tears I had no right to shed. In my most abhorrent moments – and there were many to come – I never again permitted myself such immature self-indulgence.

'I can't live with this nightmare for a moment longer. I am not yet eighteen and I have borne the brunt of more animosity, brutality, deceit, dishonesty and vindictive lawyers than most people suffer in a lifetime. No, Michael, I know Father better than you. I've lived with the troubles he's brought upon us all. He has no soft heart. He has no compassion. He is a coward, a fool, and as mad as the man he sold me to. Do you think any of his so-called friends will help him? No, he'll come crying to me. Well I don't care if he's accused of manslaughter or murder or anything else, I refuse to hold his hand another day longer!'

My brother and lover listened in silence to my inane outburst and apologised like a pair of repentant monks, though neither had any reason to apologise. After a great deal of unwarranted sympathy, I recovered sufficiently to apologise myself. I did not believe what I had said. Edmond Power was cursed with the shortcomings of every well-intentioned man.

'I beg you to forgive me, Margaret. I see now that your position is untenable. I cannot allow you to return to Súir Island. We will stay the night here. Tomorrow I shall take you to my house in Dublin and send my adjutant to Clonmel for your things.'

'That will not be necessary, I'll bring them myself,' said Michael.

'Then you are going home. Do you intend to stay?'

'It is my duty to support my family.'

'No, Michael,' I said, 'you must leave immediately. Father can support his own family. It's not beyond him. Without us he will have two less mouths to feed. Robert is perfectly capable of managing the estate and Ellen can look after Power and O'Brien.'

Michael did not reply. He turned to Thomas.

'I have been considering a career in the British army. The truth is that no one in my family has ever served in the military. I save all the money I can but I don't know the price of a commission or how to set about buying one. Perhaps there is an officer in your regiment who can advise me?'

'Commissions in the Light Dragoons are highly prized. They seldom come up for sale, and when they do they fetch exorbitant prices. But would you be prepared to serve in the colonies?'

'I would be prepared to serve anywhere except Ireland.'

'There is a dearth of officers in the West Indies. A commission there will be inexpensive if you sign up for twenty years or more. Do you wish me to make some enquiries?'

I interrupted the men's business.

'Yes, please do that, Thomas. Somehow we will find the money. Michael, I know you think it wrong to abandon our family but there is nothing more that we can do. Father must be forced to accept some responsibility. I doubt he will be arresting many more criminals.'

'If I am honest with myself, I know that it is time for me to go away and make a new life; and perhaps the further away the better. '

I never again saw my father or breathed the stale air in his house on Súir Island. Two days later, Michael brought Mother, Ellen, Robert, and Mary Ann to

Dublin with my books and clothes. We said our goodbyes. This was also the last time I saw Michael. Yet through all the tempestuous adventures of my future life I never lost touch with my family. I sent long letters, brief notes, meticulous chronicles, petty gossip, wonderful and terrible news, money enclosed – always money – whether I had it or not.

There was a time when Edmond Power might have sought out Captain Jenkins with a lucrative proposition: 'One beautiful clever daughter, a little shop soiled, a bargain at any price'. Nothing could have been further from his mind as he disembarked at Liverpool docks on a freezing evening in January 1808, a dejected refugee from Irish justice. For all the reassurances of his friends and fellow magistrates, he had always known that sooner or later he would be indicted. Now there was a warrant issued for his arrest.

For four months Edmond Power, no longer 'Beau' but still officially Justice of the Peace, lingered in a derelict corner of the poverty-infested port that handled so much of the shameless wealth of the British Empire. A defrocked priest, once a flushed face among the revellers of Súir Island, had offered Father a filthy excuse for a room for as long as he could keep them both in a state of inebriation.

Back in Clonmel, four brave magistrates, traumatised by the prospect of seeing their names on the next warrants, instructed an attorney to locate Edmond Power. The lawyer's agent, motivated by a less-than-adequate, incentive encountered little difficulty in tracing the whereabouts of the alleged murderer. He noisily pushed open the unhinged door of the rodent-infested garret where Magistrate Power lay on a heap of straw sleeping off a hard day at a quayside tavern.

'I have come to inform you, Mr Power, that if you surrender yourself your colleagues are prepared stand bail and use all the influence at their disposal in your support. They have asked me to assure you that they will testify in your defence and contribute to your legal costs.'

His half-night's sleep had sobered Father enough to be suspicious of this magnanimous offer.

'Sure, that's what their so-called friends told my father-in-law and my wife's uncle or whatever he was, the blessed Father Sheehy. And what happened? Both of them ended up in four pieces with their bloody heads on spikes outside the gaol. That's what happened. Why the hell should I believe your fine clients?'

The agent's much-needed reward was at stake.

'That was many years ago, Mr Power. The circumstances are entirely different now. I used to work as a clerk to the court. I saw with my own eyes that they throw out every allegation of misconduct by a magistrate, or anybody acting in the course of duty. You have nothing to fear, sir.'

Edmond Power had everything to fear. The court might have thrown out cases in the past but would not throw out Colonel Bagwell's money.

'It is more difficult to convince the vicious that virtue exists than to persuade the good that it is rare.'

Thomas explained that he could not take me to England until he completed his military assignment in Ireland. Since this was evidently none too arduous he would use his considerable free time to cement our marital status. He would invite Dublin society and allow me to practise my natural talents as a hostess.

My new home was an architectural disaster; a rambling townhouse, no more than twenty years old and pitted with decay. The entire interior would have to be redecorated. I visited the most fashionable shops, chose new furniture, drapery, carpets, pictures and ornaments. I planned a splendid library, an extended drawing-room, an ornate dining room and luxurious bedrooms. I was especially pleased with my design for an exotic aviary in the garden. Thomas was exuberant about my ideas. Then he told me that he did not own the house and his lease was due to expire in a few months, so I put away my notes and drawings for use in the palaces and châteaux of my indestructible optimism.

Dublin was not Paris, Rome or London or even Hampshire. It was the best substitute in Ireland for a great city where the trappings of privilege blanketed privation. I met the elite, the titled, the rich and the richer, all oblivious to the vulgarities of money and ambition. We entertained with light-hearted panache and mature French wines. How different from Edmond Power's drunken carousels on Súir Island. I was so besotted with pleasure that I hardly noticed that Thomas's invitations were always accepted but seldom returned.

Thomas was as rich as his guests wished themselves to be thought. His generosity flowed in a river of love and devotion. He bought me jewellery, perfumes, gowns, shoes and bonnets: 'Dublin must see my beautiful bride at her best'. He bought me a splendid carriage: 'You cannot be seen walking in the streets with the lower orders'. He employed new servants: 'You cannot be permitted to soil your hands with menial tasks'. He bought me scholarly books and had a Sheraton writing table made for me. 'You must not waste your God-given literary talents.'

Putting my God-given literary talents to the test I created an autobiography. From Margaret I became Marguerite; a hint of French sophistication. An appropriate maiden name presented more of a challenge. The remnant of inexorable dialect prohibited me from posing as English, so I chose Desmond as my sole concession to my mother's pedigree. She would have been so proud.

Thereafter my fiction flowed as freely as the tears it earned me.

'I was born and spent my early childhood in Ireland. When I was twelve, my father, a pillar of the Established Church of England, sold his estate, one of several, in County Galway – I have forgotten the precise location. We moved to a moated castle in Norfolk, where I was educated by governesses. My father died suddenly five years ago and I was heartbroken. Earlier this year my mother brought me back to Ireland to visit her cousin, a Miss Anne Dwyer, who introduced me to her nephew, Thomas.'

Well, there had to be some element of truth.

'It was love at first sight and we were married quietly at a village church near Thomas's regimental base. The wedding was attended by my mother, Thomas's brother, Stadfast, and officers of the Eleventh Light Dragoons. Thomas will tell you about them. I have such a poor memory for names.'

I dare not think about the number of times I elaborated this preposterous concoction.

'Society punishes not the vices of its members, but their detection; like the Spartans who punished the discovery of theft and not the crime.'

On 1st September 1807, Thomas held a celebration for my twenty-first birthday - three years in advance - the accelerated aging intended to make my fictitious past more plausible. I effusively greeted my well-wishers and remembered all their names, titles and designations. In particular I remembered Lady Virginia Velinfomt and never forgot her.

'Allow me to offer my congratulations on your coming of age, Mrs Jenkins, and dare I say how much younger you look? Married life so obviously suits you. I pray that you and Captain Jenkins will always be as happy as you are today.'

I thanked her ladyship and with befitting modesty dismissed her obligatory compliments. Lady Velinfomt was not to be dismissed. A pause. I tried to move away, but she held me in an intense gaze as if trying to recognise a face from the past.

'I do appreciate that this is an inconvenient moment, Mrs Jenkins, but might we have a quiet word – in your own and Thomas's best interests.'

'It is perfectly convenient, Lady Velinfomt. You are one of our most valued and most gracious friends.' I knew her ladyship's name from Thomas's guest list but had never seen her before.

'Permit me to come straight to the point. Are you prepared to tell me that you are not Mrs Jenkins?'

'What a strange question? Captain Jenkins is in the next room. You are welcome to ask him.'

I raised my left hand so that she could ignore my wedding ring.

'That will not be necessary. Like everyone here, I am aware of the answer. You are, in fact, the wife of Captain St Leger Farmer to whom you were forced into marriage when you were fifteen – though some say younger. That would make you about eighteen now. That, in itself, is of no consequence. Dublin society is built on cupboards of skeletons and is always sympathetic to small deceit.'

'Then why are you telling me this, now?'

'Captain Jenkins is a much loved man and no one, least of all me, would wish to see him hurt. But perhaps you are not yet aware that your father, Magistrate Power, has been charged with murder and is reported to have fled the country? Dare I commend that you and Captain Jenkins follow his example and leave Ireland as soon as you can? I trust you will not think ill of me, Mrs Farmer.'

Lady Velinfomt lost herself in the glittering mêlée and I forced back my smile.

'Do have another glass of champagne. Thomas has it specially imported from Reims. What a pity the rain is preventing us from taking our drinks in the garden.'

Beneath the veneer was anger. I was not angry with the titled prophet of doom who wished me well. I was not angry with Father, the author of my misfortunes. I was angry with society's unwinnable games and the unearned fortunes that purchased the right to play them. And I was angry because I knew now that I was terminally addicted to vanity.

'Society rarely pardons those who have discovered the emptiness of its pleasures and who can live independently of it or them.'

My anger receded. I was too good for the elite of this miserable provincial town.

Thomas had no concept of intrigue or innuendo. I had to spell out the situation as if to a child.

'Thomas, do you remember what Sir Fystite's agent told you about the Dublin press sensationalising Captain Farmer's court-martial and printing scandalous fiction about me? We both thought it was long dead and buried but now my father is accused of murder and the press will resurrect all its old lies. Of course Lady Velinfomt was right; everybody thinks they know all about me.'

'But we only heard of the arrest warrant from Ellen's letter received yesterday. There has been nothing in the papers.'

'I have read nothing either but bad news spreads quickly. We cannot stay here, Thomas. Please will you now take me to England?'

Thomas would not be convinced. He said, and I foolishly agreed, that it would be cowardly to turn our backs on Dublin. We would remain until the expiry of his lease provided a good reason to leave.

'We injure ourselves more than our enemies by indulging in hatred towards them.'

8

'Come with me, gentlemen, there is someone here with whom you should be better acquainted.'

I conduct my three biographers up the grand staircase to the first floor of Hertford House. We admire works by Rembrandt, Titian, Velazquez, Rubens and Canaletto before stopping in the magnificently restored Great Gallery. I touch my forefinger to my lips to request silence. A mixed-gender, multi-ethnic group of children sit cross-legged on the floor enthralled by the vitality of their lesson. We watch their dedicated teacher inflaming passion for knowledge where the less inspired are defeated by the diversities of class, creed and culture.

'You know who she is, don't you?' I whisper.

'Indeed, we do. The only person for whom you never had a bad word.'

The pride of the Wallace Collection, Frans Hals's improbable cavalier, swaggers from his frame and blends his laughter with enlightenment through the wit and vigour of this present-day Miss Dwyer. At her school, there is no such thing as a silly question.

'Miss, you said cavalier means a sort of knight. Why isn't he wearing armour, like in the other room?' 'Miss, you said cavalier means horseman. Why's he too fat to ride a horse?' 'Do you think he's drunk, Miss? Won't those pretty clothes get dirty if he spills his beer? Who did his washing, Miss?' 'Is that big gold ball a sword? Where's the other end, Miss?'

The greatest privilege of my life was to have Miss Dwyer as my teacher. Perhaps she was as privileged to have me as her student. I do not know. But I do know that historians forget, and will go on forgetting the inspired and inspiring teachers who, like her, opened the floodgates of talent, innovation and achievement which created history itself.

The clever student who thinks he knows so much about me and his girlfriend have also come up to the Great Gallery. They pretend to be interested in a Fragonard, but are more intrigued by the simplistic techniques of the junior school teacher. We listen to their conversation unobserved.

'This woman's brilliant. She's really getting through to them. Every one of those kids will make it to university. It's a load of nonsense to say some children are naturally more inclined to higher education than others. It depends a hundred per cent on the teacher,' he says.

'But what about unskilled and semi-skilled workers? They don't need higher education,' she says.

'Look, this is the twenty-first century. There are people alive today who will still be working in the twenty-second. There won't be any unskilled or semi-skilled work then. Higher education is the only answer.'

'Downstairs you said your glamorous friend, the Countess of Blessington was the best educated woman in the country. What sort of teacher did she have? Ireland was still in the dark ages at the end of the eighteenth century.'

'Maybe, but now that you mention it, I did read something about her being taught by a remarkable woman as a child.'

'Yes, but in those days it didn't matter how well she was taught, women were barred from all colleges and universities.'

'Apparently she tucked herself away for six years and educated herself.'

'I've never been convinced by people who claim to be self-educated. Unless she was a real genius your clever floozy must have had somebody to inspire her to go on studying.'

'Genius is the gold in the mine – education the miner who elicits it.'

'I suppose she did. Somehow I always respected the teachers at my school even though they were a useless bunch who didn't know what to do with their education.'

'And what did your wonderful Countess of Blessington do with hers?'

'She got in with the right people and married for money. What else did clever women ever do?'

There is no point in trying to correct these diligent students. They would not believe that my rise to fame and infamy was rooted in higher education at the one ancient seat of learning that never practised sexual discrimination. I graduated with honours in the only subject the University of Life has ever taught – hindsight.

--

The Clonmel Spring Assizes of 1808 brought my father's time of troubles to a painful end, leaving wounds that never healed.

Defying precedent, Edmond Power JP was duly arraigned and charged with *'murder or causing death by misadventure'* the wording uninfluenced by Colonel Bagwell's generosity. Father's proven guilt would set a permanent seal on the innocence of Clonmel's most distinguished *'patriot and soldier'* and avenge his successful lawsuit. As a magistrate and proprietor of a local newspaper, Edmond Power might have sounded credible but nobody would remain convinced by insinuations published however long ago by a convicted murderer.

The *Dublin Journal* carried a shard of cheerful news: *'No less than one hundred and forty-eight persons, charged with murder, rape and robbery'* would appear before the Assizes. I presumed that the trials would therefore be short and that there would be far more sensational cases to supply the insatiable Irish demand for scandal. I was wrong on both counts.

Father's innocent fellow magistrates kept their promise and offered unlimited advice and limited money. Solomon Watson's appetite for financing courtroom adventures had astutely abated since his pyrrhic victory over MacCarthy – or was it the other way round. This time there was to be no *éminence grise* to indemnify a Henry Dean Grady or a John Philpot Curren. The magistrates funded just one inexperienced young advocate to oppose a formidable array of prosecutors.

The Attorney General, a specialist in criminal law, fully indemnified by his friend Colonel John Bagwell MP, led for the prosecution.

'... if there was no resistance made, no apprehension of a tumult, or danger of a rescue: there the wantonly taking of a life of a fellow creature, under circumstances like these, would be clearly murder.'

The court usher assisted Joe Lonergan's mother, weeping audibly beneath a knee-length funereal veil, to ascend the three steps to the witness box. Not only had she lost a son but her husband had died a fortnight prior to the trial. Colonel John and the lovely Mrs Mary Bagwell had sent moving letters of condolence and wreaths more sombre than those undelivered to my siblings' funerals. How could the jury not pity this poor hapless widow?

A second prosecution counsel asked Mrs Lonergan to identify the pitchfork that might have killed the defendant if better aimed. Her beloved boy was taking the broken implement to the blacksmith's forge for repair. She warned him, *'Joe dear, it's too late to go; maybe Mr Power and the yeoman are out'.* Nonetheless he went and did not return. The next day the blacksmith told Mrs Lonergan that *'Joe dear'* had not been to his forge. Learned counsel shouted at the jury, 'Of course he had not been there. Joseph Lonergan was arrested without cause and shot dead while on an innocent errand.'

Directed by Colonel Bagwell himself, Mrs Lonergan's performance was faultless. Jurors gasped and covered their eyes.

James Butler and Patrick Lonergan swore by almighty God that they had witnessed the gratuitous shooting of their unarmed friend and brother. The self-styled farmer, John Everard repeated the flagrant lies he told the coroner's court. The three accounts contradicted each other in every aspect.

Everard again testified that he was an old friend of Mr Power and had asked him: *'Why did you kill Joe Lonergan?'* Mr Power replied, *'I am glad of it'.* Everard claimed that he neither saw Joseph Lonergan throw a stone nor did he hear Mr Power shout stop yet he saw the fatal shot fired *'from a distance of one hundred and fifty yards'.*

At the coroner's court it was a hundred and thirty-three. Lonergan was inside the walled garden, less than a hundred yards wide, while Everard did not emerge from his cottage until after he heard gunfire. He had seen nothing.

The Attorney General, scornful and contemptuous, moulded these manifest lies with the dexterity of a master craftsman. *'Power's sole complaint against Lonergan was that the latter had thrown a stone at him.'* The blood-stained flint was irrelevant. Edmond Power was guilty of murder and must be conveyed forthwith to the gallows.

Father's defence pivoted on the evidence of his fellow magistrates. His lone underpaid advocate, fighting valiantly for his own reputation, led Jephson and Hutchinson through their meticulously rehearsed statements. They answered in monotone: the truth, most of the truth and something like the truth.

Jephson produced his letter from the Lord Lieutenant offering *'a reward of one hundred pounds for the apprehension of members of Lonergan's gang'.* Jephson himself had pursued them on other occasions and neither he nor Magistrate Power had ever in their entire careers claimed a reward for public service. Hutchinson informed the jury, *'I have for many years known Edmond Power as a dedicated magistrate* and a humane man…. [James Butler was] *highly infamous and capable of perjury* [while Patrick Lonergan's character was] *even worse than Butler's.'*

'*These men*', concluded the ambitious young advocate, '*form a most dangerous banditti*'. Paying no heed to the Attorney General's exaggerated allegations, junior counsel for the defence easily demolished the credibility of the rabble of eye-witnesses, again brought in, briefed, bribed and bamboozled until they belied each other's evidence.

The testimony of the illiterate Mrs Jane Hayden moved the jury more deeply than Mrs Lonergan's scripted sorrow. The gaoler's wife recounted how Mr Power's son carried the prisoner in, how Mr Power '*gave her a crown to buy him food*' and sent her for Dr Phillips, how Mr Power and his son went for the priest, and how, in the early hours of 22nd April 1807, Mrs Hayden herself heard Joseph Lonergan's deathbed confession:

'*He did not blame anyone but himself for that he threw a stone at Mr Power which made him fire at him*'.

His Honour Mr Justice Day coughed out the phlegm of his summing up:

'*Much of the guilt and disorder of the county is due to the negligence of its magistrates and supineness of its gentry.'*

The jury rejected the judge's direction and returned a unanimous verdict of not guilty. Mr Justice Day, serenely incensed, had no alternative but to acquit Father, yet disregarding the jury's conclusion, pronounced the blameless Edmond Power unfit to serve as a magistrate, his name to be expunged from the roll forever. The noose would have been a more humane sentence.

Never again would drunken laughter ring through the stale rafters of the house of Edmond Power.

A month after the trial, Mr Hunt mercifully died in his bed. His executor, Mr O'Brien, a beneficiary of my tuition but not of his erstwhile partner's will, reimbursed himself for all the unclaimed debts that I had never heard him previously mention. He left nothing for Mr Hunt's numerous legatees but very properly retained a small balance in order to erect a memorial befitting the firm's founder. The new sign read Hunt & O'Brien – Power expunged – unfit to serve. Mr O'Brien tore up his old partnership agreement and enticed the heir to a small estate in County Waterford, with no experience of the corn and butter trade, to inject his capital. The young gentleman declined to inspect the books of account.

Ellen did not wait to be dismissed. She demeaned herself to accept Colonel William Stewart's offer of the amenities in his magnificent bedroom at Killymoon Castle and wrote to inform me that she would not be returning to Clonmel in the foreseeable future. She would however continue to provide financial support for our parents and expected me to do likewise. Robert quarrelled violently with Father, left home and went as far away as he could afford within the bounds of Ireland. At a well-managed estate in County Donegal he found an opportunity to exercise his natural talents, which his new employer appreciated no more than Father. A charitable cousin took Mary Ann to live with his family on the west coast, a poor relation being more economical than a maid.

Michael remained traumatised for weeks after giving the only truthful evidence at Father's trial, and held himself responsible for the result. He too left Súir Island at the first opportunity. A brief letter of commendation from Thomas secured him a commission as a lieutenant in the Second West Indian Regiment. No payment or medical examination was required. Death from tropical disease was so common in the Caribbean that no sane man would serve there other than in desperation or under duress. The British Army went so far as to gratuitously provide the new officer's uniform and pay for his sea passage.

He wrote often from St Lucia glorifying his regiment and glossing over his misery until his optimism was no longer false. He became engaged to the daughter of the British ambassador, the only eligible Englishwoman on the island. He said little about his fiancée and I chose not to guess what she might be like.

Despite his former colleagues' astutely restrained generosity, Father's legal defence had taken the last of his money. Solomon Watson's inexhaustible integrity was exhausted and he called in all his loans. The bailiffs came onto Súir Island, seized his house, stables, horses, carriages, furniture and depleted wine stock; they confiscated his land at Curragheen and advertised everything for auction. Thomas said that if I had not gone with him to Dublin, I too would have been in the catalogue. This, I would learn, was what passed for wit among the English upper-classes.

I attended many sales in my life and wrote passionately of the tragedy concealed within the cherished objects made nostalgia by the snap of a gavel. When I was a buyer, I thought of an auctioneer as a parasite or a charlatan. But when I became a seller, I saw him as a hero who rescues more unfortunates from the abyss than most supposed heroes.

> *Our faults are lessons writ for other men*
> *Who, reading them, are taught at our expense,*
> *Nor thank us for the knowledge they attain,*
> *Though bought at heavy cost of woe to us.*

Edmond Power, once a sportsman, genial host, newspaper proprietor and law enforcer, finally received the recognition he so poorly deserved. Conscience-driven citizens of Clonmel acknowledged his self-promoting prodigality and unpaid policing with as much pity as appreciation. Officers, huntsmen, squires and peasants swarmed onto Súir Island: acquisitive drones, polluting the expurgated memories of my forgotten childhood. Friends and enemies came together in their numbers to acquire mementoes of the distinguished figure – a rarity in Clonmel – who, wittingly and unwittingly, had provided them with so much free entertainment. Colonel Bagwell sent his agent to acquire the land at Curragheen to be swallowed by his gargantuan estates. Lord Donoughmore sent his sincere apologies. Heavy commitments detained him in London.

Edmond Power did not attend the sale. He knew that the tangible remnant of his years of wanton prodigality was too small to block the gates of the debtors' prison. He was wrong. The bailiff settled all Father's debts and counted out a small pile of coins into his unsteady hand. It did not amount to much, but restored a fraction of his mutilated pride and a smaller fraction of my faith in the Irish.

On the same day on which Ned and Nell Power moved into a small house in a back street of Dublin, Thomas and Marguerite Jenkins moved out of a large house in its fashionable centre. It was the 25th March, Lady Day 1809. Thomas's lease had finally expired. He was convinced that by braving out the winter, we had quashed all the rumours and my past was a thing of the past. He was deluding himself. Why did he think Dublin society were declining so many of his invitations? Why did he think I asked him to sign so many tactful acknowledgments of their tactless excuses?

'We are so sorry to hear that you are suffering severe headaches.' 'Please convey our sincerest condolences to your poor grandmother on this sad occasion.' 'We do understand. Heavy commitments have such a habit of arising at the most inconvenient moments.'

'In solitude we retain our own faults; but in society we superadd those of others.'

I had never been bored nor lonely when Thomas's military duties required him to be away from Dublin for extended periods. I corresponded with my family and other remote acquaintances, pursued my studies and wrote poems and essays. I received a few female visitors but was always pleased to welcome those of Thomas's male friends who so thoughtfully enquired after my welfare, invited me to ride with them among the royal deer in Phoenix Park or to accompany them to the opera or theatre. No, I was certainly not unfaithful to my husbands, so far as I can recall.

Thomas's assignment had also come to an end and we prepared to leave Ireland. We were not bound for England. I was greatly disappointed and thrilled with anticipation. We were going to Paris where the proud aristocracy, humbled by the Revolution, would be too cultured to question our marital status or concern themselves with my past.

France was the exemplar of civilisation. Napoleon, at the height of his power, through an all-embracing legislative code, was creating the most enlightened regime the world had yet to know. Not everyone of course shared this view of the Emperor's modest aspirations. Nations, such as England, Italy, Spain and Portugal were determined to defend their ancient superiority and would never succumb to a European dictator's warlike dreams to unite them in the cause of peace.

How different it was in the twentieth century, when the dreams of a united Europe were tenuously realised by democratic consent.

After weeks of strategically resisting Napoleon's advancing armies, Lieutenant Stadfast Jenkins, serving with General Arthur Wellesley (later Duke of Wellington) in the protracted conflict which became known as the Peninsular War, was granted respite leave, on condition that he remained on the Continent. He had rented a suit of rooms in Paris and invited us to join him there and Thomas accepted fearing that it might be many months, perhaps years, before he would see his brother again.

Though I had studied the history and culture of France and spoke fluent French my knowledge of contemporary Paris was gleaned only from Bernard Wright's *mise en scène* for the *Clonmel Gazette*. I envisaged a vibrant society thriving in an elegant city of palaces, châteaux, ornamental gardens and tree-lined boulevards, but regrettably died before Baron Haussmann could realise my vision. The French capital was no Napoleonic paradigm. It was the grim legacy of 1789; destitution, dirt, despair, dereliction, depravity, debauchery and discontent. The improbable benefits of the French Revolution, like those of all revolutions, had failed to materialise and the Emperor's infallible reforms had changed little or nothing.

An aged caretaker dramatically lifted his shoulders to his ears. *'Je suis désolé. Monsieur Jenkins n'a pas encore arrivé.'*

We were generally unconcerned. Stadfast had probably been delayed by bad weather, blocked roads, inadequate horses or a temptress at a roadside inn. The interval provided an opportunity for Thomas to show me the sights of Paris and introduce me to some of its more distinguished citizens, all of whom seemed to be acquaintances of his mother. Britain and France were at war but there was no place for politics in the genteel salons of Napoleonic Paris. I was greatly impressed.

'The French possess the talent of conversation in a rare degree: their apprehension and comprehension, their flow of words ready and vivacious…' I wrote, meaning that they were more interested in the misdeeds of Parisian society than in mine.

Among those to whom Thomas wished to introduce me was Brigadier General Comte Albert Gaspard D'Orsay, a star officer of the Grande Armée and an intimate of Napoleon himself. We rode out to his château at Chambourcy, a few miles north-west of Paris. The general was not at home. His wife, Eleanore, Baronesse de Franquemont, apologised profusely, explaining that he was serving as chief military attaché to Louis Bonaparte, the Emperor's brother, who happened to be King of Holland at the time.

Despite Thomas's disappointment, I was delighted to meet the Baronesse Eleanore. She was the first person to warmly and sincerely welcome me into a truly aristocratic home; a gracious château in total contrast to the Bagwells' grotesque colossus and the vulgar manifestations of wealth to which I was not invited in Dublin. The Baronesse proudly introduced her seven-year-old daughter, Ida, and equally beautiful eight-year-old son, Alfred. This unnaturally polite little boy, in a white silk suit, excelled at everything. He addressed us in fluent English and also knew Spanish and Italian and was teaching himself Latin. He treated us to displays of gymnastics, fencing and riding and joined his sister in a lengthy piano duet. With disarming confidence, Alfred guided us through his prodigious art work and before we left presented us with remarkably accurate disposable sketches of our profiles. This *enfant terrible* exhausted every adjective of admiration in my vocabulary. When we said *au revoir* I was more than relieved to see the last of Comte Alfred D'Orsay.

'Precocious wisdom is not desirable for youth, lest like the rash blossom which ventures forth too early it should be nipped ere it has strength to resist adversity.'

Four weeks passed and still no news of Stadfast. I continued to immerse myself in the novelty of my first visit to a foreign land, while Thomas grew increasingly anxious. At last a letter arrived from his mother enclosing a formal military communication neatly edged in black ink.

'As Commanding Officer of the Eleventh Light Dragoons it is my regrettable duty to inform you that Lieutenant Stadfast Jenkins fell bravely on the field of battle. Your son died in the service of his King and Country when the enemy ambushed his coach on the road to Paris. You will doubtless be proud to learn that he is to be buried here in Lisbon with full military honours.

On behalf of the regiment, allow me to humbly offer my sincerest condolences and request you to accept the enclosed richly deserved posthumous award.

I would add that my officers and men all greatly respected Lieutenant Jenkins and have requested me to inform you that he never had a bad word for anyone.

I beg you to believe that I remain … etc, etc, etc.'

Mrs Jenkins's letter, filled with the most exquisite lack of emotion, said that she had received a standard campaign medal. Thomas was inconsolable.

'I must go to Lisbon immediately.'

'But look at the date on the colonel's letter, Thomas. Stadfast will be buried by now. Your first duty is to your mother.'

Evidently, this had not occurred to him.

'Yes, I suppose so. We will leave for England in the morning.'

At last I was going to the land of my hopes and dreams but had to conceal my joy. I had met the deceased hero only briefly and he had made little impression but I made the appropriate effort to appear bereft.

We stayed one night at a comfortless inn near the English Channel. The food was tasteless and the rough wine undrinkable in the country boasting the world's finest cuisine and vineyards. The stench of staleness, drunkards and their urine reminded me of Súir Island and the plight of my poor parents, which assisted my endeavours to feel as miserable as Thomas. The next day, as the old packet creaked and tossed across the Channel to Dover, he vomited violently and looked so debilitated that I began to wonder if I would have to tell his mother that she had lost both her sons. I was innately immune to seasickness.

The English soil worked its magic. As soon as we stepped ashore Thomas was cured and I was transformed into an Englishwoman. I was Mrs Marguerite Jenkins, as legitimate here as in Paris, where I had gloried in being addressed as *Madame Jhoncan*. No Parisian could pronounce Jenkins.

In order to quell my excitement and relieve the monotony of the road from Dover to Hampshire, I took the opportunity to broach more serious matters.

'Forgive me for asking such an indelicate question at this time, but will you now be the sole heir to your family fortune after your mother?'

Thomas had apparently never thought about his financial affairs, or needed to think about them.

'I imagine so. When my father died they said his capital would provide each of us with an income of five thousand per annum or was it six thousand, I cannot remember precisely? It was over four years ago.'

'So Stadfast's income will now be divided between you and your mother?'

'Our attorney deals with all these affairs. Mother will speak to him.'

My enquiries were clearly irritating Thomas and I quickly changed the subject.

My first impression of the picturesque hamlet of Sydmonton was of a featureless beauty blot on the Hampshire landscape, redeemed only by its location less than a day's drive from London. I had not come to England to live in a rural hermitage. My sojourn in Paris had fed my addiction to the sophistication of city life yet, surprisingly, I immediately warmed to my new home. The classical English country house stood at the centre of a pristine estate resplendent with a parkland arboretum, mown paddocks, cultivated shrubs, flower beds, artificial lakes with ornamental fountains and classical equestrian facilities. There was not a sign of agriculture anywhere.

Immediately after our arrival Thomas took me to meet his mother. He assured me that she was fully acquainted with my history but would never ask an indelicate question. She was a scholar like Miss Dwyer and subscribed to the same progressive ideas.

A butler led us into the most imposing room I was ever to encounter in a private house, and few have encountered as many imposing rooms in private houses as me. Like the estate itself, it made me feel as if a prophetic architect had conceived it as an immaculate garden to cultivate the most delicate flowers of my spirit.

From twenty feet above the nine muses in white plaster relief rained ecstasy down onto ivory-edged shelves reaching up as if to offer back the gratitude of inspired authors past and present. The library was fifty feet long and as broad as it was high. At one end the warm light of the summer day radiated through a tall window and at the other a spiral staircase, an ornamental pastiche of ironwork, led up to a mezzanine gallery dividing the four book-lined walls. There could have been no comparable literary collection in England outside of the ancient universities. I had found my rightful home, or perhaps more fortuitously, Mrs Jenkins's rightful home.

The woman in her fifties put down an open volume covering the last visible fragment of the intricate marquetry on her crowded Hepplewhite writing table. She stood up to welcome me. Mrs Jenkins – I never addressed her in any other way – had tightly bound grey hair and a complexion so colourless that I wondered if she was ill. She was tall and imposing and her face, more handsome than beautiful, exuded immense culture. Her clothes were modest but there was nothing about them or her demeanour to suggest a mother in mourning. She smiled slightly to greet her surviving son displaying no glimmer of sentiment. Thomas spoke formally without mentioning his deceased brother.

'Mother, do please forgive me. I have delayed too long but permit me now to introduce you to my wife, Marguerite.'

'I trust that you had a pleasant journey, Marguerite. We shall do our simple best to make you comfortable here.'

I insincerely apologised for imposing my presence at this sad time, offered my unfelt sympathy and uttered the touchingly sombre praise of Stadfast I had prepared in advance. Mrs Jenkins replied in a cold monotone.

'Thank you, Marguerite, but when my beloved husband was taken from me I was advised to confine my tears to my bedchamber. It proved sound advice. My grief cannot be allowed to mar this happiest of occasions. It is an unimaginable joy to meet the only daughter-in-law I shall ever know.'

I detected neither happiness nor irony in Mrs Jenkins voice, though she was undoubtedly aware that she would never know any grandchildren either. The barren Mrs Margaret Farmer did not exist. I was her son's legitimate wife and no one else.

Mrs Jenkins gestured to dismiss Thomas, who gladly left me to become acquainted with his mother. I prepared myself for a lecture on how fortunate I was to be chosen by such fine man and how I would be expected to behave as a member of her distinguished household. But Mrs Jenkins made no further reference to her family. The invasions of an eventful life had demolished her maternal instincts, if she ever had any. Now she had lost a son but gained the daughter she might have craved. Indeed, she was the mother I might have craved for myself.

'It is, Marguerite, as if I have known you since you were a small child. My second cousin Anne wrote to me many times of her brilliant student and your poetry and *belles lettres*. I shall look forward to reading them or, if you prefer, you may read them to me. But I see that you are fascinated by my simple library. This house is your home now and you are free to avail yourself of its facilities at your leisure.'

Mrs Jenkins initiated me into her catalogue, which included works by every author I knew and many more by those I would come to know, most of them in person.

'Since you have a love of poetry, Marguerite, you might wish to peruse this new anthology. It was published last year by a young man of about your age. It displays extraordinary passion, though I very much doubt that the Sixth Lord Byron has the talent to replicate work of this quality.'

I was instantly captivated by *Hours of Idleness*. The title in itself was an abstraction that would later inspire my *Idler in Italy* and *Idler in France*. In the months and years that followed Mrs Jenkins acquired all of Byron's works as they were published, and together we subjected them, word by word, to critical analysis. I memorised long passages with no preconception of how rewarding this illuminating obsession would transpire.

Thomas had described his mother as out of the same mould as Miss Dwyer. Hard as I found it to believe, it was a superior mould.

'Anne is a teacher while I am a simple student. I study here cocooned in my private academe because the enlightened thinkers of our anachronistic universities cannot comprehend the ingenuities of our gender. This is my university and shall be yours too, Marguerite, should you so desire.'

I did so desire. For six years I took my tutorials from the masters that papered the exquisite walls of my commandeered library. I tested my intellect, comprehension, memory and reason to their limits. I consumed the classics in Greek, Latin and the literature of modern languages. I absorbed the humanities, sciences, mathematics and gained an insight into the religions and cultures of the world. And I emerged the most comprehensively educated woman in the land.

'Mr Sadleir, you insult us both by implying that Captain Jenkins took advantage of my dependence upon him. You must have appreciated that it was not in his character to force me to attend orgies or dance naked on the dining table to amuse his friends. This, and a hundred other scandalous distortions were fabricated years later by vindictive journalists and envious inferiors. While his mother was alive Thomas would not dare attempt to make me do anything against my will. Vulgarity was always alien to me.'

'My research led me to believe otherwise, your ladyship.'

'Well, I might occasionally have become a little carried away at the end of a pleasant evening.'

Summer and winter, I was in the library by five in the morning. Mrs Jenkins joined me at a more civilised hour and ordered breakfast to be taken in situ before immersing herself in academic analysis. She was writing a learned thesis, as yet untitled.

'Thank you for your kind offer of assistance, Marguerite, but you will understand that my thoughts must be pure and the arguments of my original conception.'

I did not understand what she meant until I realised that Mrs Jenkins had no intention of completing her thesis, if she was writing one at all. It was a giant charade to conceal dark secrets, never to be breathed in her lifetime. She would tell me nothing about her late husband, so obviously constantly in her mind. Once she let slip that he had been a sea captain but would not volunteer a word about the source of his apparently immense fortune. It could not have been the untenanted estate consisting only of the mansion and an ornamental landscape little larger than Father's land at Curragheen. I suppressed my curiosity and Thomas extended his compassionate leave, indefinitely. He resumed his duties as master of the hunt and the purposeful life of an authentic English country gentleman. How different from my father.

115

For all her mysterious serenity Mrs Jenkins was well versed in the ways of the world and acquainted with people in many walks of life. She stretched my education far beyond the unmarked boundaries of Sydmonton and opened my eyes to an England normally forbidden to ladies of the upper classes; an England foreign to my childhood fantasies. She showed me the reality of the industrial revolution. In a foul smelling textile mill, I witnessed what would now be called a Kafkaesque illusion: regiments of looms swaying in hypnotic unison, mechanical soldiers drilled by hungry half-human female operators. I experienced the filth and sweat of a steam engine factory in Birmingham. In Portsmouth a prosperous industrialist conducted me on a tour of his ship-building yard and explained the treacherous workings of a fiery anchor forge, feigning regret for the lives it claimed. Factory owners and entrepreneurs lectured me on the complexities of manufacture. They understood the intricacies of science but not the men and women whose individuality they accelerated to a living death in their unsanitary mausoleums of perilous production.

Back in my exclusive college I studied economics and the importance of wealth creation, and read the works of progressive politicians and original thinkers. None could tell me why symbols of success, titles and birthright that signify nothing predominated, and probably will always predominate in the human psyche over the welfare and lifestyle of those deemed inferior.

'It is doubtful whether advantage is derived from a constant intercourse with superior minds. If our own be possessed of power, the collision is likely to excite it into action and original thoughts are consequently elicited. But if inequality exists the inferior mind is quelled by the strong.'

That first enchanted autumn and winter in Hampshire marked the beginning of the end of the Captain Thomas Jenkins with whom I fell in love in Clonmel. The change was invisible. Why must love be blind? Thomas's mother raised no discernible objection when he filled her home with parasitic house guests who overstayed their welcome, and formed peripheral friendships with me. As far as I knew, none of them was aware of my past or true marital status. Thomas's invitations were always returned. He often took me to London where we were received in luxurious homes and provided with all we could desire. Yet even in London I was never entirely free of Ireland. At a private reception I was introduced to the twenty-one-year-old Member of Parliament for Cashel. This charming rotten borough just ten miles from Clonmel had a count of just twenty-four eligible voters. Thomas had met this extraordinary young politician when he was visiting his constituency to distribute tokens of appreciation in anticipation of a unanimous victory at a forthcoming election. Like its parliamentary representative, I had been to Cashel only once but we happily reminisced together about the picturesque idyll of my invented childhood. The brilliant youth expounded the Tory philosophy with the eloquence of an elder statesman. I was unconvinced, but we remained loyal friends throughout his long career, even after I began to support his party. As one of the most prolific prime ministers in British history, Sir Robert Peel always found time to respond to my correspondence and sometimes heed my advice.

I found London, like Paris, the antithesis of the urban paradise. The Thames was an open sewer over which the smoke of a million chimneys wafted eastward blackening a dead sea of infested slums. Not only London Bridge but half the city was falling down; buckling beneath the weight of miners of the gold that never paved its streets. Self-deluding labourers, the unenlightened of trade, were everywhere in evidence. Some slaughtered cattle, pigs and sheep, clogging the gutters with blood and entrails. Some milked cows in stinking dairies polluting the human habitation on their doorsteps. Some hawked clothes sewn from rags in stifling sweatshops, while others offered their emaciated bodies to prostitution. Napoleon's picture of England as a nation of shopkeepers was indeed the most incisive of insults. But for me there was another nation of shopkeepers unsullied by Napoleonic hyperbole.

Thomas initiated me into the fine art now called conspicuous consumption. Together we patronised pioneers of market perception purveying merchandise unmatched by the pretentiousness of Dublin or even Paris. William Fortnum, Hugh Mason, John Hatchard, George and Henry Berry, Hugh Rudd, Thomas Twining, John Lobb, James Lock, James Grieves and Thomas Hawkes welcomed us to their houses of quality, which to this day thrive to applaud the discerning of the moneyed classes and affront the retrospective sages who still defame trade and commerce.

London, then as always, offered more diverse culture than any city of the world. Despite the addiction to luxury embedded in my ego, I derived gratification from some of its cheaper diversions. I visited historic sites, galleries, museums and attended free lectures at the learned societies. I was even enthralled by the ubiquitous musicians, freak shows, acrobats and illusionists that energised the streets. I recorded all I saw, and many years later published *The Magic Lantern*, my perceptive observations whittled down to four innocuous essays: visits to Hyde Park, the Italian Opera, the Egyptian Tomb, and the tragic auction of the possessions of a hapless debtor.

'Well done, Dr Madden, Mr Sadleir and Mr Malloy. How clever of you all to point out the uncanny prophecy in the last, and how careless of you to have omitted the inspiration of my father's experience.'

'Indeed, Lady Blessington, undoubtedly you will have more to tell us about your experience of auctions. But first we would like to know more about Captain Jenkins. How did you find time for him while you were studying so intensely, touring with Mrs Jenkins and engaged in so many social pursuits?'

'I presume, Mr Sadleir, that as usual you are talking about sex. Why not say what you mean? I never neglected Thomas or denied him his illegitimate rights. And contrary to your poor opinion of my femininity, these were activities in which I participated willingly and with unequivocal pleasure.'

One morning before sunrise I was alone in the library reading by lamplight, when I was startled by an apparition. The ghost of my living father: Edmond

'Beau' Power in all the splendour of his hunting attire: scarlet coat, lace-fronted shirt, high cravat and gleaming boots: the same height, the same manly build and the same handsome features. It was of course Thomas, who was nothing like my father.

He had come to accept my seal of approval on his proud appearance. My approbation was as important to him as my love. Thomas was to host the most prestigious meet of the season that day. Unlike the mundane Irish hunts in which Father competed, this was an occasion when no rider would dare dress other than as tradition dictated. In England hunting was a rite not a sporting event. Its object was the barbaric slaughter of a miniscule proportion of the wildlife posing a threat to agriculture.

Fifty mounted huntsmen assembled on the mansion forecourt creating a splendid spectacle as they toasted success to their inconsequential endeavours in the vintage champagne traditionally provided by the master of the hunt. At midday, there was a lavish banquet for which I emerged from the library inappropriately dressed to congratulate the fearless hunters. I thought *Winter* from Vivaldi's *Four Seasons*, with its allegorical depiction of a hunting scene might be a suitable entertainment for Thomas's friends. I excelled at the violin. Thomas however had engaged a band of minstrels whose music was less lively and more cacophonous. Apparently this was part of the ritual and my recital was not required. I returned to the library where the trumpets, tambourines and raucous singing resounded from the great hall so loudly that the books vibrated on their shelves. Three fell on the floor. Mrs Jenkins overtly displayed her unawareness of the disturbance.

'Marguerite, perhaps you can assist me to interpret these lines of Horace: do you consider them well chosen to their context?'

Mrs Jenkins was deceiving herself. Was I deceiving myself too? Was Thomas a fallible human being no better than my father? No, I was being ridiculous. Edmond Power had been a magistrate striving to defend an Irish wasteland from petty insurgents. Captain Thomas Jenkins was an officer striving in rural Hampshire to defend the British Empire from the tyranny of a continental dictator. Edmond Power aspired to be a sportsman and a gentleman. Thomas Jenkins was born a sportsman and a gentleman. Edmond Power's beloved stables were an overused extravagance. Thomas Jenkins's pristine stables were an underused necessity. Edmond Power entertained for social advancement. Thomas Jenkins entertained as expected of the class of his birth. Edmond Power was half-educated. Thomas Jenkins was a product of the finest education money could buy who carelessly lost his taste for learning on the road from Oxford.

Thomas was first and foremost an officer of the British Army. When the hunting season of 1809 finally ended, ignoring my forebodings, he set sail to replace his brother in the latest Anglo-Portuguese offensive in the interminable Peninsular War. None of the officers of the Eleventh Light Dragoons serving in Portugal could recall a Lieutenant Stadfast Jenkins.

I dare not think about the dangers Thomas was facing but Mrs Jenkins neither showed nor expressed concern for her son's welfare. She sent him brief and prosaic notes while all my letters were expansive and emotive. I praised his courage and with suspicious sincerity wrote of my undying love and devotion. I sent amusing anecdotes, news of home and poetry bemoaning my loneliness. Thomas's replies added a little fuel to the winter fires.

Captain Thomas Jenkins served with the Duke of Wellington for over two-and-a-half years, during which I was never despondent for a day. I cannot honestly say that I missed him. Mrs Jenkins passively propelled my academic pursuits: guiding without teaching and advising without preaching. She and her library provided all the companionship I needed; well, almost all. In Thomas's absence, life in Hampshire was tranquil but not silent nor dull. The uncommunicative Mrs Jenkins proved remarkably gregarious inviting an exclusive circle of friends. She always introduced me as her daughter-in-law reciting my fictitious past more convincingly than I did myself. By example, she taught me how to put visitors at their ease by encouraging inconsequential conversation; a practice of which I disapproved and was never to permit in my own homes. She condoned no gossip, intrigue or indecorous behaviour and was particularly sensitive to personal or commercial promotion. I deplored these too but I had learnt the necessity of freedom of speech from the glorious oratory of John Philpot Curren and reserved my rational cynicism for the mature journal that I now kept in secret in deference to my situation. Though I acted as Mrs Jenkins's co-hostess she never allowed me to forget that I was a guest in her house.

'I trust, Dr Madden, that you and your ill-informed imitators now appreciate that *all* my time in Hampshire was occupied constructively – dancing naked on the table indeed!'

On 12th September 1810, Mrs Jenkins accompanied me to London to attend a truly aristocratic wedding. The Honourable John Hume Purves married Miss Ellen Power at St Mary's Church, Marylebone. I was the only member of my family invited. The bridegroom's family was also sparsely represented. His father, the fourth Baronet Sir William Alexander Hume Purves and his fourth wife were heavily committed and unable to make the journey from Scotland. It is a pity that the camera had not yet been invented. The wedding party would have made such a splendid photograph. John Hume Purves in the kilted dress uniform of the Scots Greys and his best man Colonel William Stewart in the bright red of his Irish family tartan, flanked the beautiful Ellen in the virginal white gown elegantly camouflaging the early stage of her pregnancy. After the ceremony she left for her honeymoon at Killymoon Castle, County Tyrone, Ireland, while her new husband returned home to Purves Hall, Berwickshire, Scotland.

Before she left, I promised Ellen that I would always take care of Mary Ann. This was an embarrassing mistake. Mrs Jenkins overheard, apologised for being so remiss and insisted on giving me an allowance to support my family. Mary Ann wrote from our charitable cousins' address thanking me for the money and saying nothing more than that she was well, which meant that she was desperately unhappy. I considered bringing her to Hampshire but changed my mind. She had such a dreadful Irish accent. Months passed, Mrs Jenkins grew paler and her energy waned. Her appetite for both the reclusive and gregarious life diminished and her intentionally purposeless research abated into apathy. She ceased issuing invitations and walking and riding with me in the country. Eventually I felt compelled to confront her.

'I fear you are unwell, Mrs Jenkins. Would you not be wise to consult a doctor?'

'Doctor? I have never consulted a doctor in my life. There is absolutely nothing wrong with me, Marguerite.'

'I am sure it is nothing serious, but it is possible that you have contracted a debilitating condition which can be treated before it grows worse.'

'And if I have some form of disease, what do you imagine a doctor will do? You know full well that medical science has not advanced one iota in two thousand years.'

I was not sure that this was true, but I was sure that Mrs Jenkins knew exactly what was wrong with her, yet she denied ill-health until the inevitable end.

Mrs Jenkins became weaker and her pain intensified. Hardly able to walk, she could no longer maintain the fruitless aesthetic standards of her hermetic estate and passed me the mantle of mistress of the house. I enrolled myself into a new faculty at my private university and studied the art of dissemination of limitless wealth. I learnt how to delegate to a hierarchy of servants, how to supervise the maintenance of the landscape and ornamental gardens, the stables and stud and to how stock the larder and wine cellar with the finest of the fine. In short I made myself indispensable. Those who make themselves indispensable must be dispensed with immediately, was a tenet to which I had strictly adhered to the benefit of Power & O'Brien. Mrs Jenkins was unaware of this unassailable business principle and in her deteriorating eyes I could do no wrong.

I did wrong. I had been separated from Thomas for longer than we were together. Often there was no word from him for months. His mother was formally his next of kin and she would probably have mentioned it to me if she were informed that he died or been killed. I therefore surmised that he was alive and amusing himself with some Portuguese or Spanish mistress. I of course remained loyal, patient and charitable.

On 1st September 1811, I celebrated my twenty-second birthday by ending my loyalty, patience and charity. Mrs Jenkins turned an almost literally blind eye while I entertained her son's friends. She was more experienced in the ways of the world than she failed to disguise. The secrets of her past festered and rotted within her body and mind until they could contain them no more.

The doctor shook his head in despair and wrote out the death certificate: 'Widow, age fifty-nine years and nine months; died of natural causes, 15th June 1812'.

'Had Mrs Jenkins not been so stubborn and consulted me when she first felt unwell, her life might have been prolonged by twenty years.'

I wrote immediately to Thomas.

Bad news travels fast but not always fast enough. Thomas was not home in time for his mother's funeral. Defying my for once totally sincere grief, I made the arrangements alone. All her servants attended the interment in a nearby churchyard. Without exception they loved their employer and respected her uncompromising standards. It was of no consequence that their wages had remained static since the death of her husband. Mrs Jenkins never had a bad word for anybody, was confirmed by the remarkable number of friends and acquaintances who came to her funeral from every corner of the land and from France and Italy. Complying with what I presumed to be her wishes I accommodated and entertained them all in befitting luxury. And that was the last I heard of any of them. That is not quite true; I received several thank-you letters.

Miss Dwyer sent me a letter of condolence and an apology for being unable to attend. I observed a tremor in the faultless handwriting in which she had corresponded with me since I left Ireland. Two months later she followed her second cousin to the grave. My beloved teacher was buried without religious rites, as instructed in her will, before the news of her death reached me. There was no one to pronounce a eulogy or set a gravestone.

Her attorney traced Thomas via his regiment and wrote to inform him that as the nearest living relative of Miss Anne Dwyer of Knockbrit he was the sole beneficiary of her estate. Thomas instructed him to sell all Miss Dwyer's possessions, except her books which he had transported to Hampshire as a gift for me. By pure coincidence, the cottage and its contents realised the precise total of the shipping cost and the attorney's fee. The light of my childhood was delivered three months later. I left the sad old books in their crates in a corner of Mrs Jenkins library, where there were superior copies of all of them.

I met Captain Thomas Jenkins from his ship when it docked at Southampton. Again I was confronted by an apparition, not of the dandified sportsman Edmond 'Beau' Power in his heyday, but of my father as I imagined him then, an aging man in tired civilian clothes. Thomas had not come home simply on compassionate leave. He had been discharged in disgrace having left four men dead and ten others permanently injured in a blundered manoeuvre. Wisely, he had acknowledged his error, forfeited his commission, and left the Duke of Wellington to win the Battle of Salamanca without him. I did not ask for more detail. I no longer cared.

After thirty months of separation, and without Mrs Jenkins, I saw no future in our marriage of deceit. Thomas would never receive a peerage or even a knighthood. I was not destined to be Lady Marguerite Jenkins although it was just possible that I was Lady Margaret St Leger Farmer. It was eight years since I left my legal husband and Sir Fystite might now be dead. And there was always the hope that Maurice himself might be dead.

With indecent haste, Thomas recovered from both the loss of his mother and the men under his command and resumed the life of a gentleman. He was no longer a gentleman. The horrors of war, blood, death and disaster had hardened his character. Now he gambled, drank and preferred the company of his hunting cronies to mine. He began entertaining again but without the noble panache I once so admired. Fewer of his invitations were reciprocated. He continued to buy me gifts – spending was in his blood – with decreasing generosity. He stopped Mrs Jenkins's allowance for my family. Sometimes he took me to London, and once there would leave me with friends and go off to deal with unspecified heavy commitments. I did not exert myself to presume their nature.

On one such occasion, I found myself in the house of the Reverend Francis Lee. This Christian gentleman held the exalted position of chaplain to the Prince of Wales. Since the Prince's interests were, to put it mildly, sacrilegious, I imagined the appointment to be singularly undemanding. And I was soon to learn that this was indeed the case. The royal chaplain spent most of the year with his mistress in Madrid.

Thus I was entertained by his wife, with whom I discovered an invaluable affinity. Mrs Catherine Lee was like me extraordinarily vivacious, loved society and scholarly pursuit, and destined to a life of turmoil of her own making. She too was disillusioned by religion, particularly as practised by the pious Reverend Lee, who she was about to leave for her lover, Captain Georges de Blaquiere, heir to the fabulous fortune of the Barons de Blaquiere, and father of two or possibly all three of her children.

Catherine expostulated her husband's unreasonable jealousy. When in London the Reverend Lee lived in a separate house from which his children, who he insisted were his own, were prohibited. The devout man of the cloth was pursuing a protracted lawsuit against de Blaquiere for 'criminal conversation' or usurping his home and family - an indictable offence in English law until the mid-nineteenth century – and expecting to win disproportionate unhallowed damages.

Thomas, for reasons that I had yet to learn, greatly sympathised with Georges and Catherine, and invited them and her - or their - children to shelter from the chaplain's holy wrath with us in Hampshire. For the next six months Thomas provided the wealthy fugitives with appropriate accommodation, supplied their every need, and naturally declined their polite offers of recompense.

From time to time Captain de Blaquiere returned to London in search of a permanent home and once on military duty, leaving his mistress and adopted family in my care. I seldom had the opportunity to talk frankly with another woman. Catherine excelled at talking frankly. With little inhibition she disclosed the intimate details of her, to say the least, adventurous life; that is the version of those intimate details she wished me to hear. And not to be outdone, I disclosed my marital status and deteriorating relationship with Thomas. This was a mistake.

'My dear Marguerite, how fortunate you are to be without the burden of children. If you have overstayed Captain Jenkins's welcome, what is there to prevent you doing as I have done?'

'If only it were that simple, Catherine. Where is there for me to go? I have no money of my own.'

'Nonsense, Marguerite, you cannot seriously tell me that you have no rich admirers?'

'Catherine, I have hardly anything else but if I leave with another man Thomas will have no compunction about disgracing me in society. Or he might do as the Reverend Lee has done and claim retribution from my intended guardian through the courts.'

'Don't be too certain of that, Marguerite. A fine-looking man like Thomas is bound to be keeping a mistress of his own, or more than one. Why not confront him? Perhaps he will be happy to be rid of you.'

'Possibly, I cannot tell.'

On the very day that I decided to take Catherine's advice and leave Thomas, I received news of yet another visitation from the Angel of Death. I shall not be hypocritical and say that I was unduly saddened to hear of Mother's demise. She had never liked me from the day I was born and I never grew to like her. Nonetheless, I found it distressing to think of her dying alone in a derelict lodging in a Dublin backstreet.

Some months before, Father, unable to cope with Mother's serene ability to weather the storm of disgrace, had left her and moved in with a fancy woman – the term mistress being inappropriate to her class – called Mrs Hymes, a widow with a house in Clarendon Street near Trinity College and the fashionable centre of Dublin. I therefore presumed that she was well off and keeping him in the taverns to which he was accustomed.

With some reluctance, I requested Thomas to take me to my mother's funeral.

'Of course it is your duty to attend, as it is mine to accompany you. And while we are in Dublin, we can take the opportunity to call on some of our old friends.'

I had no friends, old or otherwise, in Dublin but throughout the excursion Thomas treated me with more consideration than at any time since he returned from Portugal. His good humour emboldened me to ask the reason for his increasing economies.

'Perhaps I can be of some help? Unlike you, Thomas, I am no stranger to financial problems.'

I had suspected that Thomas had always been aware of the source of his family wealth, but I was unprepared for the story that he then related with all the laudable dispassion of his upbringing.

When Mrs Jenkins had mentioned that her husband had been a sea captain, I envisaged a courageous officer of the Royal Navy at the peak of its prestige. But while every man in Nelson's navy was doing his duty as England expected, the self-styled Captain Jenkins had more propitious seas to sail.

Lenshark Jenkins was born the only and, needless to say, illegitimate son of a notorious privateer. At the age of twenty, off the island of Martinique, he witnessed his father justly disembowelled and beheaded by the rightful owner of his contraband cargo, and thrown to the mercy of the deep. Having surprisingly little taste for this implicit hazard of his family profession, Lenshark commandeered his father's ship, sailed it back to England and refitted it for a more magnanimous purpose. The bright young entrepreneur then advertised the aging galleon as available for the transportation of emigrants to the newly created United States of America. He painted a utopian picture of the New World and guaranteed safe passage for dramatically less than any other shipping line – subject to just one undemanding condition.

Lenshark showed his prospective passengers an enticing plan from which they were obliged to select a plot of arable land at an unidentified location and purchase it at a bargain price. The benevolent captain asked only that they pay for their passage and entrust him with fifty per cent of the cost of their idyllic homestead, as an irretrievable deposit.

This unique opportunity proved irresistible to optimistic young families keen to gamble all they possessed on an invisible gateway to prosperity, and Captain Jenkins was soon overwhelmed with applicants. To ensure that his passengers enjoyed a comfortable crossing, the captain thoughtfully provided meals, water, rum and even medicines on board, at unreasonable prices. He offered austere private cabin accommodation to richer passengers and allowed those of lesser means to hire hammocks by the hour and sleep peacefully amidst the stench of the crew's quarters. The generous captain permitted the remainder to huddle together exposed to the elements on deck, at no additional cost.

When the ship docked at its uncharted east coast destination. Lenshark Jenkins proved as good as his ambiguous word. Those exhausted passengers who had survived the voyage were surprised to discover that their captain had left to attend to heavy commitments elsewhere. They were however greeted by a helpful agent, well versed in the law of land purchase. This American criminal advised them of their liabilities and charitably settled for whatever money they had remaining. Thus with naivety in their hearts, dust in their pockets and free maps and fraudulent documents in their bags, the young pioneers set off on foot to find happiness two hundred miles inland.

Lenshark received no complaints. His maps were drawn so clearly that his brave passengers never found their way back to their port of embarkation. In any case, they had no legal redress in America. Their watertight contracts had been signed in England.

Captain Jenkins, cutlass in hand, collected all the proceeds that his accommodating agent dare not misappropriate, returned a modest percentage and sailed back to London to sell the same fertile land to another contingent of gullible settlers. Five years later Captain Jenkins, living comfortably in London, was the proud owner of a fleet of some twenty-four almost seaworthy ships based in America. He no longer sailed with his passengers, charged them for their voyage or required them to purchase land. Now builders of the American dream paid him to transport human cargos directly from Africa to the almost United States. Since slave ships were prohibited from polluting the sweat-laboured dockyards of England, Lenshark had no more knowledge of how many men, women and children perished aboard his vessels, than of what became of those who followed his maps of the unexplored hinterland of the New World.

By the age of forty, Mr Lenshark Jenkins – no longer Captain – could afford to dispose of his fleet and distance himself from its bountiful trade. He retired to a model estate in Hampshire, married a beautiful cultured impoverished woman considerably younger than himself and fathered two sons.

Many years later, I told Charles Dickens about Lenshark. Dickens, who dealt in little else but privation and inhumanity, found my carefully tarnished description so incredulous that he went himself to America and witnessed the reality he so vividly exposed in *Martin Chuzzlewit*.

How I wish that I had fictionalised the story myself; then at least one of my novels might have stood the test of time.

Thomas went on to reveal that after his well-earned retirement from the shipping industry, his father managed his financial affairs personally, drawing on his experience and commercial expertise and investing in sugar. Lenshark Jenkins's estate had been valued at two-hundred thousand pounds at the date of death. Mrs Jenkins, the sole beneficiary of his will, was unable to contemplate such an unwieldy sum and left her inheritance in the safe hands of an unimpeachably respectable attorney. This was a mistake. No reputable lawyer could be seen to invest his client's money in sugar – rumoured without cause to be a euphemism for the slave trade – and so in the time-honoured dynamic tradition of his profession practised masterful inactivity. He placed all Mrs Jenkins's money into gilt-edged bonds, which yielded neither significant income nor capital growth. In the eight years of her widowhood, legal costs and other essential encroachments had shrunk her late husband's over-laundered wealth to a whiter-than-white fragment. After Mrs Jenkins died, Thomas's bankers continued to finance his characteristic lifestyle, presuming him as creditworthy as his mother. It took them no more than a year or two to work out that this was not the case. He now informed me that he would have to realise his assets but did not explain what he meant by his assets or say how he intended to realise them.

When we reached the unimposing Catholic church in a godless suburb of Dublin, Mother's departed spirit had already been despatched into the heavenly care of the Desmonds and Sheehys. The smaller mortal congregation, including Father, had dispersed. Robert, Mary Ann, Ellen and her husband, John Hume Purves, waited for us outside the gate. Thomas and I greeted them briefly, went in and stood for a moment beside the still open grave with our heads purposelessly bowed. I muttered the obligatory eulogy. 'Mother never had a bad word for anybody.'

Thomas then left me alone with my family. His old landlord was in Dublin and he wished to pay his respects. If we are fortunate, he said, he might have some available accommodation and we could extend our stay. This was the last thing I wanted. The Honourable John Hume Purves also took his leave of us. He had heavy commitments elsewhere. He always had heavy commitments elsewhere. Ellen had travelled for more than forty-eight hours over land and sea from Berwickshire but was insufficiently exhausted to tell me her family news. She had lost her second child, Alexander, at the age of eleven months, but her two-year-old daughter, Louisa was well and already showing signs of extraordinary intelligence. Ellen, who preserved her delicate beauty, insisted that her marriage could have not been happier.

It would be four years before I saw my sister again. Only then, having given birth to another son and two daughters – the first called Marguerite – did she admit to me that her marriage could not have been less happy.

Robert had inherited the Power good looks and muscular physique but in contrast to his father remained unashamedly committed to the work ethic. He loved his job and had been promoted to assistant estate manager with no increment in salary. He told me that he was saving to get married. I congratulated him wholeheartedly, wondering how I would meet his none-too-subtle hint at a financial wedding present. I told him how much I was looking forward to attending his wedding and meeting his bride. Ten minutes earlier I had vowed upon my mother's grave never again to set foot in Ireland.

Robert had brought Mary Ann in a borrowed farm cart. Dressed in deep mourning, she looked a little more attractive than I recalled but remained unpleasantly shy. No, she had no admirers. When I promised Ellen that I would take care of her, I presumed it would only be until she found a husband. Now I realised that it might be a life sentence. The main benefit of a bereavement is that it excuses the necessity to appear over-exuberant at a family reunion.

I kept my vow and did not attend Robert's wedding. Three months later he wrote to say that his wife of four weeks had given birth to a healthy daughter. She too was christened Marguerite. My siblings were not very imaginative in their choice of names, but I sent all I could afford to reward the compliment.

I walked with Ellen to the address where Mother had died. We presumed it would be a small and squalid worker's dwelling. It was a small, clean and tidy worker's dwelling. We stopped at the nearby house of a doctor, who informed us he had done all he could for our mother, but her condition was severe and exacerbated by despair. She probably had no wish to live.

'Please do not concern yourself, Mrs Jenkins. Mr Power paid for all my attendances and medicines. His most ardent desire was that Mrs Power be made as comfortable as possible in her last hours.'

For the first time that day, I was overtaken by sincere grief, but not for my mother. I remembered the caring side of my father's crude nature; of his compassion for Edmond, Anne, and for Joe Lonergan when they were beyond hope of survival. I remembered his unspoken sympathy when he brought me home close to death. I should have made the effort to go to Mrs Hymes's house and thank him but my arrogant refusal to confront the woman who usurped my parents' unhappy marriage denied me my last chance to see my father.

Mother's cherished pedigree lay on a bedside table; a passport to a noble future proffered to her descendants by her departed soul. I added: 'Ellen Power, née Sheehy, died November 1814, wife of Edmond Power, Justice of the Peace in the County of Tipperary.' Resisting the temptation to bestow a title, I folded away the pretentious document to retain as my sole uncherished souvenir of my forebears.

A large and luxurious carriage drew up in the narrow cobbled lane outside. A liveried footman alighted and came to the door.

'Captain Jenkins awaits you without, my ladies.'

I found Thomas in better humour and more excited than I had seen him for months. His old landlord, a man called Charles Gardiner, had gratuitously put a townhouse at our disposal, complete with a complement of servants and all necessary supplies. Regrettably new tenants were due and we could stay two nights only. I was delighted. I could manage to avoid Dublin society for forty-eight hours without difficulty.

Thomas was certain that his friend would raise no objection to Ellen and John dining with us and staying the night before returning to Scotland.

'There will be plenty of room, Ellen. The house is in the same street where Marguerite and I used to live. You will remember that you came there once with your family,' said Thomas.

We collected John Hume Purves back at the church gate and the four of us were driven to the familiar terrace near in the city centre. A butler in the same livery as our coachman and footman greeted us at one of the twenty identical doors that graced both sides of the street.

'Thomas, does your friend Mr Gardiner own all these houses?'

'Oh yes, he owns this and two dozen or so other streets in this part of Dublin. You once commented on how impressed you were by the terraced mansions in Henrietta Street. That's another street Charles owns.'

'Why then did you never invite Mr Gardiner when we lived here, Thomas? He sounds like a man I might have enjoyed meeting.'

'Of course I invited him, Marguerite, but Charles is seldom in Dublin. I am not sure how many other homes he has, but he owns half of Country Tyrone and lives in London for most of the year. But don't worry, you will be meeting him very soon, in a couple of weeks in fact.'

I did not wish to meet anybody in Dublin, least of all a property speculator of no fixed abode.

'But we only have accommodation for two nights; where are we to stay for a fortnight?'

'Charles will not be free while we are here but he has accepted my invitation to come and stay in Hampshire for the season. It is the least I can do for him. His wife died suddenly about three months ago. She was very young and poor Charles has not recovered from the shock. I shall require your assistance to make his stay as pleasant as possible and take his mind off his loss. We must go back immediately make the necessary arrangements. I am thinking of bringing some people down from London to keep the house full and putting on one or two special meets of the hunt.'

Mr Gardiner's two nights of free board and lodging no longer seemed quite so generous when, in exchange, he was to receive accommodation and lavish hospitality for the entire winter. Thomas's landlord might have been in mourning, but evidently he retained the presence of mind to strike an astute bargain. This, I presumed, was how he became rich. I was wrong.

9

Two almost well-dressed, almost middle-aged and almost middle-class women, exuding the expensive perfumes of the nouveaux riches, stop by my portrait.

'It's the picture on the front of that book, the one in the shop. It was only seventy or eighty pounds. I'll have to get it next time,' says the younger, adorned with four-inch circular earrings.

'They might have sold out by then. I'd buy it now,' says the older and wiser, adorned with diamond rings and bracelets.

'I wanted to but they said their machine wouldn't take my card.'

'Wouldn't it, why not?'

'I don't really know.'

'Have you checked your balance? It only takes a second on line.'

'No it doesn't. The last time I tried, I gave up after two hours, and it took another hour to get through on the 'phone and then they wouldn't tell me because I'd forgotten my password.'

'When was that?'

'A few months ago, I suppose.'

'Haven't you paid since then?'

'Of course I have, every time they told me I was up to the limit.'

'Credit card interest is phenomenally expensive.'

'Is it?'

'Yes, but you don't have to pay. I've never paid a penny. You set up a direct debit from your current account to clear the balance before the interest starts ticking up.'

'I'll have to ask about that, when I get time.'

'If you don't have time to call the bank, when will you have time for another coffee-table book? There must be a hundred around your house and your villa in Tenerife and how many have you got in Florida? When did you last open one?'

'What a funny question. Don't you like having nice things around the house?'

I feel sorry for these discontented squanderers. Experience taught me that curbing overindulgence is invariably a mistake.

> *'Experience has taught us little, if it has not instructed us to pity the errors of others and to amend our own.'*

--

Had anyone seen us on our journey back from Dublin, they would not have believed that our relationship was in terminal decline or that Thomas was balanced precariously on the brink of bankruptcy. His only concern was that his erstwhile landlord should detect no false note in the harmony of our degenerating household and that no expense would be seen to be spared on his guest's comfort and pleasure. Together in the carriage, we drew up a programme of events for the winter season: dinners, balls, soirées, outings, shooting parties and hunts. We selected guests of befitting social status. We listed fine wines and exotic foodstuffs to be ordered from those prestigious London shops where Thomas's credit was still good.

We prepared instructions for the chef, butler, housekeeper, head gardener and chief groom, all of whom had been dismissed. We planned which of them Thomas would re-employ for the duration of the visit and listed the necessary additional servants.

Thomas became so absorbed in these arrangements that he took no account of their cost. Still he remained unusually courteous to me, while I remained suspicious of his motives. He was not a complete fool, nor was he naturally charitable. There had to be a reason for him going to such lengths for a man clearly in no need of benevolence. But I no longer cared about Thomas or his problems. I would support him through this charade, enjoy my last bow as his consort and leave him to the better nature of his creditors.

'Thomas, it would be helpful if I knew a little more about your friend Mr Gardiner. I do not recall hearing his name when we lived in Dublin.'

'Perhaps Viscount Mountjoy rings a bell?'

Viscount Mountjoy rang a peal of bells. *The* Viscount Mountjoy: my model knight of chivalry, the handsomest of the handsome, the bravest of the brave, the noblest of the noble. Could it be possible that Viscount Mountjoy would remember me? Surely not. Dare I remind him? What would he have thought of our stale house on Súir Island? And what if he discovered that I was the daughter of the murderer, Edmond Power? I soon put these matters from my mind. Viscount Mountjoy had probably forgotten all about Clonmel. The most memorable thing about Clonmel was that it was forgettable.

'How could I ever forget Mountjoy Square, the most delightful urban oasis in Dublin? I remember how I loved walking in its charming gardens on fine days. Is the name a coincidence or does your friend own the square as well as all the streets around it?'

'As a matter of fact he does, Marguerite. Charles's father, the first Viscount Mountjoy built it around 1785. They say he was an obsessive perfectionist who employed only the finest architects, builders and craftsmen. I'd wager that if you come back to Dublin in two hundred years those houses will be standing exactly as they are today.'

I have no intention of going back to Dublin but Thomas would have won his wager. The four precisely equal sides of Mountjoy Square are just as they were; plain terraced houses decorated with ornamental balconies and arched fanlights above the doors to break the monotony of the uninspired architecture. Forty-seven of the first Lord Mountjoy's Georgian monstrosities remain intact. Some of the interiors are resurrected to their original genteel splendour, but most are desecrated and divided into diminutive dwellings by discerning developers. The gardens, however, remain an urban oasis, that is, apart from the deafening traffic noise and unconvincingly camouflaged football pitch occupying half the space.

One guidebook says that the nearby Blessington Street is named after me!

Two weeks later, a stately convoy of a score or more vehicles trundled through the intricate wrought-iron gates of the Jenkins estate and proceeded majestically to the mansion forecourt, churning up the especially raked gravel. Our elaborate preparations were all in vain. The noble landlord had brought every possible amenity for his own comfort and pleasure. His servants included his valet, secretary and physician. His personal French chef, once employed by Napoleon himself, came equipped with a wagon load of fine wines and exotic viands. A specially fitted coach contained the viscount's wardrobe: the appropriate dress for every conceivable contingency. And two similar vehicles were crammed with theatrical costumes and properties.

As well as a landowner, a general and an Irish Representative Peer, Viscount Mountjoy was a leading theatrical impresario. As a modest gesture of appreciation for Captain and Mrs Jenkins's overwhelming generosity, a small troupe of players was to follow from London to present *Macbeth* – the precursor of bankruptcy in theatrical mythology – for our pleasure and for any friends we might care to invite. Mr Charles Gardiner himself would take the role of Macduff.

'Have a word with my secretary, my dear Thomas. He will see you are reimbursed for the actors' accommodation and requirements, and of course for my staff, you know.'

The cost of his guest's gesture of appreciation had not occurred to Thomas. On his behalf I breathed a disinterested sigh of relief.

I did not recognise the Viscount Mountjoy who now bowed and kissed my hand. It was fourteen years since I had last seen him, and then only for five minutes. He was hardly the prince for whose second coming I had yearned since childhood, though his civilian clothes were as overstated as the uniform that once made me believe that he was the king. Now a vacant and confused expression protruded above the wide collar of his sable coat which made him look like a disorientated brown bear. His fingers constantly danced on his unruly red hair, as if trying to feel out something to say from the top of his head. Once it was love at first sight and now it was boredom at second. Lord Mountjoy spoke only in platitudes. From the moment he arrived he pursued me at every opportunity in order to avoid discussing current affairs, politics or religion or uttering a critical word about anyone or anything. He did mention that I was almost as beautiful his late wife, which I presumed was meant to be a compliment.

One topic of conversation presented Lord Mountjoy with no difficulty. Like every man I ever met, he excelled at talking about himself.

'I was so sorry to hear about Lady Mountjoy. You must be heartbroken. For a man to lose his wife is always a tragedy, but to lose one so young is … '
I completed the sentence by miming despair. To a man of the theatre I feared I might seem like a desperate actress at an audition, yet this brief performance

reduced the noble lord to tears. He dropped his head into his hands, lifted it, opened his mouth and in hushed tones began to speak about himself.

'I am more than heartbroken, Mrs Jenkins. I am bereft, you see. I have lost my one and only true love. How am I to live without Mary? My children could have been blessed with a no more devoted mother, you know. Little Luke is just one-year-old and already an orphan, you see. There will never be a more beautiful woman than Mary, you know. She was unique. She never said a bad word about anybody. What am I to do?'

What was he to do? There must have been a thousand equally unique society beauties only too willing to step into the unique Mary's uniquely expensive shoes. I naturally had no intention of being number one thousand and one. I never joined a queue in my life. To relieve the tension, I said:

'I would love to hear more about Lady Mountjoy and your family.'

I prepared myself for more waterlogged tragedy. Instead our noble guest treated me to a rambling repetitive confessional.

'Mary was so sweet, so delicate, you cannot imagine how lovely she was, Mrs Jenkins. Well, actually you don't have to. A friend of mine, Sir Thomas Lawrence, he is a portrait painter, you know, captured her to perfection. I must show you his work. She was the most beautiful bride who ever lived. We were married in church, three times, you see.'

'You were married in church three times, your lordship?'

'Well yes, I wanted to be sure my children were legitimate, you know. It could cause problems for them in the future if they were not. You see, Mary was married to Campbell Browne.'

'Campbell Browne?'

'Oh yes, I should explain. Campbell was Mary's family name. She was Scottish, you see, with such a sweet accent. Major Browne added her name to his when they were married. He was the best friend I ever had in the regiment, you know, possibly the only friend.'

There was a pause. I tried to make some sense of this explanation. Was Thomas's friend grieving for Major Browne or Lady Mountjoy? Ready to be further confused, I asked his lordship to continue.

'You see, Mrs Jenkins, they posted Campbell Browne to the Continent to fight old Bonaparte; terrible business, you know. That would have been about 1806. Yes, it must have been, you see, because by then I'd resigned from active service. They made me deputy Lieutenant of County Tyrone, you see.'

'I didn't know you had been a soldier, Lord Mountjoy', I lied.

'Oh yes, I am still a soldier, but I fear not a very good one. You see, my father was killed in 1798 when I was sixteen and the Tyrone Militia gave me his rank as Lieutenant Colonel. It's some sort of regimental tradition; they love that sort of thing in the army, you know. I owed it to him, in a way, to do my stint after Eton but I had no taste for the life, you know.'

'Surely, as a regimental Colonel, your duties were not excessively arduous?'

'Actually they weren't. I spent most of the time up at Oxford. I read English literature but I only got a third, you see. They refused to give me a first because I did not attend the exams. They would insist on holding them on the one day

I was called away on military duty. It was all a bit unfair. I made the customary donation, you know. Forgive me, Mrs Jenkins, I digress.'

'I assure you this is all most fascinating, Lord Mountjoy. You were telling me about your weddings.' What else could I say?

'Oh yes, you see, Campbell Browne had only been married a month or two. He'd had no time to find a place to live or anything, so he asked me to look after Mary while he was abroad. Well, I was best man at their wedding, you know. How could I refuse?'

'This was surely a somewhat unusual request, your lordship?'

'Yes, I suppose it was, but you see Campbell Browne didn't have a living relative in the world and he trusted me implicitly. Then we didn't hear another word, you know. I made enquiries through the regiment of course – not a thing – vanished.'

'Had he deserted?'

'Good heavens no, Campbell Browne would never do a thing like that, Mrs Jenkins. He was the very soul of decency, you know.'

'So what did you do?'

'I was obliged to keep my side of the bargain, you see.'

'Did Major Browne make provision for his wife's maintenance, Lord Mountjoy?'

'Do you know I am not sure that he did? Anyway, I thought some sea air would agree with Mary, so I put my little house at Worthing at her disposal. She was terribly happy there, you know, but I owed it to Campbell Browne to go down occasionally to see that she had everything she needed.'

'Major Browne was indeed fortunate to have a friend like you, Lord Mountjoy. Few men would have been so honourable.'

I guessed where the story was leading but it would have been disrespectful to interrupt a penitent in full flow.

'I have to confess, Mrs Jenkins, I was not as honourable as Campbell Browne had every right to expect. You see, Mary was so alluring I somehow found myself yielding to temptation. And then, you see, before I knew where I was she was expecting young Charles. We thought Campbell Browne was either dead or, if not, no longer wanted to be married. It was only right for my son to be born in wedlock and take my name, you see. So I arranged a church wedding.'

'And you did the most honourable thing in the circumstances, Lord Mountjoy. But do tell me what prompted you to repeat the ceremony? Did you discover what became of Major Browne?'

Haunted by memories of Captain Farmer, I guessed the answer to both my questions.

'It was a most extraordinary thing, you see, Mrs Jenkins. One evening a few months after Mary's second baby was born, that is little Emily, you know, the butler opens the door and in comes old Campbell Browne, large as life, as if he had never been away. What could I do? I told him the whole story, you see. Was he upset? Not a bit of it. Couldn't thank me enough for looking after Mary. He cheerfully agreed to a divorce and off he went again. Well, a small consideration was involved, you know.'

I did not know and dare not ask what constituted a small consideration. Later I heard mention of eight thousand pounds, which was probably an underestimate.

'How gallant of the Major, and how romantic of you, Lord Mountjoy. So now Mary Campbell Browne was free to become your lawful wife.'

'Well no, actually she wasn't. You see, my lawyer tried to sort out the formalities for a couple of years, but couldn't trace hide nor hair of any Major Browne. Lawyers are not always terribly practical people, you know. Eventually we came to the conclusion that he must be dead, so Mary and I went back to the church. And no sooner were we home from our second honeymoon when Mary received the standard letter from the regiment advising her that her husband had been killed in action. Wonderful man, Campbell Browne, unique, never had a bad word for anybody, you know.'

I did know. Heavenly conversation must be exceedingly dull.

'How sad,' I said, thinking that the purchased widow had no reason to be at all sad, and wondering if the gallant major had left some remnant of his small consideration to his wife.

'Naturally we had to be married again to be certain that all the children were a hundred per cent legitimate. And they all are, you see. That is, I am fairy confident Harriet and baby Luke are. Everything had to be perfect for the wedding, you know. I had my little town house in Henrietta Street redecorated throughout with new white and gold furnishings and had Mary's wedding gown made in Italy to match. Twenty peasant women worked on it for a month; intricate white lace with gold embroidery, exquisite craftsmanship, you know. I held an intimate banquet in the little ballroom for three hundred people. They all gasped at her beauty when the footmen flung open the doors and I walked in with her in on my arm, you see.'

I marvelled that the poor woman did not die of embarrassment.

'Lady Mountjoy must have loved Dublin. Its society is always so friendly and considerate.'

'Actually I don't really know. She wasn't there very long. You see, Mrs Jenkins, immediately after the wedding we left for our third honeymoon on my little estate in County Tyrone. We were very much in love, you know, though I must admit that I did get the impression that Mary was never entirely happy in Ireland. I think, possibly because she was Scottish.'

I began to feel a certain affinity with the late Lady Mountjoy.

'Did you never live together in Ireland?'

'We might have lived there for a short while after we were married – for the first time, that is. But, you see Mrs Jenkins, they had made me an Irish Representative Peer by then and I had to be in London a good deal, so I bought little Seamore Place. I still use it myself but Mary never really liked it, you know. She thought it a bit old fashioned, so I bought her a little place in Manchester Square. That's where Harriet and Luke were conceived in legitimate wedlock. It's quite charming, but now cold and empty without her, you know.'

Anticipating another tearful outburst, I tried to divert the conversation.

'I am slightly familiar with Manchester Square, Lord Mountjoy. It's a great pity to leave one of its splendid houses unoccupied. But where do your children live?'

'My children, Mrs Jenkins? Oh yes, they would be in little Mountjoy Forest, you see. London is no place to bring up children – filthy air, you know. Children need a little space to run around. My stepmother, the dowager, and my sister Harriet look after them, with the nannies and governesses down at the little Cottage. It's a beautiful place but I am thinking about making some changes there, you know. I must ask Thomas to bring you over. Did I mention that my parents are deceased?'

I was to discover that the little Cottage might more appropriately have been called the Great Mansion, and that all the children in the country could run around and quite easily be lost in a small fraction of the little space at Mountjoy Forest.

I was beginning to find the noble thespian's tedious dramatics quite entertaining.

'Perhaps it will be of some comfort to you, Lord Mountjoy, to tell me how your poor wife was taken from you?'

The Tragic Death of Lady Mountjoy was Mr Charles Gardiner's most accomplished role as an actor.

'I have again to confess, Mrs Jenkins, I hold myself entirely to blame. I am not a selfish man, you know, but my second daughter, Harriet was my only legitimate child. I was desperate for a son and heir, you see.'

I did not see. The viscount's first son, Charles, was the child of a marriage three times blessed in church. Surely his right of inheritance was indisputable.

'I fear, Mrs Jenkins, that Mary was too weak to bear another child in such quick succession. I shall never forgive myself. She was ill from conception to birth, terrible sickness, you know. It is a miracle that little Luke was born healthy.'

Mr Gardiner mimed being overcome with emotion. It was one of his better unconvincing performances. When he had dried his forced tears, I asked: 'Did Lady Mountjoy die in childbirth?'

The actor's expression implied that the idea had never previously crossed his mind.

'No, no, no, Mary was living in London, you see; bad atmosphere, the smoke and so on. I thought she needed a change of air, you know. So we arranged a wet nurse for the baby and I took her away. But what made me choose Paris? I shall never forgive myself.'

What indeed? What was wrong with Worthing? These were not questions I felt free to ask, especially as Lord Mountjoy now had his hands together and eyes closed in a theatrical rendition of prayer. When God had finished forgiving him, I said: 'Your intentions were only for the best, Lord Mountjoy. Who is to say that the sea air would have been more merciful?'

'The sea air was not more merciful, Mrs Jenkins. You see, Mary suffered severe sea-sickness on the Channel and we never reached Paris. She passed away on the ninth of September at a country inn near Saint-Germain-en-Laye. I do not suppose you know it?'

'I believe it is close to the village of Chambourcy. Thomas and I were there once. It is not a place where anybody would wish to be buried.'

At this time, I was naturally unaware of the place where my own remains would eventually be interred.

'Indeed it is not, Mrs Jenkins. I arranged for her to be brought back to Dublin to be laid to rest in the Gardiner family vault at St Thomas's, Marlborough Street; splendid Church, finest Corinthian facade in the city. All our weddings were held there, you know. Mary died on her twenty-eighth birthday, you see, it was my dearest wish to give her a last present.'

A present in simultaneous celebration of birth and death sounded rather macabre.

'I cannot imagine a nobler gesture, Lord Mountjoy.'

'I felt so humble, you see Mrs Jenkins. Possibly you will not remember the catafalque the Emperor Napoleon had built for Marshal Duroc's lying in state last year? It was a most magnificent object, you know, covered by a great tapestry in gold and silver. It reminded me so much of poor Mary's wedding gown that I bought it and shipped it over to Dublin. I had it set it up in the ballroom at little Henrietta Street and all the walls in the house draped in purple and black velvet. Sixteen professional mourners attended the coffin, four at a time for a fortnight. It took a whole week to scrape up the congealed candle grease from the floor, you know.'

A hundred carriages containing the cream of Irish society had followed Lady Mountjoy's coffin to her fabulous funeral at St. Thomas's Church, and for the next three decades Dublin society spoke with solemn reverence of the four-thousand pounds that Viscount Mountjoy spent on the most vulgar and ostentatious spectacle the city had ever known. Today, Lady Mountjoy is forgotten. In fact, St Thomas's Church is forgotten. It was destroyed in the Irish civil war of 1922 when the remains of the Gardiner family were removed to the Dublin Glasnevin Cemetery where they can still be found with some difficulty. The St George and St Thomas Church now occupying the site is more in the true Christian tradition, modest and nondescript.

The bereaved Lord Mountjoy declined to attend Thomas's welcoming banquet or the special hunt convened in his honour. He showed no interest in sightseeing. He neither drank nor gambled. But very soon the inexorable trauma of his tragic loss slipped his mind and his company became almost tolerable. I began to find his long aristocratic nose, weak chin and sublime English public-school accent inexplicably attractive.

Two days after his arrival Lord Mountjoy commenced an unimaginative transformation of Thomas's great hall into a theatre. His servants hung curtains to create a stage, piled up tables and cushions and covered them with black sheets. 'They represent the blasted heath, you see,' explained the noble director, who commandeered so much of the furniture that the house began to look as if Thomas was in the throes of moving out, which in the circumstances, might have been a more appropriate exercise. When the stage was set and the chairs arranged, Mr Gardiner's valet read *Macbeth* aloud in a dreary monotone, while the most elaborately attired Macduff ever to tread the boards, wielded a wooden sword and fought valiantly with his lines. Poor Macbeth!

Mr Gardiner's small troupe of players arrived later that day. They had no need to rehearse *Macbeth* or indeed any of Shakespeare's plays. The title role was to be taken by Mr Edmund Kean, the most acclaimed actor in the land. Banquo would be played by John Philip Kemble and his sister, Sarah Siddons had been lured from recent retirement – at unwarranted expense – to perform her most celebrated role as Lady Macbeth. Other parts were to be played by the resident actors and actresses of the Drury Lane Theatre, all of whom were on first-name terms with their patron. Mr Gardiner insisted that I too address him as Charles and I permitted him to call me Marguerite. All the players praised Charles in the most extravagant terms for his acting, and also for his financial support. 'An extraordinary stage presence', was their general consensus. The portrayal of sincerity is an essential element of a professional actor's discipline, like disguising the deficiencies of a fellow performer.

A full house awarded the play a standing ovation.

'Mrs Jenkins, you will be kind enough introduce me to Mr Kemble? I am among his greatest admirers.' 'Mrs Siddons is as vivacious as when I first saw her thirty years ago.' 'It is such an honour to be in the same room as Mr Kean.' Some of Thomas's friends also wished to meet Mr Gardiner.

After the performance, feeling much like Lady Macbeth herself, I presided over a banquet together with my soon to be vanquished husband. The small troupe stayed a week, during which Thomas acquired a large number of new friends who he never saw again. On their last night the Drury Lane company lightened the tone with Sheridan's *School for Scandal* followed by an impromptu pantomime: *Cinderella*, what else? I laughed uproariously unaware that that I was playing a leading role in parodies of both.

More houseguests arrived and I dutifully ensured that they were entertained, boarded, wined and dined in the utmost splendour and introduced to Viscount Mountjoy. But as the weeks went by, I found the whole purposeless charade more and more bizarre. Certainly it distracted me from my uncertain future and was, I presumed, similarly beneficial to Thomas and Charles. Indeed, his lordship seemed increasingly relaxed and enamoured by new opportunities to enchant our guests with a variety of melodramatic renditions of *The Tragic Death of Lady Mountjoy*. He remained pretentiously disinterested in any serious matters of business or current affairs, but soon I observed him indulging in long and profound conversations with Thomas. I wondered what they had to talk about. Surely Thomas could not have been thinking of renting another townhouse in Dublin. However, I too had profound matters to discuss with Lord Mountjoy.

'Dare I ask you, Charles, to be kind enough to glance at these notes and sketches. I made them when we were living in your delightful little house in Dublin?'

The house is now converted into five family apartments, but I thought it polite to do as he did and always employ the adjective *little* when referring to his properties.

'Yes, of course; my dear Marguerite, what are they?'

'They are just a few simple ideas. This is a rearrangement of the ground and first floors. You will see that it creates fewer but more spacious and imposing rooms. Here is my improved layout for the garden: the exotic aviary makes an enchanting centrepiece, don't you agree? And this is my list of appropriate furnishings and ornamentation.'

As well as the theatre, Charles was passionate about every form of art. He scrutinised my work with the eye of an experienced connoisseur, maintaining intense concentration for almost three minutes.

'These are magnificent, you know, Marguerite. You capture precisely my own concepts for the interiors of all my little houses. You see, creativity was never Norman's forte.'

'Norman?'

'Luke Norman, my property agent, excellent fellow, you know.'

'Perhaps, Charles, you think my interiors too grand for a house intended only for letting?'

Charles Gardiner had never set foot in my former home or in the majority of the little houses that generated his gigantic unearned income.

'Quite the contrary, Marguerite, it is a disgrace if my tenants cannot live as befits the name of Mountjoy. I owe Thomas a sincere apology, you know. I shall instruct Norman to refund the rent. He is an excellent fellow, you see, but constantly hampers himself with practicalities. He is interested in profit, over-economical, you see.'

The excellent Mr Norman did not hamper himself with practicalities, nor was he interested in profit or over-economical. He was interested in lavishing his employer's money on the six-bedroom house he occupied as a perquisite of his much envied position.

'Charles, it is quite unnecessary to repay Thomas. We are both eternally grateful for your generosity when we came to Dublin for my mother's funeral.'

'Your mother's funeral! Really? I cannot recall Thomas mentioning it, you know. But do please accept my belated condolences. Your mother must have been a remarkable woman to have bequeathed such beauty and talent to you.'

Fearing that acting unfelt grief might incite another eulogy of the unique Mary Campbell Browne, I quickly thanked Charles for his sympathy, and returned to the more pressing topic of interior decoration.

'If you will permit me, my dear Marguerite, on my next visit to Dublin I shall take your plans and ask Norman to follow them throughout the estate. It should present no difficulty. You see, he worked for my father and only employs the finest builders and craftsmen. My six little warehouses are full of hand-made furniture, ornaments, sculptures, paintings and so on. They are always at his disposal. The experience will be of great benefit to him, you see.'

The excellent Mr Norman invariably benefitted from his experience. He was the richest property agent in Ireland.

'Are all your little houses in need of refurbishment, Charles?'

'I don't think so, but I am always interested in new ideas, you know. Perhaps you would like to come over and take a look at little Henrietta Street, with Thomas of course. I am sure you will enjoy it.'

There was nothing I would have enjoyed less than another visit to Dublin.

'Thank you for your kind invitation, Charles, I cannot wait to see the interior of your little house. I admired it so many times from the outside. But would it not be simpler if you were to first show me one of your London homes?'

'Yes, of course, Marguerite, but little Seamore Place is adequately furnished for my modest needs, you know. On the other hand, there is little Manchester Square. I have not returned there since poor Mary ... I believe in ghosts, you see.'

I did see. I also believed in ghosts and Mary Campbell Browne was the sort of ominous spirit I believed in most.

'Charles, Mary would not have wished her home to be neglected. The most virtuous thing you could do for her is to revive it in her memory.'

I did not of course consider that it might be equally virtuous if he were to revive it for me. I fell in love with Lord Mountjoy as a youth and now I was falling in love with him as a still comparatively young man with the means to provide all the security I could desire.

'You are quite right, my dear Marguerite, that is the least I should do for her, you know. Perhaps you and Thomas would prefer to come and stay with me at Seamore Place, and then I can take you over to little Manchester Square. It's just an ordinary little terraced house, you know, ten bedrooms, stables in the mews and a little back garden, very pleasant when the roses are in bloom, you see.'

I knew the house. It might have brought five hundred pounds if offered for sale but Charles proposed spending five thousand. His eccentricity was becoming increasingly seductive and I wondered how best to reciprocate.

On the day prior to his departure, Charles sent his valet to my room with a note to reassure me that I had achieved my object.

'My dear Marguerite, I have been considering your comments regarding the refurbishment of Manchester Square and would be honoured if you will permit me to go over a few points with you before I leave.

If it is convenient to you, might we meet in the library at eight this evening?

Charles.'

'Ninon de L'Enclos observes that if 'a man gives a woman wealth, it is only proof of his generosity; but if he gives her his time it is proof of his love.' This however cannot be considered as a conclusive proof, for in giving their time many men give that which is of no value to themselves or others.'

In the library? No one but me ever went to the library in the evening. Charles wished to be alone with me. I put Madame de L'Enclos's observation to the test.

It was almost nine-thirty when I swung open the double doors and made my entrance, dressed as I imagined the late Lady Mary Mountjoy. My impersonation had no effect whatsoever. Charles sat facing me in one of the armchairs I had ordered to be placed by the specially lit fire and judging from the number of books on the table beside him, he must have been there for some time. He had passed my test. He had not come to talk about interior decorating.

And so began my audition for the role of the next Lady Mountjoy, for which I had assiduously rehearsed my terms of acceptance.

I gestured delicately with my forefinger and Charles quickly closed the book he was holding upside-down: *The Collected Works of Lord Byron.*

'I see you are an admirer of Byron, Charles. In my opinion he is the most accomplished poet of our time.'

'Well, you see, I cannot claim to understand everything he writes but I do love dear Noel. Not long ago I went over to congratulate him on completing another canto of *Don Juan.* An immense work, you know; sometimes I fear he'll never finish it. I took him a few verses of my own and he was terribly complimentary. Noel is always so agreeable, you know.'

I did not know. From all I had read of Byron, he was anything but agreeable. Nonetheless, I was startled to discover that I was not only in the presence of an intimate friend of a living legend, but that Charles himself was a poet.

'I am led to believe Lord Byron lives as a hermit in an ancient castle somewhere in Italy. They say he hates England and the English. Do you know him well?'

'Oh yes, Noel and I have been friends for many years. He is a little younger than me, you see, but we always keep in touch. He is so terribly famous now, you see. I don't think he really hates England; he just thought it best to leave for a little peace and quiet. There was some sort of problem with his wife, you see, but he's always keen to hear the news from London. We know many of the same people, you know.'

'Are you planning to see Lord Byron again, Charles?'

'As it happens I am thinking of going over to Genoa in the spring. Perhaps you – and Thomas, of course – would care to join me. You will find dear Noel a most interesting companion, you know.'

The chance to meet my literary idol was worth as much as Charles's fortune. Well, perhaps not quite as much, but enough to make me conclude that my love was completely sincere. I would marry Lord Mountjoy and be happy forever – whether Maurice Farmer was alive or not.

A single sentence shattered my illusions.

'Thomas tells me you are dear old Beau Power's daughter. What a small world we live in.'

In my mind I yielded to anger and swore vengeance. I did not believe in anger or vengeance. What possessed Thomas to do this to me? Why had he betrayed my past to this weak man? Weak men always gossip. My digested past would now be regurgitated and spat out with venom a thousand times over.

I was wrong. Charles was not a weak man; he was a man with weaknesses and gossip was not among them. Oblivious to my fury, he launched into cheerful reminiscences of Súir Island. He would never forget the entertainment and camaraderie at *dear old Beau Power's* stale house. 'A sanctuary from the army camp; a breath of fresh air, you know.'

And he remembered Mother.

'What a tragedy dear Mrs Power is no longer with us. A beautiful lady, I would have loved to have seen her again. Now that I am reminded, Marguerite, I do recall a number of children and being struck by the exquisite features of one of the small girls, you know. That of course would have been you.'

That would not have been me. My childhood was marred by the consumptive features that vanished with puberty. The small girl Charles remembered was Ellen who was more beautiful than me from the day she was born. I chose not to disillusion him.

'And so how is dear old Beau, bearing up? The loss must have been a terrible blow, you see. Do pass on my sympathy.'

'Father will be most honoured to hear that you remember him, Charles. But no doubt Thomas also informed you why I cannot entirely share your high opinion of him.'

'You mean the business with Captain Farmer. I'm sure it was all a misunderstanding, you know. The poor man must have had some sort of illness of the mind. Doctors don't understand these things, you see. I think Campbell Browne might have had a similar problem.'

'Yes, Charles, you mentioned that.'

'Well it's just the same, you see, Marguerite, Farmer has been away so long that by now he probably no more wishes to be your husband than you wish to be his wife. Perhaps we should make some more enquiries. When we find him, I'm sure we can persuade him to be reasonable, you see.'

I was astonished, not only because Charles was unconcerned by the revelation that Thomas was not my husband, but because he used the word *we*. He was prepared to buy Maurice off and possibly marry me despite having been informed of my repugnant history?

I resumed the persona of Lady Mountjoy elect.

'I fear that you will find Captain Farmer as elusive as Major Browne. Thomas made a thorough search but there has been no word of my husband for years.'

'We can but try, you know. He must be somewhere, unless he has departed this life.'

'Charles, I am his next of kin. I would have been informed of his death.'

'Excellent, that means he's still alive, you see, and we can do things properly. Forgive my indelicacy, but Thomas implied your marriage had never been consummated. I believe it can therefore be annulled, you know.'

Thomas had revealed everything. To what end? I could no longer contain myself. I had to clarify my position once and for all.

'I am deeply grateful for your concern, Charles. You must think very well of Thomas to go to so much trouble and expense, so that *he* might be free to marry me.'

My emphasis worked. Charles paused for a full minute. He looked confused. I wanted to help him out of his dilemma but this was something he had to do for himself. Eventually he floundered on.

'Yes, of course, forgive me, Marguerite, I did not explain, you see. I have a rather delicate duty to perform. Well, you see, Thomas has confessed his undying love for you. He endlessly praises your exquisite tastes in – well, everything I suppose – and has told me how graciously you accepted his hospitality over the last five or six years. He cannot bring himself to tell you, but due to circumstances beyond his control, Thomas has fallen upon hard times. It turns out that his late mother was terribly extravagant, you see. He is desperately ashamed, but the fact is he's no longer in a position to support you in the style you have every right to expect.'

I permitted a gentle tear to dissolve my expression of concern into one of incredulity. Sarah Siddons had taught me a great deal but Charles seemed unmoved by my sensitive melodramatics.

'You see, Marguerite, Thomas will have to dispose of this estate. He intends to rejoin his regiment, poor man. I cannot imagine why but he tells me he loves the army life. Oh, and he did ask me to stress that he loves you too.'

I tried again.

'Oh this is most disturbing news, and so sudden. I had no idea that poor Thomas was in difficulties. How am I to live without him? What am I to do? What is to become of me?'

And what was to become of *poor* Thomas? One thing was certain; the army would never take him back.

It was Charles's turn to look incredulous and he was not acting.

'Again I have to ask your forgiveness, my dear Marguerite. You must think I brought you here to the library under false pretences; little Manchester Square and so on. I was quite sincere, you know. I intended to tell you that I have arranged for a few artisans and servants to go over there and make the little house comfortable for you.'

'For me, Charles?'

With those three words, I discovered that I was irredeemably addicted to hypocrisy, as well as vanity.

'Well yes, I still have not made myself clear, you see. My idea was to request that you stay at little Manchester Square and direct the refurbishments. And perhaps you will be kind enough to help me purchase a few ornaments and pictures. I thought you might enjoy that. I was about to ask Thomas for his consent, when he told me about the army, and so on. So I offered take over as your guardian while he was away, you see. I mean I did it for old Campbell Browne, you know, so why should I not do it for Thomas – and I suppose, for Captain Farmer too, in a way?'

'And what was Thomas's reply?'

'At first he was most reluctant, you know, but in the end I persuaded him to let you to come with me tomorrow. I am sure you'll like little Manchester Square. I must introduce you to some of the neighbours. Hertford has a splendid mansion there, you know. And I understand you are slightly acquainted with my dear friend Donoughmore. His town house is just round the corner.'

Under the guidance of Mrs Siddons, gratitude flowed from my every pore. I mimed humility, anticipation, delight, love and devotion, and mentally prepared myself for a very different role.

'Thomas must be distraught. Charles. Do please forgive me, but I must go immediately and thank him, however inadequately. He has been so generous and understanding. I shall never be able to repay him.'

Charles agreed that this was my bounden duty and wished me goodnight. I said I hoped he would sleep well, picked up an oil lamp and went straight to Thomas's room. It was in darkness. I returned to my own room and requested my maid – a simple honest girl, whose name I think was Ruth – to lay out my travelling outfit. I gave her the rest of my clothes and the less valuable of the jewellery Thomas had given me. It would have been quite unseemly to refurbish my new home without replacing my wardrobe.

It was almost midnight when I found Thomas in the long gallery playing cards with Catherine Lee. Catherine was also due to leave next day after her six-month sojourn. Georges de Blaquiere was in London completing the purchase of a permanent residence and was due to return in the morning to take Catherine and her/their children from the gratuitous tranquillity of the Hampshire countryside to the extravagant turbulence of a Mayfair mansion.

I pushed open the polished oak door at the end of the long gallery. Catherine sat facing me by the stone fireplace some thirty feet away. Thomas, opposite her, was lounging on an ornate chaise-longue and I could only see the back of his head. He must have heard me come in, but did not stand. Catherine instinctively appreciated that her presence was not required and motioned for me to stay where I was.

'Do excuse me, Thomas, I have a busy day tomorrow. I am very tired and Georges will expect me at my best,' she said loudly for my benefit gathering up the playing cards. 'Oh, and Thomas, that is one hundred and twelve pounds you owe me. You will settle before we leave, won't you? Good night. Oh, and thank you so much for allowing us to stay in your delightful house.'

Catherine got up and walked intently through the dark panelled gallery to where I had stopped. She was not at all tired. She embraced me and whispered: 'My sincerest congratulations, Marguerite: how I envy your good fortune. I shall look forward to calling on you at Manchester Square'.

Not only had Thomas betrayed me to Charles but also to my dearest confidante, and now I presumed, his too. What is more he had gambled away the unaffordable sum of one hundred and twelve pounds. By the following afternoon his house would be empty of guests and full of creditors. Thomas was a broken man.

I stormed past the mesh-fronted bookcases encasing the overflow of Mrs Jenkins's library, to where Thomas remained seated nursing a large brandy bubble. I stepped round the chaise-longue

At the other end of the gallery a Tompion longcase struck midnight. And at that befitting moment Thomas glanced up and ended my Cinderella-like preview of the prince so enamoured that his sole desire was to carry me away to his realm of eternal happiness.

Charles Gardiner, Viscount Mountjoy, knew only one form of persuasion. Like the clock and other redundant furniture soon to be subjected to the auctioneer's hammer, I had again been sold, and this time the catalogue read true. Sane and sober, Charles had successfully bid – no doubt a fortune – for a barren bride ineligible for marriage, for a blue stocking out of his intellectual league, for a ruined Irish nobody despised by the whisperers of society. The traders of Clonmel market would not have offered a penny for such a defective lot.

'Ah Marguerite, my dear, I've been expecting you. I trust you have spent a pleasant evening with Lord Mountjoy.'

Thomas refilled his brandy bubble and pointed to the bottle. I ignored the invitation and remained standing.

'Eat, drink and be merry, for tomorrow you die! You appear in remarkably good humour for a man expecting the bailiffs, Thomas.'

'My clerk will deal with them.'

'Your clerk is leaving with the rest of the servants.'

'Well, I have changed my mind. Without you, my dear Marguerite, my expenses will be substantially reduced.'

'I take it you have sold me. Dare I ask my price?'

'Nothing so vulgar. I am not in the habit of indulging in trade. Charles has simply reimbursed me for your board and lodgings and for the baubles I bought for you over the years; a mere ten thousand, plus a few hundred to cover his visit. Your old friends in commerce might call it a storage charge. Do you not agree?'

Ten thousand pounds – four or five a million today! How could Charles have been so blind? Could he not see that I would have been overjoyed to go with him for nothing? But then perhaps he was so rich that ten thousand pounds was like a shilling to a poor man.

'I wish you a happy and prosperous future, Thomas. Until we meet again.'

And we did meet again, some years later.

10

'Welcome back, Sir Thomas. Where have you been?'

'Good afternoon, your ladyship. I took a stroll down to the National Portrait Gallery to have another look at a small portrait that I hoped might show me what attracted you to Lord Blessington, apart from his money.'

'I know the picture you mean. I often wondered how James Holmes managed to keep a straight face confronted by that ridiculous fur coat.'

'He must have done, because it is a remarkable work. On a canvas just six inches by five Holmes has not only captured the texture of sable but demonstrated a more astute appreciation of his sitter than I managed to do.'

'Indeed, Sir Thomas, I well remember your pretentious attempt at a full-length portrait of Lord Blessington in the gorgeous robes he had made for George IV's coronation.'

'I'm ashamed to admit that I was in desperate need of money, as I often was, and his lordship always paid promptly. I did as he asked and concentrated on the costume instead of the man wearing it.'

'You came to our house many times, Sir Lawrence. You knew my husband well enough to have imparted something of his character instead of slimming him down, giving him lifeless eyes, a weak chin, a soft upper lip, not to mention a nose like Cyrano de Bergerac.'

'Lord Blessington's character was an enigma, your ladyship. He was perpetually acting, off and on the stage. For his portrait he affected an exaggerated pose and I painted him as I presumed he saw himself. I think he was pleased with the result.'

'You were capable of better. Holmes painted his face as it was; eyes that saw only rectitude, ears that heard only truth and a mouth that spoke only benevolence. Holmes saw what you did not see – that rarest of creatures, a good man.'

'Perhaps I painted too many bad men, your ladyship.'

'Well, Sir Lawrence, if that was your forte then you will have no difficulty in capturing the characters of my first two husbands.'

'Lady Blessington, you are asking too much. I have yet to start my portrait of Mr Power. Nonetheless I will accept your commission in memory of my most generous client. '

'Thank you, Sir Lawrence. Again no images survive and you must rely on my verbal depictions. Portray Captain Jenkins as he saw himself, a young officer resplendent in the dress uniform of the Eleventh Light Dragoons.'

'And your first husband?'

'This is a more formidable challenge or perhaps not, Sir Lawrence. Clearly you are capable of painting lifeless eyes and weak chins, but I shall leave it to you to decide how Maurice Farmer saw himself. Don't forget the military moustache. He must have been more than an insane non-entity. No man or woman, however mentally sick or misguided, is without redeeming features. Maurice took pride in his appearance, as did all my husbands. Like Thomas

Jenkins, he was stripped of his commission, but portray him in the uniform of a Captain of the 47th Regiment of Foot. You do understand, different but the same. Think of a deft cartoonist merging them into a single personality through a progression of three or four drawings.'

'It was bad enough that I left a studio full of half-finished works when I died in 1830. How can I complete portraits of Mr Power, Captain Farmer and Captain Jenkins who are all dead too, your ladyship?'

'It might not be as difficult as you think, Sir Thomas. Read my novels, you will find them resurrected time and again.'

--

What was I to make of this self-obsessed viscount who paid a fortune for nothing but the privilege of spending another fortune on me? I will not deny that I was often critical of Charles's unpredictable assortment of volatile virtues and failings, or that I loved him for his money. But yes, I did love him.

Some men become rich by their own endeavours and others are born to be rich. Charles was in the latter category, therefore the more romantic.

'Men who devote their lives to money-making seldom retain a romantic spirit.'

Charles did not devote one minute of his life to money-making, unlike his great-grandfather, Luke Gardiner, who was an exception to my rule. Luke was not only a romantic spirit; he was a kindred spirit who exploited the poverty of his birth, and both made and married money. Now he was a man I would have loved to have met. Having stolen the necessary capital, he founded the London merchant bankers Gardiner and Hill and was a millionaire while still in his twenties. Poor Mr Hill! Quite unethically Luke fell in love with one of his customers; a young lady called Anne Stewart. And why wouldn't he? Anne was heir to both the fortune of her maternal grandfather, Murrough Boyle, first Earl of Blessington, and the equally obscene wealth of her paternal grandfather, William Stewart, whose estates included Mountjoy Forest. Stewart assumed the title Viscount Mountjoy but neither he nor the second Earl of Blessington, Charles Boyle, was blessed with a son. Thus both their lines became extinct on death, sadly leaving a mere woman to inherit their estates.

After his marriage to Anne Stewart, Luke Gardiner disposed of his tainted banking interests and devoted the rest of his career to a far more respectable trade - property development. The legacy of his romantic spirit can still be seen today in the questionably elegant but unquestionably lucrative architectural masterworks of Dublin: Henrietta Street, Parnell Street and the city's most celebrated thoroughfare, O'Connell Street, originally Gardiner's Mall. Due to the practical nature of his services to the nation, Luke was never honoured with a title.

I would have had no wish to meet Luke's son and heir, the first Charles Gardiner. True, he did not devote his life to money-making but neither was he a romantic spirit. He did not even squander his inheritance on a luxurious lifestyle.

On the other hand, I might have been enamoured by his son, the second Luke Gardiner. My deceased father-in-law to be, was not simply a self-opinionated romantic spirit and entrepreneur, he was also clever. He was awarded a double first at Cambridge for a very reasonable consideration. Thereafter Luke served briefly in the army and, unaided of course by his shameless wealth, rose to the rank of Lieutenant-General before being elected Member of Parliament for County Dublin. Luke supported the hopeless quest for Catholic emancipation and in 1795, the title Viscount Mountjoy was resurrected for him in recognition of his services to the enhancement of his own fortune, notably building Mountjoy Square and expanding his estates in County Tyrone.

My new guardian's father was widely travelled and acquainted with all the most distinguished figures of his day, a patron of the arts and a devotee of the theatre. When London's Drury Lane Theatre burnt down he selflessly financed its restoration, giving no thought to its investment value.

In 1798, at the age of 53, retired Lieutenant-General Luke Gardiner was stirred to defend British rule against the Irish Rebellion. He wrote his last will and testament, resumed command of his regiment and was promptly killed at the Battle of New Ross - a heroic victory for the professionally trained and equipped British army which lost one soldier for every twelve poorly armed rebels it slaughtered.

Viscount Mountjoy had drafted his will in such haste that he omitted to mention his second wife and six daughters by his first marriage. He simply bequeathed his entire estate to Charles, his youngest child and only living son. Charles idolised his self-obsessed father, a man who never had a bad word for anybody, and never had a word of any kind for his children.

Charles's mother had died when he was twelve months old. Thus after the demise of his father he found himself an orphaned sixteen-year-old with only the sensitive compassion of the boys of Eton College to comfort him. He also found himself the second Viscount Mountjoy and one of the richest men in the United Kingdom.

Charles very properly accepted his outright inheritance and assured his stepmother, the dowager Lady Margaret Gardiner and his sisters, that he would always provide for their welfare. Like Mary Campbell Browne before me, I was to bear the brunt of their enduring appreciation. Regrettably, Charles had no concept of a family feud.

'They do mean well, you see my dear Marguerite. Since poor Mary passed away, my sister Harriet and Lady Margaret have derived enormous pleasure from looking after the children at Mountjoy Forest, you know.'

Of course they had. It was hardly a demanding task. Charles employed nursemaids, governesses, servants and provided every conceivable necessity for his family to wallow in the depths of an unmitigated luxurious country life.

Charles also had no concept of a white lie. He considered it disrespectful for me to call myself Mrs Jenkins and insisted that I revert to Mrs St Leger Farmer. I had no desire to be respectful to my legal husband but had to accept that no one would be convinced by my fraudulent autobiography. In London I was presented as the wife of the Honourable Captain Maurice St Leger Farmer, missing presumed dead, and lived quietly at Manchester Square, while Charles maintained respectable decorum a mile away at Seamore Place. When he visited me, always by appointment, he was accompanied by male friends, who he wanted to impress with my meticulously procrastinated refurbishments. Sometimes he brought experts on extravagance to offer their helpful advice. At other times he suggested inappropriate ideas of his own but made no further demands upon me. Meanwhile the well-informed ladies of London resumed their own procrastinated refurbishment of the adventures of the mistress of the debauched Captain Jenkins, with only the vaguest implications that she was now Lord Mountjoy's mistress. There was of course no truth in the latter. Charles was simply afflicted with prodigality. He employed servants for me, put the finest horses and carriages at my disposal and bought me so many gifts that cataloguing my jewel boxes became quite tiresome.

My, that is Charles's house at Manchester Square was in an excellent state of repair but I thought it would do no harm to replace the rich silk wall coverings and draperies with richer materials. In deference to Charles's sensitive disposition, I ordered everything that might have reminded him of the late Lady Mountjoy to be removed from the house. George Morant, Thomas Sheraton's former partner, designed and made upholstered chairs and sofas for me, while other new furniture was by Chippendale and Hepplewhite. My pièce de résistance was the conversion of the largest first-floor bedroom into a bijou version of Mrs Jenkins's library. I am sure that Mary Campbell Browne would have approved of all my unnecessary improvements to her home and agreed that my taste was superior to hers.

I had many sincere friends in London. Its ever-affable shopkeepers again opened their fashionable tills in greeting. 'Welcome back, Mrs St Leger Farmer,' they said, forgetting my previous name and remembering that my purchases were to be charged to Viscount Mountjoy. These gentlemen loved me so much that there were times when I feared that one might request the honour of lying down to permit me to walk over him. It would have been most indelicate of me to ask why their prices had risen so significantly since I was Mrs Jenkins.

My happiness was complete. Well, not quite complete. There was still the irritating question of when, where and how I would be required to compensate my guardian with services other than interior decorating. Charles had travelled extensively. Perhaps he had experienced the oriental excesses that I had found so funny in Mrs Jenkins's translation of the *Kama Sutra*. I obtained another copy and began practising painful gymnastic contortions: a wasted effort, but not, as I was to discover, because Charles was disinclined to a diversity of erotic interests.

For the time being, he only wished to impress upon me that his intentions were honourable. He introduced me to congenial friends of a Bohemian persuasion: authors, artists and actors who mocked convention, satirised religion, politics, and society and argued like Miss Dwyer in support of free love. I am almost certain that I remained unconvinced.

'Those who always take life seriously invariably make fools of themselves.'

One man stood head and shoulders above all the distinguished visitors Charles brought to Manchester Square. Thomas Moore was just five feet tall, yet could make the most arrogant look up to him. A poet in his own right, he collaborated with Lord Byron as his biographer but unlike the great romantic did not always take life seriously. Tom's rendition of his friend and colleague's gravest works reduced all my, I mean Charles's guests to uncontrollable laughter, and his sardonic wit was as sharp as my own. 'Melody' Moore was also a brilliant musician who composed practically every stalwart of the Victorian musical soirée, *The Last Rose of Summer*, *The Minstrel Boy*, *When First I Met Thee* and dozens more. And not only was he the nation's favourite songwriter, he was a best-selling author, earning the then record advance of three thousand guineas for his exotic romance, *Lalla Rookh*. This highly original and imaginative novel has been out of print for many years.

While I savoured the company of the talented and the erudite, I could never resist the magnet of the beau monde. I saw no reason for the highest echelons of society to reject me. I was a respectable presumed widow and ward of the noble Viscount Mountjoy.

'Charles, I am most curious to meet the Marquess of Hertford. You have talked so much about the magnificence of his collection of art and antiquities in his mansion across the square. It must indeed be remarkable to attract the Prince Regent so often. I see him arrive several times a week in his yellow coach.'

'Alas, I am unable introduce you, my dear Marguerite, the second Marquess is in his seventies and unwell. He no longer entertains or goes out. The Prince comes to visit his second wife, you see.'

I did not see. 'What on earth for, Charles? Lady Isabella is enormously fat and must be old enough to be the prince's mother.'

'You are not the first to be baffled, my dear Marguerite. Hertford's son Francis, Lord Yarmouth, is an old friend of mine and even he cannot explain. He is also an art collector, you see, and spends a lot of time with the Prince down at the Brighton Pavilion; a most cultured man, you know.'

'In that case, I should very much like to meet Lord Yarmouth. Perhaps you could ask him to dinner?'

'You are quite right, my dear Marguerite, I'll send a messenger over to Piccadilly. You might know his house, number 105 opposite the park.'

'Thank you, Charles. And will you also invite Lady Yarmouth?'

'I fear not. Dear Mie Mie lives in Paris and refuses to come to England. It seems the couple have separated, you know. I cannot imagine why; they are such sensible people. They must be dreadfully lonely without one another.'

I prepared myself to be introduced at the royal court and to meet the Prince Regent.

Francis Seymour-Conway, Lord Yarmouth, future third Marquess of Hertford was unimpressed by my elaborate dinner party at Manchester Square. He was more accustomed to dining at the Brighton Royal Pavilion where sobriety and polite conversation were exceptions to the rule. In his early forties, though looking older, the royal Vice-Chamberlain showed few signs of being cultured, sensible or dreadfully lonely.

Two bottles of Charles's vintage Bordeaux cascaded over his lordship's tongue and rebounded in a stream of bluster. He was not trying to shock or impress. He simply wished to reassure us that our evidently notorious debauchery was no more reprehensible than his own. I could hardly imagine anyone, least of all Charles or I, equalling his remarkable accomplishments in this field.

He considered it important for us to be aware that he had defied his family and married Maria (Mie Mie) Fagnani, the illegitimate daughter of an exotic dancer of dubious background, who, he claimed, had seduced him and deceived him into believing that she was an Italian aristocrat. Lord Yarmouth did not strike me as a man easily deceived, and indeed he was not. Having drained his third bottle, his lordship revealed that his wife's biological father was none other than the Duke of Queensbury who, he explained proudly, he had effectually blackmailed for the fortune he was now lavishing on his art collection and wider interests.

With inappropriate expletives, the next Marquess of Hertford misinformed us that the father of Mie Mie's third child was Le Comte de Montroud, apparently one of her numerous French lovers. He had similarly unsubstantiated evidence that Montroud was also the father of his daughter, Frances Maria, and son, Richard.

'I'd have her back tomorrow but she says she wants to bring up her bastards in Paris. I acknowledge them as my own. I pay the bills. What more can she ask?'

I very much hoped that one day I might hear Mie Mie's version of this charming story.

Before draining his next bottle our guest of honour boasted that his son - the future fourth Marquess - an eighteen-year-old student at Cambridge, had already maintained the family tradition by fathering an illegitimate son of his own.

'I've had Richard's little bastard packed off to Paris. The old whore should know how to bring him up. She's a bastard herself, by birth and by nature. No, I've no idea how she is. I haven't seen her in years.'

Our guest went on to treat us to tales of lechery, intrigue and over-indulgence, most of which slandered the man who in two years would ascend the throne of England. One of George IV's first acts on becoming king would be to honour his friend Lord Yarmouth with the Order of the Garter – in recognition of his services to the arts.

I had seldom encountered any man so uninhibited in his cups. Having reeled off the names of his favourite prostitutes and detailed the amusements they provided, ignoring Charles's presence, the son of my reclusive neighbour went so far as to make me an immoral proposition. I tactfully declined and thereby lost my one and only chance of meeting the Prince Regent or any member of the British royal family.

I did not again have the displeasure of the Third Marquess's company before he contracted chronic venereal disease and died insane at the age of sixty-five. On the other hand, I enjoyed a long and pleasant acquaintanceship with his possibly illegitimate son, the fourth Marquess, Richard Seymour-Conway. Richard's son, who I also came to know well, was a bastard by birth but unlike his grandfather far from a bastard by nature. Sir Richard Wallace - who adopted his natural mother's maiden name - is deservedly remembered for compiling the magnificent collection accumulated by four generations of his predecessors and, contrary to their wishes, opening it to the public here at Hertford House.

Although Charles was a member of all the most prestigious gentleman's clubs in London he preferred to socialise in the less contentious atmosphere of the House of Lords. He took politics seriously provided they involved no controversy. When Lord Donoughmore was in London, Charles often spent many hours at his town house near Manchester Square debating topical issues, including the potential repercussions of the Prince Regent's separation from Caroline of Brunswick, or so I presumed. I knew of no other reason for the two Irish Representative Peers to spend so much time together.

Lord Donoughmore conveyed his regards to Edmond Power and his apologies for being unable to renew our acquaintanceship, due to heavy commitments. His lordship's heavy commitments never permitted him to either renew or pursue an acquaintanceship with any woman.

Charles, as promised, instructed his lawyer to find Maurice St Leger Farmer and procure an annulment of my marriage. John Allen Powell, the most illustrious attorney in London, whose clients included the Prince Regent himself, employed an investigator who, through the winter of 1815-1816, made exhaustive enquiries and discovered nothing. This was the result I anticipated and it did not occur to me that such a reputable pillar of the law might extend this hopeless quest in order to boost his outrageous fee.

In the summer of 1816, Ellen seized an opportunity to escape her remote Scottish castle and brought her three small children to stay with me at Manchester Square. The Honourable John Hume Purves - waylaid by heavy commitments – did not accompany them, yet still my sister assured me that she had made the happiest of marriages.

Ellen brought bad news from the Caribbean.

'After a long illness, caused by the debilitating sun, your dear brother, my husband, passed away peacefully at our home here on St Lucia. You will be proud to learn that one week prior to his death Michael received his long-coveted promotion to the rank of captain…'

Michael's wife did not say that he never had a bad word for anybody, though he was the only person I ever encountered of whom it was indisputably true. For weeks I was shrouded in guilt. I had murdered my gentle brother. I had chosen to forget that I selfishly persuaded him to accept a free commission to serve in a disease-ridden palm-beached tropical paradise. I had chosen to forget my invaluable adage that all that we get for nothing in this life is worth just that. I had chosen to forget that our old doctor warned me in Clonmel that Michael would never fully recover from the sickness that plagued him since birth.

I heard nothing more of Michael's widow and therefore presumed that she must have soon left the Caribbean, remarried and lived comfortably. She was my only relative who never asked me for money. No, there were no children.

Ellen also brought good news from Ireland. Robert's wife was expecting their second child. Our last surviving brother was still wasting his talent as an underpaid subordinate on a remote Irish estate and raising his family in the genteel privation of a decrepit farm labourer's cottage rented from his employer.

'Surely, Margaret, there must be something we can do for Robert.'

'I send him all I can afford whenever possible and I know you do too, Ellen, but we also have Father and Mary Ann to consider. All I can do is ask Lord Mountjoy if he can offer Robert a position on his estates in County Tyrone. '

Charles unhesitatingly wrote to Mr Norman. The excellent agent, taking no account of my gleaming commendation of Robert's rural skills, offered him a job pounding the streets of Dublin for fourteen hours a day, collecting rents and disregarding tenants' complaints. His reward was a marginally higher salary and the benefit of a small terraced house an hour's walk from the Mountjoy Urban Estate office. Robert hated the excitement of city life, the excellent Mr Norman, his virtuous corruption and worst of all, reliance on his sisters' generosity.

Robert's second daughter was born soon after he moved his family to Dublin. Naturally, she was called Ellen, forever to be known as Nellie.

Ellen, my sister that is, asked if I would take care of her children for a few hours as she had a luncheon appointment at the Houses of Parliament. Since her husband was not in London to escort her to this all-male sanctuary, I asked if her host was an honourable politician. She declined to tell me.

The children were as delightful as wild animals. I tried making up stories and rhymes and playing the piano and violin for them. Louisa and John preferred to perform gymnastics on my fine silk upholstery, while baby Marguerite employed my exquisite Persian rug for more natural functions. My maternal instincts had been too long suppressed but my cook, whose name was possibly Diana, was a mother herself and understood children. She took the three infants to the kitchen, supplied them with appropriate sustenance and dealt with their bodily demands while I pursued more constructive endeavours in my library.

On 19th July 1816 I too was invited to the Houses of Parliament, or more precisely, to the House of Lords. I was among the four hundred guests at an exclusive banquet in honour of Viscount Mountjoy's thirty-fourth birthday. Charles, of course funded the event, which also celebrated the title Earl of Blessington bestowed upon him that morning by the Prince Regent, who was unable to attend the banquet due to heavy royal commitments. Charles simultaneously relinquished the Mountjoy baronetcy in favour of his younger son, the three-year-old Luke Wellington Gardiner. I shudder to think how much Charles paid to revive the inferior family title for no apparent purpose other than to distance himself from his venerated father. The noble congratulations gushed from the Lords with such force that I feared the Thames might burst its banks. It was my guardian's proudest moment.

With cultivated courtesy, the newly created Earl of Blessington parried all questions about his marital status - well, almost all. There were no questions for me to parry, courteously or otherwise. The ladies of the Lords would rather speak to their husbands than to a woman about to snatch the London's most eligible widower from their daughters' claws, and in some cases from their own.

Three weeks after his new title was conferred, Charles sent a note to Manchester Square.

'My dear Marguerite,

Please be gracious enough to receive Mr Powell and myself at eleven this morning. I sincerely apologise for the short notice and inconvenience, but it is a matter of some importance.

Charles, Earl of Blessington.'

I became alarmed. Why was Charles bringing his lawyer to Manchester Square? I was to be evicted from my beautiful home? Had some seductive socialite succeeded in thrusting herself into the newly designed Blessington arms? I had no legal rights. Charles was my guardian only out of the goodness of his money.

My butler announced the Earl of Blessington and Mr John Allan Powell. Charles's contented demeanour did nothing to reassure me.

'Mr Powell has brought some news for you, my dear Marguerite.'

Charles, now smiling broadly, leaned back in his chair and gestured for his adviser to commence.

Mr Powell, obliged by legal convention to look grave, momentarily managed to raise the corners of his mouth, which he then opened and spoke with all the refined tactlessness of his learned profession.

'Good morning, Mrs St Leger Farmer. As you will be aware, some time ago the Earl of Blessington instructed my firm to enquire into the whereabouts of your husband the Honourable Captain Maurice St Leger Farmer, late of the 47th Regiment of Foot. I am to inform you that my investigator has ascertained that Captain Farmer was this week released from the King's Bench Prison. His precise present whereabouts are as yet unknown. However, we have reason to believe that he is residing in London.'

I was uncertain if I was expected to be pleased that Maurice was still alive or alarmed to hear he had been in prison.

'This is all most distressing, Mr Powell. Are you aware of the reason for *Mr* Farmer's conviction?' I asked, wondering why the investigator had not searched the prisons earlier. Where else would he expect to find Maurice?

'It appears, madam, that Mr Farmer was arraigned by his former employers, the East India Company.' Mr Powell now emphasised *Mr*. 'I have to inform you that your husband was convicted of fraud. If it is your wish, I shall be pleased to have the trial transcript copied for you.'

Hard as it was to believe that Maurice possessed the wit to commit fraud, it seemed irrelevant since he had not actually been found.

'Fraud! This is disgraceful, I am quite distressed, Mr Powell. Do forgive me for declining your generous offer, I really have no experience of legal proceedings.'

The lawyer's face remained set in stone. He was fully aware of my interest in Father's libel and murder cases and had been impressed by the account I had given him of Maurice's court-martial. I had no further appetite for legal insanity.

'With respect to your feelings, madam, my instructions from Lord Blessington are to find and confront your husband and negotiate a settlement in consideration of annulment of your marriage. For that I shall require your consent and co-operation. In the event that Mr Farmer declines his lordship's offer, it may be necessary to resort to the courts. First it is my duty to inform you of all we have learnt of your husband's progress since last you saw him.'

'You have my consent and may rest assured of my co-operation, Mr Powell. Please go on.'

'Thank you, Mrs St Leger Farmer. As you are aware, after his dishonourable discharge from his regiment, Mr Farmer's father procured a position for him with the East India Company. On arrival in Madras the Company judged him unfit for employment in its business but offered him a post as a foot soldier in its so-called Security Corps. This, I understand, is an unsavoury private army, where it appears that your husband came under the bad influence of a pair of boorish English mercenaries.'

'Can you be sure, Mr Powell, that it was not the pair of boorish English mercenaries who came under the bad influence of my husband?'

My spontaneous cynicism did not reach the high standards expected of legal humour.

'That I cannot say, madam, but both they and your husband were soon discharged for insubordination and disorderly conduct. With insufficient means to return to England the trio managed to secure a passage to Java. Evidently they planned to join the Anglo-Dutch struggle for control of the island, but by the time they arrived early in 1812, the British had taken power the previous year and further mercenaries were not required.'

How unfortunate that Maurice missed the opportunity to be killed, I thought, but said 'How fortunate that they missed the opportunity to benefit from the disruption'.

Mr Powell smiled coldly, warming to his unpleasant narrative.

'Like so many other English gentlemen, madam, they did indeed find an opportunity to benefit from the disruption. As you will be aware, the East India Company is engaged in the spice trade on a monumental scale in and around Batavia (Jakarta). According to the court evidence, the three fugitives, posing as Company officials, presented documents – pages torn at random from old books – to illiterate native spice farmers and demanded settlement of fictitious debts. Some half dozen of the more reluctant payers were evidently maimed for life.'

Mr Powell continued his story with the compassionless dignity of his professional training. Where would lawyers be without inhumanity?

'It is as well they were apprehended before someone was killed,' I said.

'Murder was never established, Mrs Farmer. This type of fraud was quite common in Java before the recent introduction of reforms by the present Lieutenant Governor, a bright young man called Stamford Raffles. No doubt we shall hear more of him.'

'Indeed, Mr Powell, the Earl of Blessington's friend, Mr Thomas Moore has mentioned Mr Raffles's remarkable talents to me.'

This was not strictly true. Tom had boasted of having been a lover of the first wife of the diminutive future founder of Singapore. Olivia Fancourt, a worthless adventuress, ten years older than her husband, evidently had a penchant for short men.

Mr Powell had more salacious ambiguity to justify his extortionate charges.

'It is not improbable, madam, that the Lieutenant Governor was himself influential in the arrest, that is to say, of the two mercenaries. It seems that Mr Farmer deserted his accomplices and fled the country. The men were taken into custody, flogged and tortured but no money was discovered in their possession. They alleged that your husband – I will spare you the language of the transcript – had absconded with the criminal proceeds. Six thousand pounds was mentioned but this might have been an exaggeration.'

Was it possible that Maurice had recovered his sanity?

'I am ashamed to say, Mr Powell, that such despicable behaviour is characteristic of my estranged husband.'

'That may well be the case, madam, since he was subsequently observed in Bali, Sumatra, Malaya and so on indulging in bawdy revels, until, as you put it, his despicable behaviour was brought to the attention of the Company. But again Mr Farmer avoided arrest and boarded an independent vessel bound for England. His voyage was, he claimed, greatly impeded and the ship was soon overtaken by a swift East Indiaman. Almost a year later, your husband was apprehended on disembarkation at the London docks. The trial transcript reveals little of further interest, other than that Mr Farmer was sentenced to a year in the Fleet and that no money was recovered by the Company.'

Up to this point I had listened patiently to Mr Powell's implausible narrative, and with considerable effort restrained myself from asking the conscientious lawyer precisely for what services he was charging Lord Blessington other than blindly reciting the words of a document in the public domain.

'Is it not surprising, Mr Powell, that your investigator was unable to locate my husband while he was serving an entire year in London's most prominent place of incarceration?'

'Allow me to assure you, madam, that my agent has been most diligent. Mr Farmer, in fact, served just two months.'

'Two months? I am led to believe that serious crimes of this nature are usually punished with a life sentence or even execution.'

'It is most embarrassing but I have to admit to you, Mrs Farmer, that certain members of my profession – I hasten to add very, very few – have been known to stoop to malpractice. My investigator ascertained that Captain Farmer entrusted the remnant of his ill-gotten gains to one such charlatan, who disseminated the necessary inducements to secure an early release or an unobserved escape; there is little difference in practice. He also humanely mitigated his client's internment by arranging for large quantities of alcohol to be smuggled into the Fleet.

I have concluded, madam, that the cost of these contemptible services has absorbed most of Mr Farmer's remaining spoils, and therefore he cannot afford to leave London.'

It was common knowledge that all prison guards were open to corruption. Nonetheless, I found Mr Powell's intelligence completely unconvincing.

'It is probably of little consequence, Mr Powell but dare I ask why Mr Farmer required large quantities of alcohol. From my own observations, a tiny drop was sufficient to reduce him to a state of total inebriation.'

'I regret I cannot tell you that, madam, but it is possible that he was advised to nurture his fellow prisoners to assist his release. As we speak my investigator is at the gaol questioning those who served with your husband. I am totally confident that Mr Farmer will soon be located.'

A lawyer's total confidence is the kiss of death – in this case literally. Before Mr Powell's investigator located my husband, he was cold in his grave. It was the happiest day of my life. I was a widow at last.

'No, Mr Sadleir, I did not have Maurice murdered. Who gave you that idea? A gentleman of the press or a lady of society? As I have told you, vengeance was not in my nature.'

'Forgiveness is a salve for wounds inflicted by unkindness; while rancour but serves to keep them unhealed.'

The only recorded account of the last hours of Captain Maurice St Leger Farmer appeared in the *Morning Herald*. It was nothing but speculation by a hack reporter who scavenged the gaols by night for jettisoned scraps of rotten news.

There were no unbiased witnesses to the dark deeds in the demonic dungeon where my first husband met his death. But now I can for the first time relate the truth of what occurred that night.

After Maurice Farmer made his daring escape behind the turned backs of the Fleet guards he reclaimed more of his plunder than Mr Powell considered that any lawyer, corrupt or otherwise, would return to a convicted client. With it he planned to sail to Spain and enlist as a mercenary for the patriots.

Two days before he was due to leave, Maurice received a note from his two former cellmates inviting him back to the Fleet to celebrate their own imminent release. Unaware that these men loathed their deranged fellow convict but knowing no one else in London Maurice concluded that the Fleet was the safest place to spend his last night in England. No one would think of looking for him there. He paid the customary toll and was admitted through the impenetrable armoured gates. Dragging with him a four-quart flagon of rum as a final token of gratitude for his friends' co-operation, he climbed the dark stairs to his old cell on the third floor, where together with his cellmates two unexpected visitors were waiting to welcome him.

Maurice's partners in crime had also escaped from prison in the Far East and had crossed the world to pay him their belligerent respects. Unlike Mr Powell's professional investigator, London's gaols were the first place they searched. At the Fleet an amenable guard, with their knives at his throat, informed them of Farmer's whereabouts and agreed to take him a note ostensibly from his cellmates.

The reunion commenced amicably with the visitors tearing off their shirts and turning their backs.

'Look Farmer, you bastard, this is what a hundred strokes of the cat does to a man. Give us our money, you thieving lump of cowardly shit or you'll find out just what you ran away from.'

The men removed their wide leather belts and began slapping them on the palms of their hands. Maurice gave them all the coins in his pocket.

'My lawyer has the rest. I'll go and get it for you straightaway.'

This of course was unsatisfactory. Even ex-mercenaries knew that no lawyer worked so late at night. Aided by the other prisoners, they forced a quantity of Maurice's own rough liquor down his throat, presuming that it would serve as a primitive anaesthetic until the following morning when they would escort him to his lawyer's office. The alcohol had a more predictable effect. Suddenly Maurice grabbed the heavy stone flagon and lashed out with it like the madman he was, soaking himself in spilled rum as the four ruffians relieved him of his weapon.

Since the alcohol did not immediately make Maurice pass out the escaped mercenaries offered some assistance. 'Listen Farmer, get this into your stinking drunken head. You're not leaving our sight 'til we get what you owe us – meanwhile here's some of what we owe you.'

Belts swung, screams reverberated, blood flowed until Maurice's reason now perverted by the alcohol told him that he had escaped before and could do so again. With the force of a primeval barbarian, he threw off his captors and rushed to the door. It was locked and barred. He spun round and hurled his body at the closed shutters of a high window which yielded to his weight enabling him to clamber onto the sill fifty feet above the gaol's internal quadrangle. It was too dark for him to see the ground below.

'Don't worry, boys, I'll be back with your money', were my first husband's last words.

A bedraggled, barely-breathing and blood-stained body attempted to crawl over the hard, cold flagstones of the Fleet Prison. Did Maurice remember how he once left me?

Another gratuity changed hands with appropriate threats and the mercenaries vanished into the night before the guards called for assistance. Maurice was transported to the Middlesex Hospital where no doctor worked that late.

In the morning Maurice's bereaved cellmates confessed their innocence to the prison governor: 'We did all we could to stop him, sir. But Farmer would insist on climbing onto the window to show off how brave he was. He slipped and fell before we could get to him, sir. Farmer was drunk when he came in. Ask them at the hospital, sir. They'll tell you how he reeked of rum.'

Neither the governor, nor subsequently the coroner, enquired if Maurice's fall was assisted.

Mr Powell sent me a sincere letter of condolence, enclosing a copy of my late husband's Death Certificate:

The Honourable Maurice St Leger Farmer, former captain of the 47th Regiment of Foot: died 13th October 1817 at the Middlesex Hospital, Wells Street, London. Cause of death: multiple fractures sustained in an accidental fall from an internal window at the Fleet Kings' Bench Prison.

Signed …. Senior surgeon.

I considered instructing Mr Powell to claim my inheritance from Maurice's lawyer and changed my mind.

Charles also received a copy of the death certificate, whereupon he hurried to Manchester Square and made me a formal proposal of marriage. I accepted without hesitation.

At this point I must again make it absolutely clear that I loved Charles passionately from that moment until the day he died. As Shakespeare was fully aware but did not write, money is the food of love. How could I not draw nourishment from the Earl of Blessington's overt professions of love, unique eccentricities and mindless extravagance?

'There should be a decent interval, you know, my dear Marguerite. Would you think eight months too short?'

Decent interval! What did Charles expect me to do; go round in a black veil saying that Maurice Farmer never had a bad word for anybody? Did he really think that would dissolve the venom on the viperous tongues of the London quality? We compromised on four months.

'I do understand your family affiliation to St Thomas's but do you not think a quiet wedding here in London would be so much more pleasant, Charles.'

I dreaded nothing more than having to repeat the experience of the late Lady Mountjoy and be paraded like a pedigree racehorse around a paddock for the approval of the speculative Dublin elite.

Charles agreed too readily.

'My dear Marguerite, you are quite right as always, a quiet wedding is most appropriate to the circumstances – a few close friends and family, you know.'

As I was listing the few close friends and family I considered eligible for invitation, I was surprised to receive my first and only letter from my father. He was not on my guest list. I was on his. He would be honoured if I were to attend his wedding to Mrs Hymes, accompanied by the Earl of Blessington who he remembered so well as the youthful Lord Mountjoy.

My response overflowed with felicitations and good wishes for the happy couple. 'The Earl of Blessington and I are heartbroken that we cannot join you on this joyful occasion, Father. A prior commitment – I omitted the word heavy – prohibits us from being in Dublin on that date.'

The prior commitment, at least, was true. My second marriage took place by special licence at St Mary's Church, Bryanston Square on 16th February 1818, the day after my father's second marriage. A year later I mentioned the coincidence to Charles.

'You really should have told me, you know? I would love to have seen old Beau Power again and met his new wife. I'm sure she is as sweet as your late mother.'

My bridal gown employed six seamstresses for five weeks, for which an effeminate designer charged Charles more than they earned together in five years. On my bitterly cold wedding day, a thick woollen cloak concealed the magnificent gown that I wore for about an hour. The good Lord had yet to bestow the blessing of heat upon the interior of His churches. Charles paid for Robert, his wife and Mary Ann to come over from Ireland. Ellen came from Scotland, accompanied, not by her husband – heavily committed elsewhere – but by his equally dreary his brother, William Hume Purves. The nearest to a representative of Charles's family was Mary Campbell Browne's brother, William Campbell, another sullen Scot, who dutifully came to remind me that I was inferior to his late sister in every imaginable way. The dowager Lady Mountjoy and Charles's surviving sisters declined their invitations as politely as they had declined their invitations to his three previous weddings.

Charles Mathews, the nation's best loved comedian – an apt choice – acted as Charles's best man and brought some semblance of gaiety to the occasion.

I was twenty-eight and Charles thirty-six but our age difference was more than eight years. I was the more mature. We spent our first night together at Seamore Place. My bridegroom said that there would be no time to make love as we would have to be up at three in the morning to set off on the fairytale honeymoon he had planned for us in Ireland. I was now the legitimate Countess of Blessington, and if that meant travelling in a draughty coach and a storm-tossed steam packet in mid-winter to a place I had vowed never to go again, then it would be a fairytale honeymoon.

Shivering in the snow, thirty servants lined the railings outside the plain Georgian exterior of 10 Henrietta Street. I could not doubt the sincerity of their welcome or their love for Charles, who thanked them from the bottom of his pocket and introduced their new mistress. As at St James's Square, he remembered all their names, their family histories and personal problems.

'They are all so unique and talented, you know. I would be helpless without them.'

A specially employed lady's maid – I think she was called Susan – showed me to a boudoir meticulously prepared for me with outmoded soft furnishings in gaudy colours. She unpacked my clothes and lovingly arranged my bridal gown on the bed. I explained that I had worn it for my wedding and had no further use for it.

'You may have it, if you wish.'

The magnificent garment was totally inappropriate for the poor girl's improbable future wedding or any purpose whatsoever.

'Thank you, your ladyship, but Lord Blessington particularly requested that you wear it again this evening.'

Was I expected to celebrate my honeymoon by performing some unique and talented service without which Charles would be helpless? Perhaps my second husband was as mad as my first but I did his bidding and told the maid to clean off as much as possible of the mud from Bryanston Square and dress me in my virgin white. As she did so I heard carriages outside. I peeped through the rich indigo curtains of my dedicated dressing room and saw the cream of Dublin society invading the house like an enemy army - which might have been preferable.

Charles came to collect me in a newly tailored replica of the dazzling general's uniform infested with jewelled insignia that he wore for all his previous weddings. Reminded of his arrival on Súir Island similarly decorated I took his arm and together we descended the wide marble staircase and together performed the sort of grand entrance normally reserved for Cinderella and her prince in a pantomime finale.

The chandeliers blazed so brilliantly that I was grateful for the bridal veil with which Charles insisted I covered my face. So many candles had not been lit in this room since Mary Campbell Browne lay in state, but now their light was reflected in the silver and gold table adornments instead of the rich tapestry on Marshal Duroc's catafalque. A hundred nobles and their ladies rose to their feet for the unveiling of the most beautiful bride Dublin had ever seen, or possibly the second most beautiful.

Has anyone really died of embarrassment? Thinking of my predecessor, I expected it to happen there and then. Here they all were, Thomas Jenkins's old friends last encountered a few streets away in a house rented from my new husband.

'I am so thrilled to see you again, Lady Velinfomt. Thank you so much for all your kind words and generous little gift. You were of course quite right; my first *church* wedding was indeed to the *late* Captain St Leger Farmer.'

Her ladyship appreciated my emphases.

'I do hope we shall now see a great deal more of one another', she lied.

'I am certain that we shall', I lied.

Charles spared no expense. Charles never spared any expense. I joined his guests in pouring forth a profusion of praise: the preparations, the banquet, the champagne, the floral displays, the musicians, the entertainers and the servants in the new Blessington livery. I delighted everyone with my wit and charm. Well, some of the gentlemen seemed delighted.

'A woman cannot embrace any man too warmly on her honeymoon.'

I could hardly wait to leave the sumptuous scene and Dublin society to express its disgust. I did not have to wait long. Charles had more uncomfortable delights arranged for me.

'We spend too much of our time in town, you know, my dear Marguerite. I think we should go out to the country and take the air for a while.'

It was February. The temperature was below zero and the Irish sky had forgotten the sun. Throughout our forty-eight-hour progression to County Tyrone wind, rain and snow assailed our coach. And as soon as I set eyes on Mountjoy Forest I disliked it.

Charles liked Mountjoy Forest and it liked him. There, not only his servants but a small army of tenants braved the weather and lined the half-mile avenue to the Cottage, cheering and clapping as we passed. It was too cold to open my window but I gently waved my gloved hand and smiled in acknowledgement. I was now a countess and any greater display of exuberance would have been quite unseemly. Charles, however, had no compunction about leaning from his window and shouting inaudible greetings.

The Cottage stood in the appropriately named hamlet of Rash. Possibly the structure had once been a picturesque rustic homestead but now was a grotesque monument to vanity, twice the size of the House occupied by Charles's family. Again summoning the tuition of Mrs Siddons, I lauded the immense portico, the ten-foot high polished doors and the embossed painted ceiling of the forty by twenty-eight-foot drawing room. I gasped and mimed ecstasy as Charles proudly led me into the sitting room furnished for my exclusive comfort in crimson silk embroidered with gold. It was his idea of a practical necessity, I supposed.

Adjacent to the Cottage was a precise bijou replica of the Drury Lane Theatre for a private audience of two hundred, more than the population within a ten-mile radius.

'You see, Marguerite, the actors do so love coming over from London and performing with me here. The fresh air makes such a change for them, you know. Did I mention that I have arranged a little entertainment?'

Having spent two hours demonstrating the theatrical intricacies of this misplaced fragment of London's West End, Charles took me to the House. The dowager Lady Mountjoy's greeting exuded all the warmth properly due to the second usurper of her rightful inheritance. She had not shown such chilling enthusiasm since Mary Campbell Browne's last visit. She was so ecstatic when Charles introduced me that she omitted to thank me for the modest bouquet I had so thoughtfully brought for her.

'The dining room, I think, Maeve,' she said to an extraordinarily intelligent looking maid.

'Charles has told me so much about you, Lady Margaret, and now it is clear that he in no way exaggerated,' I said.

This and my equally sincere compliments for my now sister-in-law Harriet served only to harden the frost. At Charles's request the dowager summoned a governess, who in turn brought her four charges to meet their new 'mama'. I asked them to call me Marguerite and made a concerted effort to remember

160

their names. Young as they were, they greeted me with suspicion, rightly anticipating as much motherly affection from me than as they had received from their natural mother.

Luke Wellington, third Lord Mountjoy, was now aged five. Neither he nor his six-year-old sister, Lady Harriet, had any recollection of Mary Campbell Browne whatsoever. The supposed illegitimate and thus untitled Emily and Charles Gardiner, aged seven and eight, vaguely remembered her as a sort of remote angel for which I was a poor substitute. By making ardent endeavours to endear myself – reciting my poems and stories – I managed to establish an affably distant rapport with my step-children. I enjoyed no such success with their guardians.

'You will be aware, Lady Blessington, that Charles has entrusted Harriet and I with his children's care and education. May we presume that it is your intention to respect his wishes?' For a moment I was charmed by the dowager's accent. She was the epitome of a discontented English aristocrat.

'I would never dream of disputing my husband's wishes, Lady Mountjoy. His children could not be in more capable hands.'

Charles, though born in Ireland, had been nurtured in the traditions of the English aristocracy and thus held that the non-financial obligations of fatherhood ended with conception. Although he seldom saw his children, they were naturally devoted to him. He too had known little of his father and had no recollection of his mother. A similar upbringing would do his children no harm. It was not my place to interfere in such matters. I did not marry a millionaire in order to administer an orphanage.

For the duration of my honeymoon I chose to forget that I had broken my vow never to return to Ireland. Contrary to my natural instincts, I made the necessary effort to abandon responsibility and enjoy the extravagant parties, balls, outings, concerts and theatrical presentations my husband had taken such pains to arrange for me. Actors came from London and even more houseguests than Thomas Jenkins entertained in Hampshire filled the multi-roomed Cottage or were accommodated in the other houses that disturbed the natural ugliness of the forest. The round of endless pleasure and gaiety lasted just ten days. Then for reasons beyond the control of money, the theatre darkened, the musicians played their last waltzes and the fires burnt out beneath the kitchen ranges. Trunks were packed, apologies muttered and bedrooms vacated.

For a week, gale-force winds and driving rain battered the gargantuan Cottage. Thunder clapped, lightning struck and trees fell obstructing the roads to and from Mountjoy Forest. Even the House was out of reach. Left completely alone with my husband and a dozen servants, I took advantage of this fortuitous opportunity to instigate the first, and I feared last, uninterrupted conversation of our married life.

'I am so sorry, Charles, that the beautiful honeymoon you planned has turned out this way. No words can sufficiently express my thanks for all you did for me. Your romanticism is overwhelming.'

Charles looked philosophically perplexed.

'I am devastated, you know. It was all to no avail. So many more people were due to come over to meet you, my dear Marguerite, and I rehearsed so thoroughly, you see. I wanted to give my finest performance for you. But I am far from disheartened. We shall come back in the summer, you know, and you will see how beautiful the landscape is with the sun on it.'

Charles brought out some elaborate plans for the fifteenth extension to the Cottage. They were the work of Benjamin Wyatt, the most revered architect in England. Among Wyatt's more inspired enhancements was a library without bookshelves. His watercolour illustration of this immaculate room showed six twenty-foot-high casement windows spanning the front wall surmounted by intricately carved porticos from which tasteless purple draperies reached down to the floor. On the other three walls were similarly-proportioned rococo mirrors. The ceiling was intricately adorned with gilt and four huge crystal chandeliers surrounded a gruesome circular mural, which I presumed to depict the crucifixion. I imagined the blood of Christ dripping onto my book while reading in this soulless library. I shall not describe more of Wyatt's innovative conceptions. They were not simply monstrous but completely incongruous with the surrounding countryside, that I was determined never to see again.

'I am so disappointed, Charles, that the horrible weather has prevented you from showing me more of Mountjoy Forest, but from what I have seen its aspects are clearly as charming as any in Ireland. Surely it would be a crime to disturb the perfection of nature. Mr Wyatt's drawings are exquisite but would you not agree that his style is more suited to an urban setting, London, for example?'

'My dear Marguerite, I had not considered the designs in that light, you know, but you are quite right. Wyatt is a town architect. When he was younger he made an exemplary job of Drury Lane for my father. That was after the fire, you know. When we are back in London I must ask the Duke of Wellington to show you the work he is doing over at Apsley House. It is quite imposing, you see, but it is not right for the Cottage. This should be a friendly place, where people can come over and feel at home, you know.'

'Charles, do you not think that visitors from London might sometimes find the journey a little arduous or impractical?'

'Oh, the weather isn't always like this, you know.'

'Even in more clement weather, not everyone can be intrepid travellers like you and I, Charles. Have you considered that your London friends might find it more convenient to be entertained at Seamore Place or Manchester Square?'

'Good heavens, no, my dear Marguerite; they are far too small, you know. Neither can accommodate more than twenty guests. Besides, I have my theatre here. It is a unique experience, you see.'

I did not see or wish to see.

'Have you thought of acquiring a town house large enough to contain a theatre? Imagine, Charles, you could then produce plays and act in them at any time of the year, regardless of the weather. And you will certainly attract much larger audiences.'

I prudently refrained from pointing out that Charles might also save the expense of providing his audience with accommodation.

'Well since you mention it, Marguerite, a few weeks ago a fellow in the Lords said that Sir Thomas Heathcote has a lease to offer on a house in St James's Square. But, you know, I am not altogether convinced that we need three houses in London now that we are married.'

I proffered the benefit of my naïve business acumen.

'If you were to sell or lease out Seamore Place and Manchester Square, Charles, the proceeds would comfortably pay for a townhouse. I am familiar with St. James's Square. Heathcote's house will be ideal. It is quite large enough to contain a theatre.'

I thus became the mistress of the finest mansion, in the most fashionable square in London.

11

'Bet she was alright in bed.'

'Of course she was, mate. She was a bloody acrobat, I mean aristocrat. That's what they did. What else did they have to do – men, women, upside-down, right way up, backwards, forwards, three at a time, the dog, the cat, anything that moved?'

'So what did they do for condoms?'

'God knows what they shoved up; rags, leaves, snakes skins, pigs' bladders, all kinds of sticky stuff. Nothing worked; the girls always ended up having to have abortions. Don't even think about what it meant in them days. They all had VD – both sexes. Glad I never saw 'em with their knickers off.'

'What about her then?'

'Like you said, she looks like a bit of a goer.'

'She might have been a lesbian?'

'Of course she was a lesbian. They were all fucking lesbians, or gays, or AC/DC. I told you, they were acrobats - too much bloody money. They could afford whatever they fancied. They're all still the same. They make me sick, the whole fucking lot of 'em – disgusting!'

'You're dead right, mate, rich people never give a shit for anybody. That Karl Marx, he had the right idea; give 'em a kick up the arse, he said. It's us workers what make the money, not them, and it's only right we get our fair share.'

'Yeah, and if it wasn't for that lot living like lords, we'd get a darn sight more.'

The Wallace Collection attracts few visitors of this stamp, though in Britain people of every class have won the right to shelter from the rain, kill time and treat this aristocratic mansion as their own. They have won the right to disparage those who place these priceless amenities at their disposal and the right to rail against the idle rich.

When I entitled my works *The Idler in Italy* and *The Idler in France* I was not intending to extol idleness as an accomplishment in itself. I was never idle, but can empathise with these men with nothing better to do than to gape at my portrait. Making their unsolicited acquaintance might be misinterpreted but I take the risk.

'The greatest cause of animosity between individuals of different classes is lack of acquaintanceship.'

'I know a little bit about that woman and can assure you she was not a lesbian and never suffered venereal disease. But you're quite right, she did lead an active sex life.'

'Course she did, she was a lazy aristocrat. Look, it says she was a countess.'

'She was not born a countess. It was only by a stroke of luck that she enjoyed a few years of ease. Put yourselves in her position, would you say no to a life of idle pleasure?'

'Chance would be a fine thing. You don't do idle pleasure when you're on benefits, lady.'

One of the men takes a packet of cigarettes from his pocket. I point to a sign and he reluctantly puts it back. Smoking does not count as an idle pleasure.

'I overheard you say that Karl Marx had the right idea. If you won millions on the National Lottery, would you still agree with him?'

''Course we would, lady. We're workers. Always were, always will be. Money doesn't change anything. Do you think the toffs would want to know the likes of us?'

--

St James's Square is a majestic temple to the gods of Empire and Mammon. The terraced monuments of the great quadrangle, once home to the the richest of the rich, are now employed more appropriately to their dimensions; prestigious offices, embassies, clubs and luxurious apartments. In the north-west corner at number fourteen is the London Library: a million volumes in a house built for a single family, albeit now extended over lost mews, outhouses and gardens. Lost too is the ornamental lake and fountain that in my time protected wealthy noses from the stench of the fleshpots of Piccadilly. A landscaped garden now surrounds an incongruous statue of *Gvlielmus III* (William of Orange) in the heroic guise of a Roman general riding a disproportionately small horse. My once home at number ten is now Chatham House, headquarters of the Royal Institute of International Affairs, the independent brain of the Foreign Office.

'That's right, Mr Sadleir, number ten, not number eleven. I am surprised you were not more thorough with your homework.'

Sir Thomas Heathcote introduced us to his abandoned house extolling the merits of its architect, Henry Flitcroft, whose lesser works included Woburn Abbey, country seat of the dukes of Bedford. Among the enticing features the proud owner failed to point out were broken windows, rotten floorboards, missing stairs and faded paintwork. Charles therefore did not hesitate to sign a twenty-year lease at an unconscionable rent. 'A sound investment, you see,' he said. Disillusioning him would have been most ungracious of me.

Inspired by Benjamin Wyatt's Versailles-like concepts of which he approved, and my simplistic urban opulence of which he did not, Charles proceeded to spend forty-thousand pounds - yes really, forty-thousand pounds - on making the house habitable. This cosmetic transformation involved six months of inconvenience during which we took up residence in the barely adequate splendour of Charles's dated baroque mansion in the now wisely demolished Seamore Place. Manchester Square was superfluous to needs and I persuaded Charles to advertise it for sale. The practical residence for an extremely rich family which I had created attracted a legion of competitive buyers imploring me, I mean Charles, to raise the price. Having recovered the money I had spent on refurbishment, well, most of it, I think he was pleased. After we moved into

St James's Square I recommended that he also sold Seamore Place. Lacking the benefit of my enhancements, Charles's first London home attracted little interest and he soon withdrew it from the market.

'I have always been rather fond of the little place, you see, but dear Mary was never terribly keen. Apparently you're not either, my dear Marguerite, but I would not be at all surprised if the day comes when I shall be thankful that I did not sell it you know.'

That day did come. Meanwhile, Charles entrusted the house to a London agent, who leased it at a rent which precisely covered his passive services.

Charles transferred his art collections from both houses to make St James's Square look more like a home. It looked more like a museum. He covered the walls with probably valueless daubings, presented to him by the future masters he sponsored at great cost, interspersed with the possibly valuable old masters he had purchased at even greater cost. Together we planned the interior room by room, meticulously arranging the gaudy precious objects among the furniture I had ordered to complement the ambience. The most fulfilling and unrewarding facet of our project was converting the ground floor into a charming little theatre. Soon plays, pantomimes and concerts were breathing life into the staid old square. The house filled with paid actors and non-paying audiences, who came in their numbers to absorb the cultural nourishment of the champagne reception Charles provided after every performance.

Hardly a day passed when we did not provide an entertainment of some description. Luminaries, aristocrats, statesmen, the bright and erudite, regardless of political or religious persuasion, or indeed of reputation, were all delighted to accept the invitations of the Earl and Countess of Blessington. The autographs in our visitors' book will be worth an untold fortune should it ever be found.

Among the many distinguished men to whom I was displayed as the prize exhibit in the Blessington museum of showmanship were the then prime minister, Lord Liverpool, and his successors Lord Melbourne, Earl Grey (of tea fame) and my life-long correspondent, Sir Robert Peel. I was always fascinated by their indistinguishable policies and the heated arguments aroused among these comparatively young men. But I found older men who had learnt not to take social injustice and unprovoked atrocities too seriously considerably more stimulating.

The most admirable of these sages was the Lord Chancellor, Thomas Erskine, a master advocate who strove unceasingly for radical reform and class mobility but came to office too late to change the social order as he and I would have wished. And then there was the august Dr Samuel Parr, the learned schoolmaster who taught the world that I was the *'most gorgeous Lady Blessington'*. A lifelong humanitarian, Samuel's proudest boast was that he *'never beat a boy twice at the same lesson'*.

Another frequent visitor was Charles's close friend, Lord Castlereagh, then foreign secretary and leader of the House of Commons, a Whig when not a Tory. Charles was devastated when in August 1822, Castlereagh slit his own throat after a blackmailer threatened to expose his homosexuality. I never understood why he took such drastic action when he was happily married to the society beauty, Lady Amelia Hobart. Surely, I thought, nobody would have believed the blackmailer but then I had a great deal to learn about blackmail.

Charles did not attend the great statesman's funeral, not because he was heavily committed but because we had left England a few days before he died.

'It's such a terrible tragedy, Robert had no children, you see, and therefore did not leave a son, so now the title will go to his half-brother. It's all wrong, you know. Robert never had a bad word for anybody.'

Charles chose to forget the unrepeatable words that the normally impeccably mannered Castlereagh had for the short-term prime minister, George Canning, who he almost killed in a duel.

While I relished the perfunctory pleasures at St James's Square, in reality the scenario proved much the same as in Dublin and at Manchester Square. Though my marriage to the Earl of Blessington was indisputably legitimate and the last ember of my Irish accent was extinguished, London society was blessed with the grace and memory of a circus elephant. No sooner had the ladies of its self-styled *ton* satisfied their curiosity, drunk their champagne, expressed their criticisms and plagiarised my designs they accepted fewer and fewer invitations and, needless to say, returned none.

At St James's Square generosity was pretention, laughter vulgarity, wit insult and debate ignorance, or so said the grand hostesses who flatteringly elevated me to a goddess of competition. Some went so far as to send spies. Who would have suspected the ubiquitous bard, Thomas Moore? Charles, who believed ill of no one, assured me that they simply envied my beauty, intellect and charm. And he was right.

'We never more fully display our own characters than when we assail those of others.'

No one assailed my character more than Baronesse Elizabeth Vassell Holland, queen of Holland House, the most palatial private residence in the capital. As a student of architecture I feel almost saddened to find that one of Hitler's more class-conscious bombers reduced her grandiose mansion to a pathetic fragment of its former glory.

Lady Holland had no reason to envy me. On the contrary, she should have been grateful to me for providing her guests, most of whom were also mine, with so much pleasure. Who could offer a more exhilarating conversation piece than the daughter of a murderer, the child bride of a madman, the mistress of a disgraced officer and the intellectual showpiece wife of a spendthrift eccentric?

I remained unperturbed by the predominance of male company but there were times when I felt the need of the companionship of my own sex. I asked Charles if I might bring Mary Ann over from Ireland for a short visit. This, like most charitable acts, was a misjudgement, but at least I could be sure of my young sister's discretion. She seldom had a word to say for herself at the best of times.

'I am sure Mary Ann is the most delightful girl, you know, my dear Marguerite. How old is she now; nineteen, twenty? She should be married, you see. She'll never find a husband in a godforsaken village in Ireland. It's our duty, you know, to acquaint her with society. I think you should invite her to stay with us for the season. Have the bedroom next to yours redecorated and order some new furniture.'

The room had remained unoccupied since we refurbished the house and Mary Ann stayed with us for the next twelve years. Teaching her to behave as an English lady was as laborious as it was fruitless. She would make no attempt to emulate my social skills and inexplicably refused to modify her Irish accent. She had inherited traces of the Power beauty and I saw that she was always fashionably dressed, but she never responded to any of the eligible young men I introduced to her. She evidently preferred female company.

Charles remained such a perpetual whirlwind of extravagance that I began to wonder if he really could afford so much indulgence. He was certainly rich, but how rich? I never asked because he obviously had no concept of his own wealth, and his reply would have been more confusing than instructive.

Robert wrote from Dublin to tell me that he had been promoted. He was no longer required to walk the streets as a rent collector but had been given the healthier responsibility of managing the Mountjoy urban estates from an office desk - at the same salary. The excellent Mr Norman had extended his own responsibilities to a mere sinecure knowing that Lord Blessington would never dream of replacing the excellent agent who had so loyally served his father, for a short while.

I promised Robert that if he would let me have a summary of the estate's financial position I would appeal to Lord Blessington on his behalf. In desperate breach of his unwritten confidentiality obligation and self-destructive high moral principles, Robert followed my recommended precautions, stealthily copied out the essential figures and despatched them to me by private messenger. This dastardly misdemeanour remained on my honest brother's conscience for many years. But I kept my word and Charles agreed that Robert's salary should be equal to Mr Norman's, but forgot to clarify his instructions to Mr Norman.

If, and I overlooked too many ifs, all the Mountjoy rents were collected, Charles's annual income amounted to over thirty-thousand pounds. Such an abundant harvest could only be the fruit of a boundless orchard of capital. Thirty-thousand pounds was seventy-five times the income my father boasted in the days when he kept a fine stable and eight or ten servants. What is more, all Irish income was exempt from the temporary tax William Pitt imposed to fund the Napoleonic Wars.

Two centuries later income tax is still temporary and although, as a mere reincarnation, clairvoyance is not within my gift I can safely predict that it will remain temporary for the next two centuries.

Commerce was in my blood. I knew how easily its loftiest pillars can topple and crumble into dust but had no fears for the Blessington estates. They were cast in bricks and mortar and controlled by the iron integrity of the most prestigious bankers in England. I would never have to worry about money again. I always worried about money. Too many bankers, prestigious and otherwise, were and still are evidently unaware that there is no such thing as a bottomless well.

After the theatre and patronage of the arts the Earl of Blessington's favourite pastime was speaking in the House of Lords, three or four times per annum. He claimed to be a Whig but never disagreed with a Tory. He spoke passionately on Irish Catholic emancipation, invariably adding nothing to the interminable debate. More bravely, as a committed monarchist, Charles opposed the king's indictment of Caroline of Brunswick.

'It's a man's duty to be loyal to his wife, you know. Queen Caroline is not a great beauty but she has done George no harm, you see.'

Charles felt so strongly that he actually raised his voice in the Queen's defence and went so far as to criticise his trusted attorney, the King's law agent. *It is to be very much regretted that Mr John Allan Powell had anything to do with the Milan Commission,'* Charles said at the trial. He did not fully understand that an overpaid member of the legal profession is sometimes obliged to sacrifice his integrity, even when it involved gathering false evidence for a commission ordered by the monarch to justify his untenable case.

A popular Tory magazine lampooned Charles's speech. Overwhelmed by the compliment, he learnt the offensive poems by heart, and repeated them so often that my pet parrot could recite them better than he could himself.

'They show I am appreciated, you see,' he said, and he was right. Some years later Lord Byron dashed off some high-flown lines in my honour. They were equally meaningless, but taught me that a satirist's gibe is always a greater tribute than a flatterer's compliment. But Byron was a genius not a disseminator of irreverent commentary such as offered by *John Bull* on 17th December 1820:

> *Lord Blessington's a stage struck ass-*
> *-sumer of Lothario*
> *But by his talents, wit or grace,*
> *(Had he but eyes to find his place)*
> *He's fitter for Paddy Carey O!*

The poet was referring to the ballad *Paddy Carey O* popularised at the Drury Lane Theatre by Charles's friend the comic actor, Edward Fitzwilliam. The taunt was in part directed at me since the then well-known lyrics tell of a questionably innocent Irish girl who falls in love with a vain and swaggering adventurer.

In another poem the satirist employs Charles's intermittent squint to parody his indecisiveness, and perhaps more personal traits.

> *Blessington hath a beaming eye,*
> *But no one knows for whom it beameth,*
> *Right and left it seems to fly,*
> *But what it looks at no one dreameth.*

Like everything about Charles, his sexuality was ambiguous. He had fathered four children by his first wife and undoubtedly loved her. And if he didn't love me he was a more convincing actor in the bedroom than on the stage. What he did elsewhere was not my concern. I never asked why he needed to stay so late with the actors after their performances at Drury Lane. Handing a donation to the manager was I presumed a lengthy process.

'A theatrical production is a time-consuming business, you see. There are the stage arrangements, the scenery, the properties, the costumes, the cast, the music and all the rest. The directors and actors do so appreciate my observations, you know.'

'I am sure that the theatre would be much poorer without them', I said.

Charles remained sympathetic when unforeseen attacks of neuralgia prevented me from accompanying him on his quarterly visits to Ireland. So far as I knew, he went to Dublin to take lunch with the excellent Mr Norman, disregard his report and attend to heavy commitments the details of which I omitted to ask. He would stay for a night or two at Henrietta Street before being driven to Mountjoy Forest for an obligatory visit to his family.

'I do think it so important, you see, for children to have a meaningful relationship with their father.'

'Indeed Charles, it is a great tragedy that fate robbed you of the chance to know your own father.'

The late Viscount Mountjoy attached no importance whatsoever to relationships with his children.

'My dear Marguerite, you are quite right as always. Nothing of that kind must happen to my children, you know.'

Charles did not know. He had been indoctrinated from birth with the code of the English upper classes. Public schools were paid to prepare its sons to transcend the merciless world outside and governesses paid much less to prepare its daughters to espouse successful transcenders of the merciless world outside. Children of both genders were thus fittingly distanced from the distasteful facets of their parents' behaviour.

This infallible code did not work well in practice. Charles's children were no more distanced than me from the distasteful facets of his behaviour. But as a loving wife I treated his weaknesses as amiable imperfections. Unlike his dependent family I adhered to the respect he richly deserved, in private as well as in public, and more often than not with sincerity.

There was more to Charles Gardiner, Earl of Blessington, than met the eye. The eye met a blundering overdressed waster. But pride in appearance and possessions do not prove the absence of a creative spirit, as is still so often propounded by those who think themselves wise. Charles, like me, was a creative spirit before his time. We were both progressive thinkers, discerning patrons of the arts, entrapped by convention.

Together we haunted galleries, studios and garrets. We pondered, assessed, criticised and misjudged potential talent. We overpaid for drawings, paintings and sculptures by long forgotten immortals. Charles did not collect art for investment. That was for philistines and he was an amateur. Amateur means love. Charles's love of art was an enigma that only I could fathom. He was not squandering his fortune: he was creating a perpetual surreal artwork to share with the world. He, Charles John Gardiner, Earl of Blessington was himself the living essence of his own work in which he saw me as a central feature.

The meaningless epithet *champagne socialist* was a concept of the distant future which might have been coined with Charles and I in mind. Few contemporaries of our class were more sensitive to social injustice. Wherever we went we encountered poverty, hopelessness, disease and ignorance, and justified our impotence to disseminate the splendours of our lifestyle.

'You are quite right, my dear Marguerite, too many people are living in dreadful conditions. I have been on the board of the Society for the Relief of the Irish Poor for years, you know. I go to meetings and so on, but they don't seem to get anywhere. You see, it's all so terribly complicated but I am sure there is something more I should be doing.'

'Charles, perhaps you should extend your philanthropy beyond Ireland. There are remarkable people here in England working tirelessly for reform. Some even try to encourage the poor to have ambition and make the effort to claw themselves out of the abyss. As a wealthy man you are obliged support these admirable causes.'

Robert Owen, an even wealthier man, accepted our invitation to St James's Square. Over a table groaning with pheasant and fine wines he expounded his vision of an earthly paradise of social equality. He was planning villages of co-operation: communities of self-supporting, healthy, well-fed properly housed workers. I thought he was mad.

'Indeed, Lady Blessington, education is the essence our project. If it is not asking too much, perhaps you would care to donate a little of your invaluable time to one of our enlightenment programmes?'

'I assure you that I shall do all I can, Mr Owen. I have some experience of the deplorable lack of education among the lower orders.'

I did nothing. I had read about numerous similarly deluded idealists. Owen's well-intentioned concepts would come to nothing like all the rest.

Charles was not so easily convinced.

'Practical men like you, Robert, that's what this country needs. Action speaks louder than money, you know.'

Robert Owen did not know. His appreciation of his friend's overgenerous donation was spoken loud and clear. Charles was so taken in by Owen's flattery and utopian visions that he became a founder-member of the British and Foreign Philanthropic Society destined to evolve into today's international Co-operative Movement. He attended three meetings.

Most politicians of the time were generally sceptical of social reform. Every civilisation in history has divided itself between rich leaders and poor followers, with too few of the former and too many of the latter. This is the natural order of things and reformers like Robert Owen would never change them. I nonetheless applauded his practical work and did nothing.

In the real world of unreformable class distinction Charles fulfilled his obligation to present me at London's most exclusive house of entertainment. The palatial dining rooms, salons and gambling halls of Almack's Assembly Rooms abounded with aristocratic ladies, among whom I was the most elaborately attired, attractive and invisible.

'What a pleasure to see you here again, Lord Blessington. The Duke so thoroughly enjoyed your dinner party. I am so sorry I was unable join him but as I am sure he explained my poor father had a sudden attack of gout.'

The Duke had told *me* that his wife had a severe headache.

I did not condescend to honour Almack's with my presence more than once. There were other places where I could be seen and unappreciated. I was never ignored at the Drury Lane Theatre. Charles's private box was virtually on the stage, allowing the ladies in the audience to ostensibly pay attention to the play and the gentlemen to ostensibly pay no attention to me. I loved the theatre. It was a world ruled by showmanship where social equality always prevailed with the vicious invective of Almack's and the unrestrained competitiveness of fame and fortune.

St James's Square was not entirely void of female visitors. Mrs Siddons was always happy to accept our invitations with or without her husband, William, another fine actor. Sarah embraced me as her most cherished friend until she died in 1831 but of course it was impossible to tell if she was acting. When Sir Thomas Lawrence's affairs with her daughters, Sally and Maria, delayed his completion of my portrait, her concern was completely undetectable. Sarah even brought a female friend to St James's Square. Mrs Catherine Landon told me that her daughter was a poet with modern ideas in keeping with someone of my own age. I took this as a great compliment. Letitia Elizabeth Landon was thirteen years younger than me.

She was nineteen when she first came to St James's Square with her mentor, the distinguished Scottish poet, publisher and entrepreneur, William Jerdan. Apart from her privileged background, Letitia was my mirror image. In addition to her incredible beauty she had a sparkling personality, a brilliant intellect and a razor edged tongue. She learnt to read at the age of two and by the time she was thirteen had mastered Latin and Greek and acquired an encyclopaedic knowledge of the classics and fine arts.

A few months before we first met she had been awarded the *Literary Gazette's* poetry prize for *The Tale of Adelaide, A Swiss Tale of Romance, and other Poems*. The *Gazette's* editor, who by pure chance happened to be Jerdan himself, appointed Letitia as his chief reviewer and permitted her to publish her poetry and short stories at will. Scholars, literary aficionados and students queued for every edition unaware that their new idol, writing under the simple pseudonym *L*, was a young girl. The circulation of the *Literary Gazette* rocketed and established Jerdan's lifelong reputation.

Every man who met Letitia fell for her precocious cynicism, almost as astute as my own. Yet even such an enlightened spirit could not disperse the clouds of invective gathering over 10 St James's Square. A celebrated married publisher with a girl half his age visiting the unvisited Lady Blessington was a scandalmongers' dream. Jerdan's fatherly protection did not imply an improper relationship any more than it implied that Letitia was the mistress of half of Lord Blessington's friends.

Letitia always vehemently denied any impropriety with William Jerdan or anyone else. She was over thirty when she accepted a proposal from the writer, critic and editor of *The Examiner*, John Forster, almost ten years her junior. Forster discreetly announced to the world that he had *'made every enquiry within his power'* and was satisfied that she was a virgin. Letitia immediately broke off the engagement, writing to Forster, *'the mere suspicion is as dreadful as death'*. She chose more poignant expressions in articulating her opinion of him to me.

Letitia was right to reject Forster. His *every enquiry* was largely gleaned from a scandal sheet called *The Wasp* which had absolutely no grounds for its obscure sensational revelation, *'She was ordered to the country* [by Jerdan] *to gather fruit* [and] *deliver an account thereof on her return'*.

Having rejected the unrepentant Forster, Letitia expanded her nom de plume to the still genderless *L E L* and resumed her literary career to universal acclaim. Today, her poetry and prose, unlike mine, is still widely read by students of literature and discerning bookworms. Jealousy was never in my nature.

My life at St James's Square remained an intoxicating blend of sophistication and naivety. Charles continued to invite interesting men but still I craved female companionship. Mary Ann was too silent, Sarah Siddons too old and Letitia too heavily committed to literary affairs. The most inappropriate alternative was Catherine Lee who enjoyed my company as a fellow victim of envy and ostracism. When George de Blaquiere was unavailable she would come to seek my advice and remind me of how I had profited from hers. Catherine did not need anyone's advice.

'Do you have any news of Thomas Jenkins, Catherine?'

Catherine had a great deal of news.

'None whatsoever, except that I have heard that he changed his mind about re-enlisting in the army.'

'Is he planning to marry?'

'Not so far as I am aware, Marguerite. Unlike the Reverend Lee, his life is free of gods and women. You are well rid of him.'

'With good fortune, Catherine, neither of us will see him again. I should have anticipated that as soon as poor Mrs Jenkins died our sham marriage would be exposed and vilified by London society.'

'Ignore these silly jealous women, Marguerite. You have a legitimate husband, a magnificent home and are surrounded by brilliant men. What more can you ask?'

'You are of course right, I have every reason to be happy, but rumours are always rife. I am regularly humiliated.'

'Good heavens, Marguerite, scandal is a fact of life. The ton will soon find someone else to malign, if someone doesn't malign them first.'

'Possibly, Catherine but what if Charles should become disillusioned? Confrontation is not in his nature but I know he is unhappy about my refusals to go with him to Ireland. He thinks of it as his own country – and a large part of it is – but it is not my country. I abhor Ireland, its people and its politics and have no desire to revisit my past. In any case, Charles's family have made it abundantly clear that I am unwelcome.'

'My dear Marguerite, I would die of despair if I gave a moment's thought to what my husband's family think of me. Allow the sweet life of London to overwhelm your bitter memories of Ireland.'

'That is good advice, Catherine but London life would taste far sweeter if its quality added more sugar to its fiction.'

'Marguerite, you must give yourself time. Why not ask Charles to take you away for a while? I don't mean to Ireland. What about Paris? You told me that you were well received when you went with Thomas Jenkins.'

Charles welcomed Catherine's advice with restrained alacrity.

'Yes, my dear Marguerite, it is high time we took a holiday. But, you know, there is more to Europe than Paris. I must show you the Netherlands. I'm sure you will find it delightful, all the art and so on, you see. You can't compare the French artists to the Dutch masters: De Hooch, Rembrandt, Vermeer, Vandyke and of course old Frans Hals. He painted the *Laughing Cavalier*, you know? And there is still talent there. One or two young artists have written to me. They might be worth encouraging, you see.'

Our departure was delayed by a much envied invitation.

On 19th July 1821 I accompanied Charles to Westminster Abbey for the coronation of King George IV, the one occasion when I was in the same room as a British monarch and then I only caught a few glimpses of him between the stuffed ermine upholstering the crowded pews.

The garish demi-religious ceremonial was as unnecessarily long as it was tedious. The overweight new King George IV enacted the sacred formalities with unnatural dignity. We were so absorbed by the theatricality that we were unaware of the heavily armed guards posted by every door to protect the vast congregation from the retribution of the king's diminutive wife. Queen Caroline was not invited. In common with her many sympathisers, Charles and I were incensed and commended her brave attempt to take her rightful place by her husband. As the archbishop lifted the crown, outside the much-maligned Caroline created a loud and undignified royal scene and thus sabotaged most of her public support.

On 7th of August, three weeks after the Coronation, the body of Queen Caroline of Brunswick was discovered at Brandenburg House, Fulham. Her death, at the age of just fifty-three, occurred in what would now be termed suspicious circumstances. It will never be known whether she took her own life or was assassinated but Charles mourned her as if she had been his own mother. Since he had never had the opportunity to mourn his own mother he made a brief visit to Seamore Place and as the Queen of England's modest cortege passed slowly through Park Lane en route to Harwich, from there to be shipped to her last resting place at Brunswick Cathedral, Charles came out of the house, removed his hat, lowered his head for twenty seconds and went back in.

On 10th September, Charles, I, Mary Ann, six carriages and eight servants left St James's Square, crossed London Bridge, rattled along the Old Kent Road via Rochester to Dover. That same day I made my first entry in an especially purchased leather-bound notebook. A year later my *Journal of a Tour Through the Netherlands and Part of France in 1821* was published commencing with an anonymous *advertisement*:

> '*Of this journal there has been no subsequent re-writing nor have there been added any embellishments, or extracts from books already published.*'

The editor did not say that there were no omissions. How honest of him! Even my own name was omitted. '*By the author of Sketches and Fragments etc. etc. etc.*' proclaimed the title page. My small collection of essays and short stories had been published almost simultaneously as '*by the author of The Magic Lantern*' - without etc. etc. etc. Longman, Hurst, Rees, Orme, Brown & Green evidently considered that *by The Countess of Blessington* would offend their readers' prudish eyes. The firm survives to the present day but is now called simply 'Longman'. I am so sorry for Thomas Longman's five partners! I know how it feels to have my name deleted.

Longman, etc. etc. etc. wielded their blue pencils not only across my name but the names of my husband, my sister and almost all the interesting individuals I recorded meeting in my *1821 Journal*. They also mercifully erased most of my more judicious observations.

Who did they think would want to read the whitewashed scribble of an anonymous traveller? My royalties amounted to even less than I paid a chambermaid in a year. According to my esteemed publishers, the money, which I did not need, was of no consequence. Apparently I was expected to feel honoured to see my work in print. It would be many years before I again sought that honour.

Since my first, and I have to say my most delightful travelogue had not '*added any embellishments*', I shall add a few now for the benefit of the unfortunate majority who have not had the pleasure of reading the published version.

Having spent a night at the finest hotel in Dover, I noted: '*On examining our bill, we found that it was not only the exterior of the house that was imposing, for the charges were as extravagant as the accommodations were bad.*' The proprietors of many English seaside hotels, then and since, might have done well to heed my constructive appraisal. The next morning the private steam packet that Charles chartered in London failed to appear and we had to cross the Channel with the vomiting adherents of the '*regular*' service. As I have said, I was an exemplary sailor and cheerfully wrote my journal swaying gently in the discomfort of the cabin, while Charles and Mary Anne joined the other seasick passengers on deck.

In Calais the guests at the charming old Dessein's Hotel, beloved of my friend William Makepeace Thackeray who also complained bitterly of its poor service and charges, included a party of English nobility returning from the Queen's funeral. Charles knew them all well and congratulated these brave subjects on their unrecorded – other than by me – gesture of disapproval of the new-crowned king.

'The countess and I are conscience stricken, you see. We should have come to Brunswick with you and shown proper respect,' Charles told them.

'Indeed, Lord Blessington, Queen Caroline was badly wronged. I fear she died of a broken heart.'

The accounts I read of the royal symptoms implied more physical forms of breakage, which made me and many others believe that she was assassinated. I nonetheless wrote of the noble group's genuine warmth and sincerity, which I found a pleasant novelty among their class. But then they were not in England at the time.

After Calais our next stop was at *Lisle*, (Lille) where I visited its renowned library and requested access to its ancient collection of rare Latin and old-French texts. The librarian was astounded. No woman had ever before asked to see them, let alone been able to translate them and appreciate their significance. En route to Brussels we witnessed the destruction and dereliction of the glorious Napoleonic victories but also saw a more civilised facet of the Emperor's complexity when we paused to admire the *'great magnificence'* of the *Château Lacken*, (Laeken). Our guide proudly informed us that it was from this now Belgian royal palace that Napoleon made the first attempt since Julius Caesar to rule a united Europe. In fact, he only stayed there for a less than a month in August 1804.

'While Napoleon possessed empires and gave laws to half of Europe I could condemn his overweening ambition and selfishness and shrink from his hardness of heart and want of principle; but since he has fallen from his greatness I can feel no sentiment, but pity for his situation and the littleness of mind that could lead his enemies to trample on a fallen foe and abridge his days by ill treatment.'

I was yet to become a confirmed Bonapartist but with these thoughts, the heinous charisma of the great Napoleon cast an indelible spell over my mind.

At the theatre in Brussels we were disappointed with the performance of the Prince and Princess of Orange, who denied us the royal box and permitted a touch of honest criticism to slip past Longman's editors.

'The Princess seems a mild unaffected woman but is not handsome and the Prince is remarkably plain.'

Charles, a general who had never seen a battlefield, suggested an excursion to visit Waterloo in peacetime. It was six years since Wellington had defeated Napoleon there, and as an anglophile I should have felt some sort of patriotic pride, but the gruesome atmosphere again brought to mind the slaughtered young men on both sides who probably never had a bad word for anybody. Men posing as war veterans offered pieces of uniform, bones and teeth, which they airily boasted were looted from the fallen. Even Charles was not tempted. Traders in war memorabilia remain equally sensitive today.

A floral tribute on a mass grave inspired me to write:

'In search of Flowers to Waterloo don't roam
You'll find the Flower of Waterloo. at home'

Some years later I recited this brief poem to the Duke of Wellington. I am not sure that he appreciated the sentiment.

On our return to Brussels, Charles introduced me to a fabulously wealthy banker called Monsieur Daroont who conducted us through his private art gallery, which he claimed was the finest in Europe. He showed us paintings by Rubens, Vandyke, Titian, Holbein, the Flemish masters Pourbus, father and son; Teniers, father, son and grandson and members of other doubtlessly talented families. The cultured banker lectured us with knowledge and panache until all his paintings merged before our eyes into a single blank canvas. As always Charles was patient and Mary Anne silent. It was our last encounter with Monsieur Daroont. I do hope that my yawning did not upset him.

Thereafter I was more discriminating employing professional museum guides who accepted large gratuities and listened to me explaining the exhibits to Mary Anne. They were not at all upset by her yawning. Charles did no more sightseeing. He preferred to visit living artists seeking his patronage. They never yawned.

'The work here is excellent, you see, my dear Marguerite, but I think we should view some studios elsewhere before making more purchases. We don't need to go on to the Netherlands, you know. Amsterdam is terribly attractive in places, you see, the canals, the merchants' houses and so on, but artistically speaking it has passed its prime. Do you agree, my dear Marguerite, that we should go to see what the Parisians have to offer?'

I agreed without hesitation. Belgium was a beautiful country with much to commend it, I suppose. It was full of rich and cultured people unconcerned by the plight of their peasant neighbours. As always in the aftermath of war, obscene wealth and obscene poverty sat uneasily together.

On 23rd September 1821 we turned south. It was only a fortnight since we left London but I was suffering the pangs of my addiction to the opiate of the great city, and could hardly wait to be back in Paris. Rural France was no illusory paradise. Corruption was real and endemic. At the French border, entrepreneurial customs officers wasted an hour tearing our baggage apart and demanding bribes before stamping our passports. When we reached Valenciennes I discovered that they had stolen all my jewellery. Charles, with characteristic innocence, had declared everything and paid the exorbitant duties demanded. He was not at all perturbed. This minor setback offered an excellent excuse to reacquaint himself with world-renowned Parisian jewellers whose larger and inferior products were far more expensive than in London.

The remainder of our journey through northern France was similarly educational. The picturesque landscape extolled by painters and poets through the ages was, like Belgium, marred by the rewards of war and ubiquitous destitute peasants held in abject ignorance by church and state. France was just as enlightened by revolution as was Ireland.

In Paris, the legendary hotelier Monsieur Meurice came himself to the door of its grandest hotel, kissed my hand and bowed to Charles. 'Welcome back to the Hotel Meurice, Monsieur le Comte de Blessington. We are most honoured that you have brought Madame la Comtesse to stay with us'.

Twelve years had passed since my first visit to Paris came to its ill-fated end. The great city would surely have changed. Debris, stench, idleness and the uglier manifestations of commerce were still everywhere in evidence, but now a resurrected nobility blended into an animated mosaic of culture and society. I filled my journal with a fusion of delight and distaste. Little of the latter survived publication in its unembellished form.

Soon after our arrival we received an invitation to the Chapel Royal for a service in the presence of King Louis XVIII. The aging king performed the ritual without finesse, while his gorgeously robed courtiers showed little respect for his person. They evidently found their overweight king as repugnant as I found George IV. Napoleonic philosophy, for all its ugly perfectionism, was certainly preferable to this type of monarchy. On the other hand, I was again impressed by the kindness and good manners of the French ladies who made a concerted effort to welcome me into their midst; a courtesy from which their cousins in London might have greatly benefited.

Unquestionably, the most fascinating individual I recorded meeting on my *Tour through the Netherlands to Paris in 1821* – disregarding those I was too sensitive to record – was the Baron Vivant Denon; an old friend of Charles. In Paris as elsewhere, everybody who was anybody was an old friend of Charles. The Baron was the personification of exploitative scholarship and my description of his château as *'an encyclopaedia of the fine arts'* deprecates the treasure with which it was filled.

The elderly Baron was captivated by my knowledge of both his exquisite illustrations and the thesis of his authoritative *Travels in Lower and Upper Egypt*, and in other ways too. In response I was captivated by his tales of archaeological expeditions as Napoleon's personal antiquarian. Denon's scholarly appreciation of the Emperor's ignorance of ancient Egypt qualified him to be appointed first director of the *Louvre Musée Napoléon*, an unassailable sinecure that he retained until his patron was forced from power.

I was shocked and dispirited by our host's depiction of the Bourbon monarchy's barbaric demand for every Napoleonic symbol to be removed from the Louvre. It however crossed my mind that the learned director might have personally assisted with the removal before being removed himself, but I quickly retracted the thought.

When we ceased to marvel at his Napoleonic souvenirs, Baron Denon took us to the neighbouring château of a Monsieur Thedenet Durant, who conducted us through another journey into the past. He too was an obsessive Egyptologist and described life and death – mainly death – in the kingdom of the Pharaohs in excessively lurid detail. He uncovered mummies he had dissected himself and displayed the cadavers preserved for thousands of years. I extolled the sublime beauty of these miracles of ancient civilisation until I vomited.

Over dinner in the fresher atmosphere of his own château, Baron Denon elaborated on his relationship with Napoleon. The late Emperor, he claimed, was the kindest natured of men. He was always respectful to women, enjoyed playing with children and it was impossible to be in his company without being affected by the warmth of his personality. The same would be said of Hitler.

Drawing on the favours of a corrupt acquaintance, Baron Denon procured our entry to the unoccupied Château de Malmaison, once home to the Empress Josephine. The caretaker, now bordering on dementia, had served Josephine from divorce to death and worshipped her like a goddess. '*L'impératrice n'a jamais eu un mauvais mot pour personne*, he said fawning with such exuberance that I began to wonder if he thought that I was his deceased mistress returned to taunt him. He begged me to accept a velvet tablecloth with the Empress's initials woven in gold, which of course he had no right to give away. It would have been very rude of me to refuse.

'I do believe that had Napoleon never divorced Josephine he would have died Emperor of France'.

I was probably being a little over pessimistic when I wrote this. I had the greatest respect for Napoleon's first wife who shared his and my commendable obsession with vanity.

Two of my most remarkable encounters were completely excluded by the judicious publishers of my *1821 Journal*.

I had been curious to meet Maria Emilia, née Fagnani, Mie Mie, Marchioness of Hertford since my illuminating dinner with her noble husband. In France as in England, the Blessington title opened every door and the door to the Marchioness's residence in the rue Laffitte was well worth opening. Its spacious rooms were filled with magnificent works of art collected by the third Marquess, Lord Yarmouth, still in London yearning for his beloved father to expire. Although the second Marquess obliged a few months later, the collection remained in Mie Mie's care for twelve more years. In 1835 Yarmouth acquired the grand Château Bagatelle in the Bois de Boulogne and moved his family and collection there.

As anticipated, the estranged Lady Yarmouth was not the scarlet woman her husband portrayed so delicately. Mie Mie and her son, Richard Seymour-Conway (fourth Marquess from 1842) were both highly cultured and educated. Richard was then twenty-two and unashamedly proud of his illegitimate three-year-old son, another Richard, while Mie Mie in her fifties possessed all the natural instincts of a mother and grandmother.

I made some simple drawings to amuse the little boy, who burst into tears and tore them to shreds. Even at such a tender age, Richard appreciated their lack of artistic merit. Apart from this he seemed a remarkably normal child, destined for an outstanding career in the edifying tradition of his family – in so far as it was his family. I never met his birth mother, the daughter of Sir Thomas Wallace of Craigie but I am sure she was as irreproachable as her paramour, who would have certainly married her had she not been the wife of a certain Mr Jackson. In the event, the fourth Marquess never married, but remained living in splendid eccentricity at the Château Bagatelle with his mother, Mie Mie, who died aged eighty-five in 1856. Mrs Jackson never acknowledged her son who adopted her single name, and was knighted after my death for, among other virtues, services to the Wallace Collection.

Both the fourth Marquess and Richard Wallace remained my loyal friends, literally, until the day I died.

The second encounter unreasonably deleted from my journal would prove more consequential.

There was another associate of the late and, as I had begun to appreciate, much lamented Emperor Napoleon who Charles was anxious to meet while in Paris. This, for once, was someone to whom my name rather than the Earl of Blessington's provided an introduction. I sent a message to Chambourcy and was pleased to receive a positive reply:

'General Count Albert Gaspard D'Orsay will be highly honoured to welcome his fellow officer, the noble Lieutenant Colonel, Earl of Blessington and the Countess Marguerite to his humble château, but regrettably has a number of heavy commitments throughout this week.

The General therefore requests me to convey his sincere apologies and to say that he looks forward to making Lord Blessington's acquaintance in the near future.

However, Madame la Baronesse is planning to be in Paris tomorrow afternoon and will be pleased to take tea with the Countess of Blessington in her hotel at 3pm. Please be good enough to advise should this be inconvenient.

Signed ... Private secretary'

This is an inexact translation. In the original French the underlying nuance of censure is more pronounced. While I had no doubt that General D'Orsay's commitments were too heavy to postpone, I must admit to being as disappointed as Charles, if not as philosophical. On my prior visit to Chambourcy with Captain Jenkins, the general had been in Holland serving the temporary king, Louis Bonaparte, husband of Hortense de Beauharnais, the Empress Josephine's daughter by her first marriage. Since acquiring her precious tablecloth I had been curious to learn more about the Empress, and thought that I might induce General D'Orsay to impart some enlightening information. I consoled myself with the thought that the loyal Bonapartist's wife might be more likely to disclose some interesting details of his commander's mother-in-law's scandalous life. I thus accepted La Baronesse Eleanore de Franquemont's invitation to take tea at Charles's expense.

La Baronesse spoke perfect English and I had no need to concern myself with the nuances of her meaning. She well recalled my visit to her château but was too well-mannered to inquire about Captain Jenkins. Thomas himself had told her all he wished her to know.

'And how are your delightful children, Madame la Baronesse? I shall never forget the wonderfully talented little boy and girl who performed for me in Chambourcy. They must be quite grown up by now.' I tried desperately to remember their names, while envisaging adult versions of the spoilt prodigies to whom I had been so delighted to say *au revoir* twelve years earlier.

'Indeed, Lady Blessington, it is a great joy to tell you that my children are well and prosperous. Ida has grown to great beauty. When she was just seventeen she married the Duc de Guiche, the eldest son of the eighth Duc de Gramont. Antoine is an excellent young man. General D'Orsay and I could not have wished for a more brilliant match.'

The Baronesse's son-in-law was a direct descendent of the Comte de Guiche, later immortalised by Rostand as the cruel and deceitful adversary of *Cyrano de Bergerac*. The de Gramonts were one of the most aristocratic families surviving in France and Antoine stood to inherit a fortune as large Charles's.

'My sincerest congratulations, Madame la Baronesse, and does Ida yet have children of her own? You are surely too young to be a grandmother.'

'You are exceedingly kind, your ladyship, but my youthful appearance is deceiving. In fact, I have three grandchildren. Ida is blessed with two sons, Agénor and August and a baby daughter, Antonia, born just this July. Alas, I do not see them as often as I would wish as they are at present resident in London.'

'In which case Lord Blessington will certainly be acquainted with the Duc de Guiche. I shall ensure that he invites him immediately on our return. I am so looking forward to meeting your grandchildren.'

With fascinated trepidation, I envisaged duplicates of the Baronesse's own precocious offspring.

The Duc de Guiche, Antoine Geneviève Héraclius Agénor de Gramont, a rising star of the French army, assigned to London with ambassadorial credentials, was born at Versailles in 1789, the year of my own birth. It was also the year of the French Revolution when his family fled to England where Antoine was educated at a public school, graduated from Oxford and forced to serve a short term with the 10th Hussars. Returning to France he rose, entirely by his own merit, to the rank of Lieutenant-Général in des Armées du Roi and was awarded the Légion D'Honneur for bravery and family connections.

I never discovered why all the D'Orsay and de Gramont male names began with A but it proved a useful mnemonic. I suddenly recalled the name of the Baronesse's son.

'Madame la Baronesse, will you not tell me the news of your brilliant son, Alfred?'

Nothing could have interested me less but my inquiry lit up the Baronesse Eleanore's eyes and simultaneously set her mouth in motion.

'Alfred is now twenty and he too has grown beautiful. He stands six feet three inches tall has the physique of an Apollo. What is more, he is fulfilling all the promise you witnessed yourself, Lady Blessington. Every gallery in Paris pleads to exhibit his portraiture and the critics predict that he will be as celebrated as your English artist, Sir Thomas Lawrence. You are aware of Sir Thomas's reputation?'

'Indeed, Madame, I know Sir Thomas well. He is painting my own portrait as we speak. He has been painting it for more than two years. Dare I commend that Alfred works rather more quickly if he wishes to succeed as a professional artist?'

'Oh no, he would never so demean himself. He is a professional soldier. Two years ago the Garde Royale honoured him with a commission, since when he has proven himself to be the finest athlete, and the most skilled swordsman, marksman and rider in the regiment.'

When Madame la Baronesse paused from extolling her son's interminable talents, I could think of nothing better to say than: 'The General must be exceedingly proud.'

This was the wrong thing to say.

'My husband has reservations. The young officers say there is no place in the Bourbon army for the son of a Napoleonic general. They are jealous of Alfred because his commission was secured with his father's influence, as if *theirs* were secured by other means. They have tormented poor Alfred to such a degree that he is considering resignation.'

'Is there nothing General D'Orsay can do?'

'Albert served with distinction in La Grande Armée, but I fear he is a little detached from the ways of the world. He blames Alfred for the attitude of his fellow officers. Frankly, I am hoping that he will very soon leave the army and join Ida and Antoine in London and find a bride who will appreciate him for the fine man that he is.'

The more the Baronesse told me of Comte Alfred D'Orsay, the more he reminded me of the conceited child I met at Chambourcy. Conceit was always an anathema to me. Wishing to hear no more, I diverted the conversation to my aristocratic friend's own family, a doubtless more intriguing subject. For all her refined affectations, the general's wife was no more an aristocrat than I was. It transpired that she was the fruit of an illicit union between a depraved German duke and an unmitigated harlot.

The Baronesse expounded her biography with remarkable candour.

'My history, Lady Blessington, is somewhat unconventional, but involves nothing of which I have reason to be ashamed. Nonetheless, you might find it difficult to comprehend.'

I had reached a point in life where I doubted that anybody's history could be so unconventional that I would find it difficult to comprehend.

'I believe that I have heard of your mother. Is she not the exotic Madame Craufurd?'

'Yes indeed, everyone, including me, is obliged to address maman as *Madame* Craufurd, though she is not French. She is something of an institution here in Paris, loved and widely respected at the royal court. Her one fault is that she spoils my children. Like everyone else she cannot resist Alfred's angelic eyes and indulges his every whim. It is a great pity because it is so important for young people to understand the value of money. I doubt Alfred will ever have any concept whatsoever.'

'Madame Craufurd is reputed to be extremely rich.'

'Indeed, when my stepfather Quintin died two years ago he left an untold fortune which alas Madame Craufurd tends to squander.'

The more his mother boasted about Comte Alfred D'Orsay, the lower he fell in my esteem. But the more I learned about the Baronesse's stepfather the more I admired him, and the more curious I became to meet his widow.

'If you will permit me, Dr Madden, Mr Sadleir and Mr Molloy, I will briefly postpone my own history to tell you a little about La Baronnesse Eleanore de Franquemont, as related to me.'

'Thank you, Lady Blessington, while we have all read and written much about Comte D'Orsay himself due to your interesting relationship with him and I think we would like to learn more about his family background.'

Born in Scotland, Quintin Craufurd was no ordinary corrupt merchant adventurer; he was a scholar of extraordinary distinction, whose treatises ranged from Pericles, Greek art and Hinduism to an acclaimed history of the pre-revolutionary French monarchy. At the age of nineteen, without the support of his well-connected family, or so he claimed, Quintin secured a position as a trader with the East India Company at the height of its unscrupulous power. By exploiting his exuberant personality, noble bearing and talent for illicit profiteering, in just two years the young executive had been promoted to the main board. In the best tradition of all directors in the Company's chequered history, Quintin devoted the majority of his time to private business. He was so successful that by the time he was forty he had accumulated sufficient wealth to escape his exalted responsibilities. He left India for the last time in 1784 bound for France, taking with him a vivacious Italian wife, her daughter and a shipload of gold, silver, precious stones and valuable artworks. In his pocket was an indictment for the misappropriation of Company funds, which he threw overboard.

In Paris Quintin led the irreproachable life of a scholar, writer, sometime politician and courtier, while his wife, Anne, now Madame Craufurd, exploited the turmoil of the French Revolution to enhance their social status and fabulous fortune.

In June 1791 Quintin employed his intellect to help devise the master plan intended to rescue the King and Queen from the Revolution and secure their safe passage out of France. So ingenious was the plot that the royal couple got only as far as Varennes, where they were arrested and subsequently executed. Quintin meanwhile made his own escape to Brussels leaving instructions for Madame Craufurd and her daughter, Eleanore, to follow, but his plans too were thwarted and they found themselves detained in Paris.

While in Brussels, Quintin wrote *The Secret History of the King of France and his Escape from Paris*, which he did not publish until his blundered conspiracy was long forgotten. This imaginative work of non-fiction overlooks the secret history of the royal money that escaped with the author to Belgium and similar irrelevant details. Quintin, a man of catholic loyalties, wisely employed his wealth to finance the Revolutionary campaigns of his friend Charles Maurice de Talleyrand-Périgord, who out of cunning gratitude arranged for Madame Craufurd and Eleanore to join him in Belgium. With the ascent of Napoleon,

Talleyrand, another man of catholic loyalties, was appointed foreign minister. Among his first acts was to bring Quintin Craufurd back from Brussels to accept responsibility for Anglo-French relations. Given the number of his old East India colleagues who by then had returned to England, this proved, a mistake. Talleyrand did not make mistakes. He dismissed Quintin and commandeered his wealth and artworks for the benefit of the nation. Unbeknown to Talleyrand, the young mother, Madame Craufurd, had shrewdly retained all her own and most of Quintin's assets. Soon the Craufurds returned to Paris, where they befriended and became favourites of the Empress Josephine.

Napoleon also did not make mistakes and so retained the loyal and disloyal Talleyrand to lead his regime to its downfall in 1814. Louis XVIII's government, impressed by Talleyrand's astute political ineptitude, hounded him from office. This provided Quintin Craufurd with the opportunity to extort compensation for his loyalty and disloyalty to the monarchy. Louis refunded Fr 1,344,000 and returned all the artworks. By an ironical turn of fate, the Craufurds simultaneously acquired the once-revolutionary Talleyrand's magnificent château in the rue d'Anjou.

'Thank you, Lady Blessington, but we are all historians and quite aware of all of this. We were hoping that your conversation with La Baronnesse might be more revealing.'

'You might also find it more improbable, Dr Madden, although I assure you it is the truth. Allow me to continue.'

'I was devoted to my stepfather; a truly great man. He never had a bad word for anybody', said La Baronesse.

'Did your natural father die young, madame?' I asked.

Presuming the title de Franquemont to have been inherited through La Baronesse's paternal line, I was unprepared for her reply.

'My father was the King of Württemberg, and to save you the embarrassment of a discrete enquiry he did not marry my mother, nor did I have the displeasure of meeting him.'

I was horrified. Friedrich, the last King of Württemberg, was six feet eleven inches tall and weighed over four hundred pounds. The very thought of this monster making love to a normal-sized woman was quite repulsive. I was mistaken. La Baronesse's father turned out to the more respectably proportioned Duke Karl Eugen of Württemberg, remembered for little else than his abject debauchery and incredible number of mistresses.

'Now that I have revealed my secret, which I fear is common knowledge, I think it appropriate that you should call me Eleanore, Lady Blessington?'

'And you shall call me Marguerite. I doubt that I need to tell you, Eleanore, but I too have secrets that are common knowledge. Mine, I imagine, are quite prosaic compared to your mother's.'

'When you are next in Paris, Marguerite, I must introduce you to Madame Craufurd. She relishes any opportunity to reveal her secrets for herself.'

I imaged Madame Craufurd to be by then old and infirm. Probably she would be dead before I came to Paris again but it required little persuasion to encourage Eleanore to continue. She was very proud of her mother's secrets.

'The Royal Württembergs are reputed to have lived in spectacular style. You must have had a wonderful childhood, Eleanore?'

'You cannot be so naïve, ma chère Marguerite. Men like Duke Karl Eugen pay their paramours for services rendered, not for professional errors but I fear I cannot relate maman's history as beautifully as she tells it herself.'

'Then I am sure that your version will be more truthful and interesting,' I said, prepared to be disappointed. I was not disappointed.

'Madame Craufurd is Italian by birth. She claims to have been born in Lucca, Tuscany, and that her name was Anne Franchi. Apparently my grandfather was a poor Jewish tailor, though maman never mentions him. I cannot imagine why. I do not even know his real name. Franchi does not sound at all Jewish. It is a terrible cliché, I know, but when she was fourteen my mother really did run away and join a circus. She learnt to be a trapeze artist but before long discovered that she had an exceptional talent as a dancer.'

'Dancing is the most graceful of all the arts,' I said reminded of the rowdy Irish jigs at the Clonmel coteries.

'Indeed, Madame Craufurd must have been more than graceful as a young girl. She possessed and, in a way, still possesses a fascinating allure and thus very soon found herself much in demand for, shall I say, private performances. It is said that she chose the stage name Anne Franchi to legitimise a short-lived liaison with an actor of that surname. However, it amused her client the Duke of Württemberg to extend Franchi to *de Franquemont* by adding part of the name of his most despised adversary, or in his reported phrase, another bastard. Thus I was endowed with the title La Baronesse de Franquemont.'

'I am unfamiliar with Franquemont. Where exactly is it, Eleanore?'

'I am not sure. I have never been there. It is unimportant because when I was no more than a few months old, a dancing enthusiast called Le Chevalier d'Aigrement relieved Württemberg of his obligations by falling in love with maman and bringing us here to Paris. Le Chevalier turned out to be even less honourable and considerably meaner than the duke and so maman left him, returned to the stage and caused a sensation touring as *La Belle Franchi*.'

'Lord Blessington is a great devotee of the theatre. He will be able to tell me more about her.'

Charles had never heard of the sensational dancer. His interest in the theatre was, he said, entirely cultural.

Eleanore went on – and on.

'While touring in London maman met a young man called Sullivan, the grandson of Lawrence Sullivan.'

'Oh yes, I have read about Lawrence Sullivan, the legendary chairman of the East India Company who indulged in an unsavoury five-year feud to outdo the excesses of Robert Clive. I was never convinced that either was a hero.'

Eleanore's expression implied that she was not interested in my historical conjectures.

'Maman fell deeply in love with Sullivan's prospects and accepted his proposal of marriage but his prudish grandfather disapproved of the match and ordered him to go to China on Company business. John insisted that maman accompany him posing as his wife and for five years the three of us toured the Far East as a family. We were attended by innumerable servants and accommodated in the soulless luxury of the mysterious East. I was miserable for the entire time. Eventually, we arrived in India, where my unmarried stepfather was immediately appointed Governor of Madras, a position for which thankfully he was totally unsuited. In less than a year John Sullivan was promoted for mismanagement and, still in his twenties, joined Quintin Craufurd on the main Company board in Calcutta.'

'As the grandson of the chairman, Mr Sullivan must have done as well as Quintin Craufurd in India.'

'No, he did not. He was overshadowed by his two brothers. Nepotism was strictly prohibited by the Company's constitution but members of the Sullivan family were obliged to exploit their sinecures. *La Belle Sullivan*, as the more courteous referred to maman, presumed that John would soon fulfil his obligation to become rich. On discovering that she was mistaken, she employed her terpsichorean talents to accelerate the process. Among those who assisted her endeavours was Quintin, which naturally incurred John Sullivan's displeasure. He thus terminated his unblessed marriage and, on behalf of the Company, charged Quintin with misappropriating an average of fifteen thousand pounds in each of the previous ten years.'

'Is that the reason your stepfather left India, Eleanore?'

'Oh no, Quintin could have easily repaid these trivial sums. Maman, however, was determined to remove me from the unhealthy climate of the uncivilised Indian Continent. The happy couple chose to go to Paris, where the Company was held in utter contempt and people like Quintin and Madame Craufurd were properly lionised for depriving the British Empire of the wealth which they had brought to France.'

'And what happened to John Sullivan?'

'He returned in England and became a Member of Parliament. The Sullivans were so ashamed of him.'

'Dare I ask, Eleanore, did Quintin Craufurd marry your mother?'

'Oh yes, it was a true love match, Marguerite. Maman would not leave India without a marriage certificate. Württemberg, D'Aigrement and Sullivan all let her down and she refused to make any further pretence. Quintin had their marriage blessed three times: at the British Embassy, at the Calcutta English Church and at a Catholic cathedral in Paris.'

'And was the marriage blessed with children?'

'Fortunately not, ma chère Marguerite.'

There were so many parallels. Maurice Farmer cheated the East India Company. I lived with Thomas for five years as Mrs Jenkins. Lord Mountjoy married Mary Campbell Browne three times. Madame Craufurd ascended from the abyss to the pinnacle of society, combined beauty with brains and married a flamboyant millionaire.

Madame Craufurd was the portrait of the Countess of Blessington that Lawrence never painted.

We passed our last few days in Paris viewing inappropriate châteaux for sale in fashionable areas and I tried to persuade Charles to acquire one as a regular retreat. Unexpectedly, he procrastinated and declined. He could not believe that I would always be accepted by French society. He was wrong. I was disappointed yet heartened. La Baronesse Eleanore's mesmerising picture of her prostitute mother rekindled my highest aspirations. I was ostracised by the grand hostesses of London but with Madame Craufurd as my hallucinatory mentor I would ostracise them. From now onwards the lords and luminaries who flocked to St James's Square would gladly bring their wives, sisters and daughters. An invitation from the Countess of Blessington would be the most sought after in London. I was better than Lady Jersey who pronounced me persona non grata at Almack's, or any of her rivals who indulged their God-given right to slander the innocent.

As I filled my head with these ridiculous illusions, I filled my journal with an exuberant account of our journey back from Paris to Calais. In reality it was dull and uneventful until we boarded the packet. A mile out to sea the boat was again overtaken by a raging storm. Gale-force winds whipped up thirty-foot waves. On deck drenched passengers clung to rails as they polluted the Channel. In the cabin men reeled like drunks and women lay pale and lifeless on wooden benches.

I felt perfectly well. Well enough to compose a poem, which I claimed to be 'the first ever attempted during a heavy gale and by a very timid sailor'. Here is just one of my three verses. I would not wish to cause further mal de mer by quoting them all.

> Is there, O Lord, in this dread hour,
> One stubborn heart that doubts thy power;
> When nought but clouds and waves appear
> And howling tempests fright the ear?

I was no timid sailor. And at that not at all dread hour, my faith was not in the power of the Lord but a complacent captain called Tom Burnet. I staggered up to the bridge – the only place on board free of the reek of vomit – where Captain Burnet calmly reassured me with tales of shipwrecks and mass drownings' that we were perfectly safe. When we docked I sincerely thanked the captain and commended his excellent seamanship. He stared at me in amazement. I was the first passenger to do so in his thirty-year career.

I am particularly proud of the last entry in my *Journal*. It is one of my finer examples of blatant hypocrisy:

'We reached home on Tuesday evening the 24th of October [1821]*; and the pleased countenances of the domestics, who greeted us with looks of cordial welcome, and the air of elegance and comfort which pervades an English house, brought all the*

comforts of home — dear home! fully before us: comforts that we prize more dearly,
as contrasted with the scenes which we have recently left.'

How romantic! I prized the elegance and comfort which pervaded the Hotel Meurice a great deal more than those which were never to pervade 10 St James's Square.

12

A woman in her eighties sits down beside me. At first I do not recognise her. Her features are heavily lined but her lustrous eyes define that genderless beauty that blends timeless maturity with wisdom. Her English, pitted with genteel French, is an affectation proclaiming a false affinity with her adopted home. France begins and ends in the grand salons of Paris, and is, for her, the exemplar of culture and sophistication.

The old lady knows who I am but opens our conversation with self-assured caution.

'*Vous êtes la seule personne* I have met in this beautiful château who shows *le respect ce qu'il meritait.*'

A hint of Italian in her strange accent reveals her identity.

'You are too kind, madame.'

'We are both wearing the *le même* parfum, *n'est pas, Madame la Comtesse*? I have not come across *Etiquette Bleue* in England. *A Paris, bien sûr* '

'*Etiquette Bleue* is the only perfume I have ever worn. It was specially created for me,' I reply.

She holds up a small box to display a picture of an exquisite horseman in late Georgian dress. There is a hint of irony in her still captivating voice.

'*Pardonnez moi, madame*, you are mistaken. *C'est l'image de Comte Alfred D'Orsay. Etiquette Bleue* was not created for *une belle dame* like you.'

'What makes you say that, madame?'

'*Le Comte was un dandy, comme votre Monsieur Beau Brummell, et aussi un perfumier très célèbre. La Maison de Parfum D'Orsay* explains that the *Comte* created *des parfums pour les dames. Mais vraiment*, he created them for himself and other gentlemen.'

This information does not appear in the potted history of the company enclosed with its perfumes. I point to my portrait.

'As I think you know, madame, Comte Alfred was unable to exploit his gifts commercially. Had he done so my picture and not his would be on your box. '

'*Ah oui, tu est très belle, mais* Alfred was *le perfumier et aussi la mannequin.*'

The old lady is simultaneously mocking and admiring a man who deserted his country and jettisoned his talents to idleness and debauchery. She cannot distinguish his faults from his virtues which she sees only through the tainted blue blood of his forebears. Her exoneration of the paradox of his sexuality rejects the woman who loved him to the end of her days and time and again protected him from the consequences of his indiscretions and the onslaughts of ruin and disgrace.

'It would have been impossible, madame, for Comte Alfred to be resentful when his image and inventions were purloined by his sister's family. He was the very embodiment of nobility. He beguiled both genders yet deserted all his admirers except one, to whom he remained devoted until beyond my grave.'

I check myself.

'I beg you to excuse me, madame. You must think I am mad.'

The woman forgets her French affectation and clutches my arm.

'You are very far from mad, Marguerite. I have been a beggar, a courtesan, a criminal and an aristocrat. I have lived in many lands and encountered people of every class, race and religion. How dull my life would have been without its blemishes. Is it not wonderful that we are all created different from one another and all fall short of perfection?'

'That is true but if you have come here to justify your misdeeds or to receive my pardon, you have come too late, Madame Craufurd.'

--

Returning home with renewed confidence was the anti-climax I should have anticipated. The servants dutifully lined the railings of St James's Square in the rain, as they did in the snow at Henrietta Street. There were more of them but their welcome was as exuberant. They were devoted to Charles and on occasions such as this he was devoted to them. And as in Dublin, he remembered not only their names but their wretched spouses, children, relatives, dogs, cats and canaries.

'Daniel, do tell me, how is dear Nadezhda. And have little Felix and Harry recovered from the measles? The Countess and I were terribly concerned while we were away, you know.'

I did not recognise Daniel and had no idea that he had a Russian wife let alone two sons suffering common childhood diseases. I was a vehement believer in social equality and the duty of an employer to treat servants with humanity, though I admit that in practice such fine theories tended to encounter unavoidable obstacles.

Our butler – whose name might have been Brian – had neatly arranged a month's correspondence on my Sheraton bonheur du jour. Longman forwarded copies of both the favourable critiques of *Sketches and Fragments* and *The Magic Lantern*, without saying what happened to the unfavourable. The Prime Minister requested me to remind Lord Blessington to cast his vote at the Lords. An up-and-coming painter sought my advice; 'personal difficulties' were impeding his inspiration. If he wanted money, why didn't he say so? The patron of a charity, a duke with a string of letters extending his name, humbly begged leave to present his compliments. If he wanted money, why didn't he say so? The relative with whom Mary Anne had lodged could not afford to take her back. If she wanted money, why didn't she say so? I responded to every communication, apologised for my tardiness and sent commendations, commiserations, congratulations and contributions. There were no invitations to accept or reject.

In a long letter from the Scottish borders, Ellen at last acknowledged the broadening cracks on the thin shell of her marriage. I had never understood what she saw in the dour laird. She should have listened to my advice and not married a man simply because he was rich, the heir to a title and not Irish.

Having recovered from his most recent attack of hypochondria, John Hume Purves had suffered another attack of heavy commitments in London and Ellen would be coming with him. Again she asked me to look after her children while she took lunch at Westminster. This time she disclosed that her host was none other than Charles Manners-Sutton, speaker of the House of Commons and son of the Archbishop of Canterbury. I replied inviting Ellen and her family to stay with us at St. James's Square. I always loved having children in the house, for short periods. Ellen now had three daughters; Louisa aged eleven, Marguerite four and Mary Anne two. Her surviving son, John, had just turned six.

I was surprised by the familiar return address on the back of a small envelope. Father had never responded to my letters before. Was he at last going to thank me for all the conscience-driven daughterly devotion I had dutifully despatched for a decade and more?

The letter was signed Mrs Edmond Power. This homely Irish lady advised me:

'I have kept your filthy drunken father long enough. He's been sick on my nice clean floor just once too often. You're supposed to be a countess, so you can afford to look after him from now on. This is where you will find him and good luck to you, your ladyship.'

Had the former Mrs Hymes really believed that Father would make an ideal husband? After I stopped laughing, I sent more of Charles's money to the given address and continued to do so for the rest of Edmond Power's purposeless life.

The next request was less amusing . It was a plaintive cry from my brother Robert whose relationship with the excellent Mr Norman was deteriorating rapidly. Tensions were rising. His previous employer had been a hard taskmaster who had at least attended to his own affairs, whereas Charles was properly brought up to appreciate the undeniable merit of detached delegation. Robert was finding it harder and harder to fulfil his urban responsibilities and, not without reason, feared that he would be held responsible for the declining income from the Dublin properties.

'May I beg you, Margaret, ask Lord Blessington to order Mr Norman to transfer me to Mountjoy Forest? I have always worked in the country and I am sure that I can improve the yield from his lordship's lands.'

I did wish that my family would stop calling me Margaret.

I thought of suggesting to Robert that he should follow the example of the excellent Mr Norman and assert his self-interest. It was not in my self-interest and I did not waste my ink. My poor brother's innate sense of decency had convicted him to permanent privation.

I was not only concerned for Robert. I was concerned for Charles who continued to pursue prodigality with unconscionable enthusiasm. And I was concerned for myself. I had not spent years clambering out of the abyss in order to see my future scattered to the Irish winds by an unscrupulous agent, an inept brother and an uxorious husband. As Lord Byron once told me in a less poetic moment *money is wisdom, knowledge and power all combined*.

I spoke to Charles and Charles spoke to Nathan Mayer Rothschild. Mr Rothschild inspected the deeds of the Blessington properties and without hesitation offered almost but not quite unlimited credit, at a steep but not extortionate rate of interest. Mr Rothschild always anticipated dealing with his clients on a recurring basis.

'You see, my dear Marguerite, the bankers are perfectly satisfied that the estate income comfortably covers their charges,' Charles explained.

'Can you be certain that it will continue to do so?'

'Norman reported that some of the tenants are a little in arrears but they'll catch up. They always do. The Irish are sober, law-abiding, industrious folk, you know.'

I did not know. 'Would it not be wise for you to visit Ireland and inspect the situation for yourself, Charles?'

'That is a good idea, my dear Marguerite. We must go over there at Christmas, you see. It has been a while since I saw the children. I must take them some presents. It is a tradition, you know. And while we are there I shall get Norman to introduce me to the tenants who are experiencing difficulties so that I can offer them the necessary assistance. It's the seasonable thing to do, you see.'

Somehow I did not think that it was in Mr Rothschild's blood to finance Christmas presents.

There was also correspondence for Charles to deal with. Like mine, the majority was trivial and soon disposed of. But there were certain letters over which he uncharacteristically pondered long and hard. Most he destroyed but when he chose to reply discarded draft after draft, exerting every sinew to be assertive without causing offense. Only I could have been the subject of this distressing labour.

Charles had never enjoyed robust health and after our invigorating continental holiday he began to grow increasingly lethargic. He rode for exercise less frequently. His passion for the theatre waned. He seldom attended the House of Lords and lost some of his gregarious spirit. Sometimes he would leave me to entertain alone while he spent the night at one of his clubs. His private physician diagnosed excellent health and prescribed luxurious medicines. But neither these nor anything I could do seemed to relieve his depression.

In desperation, I proposed another short holiday: just the two of us, no parasitical guests. In November 1821 we rented a house overlooking the sea on the Isle of Wight. The weather was as bleak as at our honeymoon at Mountjoy Forest making it impossible to ride or walk on the downs and talk quietly about our future as I had planned. We stayed indoors, where the incidental music of lightning flashes, thunderclaps and booms of dislodged boulders crashing into the breakers from the nearby cliffs created an ambience conducive to confession. I was first to confess.

'Charles, I shall be eternally grateful to you for disregarding all that Thomas Jenkins told you about my sordid past but there was one thing he deliberately omitted. Forgive me for not telling you before but you should be aware that Maurice Farmer's brutality left me sterile. I can never give you a child.'

Given Charles's usual reaction to bad news I presumed that he would brush aside my emotive revelation. He had four children, alive, well and, at least in my opinion, born in wedlock. Charles never criticised but he was critical. He never displayed anger but he was angry.

A long silence – another credit to Sarah Siddons and Edmund Keane. It was Charles's turn to confess. He confessed his love for me and I permitted myself to believe him but not to be deluded. Had he loved Mary Campbell Browne? Or had she too been a beautiful ornament in poor taste like all the other purchased treasures in his houses?

'My dearest Marguerite, you are my one and only true love. If we are not to procreate it is by the will of God, you know.'

Another theatrical interlude. Charles had more to confess.

'But there are also things I should have told to you, you see. My mother died soon after I was born. I have mentioned that before, you know. My father sent me to a boys' boarding school and then on to Eton. Well, you know, there are no girls at Eton. In fact, the only girls I ever met were my sisters and none of them were very pretty, you see. Some of the boys at Eton seemed far prettier. When I left I had to take my father's place in the militia, you know. He was killed. I've told you that too. It was all quite ridiculous, you see, I was only about seventeen. It would have been unbearable if it hadn't been for one or two of the young officers – Campbell Browne, for instance. It was much the same story up at Oxford, no contact with girls, you know, and like at Eton some of the students were extraordinarily handsome. Their companionship was most gratifying, you see. Then, while I was looking after Mary down at Worthing I tended to lose interest in such diversions. But it is only fair to explain, you see, that from time to time, I still experience leanings towards my own gender.'

Charles's confused clarification of his bisexuality came as no surprise. His effeminate traits were obvious enough. His love of posing in gorgeous costumes was not entirely for the theatre.

How should I react? Make a joke – 'An aristocrat without sexual deviation is like a soft-boiled egg without salt?' Be practical – 'Do not concern yourself, Charles, it is a common ailment that your physician can help you overcome.' Be angry – 'How can you say you love me, when your preference is for your own sex?' Or should I simply look demure and incredulous? None of these seemed in any way appropriate, so I again apologised for my deceit and promised my husband that his diversions would never affect my love for him. His unreserved appreciation of my understanding and support was one of his better theatrical performances.

I found Charles's confession most reassuring. If he was distracted by a man then he would not abandon me for another woman, I almost convinced myself.

'No human being is exempt from faults nor destitute of virtues. The wicked, who are many, will quickly detect the first and the good, who are but few, will alone discern the second. Hence men's faults will always be more known than their virtues.'

The weather imprisoned us on our island retreat for one more day. Reluctant inactivity permitted further impaired thought. If Charles were to fall in love with a man, then he would buy him just as he bought me as a gift to the gossips and gutter press. Could I protest, prepare or protect myself for that event, or did I have to accept it as an unrelenting ingredient of the noble lifestyle I never wished to forsake?

Charles found another confession to distract my meditation. Grave, if more encouraging matters were weighing on his conscience.

'I fear, my dear Marguerite, that my relationship with my family is not all that it should be, you know. From their point of view it was quite inconsiderate of my father to leave everything to me, you see. His second wife, Margaret Wallis, the dowager Lady Mountjoy – you met her over at the House, you know – has never got over it. Sometimes I feel her disapproval is not entirely unfounded but I wish her well, you see. I ensure that she has everything she needs, yet it never seems to be enough. And then there are my sisters, you see. Originally, we were six siblings, seven counting the dowager's poor little daughter. She died, you know.'

'It seems that the Angel of Death has an inordinate propensity to visit your family,' I said, since sympathy did not seem at all pertinent.

'Yes, I fear that does appear to be the case. My older brother, Luke, passed away when I was about five. He was nine at the time, you know. My father was so distraught that I think he lost part of his sanity and never recovered it, you know. Yes, I'm sure he did. I suppose it's a sort of macabre blessing that only Harriet and Louisa are still with us.'

'I don't think you have mentioned your sister Louisa, Charles.'

'Haven't I? Well actually I don't see her very often. Louisa is married to the Bishop of Ossery, you know. Charming man, extremely pious. I like him immensely but I don't think he approves of my attitude to Christianity. He imagines my lifestyle abuses certain of its tenets. Apparently Jesus thought poverty a virtue, you see. And then there is Harriet. She is unmarried, you know. I really cannot understand why. I've told her many times that nothing would make me happier than to provide her with an adequate dowry. She's perfectly capable and attractive, you see.'

I could not imagine what Harriet Gardiner might have been perfectly capable of, but she certainly was neither attractive in appearance nor by nature. I greatly doubted that her brother would be called upon to provide her with a dowry, adequate or otherwise.

'You said that Harriet and Lady Mountjoy enjoyed bringing up your children in Ireland. Are they not content?'

'Well, you see my dear Marguerite, I thought they were. But now they seem to want you to take responsibility for the children but, you see, they are so very young. The upheaval might upset them terribly. I have no wish to overburden my family but I see nothing wrong with the present arrangements, you know.'

I did know. Even at our one meeting, Lady Mountjoy and her stepdaughter had made it abundantly clear that they subscribed to all the scurrilous rumours that found their way to County Tyrone. Telling Charles that they wanted me to look after his children was nothing but a contemptuous taunt. They would never let them anywhere near me. I might not have been blessed with my in-laws' unnatural maternal instincts but I could have given their charges a happier childhood, and a much more thorough classical education.

Charles then came to his last and most devastating confession. Lulled into false security my unflinching acceptance of his sexual aberrations he disclosed his darkest secret, to remain forever unspoken until he announced it to the world. Luke Wellington Gardiner, third Lord Mountjoy, sole legitimate male heir to the Blessington fortune was born with a fatal affliction. He would never reach maturity.

Since our legitimate wedlock could not provide a legitimate heir, like Scheherazade, I was damned to never give my lord cause to tire of me, not for *A Thousand and One Nights* but forever and a night. I excelled at making up stories.

The ominous confessions of those autumnal days on the Isle of Wight had a remarkably therapeutic effect on Charles's health and spirits. He resumed his interest in the theatre, the arts, philanthropy, politics and other fruitless extravagances, while I pursued my quest for social acceptance. My messengers trudged the slimy cobbles of London's most elegant thoroughfares bearing formal requests for the pleasure of the company of those worthy of the house of Blessington. As previously, they returned with polite acceptances from gentlemen of note and polite notes from their ladies, who did not visit the unvisited.

'We must learn to bear with society, or to live without it. The latter appears to be the least difficult to pursue.'

One invitation was nevertheless accepted by an unquestionably noteworthy couple. Antoine, Duc de Guiche and the Duchesse Ida were paragons of the French nobility and thus possessed infinitely more refined manners than their English equivalents. The young duchesse requested permission to introduce her brother and I acquiesced with some foreboding. I could not close my door to the exuberant prodigy of whose behaviour even his own father apparently disapproved.

The Duc de Guiche, in London on a diplomatic mission at the behest of King Louis XVIII, was the epitome of a French aristocrat, handsome, upright and unpalatably arrogant. The vivacious Duchesse Ida was as I pictured her grandmother in her youth – delicate, delightful, dangerous and devious. Both spoke perfect English.

The young man who arrived with them spoke even more perfect English. Ida's brother had been a frequent visitor to England and since early childhood had been required to address his learned grandfather in his native language. Unlike the Duc and Duchesse he had cultivated an amusing French accent which he would summon at will to emphasise his superiority. Thoughtfully, our uninvited visitor relieved the butler from his losing conflict with French pronunciation and announced himself - Gillion Gaspard Gabriel Alfred de Grimaud, Comte D'Orsay et du Saint Empire. On observing Charles's bewilderment, the youth graciously granted us leave to call him Alfred.

Some years later, my friend Walter Savage Landor expressed the situation with singular precision:

'What poor animals other men seem in the presence of the Duc de Guiche and D'Orsay.'

'No, Mr Sadleir, the Comte D'Orsay did not drop his aitches or stress adjectives after nouns like a comic stage Frenchman. Nor did he cover his face with paint and powder as suggested by Doris Leslie in her little potboiler, *Notorious Lady: The Life and Times of the Countess of Blessington*. Where on earth did she get that idea? Alfred's natural complexion was the perfect complement to his masculinity, he told us.'

Alfred, Comte D'Orsay was a mobile museum of affectation, a living work of art that outstripped Charles's self-delusions at their most eccentric. The youth's auburn hair and beard were shaped by a master of accentuation of the noble feature, while his coat was meticulously cut to emphasise his God-given physique and self-perfected deportment. The most attractive of all Alfred's imperfections were the conspicuous gaps between his brilliant teeth. I exhausted my stock of superlatives in praise of the Comte's preposterous pride in his appearance.

With farcical panache, Comte D'Orsay presented me with a small gift. He bowed as low as his sartorially shrunk breeches would permit and placed a tiny vial in my hand. He said it contained an invention of his own inspired by the elixir of love. I never wore perfumes, they all smelled like urine on me. I suspected the aroma emanating from Alfred's person was the same invention. It smelled like urine on him. I exuded my sincerest gratitude and next day gave the vial to my maid and told her not to wear its content in the house.

'But if you are not completely captivated, Madame La Comtesse, I shall not sleep again until I have created a fragrance to your exquisite taste.'

Alfred must have suffered chronic insomnia since it was ten years before he finally created an essence of which I approved. He called it *Etiquette Bleue*. I wore it once, I think.

The dinner party was among the most memorable we held at St James's Square. Alfred was a natural entertainer. The table resounded with laughter at my determination to crush the over-confidence of the twenty-year-old peacock. Sarcasm is the highest form of wit. Like a cryptic crossword clue, it says what it means without meaning what it says.

'May I take it, Alfred, that your civilian attire is a deliberate affront to the Earl of Blessington's house? Or are you unaware that in England a serving officer is expected to wear his dress uniform at dinner?'

'Were I in the uniform of the Garde Royale, madame, my hypocrisy would be an affront to the noble Earl's house. My esteemed brother-in-law is dressed to signify his sworn allegiance to the Bourbon king. But I shall never wear the uniform of France until its fat immoral monarch is overthrown and the perfectly proportioned Napoleonic constitution restored.'

'And are you here in London to play an active role in its restoration?'

'That is my intention, your ladyship.'

'Then we will doubtless be honoured by your presence for many years, Alfred.'

'I do not think so, madame. I intend to remain in exile only until a government comes to power which respects the will of the people of France and my conscience permits me to accept high office.'

Comte Alfred D'Orsay had no conscience. He was also lying. As his mother had hinted, he had applied to be relieved of his commission because he was the most despised officer in his regiment. His fellow officers mercilessly derided his effeminate affectations and were unsportingly envious of his athletic achievements. Most justly of all he was condemned for his overt disloyalty to the monarchy. Such unrelenting adversity would have destroyed a lesser man but to Alfred, Comte D'Orsay a fleck of dust on his cravat was an infinitely more distressing humiliation.

'Undoubtedly you are finding England to your liking, Alfred. Our beloved King George IV could never be described as a fat immoral monarch. And as you might possibly have heard, not long ago your perfectly proportioned Emperor Napoleon was vanquished at Waterloo by the Duke of Wellington. It is now widely predicted that the Duke will soon be Prime Minister. If the house of Bourbon should still hold power in France, will your conscience then permit you to accept high office in a government which respects the will of the people of Britain? '

Everyone at the table, especially the Duc de Guiche, laughed at my innocent jibes. Alfred simply smiled his beatific smile and responded seriously.

'Indeed, Lady Blessington, when the noble Duke comes to power his most certain means of achieving enduring peace between our two great nations shall be to call upon my talents. The Napoleonic army was denied victory at Waterloo but the spirit of Bonaparte is indestructible and shall rise again.'

I had to concede that Alfred's ridiculous audacity was more amusing than my acerbic wit. Charles appreciated neither.

'The Duke of Wellington is a great friend of mine, you know,' he said. 'If you wish, Comte Alfred, I shall effect an introduction. I am sure Arthur will be most interested to meet you, you see.'

'Thank you most sincerely, Lord Blessington, but I have been acquainted with the Duke of Wellington for a great many years. I first met him at the Royal Staghounds in the Bois de Boulogne when I was thirteen. He commended my superb horsemanship, as I recall.'

'That would have been about 1814. It was the year before Waterloo, you know. What on earth would Arthur have been doing in France then?'

'It was the occasion when Marshal Ney so diplomatically invited the Duke of Wellington to France on a peace-keeping mission. As the gracious Lady Blessington has so knowledgeably pointed out, his mission failed. The Duke, however, respected my father's friend and colleague until the day he was executed for treason by the cruel and ignorant Louis XVIII.'

'Treason is a serious crime Alfred. It's not at all patriotic, you know.'

'Lord Blessington, Marshal Ney was the greatest French patriot since Joan of Arc. The Bourbon monarch would not recognise a patriot if he laid down his life for France at his royal feet. I have informed the king that I shall not easily forgive him.'

Charles was so enthralled by the beauty of Alfred's political stance that I had to remind him several times that there were other guests at the table. Eventually the astute Duchesse Ida intervened.

'I observe, Lord Blessington, that you are a connoisseur of the finer manifestations of femininity.'

Charles accepted the compliment presuming that she was referring to me and continued to allow Alfred to dominate his attention. By the end of the evening he had become positively enchanted by Ida's overdressed brother. For some inexplicable reason, I was as disappointed as my husband when Alfred informed us that in a fortnight he would have to return to France to conclude his discharge from the Garde Royale and accept his grandmother's contribution to his indefinite future.

Every morning for the next two weeks Alfred called at St James's Square to receive our approval of the latest delivery from his tailor and to invite us to ride with him in Hyde Park. I could not imagine why? He was just twenty. I was thirty-two and Charles approaching forty. Was he in love with me, as were many younger men, or with Charles, as were few? Alfred was in no need of entrées. His impeccable credentials and self-assured panache procured him a surfeit of invitations. Among the first he accepted was to Holland House. Lady Holland disapproved of her narcissistic young visitor – I don't think she approved of anybody – but, legend has it, that for the pleasure of her other guests she put Alfred's charms to a frivolous and, dare I say, highly uncharacteristic test. At dinner, she sat him by her side and proceeded to deliberately drop a succession of objects: cutlery, glasses, crockery, serviettes and so on. One by one the gallant Comte retrieved and replaced them. Alfred is supposed to have told me: *'Eventually I turned to the footman and said, "Please put my couvert on the floor so that I may finish my dinner there. It will be much more convenient to milady".'*

'Dr Madden, Mr Molloy, Mr Sadleir, you like all Alfred's equally incompetent biographers repeat this improbable anecdote in your works. Perhaps one of you can tell me milady's response?'

'The Comte D'Orsay described the event to me after your death, Lady Blessington, but I cannot remember him telling me what Lady Holland said.'

'Well, Dr Madden, do you seriously think that I believed the formidable Lady Holland was so easily crushed? She probably ordered her footman to do as Alfred said and to put his dinner in her lapdog's bowl.'

'Are you saying that the story is untrue, your ladyship, I read numerous accounts of Comte D'Orsay boasting of his triumph?'

'Surely, Mr Molloy, even you could not have been so gullible that you believed *all* the childish escapades of which the Comte boasted.'

Alfred, in fact, possessed a remarkable intellect for a man who expended so much of his energy on appearing blasé that it was surprising that sufficient remained to open a book. With nonchalant zeal and impeccable discretion, he declared that his knowledge of literature was inadequate to comment on my amateurish poetry and prose. Instead he suggested that I might be interested in the opinion of a young friend, who he claimed was an outstanding author.

'No, he has not published anything yet, but one day, your ladyship, this man will change the world.'

The following afternoon my butler – whose name was possibly Paul – threw open the double doors to my private salon and announced 'Comte Alfred D'Orsay and Mr Benjamin D'Israeli.' I wondered if Charles had started the pantomime season earlier than usual. Alfred had extolled his friend's wit but I had scarcely expected to burst into uncontrollable laughter at first sight. The incongruous couple entered arm-in-arm. Alfred, as usual, posing to invite my admiration for his *costume du jour* while his companion wore green pantaloons, a waistcoat covered in a mesh of golden embroidery and a stove-pipe hat the top of which barely reached Alfred's shoulder. With a sweeping gesture the smaller man removed this absurd headdress and bowed so low that his long black ringlets, doubtless the envy of many young women, touched the floor.

Alfred's friend was either too young to shave or, indeed, was the principal boy from one of Charles's pantomimes. Was London becoming entirely inhabited by men of questionable sexual leanings? This one could have been no more than seventeen.

'And what do you plan to do when you leave school, Mr D'Israeli?'

My sarcasm cut the young man's flesh no deeper than Alfred's. He smiled at me with the most brilliant eyes I had ever seen or would ever see.

'My dear Lady Blessington, I am my own school and my standards are higher than any in England. In response to your gracious concern for my future, I intend to become prime minister, reform the British Empire and make this nation the most prosperous the world will ever know.'

Again I laughed aloud but it was clear that he meant what he said. His every word blended sagacity and charisma with an indiscernible hint of irony. Alfred was almost self-effacing by comparison.

'I was unaware that you are a politician, Mr D'Israeli. Alfred mentioned only that you are a writer.'

'I am both, your ladyship. My fictional work is a mere vehicle to my political philosophy. I write because literature is in my blood. You, Lady Blessington, enjoy the deserved reputation of being the best-read lady in the land. You will therefore be familiar with my father's inspiration.'

Benjamin D'Israeli, like all good politicians, possessed the impeccable command of language which ensured that he would never fail to make himself obscure. He elevated flattery to a fine art. I had not until then been aware that my wider reputation included my academic attainments, nor had it occurred to me that this absurd dandy was the son of my most revered mentor. I had studied the works of Isaac D'Israeli in depth and considered him the purest of scholars.

I rapidly revised my opinion of this extraordinary young man, destined to be my lifelong friend, and also to become prime minister.

At the beginning of December Alfred returned to France. He neither succeeded in securing a discharge from the Garde Royale or charming his aged grandmother into funding a further sojourn in England. The army claimed to be in need of officers and Madame Craufurd claimed to be in need of money. Neither was true. The Garde Royale had far more officers than it required but strategically ordered the arrogant Comte to fulfil his patriotic duty and be tortured for another year. Madame Craufurd had more money than she required but like many elderly people had unwittingly descended into parsimony. She did however give Alfred a huge elaborately-crafted silver vanity case for the other retained officers to ridicule, as well as advice on how to marry into a rich aristocratic family.

The Duc de Guiche was also recalled to France that autumn. The Duchesse Ida came to St James's Square to bid me farewell and promise that Charles and I would always be welcome at the de Guiche residence in Paris. No, we were never invited.

I cannot deny that Charles had every right to expect me to accompany him to Dublin and on to Mountjoy Forest to celebrate Christmas. Returning to Ireland was unthinkable. Still I suffered nightmares glutted with spectres of the unjust dead: my brothers Edmond and Michael, my sister Anne, Mother, Miss Dwyer, Maurice Farmer, Mr Hunt, Joe Lonergan, my grandfather Edmond and Father Nicholas Sheehy. Embittered antagonists thrust spikes into my head. Silver and acid tongued phantom lawyers spat out the names Bagwell, Donoughmore, Watson, MacCarthy and Power. In dreams the good and the bad are indistinguishable.

'Some memories are powerfully retentive of injury, but totally oblivious of benefits.'

I remembered the pretentious ladies of Dublin society and pictured them reviving old scandals and repackaging them for delivery to London. I dreaded confronting the inebriated wreck of Edmond Power marooned on the sawdust floor of a squalid alehouse, or finding Robert a slave to the detested job I procured for him. Nor did I wish to invade my husband's stepmother and sister's palatial country alms-house, or give his children cause to resent me by endearing myself to them and then vanishing like their mother. The will of the first Viscount Mountjoy might have been a noble travesty, but it was not of my making and, hard as I barely tried, I felt neither guilt nor sympathy for my husband's family.

Charles still never openly expressed concern about his financial affairs but I would have felt much happier for him in the knowledge that they were being properly administered. Using the figures reluctantly smuggled to me by my brother I experienced little difficulty in calculating that inefficiency and dishonesty were rife in Dublin. I should have overcome my cowardice, gone to

Ireland with my husband and asserted my experience and acumen, but all I did was compose an aide memoire for his meeting with the excellent Mr Norman:

'My dear Charles, while I applaud your most enlightened policy of never enforcing rent collection with violence or by recourse to the law, a good tenant invariably respects a businesslike attitude. Suggest to Mr Norman that a firmer though always fair approach will painlessly eliminate your rent arrears.

On the other hand, bad tenants invariably presume waiver of rent, once granted, to be a permanent right. Instruct Mr Norman to extend additional credit only in the most deserving cases.

Insist that Mr Norman obtains competitive quotations for major expenditure and presents them to you for authorisation in future. I know you find such decisions distasteful but if you will permit me I shall put my experience at your disposal and help you to choose the most economical.'

I had many more recommendations to offer but thought it would be close to a miracle if Charles remembered to convey one of these three. Nonetheless, I added one more over-optimistic reminder:

'Your children are at an age when they should be sent to the best preparatory schools in Dublin. Your house in Henrietta Street would make an ideal home for your family. And if Mr Norman were to take advantage of Robert Power's land management skills and move him to Mountjoy Forest the vacated House at Rash would be most convenient for his family.'

Charles agreed without reservation. I thus expediently made copies of my reminders and placed one in the pocket of each of the eight necessary overcoats he required for his three-week visit.

Before leaving, Charles regaled me with his latest delusion. To my relief it involved nothing more than an epic novel. Novel writing absorbs time not money. Everything that Charles did absorbed money.

I managed to stay awake through the hackneyed clichés of his fifty-page synopsis of *Reginald de Vavaseur: A Tale of the Fourteenth Century* for long enough to appreciate its lack of literary merit. The inspiration for this magnum opus, he said, was not to be found in the prosaic streets of London or indeed anywhere in England. An author of the calibre of the Earl of Blessington needed to personally inhale the poetry of times past at the precise locations of his medieval hero's fictitious adventures. He intended to make a quixotic tour of the ancient domains of France and Italy, drink in their mysteries, sojourn in their palaces and commune with the spirits of their learned past and present. However long the journey and however arduous the work, the name of Charles Gardiner, Earl of Blessington would dwell forever among the giants of literature. Of course it would.

'Charles, this is the most wonderful idea. You are so clever and imaginative. You were born to be a writer. I'm so proud of you. I shall look forward to serving as your amanuensis and as soon as you are back from Ireland, I shall begin helping you to plan your research.'

I did not need to wait for Charles to return from Ireland. By pure coincidence *Reginald de Vavaseur's* ancient travels passed only through towns and cities I wished to visit and where there were distinguished people I hoped to meet. Naples, for example, was not only awash with history but European aristocrats, diplomats, writers and artists. Lord Byron lived at Genoa. In Paris, I would renew my acquaintance with La Baronesse Eleanore and at last meet the legendary Madame Craufurd, who would effect my introduction to the French court, the king, queen and the royal family. Of course she would.

Acquiring one of the châteaux and grand apartments we viewed at our prior visit to Paris was crucial to Charles's research. The gallant *Reginald's* last act of chivalry would be to liberate me from London society. I drafted the first two chapters, hoping against hope that the itinerant hero would not be forgotten when his creator returned from his own courageous travels.

Meanwhile a few livelier adventurers of both genders were brave enough to cross the forbidden threshold of 10 St James' Square. Letitia Landon and William Jerdan came to entertain me with judicious literary critiques. Both were so heavily committed to delicately dismembering and defiling the most meritorious recent publications that I missed the chance to tell them about *de Vavaseur.*

Another regular caller in Charles's absence was Catherine Lee, who delighted me with equally cynical news of society – never gossip – and genteel diatribes in appreciation of its most accomplished intriguers. Catherine's open cohabitation with de Blaquiere bred endless salacious rumours, few of which were without foundation. The estranged wife of the royal chaplain was not only celebrated for her amorous exploits and disastrous marriage, but for being the granddaughter of the almost famous Admiral Edward Hughes who left his fortune equally between her and her younger brother, Edward Ball Hughes. Edward had prudently invested his share at the roulette wheel on which he invariably won vast sums and earned the sobriquet 'Golden Ball'. One night at the theatre, the wild young millionaire is said to have snatched a sixteen-year-old dancer from the stage in mid performance and married her the following day. Surprisingly the marriage did not last and the fortuitous Golden Ball was thereafter frequently to be seen in the company of the Comte D'Orsay.

I told Catherine about my, that is Charles's plan to tour France and Italy. She was thrilled for me and asked if I would be kind enough to meet her in Paris and provide my opinion of several châteaux that she was considering purchasing. Since marrying a man of property I had become something of an authority on this form of investment and obliged my friend by making the necessary amendments to *de Vavaseur's* fourteenth-century travels.

Charles accomplished more than I had dared to hope in Ireland. He had found my notes and conveyed my recommendations to the excellent Mr Norman who readily complied with characteristic reluctance. He was particularly happy with the permission to employ a businesslike bully to terrify the tenants into submission and thereby enhance the estate's income, but of course not his own. He was similarly happy with the chance to be rid of his employer's brother-in-law and his transparently clandestine spying.

The excellent agent remained happy until he discovered himself under the all-seeing eye of the much-wronged Lady Mountjoy and her stepdaughter. Both were naturally loath to move to Dublin, which had nothing to offer other than Ireland's finest schools for Charles's children, the luxuries of Henrietta Street and a sympathetic audience for their opinions of the Earl of Blessington's iniquitous wife.

Robert wrote to thank me for his release from his city office and my failed attempt to procure an increase in his salary. He and his family were pleased to be settled back in the country. In fact, he was so pleased that he omitted to mention that managing an estate as big as Mountjoy Forest was beyond his ability or that the House was now occupied by the family of the excellent Mr Norman, who was finding it expedient to make increasingly frequent supervisory visits. Robert however was nicely settled in a cottage somewhere in the Forest just a little smaller than the house he had left on the outskirts of Dublin.

There was nothing more I could do for my brother; he would insist on staying in Ireland.

In January 1822, Benjamin Wyatt called at St James's Square with revised plans for a magnificent extension to the Cottage. Had I not been a countess I would have screamed with frustration. Charles would now forget the fourteenth century, cancel my, that is his continental tour and indulge his new gargantuan delusion. It would not only cost tens of thousands of pounds but serve no practical purpose whatsoever. His family would never leave Dublin and under no circumstances was I prepared to live in a grotesque pleasure palace in an uncivilised Irish wasteland. Astonishingly, Charles agreed with me – well almost.

'My dear Marguerite, you are quite right, as always. Wyatt is a fine architect, you know, but he doesn't listen to me. You see, he's a little old-fashioned. I need a younger man with modern ideas.'

To Charles modern ideas meant those that reflected his old-fashioned eccentricity. Soon some fortunate young architect would be given the opportunity to make his name and fortune by prostituting his creativity to Charles's bizarre whims.

Benjamin Wyatt was not pleased. Despite his reputation and prestigious clientele, like many great artists, money was not his forte and he was continually in debt. This was particularly surprising since he was credited with having conceived the imaginative financial tenet which stands his profession in good stead to the present day. The Earl of Blessington might well have been the first architectural client to be charged a rejection fee based on the estimated cost of the project. Estimating was not Wyatt's forte either, though calculating twelve per cent of an erroneous sum apparently presented little difficulty. Charles paid without question. Others did likewise, but their gullibility failed to save the great architect from the court of bankruptcy and a spell in the debtors' prison. Presumably the prison governors declined to pay a rejection fee for his plans for enhancing their premises.

The weather remained cold and bleak for the rest of the winter and Charles again became depressed, and as I feared, abandoned writing his novel. Neither his achievements in Ireland or anything I did or said brought him peace of mind. Normally he never gambled or drank heavily. Now he wasted his evenings at White's or Brook's, returning late and not rising until the afternoon. He again stopped attending the House of Lords or uncharitable board meetings of philanthropic societies. At Drury Lane his box stood empty and the show went on without his interference.

Worst of all, I was unable to satisfy my husband's fluctuating sexual impulses. In desperation, I hinted that I would raise no objection if he employed prostitutes of either or both genders. He ignored my remedial advice. According to the *Arabian Nights* Princess Scheherazade coped admirably with her prince's unpredictable mood swings by telling him fairy stories. If only it had been that simple for me!

I was guilty. I was the cause of Charles's problems. I had made him a laughing stock. Whereas he had always accepted the onslaughts of the satirical press as personal tributes, now that society so openly rejected me he shrank from confrontation. As our invitations were less and less accepted, Charles absented himself more and more often. All my fervent aspirations froze in the over-furnished rooms of St James's Square.

Then suddenly in March the ice melted. It was spring and Charles burst from his depression like an overgrown flower from a weeping bud.

'We are to have a visitor, my dear Marguerite: someone we have not seen for a while, you know.'

'Charles, I am really too heavily committed to receive anyone today.'

I was with Mary Ann wasting my time writing to my brother and father in Ireland; as always dispensing charity and easing neither my conscience nor their plight.

Charles handed me a pale pink visiting card. A sweet fragrance rubbed onto my fingers and made them smell of urine. Across three lines were printed all the names and titles of Le Comte D'Orsay. Delight overwhelmed my desperate effort to appear indignant.

'Mary Ann, instruct the butler – whatever his name is – to serve afternoon tea in the grand salon. And request my new Swiss maid (who really was called Antoinette) to come to my boudoir immediately. I must change out of these hideous clothes. And for goodness sake get her to find something presentable for you to wear yourself.'

Charles sent for his valet – who I think was called Barry – and requested a suitably flamboyant outfit.

Compared to Alfred, the three of us all looked positively shabby in our finery. He was in London to be measured by his tailor and to fulfil certain social obligations, the details of which he chose not to reveal. He would be able to stay only until his two-dozen bespoke coats, jackets and breeches were completed to his satisfaction. Comte D'Orsay would therefore be with us for some time.

'There is not a craftsman in all Paris to be compared to the inestimable Mr Schwartz, Lord Blessington. Allow me to commend him when you next replenish your wardrobe.'

Mr Schwartz was not the most skilled tailor in London but could afford to be the most expensive. Every morning Alfred called at St James's Square to model his latest delivery and lecture us on the minutiae of fashion. I had not previously appreciated that there were so many shades of every colour of the spectrum or so many divergent designs of collar, cuff, pocket, lapel, belt or button.

This daily discourse on dandyism revitalised both Charles's spirits and his passion for *Reginald de Vavaseur*. While he acted out scenes from his forthcoming novel in his private theatre, Alfred, an authority on medieval European history, interpreted the rites and rituals of the fourteenth century. Employing his expert intuition, discretion and affectation he made invaluable amendments to my itinerary – in the interests of literature – from which he assured me that I would derive great intellectual benefit.

'I trust that my simple annotations will assist your scholarly research for the excellent *de Vavaseur*, Lord Blessington.'

'Mr dear Alfred, you make novel writing sound so straightforward, you see, but I do fear that I might encounter some difficulties with the detail. Your observations are remarkably interesting, you know. Perhaps you will consider travelling with us for part of the journey?'

'I thank you with all my heart, Lord Blessington but I am still an officer of the Garde Royale and heavily committed. My request for decommission has alas been declined and I cannot anticipate receiving my freedom for many months.'

'My dear Alfred, you should have told me before. I am a Lieutenant Colonel of the militia, you see. The military hierarchy of our two great nations traditionally cooperate on small matters of this kind, you know.'

Alfred and I interpreted this to mean that Charles intended to bribe another general to liaise with his French counterpart.

'In that case I shall look forward with great pleasure to joining you en route, *mes chère amis*.'

We were both thrilled by the prospect of travelling with Alfred, for the same reasons. I knew that Charles's military strategy could not be implemented quickly but I was determined not to delay our departure for a day longer. I had had more than my fill of England and English bores, parasites, petty politics, intrigues and scandal.

Charles's loyal servants covered the furniture with dustsheets and equipped us for a long and luxurious continental adventure. Then he dismissed those we did not intend to take with us or leave to maintain the empty house. On 25th August 1822, I made my first entry in a new journal:

'What changes, what dangers may come before I again sleep beneath its roof?'

My question was well put. The changes and dangers that came in the eight years before I again slept beneath the roof of 10 St James's Square were indeed unpredictable.

13

An imperious individual flops down on the settee next to me and sneers rather than looks at my portrait. His red and white striped blazer and gangrenous white trousers hang loose on his emaciated body and his frayed pink shirt is several sizes too large. The man is in his late thirties, once handsome but prematurely aged. He is highly educated, yet his incessant flow of words is as foul as the breath that informs me that he has emptied more than one gin bottle before midday.

'Look at this woman, Irish nobility, quite good-looking I suppose but stuffed with laziness – fat. I despise fat women and fat men too for that matter. I fuck thin people. I left my wife when she got fat after she had our daughter – haven't seen either of them for years. I've only got one life; do you think I'm going waste it chained to a bloody spouse, a family and a nine-to-five job? Passion is my spouse, the world is my family and creativity is my job. I am an artist. An artist must be thin. I've no time for eaters, drinkers and sleepers. Old Lawrence here, was he fat? He must have been; he was no artist, all he ever did was paint portraits for money. What sort of creativity do you call that? And for that matter, who did this fat Countess of bloody Blessington think she was? It's perfectly obvious she's from the lower orders, like this lot here idling away their time. They ought to be working. Look at them, eaters, drinkers, sleepers; all bloody fat. In this country, eating is the opium of the people. I was born a peer of the realm for God's sake and now I have to work myself to the bone because these fucking left-wingers think it's clever to ban us from the House.'

I refrain from amputating this fasting anachronism's obese ego, with a swift cut of repartee. But out of compassion for a man drowning in his own superiority, I do not rise to the bait.

--

My second journal, when published many years later as *The Idler in Italy*, was purged by the editor's pencil in the same way as my *Journal of a Tour through the Netherlands*. Again my most salacious observations and embellished anecdotes withered beneath the acidic blue lead. Did these Mammon-worshiping puritans seriously think their readers preferred prosaic pen pictures of old churches and monuments to candid accounts of colourful characters spiced with a little inoffensive piquancy? Prudery prevailed as always but my meticulous censors did manage to overlook a few pragmatic comments, such as my advice on travelling with servants:

> *The greater the number of domestics one is compelled to keep, the greater the torments they inflict: for they are so incapable of submitting to aught in the shape of torments... They are generally found to be more trouble than useful out of England.'*

Charles's preparations for our departure were practical and over-elaborate. He sold the vehicles that made such a profound impression on me in Hampshire – at a loss – since a grand tour of Europe required more regal if less functional forms of conveyance. His once Napoleonic chef reminded him that French cuisine, though the envy of the world, did not always involve the highest standards of hygiene. Charles therefore purchased all the cutlery and crockery from a club of which he was one of two hundred members and ordered a new wagon fitted to accommodate it.

My own custom-built day coach was equipped with a plump cushioned sofa, a writing table and mesh-protected shelves for the works on fourteenth-century history and less enthralling subjects for me to read en route. The delicate primrose velvet that lined the interior of my night coach was so finely woven that the lightest stain proved indelible. Beneath my heavy brass bedstead was a discrete fitment for my personal chinaware, while the Earl of Blessington's coach was equipped with a mahogany cabinet holding twenty bottles and twelve wine glasses. Charles never drank while travelling. A pleasant little carriage was acquired for Mary Ann. Three large wagons carried our wardrobes while a more compact vehicle provided accommodation for Charles's clerk, valet, butler and two footmen. My maids, seamstress and laundress, so far as I know, were to travel in similar comfort. As I noted:

'I have observed that persons accustomed from birth to the utmost luxury can better submit to the privations occasioned by travelling than can their servants.'

When Lord Byron travelled in similar style, Charles explained, he transported his own livestock for slaughter en route. With difficulty I convinced him that his friend's precaution was possibly unnecessary. I anticipated enough hindrances on the continental roads without the added stench of a mobile piggery.

Our coachmen and footmen, resplendent in the new Blessington livery, led twenty laboriously groomed matching black horses into St James's Square and assembled a splendid convoy. A pageant of colour and polished brass gleamed in the morning sun. All at last was ready for me to travel to the fairyland of my threadbare childhood fantasies.

'What's old Blessington up to now? Set up a ruddy travelling circus, 'as he? It'll take me all bloomin' day to clear up this muck,' said a good-natured street cleaner. The unhoned wit of the London cockney is unparalleled.

Two days later, our party of historical researchers trundled back into Dover. Charles declined to visit its famous castle as it dated from the twelfth century while the fictitious *de Vavaseur* dwelt in the fourteenth. There had been too many vital developments in the two intervening dark-age centuries. Mary Ann and I climbed the steep hill to inspect the ancient fortress while Charles disposed of all his splendid horses – at a loss - since he believed it cruel to expose animals to the sea. He then chartered a steam packet large enough to cram in our vehicles and all the servants. As previously, a private ferry was unavailable, leaving us obliged to cross the Channel on the public packet which, yet again fell victim to gale-force winds. Everyone on board, apart from me and the crew, suffered severe seasickness. *'What a pitiable sight did the passengers present,'* I observed feeling particularly sorry for a young honeymoon couple:

> *'It is difficult for a man to believe in the divinity of a beautiful woman after he has seen her heaving, like a Pythoness, with extended jaws, upturned eyes and...'*

We reached Paris on 31st August 1822. It was my third visit to the golden metropolis of my dreams. It was as squalid as ever. Charles engaged an entire floor of a fashionable hotel, where each night a succession of porters, waiters and pageboys entered my room unbidden, hesitated without cause, apologised and left slowly. This helpful amenity was apparently offered gratuitously to every attractive female guest. I suppose the readily-available pornography of the twenty-first century does have its benefits.

The next day, Sunday, was my thirty-third birthday which Charles planned for me to celebrate in resplendent reluctance.

> *'Youth is like health, we never value the possession of either until they have begun to decline.'*

He had arranged a surprise. Thomas Moore joined us at dinner, entertained us with refined racy wit and sang a selection of his latest popular ballads. He too was on a research expedition. He was on his way to Genoa to obtain material for his forthcoming biography of Lord Byron to which Charles offered an excludable contribution. He regaled Tom with tales of the poet's youth in London and how he lent him money to enable him to live, gamble and fornicate like the lord he was. No, the loans were never repaid.

'Tom, do convey my compliments to dear Noel and inform him that I shall be bringing my dear Marguerite to meet him as soon as we reach Genoa.'

'As you know, your lordship, Byron is currently engrossed in composing the sixteenth canto of *Don Juan*. When the muse is upon him even I dread the prospect of his temperament. Might I therefore commend that you postpone your visit until he is finished? It shouldn't take him more than a month or two.'

'Tell me, Tom, is Lord Byron as handsome and dashing as he appears in his portraits? I asked.'

'It's some while since I've seen Lord Byron, Lady Blessington. Possibly you will find him rather more plump than you imagine but I do not think you will be entirely disappointed.'

I was already disappointed. I had waited for so long to meet Byron in the flesh, not in a surfeit of flesh. Nevertheless, I employed our considerate adjournment to prepare myself to impress the great poet with my appreciation of the underlying philosophy of his work - as opposed to my own more modest flesh.

There was to be another disappointment. Catherine Lee, who was due to meet me in Paris, had been detained in London on what her apologetic note described as family business, meaning further manifestations of her reverend husband's sacred wrath. I assessed the châteaux in which Catherine was interested and sent her reports of those which I did not try to persuade Charles to purchase. He agreed but sensibly decided to postpone acquiring our Parisian residence until the return journey. Within a year I would begin my new life in Paris. This was a mistake

And there was to be a third disappointment. Again I was deprived of the opportunity to meet Madame Craufurd. I had been so looking forward to seeing the interior of her magnificent château in the rue D'Anjou, which Alfred had depicted with exaggerated precision. She had rented it to Henry Fox, the nineteen-year-old son of Lord and Lady Holland and grandson of the renowned statesman, Charles James Fox. The young aristocrat inherited his mother's insolence but not his grandfather's eloquence. The legitimate heir to the Holland millions was to die without issue in 1859, bringing the line into extinction. This was undoubtedly a great loss to history.

In response to my cordial enquiry, the noble tenant replied:

'Permit me to inform you, Lady Blessington, that I am neither accustomed to conducting tours of my private residence, nor am I at liberty to disclose my landlady's whereabouts.

Yours etc., Fox.'

This was as close as Henry Fox would ever come to writing anything polite to or about me. I had little difficulty in locating the whereabouts of Madame Craufurd. La Baronesse Eleanore de Franquemont happily informed me that her mother was temporarily residing at her château and invited me to meet her there. She also invited Charles to meet General D'Orsay who had strategically retired from military service with the fall of Napoleon.

Before going out to Chambourcy, we could not resist returning to the château of Le Baron Vivant Denon. Now aged seventy-five, the baron again resurrected the ancient world through a dramatic discourse distorting both the history and the discovery of his unique collections. The former custodian of the Louvre conducted us in silence to a secret vault, unlocked a fortified chest and ceremoniously extracted diamond encrusted bracelets and tiaras made for Louis XV as gifts to Madame de Pompadour. He showed us brooches and necklaces that he himself designed for Napoleon to present to his wives Josephine and Marie-Louise, and granted me the privilege of trying on some of these priceless pieces. They were far too gaudy for my taste but since I was the first person to wear them since their original owners, it would have been impolite to ask Baron Denon how these imperial treasures came to be in his possession.

The aging scholar did not seem as engaging as previously. He exhausted us with quite possibly unembellished memoirs of his time with Napoleon, who evidently was so heavily committed to archaeology, antiquities and all matters artistic that I wondered how he found time to deal with lesser concerns, such as ruling France and conquering Europe. Baron Denon then moved on to his

Russian exploits. He had been among the many experts Catherine the Great had invited to St Petersburg to advise her on acquisitions for the Winter Palace, and satisfy other demands. Again the retired connoisseur omitted to explain how he acquired certain elegant items that the Tsarina evidently did not need. When, three years later, Baron Vivant Denon died his collection was sold at a weeklong auction the auctioneer offered no guarantee of provenance but I recommended Charles to purchase many pieces of jewellery in his friend's memory. I greatly valued these wonderful objects, as I did all Charles's gifts, but neither of us lived to discover what incredible bargains they were to prove.

Although Le Baron Denon was an authority on the history of fourteenth-century Europe he could tell Charles nothing pertaining to the adventures of *Reginald de Vavaseur*. Our visit was nonetheless far from fruitless. We left armed with letters of introduction to half the nobility of France and Italy.

The following day we accepted La Baronesse Eleanore's invitation to Chambourcy. She and General D'Orsay greeted us warmly and conveyed Madame Craufurd's apologies. She was confined to bed with a severe cold. Without contemplating that this grand lady might have been deliberately avoiding us, I proffered the appropriate words of sincere sympathy.

There was no sign of Comte Alfred either. Unexpectedly, Charles's petition as an honorary colonel-in-chief of an obscure Irish militia did not impress the commanders of the most prestigious regiment in France. Le Garde Royale had posted its most unpopular officer to Avignon where the last dauphin of France, the Duc d'Angoulême, eldest son of Charles X was assembling an expeditionary force to invade Spain in support of restoration of absolute monarchy under King Ferdinand VII. Every man in uniform was essential to victory in this glorious unnecessary campaign.

Jean François Louis Marie Albert Grimond, Comte Général D'Orsay who, according to Baron Denon, Napoleon had called '*Le Beau D'Orsay, Aussi brave que beau*', was indeed among the most handsome men of his age I had yet encountered. The retired Napoleonic stalwart retained his thick silvery hair, stood as tall as Alfred and like Charles was a general and the son of a general.

'Many generations of my family have served in the Tyrone Militia, you know, Monsieur le Général. Possibly the regiment is little known here in France but I can safely say that it is the best equipped in Ireland. I finance the equipment myself, you see. If you would care to come over one day, I shall order the brigadier to arrange a special parade and you can take the salute.'

'My sincere thanks, Lord Blessington, I shall be most honoured to inspect the Militia *de Tyro*', if I am pronouncing it correctly, when my heavy commitments permit. Meanwhile, while you are in France, perhaps you would care to come back alone when you have some time to spare. Since my retirement, I rarely get the opportunity to speak with another senior officer man to man and I am most interested to hear your views on some inconsequential matters of strategy.'

Before Charles could reply La Baronesse turned to me. 'I shall be in Paris tomorrow, Marguerite. If you wish I could meet you and introduce you and Mary Anne to some of my favourite boutiques and galleries while Lord

Blessington comes to see Albert. You will not want to listen to the gentlemen's dreary conversation.'

Charles was elated to accept his invitation to talk to another non-combatant soldier. And since shopping in town seemed more appealing than another day in the country I readily accepted Eleanore's suggestion. This was a mistake. General D'Orsay did not wish to speak to Charles about strategy. His inconsequential matters were more in the nature of shopping but not of the sort accessible in the boutiques of Paris. Nor was it the general but Madame Craufurd herself, who having made a miraculous recovery wished to speak to Charles 'man to man'. In her confused mixture of French and English which I shall make no attempt to imitate, the aging socialite expressed herself with perfect clarity.

'Lord Blessington, it is my understanding that you and the Countess have struck up an admirable friendship with my beloved grandson, Le Comte Alfred. He informs me that he is assisting you with your travel arrangements and that you have invited him to act as your guide to Europe – for the purposes of research. Doubtless he has mentioned that I am in a position to provide you with access to the royal households and highest echelons of the French and Italian courts.'

'Well, yes he has, but you see, Madame Craufurd, Comte Alfred has also told us about his disillusionment with the Bourbon regime and that he desires to leave the army in order to develop his artistic vocation. The Countess and I take a great interest in the arts, you know. Travelling with us will offer Comte Alfred an exceptional opportunity and set him on the path to a fruitful career. A sort of apprenticeship, you see.'

Madame Craufurd did not see. General D'Orsay replied on behalf of his mother-in-law.

'Quite right. The boy has the makings of a first-class soldier, Blessington, but to my great chagrin he has no stomach for the job. The hour of the great Napoleon has passed and sadly it remains the duty of every patriotic Frenchman to defend his king and country, right or wrong. But Alfred cannot be allowed to simply abdicate on a whim.'

Charles had no idea what the general was talking about.

'Be that as it may, General D'Orsay, your son tells me that he has already petitioned for his discharge, you know. After it is procured, I have offered to support him until his great talent is recognised internationally.'

'That is most generous of you, Blessington, but it is quite impossible for a discharge to be effected in the present circumstances.'

'In the British army, you know, these matters can usually be expedited quietly and amicably. If it is a matter of money…'

The sound of the word she most despised exhausted Madame Craufurd's exceedingly limited patience to such an extent that she suddenly remembered how to speak perfect English.

'Of course it is a matter of money, Lord Blessington. Apprenticeship, indeed! Let us stop beating about the bush. In my long life I have travelled the world and experienced human weakness in its every manifestation. Now I have reached an age where it is of no consequence to me who knows – and apparently there are very few who do not – that in my youth I sold my charms to frustrated men of means like yourself, Lord Blessington. Do you imagine I do not understand the perverted desires that have prompted you and the Countess to request Comte Alfred to become involved in your so-called research? Your vulgar parade of mobile bordellos is already the talk of Paris.'

'You see, Madame Craufurd, I think you misjudge me. I am a happily married man and very much in love with Countess Marguerite. I was also very much in love with my late wife, Mary, the mother of my four children, you know.'

'As you are aware, Lord Blessington, I and my family are well acquainted with Captain Jenkins – I knew *both* his parents well - and thus I am reliably informed of your propensities and that you purchased *both* your wives. It is beneath my dignity to stand in judgment, but should you wish to add my grandson to your collection of personal adornments, I must remind you that his circumstances are, shall we say, more complex than those of a young woman seeking the security of marriage.'

Charles had never experienced such blunt speech at Eton, Oxford or even in the militia. Before he could think of a slow-witted response, Madame Craufurd continued.

'Comte Alfred's commission in the Garde Royale was acquired, not by virtue of the General's unrewarded bravery but through my influence. Regrettably, I am no longer in a position to maintain my generosity, not least due to my grandson's exquisite lifestyle which you will agree, Lord Blessington, it is essential to preserve. I trust we understand one another?'

'Alas, Madame Craufurd, I do not entirely understand you, you see. Tell me what you wish me to do for you?'

'For myself, I desire nothing other than to return to my modest château and live out my days in the manner to which I have long been accustomed. General Albert, on the other hand, is too proud to tell you himself but is unable to live on the derisory pension earned in the service of the great Napoleon. Twelve thousand pounds and reimbursement of the necessary inducements to secure Comte Alfred's release would be sufficient to enable the general to retain this château which has been his family home for so many generations.'

Charles was unaccustomed to the nuances of bargaining, but felt that some comment was expected.

'That does sound rather a lot, you know, Madam Craufurd.'

Madame Craufurd glanced around at the decaying grandeur of her son-in-law's salon. The cracked murals, peeling gilt relief and faded furnishings invigorated the spirit of the robust octogenarian who only that morning had staggered from her sickbed.

'Lord Blessington, my late husband, Quintin, was like you a zealous patron of the arts. He too was privileged to sponsor a generation of artists who posthumously rewarded his investments. Alfred's talents, as you have observed, are extraordinary and I can confidently predict that you will not have to wait for his demise to be repaid many times over.'

Quintin Craufurd invested only in old masters and never sponsored an artist in his life.

Charles looked for support to General D'Orsay, now striking a pressed and polished military pose between the fire dogs on his massive stone hearth, a picture of Alfred thirty years on. He could barely wait to be rid of his son's embarrassing affectations but even a French gentleman betrays no emotion in tense situations.

'I must concur with Madame Craufurd, Blessington, and with the greatest reluctance accept that Alfred's artistic temperament is more suited to civilian life.'

'You need have no concerns, D'Orsay. Countess Marguerite and I shall ensure that your son enjoys a life entirely befitting his artistic temperament, you know.'

'I have no doubt of that whatsoever but you and I are military men, Blessington. We are trained to do things properly. You will have no objection to a legal document, in case, heaven forefend, of your premature demise?'

Charles was too relieved to have concluded the unpleasant dealings to think clearly about the consequences of a binding contract.

'You are quite right, D'Orsay, that is most important, you know. Who can tell what might happen? My own father fell in the Irish Rebellion when he was not much older than I am now; dreadful business, you know. What do you have in mind?'

This question called for Madame Craufurd's expertise.

'Lord Blessington, I take it that you have made a proper will with provision for your children?'

'Madame Craufurd, Mr Powell is the finest attorney in London, you know. I instructed him to redraft my will after poor Mary so sadly passed away.'

'I am delighted to hear that, Lord Blessington. We are all naturally concerned for Alfred's future but there is one more thing that you can do to put all our minds at rest.'

'And what is that, Madame Craufurd?'

'Will you honour the D'Orsay family heritage with your consent to Alfred selecting the hand of one of your daughters when she comes of age? It will be unnecessary to alter your will, Lord Blessington; a simple letter of intent will suffice.'

Charles was thrilled by this outrageous suggestion.

'That is a splendid arrangement, you know, Madame Craufurd. If it is God's will that our noble families shall be united then it is also a symbol of accord between our two great nations, you see. The Countess will be overjoyed. She has taken such a great liking to the Baronesse Eleanore and to Ida and Antoine.'

The ever-practical general requested the present ages of the ladies from whom his future daughter-in-law was to be selected.

'As I recall, Emily has just turned twelve and Harriet will soon be ten, you know. When you come over to Ireland, D'Orsay, remind me to introduce them to you.'

There was of course no mention of any feelings the intended couple might have for one another.

Meanwhile a warm August sun shone from a cloudless sky upon the pristine streets of Paris, that is upon those streets sufficiently fashionable to be kept pristine. Avoiding airless galleries and museums, Eleanore led me and Mary Anne on a gentle stroll through the celebrated boulevards and treated us to a guided tour of the faults and failings of their aristocratic residents. We then visited the exclusive *magasins et boutiques* where Eleanore introduced me to their genteel proprietors, who knew and loved her as much as their brothers in London loved me. By early evening I had filled a hired carriage with gowns of silk and fine fabrics, shoes, bonnets and accessories for myself, two simple dresses for Mary Ann and a tasteful cravat for Charles.

When later that evening he returned from Chambourcy, Charles was so eager to tell me all about his purchase that I was unable to show him mine. I was furious and not simply because he paid no attention to the cravat.

'Anger banishes reflection, but its consequences recall it.'

Major Browne cozened Charles out of an untold sum. Thomas Jenkins cheated him out of ten thousand pounds. Now he had allowed himself to be overtly swindled out of another twelve thousand. And I am speaking of a time when twelve hundred pounds would have bought a score of large houses in central London.

Charles had acted from the highest philanthropic motives but a sly preening general and an aging social-climbing whore pleading privation were not my idea of the deserving poor. How could Charles have been so easily deceived? Alfred, like any other young man, would have leapt at the chance of a life of uncommitted luxury and the expectancy of a fortune on marriage to a daughter of a landed aristocrat. Did my husband really think that a self-obsessed youth like Comte Alfred D'Orsay would ever make a living from art or any other work? I composed myself.

'But this is the most wonderful news, Charles. You are always so perceptive in these matters. Alfred is the ideal person to help with your research.'

'You are absolutely right, my dear Marguerite, but first we shall have go to meet him at Avignon, you see.'

All I had seen of provincial France had been prohibitively uninspiring.

'I would love to visit Avignon, Charles, it will make such a change from Paris. But first I must write to Madame Craufurd, General D'Orsay and La Baronesse Eleanore and express our deep indebtedness for their kindnesses.'

My letter to Alfred's mother contained not a hint of my opinion of her brilliantly played role in the conspiracy to defraud my husband. I excelled at insincere correspondence.

'You see, my dear Marguerite. General Albert explained that in France things take a little longer than in the British army. On the eve of battle all the colonels, brigadiers and generals tend to be heavily committed, you know. Meanwhile, there will be no point in us going straight to Avignon. I think we should first see Switzerland; snow-capped mountains, lakes, cows with big bells and so on, you know. That part of Europe is full of fourteenth-century history, you see.'

I thought that I would never tire of the enchantment of Paris but now could hardly wait to leave it for another form of enchantment. The absent Comte D'Orsay had lured not only Charles but me too into a complex labyrinth of desire from which there was to be no exit.

On 12th September 1822 our diminished but still cumbersome convoy crept unsteadily out of Paris in the direction of Switzerland. The weather was fine and the journey nondescript. I struggled to find enthusiastic observations for my journal. I wrote of places I did not see, people I did not meet and folklore I did not believe. A day here, two days there: Geneva, Lausanne, Berne, Zurich, snow, mountains, pine forests, rivers, lakes: sleeping beauty my pen could not awaken.

'Half the beauty of Switzerland would be lost were its inhabitants to change their national costume.'

This was my portrayal of the landlocked state indisputably laying claim to the most inspiring natural scenery on earth. *De Vavaseur* began to evolve from the ridges and peaks into a passable novel. I wrote only the occasional twenty or thirty pages for Charles and he might have finished the endless saga had his attention not been so often diverted by local entrepreneurs eager to welcome any prosperous traveller. Among these colourful charlatans was a certain Comte d'Houtpoul who extracted an outrageous price for a magnificent black charger called Mameluke.

'My dear Marguerite, I am sure you will enjoy riding him in the mornings, you know. It will do you good to spend more time out of your carriage. Our health is important to us, you see.'

Charles seldom rose before midday and even more seldom took unnecessary exercise.

On we went, Switzerland, France and back to Switzerland where we stayed at Baden, famed for its health-giving baths.

'A more disgusting scene I never beheld; for the faces of the bathers bore as visible signs of impure blood, as the ribaldry of their conversation and songs afforded impure lives. The odour of the baths is detestable...'

And this, remember, was the published version. Re-reading it reminds me of *Lady Blessington's Bath* in Clonmel.

On Lake Geneva a boatman called Maurice, heaving his oars into a headwind, prattled endlessly about the time when Lord Byron employed his questionable skills. Maurice spoke only French, more in quantity than quality and the following must be accepted as a very loose translation.

'Very strange man, his lordship: only came on the boat when it was pouring with rain. He'd sit there all night, just where you're sitting, soaked to the skin, gazing up at the sky and always with a loaded pistol in each hand. I didn't dare ask, but I used to wonder if he expected to be attacked by pirates. I don't mind telling you, Lord Blessington, he frightened the life out of me. And he always argued about the fare. If you see Lord Byron, sir, please remind him he still owes me five francs.'

'Did he never speak to you, Maurice?' I asked.

'Oh, yes, your ladyship, sometimes you couldn't shut him up. I never understood a word he said. He was always going on about something called cant, whatever that is. He certainly hated cant.'

'Tell me, Maurice, did Lord Byron write poetry while on your boat?'

'As I said, Lady Blessington, his lordship would only come out when there was a storm. The lightning's spectacular round the lake. It goes on for hours sometimes. I was always scared we'd be struck, especially when he'd suddenly dive in for a swim; very good swimmer, Lord Byron. But no, he couldn't write while he was hanging on to his guns. His friend, the other poet, Mr Shelley, he used to write, but then he only came out on nice days. Lovely man, Mr Shelley, always paid his fare. I heard he was drowned recently when his schooner went down; couldn't have been more than thirty – terrible tragedy. Not at all like Mr Shelley to go out in bad weather. Anyway, Lord Byron said he's also got a schooner, the *Bolivar*, down in Genoa. Apparently, he sometimes goes on that to do his writing; proper gin palace I've been told.'

'Thank you Maurice, you have given me an excellent idea, you know,' said Charles. 'I'm a writer myself, you see. A schooner is the very thing for the peace and quiet I need, you know.'

We reached Avignon on 20th November 1822. Alfred had thoughtfully booked accommodation for us at the most uneconomical establishment in the town. *L'Hotel de l'Europe* was once a sixteenth-century Rhône château and the five-star hotel of the same name that now occupies the site boasts original and unoriginal features. Its legendary proprietress, Madame Pierron, informed us that she had converted the ancient ruin herself and that her venture had been financed by Napoleon. I am sure that this was true. Though no longer young, the shrewd hotelier's seductive smile suggested that she would have had little difficulty in interesting the cultured Emperor in architectural preservation. Madame Pierron, a Revolution profiteer of the school of Madame Craufurd, had every reason to smile. Alfred had engaged her hotel for the entire winter without asking her charges.

'*Le magnifique Comte Alfred* dines at my humble hotel whenever my guests invite him *et le Général Albert et la belle Baronesse Eleanore* always stay with us when they are in Avignon. *Bien sûr*, Lord and Lady Blessington, for friends of *mon cher Beau D'Orsay* I shall make a special price.'

Madame Pierron did not specify whether her special price was above or below her normal tariff but she did provide a special welcome without charge. She employed '*the Poet Laureate of Avignon*' to compose lines in our honour and deliver them from the hotel steps. After the laureate's polished performance, I asked him if poetry was his profession. '*I live by my wits*,' he replied. In *The Idler in Italy* I commented '*I wonder how he could exist on so slender a capital?*' The original wording of my journal entry offers more astute criticism.

Camped outside Avignon, the sixty-thousand men of the French army who comprised the Dauphin's '*Hundred-thousand Sons of Saint Louis*' were training for a mass assault on Spain. Each day more and more officers in colourful uniforms were to be seen in the town. Junior officers were billeted in private homes while the higher-ranked rented large houses and brought their wives and families as if it were a holiday. Some might well have considered the bold invasion to be a holiday. Having enjoyed their excursion across the Pyrenees, the hundred-thousand sons were joined by a legion of supporters of the Spanish monarchy. The two armies marched forth in unison and gloriously slaughtered the small and poorly armed rebel resistance. Indeed, the campaign might be said to have been among the more literal examples of overkill in the history of warfare.

As Avignon filled with noble military families, it took on an ambience of Parisian elegance complete with *le beau monde*.

> *The more I see of French society, the more I like its ease and agreeability. The ladies are more spirited than their English sisters yet, in public at least, adhere to a stricter code of decorous conduct, to which I wholeheartedly subscribe... Their robes conceal much more of the bust and shoulders and* [I approve of] *the French waltz in which the gentleman does not clasp his fair partner round the waist with a freedom repugnant to the modesty.'*

I excelled at sanctimonious commentary.

We stayed in Avignon for three months. For the first time since before my first marriage I felt completely cleansed of slander and ostracism. I never wished to see London again. Almost every evening we were invited – yes invited – to a ball, party or dinner. The French were so polite that some even asked Mary Ann to join us. I thus rechristened her Marianne – the symbol of the French Republic – and tried to teach her a little of the language in the vain hope that she might attract an uncomprehending French gentleman. Alfred arrived late for every social event to which he had procured us an invitation.

His habit was to pause framed like a picture in the doorway while all his names and titles were read to the assembled guests. He invariably appeared in civilian dress, never the same twice, proclaiming to the world: 'I am the embodiment of masculine beauty. Do I not shine like a beacon upon this sea of uniforms and uniformity? Ignore me at your peril!'

One evening we dined at the château of the fabulously wealthy Brigadier Emmanuel, Duc Caderousse de Gramont, a cousin of Alfred's brother-in-law, Antoine. The retired brigadier had served alongside General Albert D'Orsay for many years and was now in Avignon only as a spectator to the warlike sport. Like Alfred's father, Caderousse de Gramont swore allegiance to the king while in his heart was still loyal to Napoleon, under whom he had served while the Duchesse was lady-in-waiting to Empress Marie Louise. The Brigadier considered it outrageous of the Bourbon Army to oppose Alfred's discharge. Taking the twenty guests at his dining table into his confidence, the old soldier joked about the absurdity of the present campaign. The Duc D'Angoulême had requisitioned ten times the number of necessary officers. What did he imagine he was going to do with them? No, he could not help Alfred.

At Christmas we were introduced to another member of Alfred's extended family. The garrison commander, Colonel Horace François Bestien Sebastiani, married to the Duc de Guiche's sister, Aglaé Angélique. Sebastiani, too heavily committed to the niceties of his mindless strategy to waste time on family matters, raised no objection to Alfred being relieved of his commission. The French army, like the English, never condoned nepotism.

Alfred, his family and other superfluous sons of Saint Louis escorted us on a fascinating series of outings. Avignon was an oasis of industry, innovation and history in the cultural desert of provincial France. We were shown the tomb of Laura, the temptress of Petrarch, which inspired me to compose a discourse on his sonnets and philosophy. I was not the first to argue that Laura was nothing but a child of the poet's imagination, her story a myth and that her celebrated headstone marked an empty grave. Charles was convinced that the sham tourist attraction actually held the soul of *Reginald de Vavaseur* and employed a local historian to research the seven fourteenth-century popes of the *'Avignon Papacy'*. The learned gentleman, having scanned the archives for three weeks discovered nothing of relevance, for which Charles paid him more than he normally earned in three months.

Another tour took us to a depressing iron foundry that manufactured *'the implements of destruction with which civilisation has enriched us.'* I was therefore more than pleased to discover that Avignon also possessed constructive implements with which civilisation has enriched us. The vast and imposing *Ancien Grand Hôpital St Bénézet* even then accommodated as many as seven hundred patients in clean, spacious, ventilated rooms on the same site where pious Christians had cared for the sick since 1177. The round-the-clock dedication of the nuns and monks could not have been more praiseworthy but I was at a loss to understand how such educated medically trained people could think that making all their patients praise God and sing hymns from four to six hours a day might assist their recovery. Charles himself provided more practical assistance in the form of an unhealthily large donation.

Avignon also cared for its mentally sick. At the *L'Hospice des Insensés* a supposedly mad patient asked me:

> *'Why come here? Can't you find enough madmen in the world outside? The world is only a madhouse on a larger scale, where the lunatics follow their own caprices, instead of in an asylum like this, being compelled to follow those of others.'*

I thought him the sanest man I had ever met.

Four weeks after our Christmas dinner, Garrison Commander Colonel Sebastiani granted his wife's brother-in-law by marriage an honourable discharge from the Garde Royale. In view of Alfred's fellow officers' congenial appreciation of the accelerated process, he proposed that we left Avignon immediately.

Charles wanted to proceed south in order to take the fresh air of the Côte d'Azur, while the ever-practical Alfred pointed out that in midwinter the hill roads would probably be impassable and at best unsuited to heavy vehicles.

Disregarding this native advice, Charles sold more of our carriages, at a loss, dismissed the servants thus rendered redundant, wrote exuberant references and bade them farewell. As an enlightened employer he even paid for their journey home. The concept of redundancy compensation remained beyond the wit of man for another century and a half.

On the freezing morning of 8th February 1823 our lighter cavalcade – I retained my comfortably fitted coach – was assembled for us in the courtyard of the L'Hotel de l'Europe and we prepared to leave for the coast. Madame Pierron came out in person with a parting gift of *'cakes, bonbons, orange flower water and bouquets of flowers'*. This was, literally, the least she could do. Charles settled *l'addition* without so much as a glance at her six-page schedule of extra charges for accommodating servants, stabling, laundry, parties and banquets. Before the invention of the humble ready-reckoner, let alone the computer a simple woman like Madame Pierron could be forgiven the arithmetical errors in her favour. While Charles distributed excessive gratuities, I expressed my appreciation for her hospitality, as unreservedly as she wished us bon voyage. With miraculous good fortune, we completed the normally three-day journey to the Mediterranean coast in under a fortnight. Teeming rain made the trails and passes so rough and slippery that I might have pitied the poor horses, were I not pitying myself. Slowly we proceeded along the deserted, yet to be celebrated coast road via Marseilles, Toulon, Antibes, Cannes and Nice spending comfortless nights as the only guests at the few inns still open in winter. The romantic scenery and interesting places I describe in *The Idler in Italy* were largely plagiarised later from writers sensible enough to travel in summer.

When at last we found a civilised hotel in Mentone (Menton), I noticed a familiar name in the guest book. After so many dreary and uneventful weeks even the prospect of meeting Henry Edward Fox seemed like a treat. Since crumpling his note in Paris, I had done my best to forget Madame Craufurd's self-opinionated tenant but Charles unhesitatingly invited the noble traveller to dine with us. This was an enduring mistake.

By removing their son and heir from the rue D'Anjou and sending him on a protracted tour of the Continent Lord and Lady Holland had, for the hundredth time, succeeded in avoiding a family scandal. On the surface Henry might have been a second Alfred. He was as tall, undeniably handsome, fastidiously dressed and exuded all the tactless self-assurance of a born aristocrat. He too was an articulate conversationalist but, unlike Alfred and myself, lacked the talent to express biting cynicism without conveying offence. He was however a liar of contemptible accomplishment. Beneath the surface Henry was a mass of complexes, partly due to the ever-present shadow of his indomitable mother, and partly to the slight hip impediment which his greatest ambition – possibly his only ambition – was to conceal. His sexual orientation involved further complexities.

'I was sent down from Oxford before the end of my first year because it was impossible to study. I was in love. According to my parents, it was an inappropriate relationship. They insisted that I break it off and resume my education abroad. As you know, D'Orsay, your dear grandmother put her place at my disposal for the summer, but then some French duke became a bit too keen to snatch me up for his daughter - a very nice girl. We spent a couple of days together. She fell in love with me of course but I'm far too young for marriage, so I decided to skip Paris for a while. What about you D'Orsay? I don't expect you are thinking about marriage just yet?'

Henry Fox's pitiful verbosity failed to conceal the assorted genders of his numerous paramours. Charles began to look anxious, irritated by our guest's fascination with Alfred. I too became anxious and quietly warned Alfred that everything he said would be noted and embellished for the benefit of Lady Holland. Henry's mother was no friend of the impertinent Frenchman who might well have dared to attempt to outwit her at her own table. I replied on Alfred's behalf:

'Indeed, Mr Fox, the Comte D'Orsay fully intends to marry. In fact, he is soon to be engaged to Lord Blessington's daughter.' This was another enduring mistake.

'The knowledge of the world that enables us to escape from errors can only be acquired from an experience which costs us many of our most cherished illusions.'

'My apologies, Lady Blessington, it appears that I was under a misconception. My heartiest congratulations, D'Orsay: as your dear mother once told me, Madame Craufurd is the most prolific matchmaker in Paris. And, Lord Blessington, allow me to also offer you my congratulations. You could wish for no finer son-in-law than D'Orsay or indeed a more appropriate union between your two noble families.'

'Thank you, Fox. Alfred is already like another son to me, you see.'

'Oh, I do see, Lord Blessington. La Comtesse Eleanore is like another mother to me.'

I was about to learn that the future fourth Baron Holland's volatile sexual repertoire included older women as well as younger men. Of that particular evening his diaries observe:

'Dined with the Blessingtons; D'Orsay is established with them, and, she says, is to marry Lord B's daughter, whom he has never seen and is only thirteen. This I suppose is a blind. She (Lady B.) is not at all pleasant, very vulgar and very abusive...'

Henry's publishers must have been considerably more permissive than mine, though they did take the precaution of delaying publication until the author was long dead.

As I have made perfectly clear, I was never vulgar or abusive in my life. Henry had no reason to be so rude. After two centuries of reflection however I appreciate how his displeasure was incurred. To him I was another attractive older woman but neither I nor Alfred responded to his gauche vanity. We were both too polite and Henry was sufficiently prudent to boast, while out of earshot, that he was the most favoured of Eleanore de Franquemont's lovers.

He was a year younger than her son. I now believed nothing that the elegant wife of the Napoleonic general had told to me, except that she was certainly the daughter of Anne Franchi Craufurd.

Although relieved after Henry Fox left us, Charles became strangely withdrawn. Nothing Alfred or I could do amused him or would revive his spirits. At first we thought that he might have been depressed by the delays, the poor accommodation or the anticlimax after the gaiety and distractions of Avignon. It soon became clear that there was something else playing on his mind, and for all our sakes, I confronted him.

'You see, my dear Marguerite, just before we set off from Avignon a letter was delivered to the hotel from old Montgomery in Edinburgh. You remember Montgomery, poor Mary's brother-in-law? I suppose he is still my brother-in-law, you see. The letter was dated 20th December 1822, which means it took about six weeks to reach me. Edinburgh is a long way from Avignon, you know. Anyway, it seems Montgomery and his wife, that's poor Mary's sister, you see, took little Luke up to Scotland for Christmas. They thought the change of air would be good for the boy's health. The letter said he is quite well... but...'. I had seldom seen Charles resort to tears since he told me the tragic tale of his first wife's funeral. But now he looked pitiful and helpless and I knew he was not acting. My words of comfort had a hollow ring.

'Why be so upset, Charles? If Mr Montgomery tells you that Luke is quite well then I am sure it is true. What reason would he have to deceive you?'

I had no recollection of a previous mentioned of Mr Montgomery. I did not even know that Mary Campbell Browne had a married sister. Charles remained silent, his thoughts as transparent as his brother-in-law's discretion. He was torn between fatherly love, the love of a man and the love of a wife urging him on to Genoa to be reunited with his once intimate friend, Lord Byron.

Late at night on 26th March 1823, our last night in Mentone, I was woken by a terrifying scream. Charles was shaking violently, sweating in his sleep as if confronted by an apparition, shouting his father's name, Luke Gardiner, Lord Mountjoy, Luke Gardiner, Lord Mountjoy, over and over again. I got up – yes, we did share a bed, sometimes – and lit the lamp. Charles's face was as white as if he had indeed seen the ghost of his father.

'Whatever is the matter, Charles?'

He hesitated for a long while.

'Well, it seems I might have had one of my bad dreams, you see. The trouble is, you know, I always forget them the moment I wake up.' Charles was a bad liar.

'It is nothing to worry about. You will be all right now. No one has the same nightmare twice. Go back to sleep.'

Charles did not go back to sleep. He had had the same nightmare before.

'Destiny is a phantom of our own creation, like the monsters children first imagine and then fear.'

We progressed along the windswept Mediterranean coast into Italy. On our arrival in Genoa there was a marked improvement, if not in Charles's demeanour, at least in the weather. Bewildered fishermen and sailors watched as we traversed the quayside, the morning sunlight glistening on the scratched paint and brass harnesses of our travel-worn carriages. Alfred rode ahead on the whiter-than-white stallion Madame Craufurd had bought him to celebrate his commission in the Garde Royale, while I rode the magnificent Mameluke, jet-black as my hair. Charles lounged mournfully in his carriage and Marianne was somewhere.

We engaged a floor of the Alberga Delta Villa, an illusion of luxury compared to the half-functioning inns endured through our ill-advised wintry journey along the Côte d'Azur. The rooms were acceptable and uncomfortable, the harbour views captivating and uncharismatic and the Italian cuisine pleasant and unpalatable. The hotelier lacked the panache of a Monsieur Meurice or a Madame Pierron though possessed the expertise to match their idiosyncratic arithmetic.

Ten years later I published my memoirs of our nine-week sojourn in Genoa, *Conversations of Lord Byron*. That's right, '*of*', not '*with*'. In essence Byron's conversation flowed in one direction which was perhaps as well, since his dramatic eloquence could perplex the most intelligent. I was never perplexed. I excelled at eloquence – apart from on paper.

The Conversations of Lord Byron has been judged the most authentic depiction of the poet's character and might also have been judged the most personal had it not been another victim of prudish and prudent censorship. I did not embroider Byron's words. He was perfectly adept at doing that for himself though I am not certain if all my quotations were verbatim. It would have been easier for a pugilist to record a blow-by-blow account in the heat of a bout than for me to take precise notes through our long and intense exchanges. In the evenings I scribbled down all I could remember to be later purged for publication in the golden age of pretentiousness. Byron was, like me, an industrious idler in Italy, a fugitive from his past and the ill-willed tattlers of London.

The Casa Saluzzo '*a fine old palazzo commanding extensive views* [over Genoa]' concealed in the foothills of the Apennines near the hamlet of Albano, served as the poet's hermitage. Neither he nor his married mistress, Contessa Teresa Guiccioli, fitted my idea of a hermit. It was easy to understand how Charles and Byron came to be on such intimate terms. They had nothing whatsoever in common yet for many years had corresponded on a variety of serious trivial matters. Charles was among the highly-favoured few permitted to address the greatest living poet by the third of his forenames, Noel. Everyone else was required to use his title and pronounce his name *Biron*.

Lord Byron, like so many of those whose livelihood is wholly dependent on publicity, possessed a pathological dread of the public. A footman requested Charles to vouch for his companions before unbolting a pair of solid iron gates to admit our carriage into the casa's picturesque neglected gardens.

Eventually, the Lord of the rented manor emerged. The thirty-five-year-old paradigm of the romantic hero shuffled towards our vehicle and greeted us as we alighted. I tried to ignore the repulsive tang of vinegar on his breath as he bowed and kissed my hand permitting me a glimpse of the greying remnant of the luxuriant hair so glorious in his portraits. I was reminded of Shakespeare's Autolycus: *'His garments are rich but he wears them not handsomely.'* Tom Moore was exercising his talent for sarcasm when he said that I would find Lord Byron rather more plump than I might expect. I doubt he weighed nine stone. Byron's obsession with the absurd notion that obesity impedes creativity convinced me that his alleged insanity was not entirely unfounded. It was his habit to wash down the few crumbs that passed his lips with diluted vinegar, in the equally baseless conviction that its acidity would dissolve any intake of fat.

It was 1st April, All Fools Day, and the noble poet fell victim to an unwitting practical joke that only I could see. Byron was as beguiled by the appearance of his four visitors as I was disappointed in his. His head swung like a pendulum, to Alfred and back to me, to Charles and back to Marianne who I managed to dress attractively for the occasion. The muses had proffered a selection of prizes for completing the sixteenth *Don Juan* canto: a carnal conundrum baffling even to a roué as accomplished as George Gordon Noel, Sixth Baron Byron. Who is who? Who is what? Who is whose? Who is first?

'You may have thought me as ill-bred and 'sauvage', as fame reports, in having permitted Your Ladyship to wait a quarter of an hour at my gate, but my old friend Lord Blessington is to blame; for I only heard a minute or two ago that I was so highly honoured.'

This was the first of the many lies that Lord Byron was to address to me. Tom Moore had long since heralded our arrival and as usual abused his poetic licence by betraying his knowledge of my past.

The Casa Saluzzo was divided into separate apartments for its resident hermits, the poet himself, his mistress Contessa Guiccioli and her brother, Byron's secretary Count Pietro Gamba. Again I was disappointed. I had been curious to meet the infamous natural blonde Italian beauty. I cannot imagine why but the twenty-three-year-old Contessa studiously avoided me throughout my time in Genoa. Byron's fiery mistress surely could not have been inflamed by his over-zealous affection for my intellect. She had no reason to be jealous. The master of words thought it amusing to refer to me as an *'Irish Aspasia'* which I considered extremely offensive.

After my *Conversations* was published ten years later, Teresa claimed that Byron met with me on no more than six occasions. The intended insult was a great compliment, since she must have thought very highly of my creative talents to believe that I had invented such convincing fiction. In fact, the romantic poet sought my company almost every day. Numerous witnesses expressed their disapproval on observing us riding together and at social gatherings. My *Idler in Italy* is full of embellished descriptions of Byron himself conducting me on sightseeing outings. Did Teresa think that these too were invented? In later life we were to be reconciled. No, she never apologised.

My first encounter with Lord Byron was interrupted when an unexpected arrival entered the study unannounced. This was an unforgivable liberty but the reclusive poet made no protest. The newcomer was, after all, an undisputed aristocrat and there was no more amiable emissary of the type of petty gossip beloved of Lord Byron than Henry Fox. Together they formed a picture of a delinquent son humoured by an indulgent father. Henry stayed all day and probably all night after we left. Charles invited him to dine with us and Lord Byron at our hotel. Naturally I was most disappointed to learn that he had to leave Genoa the following morning. It was the last time Henry missed an opportunity to abuse Charles's hospitality. Of our unexpected meeting he wrote:

'To my great dismay the family of Blessington were forcing their way, and his Lordship had already gained admittance. I found Lord Byron very much annoyed at their impertinence and rather nervous... While the B's stayed the conversation rather flagged. As soon as they were gone he talked most agreeably on every subject.'

Byron apparently told Henry, nothing if not a dandy himself, that he was *'sorry not to have conversed with D'Orsay; it was rather an amusement to see what sort of animal the dandy of the present day is.'*

Henry's fabrications were never prompted by envy. The sly Fox, overawed by the charm of my wit and Alfred's panache, was apprehensive that he might soon be replaced in Lord Byron's many facetted affections.

Byron claimed that Charles's dinner invitation was the first he had received in two years. This might well have been true. Despite his celebrity, he was not a man with whom everyone would have wished to share their dinner table. He ate as if he would never see food again, gulped down fine wines like water and then in Roman fashion went outside and forced himself to vomit. Throughout the evening, the great patriot entertained us with anti-English diatribes, blended with sarcasm, scandal and poetic expletives. At two in the morning Charles ordered, and of course paid for a carriage to transport him home in a state of inebriation. Thereafter when I was with Byron, Charles was with Alfred and when I was with Charles, Alfred was with Byron, drawing his portrait; a time consuming labour of love. I cannot imagine what Marianne was doing.

'Dr Madden, were you really so naïve that you actually believed that there was no sexual side to our relationship? I would have been highly offended if a man of Byron's reputation had not at least attempted to seduce me. I was a titled lady.'

'Judging from your present impressions of Lord Byron, Lady Blessington, I find it surprising that you, or any other lady, found him at all attractive.'

'Dr Madden, Lord Byron was a genius. He could conjure poetry at will and transform his unpleasant odour, emaciated body and manic indiscretions into irresistible aphrodisiacs. And he had far straighter teeth than either Charles or Alfred.'

I more or less spell our relationship out in *The Idler*. I even describe the poet's bedroom and his bed: *'the most gaudy and vulgar thing I ever saw.'* And if this was not evidence enough, Tom Moore's *Life of Byron* leaves little to the imagination. Lord Byron, he relates, wishing for me to extend my stay in Genoa, accompanied me to view a vacant villa called *Il Paradiso*. While there he requested me to partner him to a masked ball in the character of Eve – yes, Eve, as she appears in the Bible – while he would be Satan. Tom omits my precise response which inspired following lines from the world's most renowned poet:

> *Beneath Blessington's eyes*
> *The reclaimed Paradise*
> *Shall be as free from the former from evil;*
> *But if the new Eve*
> *For an apple should grieve,*
> *What mortal would not play the devil?*

Lord Byron did not publish this romantic rhyme in his lifetime.

Charles had become too submerged in morbid depression to be concerned by his once lover's satire. I had been blinded by Byron's brilliance for less than a week when the shadow of death spread over our two month stay in Genoa. In the small hours of the morning of 5th April 1823 an exhausted courier was admitted to the Alberga Delta Villa. In just eight days he had covered the ground between Edinburgh to Genoa bearing the news of the passing of Luke Wellington Gardiner, third Lord Mountjoy. Charles's anointed heir had died on 26th March, at the precise moment when, in his sleep, he had shouted his son's name. Morning and night Charles sat in silence, never leaving his room. When he spoke at all, it was to bemoan the prophetic nightmare in which I believed that he had seen the ghost of his father.

I understand that I might be considered callous but I felt nothing. I only met the boy twice and could scarcely remember what he looked like. Charles knew him little better than me. I doubt that if all the time he spent with his precious son and heir were added together it would have amounted to more than a day. *'A child who gave promise of every virtue,'* I wrote uncertain of what I meant; 'He never had a bad word for anybody' seemed so inappropriate for a nine-year-old boy. I tried everything I could think of to comfort my bereaved husband. I even tore myself away from Lord Byron once or twice, but after ten days of heavily committed sympathy Charles's affectation of symbolic mourning was becoming intolerable. I offered sound advice.

'You cannot go on sitting there in your black coat looking miserable. You know it will not bring the poor boy back, Charles. You really must take some fresh air. Go out and talk to people. It will take your mind off your tragedy.'

'My poor, poor Luke: he was my only legitimate son, you know. I blame myself. I should never have bestowed the Mountjoy title upon him. It's the curse of the Mountjoys, you see. There is always a portent and then an unpredictable death. It struck down my dear father, my sisters, my brother Luke – he was also only nine, you know, and now my own little Luke. Who will be next?'

I certainly did not hope that it might be the dowager Lady Mountjoy.

'You should not believe such nonsense, Charles. Mr Montgomery forewarned you that the little boy was dying. You told me that the doctors held no hope of Luke reaching maturity. He outlived their expectancy by many months. You must take heart from your good fortune. You have another son in good health.'

'But young Charles is not legitimate, you know. I no longer have an heir. We must go back to Dublin. Little Luke must be given a funeral befitting the last of the Mountjoy line.'

I considered it an insult to the memory of Mary Campbell Browne, three times married in church, to label her children illegitimate. How much more legitimate could they be? It was not in my interests to force such ethical questions upon the bereaved as in the absence of a male heir I was now first in line to the accursed fortune that might be severely dented by Charles's idea of a funeral befitting the last Lord Mountjoy.

'I am so sorry, Charles, but I fear we shall be too late. It is now more than three weeks since Luke passed away, and it will take us two more to reach Dublin. You have no need to concern yourself, your sister and stepmother will undoubtedly have made the necessary arrangements for transporting his coffin for burial at St Thomas's. You said you were thinking of going back to Ireland when we leave Genoa. You will have plenty of time then to visit the Gardiner vault and dedicate a memorial, a stone tablet or something.'

'No, no, my dear Marguerite, it is only right that we go straight to Dublin, you see,' said Charles.

Again he said 'we'.

'But Charles, we cannot possibly let Lord Byron down, after all the trouble he has expended for us? I shall never forgive myself if we leave him now.'

Alfred too had no wish to leave Genoa. He would have cut off his right hand or even soiled a silk waistcoat to please Charles but attending an Irish wake for a boy he had never met was really asking too much. Still less did he wish to risk meeting his future wife. We did all we could to help Charles mourn as effectively as possible, whatever that meant, and managed to persuade him to reluctantly postpone his compassionate journey. He remained disconsolate until my patience was totally exhausted.

'Charles, I really must ask you to be more sociable. It's bad enough having Marianne hovering around like a mute vestal virgin without you wallowing in your misery. What will your dear Noel think?'

His dear Noel thought Lord Blessington *'much tamed since I recollect him in the glory of gems and snuff boxes and uniforms, and theatricals.'* No doubt he also recollected the preposterous poses, passions and pantomimes that I had tolerated through five years of marriage. Charles had long forgotten his loans to the handsome young lord, but to assist his friend at this sad hour, Lord Byron repaid his debt – in his own unique currency. He tortured himself – Lord Byron excelled at torturing himself – by ploughing through five hundred pages of *De Vavaseur*, and as many again of Alfred's *London Journal*. The bedraggled literary genius responded to the former with the utmost tact, a string of clichéd compliments and a non-committal professional opinion. For the latter, his praise was more cautious, suggesting to Alfred that *'by changing the names, or at least omitting several and altering the circumstances indicative of the writer's real situation* [Alfred could make it] *a masterful history of our times.'* Overawed by this high approbation, Alfred entered into a tedious correspondence on the specific merits of his work. Finding Byron's invariably positive responses brief, obscure and too flattering even for his taste, Alfred foolishly put them to the test. He offered to present Byron with his autographed manuscript. The great poet rightly believing that it would be highly embarrassing should it be found in his possession, told Alfred that he could not possibly accept such a valuable document. Alfred took this as a personal affront, burnt his *London Journals* and never again attempted to write for publication. An irredeemable loss to literature.

Alfred's masterpiece was a chronicle of scurrilous revelations, many of which Byron committed to memory. The great romantic enjoyed nothing more than scurrilous revelations. According to Ernest Lovell's scholarly treatise on my *Conversations* we had at least thirty-six mutual male acquaintances. There were a lot more. Byron constantly asked me for personal details of which I was unaware but happy to concoct. But one day he surprised me by mentioning the name of a mutual male acquaintance whose name does not appear on Professor Lovell illustrious list.

'Did you know Curren? He was the most wonderful person I ever saw. In him was combined an imagination the most brilliant and profound with a flexibility and wit that would have justified the observation that his heart was in his head.'

My heart and head unreservedly concurred with Lord Byron's sentiment. Of course I knew John Philpot Curren. How could I ever forget the sublime oratory that simultaneously defended my father from the rapacious Colonel Bagwell, and the rights and freedoms of the world's press? The same rights and freedoms that so many sanctimonious champions of the abused wish to see suppressed to the present day.

'No, Lord Byron, I did not know Mr Curren personally but I have read of his reputation. He is an Irish lawyer, if I am not mistaken.'

I fully understand why the authenticity of my *Conversations of Lord Byron* is still debated. Byron's articulation was so masterful that the responses I cite and my fluent commentary is far superior to my usual literary style. If only I had been able to sustain this use of language, today I would be as famous as he. Well, perhaps not quite so famous.

I was not the only well-read woman in Byron's life but the only one who could match him in knowledge and intellect. Only I could entice him from the seventeenth stanza of *Don Juan* and his obsession with fighting alongside the heroes of Greek mythology. For those two months, our minds and at times our bodies were intertwined. I indeed came to appreciate Byron better than any of his contemporaries. As William Maginn later wrote in the *New Monthly Magazine*: *'Lady Blessington's Conversations of Byron do more to explain and illustrate his mental and moral character than all the "Lives" of him put together.'*

One facet of Lord Byron's mental and moral character that the other lives inadequately explain or illustrate is that he was, as I put it, *'certainly fond of money'*. No one extolled the marriage of my equestrian grace and the magnificent charger Mameluke with greater eloquence than Byron. The poet-adventurer invoked a passionate picture of the noble steed carrying him to be hailed by thousands as the triumphant liberator of the Ionian Isles. Perhaps! Despite his undiminished personal magnetism, Byron was no longer the picture of a dashing hero. Now riding my thoroughbred stallion only served to emphasise his scrawny and premature aging. Yet somehow Byron cajoled me into selling him the cherished Mameluke that Charles had bought as an expression of undying devotion. Defying reason, I asked a hundred guineas, accepted eighty and instantly regretted the decision. That night I noted, with intense restraint: *'How strange to beg and entreat to have the horse resigned to him and then name a price less than he cost!'*

Lord Byron invited us aboard the *Bolivar*, the schooner he had had built for the near impossible purpose of composing poetry while buffeted by the arrhythmic waves of the Ligurian Sea. The boat's seldom-used interior smelled as musty as it was gaudy. The poet's cabin reminded me of his bedroom at the Casa Saluzzo. It was fitted with a solid marble bath which must have weighed half a ton. Lord Byron's knowledge of yachting was sadly lacking. Charles too knew little about yachting but was captivated by the schooner. Envisaging himself completing *de Vavaseur* at the very table stained by the poet's own spilled ink, he offered the outrageous price of three hundred pounds. Dear Noel amiably agreed to four hundred. Charles ordered Captain Mathias Smith, a liability acquired with the *Bolivar*, to carry out all necessary restoration and sail her down to the Bay of Naples and await our arrival. Unwilling to display his ignorance of seafaring convention, he avoided asking Captain Smith to estimate the cost of the work.

On June 2nd 1823, the day of our departure from Genoa, Lord Byron descended from the Apennine Hills to bid us an emotional farewell. I was so moved by this magnanimous gesture that I took a diamond ring from my finger and gave it to him as a keepsake. In return Lord Byron removed a cheap cameo brooch from his coat and pinned it to mine. He said that I would live forever in his heart or some such nonsense. He also brought me five verses composed in my honour, to which he had devoted more than twenty minutes of his invaluable time:

> *You have ask'd for a verse: - the request*
> *In a rhymer 't were strange to deny;*
> *But my Hippocrene was but my breast*
> *And my feelings (its fountain) are dry.*
>
> *Were I now as I was, I had sung*
> *What Lawrence has painted so well;*
> *But the strain would expire on my tongue,*
> *And the theme is too soft for my shell.*

I am ashes where once I was fire,
And the bard in my bosom is dead;
What I loved I now merely admire,
And my heart is as grey as my head.

My life is not dated by years –
There are moments which act as a plough;
And there is not a furrow appears
But is deep in my soul as my brow.

Let the young and the brilliant aspire
To sing what I gaze on in vain;
For sorrow has torn from my lyre
The string which was worthy the strain.

Lord Byron: To the Countess of Blessington (1823)

Byron also gave me his Armenian grammar; apparently an item of great sentimental value. I remain at a loss to understand why he believed that I might wish to learn the obscure tongue of a country I was never likely to visit. Either he thought it was the only language in which I was not fluent or he simply wanted to be rid of an old book.

Just as we about to set off, Lord Byron's butler ran up to my carriage. His lordship had remembered that the pin he had given me was a present from the Contessa Guiccioli and with deep apologies requested its return. As a replacement the messenger brought a silver chain that might have looked well on my maid, though I never saw her wear it. No, Byron, by then almost as rich as my husband, did not return my diamond ring.

'Charles, I know that Lord Byron is one of your oldest friends but do you not think four hundred pounds is excessive for his old schooner. Its restoration will probably cost twice as much. Besides, you have lent Lord Byron a great deal of money which I am sure he can afford to repay. Dare I suggest that you reconsider your purchase?'

'Well, you see, my dear Marguerite, it might be too late. This morning I instructed my banker, Mr Barry, to have a draft delivered to dear Noel.'

'Then send at once and request Mr Barry to stop the payment.'

Incredibly Charles accepted my advice and never again heard from his dear Noel. In less than a year, the life of the Right Honourable George Gordon Noel, Sixth and last Baron Byron, romantic poet and heroic liberator, came to its unremarkable end. The doctors at his post-mortem were unable to identify that the cause of death was an excess of debilitating medicines, unhealthy diets and carnal pleasures.

Perhaps the clearest evidence that I had irredeemably succumbed to the addiction to hypocrisy, for which I was punished until my dying day, are the consecutive ending and beginning of two paragraphs of my journal entry on the day Charles received the news of his son's death:

'… *one would have the air, the clouds, all nature grieve when one is in sorrow and we return from the sunshine with a feeling of reproach at its want of sympathy with us.*'

Rode out today [with Lord Byron] *and found Mameluke as fresh and lively as…*'

14

'This is the greatest delight of my death. You are exactly as when we first met, *ma chère* Marguerite.'

'Alfred, you are late as usual. Are you still trying to make your grand entrances? And look at the size of you. Have you have done nothing but eat since I last saw you? And when did you last change your clothes? They're all worn out and filthy; and for goodness sake, stand up straight.'

'As you see, Marguerite, I neglected my appearance and my deportment and as a result became bloated and suffered an acute disease of the spine.'

'I trust you have not come here for sympathy, Alfred. You could never look after yourself for five minutes at the best of times. Your valet must have had the patience of a saint. Let me introduce Mr Sadleir and Mr Molloy. Dr Madden, you already know. Don't just stand there leaning on that crutch like an advertisement for a disabled charity, sit down and talk to them. Tell them about our relationship that they thought they understood. Excuse me, gentlemen, I've been here for rather a long time. The Wallace Collection toilets are quite luxurious, I am told.'

'How do you do, Comte D'Orsay? I am Michael Sadleir, author of *The Strange Life of Lady Blessington* and *Blessington-D'Orsay: A Masquerade*. But before you say another word, sir, I agree, my second version was a bigger mistake than my first. My publishers thought they could resurrect the old gift book market and made me over-simplify Lady Blessington's biography and add a lot of sepia tints to give a feeling of times past, I suppose. Then in 1983 another publisher celebrated a half-century of disinterest by reviving *Masquerade* in a pretty pink and green box. How nice! That did not sell either.'

'But Monsieur Sadleir, you are too modest. You were perfectly correct. Our relationship was nothing if not a masquerade. But did you, or any of you, guess what was behind the masques?'

My three biographers look to one another for guidance. They are as confused as they were when they attempted to elucidate Comte D'Orsay's sexual propensities.'

'I am sure I did,' says R R Madden. 'We met on a number of occasions while we were alive. It seemed obvious to me what sort of man you were but feel free to correct what you imagine are our misconceptions, Comte D'Orsay.'

'I am sorry to disappoint you, messieurs. Lord and Lady Blessington and I were simply people of our times. In fact, we epitomised our times to such perfection that we caused envy wherever we went.'

'But, Comte D'Orsay, you and Lady Blessington could not have come from more opposing backgrounds,' says J Fitzgerald Molloy.

Alfred mimes the removal of a mask from his once angelic face to reveal the ugliness of his over-exposed features.

'Think again, Monsieur Molloy. The only difference between the families of General Albert 'Beau' D'Orsay and Edmond 'Beau' Power was class.'

'You were obsessed with class.'

'I taught Lady Blessington its conventions and niceties and she taught me that class is synonymous with money, and that neither respects the other. As the Countess said herself: *"Money is the direct or indirect cause of nearly all crimes: by the possession of it the rich are able to commit them and through the want of it the poor are excited into the adoption of a similar course".*'

'Are you saying that you were a criminal?'

'*Bien sûr*, but I confess to nothing.'

'If you will not confess, then perhaps you will explain, Comte D'Orsay?'

Alfred is unable to explain and so confesses.

'From earliest childhood I was applauded every day and told that I was destined for greatness. People stood in awe of my intelligence, my talents, my suave demeanour, my good looks and athletic physique. I accomplished so much and so easily that I thought I could defy the laws of gravity. I developed a gargantuan ego which I retained until too late I understood that it pivoted on an inverted pyramid of crime. When the great criminal Napoleon died, my father's wealth and honour died with him yet he and my family remained French aristocrats by virtue of the bounty of the British Empire, misappropriated in India by my grandfather, the revered Quintin Craufurd and his temptress wife.

Lord Blessington adhered to tradition and was proud to be an Englishman of his time, whatever that meant. Yes, I accepted his generosity but also appreciated his finer qualities. He loved me because he saw me as the man he might have been had he not been crushed under his own father's abominations. His criminal wealth played upon Lord Blessington's conscience until the day he died.

His extraordinary will was not, as you gentlemen seem to think, full of ill-considered blunders. He never said so, but Lady Blessington bitterly disappointed him by her behaviour with Lord Byron and her failure to share his grief when he lost his heir. So he pinned his hopes on me. Only I did not prove a disappointment to him in his lifetime.'

'But you were an idler, a reckless gambler and a spendthrift, Comte D'Orsay.'

'I came to England in protest against the Bourbon regime, with my bag full of illegal money and introductions to the richest and noblest. I was embraced everywhere by parents who saw me as the ideal match for their daughters. I was not disinclined to marriage or even to following a mundane career but was too easily seduced by the English social scene: hunts, shoots, horse races, gentlemen's clubs, parties and balls. I became a dandy: the living artwork that my friend Jules Barbey d'Aurevilly enigmatically explained so thoroughly in his study of that Regency phenomenon. I was not just any dandy. I was the dandy of dandies, as impossible to ignore as a circus clown. The English nobility bowed to my wit, my charm and above all my bravado. They gasped at my sang-froid when I staked a fortune on an unskilled card game and the queen of spades raised her fatal head. They laughed when I said that I always won. But I always did; not money of course but a treasury of blind admirers. My greatest prizes were Lord and Lady Blessington. They too were living artworks who, with me, portrayed the image of our times. Unlike most of the French and English nobility they were decent and law-abiding people. They were the honourable family I never had. I loved them both, not simply for sexual gratification, but because they were the parents I never had. And they loved me as the son they never had.'

--

CODICIL

To the Will of Charles John Gardiner, Earl of Blessington

Made at Genoa, 2nd June 1823

Having had the misfortune to lose my beloved son, Luke Wellington, and having entered into engagements with Alfred, Comte d'Orsay that an alliance should take place between him and my daughter, which engagement has been sanctioned by Albert, Comte d'Orsay, General, etc. in the service of France, this is to declare and publish my desire to leave to the said Alfred D'Orsay my estates in the city and county of Dublin (subject, however, to the annuity of three thousand pounds per annum, which sum is to include the settlement of one thousand per annum to my wife, Marguerite, Countess of Blessington, (subject to that portion of debt, whether by annuity or mortgage to which my executor and trustee, Luke Norman, shall consider them to be subjected), for his and her use, whether it be Mary (baptised Emily) Rosalie Hamilton or Harriet Anne Jane Frances, and their heirs male or to the said Alfred and said Mary, or Harriet, for ever in default of issue male, to follow the provisions of the will and testament.

I make also the said Alfred d'Orsay sole guardian of my son Charles John and my sister, Harriet Gardiner, guardian of my daughters, until they, the daughters, arrive at the age of sixteen, at which age I consider they will be marriageable.

I also bequeath to Luke Norman my estates in the county of Tyrone, etc., in trust for my son, Charles John, who I desire to take the name of Stewart Gardiner, until he should arrive at the age of twenty-five, allowing for his education such sums as Alfred d'Orsay may think necessary, and one thousand pounds per annum from twenty-one to twenty-five.

Done at Genoa, life being uncertain, at eight o'clock, on the morning of Monday, June the second, one thousand eight hundred and twenty-three

Blessington

'You do have this perfectly clear, gentlemen?'

--

'Poor Byron, I will not allow myself to think that we have met for the last time; although he has infected us all with his superstitious forebodings.'

Charles was the most deeply infected of us all by his superstitious forebodings. These, added to the loss of his son had made him so melancholy and lethargic that he had not even stirred from his bed to greet Lord Byron when he came bearing gifts to bid us farewell – or so I thought. I asked the doorman to fetch him from his room and was told that Lord Blessington had left the hotel at six in the morning and been driven to Mr Barry's house. What possessed Charles visit his banker at that hour? He seldom rose before midday and we had not planned to set off until the afternoon.

I had been married to Charles for over five years, yet at times he was a perfect stranger. He was an actor, and it was all too easy for me to forget that he was perpetually acting. I had long ceased trying to separate his emotions from his improvisations, but I knew clearly enough that my inability to mourn with him over little Luke's inevitable death and my refusal to leave Byron had incurred his wrath. I justified myself with the false premise that Charles himself had lured me into a realm of delusion, where money rules and the laws of decency and morality bow to the whims of the nobility. This was a poor defence. Nothing in this world is as it seems, it is as we would wish it to seem.

In the morning twilight of our last day in Genoa, Charles John Gardiner, Earl of Blessington dictated the insane codicil destined to shape the rest of my life. His banker witnessed the document and despatched the original to Mr Powell's office in London. My husband's last will and testament was carved in granite. No duplicate was made for me but Alfred showed me his, unappreciative of its horrible implications.

'This is wonderful news, Alfred. You must be elated. Lord Blessington has confirmed his desire for you to choose one of his daughters as your bride?'

'There is no question of choice, ma chère Marguerite. I am a D'Orsay. I cannot dishonour my family name by marrying an illegitimate woman. What does it say the legitimate one is called, Lady Harriet or some such? I intend to marry her.'

'How magnanimous of you, Alfred, but have you considered the possibility that Lady Harriet might object to marrying you?'

'No. The lady who would object to marrying me has not yet been born. You would marry me yourself if you were free, *ma chère* Marguerite. What do think of these kid gloves? A fellow in Genoa made me a dozen pairs in different tints of blue and grey.'

Alfred believed untold or at least uncounted wealth to be his God-given right. He did not regard it as in any way extraordinary that he had been created the effectual heir to the Blessington fortune. It was already at his disposal and he saw no pressing reason to be concerned about his future. Charles would probably live another three or four decades, while Lady Harriet had just turned eleven and thus would be ineligible for marriage for five years. I remained outwardly unperturbed and inwardly enraged. Despite this impetuous attempt at cushioned posthumous vengeance, I was sure that my husband still loved me.

And if he did not, I was equally sure that he would never risk the scandal of a separation. I gritted my teeth and resigned myself to the status quo but only until I had persuaded Charles to amend his will.

Before turning south to join Captain Smith and the *Bolivar* in Naples we made an essential diversion to explore *Reginald de Vavaseur's* exploits in Tuscany. The fourteenth-century adventurer's itinerary still ran parallel with my own interests. The ancient city of Lucca was a miniature Paris, brimming with energy by day, aglow with gaiety by night and perpetually darkened by a mysterious past. It was the birthplace of Madame Craufurd.

In a casual endeavour to explore a less exalted aspect of his family history, Alfred found his way to a bustling Jewish quarter filled with tailors and bootmakers of every description. None of them knew of his grandmother's family or of anybody called Franchi, but they all knew an extravagant customer when they saw one. They measured Alfred for four pairs of custom-made boots, six double-breasted tailcoats, a dozen embroidered waistcoats and a tweed greatcoat for the sweltering heat of the Italian summer.

The outstanding natural beauty of Tuscany has received the accolade of every travelogue ever written, except *The Idler in Italy*. The road from Sienna to Florence, they imply, undulates through a tapestry of lush olive groves and vineyards serenaded by martins and nightingales. The panoramic landscape of green and gold which has inspired poets and painters since the ancient Romans I, more honestly, describe simply as *'tedious'*. When we reached Florence on the 8th June, the first English person to whom I presented my visiting card was Lady Sarah Burghersh, wife of the British ambassador and daughter of the banker Sir Robert Child. Her ladyship was indisposed. The cause of her unprecedented ailment was her husband's sister, the revered Lady Jersey, queen of Almack's who had courteously warned her of my arrival.

While in Florence I caught only a single glimpse of Lady Burghersh driving past me in an elegant white calèche with green and crimson wheels. The beautiful vehicle created a more favourable impression than its occupant, whose back was unintentionally turned. Regardless of Lady Burghersh, the city was an overdose of opiate to feed my urban addiction. For three weeks I gorged myself on its compendium of culture and expounded its history and the merits of the Florentine galleries, cathedrals, monuments and libraries for the benefit of Marianne. She was overwhelmed with indifference.

In Rome, I dragged my sister through another fortnight of fascinating lectures on the lost civilisation. The treasures of the Eternal City even encouraged Charles to add a few more pages to *de Vavaseur*, while Alfred, when not modelling for the edification of the local dandies, said that he won extraordinary sums at the type of clubs where he would never be seen in London or Paris. I am uncertain how they occupied the rest of their time.

We reached Naples on 17th July 1823. The Gran Bretagna was commended to us as the city's finest hotel: a reputation its proprietor took little pride in preserving.

'Dr Madden, since you had not yet met me at that time, may I ask why you took such a judgmental attitude to my reaction to that dreadful hotel? Do you remember what you wrote?'

'Her Ladyship had become exceedingly fastidious in her tastes. The difficulties in pleasing her in house accommodation, in dress, in cookery especially, had become so formidable and occasioned so many inconveniences ...'

'Was I not right, your ladyship?'

'For once, Dr Madden, you were right. I had become far too blasé, which I suppose was another reason for Charles's vicious codicil.'

If little else, the best room in the Gran Bretagna boasted a breath-taking view from five hundred feet above the Bay of Naples which, like the Tuscan landscape, I considered tedious. Through my diamond-encrusted spyglass I could clearly see the *Bolivar* among more functional vessels becalmed in the historic harbour below. My lens was however too weak to show me the exorbitant restoration that Captain Smith had completed at Charles's request.

These imperceptible improvements inspired Charles to learn the art of sailing on weeklong cruises in the Tyrrhenian Sea, to which Alfred, Marianne and I were invited to share the experience. We all declined. I was unprepared to exchange my comfortless bed at the Gran Bretagna for Byron's monstrous couch on the *Bolivar*. Marianne did not wish to be exposed to the obscenities of a male crew and Alfred, a soldier not a sailor, advised Charles that training is more rewarding when undistracted.

On dry land, I explored the Kingdom of Naples's fascinating history of unmitigated overindulgence. The city-state ruled by King Ferdinand I had been reconstituted as one of 'The Two Sicilies'. It was an earthly paradise. The health-giving properties of the dry summer heat attracted distinguished Europeans in their numbers, who brought a profusion of wealth, vitality and a modest measure of constructive industry.

We were weighed down with invitations from the Neapolitan elite. Here was a city completely untainted by my past. In Naples I was indisputably the Countess of Blessington and treated with befitting courtesy. Charles too was enamoured of the city and agreed to suspend our travels. We encountered little difficulty in locating a suitable residence. Among the first Neapolitan nobles to present his compliments was a certain Prince Belvedere. This amiable scholar, through piety and diligence, as opposed to family connections, was celebrated as one of the youngest men ever to be ordained a cardinal. His ecclesiastic career had however sadly been prematurely aborted on inheriting an inconsequential royal title, a diminished family fortune and the estate known as Palazzo Belvedere. The cardinal piously donated half his inheritance to the Pope, whereupon he was permitted to relinquish his celibate office and marry his long-standing mistress. Burdened with an unaffordable palace and no further source of income, the Prince discovered that it was a short step from the passion of the pulpit to the loquacity of the landlord.

'You will find the Palazzo Belvedere among the finest examples of Italianate architecture in the kingdom. I understand, Lord and Lady Blessington, that you are learned in the arts and will thus share my devotion to the many works my forebears have acquired and conserved since they built the house in 1670. In recent times its cultural ambience been favoured by everyone from foreign dignitaries to royalty. Maria Carolina, Queen of Naples spent her last six summers here. She particularly loved the gardens, where Lady Blessington will find a unique collection of exotic tropical specimens. The ground floor has five grand salons, a billiard room and a dining room for forty guests. On the first floor you will find some twenty spacious bedrooms, all commanding unparalleled views of the city and the Bay. There are also servants' quarters I am told.'

An observant tourist might today spot the remains of the historic palazzo sandwiched between the apartment blocks in the residential suburb of Vomero.

Charles agreed to the onerous lease drawn up by the prince's lawyer, who conveniently acted for both parties; conflict of interest being a yet unknown concept in the Kingdom of the Two Sicilies.

Our carriage was driven into the palazzo through a pair of gilt-emblazoned gates, well not quite a pair – one had fallen off its hinges – via an avenue lined irregularly with slim cupressus pines, some of which appeared to be quite healthy. We drew up in a stately if unkempt gravelled courtyard. At the front of the house five paved terraces with broken balustrades spanned the width of the building and swept down to the semi-tropical gardens about which the Prince had so enthused. Even from the top terrace the overgrown plants obscured most of the unparalleled view of the city and Bay. The Prince had explained that all his tenants desired that the estate be preserved as it was when Queen Maria Carolina, consort of King Ferdinand and sister of Marie Antoinette had holidayed there. The nostalgic landlord had therefore carried out no maintenance whatsoever since the queen died ten years earlier.

This neglected palace could have been the Italian backdrop to a Shakespeare comedy. All it required was a small army of skilled artisans and labourers to correct its handsome imperfections. I had the ornamental gazebos, sculptures, and fountains cleaned and the gates repaired. I replaced the prince's worn out furniture with fashionable designs and had his overgrown prize botanical specimens severely pruned. This was a mistake.

The re-blossoming of the baroque perennial revived Charles's deluded visions for the future of the Cottage at Mountjoy Forest. He asked me if I could remember what had happened to Wyatt's plans. When I replied that they were stored away safely at St James's Square he said that he would go immediately and find them. He could of course have saved himself a great deal of trouble by sending a courier but he was yearning to be back in London and to visit his son's grave in Dublin. It was quite impossible that he wanted to get away from me for a while, I was greatly distressed. Charles would be gone for several months, which was particularly upsetting as the Palazzo Belvedere seemed the ideal place for me to convince him of the error of his will. More optimistically, his absence would permit me to complete my refurbishments with no interference except from Alfred, whose captivating knowledge of the aesthetics of a noble continental home I would have all to myself.

When he arrived in London, Charles found St James's Square desolate and empty apart from half a dozen servants and caretakers. To enliven the atmosphere, he invited his former best man Charles Mathews to join him at dinner. The great comedian, now at the pinnacle of his career, an impresario and half-owner of the Adelphi Theatre, brought his son Charles James and the three Charles's enjoyed an evening of riotous hilarity, mainly in homage to their mutual Christian name.

To avoid confusion, I will from here on refer to Charles James Mathews simply as Mathews, which in fact was how we always addressed him.

The twenty-year-old Mathews, almost as handsome as Alfred, told Charles that he was studying architecture as an apprentice to Auguste Pugin. This greatly impressed Charles who knew Pugin's work on Regent Street and the Regent's Park terraces in co-operation with Nash. Mathews was working with Pugin's son, who he considered more talented than his principal. Indeed, Augustus Welby Pugin was to become the most venerated architect of his time, remembered for his majestic interior of the Palace of Westminster. Mathews in reality was an architect of limited talent who had learnt little from the Pugins, father or son.

'Mathews, might I take advantage of your professional expertise? You see, I have the little Cottage over in Ireland which I have been thinking of extending. I had Benjamin Wyatt draw up some plans a while ago, you know. I would be most grateful, if you would care to glance over them and let me have your opinion.'

The caretaker in charge of the storeroom, who had failed to burn the plans with the other extraneous rubbish as I had requested, laid them out on the long dining table for Mathews to inspect.

'Fancy old Ben Wyatt having a sense of humour; a medieval castle in the middle of a wood in County Tyrone, you would have to be…' The elder Mathews made a slight downward movement of the middle finger of his left hand, a well-known secret theatrical cue. '…a great visionary to appreciate how a structure of this magnitude will enhance the landscape.'

'Exactly, Mathews, that's it. It's so important to enhance the landscape, you see. But Wyatt is inflexible, you know. He is too concerned with the appearance and practical amenities – light and space and so on. He never pays enough attention to the outlook, you see.'

'You are absolutely right, your lordship. That's the trouble with Wyatt's generation; they never pay enough attention to the outlook. The modern architect plans the outlook first and *then* perfects the picture with his building. It works every time, Lord Blessington.'

Charles Mathews senior later wrote one of his funniest sketches based on this spontaneous inspiration.

'That's the point, you know. You're exactly what I need, a young man with modern ideas.'

He turned to the older comedian. 'Look, Charles, I have some business to attend to while I'm in London but in a day or two I shall be going over to Dublin and then up to Mountjoy Forest, you see. Would you raise any objection to your son coming over and taking a look at the little place?'

The following day, Charles — that is, my husband — called on Lord Donoughmore unwittingly for the last time. Another Catholic emancipation bill was due to be debated and he wished to entrust his old friend with a proxy to vote in the House of Lords. Both were conscientiously in favour of the bill which, like its numerous predecessors, was defeated.

Then he kept an appointment with John Allen Powell, who formally redrafted his will and provided the necessary copies for him to take to Ireland. On 31st August 1823 Charles John Gardiner, Earl of Blessington's Last Will and Testament was registered at the Irish court in Dublin. Its provisions were in line with the Genoa codicil with a few added conditions and bequests, in complex and incomprehensible legal terminology which clarified Charles's intentions perfectly.

'I give to my daughter, Harriet Anne Jane Frances, commonly called Lady Harriet... all my estates in the county and city of Dublin, subject to the following charge. Provided she intermarry with my friend and intended son-in-law, Alfred D'Orsay, I bequeath her the sum of ten thousand pounds.

I give to my daughter Emily Rosalie Hamilton, generally called Lady Mary Gardiner... the sum of twenty thousand pounds... [But] In case the said Alfred D'Orsay intermarries with the said Emily I bequeath to her my estates county and city of Dublin ...

I give to my son Charles John, all my estates in the county of Tyrone, subject to...'

Charles's Dublin properties were worth ten times more than his estates in County Tyrone which his son would inherit at the age of twenty-five.

The annuity bequeathed to the testator's *beloved* wife was reduced from £3,000 to £2,000. I was to inherit the lease of 10 St James's Square but on its termination the contents were to be transported to the Cottage at Mountjoy Forest. I was also to receive Charles's *'carriages, paraphernalia and plate'* and be permitted to keep the jewellery he had given me, provided I returned to his daughters any which had belonged to his first wife. How could he imagine that I would dream of doing otherwise?

The Earl of Blessington's last will and testament, like the now discarded codicil, implied that Alfred had a free choice of bride, but since the higher legacy was to go to the supposed illegitimate Emily provided she did *not* marry him, it was clear that Charles intended that Alfred should marry Lady Harriet.

Characteristically, Charles added the settlement of some debts of conscience. He left Marianne and Robert Power £1000 each. Charles had always appreciated Marianne's simple deference but his posthumous recompense to Robert could only have been motivated by conscience. Charles's sister, Harriet, was to receive an annuity of just £500 but the will made no mention whatsoever of the dowager Lady Mountjoy. Possibly this was an oversight, since Charles never openly subscribed to my suspicions of his stepmother, who since being disinherited herself had always lived and continued to live in a style befitting the widow of a viscount.

Having completed his business in London, Charles left for Dublin, where he very properly performed his duty as a Christian father; removing his hat and silently bowing his head before the as yet unmarked resting place of his lost heir apparent, for almost a minute. He then met Luke Norman, and received his bi-annual report. Despite the excellent agent's neatest numerical embroidery his results were so poor, that any other employer might have dismissed him there and then. Charles however thanked Mr Norman for all his hard work, shook his hand warmly and informed him that he had been named as one of his executors. At Henrietta Street, Charles briefly paid his respects to his stepmother and sister, gave presents to his three surviving children and forgot to tell his daughters that one of them was engaged to be married. Finally, before moving on to Mountjoy Forest, he wrote to Charles Mathews senior offering his son *'the opportunity of making his debut as an architect'*. According to Mathew's *Chiefly Autobiographical Life – 'Father jumped at the idea and I jumped twice as high as Father, for my heart bounded as well as my heels.'*

After describing a journey to Mountjoy Forest so horrific it is remarkable that he arrived at all, the mediocre apprentice informed his proud parents:

'For a couple of months, I led a charmed life; the pleasant task of planning and surveying my fairy palace was not my only resource. Stag hunting, rabbit shooting, fishing and sightseeing formed not the least part of the severe duties I had to perform... I was shrewd enough to discover that my chief charm lay in my acquiescence with his [Lord Blessington's] whims and patience with his vacillations... The fact is that he wanted to design the mansion and suggest all the arrangements, and only required someone to put his ideas into shape... I was just the person for him.'

Mathews was not simply talking about drawing. Charles insisted on a more practical approach. He instructed his keen young architect to cut furrows into the turf in the shape of the three-hundred-foot wide extension and pile stones to a height of six feet at the location of each window. Both then climbed onto the piles one by one and surveyed the outlook. Mathews again wrote to his parents:

'I was not able to get a view of certain pieces of river and a stone bridge which I had calculated upon... However all difficulties are instantly removed here, and I am going to set them to work to turn the course of the river by which means we shall get the most beautiful view imaginable. On the other side is a mountain, which is very much in our way, so orders are given to shave it all away. A whole plantation is already cut down, and a large bare mountain, very disagreeable to have staring us in the face, is to be planted with firs and larch, for which 150,000 are already moved to the spot. Are these not grand doings?'

Mathews was possibly a little prone to exaggeration.

Meanwhile I too was immersed in grand doings at the Palazzo Belvedere. Having completed my refurbishment, I recruited and trained a complement of Italian servants to entertain the cream of Neapolitan nobility - including royalty - to the standards expected of an English household. This caused a minor difficulty since the male servants insisted on wearing large gold earrings, apparently of some significance to their primitive national tradition. As always I was tolerant of idiosyncrasies but incurred some discontent by demanding that the men remove all jewellery before it offended my guests. I raised no objection to them wearing their hideous earrings in private, if they so wished.

Among those to whom I was introduced while Charles away was Sir William Gell, England's most eminent classical scholar and Chamberlain to the late Queen Maria Carolina. Gell, an eccentric bachelor who spent most of his year in Naples, was researching his immortal and largely forgotten masterwork, *Pompeiana: The Topography, Edifices and Ornaments of Pompeii*. Both Byron and Tom Moore had commended him to me as a kindred spirit and I was not disappointed. Sir William was disappointed. He was unaccustomed to dealing with women, and my ready comprehension of his work annoyed him immensely.

Carried in a sedan chair due to his severe gout, Sir William conducted me, Alfred and Marianne on a tour of the archaeological excavations at Pompeii. He lectured us zealously through the window, defying the calendar and transforming us into live denizens of the ancient town. We dwelt in its villas, walked in its streets, engaged in its politics, trade and culture until we felt the pain of being consumed by the white-hot lava flowing from Vesuvius. We were all greatly relieved when we discovered that we had survived the boring lecture.

By early September 1823, Mathews had completed fifty-five different sets of plans for the Cottage extension and Charles had approved none of them.

'Your ideas are most original, you know, Mathews, but they are too modern, you see. Take another look at Wyatt's work. He's older and more experienced, you know.'

Finally, the younger and less experienced Mathews presented a drawing which more or less complied with his client's own concepts. The outlook in every direction was a work of art and the Cottage a larger replica of Wyatt's original plan, incorporating less amenities. Mathews knew enough about architecture to realise that such a structure would be impossible to build.

'Lord Blessington, you mentioned that her ladyship has remarkable aesthetic taste. Dare I suggest that you return to Naples, and obtain Lady Blessington's approval before we lay the foundations? Meanwhile I shall to go back to London and find the most accomplished builders and craftsmen to come over and complete the project for you.'

'You are quite right, Mathews, my wife has a natural talent for the decoration of interiors, you know. And we have a young artist called Comte D'Orsay staying with us, I would like to take his advice too, you see. Make another copy of each of your drawings for me to show them and when I return, you can come back here from London and make the revisions they suggest, you see. Then I shall take your amended designs back to Naples, obtain Lady Blessington and D'Orsay's final approval, return them to you and we are ready to start building, you know.'

Mathews estimated that this would take about two years.

'Lord Blessington, would it not be a little quicker if I were to accompany you to Naples, just taking the draft which most pleases you. Then we could show it to Lady Blessington and Comte D'Orsay, make the changes they suggest on the spot and you can all approve the final plan at the same time.'

'That's a splendid idea, Mathews. I really do like your sensible approach, you know.'

'Thank you so very much, Lord Blessington. It has always been my ambition to see Naples. I am told it has some of the finest architecture in Europe, but you will understand that I feel obliged to obtain my parents' consent before going away for so long.'

'That is absolutely right, Mathews, you know. I am going to London myself next week in order to see your father about a new production he has asked me to finance at the Adelphi. I shall take the opportunity to speak to him then.'

Charles Mathews senior brought his wife Anne, herself an acclaimed actress, to dinner at St James's Square. Both put on a dramatic show of unfelt enthusiasm and agreed that the experience abroad would be a great boon to their son's career. Having secured his wholehearted suspicious parental consent, on 21st September 1823 the young architect set off for Naples together with his employer.

Mathews had with him a letter addressed to me from his mother. I am uncertain of exactly what the fond Mrs Mathews expected, but I replied assuring her that Lord Blessington never permitted anyone to be led into temptation beneath his roof. I would attend to his every need, while Alfred, who was a similar age to Mathews, would make an amiable companion. No man of any age made a more amiable companion than the Comte D'Orsay. Thereafter Mrs Mathews wrote to me every week expressing her anxieties to which I invariably responded with insincere reassurance and considerate omission of intimate detail. As an actress Anne Mathews had lived a far from sheltered existence and thus disbelieved every word I wrote. We became lifelong correspondents.

She later published an outstanding biography of her husband, also appropriately purged.

Keen to impress Charles with his limited knowledge of Continental architecture, Mathews suggested an instructive route through France and Switzerland. Many years later, after wisely abandoning the drawing boards for the theatrical boards, Charles James Mathews, actor, comedian and playwright, recounted the hilarious detail of this educational detour in his autobiography. On 30th September stopping at, as Mathews was to put it, *a fashionable bad inn* outside Geneva the travellers were surprised to come across the Speaker of the House of Commons and his wife. Mrs Manners-Sutton transpired to be my sister, Ellen, endeavouring to deny the press its right to exaggerate the significance of the son of the Archbishop of Canterbury sharing a continental hotel room with a married woman of Catholic extraction. Manner-Sutton was a perfectly respectable widower, simply enjoying a relaxing break from his heavy commitments, together with Ellen, her now four children, his two sons, a governess and a nursemaid.

Ellen's marriage had finally broken down. It was miraculous that it survived so long given that Hume Purves had received less than magnanimous compensation for acknowledging her children as his own. Rather than risk pleading that he was the injured party in a contested divorce, the dour aristocratic Scot had accepted an appointment as British Consul to Florida and Ellen very properly refused to expose her children to the disease-ridden climate of an uncivilised American backwater.

Charles of course knew the Speaker well. They had met many times at Westminster.

'Good to see you again, Sutton. I think the last time we saw one another was when you came over to the Lords for the King's speech, you know. Are you still Speaker?'

'Indeed I am, Blessington, but one of these days you will be seeing me in the other place. Every Speaker is assured of a peerage but, I fear, little else. Frankly, I have held the post for too long but I am in no position to resign. And, as you see, the number of my dependants has somewhat grown recently.'

'Yes, I see. I imagine the Speaker's House must be quite crowded, you know.'

'No, not at present: I live there only with my sons. You will understand that some MPs tend to be a little self-righteous and might consider Ellen and her children living at my official residence an abuse of privilege. I shall have to find somewhere to accommodate us all when we get back. The trouble is, Blessington, the larger residences in London are all well beyond my reach.'

'You know, Sutton, I think I might have just the solution for you. Ellen always loved staying with Lady Blessington at St James's Square. Well, you see, the house is vacant at the moment. It needs to be occupied, you know. We would be delighted if you would look after it for us, just while you sort out your affairs, you see.'

'Thank you, Blessington, but as I said, my salary would never stretch to such a splendid house.'

'Good heavens, Sutton, you are almost a member of the family now, you know. There will be no question of rent.'

Charles thought it would be a charming surprise for me, if Ellen and Manners-Sutton were to accompany him back to the Palazzo Belvedere. They readily agreed, but before reaching Milan the liberal-minded speaker and his mistress concluded – I cannot imagine on what basis – that my household was inappropriate for their well-brought-up children. Apparently they misinterpreted Mathews's excessive interest in Ellen's pretty daughter Louisa, then aged thirteen.

'Sorry, Blessington, we have to turn back. These hired horses really cannot cope with the mountain passes but we are most grateful for your offer of St James's Square. We shall move in immediately we get back. Do feel free to call on us whenever you are in London.'

For the next two-and-a-half years Charles Manners-Sutton, Ellen and their six children all lived happily together at 10 St James's Square. That is, I think they all lived happily.

Charles and Mathews arrived at the Palazzo Belvedere in early December 1823. I was naturally devastated at having been denied the chance to see Ellen again but the handsome young architect proved as adept at helping me get over my disappointment as at adapting to his new surroundings. He described the Palazzo, with the benefits of my opulent improvement, as:

'The perfection of an Italian palace, with its exquisite frescoes, marble arcades, succession of terraces one beneath the other, adorned with hanging groves of orange trees and pomegranates.'

Alfred he portrayed as:

'The perfection of a youthful nobleman; the best fencer, dancer, swimmer, runner, dresser, shot, horseman and even draughtsman I have ever seen.'

Mathews was as witty and gregarious as Alfred. They took an immediate dislike to one another. Alfred did not make friends; he collected admirers, disregarding gender but not class. For that reason alone, I am confident that there were no improper relationships between the young men, or involving Charles, though the delicacy of my nature prohibited me from making undue inquiries. The men were all invariably courteous to Marianne who displayed no interest in relationships improper or otherwise. Charles's only desire was for us to all be content. It was in none of our interests to question his definition of contentment.

'In seeking happiness we overlook content, which is always attainable, while happiness, though sometimes in view, is never within reach.'

Mathews laid out his latest plans for the Cottage on the polished mahogany of Prince Belvedere's refractory table. They were grander than Benjamin Wyatt at his worst. Not daring to think about the fifty-four rejected versions, I slowly raised my eyes to the restored plaster relief and Mathews returned to his geometrical implements to amend his designs for my further disapproval. Mountjoy Forest was never to be graced by a monumental mansion, and the outlook from its marked-out location destined forever to remain as conceived by nature, more or less.

Mathews was not a good architect. He was a good comedian, and like all good comedians was no fool. He fully appreciated that he had not been brought to Naples simply to draw fantasy castles. Like the jesters of old, his function was to amuse Charles, Alfred, me and even Marianne when, and in such manner as we deemed appropriate. He never complained. Who would complain at an overpaid sinecure in the luxury of a palace in the enduring warmth of the Neapolitan sun?

The warmth of the Neapolitan sun did not endure. In striving for excellence I had overlooked one insignificant practicality – keeping the house warm. With the onset of winter, the heavy draperies I had installed were defenceless against the refreshing sea breezes that scaled the cliffs, pervaded the Palazzo's gargantuan reception rooms and caused Charles untenable discomfort.

'My dear Marguerite, this morning I had to cut my own hair, you know. The wretched Italian barber with the gold earrings said he couldn't shave me unless I removed my cravat. But, you see, had I done so, I might have caught my death of cold. How many people have you invited for Christmas and the New Year? We really cannot have them all freeze to death, you know.'

Among those invited to freeze in the festive season was our landlord, ex-cardinal Prince Belvedere who brought his glamorous princess.

'You must accept my humble apologies, Lord Blessington, I should have mentioned that the old chimneys have been blocked for years. Being from England, I presumed you would find our winters comparatively temperate. But do not concern yourself, sir, I shall see that they are cleared immediately. Oh, I would like to take this opportunity to tell you that the princess and I greatly appreciate Lady Blessington's authentic redecorations. The late Queen Carolina would have approved unreservedly.'

Prince Belvedere did not see that the chimneys were cleared immediately or at any other time. He, like all our guests, did not feel the cold because Charles had fifty braziers installed and employed eight local labourers to keep them stoked by day and night. Cinderella's prince kept his palace warm with love, I suppose.

Regardless of the temperature, the Palazzo was the perfect venue for pretentious hospitality; a continental St James's Square, except in Naples my invitations were accepted by both genders and often courteously returned. As in Paris, the Neapolitan ladies displayed more kindness and grace than the ladies of London whose affectionate memories of me remained as belligerent as ever. As one observant Contessa asked me:

'Why do English people tell such ill-natured stories of each other? They relate such tales with spiteful pleasure. If founded in truth, they ought, from a patriotic feeling, be concealed.'

Indeed they ought, but even in Naples the open ghetto of English socialites did not consider itself obliged by patriotic or any other feeling to conceal their spiteful pleasure. One lady insisted on referring to me as the Countess of Cursington, an astutely ignorant play on my married name which did not translate well into Italian. I never cursed anybody in my life, and if I did, it was the least they deserved. I generally avoided these envious British fugitives and ensured that the pleasures of the Palazzo were neither spiteful nor unpatriotic. On two or three evenings each week, we held dinner parties, receptions, balls and a variety of other entertainments, filling the house with noble Italians attracted by my, Alfred and Mathews's conviviality and Charles's generosity – especially the latter. Often uncertain of exactly where Ireland lay on the map, some also enthralled Marianne with stilted conversation and I believe she picked up a word two of their language. No, I never heard her speak Italian.

Mathews's youthful enthusiasm revived Charles's love of the theatre. The Palazzo's wide marble staircase spread down into the grand hall like the setting for a classical opera and served as an almost credible stage. The bewildered Italians, who of course loved the classical opera, encountered little difficulty in appreciating the champagne reception that followed the light-hearted charades, pantomimes and comedies in which Mathews directed us all to act - with some guidance from Charles. Mathews was a master of improvisation. Comedy was in his blood. With deadly accuracy he mimicked us, our visitors, local personalities and international celebrities: George IV, Wellington, Napoleon, Talleyrand, Louis XVIII. He even did female impressions: Marie Antoinette and the Empress Josephine. He and Alfred reduced me to nauseating laughter with a devastating duet of impersonations of the social graces of Lady Holland and Lady Jersey.

'We never respect those who amuse us, however we may smile at their comic powers. A considerable distinction exists between the amusing and the entertaining man. We laugh with one but reflect with the other.'

Entitling my record of these events *The Idler in Italy* was a poor test of my own comic powers. I was never idle in Italy. I managed *my* noble estate, instructed *my* servants, received *my* visitors, pursued *my* studies and corresponded with *my* friends in England and *my* brother and father in Ireland. I devoted the remainder *my* time to interpreting Charles's notes – his handwriting was immaculate – and transmuting them into a readable novel: a Herculean labour of love and a Lilliputian step towards a revision of his will in *my* favour.

In spring the Neapolitan sun again blazed upon the bizarre botany of the Palazzo Belvedere and I took to working in the airless tranquillity of its ornamental gardens, disturbed only by the rustle of tropical foliage gently swaying in the warm sea breeze, and the roaring of lions and trumpeting of elephants imprisoned in a nearby private zoo. As I penned my picturesque portraits of the diverse peoples of Naples - mostly too factual for publication - amidst the wonders of nature, my love of the city intensified.

Alfred too was never idle. Naples offered every amenity essential to a nobleman of his standing. He rode, reclined, imbibed Classico Chianti, won at the tables, enhanced his wardrobe, socialised and socialised. No one was more sociable than Alfred. He was introduced or introduced himself to every figure of note in the city – British, French, Italian or any other nationality of which he approved – and with impeccable courtesy, brought the city's notable figures to the Palazzo Belvedere to return their hospitality at the Earl of Blessington's expense.

Charles similarly filled his days with activity. He passed the mornings in bed reading out-of-date English newspapers. In the afternoons he made revisions to his novel, modified Mathews's plans, rehearsed dramatic roles and when the bay was calm enough for Captain Smith to take the risk, sailed the *Bolivar*.

Marianne too was seldom idle. She was a hopeless lady's companion but I trusted her apathetic loyalty and permitted her to accept responsibility for the more mundane aspects of managing the palazzo. Had I supervised her more closely I might have observed that she was not as naïve as I imagined. She was better than me at winning Charles's favour and at accepting her just rewards. She was also more patient than me with his banal chatter, while he appreciated her simple Irish interjections more than my sardonic wit. Alfred and Mathews also sometimes sought Marianne's company, not because they found her attractive but, for some unfathomable reason, felt sorry for her. I am sure she was very happy in Italy.

Throughout the winter of 1823 and summer of 1824 just one incident threatened the harmony of our household.

'Do you recall the occasion, Dr Madden?'

'Indeed, your ladyship, I never forgot it but do please recount it for the benefit of Mr Molloy and Mr Sadleir.'

'Allow me to use your words. This how you record the dispute:

'You claim to be a student of architecture, Mathews. You constantly walk around with a sketchbook and pencils but I have never seen you draw anything.'

'And you, Comte D'Orsay, claim to be a student of portraiture. You too have a sketchbook and pencils, which I have never seen you use other than to gain the favour of some prospective paramour.'

'You're a humbug, by God, the biggest humbug and bogey I ever met, and the first time you speak to me like that I'll break your head and throw you out of the window. … If you had any idea of the world you would know it is indispensable to know your place.'

On that overbearingly hot day Alfred's sophisticated restraint escalated into childish bickering. Accusation followed accusation until Mathews became so incensed that he impulsively challenged Alfred to a duel. This was a mistake. Alfred was not only a champion swordsman and pistol shot but while in the army had walked away unscathed from at least three duels. Regardless of class protocol Alfred accepted the challenge and in accord with noble tradition invited his antagonist to choose a second. Mathews, ignorant of duelling etiquette, took this as a further insult and in a fit of pique stormed out of the palazzo. Alfred presumed that he would not get far, since the heat and the argument had clearly exhausted him, but he neither returned that day nor the next. I was beginning to wonder how I would explain to Anne Mathews that we had mislaid her beloved son, when a grim-faced medical student appeared, soaked with sweat from riding too fast in the heat of the afternoon.

'Dr R R Madden, your ladyship,' announced my butler.

'Good afternoon, Lady Blessington, I trust I find you well.'

'I thought I was perfectly well, Dr Madden but perhaps I am suffering from amnesia. I have no recollection of sending for a doctor.'

'Sadly, your ladyship, I am not here in a medical capacity. I am here on behalf of Mr Charles James Mathews. It is my duty as his second to request that the Comte D'Orsay retract his insulting accusations and offer my friend an unreserved apology. Their dispute will then be settled honourably and without the risk of having to call upon my surgical skills.'

'Dr Madden, are you still listening? I am reminding you of our first meeting.'

'My apologies, Lady Blessington I well remember the occasion. Then as now, I should have paid more attention but I was anxious to get back to my research at the Naples hospital and worried about Mathews, who was at my lodging drinking more than was healthy for a young man.'

'Well, you had better tell Mr Sadleir and Mr Molloy what happened next.'

'Yes, your ladyship. Comte D'Orsay was asleep on a divan outside and you asked the butler to go and wake him. When he came in, you said something like, "Alfred, this is Dr Madden, Mathews's second. He has requested that you apologise and retract your remarks. I think you should do as he asks". Comte D'Orsay ignored your wise advice and told me to inform Mr Mathews that Lord Blessington would be acting as his second. He then abruptly dismissed me, saying that he had to change for dinner. I think it was then about three in the afternoon.'

That evening Charles, a lieutenant colonel who recoiled at the mere thought of blood, abjectly refused to have anything to do with the proceedings.

'The following day Lord Blessington sent you a message, Dr Madden. Do you recall what he said?'

'He said that as a second I was honour-bound to broker an amicable truce.'

'And what did you do?'

'I did as his lordship said and made another attempt to persuade Comte D'Orsay that it was beneath the dignity of a nobleman to accuse the mere son of an actor. I suggested that he make *"a trifling atonement for a hasty injury".'*

'That would have been quite sufficient. But no, Dr Madden, you had to write a forty-page treatise on the history and manifestations of class distinction. Did you really think that would convince a man like Alfred D'Orsay, any more than your other verbose writings convinced anyone else? You would have done lot better to have stayed with surgery.'

Charles asked me to interpret Dr Madden's peace-making diatribe. I glanced at his confused thesis, swooned onto a chaise longue and sent for my smelling salts. Charles sent for Alfred and, with uncharacteristic assertiveness, demanded that he apologise to Mathews. As a French aristocrat Alfred could not so demean himself but my over-acted dismay provided him with an honourable pretext to withdraw his remarks and offer his gloved hand for Mathews to shake. Thereafter the two young men resumed their ongoing friendship within the bounds of class convention.

The next time I took to my couch in feigned trauma was when I learnt that Lord Byron had died at Missolonghi, in Greece on 19th April 1824:

'A thousand circumstances, trifling in themselves but associated with our séjour at Genoa and constant intercourse with him are recurring in my memory.'

I do hope that it was not claimed that the world's most romantic poet never had a bad word for anybody. Byron's most endearing quality was precisely the opposite. I was devastated. I mourned for a lost kindred spirit. For all Alfred's panache, Mathews's wit and Charles's bumbling tributes to his old friend I could not be comforted for almost the entire day.

The serenity of that summer was to be further marred. In accordance with the lease that Charles had signed but not read, the noble Prince Belvedere exercised his right to double his rent from the first anniversary, and promised again to unblock the chimneys. I, that is Charles, had spent a fortune on restoring the bogus prince's excuse for a palace, while the defrocked cardinal and the whore he claimed to be his wife, had on numerous occasions accepted our invitations to piously disapprove our lifestyle. What is more, he had not the slightest intention of unblocking the chimneys. I was not in any way perturbed. I simply advised Charles to decline his devout landlord's avaricious terms.

After a month seeking a home of similar splendour, I came across the Villa Gallo at Capo di Mont, owned by Lord Dudley and Ward, one of the richest men in England. His terms were similarly exorbitant and his estate a little smaller than the Palazzo Belvedere but his chimneys functioned properly and there were no private zoos in the vicinity. All that was required to bring the house up to my modest standards was a few thousand pounds and a great deal of quibbling with recalcitrant Italian artisans. In early autumn I threw open the villa's exclusive doors to all the Neapolitan elite and we resumed our life of tranquil hedonism.

Anne Mathews's letters continued to express her concerns, and I continued to reassure her that her son would return to London an established architect and a great deal richer. Mathews's own letters to his mother were so enthusiastic and complimentary to us that she and her husband demanded that he return home immediately.

Mathews left us before the year end. Charles, who had decided to again instruct Benjamin Wyatt, was greatly relieved to let his incompetent young protégé go. Alfred, on the other hand, was devastated. He had permitted Mathews to join his collection of admirers, or perhaps it was the other way round. Overlooking his erstwhile bête noire's social inferiority and indecipherable sexual preferences, Alfred bombarded him with affectionate correspondence for many years thereafter.

Back in London, financed by Charles's parting gift, Mathews abandoned architecture and followed his parents onto the stage, where despite his impeccable family connections, he was obliged to serve the traditional theatrical apprenticeship, in particular the art of resting. For Mathews the most convenient place to rest was 10 St James's Square where the comforts included Louisa

Hume Purves from who he had been abruptly parted at the Swiss border. My niece, now just fourteen, had succeeded to the Power beauty and Mathews spent so much of his resting experience benefitting from her mature intellect that Ellen barred him from the house. Undaunted, the resourceful Mathews continued to meet Louisa furtively until she eloped with a less appropriate man – an ill-fated event to which I shall return in due course.

1825 passed comparatively quietly at the Villa Gallo. Charles, Alfred and I as a harmonious ménage á trois lavishly entertained perplexed Neapolitans, and Marianne made herself useful. The fascinatingly purged accounts of the events of that year can be read in *The Idler in Italy* and I have no need to repeat them here. Suffice it to say that I was so content that I forgot to worry about Charles's will, while he became increasingly despondent. Devoid of Mathews's sycophantic fervour, he postponed the Cottage extension and lost interest in amateur dramatics. Sir William Gell's inspirational lectures, in and out of his sedan chair, bored him to distraction. He lethargically completed the last chapter of *Le Vavaseur* and asked me to make copies of his two thousand-five-hundred-page manuscript, a task I undertook zealously, apart from omitting my name from the author's acknowledgements. When the following year Charles's novel was published - mercifully condensed to fourteen hundred pages - many of his friends and acquaintances thanked him for their gratuitous copies.

The *Bolivar* was another victim of Charles's despondency. He became obsessed by the ghost of Lord Byron haunting the decks and cabins of his old schooner like the legendry ancient mariner. Alfred too refused to board the *Bolivar*. He did not fear ghosts. He feared Captain Smith's salacious stories which irritated him as much as Mathews's pitiless impressions of the real-life ancient mariner had reduced him to convulsive laughter. Like Charles, Alfred became increasingly despondent. Even consistently winning at the gaming tables became too monotonous to raise his spirits. He might have been happier if he occasionally invented some losses to boast about.

Among the beneficiaries of Alfred's unfailing luck was the ubiquitous Henry Fox. Henry had moved on to Naples with the tempestuous blonde Contessa Teresa Guiccioli who had forgotten Lord Byron with aristocratic haste. As always, Henry's journal is as explicit as it is gracious:

'*She* [the Contessa] *received me as those females receive one, who make such occupations not their pleasure but their trade.*'

Having boasted of having spent '*every night for a month in her bed*' Henry judged Teresa '*coarse and far from being to my taste the least attractive*' and '*too gross and too carnal*'. Then, contradicting a raft of offensive compliments he conceded that '*Teresa has a pretty voice, pretty eyes, white skin, and strong, not to say turbulent passions*'. After being too often at the receiving end of the Contessa's pretty voice and turbulent passions, Henry recorded the termination of their relationship with the astute observation: '*Poor Ld Byron! I do not wonder at his going to Greece*'.

Years later when Teresa finally realised that, since Byron was dead, there was no reason for her to be jealous of me, we became good friends. Meanwhile, she had left Naples to pursue her next amorous adventure.

On the 22nd August 1825 Charles's intimate friend and political ally, Viscount Donoughmore died at his house near Manchester Square after a long illness. Due to heavy commitments and another unforeseen attack of nostalgia, I was unable to accompany Charles to Ireland to attend the memorial service. Curious as I had always been to see the inside of Knocklofty House, I had no wish to see it filled with the familiar faces of Irish society mourning the distinguished peer, or to join them in conveying hypocritical sympathy. Doubtless it was said of the late Richard Hely-Hutchinson that he never had a bad word for anybody. Perhaps, I mused, it would be more appropriate to say that he never had an honest word for anybody.

The first Viscount Donoughmore never married and left no issue. His undistinguished brother John, another ailing bachelor, succeeded to the title. John survived only until 1832 when his nephew, another John Hely-Hutchinson – whose first wife was the Honourable Margaret Gardiner, one of Charles's deceased sisters – became the third Viscount Donoughmore and the descendants of their only child, Richard, continue the line until the present day. This wafer-thin link between the family of Edmond Power, once an aspirant peer, and that of the man who caused his downfall was among his proudest boasts in old age.

Here, I must repeat that there is not a scrap of evidence to support the ridiculous rumours, which incredibly still circulate in Clonmel, that I was the first Viscount Donoughmore's lovechild by a mysterious mistress. Charles, who knew him better than most, left me in no doubt that he never had a mistress.

When in November Charles arrived back in Naples, he was disturbed to find a prostrate additional resident at the Villa Gallo. Having thrown over the piquant Teresa Guiccioli – or was it the other way round – and having been unable to seduce a suitably adventurous replacement of either gender, Henry Fox was now our most regular visitor and student of our household. As he gratefully commented:

'The whole family bore me to extinction. My Lady has taken to be learned...
She writes on life and manners. I wish she would acquire some of the latter before
she criticises. Her whole notion of showing her judgment is by violent and almost
Billingsgate censure.'

I was, as always, courteous to Henry, considering him *'lively, playful and abounding in anecdote'*, though adding the cautiously understated retraction: *'Such a forced plant as might be expected from the hot-bed culture of Holland House.'* Apparently Henry was developing an absurd obsession with Alfred:

'D'Orsay I am extremely fond of – he has great frankness, openness and warmth
of character – quite unlike the race of die away effeminate selfish dandies whom he
resembles in being recherché in his toilette .'

Henry's most ardent ambition was to match Alfred in sartorial elegance and immaculate horsemanship. Preened like a counterfeit copy, he pitifully competed every day with his dandified hero, racing and jumping over forbidding hedges until one morning he was thrown by his overtaxed horse, causing acute fractures to the shin and ankle of his one good leg.

'Do you remember, Dr Madden, the morning when Alfred carried Henry Fox back to the Villa Gallo and I sent for you to attend him?'

'Yes, your ladyship, I performed the operation on your dining-room table. It was my first after being elected a member of the Royal College of Surgeons. In those days there were of course no anaesthetics. As I recall, despite a whole bottle of brandy and six more of Lord Blessington's most mature wine, it required the combined strength of Comte D'Orsay, Lord Blessington himself and three male servants to hold Mr Fox still. Fortunately, I prescribed a lengthy period of rest before he could walk again.'

'I do wish that you had prescribed Mr Fox's lengthy period of rest to be taken elsewhere. You might have saved us all a great deal of trouble and expense. But then a surgeon is not expected to concern himself with practicalities is he, *Mr Madden?*'

For six weeks Henry Fox rested, ate and drank, while Alfred, Marianne, our servants and I danced attendance. Charles paid for the operation, medicines and subsequent attention while Henry amended his opinion of me, temporarily.

'The kindness of my hostess towards me and the extreme partiality she either feels or professes for me prevent my saying anything in disparagement of the beauty, talents and good qualities which far better judges than I am see and admire in her.'

Alfred was the best of my far better judges. He shunned Henry's incapacitated advances and his admiration for me escalated. Henry reluctantly recovered from his injury and deigned to thank us for our concern. He then went to Rome in over-optimistic pursuit of the Contessa Teresa.

Shocked by Henry's tales of Neapolitan licentiousness, Charles concluded that we should resume our travels before being affected by its unsavory influence. In February 1826 we drove out of the Villa Gallo for the last time, our carriages loaded with small tokens of appreciation from the less decadent Neapolitans who had enjoyed our prodigality in the previous thirty-two months.

15

A gaunt middle-aged Victorian gentleman leaning on an unnecessary walking stick to emphasise his indiscernible limp stops by my portrait. He exudes that haughty over-confidence that comes only from a life of excess wealth and abject failure. Recognising me, he makes no immediate acknowledgement but, ignoring the gallery rules, touches my painted features excited by the imaginary feel of my flesh. He turns but cannot bring himself to look directly into my eyes and so sits by my side. He is Henry Edward Fox, fourth and last Baron Holland.

'This portrait was always the first thing I saw in all Lord Blessington's houses. He had it hung opposite the front door so that no one could miss it as they came in. He was so proud of you that he wanted everyone to see that you were more beautiful than the painting. And here you are; the resurrected proof that he was right.'

'Beauty is neither paint nor flesh, Henry, it is in the mind. Did you never have a beautiful thought in your life – a thought of love, perhaps?'

'I was in love with you, Lady Blessington?'

'Of course you were, Henry, why else would you have written all that hateful nonsense about me?'

'I was young and conceited. I had a string of conquests of both genders to my credit but you were different from the others. Your intelligence, sarcasm and cynicism thrilled and challenged me, yet you were always an inch beyond my reach. You were thirteen years older than me but spurned my advances which made you all the more desirable.'

'This is very complimentary, Henry, but it hardly explains your contemptuous lies and vitriol.'

'When I wrote your name I meant my mother. The old whore embodied all the faults and failings of which I accused you and many worse.'

'I am sure Lord and Lady Holland loved you, Henry. You were their only legitimate son.'

'I told them what I thought of my so-called legitimacy. My father's only virtue was his money and that came from unmitigated exploitation of the colonies, like the rest of our fine upstanding British aristocracy.'

'Is that why you were sent to the Continent?'

'I was an embarrassment. All my parents cared about was maintaining their position in society and avoiding scandal. My mother wanted me out of sight but would never leave me alone. I had to keep moving to avoid her spies. I wrote what she wanted to read. And there was nothing she wanted to read more than the Blessington love triangle.'

'Then you can hardly blame me for being wary of Lady Holland, Henry. She went on spreading malicious rumours when I was hundreds of miles away and not expected to return for years.

'She was jealous. That's all.'

'And is that why she told everyone that Charles, Alfred and I spent our lives wallowing together in a mud pool of perpetual depravity?'

The aging roué laughs angrily.

'You have to admit that she was good at it. But who was Lady Holland to accuse you of immorality? She was unfaithful more times than you, Lord Blessington and D'Orsay together. Her first husband, Sir Godfrey Webster knew full well he wasn't the father of her children. Did you know that when she petitioned for divorce the court awarded him custody of the three who survived and would not order him to provide financial support because she was pregnant by Lord Holland?'

The anger in Henry's laughter dissolves into bitterness.

'Yes, of course I knew. Everybody knew. But I wish I had known how your mother always managed to avoid scandal.'

'Sir Godfrey was a decent man, a church-going Christian I was told. He couldn't face the judgment of the pious and so shot himself dead. My mother made a great show of mourning and slyly won the sympathy of Lord Holland and her other men friends.'

'Now I am beginning to understand why Lady Holland tried so hard to divert attention to me. Tell me, Henry, what became of her first family?'

'My eldest half-brother, Godfrey, was supposed to be legitimate so he inherited the Webster baronetcy. He became an MP and did very well for himself but that's all I know. After my mother married Lord Holland, the name Webster was never spoken in the house. Sir Godfrey left her nothing and that was more than she deserved.'

'Then did your mother marry Lord Holland simply for his money, to legitimise their offspring or were they really in love?'

'All three. My parents became pillars of respectability. They would swoon at the mildest hint of infidelity. Irony of ironies, they disinherited their first son, my older brother Charles because he wasn't conceived in wedlock, poor man. They went on to have four more children together but I was the only legitimate son who survived. So here I am, the last Lord Holland.'

'Did you never marry, Henry?'

'Oh yes, I was happily married to Lady Mary Coventry. We had three children. Unfortunately, there was something wrong with her womb. They were all born dead and the Holland line died with them.'

'Do you expect me to say that I am sorry to hear that, Henry?'

'If my brother had inherited the title there might still be a Lord Holland today.'

'Yes, Henry, the importance people used to attach to wedlock was sheer lunacy. There might still be a Lord Blessington today if my husband had acknowledged the legitimacy of his surviving son. His name was Charles too.'

--

I had lived in Naples for so long that I had come to regard it as my home. I was sad to leave but far from prepared to again compete in the spiteful sport of the London hostesses. In Naples, I was never openly ostracised, snubbed or told to my face that a quartet of over-privileged foreign misfits luxuriating in the grotesque splendour of the city's finest palazzos was an open arena for the city's energetic minds and tongues.

'The vain and pretending are ever the most prone to envy; for they covet that which they would fain make people believe they possess.'

I was deaf and blind to envy. I was still a fairytale princess and all Europe was my realm. I would bask in its culture and vitality forever, and sometimes in its sunshine too. Of course I would.

We retraced our steps to Rome where I again visited Sir William Gell who introduced me to a friend called Edward Dodwell, another authoritative antiquarian, archaeologist and artist. Like Sir William at Pompeii, Mr Dodwell transported me back in time, engaged me in debate with Cicero, Marcus Aurelius, Claudius, Caligula, Caesar, Antony and Cleopatra, revitalising the dreariest of my Latin studies. For three glorious weeks I was immersed not only in the past but the present of the Eternal City. I discovered that there were more English people in Rome than Naples, attracted, according to Mr Dodwell, by the murky health-giving waters of the Tiber. His wife, Theresa, a *'Roman lady of noble descent'* almost old enough to be his daughter, argued more realistically that the attraction was the murky health-denying local wines. Charles did not share my infatuation.

'You see, my dear Marguerite, the problem with Rome is that it is too full of ancient history. Florence is full of art and there's the theatre and the opera, you know. Besides, there are far more interesting people there.'

I recalled nobody in Florence nearly as interesting as the Dodwells and Florentine art was dominated by religion; half-naked blood-soaked martyrs intended to lift the spirit. The few available palazzos were equally depressing. Again I had become determined to persuade Charles to revise his will and so accepted his wishes and agreed to move to the majestic Casa Pecori, once home to Elise Bacciocchi, Duchess of Tuscany. Set high on a hill above the Arno, the baroque mansion was in much the same architectural style as the Palazzo Belvedere and similarly adorned with crumbling balustrades, cracked marble terraces and overgrown ornamental gardens sweeping down towards the city.

Charles was right. Florence was full of interesting people. Constantine Phipps, Lord Mulgrave, for example, an absentee Member of Parliament with little or no concern for politics. During a very brief and undistinguished term as Home Secretary, Constantine, by then Viscount Normanby, became known as 'Mantalini' Normanby after Dickens's narcissistic fop in *Nicholas Nickleby*. A man less suited to public office was hard to imagine but to have him acting as British Minister was certainly preferable to the judgmental Lord Burghersh, who Lord Mulgrave was relieving for the duration of a sabbatical in England. Constantine was another self-deluding author who shared Alfred's passion for sartorial affectation and Charles's for the theatre. I warmed to him less than to his brilliant wife, Maria.

Constantine had become extremely popular in Florence, not only for his insouciant attitude to matters diplomatic but for the extravagant banquets, receptions and theatrical performances held – at public expense – at his unofficial residence, Palazzo San Clemente. At these glittering events I met many more interesting people including Lord John Russell, another future prime minister to add to my ever-widening circle of adherents. I also added a future, if brief, French prime minister, the then Florentine Chargé D'affaires, le Marquise d'Esmengard, Alphonse de Lamartine and his English wife, Mary-Elisa. I described De Lamartine as *'the not common union of a man of business, a well-bred man of society and a poet'* and these were just some of his talents. We had a great deal in common.

My perspective of Florence from the balustraded terraces of the Casa Pecori soon began to appear far more agreeable than at my previous visit. I could have happily remained immersed in the city forever, but after about nine months, Charles suddenly tired of Florence and decided to return to Genoa. My heart heavy with ominous optimism, I said farewell to my new friends and the Casa Pecori. We travelled slowly north and reached Genoa in December 1826:

> *'Every object around recalls poor Byron so vividly to my recollection that I can hardly think that he whose image is identified with all I view is sleeping in his English grave.'*

This flowed well on the page, but Byron's demise had already engendered too many expurgated eulogies without my morbid reflections. My true recollections were not so sentimental.

In Naples and Florence, I had intensified my endeavours to fire Charles's enduring love in the traditional and every other way. I had even appeared with him in a pantomime at Constantine's Palazzo St Clemente – no, not as Cinderella. Off the stage I continued like Scheherazade to beguile my prince with satirical tales of romance, betrayal, intrigue, injustice and retribution, featuring heroes and heroines bearing uncanny resemblances to individuals we knew in London or had met on our travels. Charles did not recognise any of them.

Two years later the internationally acclaimed comedian, Charles James Mathews, once an architect, caused a sensation at the St Clemente theatre with a play ruthlessly ridiculing the British Florentine elite. How I wish I had been there to see it. I would have laughed loudest of all, because by then I knew why Charles decided to leave Florence.

It seldom snows in Genoa but on the morning of our arrival our visibility was impaired by fierce flurries of fleecy flakes. The biting wind served as a sharp reminder, not only of the deceased Byron, but the icy wording of Charles's will: like all wills, a spurious illusion of the power to influence life from the grave. Surely this was the reason why Charles had torn himself from my beloved Florence and left Constantine Phipps's unique theatre. He had come to Genoa to instruct Mr Barry to redraft his will. Mr Barry was no longer in Genoa.

Charles again engaged rooms at the Alberga Delta Villa. This was a mistake, not only because of the hotel's haunting reminders the death of his son but also because of its appalling food and inferior wine. Within a week Charles was complaining of headaches, stomach and chest pain and had entered another period of irritating depression. A droning political monologue delivered by the sagacious Lord John Russell, who too had moved on to Genoa, briefly revived his spirit. *'When the reserve peculiar to him thawed he can be very agreeable'*, I charitably observed. Russell's thawed reserve was a no more enduring remedy than the concoction mixed by Genoa's most respected doctor. Alfred thus suggested that a more effective cure would be to return south along the coast road and visit his sister and brother-in-law who were staying at their country residence just south of Pisa.

In the spring of 1827 our party of four joined the Duc and Duchesse de Guiche at the Casa Chiarabati. Ida was

> *'... still in the bloom of youth surrounded by her three beautiful boys and holding in her arms a female infant strongly resembling her... I never saw parents and children so highly gifted by nature, and this opinion is generally partaken, if one may judge by the attention excited when they appeared in public.'*

What a charming picture of domestic bliss. But all was not as pictured in the house of de Guiche. Just two days before our arrival Antoine had discovered the Duchesse — *'considered one of the most lovely and fascinating women of her day'* — in bed with a secretary from the British Embassy. We had chosen a fortuitous moment. Alfred was a master of diplomacy on the rare occasions when he put his mind to it. Having learnt nothing about the futility of class distinction from you, Dr Madden, or his encounter with Mathews, he reminded his brother-in-law that a nobleman does not demean himself to challenge a lowly secretary. This rational tenet of chivalry saved both Ida's marriage and Antoine the inconvenience of having to evade execution for murdering her lover. Alfred's virtuous intervention was unquestionably beneficial to the De Guiches, but not from my point of view. Without it, Charles might have seen the noble family into which he had pledged his daughter in a less-favourable light.

At the Casa Chiarabati life was *'more rational than most other places ... the mornings are not broken into by visitors.'* By this I meant that the atmosphere was distinctly cool and our hosts were in no mood for socialising. *'Politics are never discussed and scandal is banished'* meant that my helpful opinions and tactful peace-making comments were, to say the least, unwelcome. Whenever possible we escaped to the coast at Livorno — then Leghorn, which *'sounded barbarous'* — where the main attraction was a dock-side market purveying preserved foods imported from England, which made a pleasant diversion from the tasteless Italian pastas.

Much as we all loved Antoine, Ida and their highly gifted children, in less than a fortnight we agreed to leave the Duc and Duchesse to repair their rift in accord with aristocratic protocol. We rented the nearby Casa Chiesa, an Italianate country mansion sadly lacking in the amenities of our previous residences which in *The Idler* I transform into a charming pastoral paradise.

'Though gaiety does not prevail, rational society is to be had, books can be procured; and what more is needful to constitute the amusement of sensible people.'

Rational society, in a tedious Tuscan wilderness? There was hardly a prince, duke or count, let alone a scholar within a twenty-mile radius. Charles, Alfred and Marianne, sensible people? Within days we were squabbling like bored children and the tired old books discarded by the Casa's owner scarcely constituted my idea of amusement. Charles consistently complained of his inconsistent ailments, until at last he received some propitious news. An old friend was on his deathbed. We thus quickly left the tranquillity of our rural retreat at the Casa Chiesa and returned to the comparative insanity of Florence and the Casa Pecori. Walter Savage Landor later recalled:

'I should not have remembered Lord Mountjoy. He used to be somewhat fat for so young a man; he had now become emaciated. In a few days he brought his lady "to see me and make me well again". They remained at Florence all that year [1827]. *In the spring and until the end of autumn I went every evening from my villa and spent it in their society.'*

It was actually Charles who made his ailing friend well again by taking him for a two-day cruise on the *Bolivar*. Savage was an apt name for a man whose life had been a catalogue of controversy and excruciatingly mitigated crime. Now in his fifties, he had escaped to the Continent leaving a trail of destruction in all parts of the British Isles. What Walter referred to as his villa was a huge fourteen-room apartment spread over two floors of a sixteenth-century palazzo too small to contain his temper, his belligerent wife Julia, eighteen years his junior and their four spoilt children. With the autobiographical foresight of a true genius, his first play *Count Julian* (1812) told of a noble Spaniard who brought a long series of imaginative woes upon himself by recklessly defying his peers and compatriots. Since no other impresario had the imagination to envisage this dark tragedy appealing to an audience the young author turned to Charles to finance its production at Drury Lane, where it played to an empty house for two performances. Walter never forgot Charles's blind faith. He forgot to reimburse him.

'The infirmities of genius are often mistaken for its privileges.'

Charles introduced me to the dying firebrand propped up on a sofa trying hard to look weak and dejected. I recited passages from his Latin poetry memorised for the occasion and discovered that I was the first woman he had met – possibly the first person – who had read and translated the whole of his Latin epic *Gebir*. I further surprised him with my familiarity with all the mythical, historical and contemporary protagonists in his two published volumes of *Imaginary Conversations* – well, most of them.

'Of Landor's genius his "Imaginary Conversations" had, previously to our meeting, left me in no doubt of the elevation of his mind and the nobleness of his thoughts.'

The noble-thinking elevated-minded genius had on four occasions been severely reprimanded by the man I once referred to as *'our popular minister'*. Lord Burghersh, as Charles had feared when he so suddenly decided to leave for Genoa, had returned to Florence to fulfil his bounden duty to repeal every liberal innovation initiated by Constantine Phipps in his absence. John Fane, Lord Burghersh, Eleventh Earl of Westmoreland, brother of the Countess of Jersey, diplomat and acclaimed musician held the office of British minister-plenipotentiary by virtue of birthright. His traditionally indeterminate duties involved occupying an imposing official residence in the city centre, which Burghersh and his second wife, Lady Priscilla niece of the Duke of Wellington, performed with genial punctiliousness. Both were zealously committed to standing in judgement of their British inferiors. Charles and I, as passive antagonists of the Jerseys and active defenders of the Landors, were thus excluded from all the minister-plenipotentiary's mandatory invitation lists.

I was indignantly unconcerned. Florence was as previously full of distinguished people happy to accept our invitations to the Casa Pecori and often to return them. In *The Idler* I mentioned the Duc de Richelieu, Prince Borghese, Lord Dillon and Lord Lilford and had space permitted would have added the names of some of our untitled guests. Among the as yet untitled was Henry Fox who, having once again fallen foul of the Contessa Teresa, was fortunate enough to detect our whereabouts. We could always depend upon the superciliously loyal Henry to accept our invitations, drink too much and fail to shock us with slanderous tales of Holland House. Back in his rooms, our pathetic blue-blooded friend, now even offering Marianne the chance to shun his advances, scraped the depth of his talent to find words offensive enough to express his gratitude.

'Went to the Blessingtons; … The hostess was as usual very Irish and very censorious, vulgar beyond measure, and speaking the vilest French with her native intrepidity.'

'I dined with the Blessingtons. Lord B got quite drunk and said rude things to me about Holland House, which I did not answer, because the correction of a drunkard in his own house seems to me impossible for one of his guests to undertake; and when not drunk he is below contempt.'

Charles was not opposed to a glass or two of vintage Bordeaux though seldom drank to excess. I doubt he ever thought whatever Henry meant by *'rude things'* let alone said them in public. And if Henry interpreted anything that I said as detrimental to his parents or any habitué of Holland House, he was completely misjudging my respect for London society. His venomous ingenuity was not limited to us: his depictions of his fellow diners similarly displayed an original turn of mind.

'Dined at Lord Blessington's. Met Lord Caledon and M. de Lamartine – The former looks and seems very heavy. The latter is a poet, a dandy and a diplomat, in about the third or fourth classes of each. He abused ...'

The Second Earl of Caledon and Lady Elizabeth were among the most gracious of the British nobility we entertained at the Casa Pecori. While the Earl could not be called slim, I was too polite to have mentioned the weight Henry had himself gained from dining with us so often. The quintessential nobleman, Alphonse de Lamartine had taken a bold, if unrewarding lead in revolutionary France and was among the most celebrated of his nation's poets. Though he took a gentlemanly pride in his appearance, he could hardly be described as a dandy in the same room as Alfred. Henry himself was later to serve briefly as a member of parliament and in other sinecures, while his entire literary output amounted to the one journal he was too cowardly to publish in his lifetime.

Lady Harriet Gardiner celebrated her fifteenth birthday on 5th August 1827. Alfred's chosen bride was now in her sixteenth year and eligible for marriage, in accordance with Charles's interpretation of his own will. He thus sent a request for his daughter to be brought to Florence enclosing a polite message of congratulation. His sister Harriet, uninvited, bravely accompanied her niece, less concerned with exposing the child to the perils of the journey than to the influence of her evil stepmother. When they arrived at the Casa Pecori I welcomed them courteously and tried to embrace my stepdaughter who recoiled in disgust. Having made her delivery Aunt Harriet stayed on uninvited, in the dual capacity of guardian and disapproving reporter. And she stayed and stayed. Ten months later in Nimes there were still six in our party.

I had been an involuntary child bride myself and was naturally apprehensive. But that, I convinced myself, was long ago in primitive Ireland. Now in civilised Florence the circumstances were entirely different. Unlike Captain Farmer, Comte D'Orsay was perfectly sane - sexual deviation, recklessness, arrogance and narcissism were not symptoms of insanity. Unlike Captain Farmer, Comte D'Orsay was not a talentless drunkard; he was a talented compulsive gambler. Unlike Captain Farmer, Comte D'Orsay had not drawn his sword and not wounded a superior officer; he had issued a gentlemanly challenge and wounded an arrogant colonel of the Garde Royale, among others. Unlike Captain Farmer, Comte D'Orsay was not dependent on an eccentric parsimonious father; he was dependent on an eccentric spendthrift father-in-law to be. Lady Harriet was indeed a most fortunate young woman.

'My dear Alfred, allow me to introduce my beloved daughter, Harriet. She is soon to be your wife, you know.'

Alfred looked down from his six-foot-three inches and greeted his five-foot-three inch prospective spouse with all the aloof romanticism of his noble spirit.

'Comte Alfred D'Orsay, Mademoiselle.'

'I am pleased to meet you, sir'.

These were the last words the happy couple exchanged prior to their wedding. In Dublin, Harriet would have ridiculed an absurd popinjay like Alfred until unable to control her laughter. In Florence, Harriet was unable to control her tears. She was horrified by this preposterous old man of twenty-seven.

'This is a wonderful surprise, Lord Blessington,' said Alfred. 'But why am I surprised? It would be impossible for a daughter of the noble house of Blessington to be other than the personification of delicacy and loveliness. I could have chosen no more enchanting lady in all of France and England.'

'Then, Alfred, you will raise no objection to marrying Lady Harriet straight away. I would really like to get this business settled, you see.'

'My dear Lord Blessington, it is always my pleasure to fulfil your every wish.'

'Excellent, my dear Alfred, I intend to arrange for twenty thousand pounds to be placed in trust for you. A small wedding present, you see.'

'Lord Blessington, I thank you from the depth of my heart but this is quite unnecessary. I ask for nothing except your gracious permission for me and my wife to continue to reside with you in happiness and harmony. Without you and Lady Blessington my life would be but a hollow shell.'

'My dear Alfred, that is the least we can do, you know. I shall see Lord Burghersh tomorrow morning and obtain the necessary licence.'

Lady Harriet, a small, plain, prepubescent schoolgirl, listened in silence and confusion.

'Before you say a word, Dr Madden, I know full well that I should have tried to forestall this reprehensible union. And of course I felt guilty and I still do.'

'You have to admit, your ladyship, that do you seem to have been rather callous over the whole matter.'

'I had no choice, Mr Sadleir. There was nothing I could do to persuade Charles to change his mind. And Alfred's marriage, if nothing else, would put an end to the unfounded scandal about us being a ménage à trois.'

'Were you sure of that, your ladyship?'

'Of course not, Dr Madden! We were now a ménage à quatre.'

Charles was realistic enough to appreciate that it might be two or three years before Lady Harriet might produce a legitimate heir, but took no account of the possibilities of childlessness, separation, divorce or, most disastrous of all, that she might give birth to an heiress. Still less did it cross his mind to question his beloved daughter's feelings in the matter. Charles was determined for the wedding to take place without delay, not only because he attached excessive significance to a union between the Blessington and D'Orsay families but because there was always the chance that Alfred might see sense and run off to find a more appropriate match.

I too was anxious to keep the couple beneath our roof. I had come to love Alfred and feared that sooner or later my husband would become disillusioned with the French dandy. Charles however became more loving and considerate to me and shared my bed more often than at any time in our ten years of marriage - possibly to set an example to his daughter. By contrast Alfred grew more disdainful of carnal relationships of any kind and readily agreed that his marriage should remain unconsummated for four years. This, I thought, would be ample time for me to convince Charles of the immorality of leaving me in poverty simply because I was unable to provide him with an heir or because he imagined that I had been unfaithful. In any case, there was not the remotest chance of Alfred and Harriet's marriage lasting four years.

'I am astonished, Lord Blessington, to hear a man of your standing in the British nobility request my permission for his daughter to marry a penniless French so-called count. Lady Harriet is neither old enough to consent to marriage nor to understand the consequences of the union you are proposing. What is more, your unpalatable household is the talk of Florence. I do not concern myself with local gossip but allow me advise you, sir, that the spectacle of a child forced into matrimony will serve only to compound the disgust rightly felt by all respectable British people residing here.'

'But my dear Lord Burghersh, Comte D'Orsay is a member of the Catholic Church. He has the consent of the French Minister, you see.'

'And you, Lord Blessington, are a member of the Church of England, whose ceremony must take legal preference and requires my licence. No such immoral marriage will be condoned while I hold office in this city. Inform Comte D'Orsay that any appeal or further application will be a waste of his doubtless valuable time. I bid you good day, sir.'

I was quite disturbed when Charles reported this dogmatic interview to me. As always he had capitulated too easily. Lord Burghersh might have had no conscience but he was not devoid of flesh and blood. I would have to confront him myself and melt his icy male heart.

I informed Lady Harriet that she was to be introduced to a very important man and that she must look her best. Marianne set her hair in her own dowdy style, draped her in one of her unbecoming dresses and neatly applied some grotesque cosmetic. If the interior of the ministerial residence was as gloomy as its over-ornate exterior, she might pass for twenty or older.

'Young women ought, like angels, to pardon the faults they cannot comprehend; and old women, like saints, should be compassionate, because they have endured temptations, and endured the difficulty of resisting them.'

'Lady Blessington, your husband has informed me that this girl is in her sixteenth year. She looks no more than thirteen to me. I am appalled by your sanction of her loveless marriage of convenience to a foreigner twice her age. Apparently, madam, your reputation for disdaining the mores of decent society is well founded. If you will forgive me, I have heavy commitments. My attendant will show you out.'

Walter Savage Landor, who by then had caused so much justified disruption in Florence that he feared arrest and moved to the smaller and more peaceful Fiesole, seven miles north-east of the city centre, wrote on learning the minister-plenipotentiary's reaction:

'...nothing could surprise me of the folly or indecorum in Lord Burghersh... That a man educated among the sons of gentlemen could be guilty of such incivility to

263

two ladies is inconceivable... From what I have heard of him during a residence of six years in Florence I am convinced that all the ministers of all the other Courts of Europe have never been so guilty of so many unbecoming and disgraceful acts as this man...'

I agreed but why did Walter send his well-intentioned rant to me and not jump at the chance to tell Lord Burghersh himself what he thought of him? If anyone understood that age difference is no barrier to marriage, it was Walter. He married Julia Thuillier when she was sixteen and he was a good deal more than twice her age. Walter's next letter was more alarming. Two of his four children had contracted a contagious fever. I immediately despatched my coachman to bring the healthy two back to the Casa Pecori and looked after the little boy and girl until they were safe from infection. I waved to them numerous times from my window. Walter's gratitude sealed our lifelong friendship but the traumatic experience took its final toll of his long contested happy marriage. He left Julia and the children in Fiesole and returned to England.

With the benefit of our instructive encounters with Lord Burghersh Charles shrewdly decided that it would be best to leave Florence immediately and move to Rome where formal permission for Alfred and Harriet's wedding would be more easily procured. As usual the house-hunting was left to me and in the short time available I could find nothing more suitable than two empty floors of the vast Palazzo Negroni. The rent was outrageous even by Charles's standards: one hundred guineas per month with an additional charge for the furniture. The impervious landlord would not reduce the rent but offered to sell us the furniture at cost price discounted by the rental charges when the lease expired. I refused to be party to such an unscrupulous arrangement and properly purchased our requirements for cash. When we eventually left the landlord explained that my beautiful new furniture was totally unsuited to his property, but to save us the cost of its disposal helpfully offered to retain it to hire to future tenants on the terms that I had declined.

Alfred presented his compliments to the acting French ambassador to Rome. The aged, deaf and short-sighted but splendidly named Anne-Adrien-Pierre de Laval-Montmorency, Duc de Laval et San Fernado Luis considered it a great honour to assist the son of General Albert D'Orsay, who he knew well by repute. Without asking the age of the bride the ambassador pressed his seal of approval on a form of marriage licence and Alfred pressed a token of gratitude into his unsteady hand. News of this virtuous incompetence soon reached the incorruptible ears of the British minister-plenipotentiary in Florence. Lord Burghersh, who had no authority in Rome, wrote in the most unreasonable terms, again citing the precedence of the Protestant ritual and exercising his unofficial veto on grounds of morality. Laval-Montmorency summoned Alfred back to the embassy and stammered in French that he had made a mistake: the power to licence weddings did not apply to a temporary ambassador. Due to the early stages of senile dementia he forgot to return his gratuity.

Charles then heard the excellent news that another long-standing friend William Noel-Hill, future Lord Berwick, had been reinstated as British ambassador to the Kingdom of the Two Sicilies and immediately set off for Naples. Noel-Hill who had never been married himself and attached little significance to issues such as religious precedent or the age and consent of the bride, happily obliged by sealing a legal permit. Possibly a few thousand Two-Sicilian piastras changed hands.

Back in Rome we yet again encountered the indefatigable diarist, Henry Fox.

'November 16th 1827 – after dinner I went to the Blessingtons who are now established at the Palazzo Negroni where I found a whist party. D'Orsay took me aside to ask me to be a witness to his marriage, which is to be hurried up immediately. I was much distressed and could not refuse, much as I lament and disapprove of the proceeding which seems to me one of the most disgraceful and unfeeling things ever committed.'

Henry, the very model of the concepts of disgraceful and unfeeling, for once displayed a semblance of the opposite. The following morning, he changed his mind, politely declined Alfred's request and recorded what he called *'the real truth'*, meaning everything he lacked the courage to say to our faces:

'How abominably I thought he was sacrificing the happiness of a poor child to his own convenience, or rather to the indulgence of his passion for Lady B.'

The real *'real truth'* was that Henry dare not go to Naples because Noel-Hill had been recalled to London after sanctioning the wedding – for unrelated reasons, of course – and another member of the Fox family, had been appointed acting deputy. Fortunately Henry's relative arrived too late to withdraw the licence and on 1st December 1827 the Comte D'Orsay married Lady Harriet, aged fifteen years and four months. The ceremony was performed by the chaplain to the British Legation for the Kingdom of the Two Sicilies before professional witnesses. Thereafter the unhappy couple returned to Rome: the bride with her father and aunt, and the groom alone a day or two later. Alfred celebrated his wedding night by investing Charles's wedding present at an honest Neapolitan gaming club, where, as always, he was a popular winner. A week later, Charles engaged a Catholic priest and more professional witnesses to repeat the marriage in Rome. I naturally would have loved to attend but was heavily committed to accepting late delivery of new furnishings for the Palazzo Negroni. No representative of the D'Orsay family was able to attend either.

Like every proud father, Charles was anxious to host a banquet in celebration of his daughter's wedding.

'Just something modest, say three or four hundred, you know.'

Remembering my own modest wedding in Dublin, I tactlessly explained that the bride, and even the groom, might find such an event a tiny bit embarrassing. Charles saw this as a heartless denial of Lady Harriet's rights as the daughter of a noble family, but had to agree that it might be a tiny bit embarrassing for him too, since the popular Florentine minister-plenipotentiary was, to put it mildly, displeased to discover that his authority had been undermined by his Neapolitan counterpart.

'No, Dr Madden, I do not accept your implications – or yours, Mr Sadleir or yours, Mr Molloy - that none of us showed La Comtesse D'Orsay sympathy or consideration. We were civilised people of our time. We perfectly understood that an immature schoolgirl would be distressed in such an alien atmosphere in a foreign country.'

'Please accept my apology, Lady Blessington. I was heavily committed to my work at the hospital in Naples at that period, but even there heard many rumours of D'Orsay's disdainful attitude to his wife. I certainly did not intend to suggest that I believed they applied to you. My *Literary Life* cites numerous instances of your kindnesses and I have no doubts that a fine man like Lord Blessington would have been concerned for his daughter's welfare. Nonetheless...'

'Lady Harriet was a married woman, Dr Madden, and not quite as naïve as you seem to imagine. We were obliged to treat her as an adult and did our best to integrate her into our social life but, frankly, it was a hopeless task. Good heavens, she possessed less social graces than Marianne.'

'Did she not get on well with your sister?'

'No, the miserable bride, with no apparent cause, thought Marianne was my spy and refused to speak to her. Her equally virginal aunt Harriet however apparently had much more in common with Marianne and divulged more than a few unnecessary confidences.'

'Those women who are most loved by their own sex, are precisely such as are least sought by the other.'

Poor Alfred had no concept of how to deal with his young wife's cunning silence. When unable to avoid her he made pleasant little jokes in French or muttered polite platitudes which she neither understood nor made any effort to understand. I cannot blame the girl, I suppose, for not trying to win the affection of a man perfectly content to pursue a marriage devoid of financial, social or sexual obligation. She occasionally attempted to speak to her father but Charles, who knew nothing other than the tradition of his class, considerately kept his daughter at arm's length.

'[Lord Blessington and Comte D'Orsay] *have made poor Lady Harriet (who was before well educated) listen with childish pleasure to the heartless doctrines and selfish ribaldry of her heartless mother-in-law.'*

So wrote Henry Fox, choosing to disregard the countless hours I devoted to Lady Harriet's education or that I rescued her from having to endure a wedding banquet and a honeymoon with Alfred. She should have considered herself fortunate at least for the latter. While her husband and father were heavily committed to other amusements I took the young Comtesse – chaperoned by her aunt and Marianne – on edifying excursions into the captivating history of the Roman Empire. Since these bored her even more than they had Marianne, I again called on the assistance of the brilliant Dodwells. Edward's illuminating introduction to the ancient Romans was lost on Harriet, but Theresa, *'one of the most faultless models of loveliness ever beheld'* introduced us to some fascinating modern Romans, who the young student found similarly uninspiring.

I, however, was fascinated by one particularly mysterious modern Roman Englishman introduced by the Dodwells. Frank Mills possessed *'a highly cultivated mind, great suavity of manners and qualities of the head and heart that have endeared him to all who knew him'*. His Villa Palatina, to which I was invited many times, was *'a terrestrial palace that occupied the site of the Palace of the Caesars, with its spectacular views of the Roman ruins and gardens charming beyond description.'*

One morning, while Teresa Dodwell was fighting a losing battle with Harriet's obstinate distaste for the inestimable beauty of the scattered fragments of terracotta and broken bits of statuary so picturesquely visible from Mr Mills hilltop gardens, we were *'surprised by the arrival of the Prince and Princess de Montfort and their children with Madame Letitia Bonaparte, or "Madame Mare", as she is generally called'*. Madame Bonaparte, the mother of the most illustrious Frenchman in history, did not speak French. While I knew no Corsican, by employing my extensive linguistic skills, I managed to overcome some of the inhibitions of this iconic peasant and enjoy her limited conversation. The Emperor Napoleon was the fourth of the thirteen children she bore after she was forced into marriage at the age of thirteen. I sincerely hoped that my student bride appreciated that the remarkable example of this ignorant old woman was not to be emulated.

Among other British elite wintering in Rome in 1828 was Colonel William Stewart of Killymoon who I had last seen as best man at Ellen's wedding. Even so far from England, Scotland or Ireland it was common knowledge that the now aging Irish aristocrat was the biological father of her children. Though she always vigorously denied it, it might well have been true but it was certainly not true that I was also his sometime mistress. Miniatures of my three nieces and nephew seem to resemble Stewart, who himself looked remarkably like the Gardiner family. Alfred's profile of William Stewart, now in the National Portrait Gallery's collection shows a clear likeness to Charles, or would if he had not been drawn looking so agonised by the high stiff collar evidently choking him. Stewart, now Member of Parliament for County Tyrone, informed Charles that the definitive Irish Catholic emancipation bill was at last to be debated and solicited his vote in the House of Lords. Charles, as always, agreed and offered his support.

After his honourable decline of Alfred's wedding invitation, Henry Fox grew more sanctimonious than ever. He went so far as to tell Charles that he would never again enter his house while his son-in-law was present. Alfred, in no way offended, wrote to his once aspirant admirer.

> *'I return to you your souvenir,* [a snuff box given in anticipation of favour] *for I wish to keep nothing that can for an instant recall to me your ungrateful and false self.'*

Having thus forfeited his most productive source of petty gossip and free entertainment, Henry informed his mother:

'It is said, and God grant it may be true, that the Blessingtons [and the D'Orsays] *leave Rome for Venice on 3rd of May. They are pests in a town and produce quarrels wherever they go.'*

I was unaware that we had produced quarrels anywhere but quite aware that wherever Henry went he gathered fuel for the slanderous cauldrons constantly bubbling at Holland House. He sent home increasingly imaginative allegations of our immoral behaviour at the Palazzo Negroni while simultaneously harassing Alfred with letters flaunting the revival of his affair with the Contessa Guiccioli, presumably intended to incite his jealousy. Alfred was not at all interested. Lady Holland might have been extremely interested but Henry's letters to his mother tended to overlook his personal affairs.

Towards the end of 1827, Charles suggested to Alfred that they make a short trip together in order to inspect the *Bolivar*, still moored at Naples, and ensure that it was in a condition to survive the winter. It was not. They found the decaying schooner sitting idly in the Bay and Captain Mathias Smith likewise at a dockside tavern. Alfred, fearing that he might be invited to enjoy a cruise with Charles at the helm, resorted to his most persuasive to convince his father-in-law that it was time to dispose of his under-employed Byronic memento and Captain Smith with it. Not even Lord Blessington could fail to sell this unique piece of memorabilia at a profit. The purchaser of no other vessel in the world would be able sit on the very chair where the Sixth Lord Byron sat, write at the very table where he wrote a stanza or two before being seasick or turn the very wheel turned by the very hand that held his very poetic pen.

For some incomprehensible reason the sale of an authentic relic of the Byronic legend captured Alfred's imagination. He painted a stylish watercolour of the *Bolivar* in full sail and had prints advertising the auction of Lord Byron's very own ship posted on the walls of Naples for the street urchins to tear down. On the rain-swept morning of the sale the wet and miserable crowd assembled on the quayside was astonished to witness the late Lord Byron, resplendent in the Albanian dress of his most famous portrait, emerge from his cabin onto the deck of his moored schooner. In his hand was an ancient-looking scroll from which he read aloud part of *Childe Harold* in his most inspired French accent. When the captivated audience stopped applauding, Alfred stepped ashore, strutted to and fro mimicking the poet's celebrated limp and invited bids like a Crockford's croupier enticing gamblers to bet on the turn of a card. The bidding was brisk and dramatic: going for twice, thrice, four times the price Charles declined to pay dear Noel – and gone. 'Grazie, Signor, sail the *Bolivar* with God's blessing', Alfred shouted to the delighted buyer now treading the very deck once trod by the very Byronic feet. A few days later Charles, with Alfred at his side, rode back into Rome like the triumphant Caesar. He had recovered almost all the money he had lent the deceased poet, discounting accumulated interest.

Life at Palazzo Negroni resumed normality, that is the Blessington-D'Orsay concept of normality: receptions, dinners, balls, cultural pursuits and intimate friendships. Charles again produced pretentious plays and pantomimes and music echoed through the frescoed ceilings of the gilded galleries for the confused pleasures of his growing number of guests. Every day and most nights too were filled with fruitless activity. The duplicitous Harriet Gardiner disapproved and hapless Comtesse D'Orsay sat silent.

By April 1828 our winter of content had taken its toll on Charles's health. He sent for Rome's most eminent physician who was accustomed to treating wealthy hypochondriacs and justified his fee by suggesting that the local air sometimes caused nausea. Charles immediately announced that we were to leave Rome.

'I am told that the air on the Adriatic coast is so much healthier, particularly in the spring, you see. It's all that water in the canals, you know. I have never heard of a sick Venetian. And, Alfred, you also need a rest.'

From what exactly did Alfred need a rest, I wondered?

'My dear Lord Blessington, I cannot thank you enough but regrettably I shall be unable to accept your excessively kind offer. My beloved parents and grandmother have expressed their natural desire to meet the Comtesse Harriet and I am obliged to take her to Paris.'

'You are quite right, Alfred, your family must take priority but I have already thought of that, you know. Look here, I have drawn up a simple itinerary. It's a sort of round tour, you see. We shall go over to the Adriatic and as soon as I feel better, we can come back to the Mediterranean, follow the coast road and turn due north into France, you see. Before you know where we are, we shall all be back in Paris together. My dear Marguerite has suggested a few stops for the benefit of the Comtesse's education, you know. I trust that will be agreeable?'

Alfred agreed. I had drawn up Charles's itinerary with meticulous care to delay confronting the D'Orsay family and included edifying visits to some twenty cities and resorts large enough to boast comfortable hotels and facilities. Relaxation in the summer sun of north Italy and the South of France would be of infinite benefit to Charles's health and the Comtesse's studies.

On 8th of May 1828 Mr Mills hosted a farewell dinner for us at the Villa Palatina. He invited Sir William Gell, the Dodwells and a Baron Mortier, another learned historian who combined *the bearing of a "preux" chevalier with the urbanity of a finished gentleman'*. Intellectual conversation flowed more freely than the mud-clogged Tiber. The senators and orators of ancient Rome joined us in deriding international statesmen who, then as now, promoted self-destructing civilisation and waged wars of purposeless devastation.

'How easily people of different nationalities can be integrated by the bonds of friendship and common purpose.'

How sad that it can never be so easy.

I treasured that evening of enlightenment for the rest of my days but in the way of all ecstasy, it ended in sorrow. As we were leaving Mr Mills revealed that he had contracted a terminal disease and did not expect to see us again. I described him as a man *'seated in a paradise of his own creation'* and mused that in the unlikely event of there being paradise of God's creation it might prove a poor substitute for the Villa Palatina.

> I wrote of *'the pain of parting being always enhanced by the dread of never again meeting... Schemes of future meetings, too faintly spoken to cheat into hope of their speedy fulfilment furnished the general topic; and some there were, already stricken with maladies, the harbingers of death – and they too spoke again of meeting.'*

The last words in my second volume of *The Idler in Italy* were: *'Tomorrow we leave the Eternal City perhaps to see it no more'*. I was the only member of our party who thought this in any way important.

And there was more distressing news. Another of the great luminaries whose indestructible wisdom I treasured had died on 29th March 1828. Sir William Drummond had spent innumerable hours enchanting me with his classical scholarship and experiences as ambassador to the Ottoman Empire. I remembered debating his *Topography of Troy* and answering his *Academical Questions*. I remembered the outcry when he dismissed all religions as *'mischievous'* and when his undeniable remark: *'We must expect the hoi polloi to be under the guidance of some superstition or another'* shocked churches of every denomination. Much as I would have preferred to extoll Sir William's common sense, yet again my editors fearing holy retribution restrained me from adequately emphasising the futility of worship.

My third volume of *The Idler* thus commences with a visit to the grave of a much loved and understanding friend; a sombre start to a sombre journal, purged of practicalities, personalities, politics and opinions. In reality, the constant matrix of tensions and misconceptions between the six travellers on our deliberately procrastinated journey to Paris had the makings of a riveting novel in itself, most of which is left to my readers' imagination.

As a peacekeeper Charles was beyond criticism. Wherever we went he insisted on reserving the best rooms at the most comfortable hotels and dining at the finest tables. My gratitude cascaded like a waterfall. I venerated my husband's impractical idiosyncrasies like a zealot and convinced myself that I had succeeded in appealing to his better nature and revived our love. I earned the right to a befitting legacy, yet diplomatically avoided the subject. This was a mistake. I missed the vital chance to convince Charles that I was the only one of his family worthy of a deserving legacy.

Our comparatively small but still overburdened parade of coaches rolled slowly north-east via Terni and Spoleto until at last we saw the Adriatic. The sea air at Ancona relieved Charles's mysterious ailment for almost two days and so we travelled north in pursuit of the remedial ozone. Inland at Ravenna I was curious to visit the Palazzo Guiccioli, once the home of Contessa Teresa and Count Alessandro Guiccioli, her recently deceased estranged husband. The palazzo was then owned by Alessandro's son by an earlier marriage, Count

Ignazio, who detained by heavy commitments graciously invited me to tour his home guided by a forgetful old servant.

Teresa and her brother Pietro were born and spent their childhood at the nearby Palazzo Gamba. In January 1818, when Teresa was seventeen their father, Count Gamba arranged for her to marry Alessandro, then almost seventy. There was of course no financial consideration involved but the old count required a third and younger wife as, according to my apathetic guide, all his six children were illegitimate. Happily, there was to be no issue from his last marriage. Three days after her wedding Teresa met the recently divorced Byron, who as an honorable lecherous romantic, soon could not bear to be separated from the blonde Contessa. He thus moved into the same inn where we stayed. It was the best Ravenna had to offer, the sole redeeming amenity of which was its proximity to the Palazzo. After a respectable acrimonious interlude, Byron come to an exorbitant agreement with the Count who divided the Palazzo into apartments for himself, for his wife, and the acclaimed poet masquerading as her gentleman servant. A fourth apartment was at the disposal of Pietro Gamba, who the gentleman servant employed as his secretary.

This perfectly normal and proper arrangement, said the confused guide. was unsatisfactory to all parties. In due course a form of separation was convened enabling Teresa and Lord Byron to remain unfaithful lovers for the rest of his life. A less romantic love story is hard to imagine yet I managed to fill ten pages of *The Idler* with sentimental reminiscences.

'By how many various passions had he [Byron] *been influenced during the sojourn in the rooms, I loitered today! Love that guided him to this abode….'*

What nonsense! The old man who claimed to have been *Lord Byron's* gentleman servant could not even remember which rooms were the poet's, the Contessa's or her brother's, let alone where old Count Guiccioli slept with his mistress. He boasted that he had watched Lord Byron writing his greatest poems. He did not remember their titles but remembered his lordship as *'so charitable and so full of pity for the unfortunate.'* Lord Byron? The poor servant had clearly reached the age of dementia.

The dismal old Palazzo Guiccioli, I am told, is to be restored and converted into a museum dedicated to Byronic myths intended to boost Ravenna's deservedly limited tourist trade. I do hope that the new guides are better informed than mine. Charles was neither impressed by the amazing brilliance of the purported seventh-century mosaics - Ravenna's greatest most spectacular to fame – nor by the therapeutic qualities of the town's air. We moved on a few miles to Venice, where it was just possible that the air would be sufficiently fresh. Like countless visitors before and since I was captivated by the polluted canals, unkempt gondoliers, decaying architecture and dearth of fauna or flora. Shakespeare probably never visited Venice but his vision of a place of unscrupulous commerce was – and still is – remarkably close to the truth. Charles was overcharged unmercifully for totally unique pieces of grotesque Venetian glass identical to those for sale at every other street corner. I did however persuade him to overpay for a number of *objets d'art* genuinely owned by or associated with famous visitors to the Floating City, and to have them shipped back to St James's Square. This was not a mistake. I wrote of yearning to be surrounded by my souvenirs in the home I had no desire to see again and of my nostalgia for the country I wished only to forget:

> For home — blest on earth e'er found -
> Is firmest based on English ground,
> So, though fair climes awhile may charm
> To thee we turn with hearts all warm.

After four days of continual coughing, Charles concluded that the Venetian air was not having the anticipated effect. He had been told of another miraculous physician in Milan who would certainly prescribe an infallible panacea. We turned due west. Milan was a large imposing city with an overwhelming lack of culture and sophistication. There was not even a first-class hotel, nor was there anybody of interest at the La Scala opera house where the ambience was as lacklustre as at Covent Garden. We sat through the entire *Le Nozze di Figaro* without speaking to a soul.

The miraculous physician made a thorough examination and like his mortal predecessors agreed with Charles's self-diagnosis. He commended the air at the Italian Lakes and presented his bill with miraculous panache. The air at Laveno on the shore of Lake Maggiore was infested with tourists. The ferries were so crowded that I declined to visit even the world-famous Borromean Islands. Charles, who braved the tranquil waters to see the picturesque botanical gardens on Isola Bella, quickly became sick of as well as in the Italian Lakes. He was now sure that only the Mediterranean air contained the right consistency of oxygen to cleanse his lungs. Hoping that we would not all die of ennui, we crawled back along the featureless road west to Genoa. Why? We had been there twice before and the air was the same as everywhere else on the coast. Why was Charles again risking torment by the innocent spirit of his infant son and the troubled soul of the departed Byron? I clung to the last vestige of hope that the banker Mr Barry had returned and that Charles would finally redraft his will. I was wrong. There was a happier solution. He had secretly arranged a surprise for me. As I stepped from my carriage outside the Alberga Delta Villa two footmen tore away a large sheet and unveiled Lady Burghersh's beautiful white calèche with its green and crimson wheels and the Blessington arms neatly painted on both doors.

> 'The common herd of mankind mistake ostentation for generosity, passion for love and vanity for pride. Yet how widely different they are all.'

When I had admired the ostentatious vehicle in Florence, Alfred had made a quick sketch for Charles to send to the most exclusive coachbuilder in London, a Mr Barker, who delivered a precise copy to Genoa in anticipation of our arrival. I had finally rekindled Charles's passion. Why else would he have done this for me? My thousand and one nights were over. I would soon be the rightful main beneficiary of the Earl of Blessington's will. This was a mistake.

The one and only mention of my husband's name in all my literary work appears at the end of *The Idler in Italy* – '*Lord Blessington has a princely way of bestowing gifts.*'

There was another, if less material, surprise awaiting me in Genoa. One day in the street I came across a girl of twelve or thirteen walking with an adult companion. I had never seen this child before yet I instinctively knew who she was. Her whole demeanour and the intelligence that emanated through her brilliant eyes could have been the legacy of only one man. The miniature of his infant daughter that Lord Byron kept on his writing table did small justice to the extraordinary gifts of the young girl who said her name was Ada.

Byron had said, '*I am told that she is clever – I hope not; and above all I hope she is not poetical*'. Ada fulfilled neither of her father's hopes. She was not simply clever; she possessed one of the clearest scientific brains in history. And she was not simply poetical; she possessed an unnatural appreciation of the poetry of mathematics. Ada had no recollection of her father but was in Genoa with her mother hoping to discover some remnant of his motivation and I deemed it a privilege to tell her about the Byron I knew. My expurgated portrayal obviously did not convince her. Ada had been led to believe that her father was pathologically mad and she confided her fears for her own sanity. I did my best to reassure her, though I thought inherited madness was a distinct probability. Would any normal young girl be obsessed by the possibilities achievable through the symmetry of machines or be so shocked when I mentioned that her father was a confirmed Luddite?

Ada was tutored by Mary Somerville – who gave her name to the formerly all-women Oxford college – the only female scientist of the time capable of keeping pace with her student's originality of thought. Later Ada's colleague Charles Babbage called her '*the enchantress of numbers*'. I am uncertain what this meant. I did not excel at mathematics. Though she lived two doors from my house in St James's Square we never met again. Today Lady Ada Lovelace, as she was to become, is celebrated as the world's first female computer programmer. I must have been right about her madness. She was thirty-six - the same age as her father - when she died of her own genius and the pleasures of compulsive gambling. Well, perhaps she was not completely mad.

My third surprise was of a very different nature. I discovered that Lord and Lady Burghersh were returning to London for another sojourn and had stopped in Genoa en route. Her ladyship was, to say the least, incensed on hearing of Charles's magnificent gift, and particularly displeased with Mr Barker who built her original unique calèche. I did wonder how he had been able to produce such a precise replica with only Alfred's sketch for guidance. Lady Burghersh's displeasure also upset poor Mr Barker who lost the patronage of the minister-plenipotentiary forever.

Given his record, it was hardly a surprise to discover that Henry Fox had also followed us to Genoa. Alfred would have no further truck with a creature so despicable that he would dare spurn his wedding invitation. Charles thus did not invite him to dine with us. This was a mistake. Instead Henry accepted the hospitality of the Burghershs and conveyed the heart-warming news for his mother to disseminate in London society. We left Genoa sooner than planned.

The shorter continuation of my journal, *The Idler in France*, is my best work of non-fiction, or perhaps fiction as it contains little pessimism or despondency even between the lines. As my carriage wheels scraped the first rough stones of the unmade French road I was endowed with a new vivacity.

> '*We spent our first night in Nîmes. 'Our Inn, The Hôtel de Midi, is an excellent one; the apartments good and the "cuisine soignée". In this latter point the French hôtels are far superior to the Italian; but in civility and attention the hosts of Italy have an advantage.*'

It made a pleasant change to be overcharged by pretentious French innkeepers as opposed to fawning Italian hoteliers. By the time we reached Arles I was at such peace with the world that I was almost unperturbed to discover that the town had no luxury accommodation to offer at all. We lodged at '*a large, crazy, old mansion… where cleanliness and comfort pervades the rooms. … The furniture is scrubbed into brightness; the small diamond-shaped panes of the old-fashioned casements are as clean as hands can make them.*' I ran out of praise for our '*picturesque*' hostess, her '*fête dress*' and her table, '*sufficient to satisfy the hunger of four times the number of our party*'. This picturesque woman actually apologised for being unaccustomed to guests of our class and was so naïve that she asked Charles, of all people, to:

> '*Pay what you like; things are very cheap at Arles. You have eaten very little: really it is not worth charging for.*'

He insisted that she at least name a sum and she asked if '*a couple of louis would be too much? And this for a party of six, and six servants for two days!*' He gave her more than twice the cost of a first-class Italian hotel and enquired if that was enough. Frankly, my description of this absurdly honest peasant was intentionally over-exuberant in order to add colour to our uneventful journey back to Paris. The luxurious Hotel de la Terrasse in the rue de Rivoli was more to my taste than a shared bedroom in an Arles farmhouse.

Paris! Paradise misspelled? It was almost six years since I left the French capital and I could hardly wait to again bask in the reflected warmth of its *haut monde* and be content forever. This of course did not happen but there were compensations. Charles at last relieved his sister of her obligations to his married daughter. The virtuous Harriet Gardiner filled her bag with distorted reports as gifts for her step-mother and left Alfred with some helpful words of advice that he did not understand. No, she did not thank Charles for his incentive.

The Duc and Duchesse de Guiche, now unhappily established in their splendid château in the centre of Paris, were the first people Alfred invited to dine with us at our hotel and to meet his new wife. Ida and Antoine formally congratulated Comtesse Harriet and avoided asking about her wedding which they were so disappointed to have missed. Instead they entertained us with wholesome news of Alfred's parents and grandmother and happy reminiscences of their time in Italy, evading any question of the bandaged glitch in their exemplary marriage. They were the most delightful company. Antoine even teased a quickly withdrawn smile from his black-clad virgin sister-in-law.

The de Guiches impressed their noble seal of approval upon the union of Blessington and D'Orsay, which they asserted with questionable foresight would prove an enduring service to both England and France. They also assured us that Paris was invariably tolerant of human frailty and that neither I nor Charles would ever be victims of unwarranted censure. Perhaps they believed it.

Charles had reached an age where he was content to live the simple life of an English aristocrat in exile and remain as extravagant as ever. A demon within drove him to spend his money as if these were his last days on Earth. And who was I to question a demon within while I was its beneficiary?

> *'It is true that hats, caps and bonnets may be had for very reasonable prices in the rue Vivienne and elsewhere at Paris, as I and many of my female compatriots found out when I was formerly in this gay capital; but the bare notion of wearing such would positively shock a lady of fashion at Paris.'*

How could my scholarly pen have written this? There were no *magasins bon marché* in Paris. An English countess patronised *boutiques chères* and the most *chère boutique* was that of the celebrated Monsieur Herbault, *'the high-priest of the Temple of Fashion of Paris'*. The first time I visited his showroom the peerless couturier greeted me with the words: *'Bienvenue encore une fois, Madame La Comtesse de Blessington'*. Monsieur Herbault greeted every customer, new or old, with the same words.

I cleared my conscience:

> *'Beware, O ye uxorious husbands! how you bring your youthful brides to the dangerous atmosphere of Paris ... And you fair dames, beware how you indulge... and remark on the wonderfully high prices of things at Paris ... for alas, "beneath the roses repentance rears her snaky crest" in the form of a bill the payment of which, "will leave you poor indeed".'*

More practically I advised married women:

> *'The hundred pounds* [your husband] *had intended to try his good luck at the club is better spent on your own tasteful apparel.'*

Alfred too cleared his conscience and introduced his very young wife to his very old grandmother. The couple were summoned alone to an audience at the rue D'Anjou and I did not learn what transpired until later. Alfred claimed that he had convinced Madame Craufurd that Lord Blessington retained the greatest respect for her, and that he very much desired to resume his acquaintance and to present me to her.

At last I was introduced to the elusive octogenarian. I had been so often told that she looked no more than fifty-five that I was concerned that my eyesight had deteriorated. Corpulent, caked in cosmetics and passed the age of physical exertion, I felt compelled to venerate this sedentary queen of French society. She sat at the centre of her grand drawing room dressed entirely in white; a fat snowball melting over an antique throne. She was still spending the twelve thousand pounds (plus expenses) extorted from Charles and more from 'poor' General D'Orsay, gentleman officer of the *Grande Armée* and war profiteer with little need of his derisory Napoleonic pension.

Madame Craufurd had *'a bright smile and a kind word for every guest without the slightest appearance of effort.'* Of course her smiles and kind words were effortless; she had been practising them professionally since she was sixteen. The personification of benevolence, her charisma oozed through the web of fine cracks masking the wilting contours of her beguiling face. When she spoke it was in the ugliest accent I had heard since leaving Ireland; an extraordinary mixture of English and genteel French with faint hints of her native Italian.

'When *vous être* next in England, Madame la Comtesse Marguerite, *s'il vous plaît*, convey my kindest regards to *ma chère* Lord and Lady 'Olland. Is not 'Enri un garçon charmant? When he was at *ma modeste château, nous avons parlé* many times about *nos amis à Londres.'*

She never again mentioned Lady 'Olland or 'Enri Fox to me. She had no need to. Her bilingual stab pierced like the point of a sharpened needle. I was warned.

Alfred bowed and kissed Madame Craufurd's hand. Having completed this and similarly distasteful obligations, he stated that his only desire was for his beloved friends the Earl and Countess of Blessington to be presented to King Charles X and sufficiently noble and distinguished figures of his court. With a wave of her sparkling brandy bubble his obese fairy grandmother granted his wish. Her daughter La Comtesse Eleanore de Franquemont would make the necessary arrangements.

I had not forgotten Eleanore's duplicity, and I was not prepared to share further confidences with her. I was however determined to obtain full value for the unreturnable deposit she and her family had extorted from Charles. Alfred's mother now spent more of her time in Paris than with her husband in Chambourcy. I did not ask precisely where or with whom, and she did not ask me where or with whom her married son spent his time.

Madame Craufurd's word was as good as her conscience was bad. Her name opened the most exclusive doors of the Parisian elite. We were granted an audience with the aging widower Charles X that I am sure he remembered. The grandest families embraced us and welcomed us warmly to their overcrowded balls and banquets, often before we invited them. This whirl of social activity soon became quite embarrassing since the splendid Hotel de la Terrasse was no place to return such overwhelming generosity.

Charles complacently agreed to make Paris our permanent home and as always delegated the house-hunting to me. As in Naples, Florence and Rome I discovered that suitable palaces or châteaux were few and far between. Day after day, I drove the green and crimson wheels of my white calèche through the legendary streets of the city centre seeking a dream - too unimposing, too pretentious, too inconvenient, too many dire souvenirs of the Revolution, too comfortable servants' accommodation. As I was reaching the point of despair, Alfred mentioned that the home of one of his father's long deceased fellow generals remained unoccupied.

On 7th December 1815 Marshal Michel Ney, at the age of forty-six, falsely convicted of treason, had walked from the door of his château on the now Quai d'Orsay – no, not named after Alfred's family – for the last time. The internationally respected Prince de la Moskowa's unparalleled scroll of military victories and services to the nation were honoured with the unique opportunity to demonstrate that he was indeed *'le brave des braves'* by ordering his own executioners to fire. I must have driven past the Hôtel Ney a hundred times without noticing the grand château secluded behind high walls over which its first-floor windows provided unimpeded views of the Seine and the Tuileries Gardens on the opposite bank. Approached through *'an avenue of fine trees'*, it possessed *'all the quiet and security of a country house'*. Despite this excess of greenery, I immediately felt a personal affinity with this befitting monument to the revered Marshal. There could not have been a more appropriate home for me in all Paris.

Its then owner was Le Marquis de Lilliers, an unworldly aristocrat who claimed to be inundated with offers for an extortionate short-term lease which Charles signed immediately for fear of being outbid. De Lilliers had not found a tenant for the château in the twelve years since acquiring it after Madame Ney and her four young sons were hounded from Paris with no choice but to leave their belongings. The Marquis had disposed of these mementos of the dastardly traitor and left the great château devoid of furnishing. Only with an Aladdin's lamp could I prepare the palace for our noble guests in the time available. And lo and behold an Aladdin's lamp fell into my hands. Its genie, a ghost of business past, conjured a vision of the Palazzo Negroni and the generous offer I had declined. I hired *'rich and fine furniture by the quarter, half or whole year'* with an option buy it at its original price after deducting all I paid. My arrangements proved so simple and convenient that I wrote to the proprietor of a prestigious London department store and explained that:

'...if I wish to purchase the furniture the sum agreed to be paid for the year's hire is to be allowed in the purchase money which is named when the inventory is made out. ... This Aladdin's lamp should be adopted in all capitals.'

And I received a reply:

'Our most esteemed Lady Blessington

Thank you so much for your interest but regrettably the moral and ethical principles to which our long established company invariably adheres prohibit the extension of onerous terms of credit.

We look forward to welcoming you and Lord Blessington back to our humble premises, and beg you believe that we remain your ever obedient servants etc. etc.'

A century later my Aladdin's lamp was rediscovered and its summoned genie granted the material wishes of the masses. By 1938 twenty-four million hire-purchase agreements were active and seven million per annum were being signed in Britain. Yet still not everyone appreciated the wonders of my lamp. Many other metaphors were invented to disparage it, but no sustainable evidence was ever produced to support the notion that hire purchase *per se* caused hardship.

In just three weeks I furnished the entire Hôtel Ney, apart from the east wing which Charles forbade me to enter. I feared that he might be preparing another magnificently embarrassing surprise for me. I was right. On 1ˢᵗ September 1828, my thirty-ninth birthday, two footmen threw open a pair of high doors and Charles led me into a grand boudoir that he had designed himself for my delight. It was the most vulgar suite of rooms I had encountered since our honeymoon at Mountjoy Forest. By comparison Lord Byron's bedroom was positively plain.

'The bed, which is silvered instead of gilt, rests on the back of two large silver swans, so exquisitely sculptured that every feather is in alto-relievo, and looks almost as fleecy as those of the living bird... A silvered sofa has been made to fit... [From] the columns which support the frieze of the recess, pale blue curtains, lined with white fluted silk, are hung which, when drawn, conceal the recess altogether. An escritoire occupies one panel, a bookstand the other and a rich coffer for jewels forms a pendant to a similar one for lace or India shawls.

The hangings of the dressing-room are of blue silk, covered with lace and trimmed with rich frills.

The bath is of white marble, inserted in the floor, with which the surface is level. On the ceiling over it is a painting of Flora scattering flowers with one hand, while from the other is suspended an alabaster lamp in the form of a lotus.'

Credit management having never been taught at Eton or Oxford, Charles paid cash for all of this.

I thought he had gone completely mad. No sane man would spend so much on the smallest wing of a house leased for just twelve months. Charles was not mad but nor was he completely sane. A life of zealous inadequacy had deflated his mind into a grand theatre, where he was simultaneously playwright, director, actor and audience. My queenly boudoir was a scene set for an unwritten drama. I enthused gratitude until my throat was sore while Charles heard only the applause echoing from his illusionary auditorium.

'Charles, your taste is impeccable as always, divine, delectable, exquisite, the picture of perfection. Now I am sure you love me as much as I love you.'

The last sentence might have been better phrased: 'I have as much love for you, as you have for me'. I did not mean love as generally understood. I had no illusions. Charles loved me because I was the brightest star on his phantom stage and I still loved him for his English eccentricity and reckless generosity. The old Hôtel Ney was another temple of prodigality. An endless stream of courtiers, aristocrats and royalty – of both genders – accepted and returned our hospitality. For a year, I dwelt in an unreal world of balls, banquets, operas, museums, galleries, shops and more shops. Charles gave me so many love tokens that I ceased to be concerned by the terms of his will. He was waiting for an inappropriate peak of high drama to tell me that his fortune would one day be mine. There was plenty of time. He was forty-six, a young man.

There seemed to be nothing but good news. On 20th September 1827 in Pensacola, Florida, John Hume Purves died at the age of forty-two, predictably of heat exhaustion. He left nothing to his estranged wife or her children. In December 1828 Ellen married Charles Manners-Sutton at the Protestant church of St George's, Hanover Square and all the press rejoiced. For the hundredth time it revealed that the son of the Archbishop of Canterbury – the aged Most Reverend gentleman was too heavily committed to attend the wedding – had for years kept an Irish Catholic mistress.

'The vain and pretending are ever the most prone to envy; for they covet that which they would fain make people think they possess.'

Blind to the insecurity of my Parisian Xanadu, I envied my sister. Ellen had married a man who loved her only for herself and her future was assured, I thought. She had moved to a large new Speaker's residence at Westminster where she was a more popular hostess than I had ever been in London. More enviable still, she would now be presented to the obese drunken King George IV.

By the spring of 1829 unrelenting pleasure had begun to exhaust me.

'How delicious it is to shut out all this weariness with a book, or a few rationally minded friends, to indulge in an interchange of ideas! But the too frequent indulgence of this sensible mode of existence exposes one to the sarcasms of the frivolous who are avoided.'

I excelled at avoiding the frivolous. I was always a serious if cynical scholar and an assiduous correspondent. I indulged in an interchange of ideas with more than a few rationally minded friends, of whom the least rationally minded was the young Benjamin D'Israeli. Dis sent me a copy of his first published novel, *Vivian Grey*. I deplored modern fiction and this was a particularly presumptuous example. But as I informed the author, it was *'a very wild but very clever book; full of genius in its unpruned luxuriance… all the riches of a brilliant imagination… dazzling at one moment by his passionate eloquence and at another by his touching pathos.'* No writer was to have a greater influence on my work than the future prime minister, possibly that is why it had so few enduring qualities.

Seeing me reading *Vivian Grey*, Alfred enquired if I had read anything by Edward Bulwer-Lytton, another of his pretentious London friends. I had been uninspired by the splendid reviews of his novel *Pelham* but on Alfred's recommendation acquired a copy in French, presuming that it would be another piece of tedious trivia. It was another piece of tedious trivia. For all his *'pointed and pungent satire on the follies of society'* Bulwer-Lytton was no D'Israeli. I presumed that he would never be heard of again.

Two months before the lease of the Hôtel Ney was due to expire, the Marquis de Lilliers presented us with notice to quit. My improvements had enhanced the value of his château to such an extent that he no could longer afford to let it and with vacant possession could sell it for an outrageous price. Charles shrugged and returned to England, yet again leaving me to find a new home. The Duke of Wellington, now Prime Minister, had requested him to attend the Lords for the reading of the last emancipation bill. Catholics were finally to be enfranchised and eligible for election to the House of Commons and the Earl of Blessington was determined not to miss the opportunity to cast his vote in person. My friend and lifelong correspondent, Sir Robert Peel, then Home Secretary, reminded the Commons that: *'Though emancipation was a great danger, civil strife is a greater danger.'* I wholeheartedly endorsed Sir Robert's statement. Though the civil strife raging against Charles X in the streets of Paris was a great danger, the striven lionesses of London were to me a greater danger. Under no circumstances would I consider returning to England.

For the first time in six years, Charles took his seat in the House of Lords as if he had not been absent for a day and helped the 'Roman Catholic Relief Act' to be passed by a sizeable majority. Catholicism was a minority church in England but many like Peel feared its strength in Ireland and on the Continent.

Jubilant to again be among his fellow peers, after the vote Charles attended a fund-raising dinner for the Irish poor at Covent Garden. Normally he was not a large eater or drinker but this was a special occasion, and in the congenial atmosphere of the Royal Opera House he indulged both to excess. The following morning, an expensive English doctor diagnosed indigestion and recommended fresh air and exercise. Charles neither followed his advice nor dealt with any other business. He postponed instructing an agent to find a tenant for St James's Square and cancelled meetings with his bankers concerned about his securities. He did not go to Dublin to ignore Mr Norman's report or to visit his family. Possibly he also postponed an appointment with Mr Powell before hurriedly returning to Paris laden with gifts for me, purchased by a servant.

By the time he arrived I had discovered a fine château under construction at the Avenue de Matignon.

'It will be beautiful when completed but not to be compared to the Hôtel Ney. The builders seem to be as expeditious as the upholsterers and adding a room or two appears to be as easily accomplished as adding some extra furniture'.

'But, my dear Marguerite, the Hôtel Ney suits us all perfectly, you see. I really cannot understand why de Lilliers will not extend the lease, you know. I am sure he will sell it if I offer a fair price. I need the gardens for my health, you see. I wish to stay here.'

'I think, Charles, you will change your mind when you see the delightful new gardens and how well the work is progressing. Come with me now and let me show you.'

'Let us leave that for the moment, my dear Marguerite. I have not been feeling at all well recently, you know. Perhaps I shall take a ride over there later. My doctor in London recommended exercise as well as fresh air, you see.'

There was no fresh air in Paris on that hot and humid afternoon but, after lunch, I ordered Charles's horse to be saddled. Reluctantly, he rode out of the gate through which Napoleon's most illustrious general once walked to his death, cantered along the south bank, crossed the Pont de la Concorde and turned into the Champs Élyseés. At the corner of the Avenue de Matignon, he was seized by a fit of apoplexy, lost consciousness and fell to the ground.

Charles John Gardiner, Earl of Blessington, my fairytale prince, the kindest of the kind and the most generous of the generous, died in a Parisian gutter on Saturday, 23rd May 1829.

A drunken mendicant kicked his body aside and said in bad French:

'Look where you're going, monsieur, I'm trying to earn an honest living here. You aristocrats are all the same. You'd never give anybody a lousy sou.'

16

'This is most condescending of you, Mr Westmacott. Are you here to apologise for all your repulsive insults?'

'Come, come, Lady Blessington, you were reputed, I suppose with some justification, to be the best educated woman in the land. I believe you were also something of an exponent of cod philosophy. Surely you know that an intelligent person can never be insulted.'

'Indeed, Mr Westmacott, the world would be a much happier place if more people understood that. But, after all these years, you could at least say that you are sorry for your attempts to blackmail me.'

'Blackmail, Lady Blessington? I would never sink so low. I was a simple man of business. I supplied the demands of the marketplace. I offered two commodities: the candid truth and my silence. Since I had an infinite supply of the former I charged only the price of a newspaper. The latter was more precious and thus commanded a befitting consideration.'

'I was also a journalist. Yes, I too traded in the absurd and exposed one or two thinly camouflaged truths but I never deliberately used my knowledge to destroy anybody's reputation. How did you find out so much about me?'

'Do you know, Lady Blessington, I feel sorry for today's honest purveyor of scandal. He or she has to waste countless hours scanning social media, hacking telephones and so on. All I had to do was toss a few coins to a valet or a lady's maid and they'd tell me everything the public had a right to know. The so-called quality was always so discreet in front of its servants. Certain gentlemen of the press were occasionally a little unprofessional, as some still are, but I was not to blame. I was an editor. I had no time to delve into my reporters' methods.'

'Regrettably, Mr Westmacott, I must agree with you. The ambitious and the successful work hard to earn their bad press, but my poor husband was neither. Couldn't you have left him to rest in peace?'

'Ah, the virtuous Earl of Blessington; the soul of decency, friend to all and generous to a fault, the man who caused more mayhem after his death than I did in my lifetime. It is as well you did not attend your poor husband's funeral. You would have discovered the high esteem in which he was held by his family. They couldn't even be bothered to put up a gravestone.'

'Whatever you say, I shall always believe that Charles was an honourable and well-intentioned man. But is there really nothing in Dublin?'

'Not so much as a brass plate. When the bounteous Earl wrote his clever little will, he thought of everything except to provide for his own memorial.'

'Surely his children or his sisters had some feeling for him. Or did you and others like you, make them hate him because of me?'

'As I have said, your ladyship, I dealt only in the truth. But don't be too upset. Here in front of you is your husband's memorial, and in my humble opinion it's a lot better than a lump of cold stone in a graveyard. Lawrence's *Countess of Blessington* is gawped at by hundreds of nobodies every day. One or two might even ask who the Earl was. What a pity nobody can tell them. But you and I know, don't we? A pervert, a nonentity, a loser, a second-rate showman or as they say so picturesquely in the present century "all fur coat and no knickers". Now I think of it, he had himself painted in a fur coat. I suppose he thought it would make him look respectable.'

'What does a man like you know about respectability?'

'By some people's standards, I was no saint but, Lady Blessington, you of all people should be grateful to me. By exposing your husband's appalling irresponsibility and the dog's dinner he left for you to lap up, I won you many more sympathisers than antagonists.'

--

The last will and testament of Charles John Gardiner, first and last Earl of Blessington, of course made provision for his own memorial. However, in the interests of his legatees, his executors postponed construction of the grotesque pile he planned for Mountjoy Forest, permanently. With respectful disregard for his probable wishes, Charles's remains were taken to Dublin and laid to rest, not beside those of his beloved first wife Mary, but on a shelf in the Gardiner family vault beside his detested father. The funeral at St Thomas's Church, Marlborough Street was attended only by his children, Charles and Emily, his sister Harriet Gardiner and the Dowager Lady Margaret Mountjoy, who had overlooked sending out the customary notices. None of the innumerable beneficiaries of the Earl's lifelong prodigality were in Dublin that day and his loyal and devoted servants, dismissed by his stepmother, were heavily committed to seeking employment elsewhere.

'The Earl of Blessington never had a bad word for anybody,' said a clergyman who had never met him. It was the first time he had uttered these words with a semblance of truth.

In Paris, I was inundated with messages of condolence: peers, politicians, officers of the militia, industrialists, charity organisers, shopkeepers, tenants, servants, actors, artists and writers, grieving for their lost free hospitality or source of income. The fawning eulogies were as sickening as my repetitive responses. I destroyed them all but one:

> *'Often shall I think of the many hours we have spent together, the light seldom ending gravely, the grave always lightly... He told me that you were requisite to his happiness and that he could not live without you... Everyone that knows me knows the sentiment I bore to that disinterested and upright and kind-hearted-man, than whom none was ever dearer or more delightful to his friends. Tho' my hand and my whole body shake as I am writing it, yet I am writing the truth.'*

The eloquence that flowed from the pen of Walter Savage Landor was a treasure worth preserving. Walter knew no guile. To him everyone was either an unblemished saint or an unmitigated sinner – mostly the latter – with no category between. Charles might not have had a bad word for many people, but the only sincere good words for him came from an unworldly megalomaniac genius.

Had I spoken of the depth of my affection for him, I would have been neither understood nor believed. How could I go to Dublin simply to be humiliated? To Charles's family I would never be anything but the temptress who lured him to his destruction.

Marianne expressed her sympathy with all the dispassion of a devoted sister: 'You were a fool, Margaret. You shouldn't have taken Charles for granted all these years'.

At the Hôtel Ney, I mourned alone, an aging princess, in a palace decomposing around me into a desolate mausoleum. In Dublin there was no mausoleum or even a headstone. Charles's memorial was his will.

Alfred had taken Harriet to Chambourcy to visit his mother. Eleanore had contracted some sort of fever. As an invariably dutiful son, he used this as an appropriate excuse for not taking his wife to Dublin for her father's funeral. More importantly, Alfred did not wish to be in the Hôtel Ney while its contents were being removed to Avenue Matignon. Some of the dust might have settled on his coat.

On the day Charles was due to be buried in Dublin, I received a message from Alfred. It informed me that the Baronesse Eleanore's fever was worse than he had imagined. She was dangerously ill and he begged me to join him at her bedside. Charles's death had heightened my contempt for the woman who had been complicit in swindling him, but poor Alfred could expect no comfort from his disrespectful wife. Virtuously, I emerged from my house of mourning and, accompanied by Marianne, was driven out to Chambourcy.

I arrived in time to witness the illegitimate Baronesse of impure royal blood, pay the ultimate price for a life of deception, debauchery, gin and fine wines. So far as I could discern, her unavailing last words were: 'Take care, *ma chère* Marguerite, Alfred will ruin you.'

I could not decide if this unhelpful warning was intended as some form of reparation or as a last laugh at my gullibility.

Alfred was inconsolable. The fates had simultaneously snatched away both his unfaithful mother and faithful benefactor. Ida, Duchesse de Guiche, calmed as always by aristocratic detachment, knew precisely how to console her brother. Immediately their mother was pronounced dead, she sent for Alfred's tailor to come from Paris and measure him for an excessively discreet funereal suit. The duly consoled Alfred would be the best-dressed mourner ever seen at the cemetery of Chambourcy.

Madame Craufurd had also been brought from Paris to enjoy her daughter's demise. Displaying little deference to the solemn occasion, she sat in the centre of the salon like a white whale floating in a sea of black. I could detect no emotion through the greasy cosmetic which now failed to disguise the ugliness of her charisma. She smiled at me with the nauseating magnetism that throughout her life had never failed to attract unwary flies into her webs of intrigue, looked up to the ceiling and breathed a deep sigh. These encouraging gestures were intended to advise me to expect a long widowhood, and to cope as stoically as she. Presuming that I was as deaf as her, she broke the silence of the solemn occasion by shouting obligatory platitudes about Charles, and thanking me for my equally unfelt tributes to her daughter.

Death, even that of her own daughter, was of no consequence to Madame Craufurd. Soon she would be dead herself. By her side on the wide sofa sat Comtesse Harriet D'Orsay. She too showed little sign of bereavement. She had hardly known her father, let alone her mother-in-law. General Albert D'Orsay and General Antoine, Duc de Guiche stood side by side in front of the vast stone fireplace, erect like a pair of over-decorated wooden skittles reciting standard words of military condolence.

Through my black veil – worn for Charles, not Eleanore – I observed a burgeoning rapport between Madame Craufurd and her grandson's virgin wife. Even in her declining days Madame Craufurd's mind retained its honed razor edge. Harriet was approaching seventeen and habitually wore uncompromising black in memory of her lost childhood but today of all days, an inch of pale green protruded above the high neck of her dress: a statement of defiance and a signal of growing confidence. She had heeded, and would go on heeding, the wisdom of her husband's once seductive grandmother.

After Eleanore was buried, Alfred and Harriet stayed on at Chambourcy while Marianne and I returned to the sincerely funereal Hôtel Ney. Piece by piece my furniture (subject to hire-purchase), pictures and objets d'art were taken to their next resting place under construction at Avenue de Matignon. My *'expeditious builders and upholsterers'* seemed to take forever. For two more weeks I was confined to a dark theatre grieving for its lost impresario, and in my head hearing the voice of Lord Byron reciting the simplicity of his *Prisoner of Chillon's* liberation from despair:

> *But silence, and a stirless breath*
> *Which neither was of life or death;*
> *A sea of stagnant idleness,*
> *Blind, boundless, mute and motionless!*
>
> *A light broke in upon my brain,*
> *It was the carol of a bird;*
> *It ceased, and then it came again,*
> *The sweetest son ear ever heard,*

The only birdsong left to lighten my prison was the creak of the silver swans lamely supporting my bedstead. My elegant aviary designed in Dublin was now a detail of a larger and more elaborate replica designed by Alfred.

Two weeks later I moved to the Avenue de Matignon. One morning I found Alfred by the aviary feeding other birds of exotic plumage. He returned an indigo macaw to its perch and replaced his perfectly contrasting yellow kid gloves. Quite suddenly he turned and embraced me with the all passion he normally reserved for ordering a new pair of breeches, and then suddenly deflated like a pierced multi-coloured balloon.

'Marguerite, you are my mother now. You are the only mother I shall ever love.'

Alfred was twenty-eight, and I was not yet forty.

'No doubt my recent trials have aged me, Alfred, but are you saying that I now look old enough to be your mother?'

'You know that is not true, Marguerite. You look younger than my sister. Without you, what do I have to live for? Ida will not allow me near her children. The Duc de Guiche disapproves of what he calls my effeminacy but means a form of depravity that, as you know better than anyone, is abhorrent to me. Last week, Le Générale D'Orsay threw me out of his house, employing the filthy language of his common soldiers. He will never speak to me again. He ranted and raved and said I'd lost my right to call myself a nobleman because I was not a man at all. And this from a general who served the great Napoleon and now bends his aging knee before a worthless creature like Charles X.'

'My darling Alfred, you are more of a man than your father ever was.'

'I have no father, I have no mother and I have no Lord Blessington. You, my beloved Marguerite, are all I have.'

'But Alfred, remember you have a wife, and a great fortune in your trust. You are to be rich and free to live as you wish.'

'That is what Lord Blessington led me to expect but I am in desperate need of your help, Marguerite. You understand the English law. Perhaps you can explain this letter from a Mr Alexander Worthington? It says I am now Lord Blessington's executor, jointly with this agent, Norman and this Worthington, whoever he is.'

'All that will be required of you, Alfred, is to sign a few important-looking documents. Norman will continue to manage poor Charles's lands and properties and I believe Worthington is a lawyer who specialises in the inconsequential formalities of executorship.'

'But, Marguerite, you know I have no understanding of these matters.'

'I too have received a letter from Worthington. In my reply I shall request a detailed statement of the estate's position and explain it to you.'

My letter from Worthington's office had enclosed the first instalment of my paltry annuity. My dear friend Charles Dickens, through the wisdom of Wilkins Micawber, told the world that happiness is the result of an annual income of twenty pounds. But that was two decades later when money was worth a little less. This was 1829 and for me unhappiness was the result of the annual income of two thousand pounds, which Worthington implied that I could not rely upon receiving indefinitely.

I said *au revoir* to the world of the Earl of Blessington where money came from the ether, and *bonjour* to the real world where it comes from inspiration and endeavour. I threw my widow's weeds onto the compost heap of the past and ordered six bright new dresses from an over-rated Parisian couturier. Then I wrote to Worthington demanding access to the accounts of the Blessington estate.

There were no accounts.

'I very much regret to inform your ladyship that with so many pressing priorities, there can be no prospect of a meaningful statement of your late husband's affairs for some months.

I beg to remain, Lady Blessington, your ever humble and obedient servant – etc. etc,

Alexander Worthington.'

Mr Worthington's London and Dublin offices were sinking beneath a mountain of property valuations, investment validations, income assessment, unpaid bills, overdrawn bank accounts, menacing moneylenders and embittered petitions from Charles's grieving relatives. In addition, large estates were, in those days, subject to an insane set of laws known as *'the equitable and statutory apportionments'*. This accounting chicanery was meticulously designed by the legal profession to ensure fruitlessly fair distribution of capital and income arising before and after the date of death, and to guarantee lengthy delays and excessive administration costs. Charles's affairs would take not some months, but some years to unravel. Mr Worthington could expect little more cooperation from the excellent Mr Norman than from Alfred. I might have felt sorry for the lawyer had he not been so quick at extracting the iniquitous fees that he so equivocally justified and so slow at everything else.

Again I met my self-adopted son in the garden.

'Alfred, from my understanding of Charles's will you should now be in receipt of a very substantial income from the trust monies?'

'That is apparently the case, Marguerite, Worthington sent three or four hundred pounds for my present needs, but I am in no way concerned; I have already trebled it at the tables. He apologised most profusely for not being able to send more. It seems some moneylender or other is being difficult, and a few houses have to go. But there are plenty more in Dublin. Do give me your opinion of this cravat? I had it dyed to match the green parakeet. Do you see him, up there at the top of the aviary?'

I offered to assist Alfred by managing his and the legally infant Harriet's financial affairs. After all, the young couple were sharing separate suites at my château and I felt perfectly entitled to a modest contribution towards the household expenses. I approved of Alfred's cravat and matching dyed buttonhole, and he agreed to pay the rent, the maintenance of the stables and the servants' wages. Well, he had asked me to treat him as a son.

Not only was I a good mother, I was a good daughter and a good sister.

I appealed to Mr Worthington's compassion for settlement of Robert's legacy in advance of probate. My businesslike entreaty explained that my brother's wife was terminally ill and that he was unable to afford doctors and medicines. His children were suffering malnutrition and in need of food, clothing and shelter. This all might well have been true.

Worthington's office passed my letter to the excellent Mr Norman who was so moved that he immediately gave Robert two-hundred pounds on account of his one thousand pound legacy, together with a note informing him that his services would no longer be required. No, Robert never received the rest of his legacy. The Honourable Charles Gardiner, now aged nineteen, had come down from Oxford with the intention of managing Mountjoy Forest himself until he inherited it at the age of twenty-five.

The next letter I received from Robert informed me that my appeal to Mr Worthington was more truthful than I had believed.

'I know I have asked for your help too many times, Margaret, but my small legacy is almost gone and I am unable to support my family. My wife is very sick and I am desperate to find work. Can you remember any of the landowners that Lord Blessington knew who might be in need of an assistant? '

I could think of no one. Charles and I had entertained many Irish landed gentry but I had heard nothing of them for years. Those I remembered would not do their own mother a favour let alone me or my destitute brother. As a last resort I approached the Tyrone Militia, and exerting my rank as widow of its Colonel-in-Chief, respectfully ordered the brigadier to grant Robert a commission.

'You have my word that Mr Robert Power will make an excellent officer and be a credit to the regiment.'

I did not expect a reply, least of all the following, which reached Paris just four weeks later:

'My most esteemed, Lady Blessington,
    If I might be permitted to add a personal postscript to the Regiment's formal letter of condolence, not only I, but my officers and men of all ranks recall Lieutenant-General Viscount Blessington with the greatest affection and respect. We are all deeply grateful for his unfailing contributions to the regimental funds.
    The Tyrone Militia is therefore proud and humbled to be permitted the opportunity to honour its late commander-in-chief by accepting Mr Power's application with immediate promotion to the rank of Captain.
    My adjutant has been ordered to carry out the necessary arrangements.
    In deepest sympathy

Your obedient servant, etc, etc'

Nepotism was always the most powerful weapon in the arsenal of the British army. The necessary arrangements consumed all that remained of Robert's legacy-cum-severance payment and his officer's pay was less than he received at Mountjoy Forest. As an officer he was expected to have his own uniforms made and pay his mess bills from private income. I did my best to supply the obligatory private income, while Captain Robert Power proved himself as suited to army life as his regiment's late Colonel-in-Chief.

With yet more pitiful advocacy I wrung Marianne's whole one-thousand-pound legacy out of the administrators, and in order to be completely fair to her retained only half as a contribution to her keep. Normally I would not have dreamed of doing anything so uncharitable, but I was aware that she had accumulated significant savings through the years while she had lived in luxury at Charles's expense. I felt obliged to teach my still young sister the value of money.

The only member of my family to whom I felt no obligation was Ellen. Her letter of sympathy, like all the others, extolled Charles's magnanimity. She reminisced about her rent-free years at St James's Square and touchingly advised me that it was a shame to leave such a beautiful house empty. How helpful! In similar sisterly spirit, she asked what was stopping me from coming back to London. As mistress of the Speaker's house, Mrs Manner-Sutton mixed with the most prominent members of the Commons and Lords and could introduce me to any number of rich and interesting bachelors, divorced men and widowers.

She had been a victim of the same purveyors of iniquity who had plagued me but had learnt how to silence them with feminine wiles. She was confident that I could do likewise. In a postscript, she mentioned that she had missed me and yearned to see me again. I was unconvinced but knew that, sooner or later, no option would remain other than to follow Ellen's advice. Even with access to Harriet and Alfred's intermittent income, it would be impossible for me to stay in Paris. Civil unrest was rising to an untenable crescendo. Day and night the streets were crowded with angry impoverished citizens, fighting and rioting, and were becoming too dangerous for me to venture from the opulent Avenue de Matignon.

No sooner had I resolved to return to London when another Charles – would there be no end to them? – stepped boldly into my life. Charles Molloy Westmacott was the high-principled proprietor of a scandal sheet called *The Age* and proud recipient of a string of convictions for blackmail. This distinguished journalist, then sheltering from the wrath of the less grateful of his clients, sent his English devotees the news from Paris that:

'Alfred Orsay, with his pretty pink and white face, drives about á la Petersham with a cocked up hat and a long tailed cream-coloured horse. He says he will have seventeen thousand a year to spend; others say seventeen hundred. He and my Lady go on as usual.' *'What a ménage is that of Lady Blessington This young gentleman* [Alfred], *Lady Blessington and the virgin-wife of sixteen all live together. You must surely remember a lady who, some fifteen years ago, was acting wife to a Captain J. of some dragoon regiment. As he had nothing but his spurs and whiskers Mrs J. used to levy taxes on her friends according to a system here called 'les contributions indirectes'. Petersham introduced her to a lord who like a fool married her.'*

Alfred was calmly enraged at being compared to Viscount 'Beau' Petersham, later Earl of Harrington, who was twenty years his senior and had no concept of the correct way to wear the Petersham overcoat of his own design. I was even more calmly enraged. How dare *The Age* print so many beautifully embroidered facts? I immediately wrote to the owner-editor.

'Dear Mr Westmacott

I shall not stoop to responding to your disgusting fiction concerning my household, but demand that a full and thorough withdrawal and an unequivocal apology be displayed prominently on your next front page. Should this not be forthcoming I will be faced with no alternative but, jointly with the Comte and Comtesse D'Orsay, to immediately commence legal proceedings on numerous counts of libel and defamation of character.

I trust, sir, that you will not compel me to take such action. etc. etc.,

Marguerite, Countess of Blessington'

And I received a full and thorough reply.

'My dear Lady Blessington,

You cruelly misjudge me, madam. As a reputable newspaper proprietor I adhere to the highest principles of my honourable profession. Under no circumstances do I publish anything unless I am certain that it is the truth. What is more, everything printed concerning you and others of your, let us say, somewhat unconventional ménage is common knowledge in London, as it is in Paris. Were I to withdraw my harmless commentary, I should be a laughing stock. And should you publicly deny it, you will be a greater laughing stock. Permit me to remind you, your ladyship, that there are in London society correspondents far less scrupulous than I.

Until now I have been more than discreet but information has come to my attention, based on which I have drafted the attached article; the first of an intended series. Might I request that you spare a moment of your valuable time to glance through it, and do me the honour of pointing out any inaccuracies you might observe.

To spare you the effort of asking, as a professional journalist I am honour-bound never to disclose my sources. But then of course you know that, your own dear father was himself a sometime newspaper proprietor. Convicted of libel, was he not? Or was it murder, I forget? However, it can do no harm to inform you that certain ladies of quality are presently in the habit of regularly travelling between the English and Irish capitals.

I shall be in Paris for a further fortnight and will deem it a privilege should you see fit to receive me at your splendid château. Behind the high walls of the Avenue de Matignon I am sure we can devise a simple strategy to spare the blushes of a social eminence of your esteemed reputation.

Believe me, Lady Blessington, when I say that I remain your ever humble servant and obedient friend.

C. M. Westmacott'

I refused to yield to anger and forced myself to think as irrationally as Westmacott himself. He claimed to be a professional and, as such, would already have employed his expertise to penetrate the high walls of the Avenue de Matignon. Had I been honest, and who would have been honest in my position, I might have been impressed by his remarkable talents, which in the fullness of time enabled him to retire to Paris partly disabled from numerous beatings and only an immense fortune with which to replenish his diminished stock of friends.

But the esteemed journalist was trying to be too clever. His first error was to remind me of my experience of the law of libel and his second to specify the time at my disposal. I did not answer Westmacott but forwarded his letter and offensive cuttings to the London office of John Allen Powell. When the owner-editor of *The Age* returned to London, he was greeted by an inventory of counter-charges and a reminder that the penalties for blackmail included gaol and the cat-of-nine-tails. C. M. Westmacott had experienced both.

The lawyer's communication was all legal bluff and bluster but surprisingly, Westmacott succumbed and restrained from publishing the findings of his assiduous research, for a while. Other gentlemen of the press were not so negligent in their duty to ensure that I was remembered by London society. I thus bravely chose to remain in the safe haven of strife-torn Paris.

Alfred kept his promise of conjugal celibacy. When spurned by a male admirer he occasionally took comfort between my silver swans, since I was, and would remain the only female capable of arousing his passion. Though inquisitive observers frequently reported us riding together in the Bois de Boulogne, we were far from inseparable. Alfred spent his time at the race courses, boxing rings and gentleman's clubs where there was always a discerning audience to impress with his sartorial elegance and reckless gambling. He had only to boast of the Blessington inheritance and he was inundated with offers of credit to pay for his consistent good luck.

This is not to suggest that Alfred neglected his wife. Madame Craufurd would not have permitted anything so ignoble. She found the young Comtesse's burgeoning charms so potentially attractive that, possibly for the first time in her life of sin, she felt a twinge of conscience. The aged socialite concluded that atonement might be a worthwhile precaution against the improbability of finding in Heaven a being superior to herself. She thus dispensed with protocol and invited to la rue D'Anjou, a selection of more suitable husbands for her grandson's virgin wife. The blossoming Comtesse Harriet scarcely required the sponsorship of the despised royal court's most beloved matron to attract, among other noble suitors, Ferdinand-Philippe, Duc de Chartres. Fortunately for his new mistress, the probable heir to the throne of France had been properly educated at an English public school.

By the spring of 1830 it was clear that the days of the Bourbon monarchy, and of Charles X in particular, were numbered. Revolution again polluted the Parisian air and stained the debris on its streets red with blood. Patriotic aristocrats, who had seen it all before, hurriedly packed their courtly cash and noble gemstones and fled the capital, temporarily. Not even the sturdy walls of the Avenue de Matignon provided a barrier to the noise and stench of political turmoil.

To Alfred, Comte D'Orsay, nothing if not a patriotic aristocrat, this was perfectly agreeable. He flaunted the glory of his Napoleonic heritage as never before and was even applauded as he rode in the street, once or twice. But the people of France were not cheering his irrational defence of the deceased Bonaparte. They were cheering for Louis-Philippe, whose martyred father, the Duc d'Orléans, was executed for supporting the 1789 Revolution and whose handsome son, Ferdinand-Philippe, Duc de Chartres, was the paramour of the Comtesse D'Orsay. Louis-Philippe, as the popular aspirant to the throne of France was, shall I say, displeased with Ferdinand.

The time had come for me to leave Paris and face my London antagonists. A far-sighted reckless investor relieved me of the lease of the Avenue de Matignon and bought all my furniture, after I terminated my hire-purchase agreements at minimal cost. Despite the adverse market, my silver swan bed, aviary and other redundant practicalities realised significant returns which I employed to have the more valuable of my *objets d'art* transported with me to St. James's Square to add to Charles's collections.

In July 1830, literarily in the heat of revolution, Louis-Philippe seized the throne from Charles X and Alfred was overjoyed. The new king would certainly honour him, the son of a general in the Grande Armée, with high government office in the best interests of the nation. And indeed Alfred did receive a communication from the royal equerry. It advised him to immediately remove his wife from France in the best interests of the nation. Alfred thus fled his native land, less to escape the wrath of its new monarch than the threats of its accommodating gamblers, bankers and tailors. In London he would preserve his marriage and, from the fortune dependent upon its preservation raise all the credit he needed.

Neither he nor Harriet had received any remittance from the Blessington estates for many months but Alfred remained unconcerned. His late father-in-law's name was always good in Lombard Street and London was full of wealthy friends happy to lose to him at the card tables. His fellow executors, who no longer bothered to provide him with their incomprehensible reports, would soon settle their arrears, from which he faithfully promised to contribute to my expenses at St James's Square. And I believed him of course.

Marianne adamantly refused to come back to London. This was an immense relief. My sister had been my superfluous companion for far too long and I had wearied of her endless criticisms of what she called my shameless lifestyle. Whatever she meant by that, she had managed to happily accept it for eleven years while Charles had treated her with incredulous consideration. Now things were different. There was no further need for Marianne to criticise my guardianship of the innocent Harriet in the arms of her French lover. Alfred had always been courteous to Marianne, an amusing ragged Irish philistine, but since Charles died she had also presumed to find fault with his self-indulgence, unscrupulous marriage and even his mother-son relationship with me.

Our ferry docked at Dover. I mimed dejection and in a few strong words of sisterly farewell, I asked Marianne why she had rejected or repelled every young man to whom I had introduced in England, France and Italy. Presuming that I knew the answer, she simply shrugged to indicate that she did not appreciate the question, and so I asked about her immediate intentions. She planned to go first to Dublin to see Father. Then she would go to County Tyrone to assist Robert's wife who was genuinely ailing and help care for her daughters, Marguerite, aged fourteen and Nellie (Ellen), aged twelve. Since she had no need of money herself, I entrusted Marianne with all I could afford to distribute among the residue of our family, hypocritically embraced her and we parted for the last time, or so I thought.

I had not been forgotten in my eight years of absence. The free press, of which I was always an unrelenting advocate, welcomed me back to London with all its inimitable tenderness. Within days it began raining down its gentle invective upon the new trio comprising my household at 10 St James's Square.

C. M. Westmacott had fully intended that I should have no difficulty in identifying the 'certain ladies of quality, presently in the habit of regularly travelling between the English and Irish capitals'. True to his profession, he wished the revelation of his undisclosed source to cause as much pain as possible. The arch blackmailer had a wonderful sense of humour. He had almost laughed his innocent head off at Mr Powell's threats.

Of London's most illustrious society hostesses, the infinitely respectable Countess Catherine Maria Charleville stood second only in self-esteem to Lady Holland. A versatile artist of some accomplishment, the countess was intelligent, charming and kind, with a viperous tongue and a propensity to criticise her revered guests to their faces, something I would never do. She also boasted of being partially disabled in both lower limbs, though was fit enough to regularly brave the hazards of the long and treacherous road from her mansion in Cavendish Square to Charleville Castle at Tullamore, west of Dublin. I never actually met her but her husband, Viscount Charleville had often attended the dinners Charles hosted at St James's Square for the exclusive fellowship of the Irish Representative Peers, and exasperated them with the fervour of his political obscurity. Regardless of party allegiance, social or national consequence, Charleville supported every bill favourable to the unscrupulous land dealings from which he accumulated his unmitigated wealth.

Lady Charleville's closest friends and confidantes included the dowager Lady Margaret Mountjoy and Harriet Gardiner, themselves now frequent travellers between Dublin and London. Their jaundiced accounts of my misdemeanours would have been of no interest to the sixty-six-year-old grand hostess had she not been so averse to her married son's growing friendship with Alfred. As a loving mother, her greatest fear, quite unreasonably, was that the pampered young Lord Tullamore might be keeping bad company.

Like all in Alfred's circle, Tullamore was a dandy and habitué of the London clubs. When not so engaged, he sat – and did little else – as the unopposed Tory Member of Parliament for the rotten borough of Carlow in Ireland. The Whig statesman Thomas Creevey aptly described him as *justly entitled to the prize for the greatest bore the world can produce.*'

At the age of nineteen, Tullamore, on a sudden whim, had married the adventurous granddaughter of the Duke of Argyle, Charlotte Beaujolais, and it came as no surprise to anybody other than Lady Charleville that this attractive young lady gave herself to more than one lover. The protective countess regarded her daughter-in-law as abhorrent as Alfred and, incomprehensibly, comparable to me.

My immediate concerns on returning to London were, however, less social than financial. The proceeds of my possessions sold in Paris would not last long. I took stock. My assets consisted of my uncertain annuity, the lease of 10 St. James's Square, its contents, and, oh yes, Alfred's solemn promise to pay his share of the expenses. The long lease was more of a liability than an asset. Not only was the rent excessive, but I was responsible for all repairs and maintenance and a great many had accumulated in my absence. I thus offered Mr Worthington the unique opportunity to purchase the lease for the estate. He agreed, but not at the price I asked.

'Dare I suggest, Lady Blessington, that you are being a little over-ambitious,' said one of the clerks at his London office.

I was being a lot over-ambitious. I was also a little desperate until Alfred mentioned that one of his clubs, the Windham, was seeking more prestigious premises. I sent my butler, whose name, I think was Horatio, round to Piccadilly with a request for the secretary to call upon me.

'Indeed, Lady Blessington, St James's Square is the ideal location for a club of our standing. The committee has been considering several houses in the immediate vicinity for some time. Number 10 however is too spacious for our comparatively small and highly-exclusive membership. And, as you doubtless are aware, your former tenants, the Honourable Mr and Mrs Manners-Sutton, appear to have sadly neglected the fabric of the property.'

The house is yet to be built which can emerge unscathed from the ravages of six children for two-and-a-half years. Ellen and Manners-Sutton had not only lived rent free, but had spent not one penny on the fabric of the property. By feigning naivety, polite bargaining and flaunting my femininity, the best I could do was convince Windham's to accept a sub-lease at three-quarters of the rent declined by Mr Worthington, and thus secure me a much-needed, if modest, profit for the remainder of the term.

Windham's also purchased all the furniture and utensils I did not need. I retained only my library, my collection of memorabilia and the more valuable of the artworks and silver. In memory of its late patron, the Drury Lane Theatre bought all Charles's clothes for use as costumes. Everything else I disposed of through newspaper advertisements or at auction. Amidst this whirlpool of activity, the precise wording of Charles's will slipped my mind and possibly some of the *'jewellery, plate and paraphernalia'* bequeathed to his children was sucked in. In total, I realised sufficient to resume the lifestyle of a countess, or so I thought. All I required was a suitable house, in Mayfair perhaps. Charles's old mansion at Seamore Place would be ideal. By pleading homelessness and widowhood, I would persuade Mr Worthington to offer it to me on a compassionate lease. I returned to his London office. He was unavailable. He was never available there or anywhere else.

'Lord Blessington sold the house three years before he died, your ladyship,' said his clerk.

'Really, do you know why?'

'Apparently he was travelling on the Continent at the time, and it was turning out more expensive that he thought, your ladyship.'

'And did he raise the necessary funds?'

'I don't think so, your ladyship, it was sold very cheaply to an anonymous agent from Dublin.'

'And does this Irish agent still own the house?'

'No, your ladyship, he sold it at substantial profit to Lord Mountford.'

The new owner of 8 Seamore Place was as businesslike as Charles.

'Yes, Lady Blessington, I purchased the house from an excellent fellow. I think he was called Norway, or something like that. He said that the house was a prudent investment yet I had great difficulty securing a tenant. When eventually I found one, he vanished after about eight months leaving the rent unpaid and the interior in an alarming state of disrepair. As you might appreciate, your ladyship, it was such an unpleasant experience that I have been unable to bring myself to offer to lease the house again.'

'You may rest completely assured, Lord Mountford, I shall cause you no such embarrassment. This lovely old mansion is a part of my life, filled with happy memories. Ah, so many happy memories! It was my first home after I married Lord Blessington and we were ecstatically happy here for many years. Such sentiment! I trust we can come to a satisfactory arrangement.'

'It will be an honour to welcome you back, Lady Blessington.'

I had lived at Seamore Place only for a few miserable weeks while St James's Square was being refurbished.

'You are most gracious, Lord Mountford. But for your absolute peace of mind, I am prepared to offer you a whole year's rent in advance. But, as you have pointed out the maintenance *has* been somewhat neglected. A man of the world, like yourself, will be aware that it is customary in such circumstances to waive a short period of rent to permit a new tenant to render the house habitable.'

Lord Mountford, unaccustomed to the niceties of the landlord's art, accepted about a quarter of the market rent with payment to commence nine months hence. At the expiry of that time, I sincerely apologised for the tardy administration of the Blessington estates and paid by monthly instalments in arrears, whenever possible. Meanwhile I employed the rent-fee period to redecorate the entire house and replace the furnishings. The thoughtlessness of the previous tenants was quite shocking. Seamore Place was left in almost as bad a state of repair as St James's Square. Though the new house was smaller, the outlook on Park Lane was more pleasant. The wind did not carry the odours of Piccadilly westward.

Soon the fears and forebodings brought from Paris crystallised into enduring self-esteem. Since I was better educated than any high-born London hostess I would make Seamore Place a house of culture and intellect, rather than an assembly room for chattering socialites. I would invite only men of talent, distinction and achievement, and possibly some women too.

The largest room in the house was fitted with high casements opening onto an enclosed balcony, spanning the width of first floor and offering daylight until the last crescent of sunset faded. Hung with aquamarine silk draperies embroidered with gold, this was my boudoir, my workshop and my window on the animated kaleidoscope of human diversity outside. The ground floor was dominated by my library - another replica of Mrs Jenkins's cerebral sanctuary – adjoining a dining room for just eighteen guests. My dinner guests would be meticulously selected.

Having completed my refurbishments, I set out my salvaged collections for the edification of my guests – here the Empress Josephine's Sèvres-topped table, there Marie Antoinette's royal blue vases, a golden chair presented by George IV to Charles X – creating the feel of a fine art museum. As one poetic sage put it, Seamore Place was *'a house of bijoux and a bijou of a house'*.

'Mr Sadleir, what possessed you to suggest that I engineered *'a direct assault on the leisure hours of fashionable London'* and that I devised a *'plan to conquer London'*? And what did you mean by *'the suddenness of* [my] *attack had taken* [my] *enemies by surprise?'*

'To be frank, Lady Blessington, I thought this the least interesting part of your story. I was simply trying to liven it up a little by restating what others implied.'

'I am surprised at you, Mr Sadleir. You make me sound like some sort of social Queen Boadicea. You were supposed to be a serious historian, not a purveyor of unfounded assumptions.'

'I assure you, Lady Blessington, that I researched your life as thoroughly and professionally as was possible at the time and I did not commit my conclusions to paper lightly.'

'In that case, you should have known that I gave Lady Holland, Lady Charleville and the other belligerent queens of the London salon no reason to suspect that my intention was to invade their cherished little realms. Consider my position? I was an eligible widow. I knew numerous wealthy men. What was there to stop me marrying again and leaving the Gardiners and the D'Orsays to squabble among themselves over Lord Blessington's masterful miscellany of posthumous planning.'

'Yes, I often wondered why you did not do just that. I was unaware until today that Captain Farmer left you barren, and had presumed that you chose to remain unwed because you were sexually impotent.'

'I have told you in no uncertain terms, Mr Sadleir, your theories were mistaken. After two marriages ending in tragedy, three, if you count Thomas Jenkins, surely you can appreciate that the idea of taking another husband was not exactly attractive. The time had come to make my mark in the world by my own ability.'

'But why did you commit yourself to the expense of a great house like Seamore Place? You must have known a man like D'Orsay was never going contribute to your expenses. He squandered or gambled away a hundred pounds for every pound he received from Lord Blessington's estate. What is more, the Gardiner family constantly challenged his rights of inheritance. You must have guessed that he would be bankrupt before too long.'

'Of course I was aware of all that, Mr Sadleir. I was surprised that Alfred and his so-called wife stayed with me as long as they did. But I needed their money. I was a countess and poor. When you are poor you cannot afford to look poor.'

As I said at the beginning of my story, pride in appearance matters, it has always mattered and always will matter. Pride in appearance is a performing art and Seamore Place was my theatre, with no tickets for snobs, bores, boasters, prattlers or theology-spouting clergy. The haughty hostesses of London were welcome to such riffraff. Only those I judged learned and accomplished would gain entrance to my house of pretentious culture. Out went my invitations and back came my friends: Disraeli, Moore, Lawrence, Landor, Jerdan and Letitia Landon. Protected by my opulent walls, Charles's old colleagues from the Lords and Commons spoke their anachronistic minds unrestrained by parliamentary convention. After the curtains closed in the West End, actors and actresses found respite from the unreality of the stage in the fantasy of my salon. Alfred spiced his genius for rapport with wit and cynicism and introduced a raft of brilliant young men, who, like him, took pride in appearance just a little too far.

For a year I sedated myself from the unceasing whispers of the beau monde supported by taunts and torment from the Commons Speaker's now legitimate wife, guarding her reputation by deriding mine. Ellen's exalted elevation to hostess of her husband's official residence demanded that she forget the late Earl of Blessington's generosity, together with her sisterly devotion. Her guests, like mine, saw only the mask of happiness.

'There are so few before whom one would condescend to appear otherwise than happy.'

I was not the only person masking unhappiness at Seamore Place. Every day Alfred and Harriet screamed abuse and accusations at one another with a ferocity that made London's ladies of fashion seem almost civilised.

'You are not my husband. I will never let you to come near me. All you do is dress up like a woman and gamble away my father's money with your filthy debauched friends. You say you cannot consummate our marriage because I am too young, yet you can practice hideous perversions with your young men and the old woman downstairs.'

I was past forty; an old woman to a girl of Harriet's age and Alfred, despite his keen eye for portraiture, was blind to my multiplying chins and expanding waist.

'How dare you insult Lady Blessington when you yourself, madame, are no better than a whore? In Paris I had to drag you from the bed of an upstart prince. And here in London, do you think I enjoy hearing the name of the Comtesse D'Orsay linked with that miserable cuckold, Tullamore, and God knows how many others.'

I did my utmost to broker a peace but neither Alfred nor Harriet had the slightest desire to see my concept of reason. Only in one respect were we in accord: we were all growing impatient with the stagnant progress of the Blessington estate. Acrimoniously, we agreed to make a concerted endeavour to learn our financial prospects, however daunting.

'My esteemed Mr Worthington,

The Comte and Comtesse D'Orsay and I, as beneficiaries of the estate of the late Earl of Blessington, regret to inform you that we have reason to be concerned by your lack of remittances and dearth of reports. We thus demand to be informed forthwith when we can expect to receive settlement of our outstanding legacies.

Once again, I must presume upon you to forward a full financial statement.

I beg to remain your obedient servant.

Marguerite, Countess of Blessington'

Mr Worthington's studied ambiguous response was abundantly clear. The estate's affairs had become so unwieldy and perplexing, that he barely understood them himself. We were all annoyed and exasperated, and we were not alone. Charles had raised finance from so many sources that I found it hard to believe that he had concealed this absorbing pastime from me. At least thirty bankers and moneylenders were demanding repayment. From the executors' erroneous statement of affairs, I calculated that about £160,000 was outstanding, seventy-million pounds or more today, with interest compounding faster than a horse can gallop. Many properties had been sold. Could the estate cover its long-term obligations?

Uninformed bankers fawned and offered me credit. They thought I was a rich heiress and I was greatly tempted not to disillusion them but I respected English law and above all feared bankruptcy. Bankruptcy relieves debt but not conscience. Alfred entertained no such qualms. His extravagance outstripped Charles at his most profligate. He purchased thoroughbred horses, had carriages built resplendent with the D'Orsay arms and ordered exquisite boots, shoes, hats and gloves by the dozen. He had coats and breeches made to measure by the most exclusive tailors in London, none of whom he intended to pay. In fact, he expected them to *'line'* his bespoke pockets with cash to stake at the clubs, and they happily complied. The patronage of London's best-dressed man-about-town was invaluable publicity.

While, as always, I frowned upon extravagance, I never deigned to be economical. Ever-affable shopkeepers lowered their heads and raised their prices. None was more attentive to the demands of my wardrobe, kitchens and cellars than Mr Howell and Mr James. The proprietors of Regent Street's most prestigious department store invariably treated me with the utmost courtesy, and never raised the vulgar question of payment. Perhaps they were a touch too amenable?

On the 31ˢᵗ July 1831 a self-opinionated newspaper called *The Satirist*, controlled if not owned by my indefatigable penfriend, Mr Westmacott, amused its readers with a riddle:

> *My first is the reverse of a curse,*
> *My second of every great weight is,*
> *My whole is neither better nor worse*
> *Than a dame from the land of potatoes.*
> *Of her daughter-in-law*
> *She makes a cat's paw*
> *(Ask the fair virgin bride*
> *By Count D'Orsay's side)*

On 5ᵗʰ August an anonymous well-wisher sent the Comtesse D'Orsay, by then certainly no virgin bride, a copy of this ingenious verse as a gift for her nineteenth birthday. Harriet, lacking any sense of humour, found it a severe embarrassment.

I had provided my step-daughter-in-law – 'not daughter-in-law, Mr Sadleir' – with a comfortable home and shown her every kindness and sympathy. Yet the ungrateful girl sent this disgusting poem to her beloved family with an account of life at Seamore Place so horrendous and alarming that Lady Mountjoy, Harriet Gardiner and the Comtesse's sister Emily tore themselves from the grace and favour of Henrietta Street and mounted a defensive expedition to London. On the day they moved into their new residence on the far side of Hyde Park, the Comtesse D'Orsay made a hurried departure from Seamore Place. No, she did not say goodbye or thank me.

A fortnight later Alfred received a communication from a leading firm of Dublin advocates.

'Sir, As representatives of the Honourable Charles Edward Gardiner, we hereby notify you that for the protection of his financial interests and those of his sisters Lady Mary Emily Gardiner and Harriet, Countess D'Orsay, and of his grandmother Lady Margaret Mountjoy, the said Mr Gardiner has instructed us to petition the Court of Chancery for the invalidation of the last Will and Testament of his late father, the Earl of Blessington.'

A second letter warned Alfred to expect a petition on behalf of 'Lady Harriet Gardiner, presently known as the Comtesse Alfred D'Orsay', for the annulment of her unconsummated marriage, entered into under duress and without consent.

Charles Dickens was to often enchant me with his vehement diatribes against the venerable institutions of British justice, but I was long dead before it was possible to heed the immortal caution at the commencement of *Bleak House*.

'This is the Court of Chancery ... which gives to monied might the means abundantly of wearing out the right; which so exhausts finance, patience, courage, hope; so overthrows the brain and breaks the heart; that there is not an honourable man among its practitioners who does not give — or does not often give — the warning, "Suffer any wrong that can be done you rather than come here!"'

I had suffered enough legal jargon to predict the consequences of Alfred's communications. Mr Worthington, a professional executor, was scarcely malleable but now he was to be manacled hand and foot. His every act would be subjected to the consent of the Court of Chancery. And the consent of the Court of Chancery would be subjected to due deliberation. Due deliberation made the Court of Chancery slower than a weary snail. It would be years before it would reach any conclusion, and by then all the Blessington estates would have vaporised into a haze of memory.

Thankfully the term 'due deliberation' is seldom employed in the twenty-first century. It has been replaced by the infinitely more effective 'due diligence', the tremendous benefits of which are so often unappreciated by the laity.

The lawyer's letters might have turned a lesser man suicidal, but Alfred dismissed my interpretation with his invariable sangfroid.

'Have no fear, Marguerite, a will is but a blunt instrument. It therefore can be sharpened. Perhaps my wife will discover that she has no grounds for complaint. Meanwhile I always have Crockford's to rely upon. Young Tullamore mentioned he'd be there tonight. I promised to let him have a look at this silk coat that Schwarz delivered yesterday. Do you not think it an exquisite match for my shoes?'

By ten-thirty that evening Comte Alfred D'Orsay had won, or as the more negatively-minded might imply, lost five hundred pounds. To celebrate he asked his friend, Lord Tullamore, to join him in a magnum of Mr Crockford's finest vintage champagne.

'No, Tull, black is not at all fashionable this year. Observe closely, do you see the tint of ebony that makes all the difference.'

'Yes, you are quite right, D'Orsay, and the style is quite unique. You wear it so exquisitely. I do so envy your deportment.'

'Permit me to recommend the esteemed Mr Schwarz, whose cut will show your inimitable gait to perfect advantage. I shall send him to you for a fitting in the morning. Meanwhile, I wonder if we might have a quiet word on a slightly more delicate subject.'

'I am indebted for your advice and at your service, D'Orsay. Let us ask the waiter to take our champagne into the smoking room.'

'As I think you are possibly aware, Tull, I have heard nothing from my wife recently and naturally I am concerned for her welfare. Would you by chance have any news of the Comtesse Harriet?'

'I really can't tell you anything of great help, D'Orsay, except that my mother did mention that the Comtesse has visited her once or twice with Lady Mountjoy.'

'As you know, I never indulge in petty gossip but I've heard it implied you know a little more than that. Tull, we're old friends. Trust me, you have my word that whatever you say will be treated in complete confidence and will cause no offence.'

'Alright, D'Orsay, Harriet is perfectly well. And if you must have the truth, I have been seeing her recently, but I give you my word of honour, there has been no impropriety.'

'Look, Tull, I appreciate this might seem a little unusual, but I would actually prefer it if there were a little impropriety, as you put it. As doubtless the Comtesse has informed you, we have never lived as man and wife. Most women would cut off their right hand for my favours yet, quite beyond my comprehension, Harriet invariably rejects me. Be that as it may. Would you not find it a great pleasure, shall we say, to assist me in this regard?'

'This is a strange request, D'Orsay. What on earth prompts it?'

'Well you see, Tull, there are legal issues. Nothing serious: they can be eliminated easily enough by one of two scenarios. Either you will provide evidence to enable me to win a divorce settlement – total discretion, no names of course – or Lady Harriet will conceive an heir for me to acknowledge as my son. Either way, the outcome will be much the same. I shall become the unassailable beneficiary of the bulk of the late Lord Blessington's estate in accordance with the clear intention of his will.'

'My dear D'Orsay, I fear you misjudge the situation. My own wife has been unfaithful to me many times but I am determined to preserve my marriage. I have deliberately been seen with Harriet to demonstrate to Lady Charlotte that I am not the feckless cuckold she seems to think me. In any case, D'Orsay, your Comtesse is out of London. She is at present at Lord Blessington's old house at Worthing with her sister Emily taking the sea air. What else she does there is of no concern to me. Goodnight sir, I wish you good luck at the tables and with any other of your wife's paramours you might choose to approach. Oh, and please don't trouble yourself to summon Mr Schwarz.'

Lord Tullamore very properly conveyed the gist of this conversation to his adoring mother. Lady Charleville was disgusted and delighted to have her opinion of Comte D'Orsay confirmed.

'I realise now, Mother, that the man is completely unprincipled and amoral. I intend to have nothing further to do with him. I am not at all surprised that the Comtesse left a house where her husband was living openly with a mistress who is also his mother-in-law.'

Alfred, who never lost a bet, had lost the most hazardous of all. He did not tell me about his offer to Lord Tullamore but I observed a change in his demeanour. At the oddest times he would suddenly embrace me, as he did in the garden of the Avenue de Matignon, remind me that I was his mother, and profess his undying love. When appropriate I reciprocated.

'Our love was not as improbable as you surmise, Dr Madden.'

'Frankly, Lady Blessington, I could never see that you had anything in common whatsover.'

'You were never very observant, were you? Alfred and I had a great deal in common. We were both social misfits who loved the worthless prestige of luxury and opulence. And don't forget beneath his blasé pose Alfred was like me an accomplished scholar as well as a talented artist. As you know he was a star student at the Lycée Napoléon, which like an English public school, endowed the perpetual self-confidence which made him so attractive, while he in turn was attracted by the perpetual self-confidence with which I was endowed by nature.'

The artistic Lady Charleville dragged the names of D'Orsay and Blessington through the slimy mud of London society with the cultured dexterity with which she dragged her brushes through her oily paints. Scandal rose to a new crescendo. In my nightmares flocks of witches with cavernous mouths flew out of the trees in Hyde Park and consumed my house with curses, lies and abuse. Wary, longstanding adherents of my soirées, who should have known better, avoided Seamore Place as if it were a diabolical pit of evil. I ceased issuing invitations, temporarily.

Alfred had to leave and not be seen to come back. When I broke the news, he fell to his knees and confessed to extravagance, excessive gambling and debauchery as if he feared that I was throwing him out for no better reason than these commonplace gentlemanly pursuits. He even went down on his knees and begged to stay like a small child sent to bed early. I told him to go immediately. The following morning passers-by were treated to the spectacle of a magnificently dressed Frenchman directing four carriages transporting his possessions – clothes, accessories and toiletries – approximately one-hundred-and-fifty yards from Seamore Place to hurriedly rented rooms in Curzon Street.

This of course meant that I would receive no further contributions to my expenses. It was a small loss since I could not recall the last time Alfred paid me anything. My only remaining sources of income were my unreliable two-thousand-pound annuity and small profit rental on St James's Square. My capital consisted of its unsaleable lease, my collections of precious objects, and the almost exhausted remnant of the money brought from Paris. Insolvency was a quite disturbing prospect.

I was disorientated but not defeated. There was an abundance of intangible assets in my possession: my title, talents, education, acumen, stoicism, influential friends and femininity. All were there be exploited. I held my head high as I drove my white calèche with green and crimson wheels á la Lady Burghersh ignoring the acidity of her sister-in-law, Lady Jersey, her sneering friends at Almack's and my dear sister at Westminster. Alone, I reopened the door to London's most intellectual private forum; possibly its only intellectual private forum. Without the attraction of Alfred's outrageous charms, a few ladies cautiously braved their reputations to be seen and heard in my salons, while my male adherents trickled back without a hint of embarrassment.

When you are poor you cannot afford to look poor. Economies were too expensive. My hospitality had to befit a countess. I had to indulge the eminent and the erudite in constructive debate. I had to spread wisdom and understanding. I had to be bounteous to my family. And above I had to face reality. My creditors' patience would not last forever.

For six weeks Alfred kept his distance, all one-hundred-and-fifty yards. After successful evenings at the tables he began stealthily calling at Seamore Place, before returning to whatever pleasures awaited him in his rented rooms. At my house there were always influential people to introduce to his young friends from Crockford's and other clubs from which he was not yet banned. I welcomed them all with polite reluctance, and made sure that he was never seen to be the last to leave. One evening Alfred brought not a young friend but an old friend of his father's. He had won – and for once it was true – a considerable sum from this blue-blooded Frenchman, glorying in the name of Louis Alexandre Benjamin Green, Comte de Saint-Marsault et Marquis de Chatelaillont. The Comte, in a yellowish coat with a surfeit of gold jewellery to accentuate his sallow complexion, informed me that he was a brigadier of the French army. He looked respectable and upright, if a little too old to be a serving officer.

The Comte de Saint-Marsault also reminded me that we had met before at Madame Craufurd's château in Paris. I had no recollection of the occasion, but apparently Marianne had made a remarkably favourable impression on him. Marianne had never made a remarkably favourable impression on any man, as far as I knew. When I told him she was well but still unmarried, he smiled brightly through his gold teeth and asked if it would be possible to see her again. He was a bachelor who had devoted his life to military service but now as he neared retirement was growing lonely, he said. I presumed him more lecherous than chivalrous but this was an opportunity my sister could not afford to miss. The Saint-Marsaults were an old noble French family and the Comte was clearly a man of considerable means. That same night I sent an urgent message requesting Marianne to come straight to London. I had no particular desire to see her again, but out of sisterly love paid for her travel which she could comfortably afford. Marianne, pleased to be relieved of caring for Robert's sick wife, left her in the capable hands of her daughters and returned to London with optimistic trepidation. The charming old French noble welcomed her, courted her like a gentlemen and proposed marriage after Alfred, endeavouring to be helpful, led him to believe that she was a beneficiary of Charles's estate, which was not entirely untrue. Marianne accepted the proposal after Alfred, endeavouring to be helpful, led her to believe that Saint-Marsault was too old for sexual congress, which was not entirely untrue.

Marianne was now thirty and I advised her of how fortunate she was to have won the hand of a man, who with some imagination might seem fairly well preserved in his sixties - his late sixties. If she married the Comte, it was probable that he would soon predecease her and that she would inherit his fortune. It was even possible that she might give birth to a son and continue the Saint-Marsault line. She believed all of the above, except the last. In fact, Louis Alexandre de Saint-Marsault outlived Marianne by many years. He died in 1860 at the age of ninety-two, leaving no issue and ending his family line.

On 15th September 1831 Marianne, vaguely recalling the religion of her birth, married the Comte de Saint-Marsault at a Catholic church in Mayfair. As a wedding present, I permitted the ill-matched couple to enjoy an extended honeymoon at Seamore Place. The Comte took as long as four weeks to discover that his wife had less money than himself, or so she told him. After three months of matrimonial hell, her husband, who was probably as asexual as I presumed Marianne, returned to France, sold his commission and retired on a comfortable pension. As an officer and an aristocrat he honourably sent Marianne financial support for the rest of her life. Apart from that, she never heard from him again, Alfred never received his winnings and my conscience tormented me for a short while.

The Comtesse de Saint-Marsault returned to County Tyrone just in time to attend the funeral of Robert's hapless wife. Marianne sent me the sad news after returning to Dublin, where she was trying to stop Father telling anyone who would listen that two of his daughters were countesses and soon it would be all three. He also boasted that his two sons were officers in the British army, forgetting that one was dead and the other had applied to resign. My sister's letter moved me to tears, but not for Robert's wife who I had never met. I cried for the pitiful once proud Edmond 'Beau' Power, whose mistreatment I had long since forgiven, and whose noble delusions had dissolved like a hazy mirage in a desert of alcoholic despair. And I cried for my late mother, who I had also forgiven, and her glorious ambitions which had so lamentably been fulfilled.

Captain Robert Power was granted a discharge but prohibited from selling his commission since it was granted gratuitously in memory of the late regimental colonel-in-chief. Now with no wife and no prospects, all he could do was scrape a living from any agricultural work he could find. I blamed myself for making him abandon his true vocation for the glorified misery of defending the nation. There had to be something more I could do to help him.

Among my regular visitors to Seamore Place was John Lambton, Earl of Durham, the Lord Privy Seal; an important government sinecure awarded to him by his father-in-law the then Prime Minister, Lord Grey, another long-term friend and correspondent. The clever supercilious Durham was commonly known as 'Jog-along Jack' for his infamous answer to a parliamentary question about middle-class income, *'a gentleman may jog along comfortably enough on £40,000 a year'*. Of course this was intended as a joke but the press in its sanctimonious wisdom, sensationalised the remark to imply that this obscene figure was the politician's real income. The press had it wrong. Jack's income was far higher - at the time.

I presented Lord Durham with an imaginative account of talents that Robert was unaware that he possessed to digest with a few large measures of mature brandy. We then entered into a political analysis of the unemployment question, during which I discovered that while Jack knew no employers in Ireland he had powerful commercial interests throughout the British Empire. And Jack discovered that I had a more enticing nature than he had previously realised. In three months I, that is Lord Durham, secured my brother a prestigious diplomatic post in Quebec. Colonial diplomats generally only took up such posts when all else had failed and thus Robert was amply qualified. He knew nothing about Canada or Canadian politics and remained loyal to Ireland where he had no prospects whatsoever. The only way I could persuade Robert to accept the well-paid position with opportunities for promotion was by offering to bring his daughters Marguerite and Nellie to live with me in London and promising that they would receive a befitting education. This was not a mistake.

17

'Good-looking woman. Any idea who she was?'

'Yes, I know who she was. I'm a publisher; it's my business to know these things. She was an author.'

'Do you know anything else about her?'

'No.'

'You say she was an author, what did she write?'

'Let me think – silver-fork novelist – love and money sandwiches – Victorian rubbish, *The Repealers, The Governess, The Victims of Society*, loads more, they'll come back to me. Oh yes, something about Byron; that made her a few quid. Didn't last long, none of them ever did.'

'Have you read any of her books?'

'Good God, no. I told you, I'm a publisher. I haven't read a book in years. Publishing isn't about reading books, it's a business, it's about making money.'

'If you never read books, how do you know which ones will make money?'

'I don't. Nobody does. You get a feel. Half a page and I'll tell you if it was written by a professional, that is, for money, and if not, out. Authors! They all drive me mad; they think they can get away with living in the bloody ether. Well they can't. This is the real world and they have to give the punters what they want.'

'If her portrait is anything to go by, the Countess of Blessington was pretty well off. She doesn't look to me as if she needed to write for money.'

'It's a pose. They all bloody pose. They think they're human commercials. She was promoting the image of her readers dreams, pure as the driven bloody snow like her, God help them. That sort of bilge always sold and still does.'

The publisher turns to me and dismisses my nod of approval like an exasperating manuscript.

'I'm right, madam, am I not?'

He smiles smugly and goes into another gallery to look for a picture unsuitable for the cover of his next paperback. His companion, a total stranger, lingers until he is out of sight.

'Thank goodness he's gone. Did you hear all that? I'm writing a book but I certainly wouldn't ask anybody like him to publish it.'

'Unless the publishing business is greatly changed from my experience, I doubt you will have much choice,' I reply.

--

It was 1831. I had dismissed Alfred from my house and driven his wife to a life of debauchery no better than his own, yet he was still the son I never had and, in my own way, I loved him. I bore him no grudges. I never bore grudges. To have done so would have been to stoop to the level of the *ton* still ostracising me and spreading their immature rumours. I was no longer as rich as they, or as they purported to be, but had more compassion than all of them put together.

'Those who suffer their happiness to depend on the futile pleasures of society, instead of the resources of their own minds, who, with the power of soaring onto the pure regions of the sky, descend and loiter amidst the dust of the earth at the risk of being snared or destroyed by every vagrant urchin.'

Above all, I wished to make amends for my imperious attitude to my pathetic family; for letting my mother die abandoned; for treating my father as an embarrassment because we were so much alike, for sending Michael to his death in the Caribbean, for pushing Marianne into a loveless marriage, and for my well-intentioned attempts to assist Robert, who I imagined desk-bound and despairing as a doomed diplomat struggling to learn French in Quebec. His wife was dead and he would probably never see his daughters again.

Here I will repeat that I believe that the Earl of Blessington was a good man, and for all his eccentricities I loved him, just as I loved Alfred. I was prepared to accept that my punitive legacy was no more than I deserved. If I failed my husband in his lifetime, the least I could do was honour his memory by showing that I was worthy of his name and title. And the proper way to honour the memory of Charles John Gardiner, first and last Earl of Blessington, was to pursue an equally grandiose, gregarious and generous lifestyle.

Either Mr Worthington contracted a severe attack of decency or could no longer cope with my bombardment of aggressive correspondence, but he unexpectedly informed me that a special fund had been set up to guarantee my annuity. Although this was reassuring, it was still too little to fund the essential practicalities of a Mayfair mansion, its stables, carriages and fifteen to twenty servants – I forget the precise number – as well as supporting two nieces and distributing largesse to my father. I could not go on living in this style indefinitely and became increasingly desperate to find a new source of income.

Of all the great achievers who I received at Seamore Place, I welcomed none more warmly than Charles, as he now called himself of course, Bianconi on his rare business visits to London. To me he would always be Carlos, the young artist who brightened my darkest days in Clonmel and the one and only link with Ireland that I never wished to break, perhaps because he was Italian.

Carlos had long since laid up his oars, closed his corner shop in Carrick-on-Súir and ceased making popular engravings. The impractical public transport system that I had dissuaded him from abandoning had made his fortune. His fast expanding enterprise transported freight as well as passengers, owned coaching inns, improved roads and employed hundreds without obvious religious prejudice. Charles Bianconi had become a legendary Irish entrepreneur in his lifetime – possibly the only legendary Irish entrepreneur in his lifetime - and would live to see his transport network not only spread over the entire island, but serve as an exemplar to other nations. Now he owned an estate and fine house at Longfield, a few miles from Clonmel, and was widely respected for his communal work and philanthropy. He spoke fluent English with a coarse Irish accent which reminded me of my father's.

'Do you remember, Margaret, how we used to meet at the post office, when I was sending letters home. You tried to teach me English and I tried to teach you Italian?'

'Could I ever forget, Carlos? I lived in Italy for more than three years and not a day passed when I did not think of the words you taught me. *Dovremmo parlare italiano ora?*'

'No, not now Margaret it's a long time since I spoke Italian. My wife and children can't speak a word of the language. I'm Irish now, more Irish than the Irish, they tell me. I'm a member of the Clonmel council and shall be mayor in a year or two.'

'No one deserves success more than you, Carlos. Did I not predict you were destined to become a great man? And now you make me feel humble. I hardly imagine that I am very popular in Clonmel.'

'That's where you are wrong, Margaret, they adore you there. They admire you more than they admire me. Not many of our local girls get to become a rich and famous countess.'

'Yes, Carlos, I am a countess, but as I am sure you know, here in London I am more infamous than famous. And I will tell you in confidence, that I am far from rich.'

'Yes, I've heard stories. But you don't have to worry about Clonmel, we've plenty of scandal of our own to keep us busy, but how can you say you are not rich, Margaret. I thought Lord Blessington was the richest man in Ireland.'

For the first time in my adult life I was in need of a man's advice. If any man could advise me it was Carlos, a businessman who had seen Adam Smith's invisible hand and an artist who understood creativity and the human spirit.

'I have to tell you, Carlos, that Lord Blessington, on a whim of madness, all but disinherited me. I desperately need to make money.'

'Margaret, do you remember the golden rule you told me when you were managing your father's old business? Where would I have got without it.'

We recited together, 'You will never make money if your sole object is to make money.'

'Nothing's changed, Margaret. You told me a businessman must look into the mind of the market, see its desires and deliver them wrapped in expectancy. You made it sound easy, but it never is. The problem is that people don't know what they desire or expect themselves, so how can they tell you? What's more, you cannot tell them. Fortune seekers have tried to tell people what they want to buy since the beginning of time. Not one of them has made a penny, Margaret. We both learned that in Clonmel, did we not?'

'Carlos, I can hardly set up as a corn and butter merchant here in Park Lane. What can I do?'

'You can write. I'll always remember your beautiful poems and essays in the *Clonmel Gazette*. Did you know they inspired some of my best-selling lithographs?'

'Poor Bernard Wright only took them for the *Gazette* because I spoke French, and he could tell me what he thought of Lord Donoughmore without anyone understanding. A few years ago I published two books of my essays. They sold about forty copies between them, mostly to friends. I gave my royalties to charity and added a donation so as not to seem mean.'

'Might I look at those books, Margaret?'

Blowing off the dust, I took two small volumes down from a shelf. Carlos thumbed through them, quickly stopping here and there to read a paragraph.

'May I be brutally frank, Margaret?'

'It will make a pleasant change from people being brutally devious.'

'These are charming essays and a lot of people might like them, but they're anonymous and therefore worthless. Put your name on them and they become valuable. Everybody's heard of the Countess of Blessington.'

'Oh yes, everybody's heard of the Countess of Blessington, the vulgar Irish upstart, who lured a rich and gullible Earl and tried to buy her way into society. Everybody's heard how she has countless lovers and indulges in a life of debauchery and excess.'

'Don't you see, Margaret, that's just the sort of nonsense that creates demand? People will buy anything you write expecting to find some sort of titillation and, believe me, they'll find it whether it's there or not.'

'I understand what you are saying, Carlos, but have you ever had dealings with a publisher? That book in your hand, for example, *Sketches and Fragments*, would be three times the size if even some of my most modest work had not been rejected. It might have offended their prudish readers.'

'I'm sorry, Margaret, I know nothing about publishing. But before you start any business you have to research the market. Why not speak to one or two of the successful authors who, I hear, come to your soirées.'

It required little research to discover that the then most popular literary demand was for romantic fiction. I had never read romantic fiction, apart from autobiographies, and I certainly had no intention of writing my own. Carlos was right; I needed the advice of a competent writer.

Alfred had mentioned that his flamboyant friend Benjamin D'Israeli was back in London after taking a lengthy sojourn on the Continent to avoid the furore in the wake his novel *Vivian Grey*, as well as his creditors. I had read *Vivian Grey* while in Paris, and been greatly impressed by my young friend's insight into the injustices and inhumanity of a class-bound society.

Having so much enjoyed his thinly-disguised satirical portrayals of certain of my acquaintances in *Vivian Grey*, I read his second novel *Contarini Fleming*, presuming that I would be disillusioned. I was disillusioned. Surely I could write something better than the over-stated adventures of the eponymous hero, too obviously a vision of the author's own unachievable ambitions. I remembered D'Israeli as the ridiculous teenage dandy, full of his own importance, who made me laugh so much. But a clown was perhaps what I needed to divert my mind from impending ruin.

My footman – whose name might have been Peter – announced Mr Benjamin Disraeli, whose changed appearance was as disappointing as his second novel. Mr Disraeli, now in the sombre attire of a parliamentary candidate, bowed as low as previously, revealing that his effeminate ringlets had vanished with the apostrophe in his surname. He said he had been convinced of my extraordinary literary talent from the moment he first saw me. My request for his humble counsel was the greatest compliment of his life. Perhaps he had not been paid many.

Thereafter Dis, as he insisted that I address him, called regularly and we discussed politics, society, religion, science and art; everything except writing. His ideas were so far ahead of the times that I accused him of being a cabalist, a mystical Jew with the ability to read and change the future. He could not read the future but undoubtedly had the ability to change it.

I would never again be so seduced by a platonic relationship. Dis remained my friend and correspondent until my dying day but he was the worst mentor I could possibly have chosen. Like me, he was incapable of transferring the vibrancy of his personality onto paper, and his verbal brilliance was nullified by the high-flown language of convention in his novels.

The man whose advice I really needed was his father, Isaac, whose five-volume *Curiosities of Literature* I had studied with Mrs Jenkins in Hampshire. Between losing I have forgotten how many parliamentary elections, Dis found time to take me to his family home at Bradenham House in Buckinghamshire, where Isaac D'Israeli – who never changed his name or religion - spent many hours expounding his *Defence of Poetry, Essay on the Literary Character*. As were so many scholars before him, he was astonished by my familiarity with this, his other works, and the clarity of my interpretations. Isaac could not have been more encouraging but he had never written a romantic novel himself, and I learnt little of value from this greatest of literary luminaries.

It was really of little consequence. A bank or department store would foreclose long before I would have time to complete a full-length novel. Again I turned to Dis, whose advice was as impractical as his father's. He did however suggest that I spoke to Alfred's friend Edward Bulwer-Lytton, another up and coming author, recently appointed editor of the prestigious *New Monthly* literary journal. I had read Bulwer's best-selling novel, *Pelham*, in Paris. It was dreadful. Fearing that he would reject the essays I sent him with Dis and Alfred's commendation, I added the most contemptuously fawning appraisal I could compose.

> *'You possess a felicitous fluency of language, profound and just in thought, and a knowledge of the world rarely acquired at your age, for I am told you are a very young man. The work combines pointed and pungent satire on the follies of society, a deep vein of elevated sentiment, seldom if ever, allied to the tenderness which pierces through the sentimental part…. Many of the passages recalled Voltaire by their wit and terseness.'*

Edward Bulwer-Lytton did not bother to reply.

With no prospect of income from writing, I again prevailed upon Mr Worthington to buy back the lease of St James's Square, hoping that my now regularly-received annuity implied that there had been an improvement in the affairs of the estate. There had been a decline. My sinking fund had been created only under duress. After months of due deliberation, the Court of

Chancery decreed that a widow's legacy must be given preference over all other claims. The court had ordered the executors to sell certain properties and with the proceeds purchase a sound investment to fund my two-thousand pounds per annum. What sounder investment could there be for the estate than the lease of 10 St James's Square, from which my net income had diminished to less than five hundred pounds per annum? I therefore advised Mr Worthington that the Windham Club was an exemplary tenant, who always maintained the house – which I had not seen since moving to Seamore Place – in immaculate condition. Its committee – none of whom I had met – consisted of high-principled English gentlemen who would certainly raise no objection to a rent increase at the next review. The Blessington estate paid me three thousand five hundred pounds for the lease. I can scarcely describe my relief at being rid of the house, which held so many happy memories of my late husband.

At the next rent review, the Windham Club committee declined its option to renew and moved to more suitable premises three doors away, while the lease of 10 St James's Square remained a liability to the estate for the remainder of its term. Sounder investments were designated to fund my annuity, or so I was told.

I settled my most pressing debts and continued to live and entertain as my late husband would have wished, which soon devoured my Windham windfall. I had again almost reached the point of despair, when one morning my butler, Ronald or was it Roger, proffered a visiting card on his silver tray:

Samuel Carter Hall, esquire
Subeditor
New Monthly Magazine and Literary Journal

I presumed this gentleman to be an insignificant subordinate sent to return my work with a condescending apology from the editor. I was wrong.

'It is most kind of you to take time from your undoubtedly busy schedule, Mr Hall, but I was looking forward to meeting Mr Bulwer-Lytton in person. I am a great admirer of his excellent novels.'

'Bulwer! I haven't seen him in ages. Either he's cocooned writing some nonsense about *The Last Days of Pompeii*, spouting in the Commons, or most likely embroiled in one of his never-ending domestic crises. I have to do everything myself at the *New Monthly*, Lady Blessington.'

'Then your time is precious, Mr Hall, as is mine. I am expecting guests this evening. Do not let me detain you.'

'As you say, Lady Blessington, I do have heavy commitments. I shall therefore not leave you in suspense. I have read your work and am immensely impressed. I shall be happy to publish it for you.'

I made the necessary effort not to appear pleased.

'Thank you, Mr Hall, I take it there will be conditions?'

'Regrettably, Lady Blessington, some of the subscribers upon whom we depend for survival tend to be easily offended. Some of your phraseology is, shall we say, just a touch too rich for their taste. But do not concern yourself,

I am an experienced editor and have noted some amendments for you to consider.'

'As you have perceived, Mr Hall, my time is precious. If you wish me to re-write my work, I shall require appropriate recompense.'

'If twenty guineas per page is satisfactory, your ladyship, my clerk will be pleased to collect your revised manuscript on Monday.'

It occurred to me that this presumptuous young man expected me to argue for a higher fee, but given that my three previous publications had together yielded royalties of less than one guinea, I humbly accepted his offer. This was a mistake.

'Thank you, Mr Hall. Rest assured that your readers will be delighted. I must however make one stipulation. My contributions must be acknowledged as by the Countess of Blessington.'

Mr Hall looked horrified.

'Lady Blessington, the *New Monthly* has nothing to hide. We name all our contributors whether they wish us to or not.'

The Countess of Blessington, diligent lady essayist, poet and author, own pen and paper, no commission too large, was open for business. I had been a lady of leisure for too long. The discipline of regular work was an agonising wrench from which I immediately recovered. At five each morning I opened my curtains – yes, I did it myself – and, in the darkness of dawn, dragged myself to my inlaid escritoire, lit my lamp and wrote until I satisfied the unspecified demands of the *New Monthly's* unspecified readers. How simple the corn and butter trade seemed by comparison. But others lived by their pen and so would I. And I did. Mr Hall published everything I presented or what remained after he had edited out my most elegant cynicism, at twenty guineas per page.

Writing is a solitary profession but I was not a solitary person. Without Marguerite and Nellie, I could have completed nothing acceptable to Mr Hall or any other publisher. My polite young nieces had put aside the abject poverty of rural Ireland and with remarkable ease adapted to the abject luxury of urban Mayfair. I kept my promise to enhance their education. I taught them how to catalogue my library, organise my notes, proof read and copy manuscripts. Both displayed so much talent that soon they were offering naïve constructive criticism and, with my permission, composing their own essays and short stories - to be published under the aegis of the Countess of Blessington. They thoroughly enjoyed spending more time at their writing tables than I did. There is absolutely no truth in the speculation that they were virtual prisoners, responsible for the bulk of my work.

The whole system of female education tends more to instruct women to allure, than to repel; yet how infinitely more essential is the latter art! As rationally might the military disciplinarian limit his tuition to the mode of assault, leaving his soldiery in entire ignorance of the tactics of defence.'

I taught Marguerite and Nellie not only to assist me with my writing but to assume responsibility for the day-to-day management of my household. Their impoverished childhood had instilled into them that waste, far from being an essential boon to the economy as more enlightened thinkers propound, borders on criminality. They would condone no inefficiency or insubordination and mercilessly culled my devoted poverty-stricken servants. Despite my heavy commitments, I always found time to bid them farewell and write glowing references.

While we were at work, Marguerite and Ellen guarded the house like gaolers, barring the doors to all unsolicited nuisances, such as tradesmen bearing bills. In particular, they ensured that I was unavailable when Alfred called for no other reason than to gain my approval of the latest delivery from his tailor, or his shoemaker, or his glove maker or whatever was crucial to the sport of the day. I could neither afford the time nor was I prepared to encourage more salacious rumours that I was in the habit of entertaining the now celebrated dandy during the day. Among the more difficult facets of Marguerite and Nellie's education was teaching them not to laugh at Alfred. They had to learn that dandyism is a fine art to be taken very seriously.

'If you will be good enough to leave your card, Comte D'Orsay, Lady Blessington will inform you of the date of her next salon. Her ladyship conveys her compliments, and wishes you good fortune at the races.'

One morning in January 1832, my nieces perceptively allowed an unheralded visitor to penetrate their tactical defences.

'Welcome back to Seamore Place, Mr Hall. You have been much in my thoughts recently. Reading your dear wife's *Sketches of Irish Character* has been a most enlightening experience – so accurate and incisive. You must be extremely proud of Mrs Hall. Do congratulate her and tell her how I enjoyed her book.'

Anna Maria Hall's view of the Irish was as jaundiced as my own. Although she was born in Ireland she had not been there since she was fifteen, and like me, avoided the country like the devil's curse. In normal circumstances I would not have picked up her book with a pair of tongs, and had only skimmed through it because I was dependent on her husband's heavily committed goodwill.

'Thank you so much, Lady Blessington, Anna Maria will be overjoyed. A compliment from another lady author will mean the world to her.'

'I shall be equally complimented if Mrs Hall values my opinion but I have never aspired to any work so ambitious as hers.'

'I would not go so far as to say that, your ladyship. By the strangest of coincidences, I have been reading, that is, glancing through, your *Journal of a Tour through the Netherlands to Paris in 1821*. A remarkable little book: I am sure it was received to great acclaim. It's so beautifully written, so absorbing. I cannot wait to read it all, when I am free of heavy commitments.'

It is not hard to appreciate why Dickens is said to have chosen Samuel Carter Hall as his model for the arch-hypocrite Pecksniff in *Martin Chuzzlewit*. My *Journal*, published anonymously ten years earlier, had not received so much as a revue, let alone great acclaim.

'Should you do so, Mr Hall, you will join a most exclusive club, but doubtless more pressing business has brought you here.'

'Indeed it has, Lady Blessington. Your book reminded me that you once mentioned having also kept a journal of your travels in Italy, and while there you met Lord Byron. Marvellous poet, Byron; I've read every word he wrote, or as many as I could understand.'

'Lord Byron was the most extraordinary man I ever encountered. I made copious notes of everything he said to me, and however many times I re-read them he remains a complete enigma.'

'I dared hope that you might say something to that effect, Lady Blessington. Byron has been dead for seven years, and still the public is more obsessed with the man than his poetry.'

'Indeed, Mr Hall, think of the disastrous interest created by Thomas Moore's *Letters and Journals of Lord Byron* when they were published last year. Tom collaborated on Lord Byron's biography for many years and knew as little about him as anyone else.'

'I must agree that Mr Moore's work was not well received, Lady Blessington. Much to my own chagrin, heavy commitments have not permitted time to read it in its entirety, but the general consensus of my profession is that it is too lengthy and analytical for the general reader – too scholarly, in fact. '

'Be that as it may, Mr Hall, there will never be a more authentic biography, since, as I am sure you are aware, Tom was scandalously persuaded to destroy Lord Byron's own memoirs soon after his death.'

'Possibly he was well advised. Byron never shied from expressing forthright opinions or revealing the sort of unacceptable facts that Mr Moore dare not publish. But as you say, Lady Blessington, Byron's private life is a fascinating enigma. Since his own testament has perished, if you were to publish the notes of your conversations with him, they might provide some interesting clues.

I was so thrilled by the prospect that I became highly indignant.

'Mr Hall, Lord Byron's private life has been more than sufficiently defamed. It is bad enough that I am reduced to living by my pen, but under no circumstances will I condescend to writing anything derogatory to the memory of a great man and a great friend, simply to amuse your vulgar readers.'

'Forgive me, Lady Blessington, I would never ask you to do any such thing. It is the invariable policy of the *New Monthly Magazine* never to print a word, which by any stretch of the imagination might be interpreted as derogatory to any individual living or dead, reputable or otherwise. But should your ladyship reconsider, I am sure we can come to a satisfactory arrangement. Let me have a brief abstract.'

The imagination did not need to be stretched to find a word, or many words, in the *New Monthly* derogatory to individuals, living and dead, reputable and otherwise. Some editions contained little else.

As Carlos had reminded me, a businessman must look into the mind of the market, see its desires and deliver them wrapped in expectancy. Mr Hall had done my mindreading for me. We both saw the desire of the reading market. Its desire was not for fact but for confirmation of its own concepts of Byron's misdeeds packaged with those of the Countess of Blessington. Only I could deliver that package. All I had to do was to gift wrap my observations and cushion them with expectancy.

Twenty guineas per page ballooned to forty. I set Marguerite and Nellie, now comfortably settled together in a pleasant little attic room awaiting decoration, an edifying exercise in unscrambling sheaf after sheaf of the old scribbled notes I had not looked at for years. I furthered their education by teaching them that Sunday is a working day like any other, and that they could not afford to waste their God-given time celebrating mass as they had in Ireland. For seven days each week they cheerfully immersed themselves in the enlightening tasks of searching, dusting, sorting, copying, dissecting, correcting, purging and revising. I insisted that nothing must be added. Lord Byron quoted verbatim, or roughly verbatim, was abhorrent enough to entice any reader.

'Did Byron really say this to you, Aunt Margaret? It's horrible and disgusting.'

'That, as I recall, is a modified version of his phraseology. Nellie, please tear the page out of my journal and throw it on the fire. It might prove costly if it was published by mistake.'

When at last all was more or less in order, I began:

'Genoa, April 1ˢᵗ, 1823. – Saw Lord Byron for the first time. The impression of the first few minutes disappointed me, as I had from the portraits and descriptions given, conceived a different idea of him. I had fancied him taller with a more dignified and commanding air; and I looked in vain for the hero-looking sort of person with whom I had so long identified him in imagination. His appearance is, however, highly prepossessing…'

The romantic genius was an addict to scandal and a master of satire. As I put it rather well: *'he mingled sarcasms on himself with bitter pleasantries against others'*. Mr Hall fully appreciated the commercial value of Byron's scrupulously cited barbs but invariably advocated moderation. His readers would expect me to clarify precisely who Byron was talking about without mentioning their names. So many of my most interesting quotations perished beneath the prudish pencil hypocritically wielded by Mr Hall that I wondered if what remained was worth printing. But in July 1832 a special edition of the *New Monthly Magazine* was devoted to the first, and not entirely expurgated, instalment of my *Memories of Lord Byron*. It caused a greater sensation than I had dared imagine.

A week after publication, Edward Bulwer-Lytton, Member of Parliament, bestselling author, dandy and fornicator, presented his card at Seamore Place. Still in his twenties, the editor of the *New Monthly Magazine and Literary Journal* combined the autocratic airs of a born aristocrat, the arrogance of a statesman and the snobbery of the man who coined the phrase *'the great unwashed'* to describe those whose interests he compassionately represented in parliament. No one could have been less suited to the editorship of a literary journal.

'So what's my friend D'Orsay up to these days? Sorted things out with his wife, has he? Dreadful harridan, I hear.'

'Mr Bulwer-Lytton, the Comte and Comtesse have not lived in this house for many months. I rarely see them nowadays. I am told they are both well.'

'Oh, I see I have struck the wrong note. Well, Dis sends his compliments. He speaks most highly of you, Lady Blessington. I gather you are great friends. Perhaps one day you'll write your *Memories of Lord Disraeli*. I suspect they will be as fascinating as Byron's.'

'I would dearly love to be Mr Disraeli's biographer but I think it more than probable that he will outlive me. That, Mr Bulwer-Lytton, is for the future; for the present, may I presume you have come to talk about Lord Byron. Did you by any chance know him yourself?'

'I am something of an authority on Byron's works, Lady Blessington, but he never took the opportunity of benefitting from meeting me. Nonetheless we had, let us say, certain things in common and these are indeed what I am here to speak to you about.'

'Please feel free, Mr Bulwer-Lytton. Nothing you say will go further than these walls.'

'You must understand the situation is somewhat delicate, your ladyship. As you are doubtless aware – most people are – both Byron and I fell victim to the wiles of poor Lady Caroline Lamb, while she was married to Lord Melbourne.'

The editor paused, breathed a short sanctimonious sigh, and continued:

'Worse still, my dear wife, Rosina, also fell for Lady Caroline's malleable charms. It is all rather embarrassing. As a Member of Parliament I am expected to set a good example. What is more, Melbourne is now Home Secretary and my political future is dependent upon his goodwill.'

'I can safely say, Mr Bulwer-Lytton, that the minds of the *New Monthly Magazine's* readers will be far too absorbed in my scholarly analysis Lord Byron's relationship with Lady Caroline, to be concerned with your or your wife's past.'

'That may well be the case, Lady Blessington, but as you know Byron was, to say the least, prone to embellish his stories. Since both he and Lady Caroline are now sadly deceased, neither can confirm nor deny anything I publish. I therefore have to request that you omit all of Byron's references to me or my wife.'

'You are the editor, Mr Bulwer-Lytton. I am simply a humble contributor and shall do as you bid, but do not hold me responsible if your circulation suffers.'

I hardly expected my inoffensive sarcasm to ignite a political diatribe.

'I fear, Lady Blessington, that my circulation has already suffered. Your *Memories* are my last hope of saving the *New Monthly*. The publisher, Henry Colburn and his lackey Carter Hall insist that the entire content of their dreary magazine must be literary related. That is not why I accepted the editorship. The public must be told of the plight of the industrial poor, the extortion and exploitation of the colonial natives and the appalling state of our schools. Do you realise that there are children in this country who have never heard of Jesus? And the Reform Act does not go nearly far enough. Half the middle classes are still disenfranchised. Parliamentary corruption must be stamped out. This government is leading us straight back to war. What the nation needs is change, mark my word, change.'

He went on and on labouring point after point. His attitude to the *New Monthly* seemed like a frenetic version of the late Lord Donoughmore's employment of the *Clonmel Gazette*, a publication similarly ill-suited for political propaganda. I concluded that the future first Viscount Lytton of Knebworth was as devious as my father's late sponsor. I was wrong, but convinced that my *Memories of Lord Byron* were indeed the *New Monthly's* only chance of surviving long enough to pay me for them.

'While I sympathise with your politics, Mr Bulwer-Lytton, and am most interested to hear more, perhaps this is not the ideal moment. I am holding a dinner party on Wednesday: just a small gathering, two dozen or so. I shall be honoured if you and your wife would care to join us, and do ask Mr and Mrs Hall to come too. But I should forewarn you, that I welcome gentlemen of all political persuasions. I trust you are not averse to reasonable argument.'

'I sincerely apologise, your ladyship. I was carried away. I often am. But you are quite right; this is not the proper time for politics. I shall be delighted to accept your invitation and I am sure Carter Hall will be too. The quality of debate at your soirées is legendary. And should I be speaking to Rosina, I will ask her to accompany me. She is never averse to argument though not always reasonable.'

'Perhaps you have come to tell me how the first instalment of my *Memories* was received, Mr Bulwer-Lytton?'

'Yes, I forgot. I must offer my heartiest congratulations, your ladyship. The special edition sold more than three times our most optimistic estimate. Colburn was so delighted that he's authorised me to increase your rate of remuneration.'

I was fully aware of the sensation caused by the special edition and had every intention of demanding a significantly higher fee.

'This is so unexpected, Mr Bulwer-Lytton. I am overwhelmed by your praise and generosity. Please convey my sincerest thanks to Mr Colburn. I had no idea that your readers might be so interested in my boring *Memories*.'

'I can assure you they are, Lady Blessington, and I too am anxiously awaiting your next instalment.'

'Oh, there's no need to wait, I have the next six instalments ready for submission. Do take them and ask Mr Hall to cast his eye over them. I am unaware of the customs of your profession but since the instalments are to be spread over six monthly editions, may I request settlement in advance? Commencing my career as an author is proving more demanding than I anticipated.'

'Of course, Lady Blessington, I will see to it myself. I fully appreciate your situation. When I married Rosina, my own mother cut me off without the cost of a seat in parliament. I had to become an author in order to survive my domestic bliss.'

'I congratulate you on your unprecedented success. Perhaps you have some advice for a novice like me?'

'No, I cannot think of any. But don't worry, by the time the *New Monthly* is finished with your *Memories* you will be so popular that whatever you write is bound to sell. Colburn is already talking about a book version. My only advice,

Lady Blessington, is *carpe diem*; exploit your success. Why not publish your conversations with another celebrated individual?'

'Do you really think that is a good idea, Mr Bulwer-Lytton? Unlike Lord Byron, the celebrated individuals with whom I have had conversations are all still alive. I doubt they will be pleased to read their indiscretions in your magazine. But I do have in mind a novel in which some of the protagonists might be misinterpreted as bearing a resemblance to certain well-known figures.'

'Excellent, I would love to hear more about it, but regrettably must now take your leave. I'm speaking in the Commons in an hour. Allow me to put my publisher in touch. Expect to hear from Mr Richard Bentley – delightful man – you will like him immensely. And Lady Blessington, I will be honoured if in future you were to address me as Edward.'

'I will be similarly honoured if you will address me as Marguerite. You won't forget to take my manuscripts with you, will you, Edward? Oh, and here are some more poems and essays that might interest your readers.'

Edward paid me more for my mediocre poems and essays written years before than the *New Monthly* usually offered acclaimed authors. Thereafter we became close friends. As he and Carlos predicted, my reputation, that is my *literary* reputation, proved an asset to be exploited indefinitely.

I heard nothing from Edward's publisher. Presuming that Mr Bentley was unappreciative of my talents, I sent for his former partner, Henry Colburn, who had won the proprietorship of the *New Monthly* in settlement of the gentlemanly dissolution of their acrimonious partnership.

Mr Colburn's respectful reply explained ambiguously that a publisher of his standing did not stoop to attend upon a mere countess. Being in no position to protest, I ordered my coachman to take me to Great Marlborough Street where a hanging sign read 'Colburn', with '& Bentley' just discernible through a smear of new black paint. I was shown into a large, untidy and apparently empty room. Only when I approached the one shabby leather armchair in front of an enormous desk did a gnome-like head rise from behind a sea of books and papers. I wondered why the great publisher was sitting on such a low chair. Mr Colburn was standing up.

'If Henry Colburn is sitting down I am wasting my time. I pay others to do desk work,' he said.

Colburn had every portrait of himself destroyed, with good reason. Not only was Mr Colburn almost a dwarf, he was a mass of complexes and the most venerated pillar of his profession.

'We are all delighted by the reception of your *Memories of Lord Byron*, Lady Blessington. Did Carter Hall tell you that I am considering bringing them out in book form? I trust that you have not offered the rights to anyone else, *Bentley* for example?'

He spat out his former partner's name with such force that a pile the papers level with his mouth blew off his desk permitting me a full view of his ugly face.

'I have not had the pleasure of meeting Mr Bentley.'

'You are most fortunate, Lady Blessington. I wish I'd never had that pleasure. He's a blackguard, utterly incompetent. He's taken me for a fortune but under no circumstances will he take your *Memories*. Henry Colburn, and nobody else, will publish them for you.'

'That is most kind of you, Mr Colburn, but I must confess that I too have been considering a book version and I feel obliged to my previous publisher, Mr Longman, whom I understand has an interest in the *New Monthly*. As you will know, he is invariably helpful and cooperative.'

I had never met Thomas Norton Longman and felt under no obligation to him whatsoever.

'Longman! Yes, he invested a bit of money once and nobody in his firm has lifted a finger since. He's a blackguard, utterly incompetent. Don't trust Longman's, Lady Blessington, they're living off old fat. If they don't come into the nineteenth century soon, they won't be around long enough to publish your book or any other books. No, no, Lady Blessington, you need a publisher who lives in the present, someone with initiative and foresight. You need Henry Colburn, who knows a bestseller when he sees one: one glance at Pepys and Evelyn's diaries, that's all I needed. And I'm no stranger to Byron. Caroline Lamb's *Glenarvon* was a runaway success because it was published by Henry Colburn. I could have done the same for Galt's *Life of Byron* but no, he would insist on grinding out a whole-life biography of a man he never met. Take it from Henry Colburn, Lady Blessington, what the reading public wants is a personal impression.'

This cultured tirade from the legendary publisher was exactly what I had hoped for.

'As you will be aware from your unparalleled experience, Mr Colburn, a great deal of work will be required to transform a series of instalments into a book of personal impressions. I am told that you customarily honour your esteemed authors with a befitting advance.'

'Naturally, Lady Blessington, no publisher remunerates its authors more handsomely than Henry Colburn. Shall we say two-hundred-fifty guineas?'

I was unconvinced by the diminutive Mr Colburn's inflated bluster. He was overanxious. If my *Memories of Lord Byron* was really a potential bestseller, then I could do better. I humbly assured him that I would seriously consider his offer. Meanwhile, I had nothing to lose by broaching another proposition.

'Mr Colburn, I am also planning a romantic novel which Mr Bulwer-Lytton mentioned might be of interest to you.'

This lie triggered a second tirade, less charming, but more businesslike than the first.

'Bulwer! Whatever possessed me to appoint that man? He's a blackguard, utterly incompetent. Rest assured, Lady Blessington, he will not remain Henry Colburn's editor for long. He wants to be prime minister, yet he knows as much about leadership as the hind legs of a centipede. He's already lost a third of the *New Monthly's* readership with his political nonsense and now he's signed up with *Bentley* for his next three books. Yes, yes, with regard to your novel, send me an abstract and we'll talk about it when *Byron's* done and dusted. Trust me,

Henry Colburn, I shall not forget, but as you can see I am heavily committed at present. I must wish you good day, your ladyship.'

I could not see that Mr Colburn was at all committed, heavily or otherwise, but if he was right about the house of Longman living in the past, approaching them would be fruitless. My first publishers would recall the dearth of interest in my earlier works and reject their opportunity to take another risk. I needed a publisher into whose hands I could confidently place my literary future.

I had despaired of finding such a person when, towards the end of 1832, I at last heard from Edward's friend. Like his former partner, Richard Bentley was too heavily committed to call on me at Seamore Place, and I was still in no position to protest. On a cold December morning, the mud-splattered green and crimson wheels of my white calèche drew to a halt in front of a plain Georgian building in New Burlington Street. On the hanging sign above the door, the single word Bentley was just discernible through the streaming rainwater. I alighted onto this exalted London street and, carefully avoiding the horse dung on the slimy cobblestones, entered the publisher's office. Mr Bentley's room was clean and well-ordered, which made me think that I had made the wrong choice until I discovered that his business methods were as arbitrary as his despised ex-partner.

'My dear Lady Blessington, Colburn has no legal right to publish your work other than in the *New Monthly Magazine*. That esteemed journal would no longer exist were it not for the sixteen thousand pounds he extorted from me. Now he has the gall to claim that I left him in debt. He's a blackguard, utterly incompetent and in constant breach of his restraining order.'

'Mr Colburn did not mention a restraining order, Mr Bentley.'

'Of course he didn't. He wouldn't, would he? He's banned from publishing within a twenty-mile radius of London. His writes his agreements in the names of sham subsidiaries in godforsaken little towns. No, no, no, your ladyship, it cost me dearly to pick up the threads of that so-called partnership. If Colburn so much as hints at publishing your book, he shall hear from my lawyers in no uncertain terms.'

Mr Bentley's gratuitous outburst was a sweet melody in my ears. The two most eminent publishers in London would have to battle for my patronage. Mr Colburn's *New Monthly* was paying me a great deal of money, but Mr Bentley was ten years younger, tall, handsome and similarly abrasive, lecherous and unscrupulous. I therefore refused to take sides in their childish dispute, as long as Mr Bentley prevailed.

Richard Bentley claimed to represent more successful authors than he could possibly handle, yet afforded me three hours of his precious time. I was astonished by his knowledge of the published instalments of my *Memories*, as well as those Mr Hall kept secret prior to release. He quoted passages, pinpointed their weaknesses and gave me the benefit of his quibbling constructive criticism. He said *Memories of Lord Byron* was an inappropriate title for a book devoted predominately to dialogue. I did not agree but after he offered an advance of three-hundred guineas, I consented to the misleading *Conversations of Lord Byron* and similarly astute refinements.

'This is exceedingly generous of you, Mr Bentley, but I am inexperienced in matters of business. I think Mr Colburn mentioned three-hundred and fifty guineas.'

'Did he really? He must have something up his nasty little sleeve. If it's worth three-fifty to him, it's worth four hundred to me, but that, your ladyship, shall be my last offer.'

When I was confident that Mr Bentley would not change his mind, I took the precaution of alluding to my non-literary reputation.

'Yes, Lady Blessington, Westmacott's been up to his old tricks again. I've seen the pamphlet. What does he call himself this time, *'Dissector'*? I take it he is trying to blackmail you?'

'Certainly not. Under no circumstances will I have truck with any man who does not adhere to the rigid moral principles of the journalist's profession, Mr Bentley.'

'How much have you given him, your ladyship? '

'I have paid Mr Westmacott absolutely nothing: well, just sufficient to stem the most preposterous of his lewd allegations.'

'Your private life, Lady Blessington, is of no concern to me. However, the *'Dissector'* pamphlet implies that its author possesses proof that your *Memories* are copied from Byron's own unpublished memoirs. I have to ask you if there is any truth in this.'

'None whatsoever; Thomas Moore was far too scrupulous to show the manuscript to me or anyone else before he set fire to it. You have my word, Mr Bentley, that I have cited nothing other than my own conversations with Lord Byron and that the commentary is entirely my own.'

It was true that Tom had not shown me Lord Byron's actual manuscript, but he was prone to amuse me by quoting some of the more poignant passages. I excelled at mental retention.

'I of course believe you, Lady Blessington. I too have had dealings with the good Westmacott and I'm sure that his so-called proof has no foundation whatsoever, but I do fear that his pamphlet might have a certain influence.'

'Mr Bentley, a man of your experience surely knows that bad publicity is the most profitable publicity.'

'You might be surprised at how often I hear that, your ladyship. But for my complete peace of mind, I have also to ask if your work was in any degree influenced by that dreadful *Journal of Conversations* of Thomas Medwin's that Colburn was insensitive enough to bring out a few weeks after poor old Byron died.'

'Mr Bentley, Medwin's book was nothing but sensationalist nonsense; a travesty, rightly denounced by every critic in London. How can a book written so quickly have any literary merit? In any case, he was unaware that I ever met Lord Byron. Frankly, I do not believe Medwin kept a journal at all.'

'Unfortunately he did. I saw it once, but you are quite right, little of it ended up in his book. Colburn was so afraid of Byron's indiscretions, he destroyed Medwin's original journal himself. Like Thomas Moore, Colburn is a little man and a big coward.'

It took me over a fortnight to convert my *Memories* to *Conversations* in book form. My readers knew, or thought they knew, all I could tell them about Lord Byron, and only expected my book to underscore their unbiased judgment. All they required was a second chance to censure the great poet's licentious behaviour and be shocked by the indecorous utterances they expected of him. Safely secluded high in his domain in the Italian Apennines, Lord Byron had no qualms about mercilessly ridiculing and maligning our mutual acquaintances in England but still I needed every anecdote I could muster to entice my growing public. Lord Byron had told me that Teresa Guiccioli saved all the letters he sent her. Thinking that they might contain something to add a little more piquancy, I wrote to the Contessa, and she courteously responded:

> *'And also, don't you think, my dear Lady Blessington, that if I were to give you extracts and names, don't you think* [sic] *that the malicious part, at least, of your readers, would say that you were influenced by your friendship towards me, or by my entreaties to speak in honourable terms of Lord Byron's affection for me?'*

This, and similarly declined requests, ensured that I complied with Mr Bentley's condition that the *Conversations* be sourced entirely from my own records. So far as I know they were. I was really too heavily committed to supervise all my nieces' corrections and imaginative commentary.

Here are a few examples of Lord Byron's words cited from my *Conversations*. Imagine those Bentley's editors rejected!

> Of Henry Fox he told me: *'How can his mother do without his sarcasm? With his "espièglerie" and malice, he must be an invaluable coadjutor; and Venus without Cupid could not be more "délaisée" than Milady* [Holland] *without her <u>legitimate son</u>.'*

> Of Henry's father he said: *'Indeed I do love Lord* [Holland], *though the pity I feel for his domestic thraldom has something in it akin to contempt. Poor dear man! He is sadly bullied by Milady.'*

> Lady Holland herself, according to Lord Byron, was *'certainly the most imperious, dictatorial person I know... She has contrived, without any great resemblance of* [cant], *merely by force of − shall I call it impudence or courage? − not only to get herself into society, but absolutely to give the law to her own circle. She passes for being clever, this perhaps owing to my dullness, I never discovered...'*

> *'Lady* [Jersey]*'*, observed Lord Byron, *'with "beaucoup de ridicule", has many essentially fine qualities; she is independent in her principles − though bye-the-bye, like all Independents, she allows that privilege to few others, being the veriest* [sic] *tyrant that ever governed Fashion's fools, who are compelled to shake their caps and bells as she wills it.'*

Controversy raged for decades over the authenticity of my *Conversations of Lord Byron*. Scholars, critics and self-styled friends of the poet accused me of every kind of fabrication and plagiarism, though none detected Marguerite or Nellie's painstaking contributions. Even Professor Ernest Lovell, who in 1968 subjected the *Conversations* to microscopic dissection, did not raise the question. I really cannot imagine how this eminent American academic thought that I could have simultaneously completed so much work without help.

Henry Colburn, making no secret of his vexation over losing *Conversations of Lord Byron* to Bentley, glanced at the five-hundred word abstract of my first full-length novel, *Grace Cassidy*, for thirty seconds and offered an advance of three hundred guineas. Richard Bentley deliberated for a week before summoning me to back to his office

'Since your story, Lady Blessington, falls within the current vogue for so-called *silver-fork* fiction, you might wish to discuss your proposed plot with my clients and your friends, Mr Disraeli, Miss Landon and Mr Bulwer-Lytton, who are among the finest exponents of the genre. I am sure that a lady of your undoubted literary talent will not need to expend too much of your invaluable time on their guidance.'

Henry Colburn had been similarly patronising.

'This is most complimentary, Mr Bentley. Might I therefore take it you will consider my novel for publication?'

'Indeed, Lady Blessington, provided you have not offered it elsewhere, to *Colburn* for example. Your work indicates an extraordinary insight into the idiosyncrasies of certain pillars of society. An identifiable hint or two of social transgression – no names of course – are always the ingredients of a bestseller. The secret, Lady Blessington, is to say what you know best, without saying what you know best. I trust I make myself obscure?'

Mr Bentley made himself perfectly obscure. I presumed he thought I was as addicted to scandal and petty gossip as all the other female pillars of society who aspired to his patronage. I was nonetheless grateful for the opportunity to respond to some of my antagonists. Yes, I wanted that, but I wanted more to prove myself a serious writer. I wanted to talk about political and social issues: British atrocities in Ireland, Catholic emancipation, injustice, prejudice, inequality, poverty and paucity of education. My first novel had to convey these crucial messages and at the same time appeal to a popular readership. *Grace Cassidy*, my heroine, would contrast the strength and decency of a working-class heroine with the shortcomings of the upper classes of both genders. The result of course turned out to be an over-simplistic melodrama, full of clichés and a mockery of my own ability.

I am uncertain if my over-exuberant gratitude revealed my financial plight or if Mr Bentley genuinely recognised my potential as a writer, but he then asked if I would be interested in another type of literary project.

'Do you know anything about the annuals, Lady Blessington?'

'I have occasionally observed them in other people's drawing rooms, but they are not the sort of thing I would choose to read, Mr Bentley.'

'The annuals are not the sort of thing anybody would choose to read. They are not intended to be read. They are intended to be given. And they are given in abundance, your ladyship. Would you believe that nineteen different titles were published in London last year? Take a look at these.'

Mr Bentley selected some large thin volumes from his shelves. They were exquisitely bound in tooled morocco leather, velvet or watered silk and picked out in gold leaf to overstate their delicately presented lack of content. Short stories and shorter poems were interspersed with fine engravings of elegant beauties protected by transparent tissues like priceless originals: images of the superior to charm the inferior. As I thumbed through Mr Bentley's volumes, I was astonished to discover this trivial escapism was mainly the work of authors and artists I knew well.

'Do you think you could edit one of these publications, Lady Blessington?'

The annuals were not only inexplicably popular but outrageously priced. Their editor would have to be remunerated accordingly. I thus informed Mr Bentley that it had long been my ambition to edit an annual and that I possessed the appropriate experience. That I had never previously so much as opened an annual was irrelevant. I was a countess.

'At present, Lady Blessington, I am too heavily committed to publish an annual of my own, but should you so wish, I will introduce you to my friend Mr Heath. His *Book of Beauty* consists of the same prudish nonsense as all the others, but he insists on having a titled lady as his editor. I imagine you will suit his requirements admirably. But, Lady Blessington, I must warn you that editing an annual is no sinecure. If appointed, you can look forward to a very heavy commitment. I trust you are undaunted by the prospect.'

I left Richard Bentley's office less daunted by any prospect than I could remember. He had offered a unique opportunity for me to show the cynics of London that I was capable of leading the life of a countess entirely by my own merits. And editing would add another invaluable facet to my nieces' education. For the next fifteen years, I seldom allowed myself more than five hours sleep in a night, I was so heavily committed to entertaining literary gentlemen as prospective contributors, and some ladies too.

Charles Theodosius Heath was the most celebrated engraver of his time. He had acquired his first press at the age of seventeen and begun producing architectural illustrations of extraordinary quality. Adding portraiture to his repertoire, Heath exploited the vogue for prints of society beauties and established a wide following among the nouveaux riches. Now he owned London's most prestigious gift-book studio, employing more than forty designers and artists to relieve him of the drudgery of creating the ubiquitous diverse images that bore his original signature.

Heath's Book of Beauty, like its identical competitors was a vehicle of self-publicity, an illustrated annual filled with delightfully depressing poems, unoriginal short stories and uninformative articles. While certain parallels might be drawn between the careers of Charles Bianconi and Charles Heath the latter lacked the ruthless finesse of a natural entrepreneur. As anticipated, it was of no concern to him that my total knowledge of gift books consisted of a quarter of an hour's perusal of Mr Bentley's old editions, or that my first novel was yet to be published. I was the Countess of Blessington and thus London's most appropriately qualified editor for the *Book of Beauty*. Heath's main competitor, *Fisher's Drawing Room Scrap Book* – more suitable for scrap than the drawing room – had recently lost its titled lady editor. My first task was therefore to steal her readers.

Mr Heath required *'Edited by the Countess of Blessington'* to appear prominently on the binding and title page of every edition and that the frontispiece be a full-length engraving of me. I informed him that I was neither a trivial journalist nor a fashion model and under no circumstances would I accept such embarrassing stipulations. I changed my mind only when he offered the highest fee ever paid to a gift book editor. Despite his imprudent generosity, I cannot say that I warmed to Mr Heath, particularly after learning that I had replaced my cherished friend, Letitia Landon, as the *Book of Beauty's* editor. It was some years before I discovered why she had been dismissed.

'Dr Madden, Mr Sadleir, Mr Molloy, hard as you and other students of my life evidently find it to believe, I did not become a writer with no object other than to make money. As I have explained, that is an impossibility. I wrote because my conscience reproached me for luxuriating in the wealth directly and indirectly plundered from the underprivileged at home and abroad by the class for whose acceptance I strived throughout my life. I wrote because I could never escape the Emerald Isle of my birth, and the noble mediocrities who sucked its alcohol-polluted blood dry. Most of all I wrote to arouse awareness of the destructive futility synonymous with the *quality*. Do you all really think I could have become the highest paid female author in the land – briefly, that is – if I had nothing serious to say? And what did I ever say or do to make the three of you believe that I became a society hostess for no better reason than to show my superiority to the rest of that parasitic species?'

'To be listened to with attention, and to acquire the reputation of a good talker, never speak of yourself, but always in implied praise of those you address or in pungent satire of their contemporaries.'

As the circulation of my serious work increased I lured more and more men of culture and intellect from the stifling convention of the traditional salon. In the unique ambience of Seamore Place I encouraged free speech regardless of political party or religious faith, and no facet of the arts or sciences was taboo. Sex, natural and otherwise, bodily functions, economics and even trade were perfectly acceptable drawing-room conversation. I drew the line only at personal finance. I never invited the sort of people who would allude to such an indelicate subject in public.

I would have preferred to prohibit scandal and gossip too but that was inconceivable in the presence of so many clergy, academics and statesmen. I excelled at perpetuating controversy, and with tactful sarcasm always restrained acrimony within the bounds of civility - well, almost always. At the first sign of discord, I, Marguerite or Nellie would play soothing music on the piano or the violin, or I would ask Tom Moore to sing one of his ballads. My guests always left in good humour and often, I believe, quite sober.

I began my first *silver-fork* novel in February 1833. Despite my superior intellect, this immature genre transpired to be a natural forte and an ideal vehicle to expose the failings of the *ton* who I simultaneously suffered and emulated. I competed against the clock and won. I drove my pen like the whip of a jockey on a Derby loser and savoured every frantic moment.

I had a great deal to say. I said what I knew when I dare not say what I knew. I painted my flawed protagonists, such as Lord and Lady Abberville, the Countess of Guernsey and Lady Elsinore to camouflage any possible resemblance to well-known figures such as Lord and Lady Charleville, Lady Jersey and Lady Tullamore. My readers would never guess that Sir Robert Neil and Lord Key were inspired by Sir Robert Peel and Earl Grey, or Lady Yesterfield by Lady Chesterfield?

Marguerite and Nellie laughed so much at my earnest endeavours that I was forced to reprimand them for not concentrating on the educational nuances of proofreading. They said my prose was appalling. They were wrong. To a true poet grammar is optional. After just six weeks, I presented Mr Bentley with a six-hundred-page manuscript: the first two volumes of *Grace Cassidy or The Repealers* [of the Act of Union].

My eponymous heroine is an honest and upright Irish working-class woman who copes effortlessly with extreme privation and with Jim, her drunken politically brainwashed husband. Grace also excels at domestic economy and maintains her modest home in pristine condition, albeit unburdened by children or other resident relatives. Employing only kindness and common sense, Grace eventually liberates Jim from both the extremist *Repealers* and the demon drink. At the dramatic climax she proves herself a true heroine by rescuing the arrogant Lord and Lady Abberville from a politically-motivated fire started by her husband's former co-conspirators. Thereafter, all the characters resume their proper place in society. It seemed like a superb plot at the time.

The Irish working class would doubtless have preferred the likes of Lord and Lady Charleville – I'm sorry, Abberville – to have been reduced to cinders instead of being restored to compassionless normality. Correctly presuming that *Grace Cassidy* would never be read by the Irish working class I yielded to the conventions of the silver fork, in which the social order invariably prevails. The real Lord Charleville, for example, was greatly respected in Ireland for abandoning a lifetime of unrelenting anti-Catholicism to join the Wellington government in passing the Emancipation Act.

By the end of May, all nine hundred and sixty pages of *Grace Cassidy* were complete and on 19th June 1833 published in three leather-bound volumes. So attractive, I thought. Perhaps the quality of my first novel suffered a little due to my nieces' tardy corrections but it was undoubtedly my most courageous. I really cannot understand why it is not an enduring classic. Its revues fell into three categories: the frugal, the fawning and the fairly favourable.

Also in 1833 Richard Bentley brought out my *Conversations of Lord Byron*. Those critics too disinterested to allege that it was a complete fabrication were carefully noncommittal or cautiously complimentary. Most of the readers however were also subscribers to the *New Monthly* and therefore delighted when the book version augmented their prejudices. Both my *Conversations* and *Grace Cassidy* sold more copies than I anticipated but neither reached Mr Bentley's over-ambitious targets. The revenue, he said, failed to justify my advances. I really could not understand his attitude. Nothing I had said or did compelled him to pay me so much. The house of Bentley published no more of my work for the next twelve years.

I should have taken Mr Bentley's warning more seriously. Editing the *Book of Beauty* was no sinecure. Day in and day out, I corresponded with contributors, conducted interviews, appraised submissions and most tiresome of all, composed enthusiastic acceptances and courteous rejections. I wrote every letter myself by hand – the typewriter did not come into common use for another century – and slaved to make each page aesthetically pleasing within the limited capacity of Mr Heath's pedantic presses.

Hardly had I assumed the mantle of editor than I was inundated with contributions from every author and poet of note except the one I most required. Letitia Landon was at the peak of her career and unavailable. To win her favour I had worked conspicuous compliments into *Grace Cassidy*, even naming and extolling her novel *Romance and Reality*. I do not know how my appeal reached her, but she replied from an unstated address, congratulating me on being chosen as her replacement and explaining that she had resigned to concentrate on longer-term endeavours. She was too heavily committed but would have a poem or story to offer me in the unstated future. I don't think she intended to be condescending.

Anna Maria Carter Hall, according to her husband, was rightly flattered by my request for a contribution. She submitted *An Irish Fairy Fable – a Tale*. Her fable or tale was as bad as her *Irish Sketches* but I dare not reject it. Had I done so, I would have been the only female contributor to a publication directed at a feminine readership. Selecting socially acceptable male writers presented no such difficulties. Viscount Castlereagh, half-brother of the deceased former foreign secretary, produced a short story. The young multi-millionaire George Howard, Viscount Morpeth, exercised his talent as a poet and I even managed to coax a short story out of Edward Bulwer-Lytton, though the annuals were beneath his contempt. His brother Henry, another Member of Parliament and stalwart of my dining table, produced both a story and a poem. I even accepted one of Walter Savage Landor's *Imaginary Conversations*. Most of this material had been published before or rejected elsewhere. Of the twenty-six stories, articles and poems I selected, nine bore my name, including those adapted from my niece's immature compositions.

Mr Heath displayed a great affection for that most meaningless of legal epithets: 'time is of the essence'. It was imperative that his typesetters received my completed copy by mid-September. And I delivered it in mid-October. Miraculously *Heath's 1834 Book of Beauty, Edited by the Countess of Blessington*, was sale for Christmas 1833 not only in the British Isles but as far away as India and the United States of America.

In August of that year my ascendancy had suffered an inevitable setback. Late at night there was a break-in at Seamore Place. I blamed my nieces. How many times did I have to caution them against risks of economy? With so many precious objects in the house, we should have had more locks and bolts on the doors and windows.

'No, Mr Sadleir, the burglary was not arranged by the Honourable Charles Gardiner and his sister Emily. It was a pure coincidence that everything taken was bequeathed to them in their father's will.'

Some years later I received an unsigned letter from the perpetrator commencing 'My dear Marguerite' and disclosing the useful information that my property had realised six hundred pounds. This was far less than it was worth and far more than my step-children deserved.

I was too distressed by the intrusion to accompany Alfred to Paris for the funeral of Madame Craufurd, who expired at the age of eighty-four on 14th September 1833. I use the word expired as a one-word eulogy. A being as majestic as Madame Craufurd did not simply die like a mere mortal. Alfred was inconsolable. I cannot imagine why. His grandmother had given him no money since he separated from his wife. Until her last breath, Madame Craufurd had held court in the splendour of her château in the rue D'Anjou squandering away the remnant of her fortune. She bequeathed her entire insolvent estate to her great-grandchildren, who did not receive so much as a centime. The Duc de Guiche nobly undertook the role of executor and settled with those of his wife's grandmother's creditors who he was unable to evade. He also paid for a becoming funeral, attended by two hundred courtiers and aristocrats, including King Louis Philippe, Queen Maria and representatives of the royal Württemberg family. Poor Antoine!

'Elle n'a jamais eu un mauvais mot pour quelqu'un,' said the priest, in pious praise of the late prostitute, parasite and imposter.

At Christmas 1833, the *1834 Book of Beauty*, edited by the Countess of Blessington, outsold the appalling *Drawing-Room Scrap Book* by more than two thousand copies. My first annual was a triumph of the nondescript. Mr Heath was as pleased as both our bankers and possibly some of the recipients of their seasonable gift. I remained editor of *The Book of Beauty* until 1841, after which its title page read *'Edited by Miss Marguerite Power'*. I doubt anyone noticed the change.

I condescended to remain Heath's editor for a royalty instead of a fixed fee, thereby earning considerably more than he did himself. Once I had felt but did not say that I was proud to be employed in the corn and butter trade, now I said but did not feel proud to be employed in the annual and gift book trade. These overpriced symbols of status were nothing but worthless ornaments for the bookshelves of the mindless. The *Book of Beauty* proved so lucrative that I sacrificed conscience to the unconscionable by contributing to most of my competitors to further boost the revenue essential to my reputation. Longman's *The Keepsake* – of which both I and my niece Marguerite were later editors – even paid me for a satirical poem ridiculing the pseudo artistry of its own genre.

When I wrote *The Stock in Trade of the Modern Poetess* I was angry. I was angry at having been reduced to passing off sentimental clichés as poetry. Now I am angrier still because my sarcasm was not sufficiently poignant. How many gratified owners of their prestigious annuals, '*Edited* – or as I was fully aware, exploited - *by the Countess of Blessington*', appreciated the depth of irony in lines such as these, ridiculing the stylised gallantry of nineteenth-century poetry intended for female eyes only?

> *Lonely shades, and murm'ring founts;*
> *Limpid streams, and azure mounts;*
> *Rocks and caverns, ocean's roar;*
> *Waves, whose surges lash the shore;*
> *Moons that silver radiance shed,*
> *When the vulgar are "a-bed;"*
> *Star and planets shining high,*
> *Make one feel 'twere bliss to die;*
> *Twilight's soft rays are "all" too bright;*
> *Wither'd hopes and faded flowers, …*

> *Next, a hero, with an air --*
> *Half a brigand -- half corsair;*
> *Dark, mysterious in his life,*
> *Dark, mysterious in his life,*
> *Dreadful in the battle's strife,*
> *Vice and virtue in his breast,*
> *War for empire —Banish rest —*
> *Raving still of glory – fame —*
> *While dishonour marks his name;*
> *Loving one, and only one —*
> *Though he has that one undone;*
> *A Macédoine of good and evil,*
> *One part hero – three parts devil:*
> *Quite an Admirable Crichton*
> *Is the hero all now write on. --*
> *This is now the stock in trade,*
> *With which a modern poem's made.*

Whether or not my anger was appreciated, *The Stock in Trade* was the best of my mediocre poems; an exercise to remind me that the most ferocious criticism is, and will always be, impotent against the mysterious forces of commercial demand.

My literary work was adding over three thousand pounds to my annual income. I was still not rich but could afford to look rich as far as the decaying opulence of Seamore Place permitted. The simultaneous drudgery of creative writing and elite entertaining provided only surface gratification. I seldom went to be seen at the opera or theatre. I acquired a pair of fine greys to pull my white calèche with green and crimson wheels, and a groom-cum-driver - I think he was called Colin - who at the mercy of the rain, ensured that I was not forgotten in the royal parks. When time permitted, I would stop for a polite conversation with an acquaintance but, in reality, my grimy urban paradise mirrored the unjust distribution of wealth that I was striving to expose with all the restraint of a professional writer.

Alfred would sometimes deny his male friends the pleasure of his sartorial extravagance and invite me to ride with him. I declined, it would have been an invitation to London's purveyors of ill will. Nor could I afford to be seen walking out alone. As a result, I took less and less exercise and put on a little weight, which certain boorish publicists and cartoonists made it their business to exaggerate out of all proportion. I think they exaggerated out of all proportion.

My commitments also became heavier, gaining weight like spherical boulders descending a steep hillside. I offered my next novel *The Two Friends* to both Colburn and Bentley, who like all severed business partners, continued to despise one another for precisely the same reasons. I had done all in my power to retain their goodwill - I never invited them both on the same night - but although both received my synopsis with the utmost courtesy, neither offered an advance that I could afford to accept.

I again sought the advice of Edward Bulwer-Lytton. Edward was now the most popular author in the land - possibly earning more than me - yet despite his phenomenal workload and multifarious activities, continued to pursue my friendship with excessive enthusiasm. He did everything with excessive enthusiasm. He always arrived late in the evening, often when all my guests had left, yet looked as fresh and sprightly as if he had done nothing all day. I explained my predicament and he scribbled an introduction to an enterprising new firm called Saunders & Otley. I had never heard of them but Edward assured me that they as were as trustworthy as Bentley and Colburn. I thus did not bother to ask these young upstarts to call upon me, but requested an appointment at their offices in Conduit Street.

I never met Otley and distrusted Simon Saunders from the moment I set eyes upon him. He was a thorough gentleman. He declined my request for an appointment and managed to walk the entire quarter of a mile to Seamore Place. He was so enamoured by *The Two Friends* that he tripled Bentley and Colburn's identical offers. Unable to decide if Saunders was a poor businessman or if he had fallen in love with me I completed *The Two Friends* even faster than *Grace Cassidy*. The suggestion that I wrote this eight-hundred-page novel in four weeks might be a slight exaggeration, but I had it ready for publication by the end of 1834.

Like Bentley, Saunders had briefly been a partner of Mr Colburn. They were not two friends. My *Two Friends* remained friends because they never entered into a business partnership with one another. The underlying theme of the novel, like all its successors, was the faults and failings of society. I compared and contrasted the superiority of the English and Continental nobility with the vulgarity of the nouveau riches and exposed the futility of class snobbery. I excelled at exposing the futility of class snobbery.

The Court Magazine's 'Literature of the Month' column for March 1835 reviewed Saunders & Otley's exquisitely bound volumes with ungrammatical discretion.

> *'In the present novel the Countess of Blessington has given us a better and more perfect description of French society – that is to say, of that portion of French society comprising the remnant of the old aristocracy exclusively inhabiting the Faubourg St Germain at Paris – than we can remember to have read before. We could fix upon twenty persons of our acquaintance who might of* [sic] *sat for the portraits of the Comte de Bethune and the Duchesse de Montcalm… He* [the reader] *will find… the interesting and exciting story… sufficiently stirring to carry him through the three volumes at a single sitting.'*

What sort of reader was so stirred by *The Two Friends* that *he* was carried through it at a single sitting? I am sure that some people found my story amusing but *'exciting'* was going a little too far. Mr Saunders claimed, and I have every reason to believe him, that he was satisfied with the number of volumes sold. Nonetheless, Saunders & Otley did not invite me to submit my next novel, presumably because having finally lured Edward Bulwer away from Bentley, they could hardly afford me too.

I was unaware that my work was loved in the United States of America until one afternoon in May 1834 a young man appeared at Seamore Place bearing a letter of introduction from Walter Savage Landor. Walter, with faultless grammar, I suppose, described Nathaniel Parker Willis as *'the best poet the New World has produced in any part of it.'* I could not understand why Walter thought so highly of this glorified newspaper columnist when his American contemporaries included literary giants such as Ralph Waldo Emerson, Edgar Allan Poe and Henry Longfellow. All of their work is still read, whereas I doubt many people, even in the USA, have heard of Willis nowadays.

Nathaniel was just twenty-eight, touring Europe and dispatching home hasty judgments of its more distinguished figures for the edification of the American public. The overweight hirsute young poet had established his reputation by dint of being the son of the richest newspaper publisher in Portland, Maine, and I considered him brash to the point of rudeness. However, the following year I reassessed my opinion, slightly, when I read his *Pencillings by the Way*. This is how Nathaniel described our first meeting:

'In a long library, lined alternatively with splendidly bound books and mirrors, and with a deep window the breadth of the room, opening upon Hyde Park, I found Lady Blessington alone. The picture to my eye, as the door opened was a very lovely one; a woman of remarkable beauty, half buried in a fauteuil of yellow satin, reading by a magnificent lamp suspended from the centre of the arched ceiling ....'

He went on to record his conversation with me as accurately as his description of my house.

'To rich Americans, your ladyship, snobbery is next to godliness and more often practised. The Book of Beauty sells for more than your servants earn in a year, and hundred times more than a black servant earns in America, simply because it says 'Edited by the Countess of Blessington' on the cover.'

'And do the Americans like my *Conversations of Lord Byron*, Nathaniel?'

'Half the people who buy your book have never heard of Byron but they most certainly have heard of you, Lady Blessington.'

'Perhaps, I should consider emigrating to the New World?'

'I am confident that you would be very happy there. Your work is adored by American society.'

'From what I hear of American society, Nathaniel, the English Channel might provide a more effective defence from my adoring readers than the Atlantic Ocean. I doubt that I shall leave England again but should I consider doing so, my preference would be France or Italy, where I am less famous and society is too polite to comment on my work.'

Nathaniel wrote in *Pencillings by the Way*: *'She* [Lady Blessington] *rose and gave me her hand very cordially; and a gentleman entering immediately after, she presented me to the Count D'Orsay, the well-known Pelham of London, and certainly the most splendid specimen of a man, and a well-dressed one, that I have ever seen.'*

Alfred was still occupying his rooms in Curzon Street and indulging in inconsequential pleasures with the lesser dandies who clamoured to gasp at his luck at the clubs.

'People who fall into the stream of fashion, like those who tumble into the Mississippi River are seldom saved from its vortex.'

For every pound I and his bedazzled bankers lent him Alfred spent ten and added fifty to his debts. His unparalleled recklessness made him a celebrity in his own right. The Comte D'Orsay succeeded George Brummell as the nation's first arbiter of male fashion but whereas Brummell had advocated reserve, D'Orsay advocated flamboyance. It was no longer the golden age of the dandy but every young man and some not so young, who aspired to that exalted appellation deferred to Alfred. He showed aspirants how to be noticed in the salon, at the hunt, the race course and any other unsavoury venue appropriate to a gentleman. He went so far as to publish a short discourse on etiquette as a guide for those unaware that they were disadvantaged by unrefined manners.

Pending resolution of their matrimonial settlement and the Honourable Charles Gardiner's challenge to his father's will, the Court of Chancery directed the executors of the Blessington estate to suspend all payments to the Comte and Comtesse D'Orsay. Alfred was almost thirty-four, an age by which even French noblemen had begun to earn their own living. He might have made his fortune from his fragrances but would never bend his knee to the market place. The Duc et Duchesse de Guiche, though quintessential aristocrats, were to have no qualms about permitting their sons to exploit their Uncle Alfred's inventions without financial obligation.

Alfred's only other saleable talent was his ability to draw, paint or sculpt portraits, which he always presented gratuitously to their subjects. I reminded him of the indisputable but often disparaged adage: all one gives or is given for nothing is never worth more than just that. He did not understand what this meant. In common with many renowned artists, Alfred's only works to be appreciated in his lifetime were those commercially commissioned. I thus appointed myself what might now be called his agent. Most of Alfred friends were also dandies or gentlemen of similar narcissistic persuasion, and nothing could have been easier than for me to induce them to sit for him. Comte Alfred D'Orsay was soon the most expensive portrait artist in London. I never negotiated or capitulated to feigned financial embarrassment.

Among *my* first clients was Edward 'Golden Ball' Hughes. I had been curious to meet this dashing adventurer of the boudoir and roulette wheel, since I first met his sister Catherine Lee. As an irresponsible youth, Edward's over-exuberant lifestyle and incessant good luck at the tables had forced him to flee the country. In France he ceased gambling and adopted the infinitely more respectable profession of speculating in American bonds. In less than a decade he had settled his debts and returned to England a rich and reformed character. He now owned a large estate near Sidmouth on the Devon coast, and lived quietly with his second wife and seven children, the latter being the most positive of his lifetime achievements. The unprepossessing Edward, who now took offence at being called 'Golden Ball' was followed by his sister, who now took offence at being called Mrs Lee. Alfred never usually drew women but succumbed to the fee that I extracted from my cherished friend, now La Baronesse de Calabrella. The Baronesse is the only female portrait in Comte D'Orsay's series of sixty-one etchings entitled *Men About Town* in the possession of the National Portrait Gallery.

It was not long before I saw Catherine and her brother again. At the beginning of 1834, Alfred and I received a joint invitation to celebrate the marriage of the Baronesse de Calabrella, widow of the late Captain Georges De Blaquiere and Captain Thomas Jenkins, bachelor. We were not invited to a church, but to a banquet. Thomas had conducted his own wedding, just as he married me in Clonmel – and subsequently others – foregoing religious formality. The third-time bride had not set foot in a church since her unhallowed separation from the late royal chaplain.

Thomas had aged handsomely. His long silvery hair curtained the fading traces of his non-aristocratic features and his considerably heavier frame retained a semblance of his military bearing. I thought he looked well in the uniform of the Eleventh Light Dragoons he had lost the right to wear many years before. The forty-six-year-old Catherine appeared as bright and devious as ever. With the utmost sincerity I congratulated my former guardian on choosing a bride so rich that he would never be put to the trouble of finding a man to purchase her from him.

Catherine told me all that had happened since we last met – almost all. The righteous Reverend Francis Lee had considered the outrageous damages awarded against Georges de Blaquiere for criminal conversion in 1815 far from adequate. They were, nonetheless, sufficient to enable him to sue his estranged wife for divorce. In other circumstances, Catherine might have graciously consented but, not being easily defeated, vigorously defended her virtue and preserved the right to inherit her husband's enhanced fortune. In 1826, the Reverend Lee's Spanish mistress threatened to expose his numerous other affairs and in a final act of atonement, the wealthy churchman renounced his calling and gorged himself on poison leaving the good woman in abject poverty. At the funeral, the small congregation was disturbed by her uncontrollable laughter, when he said, in Spanish, that the Reverend Lee never had a bad word for anybody.

Catherine, still legally his wife, inherited not only his entire estate, including the remainder of the compensation received from Georges de Blaquiere, but a lifetime pension as the widow of a royal chaplain. She very properly erected a small gravestone 'in memory of her deeply mourned and sadly missed husband' and on the same day married Georges, who had lived with her and their mutual children for the previous sixteen years. Throughout most of that time, they had both been unfaithful and now, disenchanted with one another, married for financial expediency. Georges died after just four months of wedded misery and Catherine laughed uncontrollably. She had added the De Blaquiere millions to the Reverend Lee's estate and her grandfather's fortune invested in continental châteaux. In celebration of her second widowhood, she had changed her name to the Baronesse de Calabrella, an obsolete title acquired with one of her Italian estates. For the next three years she and Thomas Jenkins, her lover while with Georges, moved from one idyllic home to the next in France, Italy, Switzerland and the Netherlands, making occasional discreet visits to London. Hard as I found it to believe, they were extremely happy together.

Not long after Catherine and Thomas's wedding, a new Whig government replaced the Tories and removed Charles Manners-Sutton from the Speaker's chair. As a reward for his eighteen years of distinguished service, he was invested with the Order of the Bath and offered the position of High Commissioner for Canada. In the light of Robert's reports from that barbaric colony, Ellen refused to emigrate under any circumstances and Manners-Sutton opted for the less demanding House of Lords. In 1835 he assumed the title, Viscount Canterbury, in memory of his late father, the Archbishop, and was granted a pension of four thousand pounds per annum. Of course he had to concede his official residence. He and Ellen graciously retired to Southwark Crescent, Paddington. No, I was never invited there.

I really could not understand why they did not choose a more fashionable area but I sent Ellen, now Viscountess Canterbury, a polite message of congratulation. She replied, not to me, but to Father in Dublin. Edmond Power could at last boast to his cronies, who did not believe him, that all three of his daughters were countesses. He wanted to write and congratulate his favourite daughter but was so riddled with gout that he was unable to lift a pen. Lifting a tankard to his questionably successful family caused him not the slightest pain.

18

A tall man with unruly auburn hair protruding over a sable-collared coat stands with his unmistakeable back to me. He leans towards my portrait and examines it with the studied theatrical gestures of a comic sage.

'I knew you would get here eventually, Charles. You could never resist the opportunity to stare at my portrait, even when I was right next to you, as I am now. Did you expect it to change?'

Charles John Gardiner, First and Last Earl of Blessington, aged forty-six, turns and looks into my eyes. And I look into his. We both see love and apprehension.

'You know, my dear Marguerite, your picture is as fresh today as when they unveiled it at the Royal Academy in 1822. But it is not right, you see. It was never right. Lawrence could never appreciate why it was so important to me.'

'You can hardly blame Sir Thomas for thinking you wanted to show off the wife you acquired at such great cost.'

'Who to, your lovers? They didn't need a picture, you know. They had the real thing.'

Through our eleven-year marriage Charles never openly expressed annoyance or showed suspicion of my behaviour.

'But Charles you commissioned Sir Thomas just a few weeks after our wedding. I had no lovers then.'

'Possibly not, but I knew it wouldn't be long. Do you think I didn't know the sort of man I was, my dear Marguerite? Who would have believed that a woman like you could love a man like me? But I wanted to believe it, you know. Lawrence was clever, you see, he painted you, disdain and all.'

'What are you talking about, Charles? I never disdained you. Ask anyone, I loved you until the day you died? Read my journals, my novels and my correspondence. I defy you to find a word of criticism.'

'And will I find a word of any kind, least of all one of love? You, like everybody else, thought I was a buffoon who hopped from one whim to the next, squandering my fortune. Did you ever ask yourself what made me that way?'

'It was your nature, Charles, and I adored you for it.'

'Nature was the one subject that never interested you, my dear Marguerite. You loved me no more than you loved nature, you know.'

It is my turn to express annoyance.

'Are you saying that Mary Campbell Browne did not love you, and that Alfred did not love you? Your father probably loved you too. Why else would he have left you everything and nothing to his wife and daughters? Charles, please stop laughing out loud. It is embarrassing. This is a public place. And for goodness sake stop crying.'

'My dear Marguerite, at no time did you, Mary, Alfred or anybody else love me other than for my money, you know. And as for my father, he was like dear Noel; possessed by some sort of quixotic demon that drove him to his death in a battle that was none of his concern. My father hated me. His will was a diabolical joke. Every pound he left was weighted with ten pounds of obligations that he knew I was too weak to fulfil.'

'You are wrong, Charles, we all loved you in our different ways. You were a good man; a better man than your father for all his insane heroics and ill-gotten millions.'

'My dear Marguerite, possibly I was a good man, but, you know, I was a bad scholar, a bad soldier, a bad politician, a bad writer, a bad builder, a bad father and a bad lover. I was not even a good actor, but I was a better actor than you. Did you think that your ladylike attitudes convinced me of your loyalty?'

'Is that why you all but disinherited me?'

'My dear Marguerite, you only have yourself to blame, you know. It amused you to think you were helping me rebel against my father by spending his fortune. Yes, my extravagance was a form of rebellion but, you know, I knew what I was doing. I wanted to be myself, not Lord Mountjoy's inept son. That's why I became Blessington and tried to build an enduring monument to myself in County Tyrone – a long way from Dublin, you see. As you never tired of reminding me, my dear Marguerite, my ambitions, my plans, my philanthropy and even my loves all came to nothing. It might have been very different, if you had loved anyone apart from yourself.'

--

At the end of 1835, Lord Mountford died and I received formal notice to quit Seamore Place. My landlord's widow was too frail to cope with the responsibility of a Mayfair mansion, wrote her lawyer. He was instructed to dispose of it but if I vacated the premises within three months Lady Mountford would graciously consent to waive my rent arrears. Thoughtfully, the lawyer pointed out that the lease renewal was a year overdue, and therefore his client had the right to increase my rent retrospectively.

The letter added, presumably as a formality, that I could purchase the house myself, should I so wish. I did not so wish, especially at the price the frail and gracious widow had the audacity to ask. She must have seen how I had improved her house over the years. Evidently the woman was a total philistine.

Lord Mountford's death, nonetheless, proved an unwitting spur. Like mine, the magnetism of Seamore Place was losing its attraction. My mirror reflected the distortions that the cruellest caricaturists no longer needed to exaggerate. I started wearing bonnets tied with lace ribbons, which no more disguised my triple chin than my unfashionable loose dresses had my increasing weight. I was forty-six and time was not on my side. Time is never on the side of the ambitious.

'As the pearl, which is the object of universal admiration, is produced by the disease of the oyster, so do many of the illustrious actions originate in that mental disease – an overweening ambition.'

Appearance mattered, but overweening ambition mattered more. I knew that my next home would be my last, and would have to meet my most exacting specifications. It would have to be as imposing as my continental palaces, yet within fashionable London and a haven from the common horde. It would have to provide security of tenure so that I would not be evicted again. Above all it would have to be economical.

At Seamore Place members of parliament were so relaxed that they often divulged official secrets and sometimes even useful information. One member mentioned that William Wilberforce's house had been standing empty since before his death in 1833. I was familiar with the splendid mansion on the other side of Hyde Park that the legendary politician and philanthropist, immortalised for his advocacy of the abolition of slavery, built to enjoy his richly deserved retirement in inherited opulence. Wilberforce had been able to live there only for few months before he himself was enslaved by failing health and committed to die in a smaller luxurious home.

Wilberforce's executor did not share his altruistic virtues. Unimpressed by my overemphasis on the house's years of neglect, he accepted my affected under-enthusiastic offer on condition that I undertook responsibility for all repairs and maintenance. Mr Powell read the twenty-year lease and recommended that I found a more economical home. Its terms were punitively onerous and the rent over-exorbitant. I ignored his advice. Lawyers are not very practical people.

Today no trace remains of Gore House and its three acres of magnificent gardens have long since been enhanced by a field of concrete - and the Royal Albert Hall.

I worded my change of address communication to present my new house as an urban idyll set in an incongruous rural location. *'I have taken up my residence in the country, being a mile from London.'* The brick walls surrounding the gardens created a formidable defence from both the inquisitive and the acquisitive. The view from the first-floor windows was a panorama of Hyde Park's uncultivated meadows, where horses and cattle grazed free of the stench of their fellow creatures imprisoned in the elegant private stables and dairies of Mayfair mews.

The interior, a forgotten example of the work of Robert Adam, was not beyond redemption. Under Alfred's fastidious artistic direction, a skilled ensemble of patient craftsmen corrected the great architect's imperfections. When all was complete, I was the indebted mistress of the finest private residence in London - or one of them.

'Am I exaggerating, Mr Sadleir?'

'I fear not, Lady Blessington.'

'Then, do I have your permission to repeat the description of my library that you quoted from a letter to my niece Marguerite from Camilla Dufour Crosland?'

'By all means, your ladyship, but do bear in mind that my citation is incomplete.'

'The walls of this room, which ran right through the house from north to south with windows at each end, were lined with bookshelves. The edges of the shelves were painted ivory white and enamelled, a startling innovation in those days, and one of the several fashions in decoration, dress and interior furnishings of which Lady Blessington was the precursor. The interstices of the shelving were faced with looking-glass, the panels of the doors being also mirrored. The room, which had originally been two, had supporting columns part way across its centre and two fireplaces. Only one doorway was retained – that opening to the right of the front door as one entered the house, so that the southerly end of the room was secured from draughts and disturbance. At that end, beside the fireplace, stood Lady Blessington's great chair, with the table at its side littered with the usual books and bibelots. The china, statues, clocks and other treasures were disposed very much as at Seamore Place. The furniture was entirely re-covered in apple-green silk damask, and the chair backs were protected by antimacassars of muslin and lace. The curtains were of green figured damask, with fringes. A single small-patterned carpet, specially made of a shade of green rather darker than the upholstery, covered the entire floor.'

And this was just one of my reception rooms. Lord Durham, who visited me after returning from a brief and unproductive assignment as ambassador to Russia, commented:

'She has got Gore House for ten years. It costs her a thousand pounds in repairs, about another thousand in new furniture, entails two gardeners, two cows, and another housemaid; but she declares with the gravest of all possible faces she only does it for – economy!'

'Jog-along Jack' deserved to be ridiculed for having no concept of the value of money. Not only did he get the length of my lease wrong, but how did he imagine that I could maintain such a large residence for so little and with so few servants? Perhaps I should have permitted personal finance to be mentioned at my salons – but I would never condone vulgarity. Yes, of course my move from Mayfair to Kensington was primarily for reasons of economy. Had Lord Durham stayed in England long enough, my strategy might have penetrated his over-indulged skull, but in 1837 he accepted the post of Governor General of the Province of Canada. The Prime Minister, Lord Melbourne, who I must presume knew little about Durham, sent him to deal with militant rebels aiming to seize independence. After five months, Melbourne, acting on more reliable intelligence, recalled Durham just in time to prevent the vast under-populated colony from going the way of its richer southern neighbour.

Before he left, I entrusted Durham with letters and gifts to take to Robert. I do not know if they were delivered since I never again heard from either the Governor General or from my brother. Lord Durham, unable to cope with the cold political climate and even colder meteorological climate, returned the following year to recuperate on the Isle of Wight, where he died at the age of forty-eight, leaving his wife to 'jog along' a quarter of a million pounds in debt.

Alfred continued to profess his love and begged to come and live with me at Gore House. While I took pride in impressing my guests with ornamental features, I dare not risk such a colourful gift to the ever-observant satirists of the free press. With little foreseeable income from the Blessington estate, I continued to urge Alfred to exploit his artistic talent. I went so far as to offer him a free atelier at my house, whereupon he moved his residence from Curzon Street to a small cottage behind my back gate.

The high windows and casement doors of the spacious garden room which spanned the width of Gore House provided serene views of my ornamental gardens and admitted light from sunrise to sunset. At my expense, Alfred refurbished this natural studio partly as a tasteful drawing room and partly as an alchemist's laboratory. He lined the walls with shelves neatly arranged with jars of rare chemicals, phials of powders, poisons and potions like an apothecary from a gruesome children's picture book. Alchemy was not the artistic talent I had envisaged Alfred exploiting, but, with scientific logic, he persuaded himself that he could adapt his perfume-blending skills to the production of gold in a crucible. Fortunately, a globule of acid dared to splash onto one of his thirty embroidered waistcoats and convinced him to seek his fortune by less hazardous means.

Like Alfred and Lord Durham, Edward Bulwer-Lytton had little appreciation of the nuances of personal finance. Edward could not understand why '*I employed Lord Chesterfield's cook from motives of economy*'. I had to explain to him that the sixth Earl of Chesterfield, among the richest men in England, was hardly likely to miss just one cook. I ran Gore House on the most astute commercial principles and Marguerite and Nellie kept meticulous records. They disapproved of my every extravagance, though I had been to great pains to teach them that economy is the greatest enemy of profit. To my regret, their beautifully hand written account books have been mislaid.

Each year we, that is I, completed at least one new novel as well as editing and contributing poetry, articles and short stories to an ever-growing number of annuals and periodicals. I also devoted as much of my valuable time as possible to furthering Alfred's career and promoting other grateful artists and authors. I never charged for my services. These talented gentlemen simply volunteered to reimburse my essential expenses and were too polite to ask me to provide details, so far as I can recall.

'*Everybody goes to Lady Blessington. She has the first news of everything and everybody seems delighted to tell her. She is the centre of more talent and gaiety than any other woman of fashion in London,*' wrote the insane artist Benjamin Haydon, once an inveterate parasite at Seamore Place. Soon after my move to Gore House, the bankrupt Haydon accomplished the extremely difficult feat of simultaneously cutting his own throat and shooting himself. Alfred was so perturbed that he established a fund for the benefit of his friend's widow and children – for me to administer. Due to the extraordinary generosity of the Prime Minister, Sir Robert Peel, who could afford it and of Alfred himself, who could not, I collected a substantial sum. Mrs Haydon was extremely grateful for the balance after deduction of my essential expenses.

My success at attracting the luminaries of art, science, literature and politics to Gore House was benevolently resented by the Countess of Jersey and her friends at Almack's, where my name remained emblazoned at the head of its roll of the *Unvisited*. The more visitors who accepted my invitations, the more *Unvisited* I became. Indeed, to many of my resented visitors, Gore House was like a second home, a third or a fourth.

Few of my guests gave my noble critics more cause for indignation than Edward Bulwer-Lytton, whose family, like theirs, was soaked in blue blood - at least on his mother's side. His father, William Earle Bulwer, was a mere general, who dutifully died when Edward was four. Thereafter, Lady Elizabeth Lytton, deleted her husband's name and brought up her family at Knebworth House, the stately home at the vast Hertfordshire estate granted to her ancestry in the reign of Henry VII.

When, in 1827, Edward married an Irish nobody called Rosina Wheeler. Lady Lytton, renowned for her wisdom and pragmatism, quite rightly celebrated the event by boycotting the wedding, cutting off her son's allowance and advising him to go away and earn his own living. The couple managed to violate the social order for just long enough to produce a son and daughter. I never met Rosina since Edward did not bring her to Gore House for fear that she might attempt to murder me. Apparently this was not an exaggeration. I cannot imagine what gave her the idea but she was convinced that I was one of her husband's mistresses. Possibly she was as mad as Edward asserted, but then I was never entirely convinced of his own sanity.

Rosina was born at Cashel in 1802 while I was at school ten miles away in Clonmel. Like me, she was distinguished by her Irish beauty but, unlike me, had fiery red hair, a matching temper and a fervour for biblical knowledge of both genders.

Edward was always oversensitive to criticism. This ignoble trait neither helped him as a politician, writer or head of a dysfunctional family. In fact, despite his fame and fortune, the only friendships he ever formed were at Gore House, notably with Dickens, Disraeli, his future biographer John Forster and, of course, me. There was always an underlying friction between Edward and Alfred. Whereas Alfred's aristocratic vanity and rudeness endeared him to those to whom he chose to be endeared, Edward's similar qualities had the opposite effect. In fact, he was one of the rudest and most self-opinionated men I ever met. I recorded advising him on one auspicious occasion: *'You are going to meet* [Lord] *Durham and he is prepared to admire and like you. Pray do not be supercilious to him as you are to most people.'*

Had it not been for my interventions with Colburn, Bentley and Saunders, Edward would certainly not have remained the nation's most popular author, until surpassed by Dickens. *The Last Days of Pompeii*, published by Bentley in 1834, earned him huge returns but neither this nor any of his string of bestselling novels proved an enduring classic; possibly due to the influence of the arrogant literary aficionados who so intelligently deride his arch-cliché *'it was a dark and stormy night'*, and the questionable wisdom of his *'the pen is mightier than the sword'*.

Another regular fugitive from self-inflicted turbulence was Walter Savage Landor. When in London he invariably accepted my offer of *'a comfortable room and better still a cordial welcome'* at Gore House. Like Rosina Bulwer-Lytton, his wife, still living in Fiesole, was irrationally jealous of me, although it must have been obvious to Julia that my relationship with Walter was purely professional. He was over sixty and, despite my multiplying attractive matronly imperfections, I still enticed quite enough younger men.

Walter behaved like a spoilt child appealing to me for unnecessary help. Everything he wrote, particularly his *Imaginary Conversations*, proclaimed his genius, and as such was invariably spurned by publishers. Imagine trying to create interest in titles such as *Shakespeare's Examinations for Deer Stealing, Pericles and Aspasia* and *Pentameron*. Yet by the end of 1836, these and others were available from every popular bookseller. I cannot say if this was due to my influence but in gratitude Walter contributed so many wonderful poems and stories to my gift books that I felt honour-bound to pay him for some.

I introduced Walter to many of my other contributors who came to Gore House, including the author and literary critic, John Forster, who I had not forgiven his restrained treatment of Letitia Landon but reluctantly invited at Edward's request. Despite Forster and Landor's thirty-seven-year age difference and contrasting characters they formed a lifelong friendship. Long after my and Walter's death Forster completed his eight-volume *Works and Life of Walter Savage Landor*. He must have omitted a great deal of interesting detail.

I have Forster to thank for introducing Charles Dickens to Gore House in April 1836. At twenty-two, Dickens was already an accomplished journalist with a compilation of articles under the self-effacing title *Sketches by Boz* to his credit and had recently married Catherine Hogarth. Dickens readily agreed to write a short story for my next *Book of Beauty* but submitted nothing that year. He was heavily committed to Forster's friends, Edward Chapman and William Hall then publishing *The Pickwick Papers* by monthly instalments. This idiosyncratic satire was so well received that I suggested to Dickens, with some reservations, that he become a full-time novelist. He might well have listened to my advice had I not introduced him to Richard Bentley, who invited him to edit a new journal at a salary the son of a bankrupt pay clerk could ill afford to reject. For three years, Dickens filled *Bentley's Miscellany* with the work of every distinguished literary figure of the day, most of them recruited at Gore House. He simultaneously completed *The Pickwick Papers, Oliver Twist* and *Nicholas Nickleby*, and wrote scores of articles and short stories. When he resigned, at the age of twenty-seven, Dickens was the nation's most acclaimed author and *Bentley's Miscellany* its most respected literary journal. Bentley replaced him with the historical novelist, William Harrison Ainsworth, another of my regular guests and contributors.

'Mr Sadleir, speaking of Ainsworth: among your appendices to *The Strange Life of Lady Blessington* you include: *"Some Contemporary Opinions of Lady Blessington: The Enemy and Opinions either Judicious or Definitely Favourable."* Why could you not bring yourself to simply say friends?'

'Regrettably I must remind your ladyship that some of your so-called friends were not always entirely frank in their public pronouncements. I, nevertheless, gave you the benefit of my considerable doubts, and selected more of the favourable than the unfavourable. Will you not give me credit, at least, for omitting some of the more vitriolic creations of the gutter press.'

'Indeed, Mr Sadleir, you were most considerate. However, I was intrigued by the briefest of your *Definitely favourable*. Did William Harrison Ainsworth really call me *"that jolly old girl, Lady Blessington"*? If so, I shall forgive those you call *"the enemy"*.'

"Prodigals: Persons who never learn the difference between a shilling and a sixpence until they want the latter."

The years from 1836 saw the apogee of my days as the custodian – I never liked the word hostess – of what one author termed my *'intellectual gymnasium'*: a forum for the cultural *crème de la crème* that I, with some support from my nieces, worked relentlessly to maintain. I was still however constantly aware that my literary income, which today might be measured in millions, could not be sustained forever.

My contentment with my punitive schedule was interrupted in February 1836 by news of the death of my old friend Sir William Gell. I was surprised to discover that he was only fifty-eight. Despite never having been married or subjected to scandal he had looked seventy even when he lectured me on ancient Rome from his sedan chair. I liked and respected Gell but I never really considered him to be a truly great historian. Edward Bulwer-Lytton did not share my opinion. For ten minutes he wept on my shoulder for his friend whose collaboration on *The Last Days of Pompeii* had brought him fame and fortune. Sir William was buried in Naples. Doubtless the bad words he never had for anybody did not include his rants about English publishers and Italian doctors.

Nathaniel Willis wrote from America to tell me that I was held in higher esteem than ever and that my next novel was anxiously awaited. Having no reason to disbelieve him, I completed *The Confessions of an Elderly Gentleman* in three months. For the benefit of my transatlantic devotees, I filled this elderly gentleman's *Confessions* with charming memoirs of improbable romances, sidestepping all implications of sex. It was my shortest and most fictitious story. It had to be fictitious. I could scarcely publish the factual confessions of the elderly and some not so elderly gentlemen I had known. It is therefore among the most forgotten of my successful novels.

Early one morning while my nieces were thoroughly enjoying making laborious copies of the manuscript of *Confessions of an Elderly Gentleman* for the competitive attention of Saunders & Otley, Colburn and Bentley, my footman presented me with a note:

'My Most Esteemed Lady Blessington,

Allow me to introduce myself and welcome you to Kensington Gore. I have the honour to be your neighbour Thomas Norton Longman, senior partner in Longman, Hurst, Rees, Orme, Brown & Green, publishers, founded by my late grandfather.

Might I first take this opportunity of offering my sincerest compliments on the richly deserved success of your novels *Grace Cassidy* and *The Two Friends*, which so splendidly complement your excellent *Conversations of Lord Byron*.

Some years ago you honoured my firm with your permission to publish two volumes of your essays and the illuminating account of your travels in Europe. Your recent work indicates that you have more than fulfilled the promise you then displayed and justifies our faith in you.

Should you visit our premises in Paternoster Square you will find the house of Longman much expanded with enhanced facilities to disseminate our publications to the international market, in particular to the United States of America. Please do not hesitate to contact me personally if I can be of further assistance to you.

Please believe me, Lady Blessington, when I assure you that I remain your humble and obedient servant, etc. etc.'

'Flattery if judiciously administered is always acceptable, however much we despise the flatterer.'

I was flattered and irritated. How dare the likes of Bulwer and Durham tell me that my investment in Gore House was too extravagant? A neighbour, the head of one of London's largest and most prestigious publishing houses, was prepared to demean himself to gain my patronage. Men of Mr Longman's stature did not present themselves to authors scraping a living in the slums.

I waited a judicious interval of some forty-eight hours before inviting Mr Longman to call upon me. Having greeted him with befitting courtesy, I conducted a mock auction of the rights to publish *The Confessions of an Elderly Gentleman*, in which he, as the pre-determined victor, outbid the absent Bentley, Colburn and Saunders by the narrowest of margins. Mr Longman was so pleased with his overpriced acquisition that he accepted my proposal for a sister novel.

I wrote *The Confessions of an Elderly Lady* in the same formula and haste, the only significant changes being the gender and perspective of the narrator. They were so alike that the anonymous critic in the July 1838 edition of the *Edinburgh Review* was unable to differentiate between the two. I think he might have found it easier if he had managed to finish reading one of them.

'They contain much shrewd but quiet satire and much subtlety of observation, while here and there in the midst of their lively irony, there are touches of reflection, morality and unconscious pathos.'

Having exhausted his limited stock of polite epithets – *'popular in their nature'*, *'sparkling in their execution'* – this experienced reviewer made no further specific reference to either *Confessions* in his fawning nine-page critique. Frankly, I would have preferred a straightforward castigation to his pretentions explanation of the genre emulated by every female novelist of the era.

Both *Confessions* proved popular, not only in America but in Canada, India and other nations sufficiently educated by British colonialists to appreciate the prestige value of my title. The unwarranted income Longman generated from the two shallow novellas inflated my ego out of all reasonable proportion. At Gore House I was a literary giant among literary giants. I was a superwoman. And I was not the last to think so. Albert Payson Terhune, an American more interested in dogs than women, super or otherwise, certainly acceded to that view. In 1916, Terhune bracketed me with Cleopatra, Helen of Troy, George Sand, Madame du Barry and Lady Hamilton among a dozen *Superwomen* thoughtfully selected at random from world history. I might have considered this a well-deserved endorsement of my historical importance had not Mr Terhune's idea of a superwoman included contempt for the devotion of husbands and lovers, involvement in multiple affairs and intrigues, disregard for family and children, recklessness with money and creation of a trail of destruction. And if into the bargain a superwoman brought a superman or two to their knees, so much the better. Perhaps it is not entirely lamentable that so few historians and critics have shared Terhune's opinion of me.

In the light of so much approbation I concluded that it was time to write my masterpiece. Edward Bulwer-Lytton, who had written so many masterpieces, was the obvious person to turn to for guidance. Dickens might have been a better choice, but he never spent a night under my roof that I can recall.

'Edward, I am considering a chef d'oeuvre; something enduring, by which to be remembered after I am dead. Can you offer any suggestions?'

'No, I fear not, Marguerite. You must wait for the muse and create a story from whatever it throws at you. Write what you feel passionate about: unfaithful lovers, blackmailers, venomous gossips, journalists, inept politicians, unscrupulous lawyers, and so on'

'I have been victim to all of those, Edward, and they boil down to the same thing; the merciless inhumanity of society.'

'Well, there you have it. There's your novel. Write about victims of society. Who better than you, Marguerite, to show up the aristocracy for what it really is?' said the future Viscount Lytton of Knebworth.

'Madame de Staël compared the English to the favourite beverage of the lower orders – porter: the top all froth, the middle good, and the bottom dregs.'

'Am I to take it, Mr Sadleir, that when you said of *The Victims of Society*, *"Bulwer was definitely responsible for the finished work"* you were implying that Edward wrote the entire book?'

'It did not seem impossible, your ladyship.'

'It is as ridiculous as all the rest of your theories. You were Edward's biographer as well as mine. When do you imagine he found the time? Yes, he offered a few comments and suggestions, but that was all. You call my masterpiece the *"terrible story of an innocent young wife driven to death by the malicious slanders of heartless fashionables."* How could such a terrible story have come from anywhere but my own experience? You of all people should have known how prophetic my fiction would transpire.'

I put all that remained of my passion into *The Victims of Society* but, as always, pushed my pen with the speed of the hare that obviously beat the tortoise by a mile. I followed Edward's advice and waited for the muse. I waited almost an hour, filling the time with unnecessary correspondence –'your inspired poem is too beautiful for *The Book of Beauty*. I am sure it will be much in demand elsewhere.' Then the muse asked me, 'Why not write something more cynical? A little sarcasm never goes amiss.' And so I narrated my masterpiece through a series of letters, commencing with a brief preface to leave no doubt of my intentions:

> *The design of personal satire is sometimes justly, more often erroneously, attributed to those who attempt to paint the manners of the day, and through the characters of fiction, to delineate the vices or the follies of real life.*

My personal satire blended barbs with conspicuous discretion. Unfortunately, Mr Longman had a keen sense of humour. He laughed long and hard at my depictions of his friends and clients before rejecting my manuscript. Saunders & Otley, also philistines to the art of satire, however consented to publish all that remained of *The Victims* after their editors deleted every nuance they understood. My masterpiece became a victim, not of society but, as usual, of convention.

The *Edinburgh Review* critic, pronounced *The Victims of Society* 'a prodigious improvement on *The Repealers*'. By this he meant that he appreciated its merit as much as he had appreciated my two *Confessions*. His crude synopsis made my astute allegory seem like the worst type of Victorian melodrama. If it was really that bad then I can proudly claim to be among the originators of that ever-popular genre. Edward Bulwer-Lytton sent a letter of congratulation which read more like a commiseration: '*You have attacked only the persons whom the general world would like to hear attacked*'. This was what I had intended but evidently failed to achieve. As usual, my written attacks were restrained by the knowledge that the retaliation of those '*persons*' would certainly demolish my unstably restored reputation.

The Victims of Society was published in 1837, the year in which the death of King William IV made me an authentic Victorian author. Also in that year I learnt of the deaths of the two men who had even less positive influences on my life.

'My Dear Margaret,

It will probably be of little interest to you but last night Father died after collapsing at a local tavern. Mercifully, he was so drunk that there can be no possibility that he knew what had happened to him. I have arranged for him to be laid to rest next to Mother. I do not expect grand ladies like you and Ellen will condescend to attend your own father's funeral, but the least you could do is contribute to its cost.

Father has made many friends in his declining years, and some of his old cronies will be coming from Clonmel. You will appreciate that I am impoverished and cannot possibly afford the necessary supply of alcohol.

Please convey my kindest regards to dear Comte D'Orsay, and to our nieces. I trust you are all well.

Your affectionate sister, Mary Ann.'

It was a childish gesture, I know, but I could not refrain from addressing my reply to 'Marianne, Madame La Comtesse de Saint-Marsault'. How dare she suggest that I did not care about my family? For how many years did I – all right, Charles – support Robert? And was I not still supporting his daughters? And for how many years did I – all right, Charles – keep Marianne herself in the lap of luxury? Did she think that I did not know how much she had squirreled away in that time, or that the Comte de Saint-Marsault was still sending his 'impoverished' wife more of his military pension than she deserved? Her new Dublin address indicated that she was living in some style. I had even heard that she had a lover. I am uncertain of which gender.

I was so incensed that I replied enclosing enough money to pay for Father's funeral, wake and headstone. I even drafted an epitaph: 'Edmond Power, late Justice of the Peace, died in his seventy-first year, deeply mourned and sadly missed by his beloved daughters, Marguerite, Countess of Blessington, Ellen, Countess of Canterbury and Marianne, Comtesse de Saint-Marsault.' Out of consideration for my nieces, I added 'and his devoted son, Captain Robert Power' by then almost certainly dead himself. No, no one ever visited the graves of either of my parents.

Edmond Power had finally succumbed to cirrhosis of the liver. Regardless of my sister's unbecoming cynicism, I was profoundly affected by his death. My tears were sincere. How could I think ill of a man whose faults, failings and delusions I shared? I do hope the priest did not say that Edmond Power never had a bad word for anybody. For all his senseless ambitions and ill-treatment of me, he deserved better than that. My inheritance was a fairly clear conscience. Heavy commitments prevented me from going to Dublin to attend the funeral.

Six weeks later, I was morally obliged to cancel all my commitments, heavy and otherwise, and attend the funeral of Thomas Jenkins. The Baronesse de Calabrella, who had some experience of burying husbands, spared no expense and chose a beautiful summer day for the reception. The grieving widow arranged such a splendid banquet that she and the other mourners, including myself, quite forgot that it was supposed to be a sad occasion.

The Bishop of London, engaged at an exorbitant fee, intoned, 'Captain Thomas Jenkins – was a man – who in his lifetime – never once – spoke a bad word – of a living soul'. I had to suppress my laughter. It must be hard enough to compose a eulogy for the general run of sinners let alone for someone like Thomas. For a man of the cloth hypocrisy is not a sin; it is an unavoidable occupational risk. It was hardly surprising that Thomas's health had given out. His final three years as the questionably lawful husband of the Baronesse de Calabrella were spent in inordinate hedonism at her expense. In gratitude, he left his insolvent estate to Catherine who, in loving memory, declined to pay any of his debts.

The Baronesse thereafter publicly renounced prodigality and settled down to her idea of respectable widowhood at her Mayfair mansion, similarly proportioned to Gore House. Following my example and advice, Catherine took to literature and in the 1840s published a series of romantic novels as E. C. de Calabrella, including *The Double Oath, or the Rendezvous, The Tempter and the Tempted* and *Evenings at Hadden Hall*. No, I did not read any of them but was told that they were so influenced by mine that many people, especially in America, thought us to be one and the same person. Catherine also submitted numerous contributions to my periodicals, most of them essays on etiquette and refinement, such as *The Lady's Guide to Perfect Gentility, Dress and Conversation*. As an honest amateur she would never accept remuneration, though I tried my half-hearted utmost to persuade her. She was by then richer than the late Earl of Blessington in his heyday. A year after Thomas died, Catherine acquired her own magazine, the *Court Journal*, devoted to society gossip in a vain attempt to launder her reputation, now more tarnished than mine. In return for her many kindnesses, I did not request payment for my advice on the law of libel, but accepted my usual fees for the old poems and essays that I permitted her to publish.

In February 1838 Alfred informed me that the annulment of his marriage was at last formally completed and his financial concerns were all over. Either he had gone mad or had over-optimistically interpreted a misleading communication from his lawyer. He had not seen his wife in almost six years, during which her and her brother's legal actions had been in eternal stalemate, due to the Court of Chancery's due deliberation and Lady Harriet's heavy commitments in London and Paris. In consideration of agreeing to his wife's petition for annulment and relinquishing all further claims on the Blessington estate, Alfred was offered fifty-five thousand pounds: thirteen thousand to be paid immediately and the balance *'within ten years'*. He would also receive an annuity in the extraordinary sum of two thousand, four hundred and sixty-seven pounds, guaranteed by a fund similar to mine. This was a vast fortune, but it meant that Alfred would receive over a hundred thousand pounds less than he anticipated from his misinterpretation of his father-in-law's will. He received nothing. Every penny was used to pay a small proportion of his debts.

I breathed a sigh of relief. My relief lasted little longer than my sigh. I was free of the Gardiner family but I would never be free of Alfred, and Alfred would never be free of debt. I advised him to oppose Harriet's offer. His lawyer advised him that the court would judge him a callous fortune hunter, who made no attempt to fulfil his matrimonial obligations and probably award less than she was prepared to pay. Immoral as he found this, Alfred chose to accept the money and chance his arm where the odds were more heavily weighted against him. He boldly advertised his settlement and Crockford's boldly permitted him to resume winning.

When the then Comtesse D'Orsay had walked out of Seamore Place into the charitable arms of her Aunt Harriet and Lady Mountjoy, the cruelly abused child bride was so completely traumatised that six weeks later she resigned the security of a family home for the sort of life she certainly did not learn from me.

For all his denials, there can be no doubt that Lord Tullamore was one of her lovers. Others included a Lord Forester and Lord Castlereagh, the thirty-year-old nephew of Charles's ill-fated friend. But in the extraordinarily plain young Comtesse's eyes none of these virtuous Englishmen had compared at all favourably to the handsome Ferdinand Philippe. Why, indeed, would any unattractive young girl not be in love with the heir to the throne of France, who took her back to Paris and provided her with a château in the fashionable rue Tonchet? This fairytale romance continued for three years until 1837 when an appropriate royal marriage was arranged between Ferdinand, now Duc d'Orléans, and Princess Helene of Mecklenburg-Schwerin. The Comtesse D'Orsay's officially married status thus cheated the twenty-five-year-old royal mistress of her very slim chance of becoming queen of France. She thus returned to England to put her - legal - affairs in order. Financed by Ferdinand, Harriet engaged an advocate to petition the Court of Chancery to expedite its due deliberation. On settlement of the customary unacknowledged inducement, and in accord with the hallowed majesty of English Law, the Court ruled that the Earl of Blessington's will had been perfectly valid all along.

My simple, naïve stepdaughter reverted to her maiden name and having bought Alfred off cheaply and secured the bulk of his share of the Blessington estates, instructed her advocate to acquire the interests of her two siblings for an undisclosed sum. Having procured the annulment of her marriage to Alfred, the newly eligible Lady Harriet Gardiner returned to Paris and into the arms of the Duc d'Orléans, who assured her that his loveless marriage would not last long. And it did not. When in 1842 the Duc's carriage capsized at speed, he fell out and was killed instantly. He was just thirty-two. Thereafter Harriet, thwarted queen of France, deigned to marry Charles Spencer Cowper, nephew of Lord Melbourne and stepson of Lord Palmerston. The still plain but now also ageing heiress thereafter lived modestly at Cowper's Norfolk estate, Sandringham House, the palace subsequently acquired by the British royal family. I am delighted that all ended well for the innocent child who I so heartlessly abused.

I heard nothing more of my stepson, The Honourable Charles Gardiner, but understand that he did eventually inherit Mountjoy Forest, which he broke up into small plots and sold off in tranches. His late father would have been heartbroken to learn that his beloved House, Cottage and theatre were all demolished to make way for productive agriculture land. The poor illegitimate Emily married a Mr Charles Whyte and lived out her days happily in a splendid mansion in Dublin. No, I was not invited to the wedding.

Until this time, I had been unaware of the extent of Alfred's winnings. I only became alarmed when I discovered the number of bankers and moneylenders, who pounced immediately he announced the triumph of his separation. Mr Worthington's office explained that the former Comtesse's priority claims had temporarily drained the estate's cash reserves, but promised to realise Alfred's settlement as soon as possible. Then as now, in legal terminology 'as soon as possible' meant a very long time and possibly never. Alfred's entitlement was however eventually paid in full to the most vocal of his creditors.

Alfred at last understood that he had to seriously exploit his artistic gifts. He extended his range to lithographs and bronzes, while I overcoming growing resistance secured commissions for him from those of our mutual acquaintances to whom he was not in debt. Most of his sitters, like the artist himself, found it more expedient to approach Alfred's studio via the back garden gate. But towards the end of 1838, Alfred insisted that an illustrious client be admitted by the front door, and requested me not to charge Prince Louis-Napoléon Bonaparte for his portrait. Why not? Was I supposed to feel sorry for the late emperor's nephew simply because the Bourbon monarchy had banished him from his beloved Paris? Was I supposed to commiserate because his mother, the Empress Josephine's daughter by her first marriage, had recently died leaving him her millions? Or did Alfred expect me to offer charity to a poor refugee attended by a dozen servants at 17 Carlton House Terrace, one of the finest town houses in London? No, He never invited me there.

The future Emperor Napoleon III was born while his father was temporary King of Holland and General Albert 'Beau' D'Orsay his aide de camp. Louis neither recalled Alfred's father nor knew anything about him. He was simply pleasantly surprised to find an aristocratic Bonapartist with valuable social connections in London. The twenty-nine-year-old prince did not need a pencilled profile by Alfred.

'Love in France is a comedy; in England it is a tragedy.'

A notorious womaniser, before and throughout his sublimely happy marriage to the Princess Eugénie, Louis's name was linked with some twenty mistresses. I was not among these favoured ladies, despite the number of nights he spent at Gore House. He was almost two decades younger than me and presumed, like so many others, that Alfred was my devoted lover. On the other hand, I never enquired into Nellie's private affairs. She was the prettier of my nieces.

For the next two years, I spent half my literary income feeding and boarding the retinue Louis-Napoléon brought to assert the prestigious status from which he was precluded in France. He was suffering from what the modern amateur psychologist might call small-man syndrome. To make himself look less unimposing, he appeared at my soirées in boots with built-up heels and the uniform of a general of the Swiss army in which he had served for six months as a cadet. Louis believed with deluded conviction that the brittle waxed moustache decorating his diminutive upper lip was essential to the authority necessary to lead France to the glory of his imperial uncle's unfulfilled dreams.

Louis was possibly as mad as any genius to whom I introduced him: Edward and Henry Bulwer-Lytton, Disraeli, Dickens and others including Frederick Marryat, William Thackeray, and the poets Robert Browning, Leigh Hunt and Barry Cornwall. They all concurred that Louis's propensity was more to literature than leadership. They were right – almost. In August 1840 Louis-Napoléon, exercising his self-nurtured hegemony, imaginatively decided to invade France with just sixty armed men. Intelligence of this courageous campaign goaded King Louis-Philippe into excessive retaliation. When his aspiring successor's one chartered ship docked at Boulogne, instead of an army of Bonapartist patriots waiting to join him, the monarchist army was waiting to arrest him. Poor Louis was tried and sentenced to life imprisonment at the impenetrable island fortress of Ham on the Somme. In the comfortable seclusion of his penal cell he wrote poetry, political propaganda and a persuasive portrait of a paradise purged of poverty and privation. Eight years later Louis's barely comprehensible neo-socialist rhetoric would convince the electorate more decisively than any subsequent French politician. Before embarking on his suicidal escapade, Louis promised us that when he became ruler of France he would return my hospitality at the L'Élyseé Palace and that Alfred would receive a ministerial appointment. I am sure that he intended to keep his promises.

Soon after Louis's first visit to Gore House I learnt of yet another death. This time I mourned for a month with barely a hypocritical thought entering my head. I loved Letitia Landon, who died aged just thirty-six on 15th October 1838, above all else for her tender cynicism and kind-hearted repartee, as sharp as my own. Her delightful poetry and prose concealed a bad word for almost everybody. *'Whatever people in general do not understand they are always prepared to dislike; the incomprehensible is always the obnoxious,'* she wrote. Only four months earlier I had attended her wedding to the governor of Cape Coast Castle. George Maclean – as suspicious of her professed chastity as her first fiancé, John Forster – finally honoured his commitment to marry Letitia on 7th June 1838 at St Mary's, Bryanston Square, the same church in which the Earl of Blessington married me. Within weeks of arriving in Africa, Letitia was found dead with an open bottle of prussic acid in her hand. The report of her death read like a cheap detective novel, but I very much doubt that she was murdered. A nondescript Scottish civil servant like Maclean would not have had the passion of a murderer. No proper post-mortem examination could be carried out in the tiny equatorial outpost, but the general consensus was that the acid was taken as a medicinal precaution, and that Letitia died from its remedial effect. Nonetheless, she might have had good reason to commit suicide. It was not hard to imagine Letitia's feelings married to a colonial governor, who might or might not have discovered that he had separated her from her three children. Many years later it emerged that their father was indeed her married lover William Jerdan, and that the *Wasp* had been right about her retreats from London. I had long since guessed the truth but chose to put it from my mind and believe in Letitia's chastity. If there was ever a victim of society, it was L.E.L.

'*Society is like a large piece of ice and skating well is the art of social life,*' she wrote. I never learnt to skate but Nathaniel Parker Willis's *Pencillings by the Way* reads like a counterfeit certificate of merit validating my accomplishments in the art of social life. The sun's reflection on ice can be blinding.

> *I am obliged to gazette Lady Blessington rather more than I should wish and more than may seem delicate to those who do not know the central position she occupies in the circle of talent in London. Her soirées and dinner parties, however, are literally the single and only assemblage of men of genius without reference to party – the only attempt at a republic of letters in the world of this great, envious metropolis.*'

Nathaniel was not always so complimentary about members of my assemblage of men of genius.

> '*Captain Marryat's gross trash sells immensely about Wapping and Portsmouth and brings him five or six hundred the book – but that can scarce be called literature.*'

Marryat was appropriately incensed and in response wrote a devastatingly accurate critique of *Pencillings by the Way* in his own magazine, the *Metropolitan*. Nathaniel challenged the literary seaman to a duel. This was a mistake. As a naval officer Captain Frederick Marryat had often employed firearms in the defence of his country, while the wealthy journalist bore them only in obligatory compliance with the freedom of the American Constitution. I had grown fond of Nathaniel after he wrote so many flattering things about me, and insisted that he published an apology. Marryat dispassionately accepted and Nathaniel turned to publishing indiscretions about other adherents to my circle, including Thackeray, Disraeli and Albany Fonblanque, the forthright liberal editor of the *Examiner*, all more than capable of destructive counterattack, in writing. Edward Bulwer-Lytton lacking the insensitivity essential to a true literary genius, responded to the brash American with the refined restraint of an outraged Englishman. His letter was so charmingly ineffectual that Nathaniel cherished it for the rest of his life. Duly reprimanded, he wrote to me: '*A more temperate just (though severe) and gentlemanly letter I never read. He gives me no quarter; but I like him better for it.*' Nathaniel Willis produced a huge portfolio of much lauded poetry and novels, now seldom read. He remained an invaluable source of transatlantic news, but I never again risked permitting him to enter my 'republic of letters'.

In 1838 Nathaniel, back in New York, reviewed *The Works of Lady Blessington* published by Carey & Hart of Chestnut Street, Philadelphia. The two heavy leather-bound volumes contained my first five novels, the *Conversations of Lord Byron*, numerous poems and a short story called *The Honey-Moon* - possibly a version of an essay by Marguerite, or was it Nellie. Nathaniel wrote to tell me my *Works* were received with great acclaim and that my name retained its commercial value. Presumably the Americans thought I still looked like the engraving on the frontispiece. Nathaniel sent me a verse of extraordinary metaphors which, despite his exuberance, helped bolster my waning confidence.

Westward, enchanting stone and stock,
You hold all Congress fast in fetters,
And Jonathan in citron frock
Carves Blessington on every rock
And for a country sells her letters.

Jonathan here referred to *Brother Jonathan's Monthly Library*, where my novels appeared by instalments. I do not know which country the 'best poet of the New World' had in mind, but in England my 'letters' were certainly now selling for a great deal less than the value of any of which I was aware.

Saunders & Otley sold sufficient copies of *The Victims of Society* to recover their advance and costs of publishing. Discretely perturbed, Simon Saunders showed no compunction in continuing to accept my hospitality, where in the venerable tradition of commercial synergy, he blamed his partner for the poor sales. Alfred, who despised all publishers, famously retorted: *'If you are Saunders, then damn, Otley and if you are Otley, then damn Saunders'*. Since Otley was probably a figment of his imagination, Saunders took great offence and never published my work again.

I returned to Mr Longman who was still promoting my *Confessions* to a diminishing readership. He accepted my latest novel with little enthusiasm since it was my most emphatic exposure of social injustice. I was inspired to espouse the cause of exploited governesses and *'raise attention and excite sympathy towards a class from which more is expected and to whom less is accorded than to any other.'* My personal experience of this 'class' consisted of my one meeting with the two young ladies at Mountjoy Forest, who worked minimal hours, were provided with every luxury and not above supplementing Charles's generous salaries with a little ladylike pilferage. My stepchildren's governesses were even sometimes invited to dine with Lady Mountjoy and Harriet Gardiner, whose indistinguishable characters bore no resemblance to the cold and callous mistress of my oppressed heroine. Woeful revelations of this kind were among the most popular themes of the period and since it was so much like all the others *The Governess* quickly became a bestseller.

Longman, etc., etc., etc. began to pester me for another amusing tale of topical torment but under no circumstances was I prepared to prostitute my art to the whims of an avaricious publisher. I was a serious poet, possessed by the spirit of Lord Byron. Thus for my next work I discarded prose and devoted my creative energy to an epic narrative of noble love and intrigue expounded through simple rhyming couplets. The critic of the *Literary Gazette* noted: *'The versification is familiar and unlaboured (perhaps a little of the latter might have been bestowed upon it here and there with advantage)'.* I think this was rather harsh since I devoted well over four weeks to composing the two-thousand-four-hundred lines, some of which I will admit might have benefitted from a little more laborious reflection. Nonetheless, I convinced myself that *The Belle of a Season* would return me to the peak of popularity and thanks to the ten delightful illustrations by my friend the Swiss artist, A E Chalon, it earned just enough to cover my advance. The taste for epic poetry must have died with Lord Byron.

I became severely disheartened and uninspired. Marguerite and Nellie's apprenticeships were complete. They had worked hard under my tuition and were now accomplished editors and authors in their own right. I felt proud of having taught them to be undaunted by the censure of the press or the compliments of the eminent, and to trust both sceptically as I did.

'There is another letter from Longman, Aunt Margaret.'

'Who is it this time, Green, Brown or some other shade of transparent veneer? They will just have to wait. Say I have nothing for them at the moment.'

'What about your travels in Italy? We have been chopping and changing your journals since we finished *The Conversations* four years ago. We've cut out all your honest opinions and most of the names, and added lots of interesting fiction for you. Everything has been collated and copied. Why don't we send them to Longman?'

'I'm afraid we cannot do that. I have already accepted an advance from Saunders or was it Bentley. No, no, it was Colburn. Horrid little man, but if he thinks he can sell that unending travelogue, who am I to question his judgment? Can either of you think of something else to keep Longman happy?'

'What about your Night Thought Books? You said they would cause a sensation if they were published?'

'Sadly they would do just that, Nellie. As you know, they are only my succinct and unbiased observations. I do not imagine that Mr Longman would wish to invite a mountain of writs.'

'But you have also written down so many of the clever things people have said to you.'

'Yes, I sometimes make notes of intriguing remarks or interesting ideas for future use but they are nothing more than desultory thoughts and reflections.'

'In that case, Aunt Margaret, why not offer Longman a selection of your desultory thoughts and reflections – aphorisms, philosophy, that sort of thing. They don't have to be original, everything's been said before in one way or another. It will make a perfect gift book at any time of year, not just for Christmas. It will be cheaper and won't date.'

'Marguerite, you know how many note books I've filled. I sometimes wonder how I ever did anything else. It will be a monumental task to select acceptable material.'

'If we managed to sift through all your hyperbole about Byron, we can do the same with your night thoughts. We know exactly what will be rejected.'

By the end of 1839, Longman and its associates abroad were distributing my expurgated *Desultory Thoughts and Reflections* as an alternative to the annuals. But unlike the annuals it was bought for its content as well as its physical appearance. Pseudo-philosophy demanding no intellectual effort always goes down well with a certain kind of reader.

'Philosophers: — men who expect little enjoyment in life and therefore are not disappointed.'

In the wake of *Desultory Thoughts* I became the editor of a new type of gift book more preposterously devoid of substance than the traditional annuals. The firm of Thomas Ackermann asked me to compose twelve short poems to describe twelve etchings of *Flowers of Loveliness* by E T Parris. This distinguished engraver's moderately competent floral images – roses, daisies, lilies of the valley, violets and so on – were not flowers at all, but unnaturally beautiful ladies, some posed with their pretty female children, undoubtedly legitimate. Parris neatly camouflaged the real flowers into these idyllic scenes for me to elucidate through delicate improbable poetic narrative and dialogue. My poems all expounded melancholy sentiment without explaining why such attractive and evidently prosperous ladies were either damagingly scorned, dreadfully unhappy or both. I simply implied that the flowers reminded them of their misery. Then as always, the demand for misery was insatiable. Now the miserable could offer it as a gift to the miserable. I completed all the poems in two weeks.

The twenty-six-page volume was skilfully printed, bound in red and gilt morocco and too tall for the average bookshelf. *Flowers of Loveliness* was thus possibly the first true exemplar of what is now called a coffee-table book, priced at today's equivalent of about two hundred pounds but it was printed on paper of the finest quality.

Ackermann's *Flowers of Loveliness* proved a huge success. I therefore accepted Longman's more generous offer for a competitive publication. My *Gems of Beauty* retained the dejected beauties but substituted the flowers with precious stones. I excelled at extolling precious stones. Flowers tend to wilt and die so quickly. Between 1836 and 1840 I edited five annual editions, for which I wrote all the poetry myself, though some readers considered Marguerite and Nellie equally talented poets.

In 1840 E T Parris resigned after discovering that Longman paid me three times more for my verses than he received for the intricate engravings on which he laboured ten times longer. I had no difficulty finding another engraver of limited repertoire to replace him but ran out of gems to extol. I therefore introduced human metaphors for romantic misery: *'The Lovers'*, *'The Brigand'*, *'The Flatterers'*, *'The Heiress'*, etc. In an attempt to explain away the now deceptive title, I prefixed the 1840 *Gems of Beauty* with:

> *'What's in a name?' Our Shakespeare's self did ask,*
> *And I repeat when, turning to my task*
> *The title 'Gems of Beauty', I Behold -*
> *A title now some three or four years old.*
> *Applied somewhat unaptly, I must own,*
> *Since here no longer glittering gems are shown.*
> *But your indulgence, readers fair and kind,*
> *Gives value to the title in my mind.*
> *So it is retained, then be no less kind now,*

Accept our humble offering, and our vow
That it will ever be our pride and duty
To please, if we cannot we cannot give gems to beauty.

And this was the last, the best and justly least appreciated of my *Gems of Beauty*. My disenchanting swansong brought about the beginning of the end of the annual and gift book, which maintained a decreasing following for another two decades before being totally eclipsed by more pretentious alternatives. Henry Colburn honoured his long-standing commitment and published the first two volumes of *The Idler in Italy* in 1839, the third in 1840 and *The Idler in France* in 1841. These lamentably censored memoirs of my travels in Europe were to be my last commercial success. Henry requested more in similar vein but since returning to London I had travelled little further than Buckinghamshire at the invitation of Benjamin and Mary Anne Disraeli. I might have been able to offer Colburn an English travelogue, but my other grateful friends and guests tended to be too heavily committed or embarrassed to invite me to their country houses.

The events of the next three years did not bode well. I closed my eyes to the fraying fabric of my literary career while my bankers become more observant. Henry Colburn was also observant. He observed little merit in *The Lottery of Life*, yet paid me an unwarranted advance for the pleasure of my company. I shall not elaborate. My three volume novel published in 1842 was rushed as usual, the plot was as usual and the message as usual. I wrote of the injustice of birthright and unearned privilege and joined a thousand other Victorian authors brandishing their social consciences before the blind, deaf and impotent. Colburn's editor lacked my nieces' finesse. Without this semi-literate hack, *The Lottery of Life* might have sold sufficient copies to encourage Henry to enjoy my company again. It did not, and he did not. Once again I turned to the ever-more heavily committed Mr Longman. Green, Brown or perhaps it was Orme, offered a derisory generous advance which I could not afford to reject. In 1843 *Meredith* failed to fire the imagination of the reading public. Mr Longman did not call at Gore House again but his partners always sent the most considerate letters of rejection.

In 1841 a third niece joined my literary workshop. Louisa, Ellen's eldest daughter, bore little resemblance to the seductive adolescent prised from the young arms of the architect comedian, Charles James Mathews. Nor was she recognisable as the beauty painted by Sir Thomas Lawrence while Manners-Sutton was still the Speaker of the Commons. At barely twenty-eight, Louisa was thin to the point of emaciation with an ashen complexion contrasting the darkness around her sunken eyes. After Ellen banned Mathews from St James's Square, Louisa had shown every sign of fulfilling her early promise but, in defiance of her mother, soon eloped with a bright young man called John Fairlie. John was a patient and understanding schoolmaster who never resorted to corporal punishment. He had thus been dismissed and, able to find only poorly paid employment, could not support his growing family. After a strained reconciliation, Manners-Sutton and Ellen - Viscount and Countess of

Canterbury - disowned Louisa for marrying a man so immoral that he put his vocation before his income. In desperation Louisa came to me, her rich aunt, and begged for help.

It made a refreshing change to hear a tragic story for which I felt unreserved sympathy and I invited Louisa to relieve her cousins by adding the finishing touches to *The Idler in France,* my finest work of non-fiction. When she had finished very little was my work and less was non-fiction. Due to her talent for word economy my second *Idler* emerged as one short volume, more saleable than the three-volume first.

Despite her sickness Louisa was greatly talented and much loved. She composed poems and stories for my annuals and edited a gift book of her own: *Portraits of the Nobility: a series of engravings from drawings by A. E. Chalon – With Illustrations in verse by Distinguished Contributors.* Sir Edwin Landseer, a longstanding friend and contemporary of Alfred, who sometimes came to share his studio and other artistic experiences, was devoted to Louisa and provided some delightful illustrations, as did Alfred himself. The book was published by Charles Heath, whose signed engravings were genuinely his own work. I procured a small but much needed advance and some royalties for Louisa. No, of course I did not make any deductions.

Louisa always brought her little daughter with her to Gore House. The five-year-old Isabella Fairlie was a deaf mute exuding an innocent charm that penetrated the hearts of all who met her. Marguerite and Nellie loved her and taught her to read and write. Even Alfred tore himself from his work to play with her in the garden, amuse her with his tropical birds and show her how to draw. Disraeli, having no children of his own, was especially fond of Isabella. This is one of five touching stanzas he composed for her:

> *They say that those sweet lips of thine*
> *Breathe not to speak;*
> *Thy very ears, that seem so fine,*
> *No sound can seek.*
> *And yet thy face beams with emotions,*
> *Restless as the waves of an ocean.*

'B. Disraeli, *'To a Beautiful Mute: The Eldest Child of Mrs Fairlie'*

Despite all our encouragement and her absorption in the work she loved, day by day, Louisa became visibly weaker. Working long hours and coping with the demands of a family including a terminally ill child and a husband struggling to earn a miserable living by any means possible, exhausted her. Louisa continued her losing battle against the onslaughts of both for two whole years.

Which brings me to 1843, not quite the worst year of my life, but another in which death, tragedy and ill omen overshadowed all else. On 28th January of that year, little Isabella Fairlie died at home in her father's arms. She was seven years old. Of all the thousands of letters I received in my lifetime, Isabella's last effort was infinitely the most memorable and heartrending.

> *'My Dear Aunt, I am so pain* [sic] *in my breast and cough a deal. I thank you for the barley sugar and large cake. Papa gave me a flower paper. I am writing in bed at night. How kind of you to bring what I want, Mamma send* [sic] *me large round barley sugar, not like you give me. Give my love to Alfred, Margery,*[Marguerite] *Ellen,*
>
> *from I.L.F.'*

I had become so cynical that I could not prevent myself thinking that poor mute Isabella never said a bad word about anybody. I wish I had told her that. She was quite intelligent enough to have enjoyed the irony. A month later, Louisa Fairlie, nee Hume Purves, at the age thirty-two resigned her borrowed time and followed her daughter to the grave. It was another merciful release though, I believe, a great loss to literature.

The two funerals brought me together with my sister Ellen for the first time in years. With unprecedented humility, she asked if she might call on me at Gore House. The Viscountess Canterbury did not arrive in a fine carriage. The viscount's carriages had all been sold. I watched my once fabulously beautiful sister limp across Hyde Park aided by a walking stick. She was fifty-three, a year younger than me but more devastatingly aged by good fortune. My first thoughts involved no sympathy. I could not forget Ellen's haughty disdain while she was the grand hostess of the Speaker's residence. Nor had I forgotten her and Manners-Sutton's ingratitude to Charles for permitting them and their illegitimate families to live rent-free at St James's Square. Viscount Canterbury had, for years, been a pillar of national government. How could he be so inept, that he stood by and did nothing while his daughter and grandchild turned to me for succour in their dying days? And now the Viscountess was coming to ask for charity. Yet, for all my pent-up anger and ingrained cynicism, never in my life did I abandon my family at times of need. Ellen would be no exception, but first she would have to squirm and repent.

> *'Conscience is the rewarder of virtue and the avenger of crime.'*

'I passed Mr Disraeli walking in the park, Margaret. He raised his hat but I'm not sure that he recognised me.'

'Oh, Dis left about a half-an-hour ago. He does so enjoy coming to Gore House, as do so many of our most eminent politicians. I suspect you are acquainted with the Duke of Wellington, Earl Grey, Lord Russell, Lord Melbourne…'

I reeled off the names of a dozen or more eminent statesmen including the present prime minister, Sir Robert Peel. Some had never been to Gore House but it was at least true that I had met or corresponded with them.

'I know them all, Margaret. Or I used to know them. Hardly anyone keeps in touch now that we cannot afford to entertain. Our house in Southwick Crescent is too small and inappropriate. Do you know Paddington?'

'No, Ellen, it is not a part of London that I am accustomed to frequent.'

'We have lived there since we handed over our official residence at Westminster.'

'Surely Viscount Canterbury can afford somewhere better. I understand the Speaker's pension is four thousand a year.'

'That's right, Margaret but while he was Speaker he received much less and was expected to constantly receive important dignitaries from abroad and so on, even the King and Queen. He retired heavily in debt. Entertaining is very expensive.'

'So I have been told. I've also been told your husband is a compulsive gambler and has made himself exceedingly unpopular since entering the Lords.'

'Every politician makes enemies, Margaret. There have been all sorts of allegations – abuse of office, embezzlement and so on. I wish they were true and then we might have some money. Members of the Commons didn't complain in the eighteen years he held office. The Tories even proposed him for prime minister, but when the Whigs came to power they accused him of bias. They said he was made Viscount Canterbury only because of his family connections, as if any of them got into the Lords through any other means. He had the chance to become high commissioner to Canada but we were both too sick to make the journey.'

'But surely Manners-Sutton is still receiving his pension?'

'The Whig government reduced it and it's seldom paid. He was a brilliant advocate but no longer has the connections to secure well-paid briefs. Everything he earns goes to creditors and blackmailers. He says he must avoid bankruptcy at all costs to preserve our good name. He doesn't seem to realise that it doesn't matter anymore.'

'I am truly sorry to hear that, Ellen. But there are stories, not only of gambling but affairs with certain well-known ladies. Is there any truth in them?'

I interpreted my sister's downcast silence as the affirmative. I was no stranger to blackmailers but frankly surprised that a man of Manners-Sutton's experience yielded to their demands.

'When Manners-Sutton's father died a few years ago, it was reported he left a large fortune. You cannot become Archbishop of Canterbury unless you are rich.'

'He was rich, Margaret. The Archbishop was descended from the Dukes of Rutland, landed gentry with more money than the Church itself. I never met him. When his son married a low-born Catholic, Archbishop Manners-Sutton immediately disinherited him, and they never spoke again. He didn't leave us so much as a blessing.'

I studied atheism for many years and was aware that Jesus taught the virtues of charity and forgiveness. Presumably it was not obligatory for an Archbishop of Canterbury to practise Christianity outside his pulpit. The heroine of one of my novels might have shed tears, embraced her sister and cried 'all is forgiven'. My novels were fiction.

'I'm afraid, Ellen, you will not win my sympathy by talking about disinheritance, debt, blackmail or scandal. The Earl of Blessington left me with little else. I have had no choice but to work through all my waking hours. Blackmailers are just one of the demands on my resources. Yes, and I know all about gamblers, who don't pay when they lose. I've lived with one for years. Look at me. Is this the face of a healthy woman? It gets harder to smile every day. I did everything possible for Louisa and poor Isabella, but I have no money left for you.'

'I did not come to ask for money, Margaret. I came to offer an apology. It was wrong of me to distance myself from you and befriend your antagonists. My reputation was as scandalous as yours, but I was desperate to help and protect my husband.'

'We pass our lives in regretting the past, complaining of the present and indulging false hopes for the future.'

That day we talked for a long time about the regrets of our past and the false hopes remaining to us. I was not completely convinced of my sister's sincerity and we were never properly reunited. The woes of the Canterburys, like the rest of my family, were best avoided in polite conversation. I did however speak to the Duke of Wellington, through whose influence I secured a commission for Ellen's son. John Hume Purves proved an outstanding officer and rose to the rank of Brigade-Major. The most half-hearted of my endeavours for my family was the one least in vain.

On December 26th General 1843, Albert 'Beau' D'Orsay died at Chambourcy. Louis-Napoléon wrote from his prison cell to remind Alfred that his uncle, the great Napoleon, is said to have called his father as *'an admirable model for Jupiter'.* This thoughtful message of condolence did not comfort Alfred. He considered that his good looks came from his mother's side of the family. He had lost what little respect he had for his father since learning of his part in the conspiracy to cheat Lord Blessington. The fact that Alfred had given Charles so little in return was irrelevant.

Alfred begged me to come with him to France for his father's funeral. I might have enjoyed celebrating the new year in Paris but once again heavy commitments confined me to the warmer atmosphere of Gore House. I feared that had some well-meaning priest declared that General D'Orsay never had a bad word for anybody, I might have succumbed to correcting him in inadvisable French. Also the Duc and Duchesse de Gramont – Antoine abandoned de Guiche on his father's death - made no secret of their disdain for what they imagined was my relationship with Alfred. As a dutiful bereaved son, Alfred thus undertook the journey with only his valet for company. At Chambourcy he was reconciled with his sister, brother-in-law and the Parisian tailor who, at Antoine's expense, made an exquisite black suit identical to the two that had hung unworn in Alfred's wardrobe since the funerals of his mother and Thomas Jenkins.

I had no reason to suspect that a virtuous noble like the Duc de Gramont might inadvertently deprive a relative of his rightful inheritance. I simply suggested to Alfred that he might wish extend his period of mourning until the General's will had been read. In accordance with its terms Antoine was duly appointed executor and promised faithfully to distribute the depleted estate fairly among the D'Orsay family. Of course he would.

On a fine Sunday in the spring of 1844, Alfred returned to London with insufficient money in his well-tailored pockets to prevent repossession of his cottage behind Gore House. In those days, the law protected English debtors from being served with a writ on the holy Sabbath. Thus by the grace of God no lawyers, gamblers or tradesmen were waiting at the Comte D'Orsay's door to observe his valet stealthily remove his possessions and transport them to his studio through my back garden gate. Alfred was confident that at Gore House he would be safe from his creditors and antagonists. Where would they expect to find him, other than with me?

Every day my butler proffered a silver tray, neatly stacked with tradesmen's bills, menacing demands and sinister letters from lawyers. And every day Alfred tore them up and neatly replaced the pieces. Like every successful gambler, he knew that his luck was about to change. King Louis-Philippe would soon be overthrown; Louis-Napoléon would be released from prison and return to Paris in triumph. As ruler of France Louis's first act would be to send for Alfred and award him – I am not quite sure for what – with an appropriately important sounding sinecure and decree all his debts null and void. Of course it would.

'Pride and poverty are the most ill-assorted companions that can meet. They live in a state of continual warfare, and the sacrifices they extract from each other like those claimed by enemies, to establish a hollow peace only serve to increase their discord.'

Together with Alfred, the rising spectre of insolvency took up residence at Gore House. In the evenings I continued to entertain the eminent with all the grace and composure of a learned countess. I was poor and could not afford to look poor.

I ground out four long volumes of *Strathern or Life at Home and Abroad* while Marguerite and Nellie slaved as surrogate editors for the *Book of Beauty* and *The Keepsake*. They wooed contributors, designers and printers, sifted, interviewed, negotiated and created the finest annuals to bear my name. *'Edited by the Countess of Blessington'* still glittered but was no longer gold. In America superior publications edited by native socialites outshone the prestige of my English gift books.

Much as I loved Alfred as the son I never had, I tortured him to forget the noble and confront the mundane. I refused to let him order new clothes but could not be so cruel as to deprive him of his valet. Wrenching him from the gambling tables caused less anguish. He was already banned from every racecourse, cock-fighting pit and boxing ring in the Home Counties. He was persona non grata at the gentlemen's clubs that once held his patronage an invaluable endorsement. Dealers, who had overcharged him for horses and carriages reclaimed them in part payment of debt. His unique wardrobe, for which he owed thousands, had no saleable value. Dandies did not buy second-hand clothing. Having exhausted every method of raising unearned income, Alfred applied himself to his work with more diligence than ever. I managed to procure more commissions for portraits and soon, as one cynic put it, he was earning enough *'to pay for his gloves for a year'*. If only it had been that much. I retained all Alfred's fees in his best interests but they made little inroad into my unaffordable necessity not to look poor.

Among those I invited to sit for his portrait was the Duke of Wellington, now living in arrogant retirement at Apsley House a short walk across the park. He attended more sittings than necessary to reminisce with Alfred about meeting him when he was a young boy, an occasion neither could recall with clarity. I trained a parrot from the garden aviary to screech "up boys and at 'em" until the Duke developed a headache and left. I had to do something to stop Alfred continually praising Napoleon.

Alfred's portrait of the Duke of Wellington at the age seventy-six - now among the two-hundred and forty-three of Alfred's works held by the National Portrait Gallery - is widely acknowledged as his finest work in oils. It portrays the Duke in civilian clothes apparently making a strenuous effort to stand straight by supporting himself against an ornate table. He wears the Spanish medal of the Golden Fleece partly obliterated by a funereal sash over a white waistcoat with one button unfastened. I suppose it was too tight, old Arthur was never so careless. The face in profile – Alfred could only paint or draw faces in profile – exaggerates the Wellingtonian nose and a half smiling, half sneering and entirely vacant expression. The Duke is reputed to have commented *'At last I have been painted like a gentleman. I'll never sit to anyone else.'* Possibly he was in the early stages of senile dementia.

I arranged for Wellington's secretary to pay Alfred's fee directly to Mr Schwartz, who, aware of his customer's straits, had long since ceased to *'line the pockets of his coats'* as a gesture of gratitude for years of trading on the Comte D'Orsay's reputation. The Wellington portrait settled just enough of the unappreciative tailor's bill, to encourage him to postpone issuing a writ of bankruptcy

If 1843 and 1844 were bad years, 1845 was worse. Despite Richard Bentley's best efforts, the House of Colburn had gone from strength to strength. Henry became so rich that he could afford to separate from his wife: an auspicious event, which I seized the opportunity to exploit. The hard-headed gnome had always derived some sort of erotic satisfaction from my presence but, as a married man, never made an improper suggestion. By the start of 1845, I had become so desperate that I made one for him. He thought I had gone mad, and perhaps I had. Nonetheless, I succeeded in luring him into deploying a succession of editors to make my next novel marginally publishable. When they had finished all that remained of *Strathern* in my original words was the opening poem reflecting my own situation with blind intuition:

We make ourselves a pleasant home,
Deck'd out with all that's rich and rare,
As though we thought Death would not come
To tear us from a scene so fair.

As Colburn's typesetters were preparing my poem for his press, metaphoric *Death* came to all that was rich and rare in my *deck'd out pleasant home*. My dinner parties and soirées ceased. I still received a few visitors and informed those who asked that I was resting for the benefit of my health. This was true. Years of intense labour, forced happiness and scaling the slippery rock of social mountains had taken more of their toll than I could afford to admit. My doctor diagnosed no specific complaint. Nerves, he said. What sort of medical condition is nerves? There was pain in my head, my legs, my stomach and places that no lady, let alone a countess, mentions in public. I was fifty-six and my eyesight and hearing had begun to deteriorate. All my anatomy was in terminal decay.

In the sodden fields of Ireland, the anatomy of millions of diseased potatoes was also in terminal decay. Like everyone else, I did not appreciate the severity of the blight or foresee its repercussions. For seven long years, famine consumed the poverty-contaminated fat of the previous seven and many more before those. Money could buy no cure nor impede the inevitable escalation of death and destruction. In my learned ignorance, I blamed the disease on the primitive agriculture, the illiteracy and apathy I witnessed in my youth. Perhaps I was right. But it did not occur to me that I too might be thrown onto the cankerous heaps. The remnant of the Blessington estates, I reasoned, consisted of fine houses in Dublin not smallholdings in rustic backwaters. They were occupied by gentry and merchants, not potato-digging peasants. When my guaranteed annuity failed to appear I sent angry demands to Mr Worthington, whose office responded with accounts of diminishing returns. Once prosperous tenants had fled the country, taking all they could carry except their unpaid rent bills. Whole streets stood empty. Properties today worth millions could be bought for a hymn of mourning.

London journalists luxuriated in stories of the horror of impoverishment, starvation and eradication of entire communities. Their callous exploitation was outrageous yet I followed their hypocritical example and called for sympathy for the Irish. Opposing Churches preached that the same but different gods were punishing the people for their sins, and they were believed. Why did these judgmental gods not punish the Churches for failing to disseminate their obscene wealth – forfeited from the forefathers of the ill-fated faithful? I could neither forgive the over-fed priests I heard as a child preaching the virtues of humility and poverty, nor their suffering congregations, taught to deny the virtue of the pursuit of wealth.

'The pursuit of wealth is the highest expression of virtue. Nothing contributes more than money to the perpetual struggle, not only against poverty, but against all forms of suffering.'

Among the few virtuous citizens of Ireland untainted by the festering tubers was my sister Marianne, never happier than when asked to flaunt her title in support of emergency relief. Naturally, I was the first person to whom she turned for a donation. The Appeal's *printed* notepaper – then a novel and extravagant phenomenon – was headed: 'Patroness, La Comtesse de Saint-Marsault'. How could anyone refuse a patriotic Irish lady with such an impressive French name? I sent more than I could afford with a less than charitable accompanying letter. I never expected to see my sister again. But I did. It was 1845, a year of bad news.

On 18th July Charles Manners-Sutton, Viscount Canterbury suffered a sudden fit of apoplexy, and like Charles Gardiner, Earl of Blessington, fell dead, not in the Champs Élyseés but in a squalid street in Paddington. He was sixty-five. Once again, I should have felt bereaved but I had never had much respect for Manners-Sutton. Not many people had. Only his and Ellen's surviving children attended his funeral, together with the handful of retired politicians who recalled their long-serving Speaker's redeeming features. Marianne sent Ellen a letter of condolence on the Appeal's notepaper, hand bordered in black ink of course. Did she seriously think this would impress her sister? La Comtesse begged Ellen to understand that conditions in Ireland were so bad that she was unable to tear herself from her heavy commitments.

As always, I let my family tear me from the heaviest of my commitments. I not only attended the viscount's funeral, I paid for it. Ellen had no money and it was unthinkable that a member of the House of Lords could die too poor to pay for his own interment. The Church of England also reserved no funds for the deliverance of an irreligious son of an Archbishop of Canterbury into the care of his maker. The vicar of Paddington spoke briefly of the viscount's good words for everybody and read out the names of his family from my notes.

The *Times*'s lengthy obituary was cold, factual and highly impressive: educated at Eton; graduate of Trinity College, Cambridge; Member of Parliament for the University of Cambridge; Speaker of the House of Commons under four Prime Ministers; Privy Counsellor; Knight Grand Cross of the Order of the Bath; Viscount Canterbury, of the City of Canterbury, etc. etc. ... '*He married Ellen, daughter of Mr Edmund* [sic] *Power of Curragheen in the county of Waterford, widow of John Home Purvis* [sic] *Esq and sister of the Countess of Blessington.*'

An obituary writer, like his subject, never has a bad word for anybody. He omitted the distasteful detail of debt, depravity and debauchery and filled his allotted space with unsubtle euphemisms.

'His lordship's father was for four and twenty years Archbishop of Canterbury, a fact which no doubt influenced the selection of a title by the late Viscount upon becoming a member of the House of Lords, for we have no reason to believe that he had any connexion with the ancient cathedral city.'

The obituary went on to remind its readers: *'It is rather remarkable that the rejected speaker was kept some time waiting for his Peerage'*, and ended with an extraordinarily frank apology for the exclusion of *'the details* [of] *several minor and personal anecdotes floating in society'.* And this was the *Times*!

> *'As storm following storm, and wave succeeding wave give additional hardness to the shell that encloses the pearl, so do the storms and waves of life add force to the character of man.'*

The storms that had added hardness to my shell softened my zest for life. I was driven only by my conscience, my vanity and my nieces. Marguerite and Ellen were the last hope for my family and my last chance of atonement. I strove to appear happy, to appear rich, to stay solvent and to support Alfred.

Alfred strove with me, and did my bidding like a slave. This is not to imply that I acted as some sort of sadomasochistic mistress, though he did seem to relish making a prison of his studio. Without exercise Alfred put on so much weight that few of his splendid clothes now fitted and no tailor would alter or replace them without payment in advance. On fine days I instructed his valet to stuff him into his breeches, and take him for a short stroll around his old haunts. In Mayfair, if nowhere else, he would be safe from the bearers of weapons of legal destruction. Alfred's portly figure did not go unobserved.

> *'D'Orsay, is going round to the trade to see that his works of art are well displayed. He is now oft to be seen, on days other than Sunday, admiring his own portrait, which is pardonable vanity enough, for he has painted and chiselled himself not as he is, but as he was before his confinement. We dare not say that he is getting too fat to be admired by anyone but himself.'*
>
> The Satirist, 24th August 1845

I too confined myself to my work and became too fat or, as I put it, *'inclined to embonpoint'.* I clung to the belief that writing held the key to financial salvation. I completed another novel and again approached Henry Colburn, who had lost his lust for me, his derisory investment in *Strathern* – another of my finest novels – and his appointment book. Richard Bentley had managed to avoid me for eleven years although I bore him no ill-will. I humbly called at his premises and he humbly agreed to see me. Now grey, almost bald and ravaged by success, he was as enthusiastic as ever and as bitter in his rivalry with Colburn.

'My dear Lady Blessington, I read a chapter of your *Strathern*, it was another of your finest novels. You should have brought it to me. Colburn's a blackguard, utterly incompetent. He wouldn't recognise a bestseller if he saw a thousand readers queuing to buy it.'

'Mr Bentley, I shall not honour Mr Colburn with my favour again. His business methods are too personal for my taste.'

'You are quite right, your ladyship. Colburn's presentation of your image in *Strathern* was completely inappropriate.'

'Indeed, Mr Bentley, I was horrified when I discovered that he had prefixed *Strathern* with Sir Edwin Landseer's horrible little engraving. I appreciate that I am no longer young, but my American public do not wish to envisage the Countess of Blessington with a matronly figure and a triple chin.'

Sir Edwin should have confined his portraiture to animals. His picture of, *'Lady Blessington's dog'* is one of his most delightful paintings. I never kept a dog. It was a stray he found wandering in the garden of Gore House. The only Landseer portrait I like is his elegant pastel of Nellie, here in the Wallace Collection. She never told me how she managed to pay for it. Poor Edwin later suffered serious psychological problems and was eventually certified insane. When I knew him, he was sane enough to regularly accept my hospitality, gratuitously share Alfred's studio and to overcharge Colburn for his ugly caricature of the author of *Strathern*.

'Rest assured, Lady Blessington, I shall not be employing Sir Edwin. As you may be aware, he is at present heavily committed to sculpting four giant lions for some ludicrously ostentatious memorial to Lord Nelson. But you are here to talk about your *Memoirs of a Femme de Chambre*. I have read the synopsis. It should go down well enough with the booksellers.'

'Thank you for your confidence, Mr Bentley. May I expect my customary rate of advance?'

'I regret, Lady Blessington, the offer of advances is no longer within my remit. You must understand that my firm has expanded. I now have partners and must adhere to rigid policies. I am however completely confident that the ongoing royalties will handsomely reward your ladyship's pains. When shall we expect your manuscript?'

'I could have it ready before the end of the year, if I am not waylaid by too many other offers.'

'Excellent, Lady Blessington, I shall look forward to publishing it without Sir Edwin's engraving. We would not wish our readers to mistake it for an image of a *Femme de Chambre* at the age of memoir writing, would we?'

I approved neither of Richard Bentley's wit nor of his terms of business, but smiled pleasantly and accepted both. *Memoirs of a Femme de Chambre*, another variation on the theme of my *Confessions*, was not delivered before the end of the year. I was again waylaid by the Angel of Death.

Ellen had misled me. Viscount Canterbury was not suddenly struck by apoplexy in the street but had taken to his bed months before, mortified by threats of indictment for debt and deception. He was a Queen's Counsel but to cowardly to defend himself in court. Happily, he died before being thrown to the majestic mercy of the law.

I wrote to the prime minister and begged for the Speaker's pension to be extended to his widow. Sir Robert Peel declined, courteously as always. I had asked too many favours of him.

Years of anxiety had affected Ellen's health. Her doctor diagnosed no specific ailment and recommended fresh air. Where had I heard that before? I paid for her to go with her daughter, another Marguerite, to the sleepy Gloucestershire village of Clifton and settled the unpaid rent on a small house Manners-Sutton had used as a retreat in the worst of times. The Clifton air, benefitting from the pollution blown with the smoke from the neighbouring port of Bristol, claimed Ellen's life on 16th November 1845, just four months after her husband's.

Marguerite and Nellie had greatly loved their cousin Louisa and little Isabella, but had scarcely known their aunt. They nonetheless begged to attend Ellen's funeral with me, uninfluenced by their interest in the railway line opened that year, conveniently running from Paddington to Bristol. It was also my first train journey. All three of us enjoyed the experience so much that we had to make a concerted effort to appear mournful. Apart from the frustrations of stops and starts, the railway was marginally more comfortable than being dragged over the pitted roads of England by an apathetic team of horses and possibly a little quicker.

Marianne, to my surprise, dragged herself from feeding the potatoless for long enough to cross the Bristol Channel to pay her last respects to the Countess of Canterbury. I had never seen my last surviving sister so cheerful as at this austere little churchyard. The potato famine might have caused more death and enduring anguish than any event in the history of Ireland, but at least it made La Comtesse de Saint-Marsault sincerely happy for the first time in her life.

It was the last time I saw Marianne or Ellen's surviving children, Marguerite, Mary and the then Major John Hume Purves and her stepdaughter Frances Diana Manners-Sutton. No representative of either House of Parliament came to remember my sister's relentless years of entertaining on borrowed money at the Speaker's house. But the most conspicuous absentee of all was Colonel William Stewart, who did not even send his unacknowledged children a note of condolence. Stewart died five years later, still unmarried. I did not know or care who inherited his millions.

The short service could have been no more austere. Perhaps it was said that Ellen never had a bad word for anybody but I paid no attention to the dispassionate parson. Before returning to Bristol station, I left the church warden a donation for a memorial to Lady Ellen Manners-Sutton, Viscountess Canterbury. I do not know or care if it was erected.

Walter Savage Landor sent me another touchingly worded letter and I am particularly proud of my reply. It was one of the most hypocritical I ever wrote.

'Gore House, November 26th 1845

Alas! alas! of the two heads that once rested on the same pillow, one is now laid in a dark and dreary vault at Clifton, far, far away from all she loved [and] *from all that loved her… The ties of blood may sometimes be severed, but how easily they are re-united again when the affection of youthful days is recalled… And now she is snatched from me when I hoped to soothe her.'*

In some ways, I was glad that this was the end of my sister. In every way, I was glad that this was the end of 1845. I consoled myself with the thought that the new year would be better and greatly relieved when it started well.

In January 1846 Charles Dickens was appointed first editor of the *Daily News* and asked me to be his society correspondent with a brief to provide *'any sort of intelligence I might like to communicate of the sayings, doings, memoirs, or movements in the fashionable world'*. I suppose he felt sorry to me. He must have known that I was quite unsuitable for the position. Those who vicariously shared the lives of the *ton* were hardly likely to trust the word of the notorious Countess of Blessington. But I was in no position to dismiss five-hundred pounds per annum – I had asked for eight hundred – and I thanked Dickens with absolute sincerity and promised that I would not let him down. Three weeks later, Dickens let me down by resigning in favour of the self-righteous John Forster, who I suppose I must concede was wise to decline to renew my contract at the end of the first half-year.

Richard Bentley did not let me down. He distributed my *Memoirs of a Femme de Chambre* with panache and encouraged enthusiastic reviews. Given my recent disappointing returns I was delighted with my first royalty, sufficient to enable me to settle a few of my most pressing bills and even some of my remaining servants' outstanding wages. I anticipated an ongoing stream of income, but thereafter my *Femme de Chambre* paid me no more than I paid my own femme de chambre, before she was dismissed. Richard Bentley helpfully explained there had been a spate of similar popular novels which he described as of the Victorian genre. He was not at all concerned.

'To ensure that your work is enduring, Lady Blessington, you need to capture the immediate spirit of the times. Do feel free to come back to me whenever your next novel is ready. There's no hurry.'

Either he appreciated my versatile talent or was not interested in publishing an enduring work. It was the latter. The following year he brought out *Marmaduke Herbert or The Fatal Error – A Novel founded on Fact*. The novel was founded on as much fact as any of my others but was not quite a fatal error. For four or five weeks, the three volumes flew from the shelves of popular exclusive bookshops and again I received an acceptable first royalty, a miniscule second and nothing more. I sent Bentley the synopsis of a novel capturing the immediate spirit of the times. The letter of rejection was written by a subordinate – the Prime Minister always replied to my correspondence in person – but I was in no way offended. I simply did not offer Mr Bentley, or anyone else, the privilege of publishing another enduring novel for me.

I covered my library floor with discarded scribbles. *Country Quarters* was not only my last novel, but my worst. Some years later poor Marguerite and Nellie had to completely rewrite it for posthumous publication. It did not sell many copies.

On 25th May 1846 the miracle that Alfred had so long prophesied came to pass. Louis-Napoléon bribed his guards at the impenetrable Fortress of Ham, cunningly disguised himself as a workman by lifting a plank of wood onto one shoulder and walked through the prison gates negligently left open for the occasion. He then crossed the lowered drawbridge, dropped the plank into the river, stepped into the carriage that happened to be waiting for him, and requested the driver to take him to a safe sanctuary in England.

What safer sanctuary could there have been for a fugitive aspirant emperor than Gore House? Louis's recuperation from the trauma of his daring escape lasted a fortnight; long enough to add significantly to my debts. Thereafter Louis moved to a large town house in King Street St James and, undaunted by his French enemies, resumed the pursuit of a life of debauchery and political ambition. No, he never invited me there.

Disregarding the embarrassingly shabby state of my home, I resumed hosting dinners and receptions for Louis. And he resumed his acquaintance with Dickens Landor, Bulwer-Lytton, Marryat, Browning, Cornwall and Thackeray, as well as Alfred, Landseer and numerous other artistic figures. I invited Hector Berlioz, then guest conductor at the Theatre Royal, and Franz Liszt, in London on a concert tour, came and played my piano for Louis. The prime minister and other leading politicians however declined the opportunity to meet the future King of France.

Richard, fourth Marquess of Hertford and his son Richard Wallace were delighted to be reunited with Louis. They invited him – but not me – here to Hertford House and permitted him to view their art collection transported from the Château Bagatelle. Louis was unimpressed. Such important works belonged in France, he said.

The Fourth Marquess informed Louis that a Miss Elizabeth Ann Howard was anxious, to meet him, but he would be unable to effect the introduction as he had to urgently return to Paris to protect his remaining investments from the ever-escalating civil unrest. Louis, an escaped convict, considered it unseemly to invite the daughter of a bootmaker and sometime actress of dubious talent to his house in King Street, St James, and so requested that I hold a dinner for Miss Howard at Gore House. It transpired that this lady had written to Louis numerous times while he was in prison professing her love for him and Louis had replied, professing his love for her, though they had never met. I thought this extremely bizarre but am now gratified that I suspiciously agreed to effect the introduction, since their meeting was to profoundly change the history of France.

In the cheerless dungeons of the Fortress of Ham every amenity had been available to prisoners like Louis-Napoléon who could afford to pay. To help pass the time, the late emperor's nephew had taken advantage of the services of a visiting courtesan called Alexandra who, inconveniently, bore him two sons. His inveterate correspondent, the beautiful Miss Howard, conveniently offered to bring the boys up in England, together with her own son by a Major Mountjoy Martyn, a relative of my late husband. The happily married Major, evidently with the Mountjoy attitude to money, endowed the charitable Miss Howard with a grotesque inducement to deny his paternity.

Having at last met her beloved Louis at Gore House the besotted Miss Howard was to support his return to Paris to enjoy the revolution of 1848, and subsequently finance his campaign to be elected as the first President of the French Republic. In gratitude, Louis made her his longest serving mistress, and the mother of at least two more of his illegitimate children. When eventually he became Napoleon III, he discarded his loyal low-born paramour and very properly married the high-born Eugénie de Montijo. The honourable Emperor acknowledged the disillusioned Miss Howard's years of financial and erotic generosity by creating her Comtesse de Beauregard. By then she had spent her fortune on her love for him and was in no position to maintain the enormous château and estate which came with the title. I am uncertain of what became of the still beautiful matronly Miss Howard. Doubtless an immoral woman of her class would have resorted to marrying for money.

Had 1847 not been such an unhappy year for Edward Bulwer-Lytton, his influence with the London publishers might have been the saviour of my literary career. In the New Year honours list he was awarded the Knight Grand Cross of St Michael and St George for services to government – with no mention of his infinitely greater services to literature. His knighthood was not just a disappointment, it was an insult. He was a Lytton, whose mother's antecedents had been ennobled since the time of William the Conqueror. But Edward was denied a peerage since, having been sorely defeated in the 1841 general election – the first after abolition of the rotten boroughs – his political opponents preferred him to remain ineligible to sit in the House of Lords. This would prove the least of his problems. Hardly had Queen Victoria's sword touched Sir Edward's shoulder when his nineteen-year-old daughter, Emily, died of typhus fever. Nothing I could do or say would comfort him. As a good aristocratic English father Edward had seen little or nothing of his children since being awarded custody on the dissolution of his marriage ten years earlier. Emily had been brought up by governesses and her younger brother Robert, sent away to a public school. Rosina, Edward's hot-headed, faithless and brilliantly clever former wife accused the newly created knight of deliberately causing Emily's death and conducted a one-woman campaign to destroy his reputation and remaining political aspirations. And she succeeded. She arraigned Edward with allegations of numerous affairs - including with me – and unleashed a glut of publicity. Rosina not only screamed abuse at Edward during his public speeches but to further embarrass him published a bitingly satirical novel, and so with characteristic restraint, he arranged for her to be incarcerated in a lunatic asylum. The press, unreasonable as always, interpreted this as an act of lunacy in itself and vilified Sir Edward as a monster. There was a public outcry and Rosina was released after just three weeks.

The estranged Lady Bulwer-Lytton continued her attacks with all the vitriol of an innocent woman, until Edward retired to the Continent to preserve what remained of his own sanity. I corresponded with him for the rest my life but I never saw him again. Eventually he returned to England, where he was properly elevated to Viscount Lytton of Knebworth and as a close political ally of Disraeli, served a brief and unremarkable term as Secretary of State for the Colonies. I was long dead by then.

My health deteriorated and my income dwindled until finally I was forced to abandon economy and dismiss my remaining servants – well, most of them. One by one I called them into the library and offered my heartfelt thanks for their years of dedicated service. I then asked their names, wrote glowing references and expressed my sincerest hope that they would find suitable positions. Since I was never informed to the contrary, I presume that they succeeded.

I managed Gore House with only a housekeeper, a maid, a gardener, a cook and Alfred's valet. I coughed and spluttered over endless optimistic correspondence, while Marguerite and Nellie edited *The Book of Beauty* and *The Keepsake*. My devoted nieces constantly complained that they had been my slaves for years, and now had nothing to expect from the future. Yes, I suppose I could have found them suitable husbands, but given my experience of Marianne, I thought it wise to leave them free to choose for themselves. What a great pity that they were too heavily committed to my work.

Alfred did not complain. He too assigned much of his time to optimistic correspondence, writing of deluded expectancies of income from the Blessington estates and anticipated favours from Louis-Napoléon. We both received generous replies laden with helpful advice, for which we offered our thanks with unquestionable sincerity.

> *'I lost my spirits and my health,*
> *But kept my friends so did not wince*
> *Until one day I lost my wealth,*
> *And never heard of friendship since.'*

News of financial embarrassment spreads fast. Now almost as many final demands and letters with menaces were addressed to me as to Alfred. Shopkeepers, once flattered by the patronage of a countess, closed my accounts with one notable exception. Howell and James extended my credit and continued to deliver my orders from their exclusive Regent Street emporium with their customary humility. Why such experienced businessmen remained so trusting was a question that I chose not to contemplate.

19

'You don't mind if I stand in front of you and take a snap? Won't take a second – business, I'm afraid.'

The cheerful well-fed young man has come to the Wallace Collection for the sole purpose of illicitly photographing my portrait with his mobile telephone. He is dressed in a bright red t-shirt and a yellow top hat with bottle-green ribbons suspended from its brim. On the front of the shirt is printed a picture of Marilyn Monroe and on the back Elvis Presley, both surmounted by a crudely-designed golden emblem – 'F U'. I presume he is some sort of clown, a children's party entertainer perhaps. I am wrong.

'Dare I ask what F U stands for?'

'Not what a lot of people think. Fun Undertakers, that's all. Here take my card. Hang on to it, you'll need it one day, everybody does.'

'Thank you very much, Mr Reaper.'

'No, no, my name's not really Reaper, it's De'Ath. My real name's Maurice Thomas Charles De'Ath. But everybody at F U, male and female, has to be called G. Reaper. It's my partner; he's got a bit of a corny sense of humour. 'We'll be the last people in the world to let you down' and all that sort of stuff. People don't want old jokes when they've lost a loved one; they want to enjoy themselves.'

'If you don't mind, I would prefer to call you, Mr Reaper. My late husbands shared your names and in different ways all took their deaths far too seriously.'

'Strange you should say that. The photo is for a serious client. I've never heard of this Countess of Blessington, but the widow says her old man thought she was brilliant and wants me to put her picture all over his coffin. I suppose she is a bit sexy.'

'Is this sort of thing common nowadays, Mr Reaper?'

'Not yet, most people still go in for the old sackcloth and ashes, but with F U you get a choice. We always ask what the deceased liked most when they were alive. Marilyn and Elvis still are the most popular for the older stiffs, but we get all sorts. Couple of weeks ago we had an ex-zoo keeper, who's partner wanted an elephant called Gladys. She made the most beautiful coffin I've done. Broke my heart to burn her up.'

'What about religion?'

'That's never a problem. We've got our own rent-a-clergy scheme, any denomination, but our sort of clients generally think life after death lasts only as long as anybody remembers your funeral. That's got to be true.'

'And memorials?'

'Now they are a problem. The old cemeteries won't take our animated musical obelisks. We sell a few to people who like to keep them at home, but they soon get tired of them.'

It is a great compliment, I suppose, to have my image cremated with the body an unknown admirer, and I am convinced by the sincerity of the young man's vocation. I wish him many years of fun undertaking before he hurries away.

A traditional funeral serves to compound the misery of the genuinely bereaved and as a hypocrite's charter for those who care only for the living. Nothing said or done at a graveside prolongs life beyond the last breath, which should be the moment to forget the deceased and start to enjoy the life remaining.

In my lifetime I told many lies, and today I have told many more. The truth died with me and it is right that it should be forgotten.

> *'We value time, but on the bed of death*
> *When its brief sands are running to an end;*
> *O! how we then remember with dismay,*
> *Our wasted hours, which, like reproachful ghosts*
> *Of murder'd friends, rise up and pass before us!*

--

The 1847 and 1848 editions of *The Book of Beauty* and *The Keepsake*, edited in my name by Marguerite and Nellie, proved the most delightful and engaging since the time of Letitia Landon. Charles Heath, as always, did his best to justify their exorbitant price with gorgeous simulated silk covers and his charming engravings by anonymous surrogates. His best was not good enough. The sales failed to cover his costs, and he was declared bankrupt. I cannot tell if this contributed to his death in September 1848, but I have no doubt that it accelerated mine.

For an hour or longer I sat in my grand leather work chair looking blankly at the mass of figures laboriously copied by the trustees in bankruptcy; an abstract artist's impression of the death mask of Charles Heath and Company. 'Countess of Blessington, £700', I read. More was owed to me but by then it was irrelevant. I held about as much hope of recovering my debt as my health and beauty. One copperplate schedule was headed 'assets', for which I read ashes; the tools of creativity burnt to dust by inflamed 'liabilities'. Was insolvency a serial killer – Heath, Alfred, me? Not yet: The Countess of Blessington, oracle to the great and the good – more of the former than the latter – was alive, and if not kicking, still determined to recover. Drowning in a lake of sterile medicines, my only saviour was my mental strength.

Throughout the first half of 1848 civil unrest continued to rage in France. In the 'February Revolution' the monarchy was overthrown. King Louis-Philippe ended his eighteen-year reign and was driven into exile, leaving the poet-politician Alphonse de Lamartine to form a provisional government. On the day that Louis-Philippe arrived in England, Louis-Napoléon left for France. I can hardly describe my relief. I would never have to entertain the conceited young upstart again, or so I thought. Alfred begged me to go with him to Paris.

Alphonse, he said, would remember our idyllic days together in Florence and greet us with warmth and affection.

It would be an understatement to say that the provisional president did not greet Louis-Napoléon with warmth or affection. The future Napoleon III immediately turned tail and returned to the pursuit of his statesmanlike ambitions in the debauched luxury of King Street, St James. Again he took advantage of the cultured, if decaying opulence of Gore House to expound his grand designs for the benefit of the disinterested influential guests, entertained by the grace of Howell and James.

On the streets of Paris, demonstrations and riots intensified and culminated in the bloody crescendo of the 'June Uprising'. Alphonse de Lamartine calmed the revolutionaries with promises of democracy and universal enfranchisement, and made a hasty diplomatic exit before the disastrous consequences of his magnanimity were foreseen. Louis-Napoléon again returned to France, entered his name as a candidate for president, and, as a new messiah with old radical theories and timeworn prophesies, won the love of the people. In December 1848 Louis-Napoléon Bonaparte was duly elected by an eighty per cent majority and sworn in as the first elected leader of the Republic of France. A pyrrhic victory; his rabble-rousing rhetoric created great expectations that he was powerless to fulfil, even had he wished to. Louis soon learnt that the survival of a leader in a democratic socialist utopia is synonymous with tyranny, and as a responsible man of the people, took draconian measures to curb every hint of dissension.

Alfred never lost faith in the glorious new Napoleonic age. Nonetheless the triumphant president propitiously forgot to offer him a position in his hastily formed government. A more improbable democratic socialist was hard to imagine.

By January 1849, I, Alfred and my nieces had become prisoners, confined within the walls of Gore House. Gaolers bearing writs gathered daily at every entrance. My domestic staff was down to a cook, a maid and of course Alfred's valet. Marguerite and Nellie did what they could remember of domestic chores from their impoverished Irish upbringing and I tried to assist them, when I felt well enough. My experience of cleaning a small office on Súir Island with a broken besom was of enormous help in a palatial mansion.

Alfred, of course, had no concept of the practicalities of housework and, since potential sitters did not appreciate being welcomed by the custodians of my back gate, there was no further demand for portraiture. He thus turned his multifarious genius to invention.

Having taken sound financial advice, Alfred had invested half of Charles's wedding present in railway companies and like countless other cautious speculators, soon discovered that his shares were worthless. Travelling by train, he protested, was far too dangerous.

Marguerite, Nellie and I had felt perfectly safe travelling from Paddington to Bristol and back.

To ensure that we would be safer still on future journeys Alfred designed an absurd apparatus that he said would save innumerable lives and yield him untold wealth. Of course it would. He produced elegant watercolours showing a train with a rope running along its carriage roofs to the driver's cab where it was attached to a large bell. In the event of untoward incident, a rear platform guard could pull the bell rope to advise the driver to stop. Another charming pastel showed that the alarm might be activated by the passengers themselves using tastefully decorated cords linked to the rope through small apertures in the carriage roofs.

The directors of all the leading railway companies returned Alfred's drawings with exuberant appreciation of his artistic skills. As professional engineers, they explained that there was no possibility of a rear guard or a passenger observing a hazard sooner than the driver. Passengers wished to minimise rather than increase the number of stops and might be discomforted by rainwater dripping through holes in the carriage roofs.

Alfred wrote to a number of government ministers complaining of the companies' disgraceful neglect of traveller safety. They all wholeheartedly agreed and ignored the situation until 1864. In that year six passengers were murdered in a horrendous train robbery, and in consequence - after two years of due deliberation - the government made the communication cord a statutory requirement on all trains. Thereafter, Alfred's device saved innumerable lives and yielded untold wealth to manufacturers and distributors throughout the world. Alfred and I were long dead by then.

His next invention proved similarly beneficial to others. He mixed a thick cream and requested his French valet – whose name I think, was Gilles – to test it on a small selection of his shoes and boots. In less than two hours the corridor was lined with thirty pairs of gleaming footwear. Alfred immediately sent the formula with a sample of his concoction to the most fashionable bootmaker in Paris, Monsieur Henri. The unsolicited communication reminded this honourable businessman that in London – where he previously traded as Henry Hobnale – he had sued Alfred for three hundred pounds and accepted, in lieu of payment, the exclusive rights to advertise all his products in France as: *'Utilisé par Le Comte Alfred D'Orsay'*. Monsieur Henri's lawyer advised Alfred that the rights extended to the gooey mixture, and threatened him with serious repercussions should he attempt to sell it himself. The grateful cobbler exploited his former client's invention and sartorial reputation until he retired a wealthy man.

Alfred then returned to his alchemy laboratory and re-employed his abandoned collection of mysterious chemicals and potions in creating new fragrances. Alfred again sent samples to Paris, but only into the safe hands of his sister, Ida. The Duchesse de Gramont was so grateful for her gifts that she passed them to her son, Annérius, who added the unpatented fragrances to his firm's *Parfums d'Orsay* collection. I believe he later congratulated his uncle on devising products so easily manufactured.

One Saturday afternoon in April 1849 high drama came to Gore House. Instead of my modest order, Howell & James delivered a courteous communication accompanied by a dozen sheets of error-free arithmetic.

'Our deeply respected and most valued Lady Blessington,

As you will observe from the attached statement of account, the outstanding balance currently amounts to three-thousand-five-hundred pounds, one shilling and four pence. This exceeds your credit limit by one shilling and four pence. Since it is almost two years since we last received a payment from you, it is our regrettable obligation to request immediate settlement. Until this is forthcoming we will be unable to accept your further invaluable orders.

In accord with our invariable policy, the utmost confidence will be observed.

We beg you, Lady Blessington, to believe that we remain your most humble and obedient servants, etc., etc.'

A commotion upstairs disturbed my contemplation of the consequences of this long-expected thunderbolt. A few moments later, Alfred's valet ran into the library, which I found quite unnerving. I never permitted my servants to run indoors.

'A thousand apologies for interrupting you, Lady Blessington, but a gentleman is banging on the Comte D'Orsay's dressing-room door and demanding admittance.'

'Then why doesn't the Comte admit him?'

'Because, your ladyship, I locked the Comte D'Orsay's door from the outside.'

'Who is this gentleman and how did he get into the house?'

'He claimed to be from the bakers and obliged the maid by carrying a tray of cakes into the kitchen, your ladyship. Then he asked her to direct him to Comte D'Orsay's suite, and when she did so, he left the tray and rushed upstairs.'

Since I could expect no further deliveries from Howell & James, I was relieved to discover that there was some food in the house.

'I take it he is demanding money? How much does he want?'

'I could not hear clearly, your ladyship, it sounded like a hundred-thousand pounds, but perhaps it was two hundred-thousand. This made me think that the gentleman was not really from the bakers.'

'So what did you do, Gilles?'

'Your ladyship, I ran up after the gentleman and informed him of my obligation to announce all visitors. Then I asked him to wait while I advised Comte Alfred of his arrival. The Comte was most perturbed. As you know, your ladyship, he must never be interrupted while engaged in selecting his coat for dinner. He gave me a key and told me to lock the door when I went out. The gentleman seemed quite confused when I informed him that I would have to speak to you before he could be admitted.'

Silently, I thanked the traders of Clonmel market for teaching me to keep a cool head when surrounded by financial insanity. I knew full well who Alfred's unwelcome visitor was and why he was prepared go to such lengths to see him. He had come to deliver a writ of execution. Simply touching a debtor's arm with the document during business hours constituted formal delivery. Business hours ended at sunset. I glanced at the window. It would soon be dark and it was Saturday. Tomorrow was the Lord's Day when legal transactions were prohibited.

'Merci beaucoup, Gilles, vous avez bien fait. En aucun circonstance, ne laissez cet homme dans la chambre du comte. Comprenez-vous?' I whispered, although no one else was within earshot and Alfred's valet spoke perfect English.

'Je m'appelle Jean, Madame la Comtesse, mais bien sûr, je comprends'.

'Gilles, bring the man down here to the library. When I invite him to take a seat, leave us and lock the door from the outside. Here is my key. Then go back and inform Comte Alfred that he will be departing for Paris later tonight. Pack one bag and no more. Then return to the servants' quarters and wait for me to call you.'

'Will I be travelling with my master, your ladyship?'

'Of course you will. Do you imagine Comte Alfred is capable of getting to Paris alone?'

Jean, or whatever his name was, ushered in an anxious looking young man with a little flour smeared on his face. He was wearing an ill-fitting chef's bonnet and a small striped apron from which his business suit spilled out at the sides. A large folded sheet of paper protruded from his coat pocket.

'Monsieur Maladroit Clerk, madame,' announced Jules, emphasising his French accent.

I pointed to a sofa, and motioned to dismiss the valet.

'Welcome to Gore House, Mr Clerk. But since you are so clearly not a baker, will you at least confirm that Clerk is your real name?'

'It's both my name and my job, your ladyship. People often make jokes.'

'Then perhaps you had better remove your disguise. I would not wish to make the mistake of calling you Mr Cook.'

The young man had very little sense of humour.

'Yes, I have to return the hat and apron to the bakery and get my shilling back on Monday. I often have to resort to disguises in my line of work. It's the only way to get into some people's houses. You wouldn't believe the tricks they get up to keep me out, your ladyship.'

'And may I ask why you tricked your way into my house, Mr Clerk?'

'Didn't the valet tell you, your ladyship? I'm from the sheriff's office to see a certain Count Alfred D'Orsay. I have to serve him with this writ and make an inventory of his possessions for the bailiff?'

'Bailiff, Mr Clerk? This is a terrible shock. There must be some mistake. Will two pounds help?'

'Oh no, Lady Blessington, Count D'Orsay owes an awful lot more than that. It's the biggest case I've ever handled. They'll be making him bankrupt next week, that's why I must see him today. Does he speak English? I don't know any French.'

'Unfortunately the Comte speaks no English whatsoever. If you wish, I shall request him to join us here in the library, so that I might interpret for you.'

I stood up and rang for Jean.

'You have clearly had a busy day, Mr Clerk. Might I offer you some refreshment while we are waiting for Comte D'Orsay? I doubt he will be long.'

I found some cheap port, brought by one of my better-mannered dinner guests and filled a large tumbler with the disgusting liquor. Mr Clerk quaffed it down as if it were water. Observing no immediate effect, I replenished his glass.

A few minutes later, Jules unlocked the door, entered and bowed.

'*Et le Comte D'Orsay est toujours enfermé dans sa chambre?*' I asked.

'*Oui, Madame.*'

'*Merci, Gilles. Gardez-le là pendent une heure et demi.*'

'Mr Clerk, the Comte D'Orsay's valet says his master will join us as soon as he has finished dressing. The Comte tends to be a little fastidious and therefore might be a few minutes. Meanwhile do have another port.'

I anticipated great difficulty in distracting Mr Clerk until the conclusion of sunset. But having finished my port and half a bottle of brandy, he transpired to be a most interesting conversationalist. We had a great many mutual acquaintances. His lurid tales of escorting the husbands of certain society hostesses to the Fleet and the Marshalsea were especially amusing. Indeed, his adventures were so absorbing that I forgot to watch the sunset, until it was almost completely dark.

'I apologise for interrupting your story, Mr Clerk, but permit me to ring for a servant to light the lamps.'

Almost before I released the bell rope, Alfred's valet had unlocked the library door.

'*Le monsieur part maintenant, Jules. Montrez-lui à la port, s'il vous plaît.*'

'*Bien sûr, madame.* Allow me to show you out, Mr Clerk.'

The now slightly tipsy official did not notice the valet's sudden mastery of the English language.

'I'm sorry, your ladyship, I can't leave until I've served Count D'Orsay's writ.'

'That will not be possible today, Mr Clerk. The sun has set and we are outside statutory hours.'

'Then I'll have to come back in the morning, your ladyship.'

'As I am sure you are aware, Mr Clerk, here in England the good Lord does not countenance business to be conducted upon the Sabbath Day. Goodbye, and allow me to say how much I enjoyed your company.'

Jean enjoyed literally kicking Mr Clerk out of the door. He had forgotten his tray of cakes, which the valet would eat that evening.

I did not really enjoy this amusing ordeal. I felt nauseous and frail and had much to do. The predators outside left at dusk, but they would brave the wrath of the Lord and continue their vigil in the morning. Alfred would have to leave in the dead of night. I had some banknotes hidden in a copy of *Grace Cassidy* – thrift being among my heroine's many virtues – the safest place in the house, since nobody was likely to open my best novel. I gave some of the money to Gilles, Jean or Jules and told him go out and find a coachman to take Alfred to Dover.

Alfred emerged from his rooms, as always, immaculately dressed for dinner. The maid brought the last few of Mr Clerk's cakes neatly arranged on a silver platter for us to partake of a pessimistic last supper together. A last supper is by definition pessimistic. Alfred was not at all pessimistic. He was about to embark on the greatest adventure of his life. President Louis-Napoleon was waiting in Paris with nothing better to do than elevate him to his rightful destiny in the democratic Republic of France.

I handed Alfred the last of Grace Cassidy's savings. He begged me to go with him and I was greatly tempted, but I was in no immediate danger of arrest, and even in those circumstances, could think only of my irretrievable reputation. I promised to follow as soon as I reached an agreement with my creditors, a hopeless task that I had no intention of attempting. Alfred assured me that when I reached France the Duc and Duchesse de Gramont would welcome me to their château. Of course they would.

Alfred passed his last two hours at Gore House by first selecting a travelling outfit which still fitted, then returning to the library, requesting Nellie to play something by Liszt and settling down to the last of Charles's vintage Bordeaux. Marguerite played Chopin until he fell asleep.

At three in the morning, we lit lanterns and stealthily hurried across the garden to the rear gate. A driver experienced in midnight flights was waiting with a coach and four. For the first time that day Alfred expressed emotion. He would never see England again. He was leaving Gore House. He was leaving me, his adopted mother. Worst of all, he was leaving his wardrobe. I promised I would be with him in a matter of days and we would live happily together forever. I felt ill and cold, and immediately retired to bed. Fairytales only happen once.

The next day I woke up to reality. I had literally given away my last penny. Still I was too proud to contemplate accepting charity from rich friends. I would have to sell all that was saleable and raise enough money to enable me to escape the country unpursued. It was Sunday, the Lord's Day. I could sell nothing.

I walked aimlessly about the house, wrestling with my conscience, my nauseous pain and my equally unhealthy finances. I wandered into Alfred's studio. The most meticulous of men had left chaos and confusion. Strewn about the floor were discarded drawings, paintings, busts and statuettes. The tables were covered with pots of dried paint, broken pens, empty inkwells, hard brushes, blunt pencils and spoiled drawings. Instinctively I began to arrange the artwork into some sort of order. I counted twenty-seven of Alfred's portraits of me and others by Landseer and Maclise. Then I noticed an advertisement in a paint-stained old newspaper: House Sale – Apply Phillips & Co, 73 Bond Street.

William Phillips, son of the founder of the illustrious auction house lived a few streets away. He had been an occasional visitor and had admired my collections, paintings and furniture. If Mr Phillips could not sell them for me then they were as valueless as they were redundant. Marguerite and Nellie delivered my note.

'My sincerest apologies, Mr Phillips, for disturbing your day of rest but I have urgent need of your advice. I will be forever grateful if you will spare me an hour of your precious time. Marguerite Blessington.'

The auctioneer, requesting no further explanation, accompanied my nieces back to Gore House.

'The law does not permit me to work on the Lord's day, Lady Blessington, but I assure you that it is seldom my day of rest. You would be surprised at how often I am called from church to conduct urgent business. No doubt you wish me to evaluate your possessions.'

Room by room I conducted Mr Phillips through Gore House, pointing out the merits of furniture, pictures, books, silver, glassware, jewellery and ornaments. I was wasting my breath. Mr Phillips possessed the all-round vision of a magical bird, which saw not objects but value. He saw value in objects long forsaken, objects presumed worthless and objects made worthless by neglect. Quietly and professionally he took notes as fast as I wrote my novels.

'I am planning to spend my retirement in Paris, where I have been invited to live with relatives in their well-furnished house. Regrettably I shall have no space for all these baubles. Perhaps, Mr Phillips, you might be interested in arranging a small house sale.'

'Lady Blessington, that is my business, but it will not be a small sale. If it is your intention to dispose of the entire contents of Gore House, it might be one of the largest we have yet organised. The auction itself will require at least ten days.'

'As I said, Mr Phillips, I am due to go abroad. How soon can you arrange a sale?'

'We could possibly do something in six weeks.'

'No sooner?'

'You must understand, your ladyship, that a great deal of work is involved. We must make a full inventory, print and distribute a catalogue and place advertisements. For a sale of this size I would suggest five viewing days, for which it is necessary to display everything to best advantage. I must however advise you, your ladyship, that we can find buyers for anything except sentiment. Our sellers often find the disruption to their homes highly distressing. I trust you will not be too dispirited.'

None of this came as news to me. I had bid at many auctions and knew how they were conducted. My old essay in *The Magic Lantern* dramatised the fictitious heartache of a house sale, and I remembered only too clearly the factual heartache of the disposal of my childhood home. And now the cherished symbols of my delusions and attainments were to be crushed under the hard wood of an auctioneer's gavel. I made no reply but a brief glance at my face told Mr Phillips all he needed to know.

'Please do not be embarrassed, Lady Blessington. Nobody sells at auction unless they need the money. You cannot afford to wait for us to arrange a sale, can you? The truth is you need money today.'

'Today is the Lord's Day.'

'The Lord's Day is of no concern to some of my most ardent customers. Do you object to having Jews in your house, your ladyship?'

'Mr Phillips, some of my best friends are Jews, not least of whom is Mr Disraeli. His father, Isaac, who sadly died last year, was the most cultured man I ever encountered. And I am also well acquainted with the Rothschild family, who for many years were most helpful friends to my late husband.'

'You might be surprised to learn that my clients are of a different hue, Lady Blessington. They drive a hard bargain.'

'And you might be surprised to learn, Mr Phillips, that I too drive a hard bargain.'

'In that case I must explain, Lady Blessington, that when I introduce a private buyer my commission is the same as for a sale at auction. If you will permit me, I shall make a list of objects that you might wish to dispose of immediately with their estimated values. The choice is yours of course but I recommend that you retain as much as possible for the sale. My auctioneers invariably achieve the best prices.'

'I understand, Mr Phillips. I am most grateful for your advice and shall look forward to meeting your clients.'

'I shall go and speak to them now and return as soon as I can. Should any Jews arrive before me, do not be afraid to admit them. They are quite harmless and will not steal anything. They will probably disparage everything and make derisory offers, but do not accept less than I recommend. Oh, and don't bother to offer them any refreshment. Nothing ever satisfies their imponderable dietary laws.'

Within an hour four of Mr Phillips's most ardent customers, who indeed had little in common with the Disraelis or Rothschilds, appeared simultaneously on my doorstep. All wore the black costume of a Polish noble of a prior century, and did not remove their cartwheel fur hats when I invited them into the house. In so far as I could discern any expression through the forest of their beards, it was the why-are-you-are-wasting-my-time look cultivated by medical practitioners. I offered my hand to the first, who recoiled as if I had a contagious disease. To an orthodox Jew all women, regardless of their religion, are at certain times unclean but surely it must have been obvious to these prolific family men, that I was too old for such nonsense. Nonetheless, they responded with an amiable blend of suspicion and horror when I greeted them in classical Hebrew. Fearing that I might also understand Yiddish they began to speak in passable but heavily accented English.

'Strabo asserts that a species of honey was produced at Pontus which, owing to the bees having fed on aconite and hemlock, was poisonous. May we not liken flattery to this poison – sweet but destructive?'

Presuming God's chosen people to be as susceptible to flattery as those less impaired, I began by telling them that they were younger and more handsome than I expected. Since this totally confused them, I added that the Jews are known to be the most intelligent people on earth. But if, as reputed, the Jews are also the shrewdest businessmen on earth, this quartet was a poor example of the race. Bending over magnifying glasses like badly disguised detectives, they examined a random selection of my possessions, shook their heads and rejected them without comment.

Fearing that they would buy nothing at all, I held up an inferior silver chalice, pointed to the hallmark and muttered twice Mr Phillips's valuation in what I hoped was Yiddish, possibly it was Gaelic. As I did so the dealers commenced an acrimonious debate over the merits of the neither poisoned nor honeyed chalice. After a short melodramatic performance, involving a variety of languages, facial expressions and hand gestures, a victor emerged with an offer of the price I originally asked. In like manner they purchased everything Mr Phillips had marked. My new Jewish acquaintances left a pile of coins and banknotes on a side table, pronounced Hebrew blessings and relieved me of the least cherished of my belongings. Mr Phillips reappeared soon after they left.

'Surely they haggled with you, your ladyship?'

'No, Mr Phillips, they haggled among themselves. They might have been disarmed by my knowledge of their traditions, but I really cannot understand how I managed to captivate them so easily.'

'You might if you met their wives, Lady Blessington. Orthodox Jewish men do not expect their women to be scholars; they expect them to produce children.'

I felt anything but a temptress. My head ached and my body was so racked with pain that I could hardly think. I coughed constantly and sometimes vomited. My doctor said that the Parisian air had restorative qualities. I remembered that Mary Campbell Browne was told the same before she died en route, but my nieces, excited by the thought of visiting Paris, persuaded me to follow Alfred.

I handed the keys to Mr Phillips and instructed him to sell everything regardless of price and remit the proceeds to my lawyer. Then I sent all my bills to Mr Powell's office with instructions to settle them pro rata, and if possible, avoid legal action. In tactful response the ever-assiduous lawyer commended that I made a will. Having been the victim of Charles's demented posthumous directions, this was something I had vowed never to do. Nobody, however rich or well intentioned, has ever succeeded or will ever succeed in directing life from the grave. I simply wrote a letter requesting that in the improbable event that I died solvent my estate should be divided equally between Marguerite and Ellen Power.

On 14th April 1849 the three of us walked hand in hand around the periphery of the garden and through each of the rooms of Gore House as if to say our silent goodbyes. We reached Paris four days later. It was nineteen years since I was last there. My aching head filled with confused memories, and I experienced a moment of optimism. The French capital was still an urban paradise; a theatre royal of dilapidated grandeur.

President Louis-Napoléon, having made similar observations, had consulted an aristocratic architect called Baron Haussmann whose dramatic design involved disinfectant, demolition and development on a massive scale. The president, as yet insufficiently secure to decree realisation of the Baron's monumental hallucination, permanently postponed the Comte Alfred D'Orsay's appointment as Minister for the Arts, with responsibility for supervision of the project.

Alfred did not emerge from his sister and brother-in-law's château to welcome us to Paris. I never saw him again, until today. His flight from London had caused great furore, and he had good reason to fear that the arm of her Britannic Majesty's court extended to the Arc de Triomphe and further.

I took a suite for three at the Hôtel de la Ville, in the rue de la Ville de Évêque. It had a delightful view of Madame Craufurd's old château in the rue D'Anjou, which did nothing to raise my spirits. I sent a note of my arrival to Chambourcy gently hinting that I would prefer to move to the country until I found somewhere permanent. La Duchesse de Gramont responded in English with impeccable courtesy.

'Ma chère Marguerite,

Antoine and I are overjoyed to hear that you are well and have arrived safely in Paris. We are greatly looking forward to seeing you again and to meeting your nieces when you honour us with a visit.

Sadly, Alfred's recent misfortunes have overwhelmed him, and he has taken to his bed. He has, however, begged me to convey his sincerest love, and inform you that he will join you immediately he recovers his strength.

As you know we are also providing accommodation for Alfred's valet, and thus regrettably our small château is unable to accommodate .....'

A raft of compliments followed. I interpreted this charming rejection to mean that the Duc and Duchesse could hardly wait to be rid of their disgraced relative, and had no desire to entertain me or my family. There were at least twenty bedrooms in the small château at Chambourcy inherited from Alfred's father.

I dispatched numerous letters to England, most of which can today be found in libraries and archives around the world. They were all written before I left Gore House and there is scarcely a word of sincerity in any of them. To Sir Edward Bulwer-Lytton's brother, Henry, recently returned to England after five years serving as a diplomat in Spain, I wrote:

The President has not forgotten old times, nor old friendships. He has been unceasing in his kindness ever since our arrival. We dine with him tomorrow and hold communication with him every day. His old attachment to Alfred revived with fresh force the moment they met.'

'[All] *reclaimed me with open arms…'* my letter lied.

I boasted of having been reunited with numerous distinguished figures, French and English. The only one I actually met was the English ambassador Constantine Phipps, now Lord Normanby, in whose theatre in Florence Charles and I had acted with such great delight. I told him that I had very little money left and would soon be destitute but he could offer no help. What are ambassadors for, I wondered?

'Dr Madden, Mr Sadleir, Mr Molloy, let me confirm what you all doubtless suspected. Yes, it was all a pretence. Did I not make that abundantly clear in the penultimate sentence of my last letter to Henry Bulwer?

'In short I have lived too long out of the gay world and in the rational one to enjoy soirées and fashionable parties.'

Louis-Napoleon's precarious presidency was plagued with problems and pressures. How could he have found time to waste on Alfred and me? You, Mr Sadleir, wrote that Louis would not dare *"have given a lucrative post forthwith to so equivocal being as D'Orsay – a man who had lived out of France for twenty years and only returned thither in a flight from English justice".* If that were true, and it was, why would the President not also distance himself from a useless aging bankrupt woman like me? No, of course Louis never invited me or Alfred to dine. The future Emperor Napoleon III invited potentates bearing power, not fugitives seeking favours. In any case, as you all know full well, I survived just six weeks in Paris.'

'But what about your *'most famous witticism'*, your ladyship? As I put it *'in a tangle of traffic the wheels of* [your] *carriage became locked with those of the President. He turned and recognised* [you]. *Raising his hat, he greeted* [you] *politely: Vous restez longtemps à Paris, Lady Blessington?* [To which you] *replied, Je ne sais pas. Et vous?* Are you now telling me this is also not true, your ladyship? '

'Really, Mr Sadleir, is this a probable conversation between two people who you claim were *'holding communication'* every day and regularly dining together? The anecdote is true enough, but the protagonist was a much younger and prettier English lady. Who was I to engage in friendly banter with the president of France, and where would I have got a carriage in Paris? My beautiful calèche was in Mr Phillips's workshop having its white, green and crimson paintwork retouched ready for sale.'

I would have relished half a chance to confront Louis with his debts of honour, but the *Satirist* spelled out my situation with deadly inaccuracy

The powerful Countess
For beauty and bounties (?)
Has bolted to Paris – has bolted to Paris:
Bring hither some mops,
For the tears of the shops,
And for Howell of Regent Street, who in despair is!

To a place that is shady
The motherly lady
Has smuggled her nieces, a powerful resource;
And Alfred the Great
Is to find them a mate,
Or snap up the sweepstakes as clerk of the course.

Poor President Nap,
Though he's scarce worth a rap,
Is expected to harbour each one that decamps
So haste and resort
To his gingerbread court,
Levanters and demireps, shufflers and scamps!

From *The Gore House Scamper, A New Song to an Old Tune* – cited by Connely, in *Count D'Orsay: The Dandy of Dandies*

Not long before I might have been delighted to discover that I was still worthy of satire – the most coveted of all compliments – but now it only added to my pain. A French physician called Dr Simon came to the hotel and administered laudanum, which induced a vivid nightmare:

Twenty thousand people, I know them all, friends and enemies, file hand-in-hand through Gore House and marvel at my life and work. Mr Phillips waves his arms to the left and right; pendulums racing with time turn back the clock. There is no clock. The past, present and future merge into a shapeless bubble. Dickens, Byron, Landor, Wellington, Peel and Disraeli sit at my dining table. Together we pour scorn upon the injustices of society. England has become a State of discontent. The masses suffer free education, free doctors, hospitals, pensions and grants. Glued by tears to devices of instant communication they torture their fingertips with unlimited entertainment and information. They eat an abundance of cheap and unappetising food more delicious and nourishing than the viands I am serving to princes. The gavel beats with the rhythm of a percussionist. 'What am I bid for a trinket touched by the hand of the most gorgeous Lady Blessington?' The entrepreneur Bianconi and the blackmailer Westmacott lift their hands in unison. Both are millionaires and laugh together at their unparalleled achievements. I welcome a thousand familiar faces to my first and last

385

soirée. My silver reflects the brilliant light of my crystal chandeliers, and a palace of crystal grows. 'In just eighteen months, gentlemen, Prince Albert will bring the wealth of the world to London. Do not hesitate, now is the time to invest.' Alexis Soyer, the most celebrated chef in London, waves a lease from the roof of Gore House. My dining table, groaning with haute cuisine, splits into two, divides and divides again. Men, resplendent in white ties and ladies in colourful ball gowns toast Queen Victoria. A garden, blooming with herbs, fruit and vegetables turns to stone and spreads like the incoming tide across my landscaped lawns. Row after row of potatoes are harvested in Ireland. The famine is over. Marianne is crying. Mr Norman and Mr Worthington are dancing. Gore House vanishes. Its quadrangle of brick walls softens into a circle. The circle grows, tier after tier. The Queen, in deep mourning, weeps by the door of the grandest concert hall England will ever know and demands a memorial more befitting to her beloved Prince Albert. The greatest musicians, orchestras and singers perform in my drawing room, and all the peoples of the world are their audience, listening and watching simultaneously. Mr Phillips beats and bangs, louder and louder. Again and again Richard Wallace nudges the fourth Marquess of Hertford. His left hand is to his ear. He is not wearing his ring. *The Countess of Blessington by Sir Thomas Lawrence*, going, gone at three hundred and twenty guineas. The Marquess is wearing his ring. Mr Phillips throws up his gavel into a halo of light and it transforms into a golden number – £13,385, £13,385, £13,385, £13,385. Mr Howell and Mr James shake hands with old Mr Powell. 'Do not trouble yourself, sir, the Countess of Blessington, owes us nothing.' Charles Heath bows low and seven hundred pounds fall from his top hat. Manchester Square, St James's Square, Palazzo Belvedere, Palazzo Negroni, Casa Pecori, Hotel Ney, Avenue de Matignon, Seamore Place and Gore House merge into a single gigantic palace. Versailles is dwarfed in its courtyard. Louis-Napoléon, in a fit of jealousy, reaches out and ....

I awoke ailing and despondent, unfit to interpret my grim hallucination. Marguerite and Nellie were out searching for a permanent home. They had watched Mr Phillips at work on his day of rest and were confident that his sale would raise the funds to support us until Alfred recovered, and received his settlement from the Blessington estate and his rightful legacy from his father. They found some impressive first-floor rooms in the rue du Cirque overlooking the president's Palais de L'Élyseé. How charming! I would be able to wave to Louis over the heads of his mindless supporters: *'the great unwashed'*, in Sir Edward's immortal phrase.

I forced myself into a carriage and asked to be taken to the corner of the rue du Cirque and the Champs Élyseés, near where Charles had fallen to his death. The stately suite was spacious, unkempt and unsafe. The rent was therefore cheap. I told my nieces to accept a short lease, returned to my hotel bed and again sent for Dr Simon. As I waited, I designed another palace in my head. I shall have a splendid drawing room to receive the royalty of Europe, a dining room to entertain its nobility and in another elaborate reproduction of Mrs Jenkins's library I shall write beautiful poetry and novels and be remembered for ever. Dr Simon warned that his medicines might cloud my judgment. He was wrong. I was fully aware of my inability to pay the hotel bill, let alone for the restoration of a noble residence.

The doctor diagnosed an enlarged heart: what else after a life of constantly extending it? It was too late to turn back the clock. There was no clock.

At Gore House, Mr Phillips and his porters and clerks appraised the physical residue of my life. They cleared attics and outhouses of my indispensable possessions untouched since I first lived at St James's Square. They emptied cabinets, drawers and chests and, book by book, cleared my cherished library shelves. They rearranged the house like an impoverished museum, drew euphemistic pen pictures and printed a heavy catalogue: *The Costly and Elegant Effects of the Rt Hon Countess of Blessington, Retiring to the Continent.* Twenty thousand copies were bought at three shillings each. A disposable reference outsold the most enduring of my literary work.

The auction commenced on Monday 7th May 1849 and continued through every working day until Wednesday 23rd. Mr Phillips offered to send me a free copy of the catalogue – how generous – but I had not bothered to give him my address in Paris. Today I am reading it for the first time. The facsimile in A N L Munby's *Sale Catalogues of Eminent Persons* shows details of the buyers, the prices they paid and even the auctioneer's notes. I feel no sentiment. It is an ironic memorial: the worthless droppings from illustrious tables, depreciated by reckless extravagance and restored to glory by the passing of time.

Mr Phillips was a poet among auctioneers. '*Objects from the Petit Trianon, from Stowe, from Strawberry Hill, gifts from Sir William Gell, Lord Byron and Ferdinand, King of Naples; Articles formerly belonging to Madame de Maintenon* [the 'secret' wife of Louis XIV] *and Voltaire; The Countess's state bed, which once belonged to the Empress Josephine.'*

'*Grand Piano by Érard: selected by Liszt*'. Yes, Franz Liszt played at Gore House, but there were no other pianos for him to select. The unique instrument was built for me by Sébastian Érard himself, another magnificent gift from Charles unacknowledged in my works. I imagine crowds gathered around my '*pair of old Bleu du Roi Sevres vases supporting lily candelabra for five lights, formerly the possession of Marie Antoinette*', sold for seventy-two guineas, and the Empress's '*decorative Sevres clock enamelled in medallions of Cupids*' sold for £48 6s 0d. It never told the right time, even when she owned it.

Mr Phillips sold every one of the 2,232 lots, but the sale did not end there. I am speaking of a time yet untainted by the credit card and electronic transfer. A slow stream of buyers returned to Gore House, proffered their cash, and one by one removed their purchases. By the end of May my home was an empty shell and Mr Phillips had collected a total of £13,385. How many millions is that today? After withholding his fees and expenses he rendered £11,985 4s 0d to Mr Powell. The lawyer paid my bills, waited a decent interval for late claims, and despatched a swift messenger with the good news that all my financial problems were over.

The swift messenger had never been to Paris and spoke no French. He thus experienced considerable difficulty in locating the rue de la Ville de Évêque. When he found me, it was too late. I died, like so very few others, with my affairs in order.

In the night of 4th June 1849 I departed this world in a hotel room with a view of shattered nostalgia.

'Of course I took my own life, Dr Madden. It was perfectly simple. Dr Simon sold me enough medicines to stock an apothecary. What was there to live for? It was better to put an end to it all than to beg charity from the great men to whom my house had been a free depository for their pretentious troubles. My health, my beauty and my joie de vivre were beyond redemption. At best I would be tolerated by French society, and at worst mocked by English. I had seen too many of the rich and resplendent smiling through an old age of ravage, ruin and ridicule.

'Goodbye, Dr Madden, Mr Molloy and Mr Sadleir. What a pity that none of you will be able to re-write my biographies.'

Epilogue

'We make temples of our hearts, in which we worship an idol, until we discover the object of our love was a false god; and then it is not the idol only that is destroyed – the shrine is ruined.'

My death certificate read Countess Marguerite, Widow of the Earl of Blessington, died Paris, aged fifty-nine years and nine months on 5th June 1849. At the same age and on the same date, thirty-seven years earlier, Mrs Jenkins, the forgotten mentor of all my accomplishments, had died.

When the news reached Chambourcy, Alfred was overwhelmed by grief. That same day he had learnt of the success of the Phillips's sale. He broke free of his sanctuary, borrowed a horse and galloped into Paris as fast as it would carry him. This was not very fast, as the former army riding champion was now at the point of obesity and suffering chronic sciatica. At the rue du Cirque he was disappointed to discover Marguerite and Nellie, not wailing over my coffin, but acting with the sensible decorum I had taught them by example.

Alfred broke down and sobbed uncontrollably for an hour. My nieces tactfully omitted to mention Mr Powell's message, which disclosed not only the result of the auction, but confirmed that they were the joint beneficiaries of my estate. The old lawyer's letter contained other good news. He had made Howell and James cancel their writ after discovering that they had insured my life for three thousand-five hundred pounds and collected when it was legally established that I did not commit suicide. With the waning of the Potato Famine, Mr Norman had found new tenants for the remaining Blessington properties in Dublin, and settled my five-year outstanding annuity, adding ten thousand pounds to my estate. Mr Powell had also collected seven hundred pounds from the new proprietor of Charles Heath's studios, who invited Marguerite to remain editor of the *Book of Beauty*.

The Comte D'Orsay asked for nothing from my posthumous wealth. He too had lost the will to win and add to the hundred-thousand pounds he owed in England. Alfred was an obsessive romantic. His only remaining desire was to be as close to me in death as in life. He claimed it was my greatest wish to be buried in France. I do not recall this wish, but my properly educated nieces agreed that a Catholic funeral at Chambourcy would be more economical than shipping my body back to England. I don't think they really liked me.

The Duc and Duchesse de Gramont were not at all pleased when the four of us returned together to their questionably legally inherited country seat, even though one of us was a cadaver and unlikely to cause them any trouble. As a truly compassionate aristocrat, Ida provided two night's accommodation for Marguerite and Nellie in the room occupied by Alfred's valet, Jules, before he was dismissed for being unable to fit his master into any of his clothes. Alfred prevailed upon his brother-in-law to pay for my funeral, which he did on condition that no one was invited from England to be told that I never had a bad word for anybody.

After my interment, Marguerite and Nellie, thanked the Duc and Duchesse de Gramont profusely, recovered their deposit on the lease at rue du Cirque and returned to London. My last loyal friend, La Baronesse de Calabrella invited them to live at her Mayfair mansion and enjoy her genteel lifestyle there and in Paris, Switzerland, the Netherlands and Italy. Catherine soon found Nellie (Ellen) Power who was beautiful, as portrayed by Landseer (Wallace Collection), a suitably rich husband, while Marguerite Agnes Power, as portrayed by William Henry Egleton (National Portrait Gallery), never married, as far as I know. Marguerite remained editor of *The Book of Beauty* and *The Keepsake* until there was no further demand for the genre. Thereafter, with the help of friends and contributors to whom I had introduced her, such as Dickens, Thackeray and Forster, she published a series of novels including *Evelyn Forester, The Foresters, Nellie Carew* and *Sweethearts and Wives*. Today the works of Marguerite Agnes Power, died 1867, merit about as much attention as mine.

Gillion Gaspard Gabriel Alfred de Grimaud, Comte D'Orsay et du Saint Empire, at his brother-in-law's expense, built the ugly pyramid mausoleum, now evidently the pride of Chambourcy. How sad that this Parisian suburb has no greater attraction to offer its tourists, especially as my memorial was not, as is invariably claimed, designed by Alfred. It is simply a cheap copy of the tomb of his grandfather Quintin Craufurd, in the Père Lachaise Cemetery in Paris.

Soon after my death, Antoine, Duc de Gramont granted Alfred a loan, which he did not expect to be repaid and escorted him from his château. In the best traditions of a declining dandy and artist Alfred resorted to the Bohemian life of a Parisian garret. His remaining friends in high places provided occasional donations and invitations, and sometimes commissioned a portrait. Unable to dress appropriately for the Parisian clubs, Alfred foreswore gambling and devoted the rest of his life to feeling sorry for himself, mourning for me and writing to Louis-Napoléon to remind him of the promises he never made or intended to make. The great reforming President had enough troubles without sworn allies desperate to help him. Having won a ninety-two per cent majority in the national referendum of December 1851 – in which there was no corruption – Louis approved a new French constitution and in effect made himself an absolute potentate.

Comte D'Orsay's plight was at last brought to Napoleon III's attention. Like all ruthless dictators, Louis desired only to be seen as man of honour. He therefore appointed his old friend Director des Beaux Arts. By then Alfred's acutely diseased spine unable to support his bloated torso prohibited him from taking up the office. He died on 4th August 1852, at the age of fifty-one, having outlived me by just three years.

Since the Comte D'Orsay was, in theory, a favoured member of the newly constituted government, the Duc and Duchesse de Gramont arranged a splendid funeral for him at Chambourcy. It was attended by a large number of French nobles, most of whom had not known Alfred and a few mutual friends who came over from England with belated tributes to me.

For reasons of convenience he was laid to rest next to me in the ugly pyramid and later two stone plaques were later erected inside in my memory. On one is a poem (I think) in my honour by Barry Cornwall, once a regular contributor to my annuals:

> *In her lifetime*
> *She was loved and admired*
> *For her many graceful writings,*
> *Her gentle manners, her kind and generous heart,*
> *Men famous for art and science,*
> *In distant lands,*
> *Sought her friendship:*
> *And the historians and scholars, the poets, and wits, and painters,*
> *Of her own country,*
> *Found an unfailing welcome*
> *In her ever hospitable home.*
> *She gave, cheerfully, to all who were in need,*
> *Help, sympathy and useful counsel;*
> *And she died*
> *Lamented by her friends,*
> *They who loved her best in life, and now lament her most,*
> *Have raised this tributary marble*
> *Over the place of her rest,*

Not very good, is it? Lord Byron did better in twenty minutes.

On the other stone is a Latin eulogy by Walter Savage Landor, together with his own translation:

> 'Underneath is buried all that could be buried of a woman once most beautiful. She cultivated her genius with the greatest zeal and fostered it in others with assiduity. The benefits she conferred she could conceal, – her talents not. ....'

This was not as I would have wished either.

I do recommend a visit to the Wallace Collection. You meet the most interesting people here.

Appendix A

HISTORICAL NOTES

Bagwell v Power: see Appendix B. Judging by the number and seniority of the counsel involved this must have been an important and seminal case.

Blessington, Earl of, Viscount Mountjoy: appearance - Lawrence's portrait of Lord Blessington in his robes for George IV's coronation, now in a private collection, is clearly a romanticised pose and probably not a good likeness. Holmes's miniature oil held by the National Portrait Gallery is seldom on public display but a close copy can be found among the two hundred portraits in Sir George Hayter's monumental Trial of Queen Caroline (1820). The earl's vacant profile turned away from the animated protagonists might suggest lack of comprehension or deliberate inattention to the distasteful proceedings. D'Orsay's later profile, also at the NPG, is probably a more accurate likeness and similarly portrays a rather vacant expression.

Craufurd, 'Madame' nee Anne Franchi: (c1749 - 833) had two children by the King of Württemberg. Since nothing has been discovered about Eleanore de Franquemont's sibling, he or she is omitted from the narrative.

De Guiche (Gramont) family and Parfums D'Orsay: The Duc de Guiche (later de Gramont) and Ida Comtesse D'Orsay had one daughter Antonia, who died aged 5, and three sons. The eldest Agénor inherited the title on the Duc's death in 1855. The mounted image of Comte D'Orsay is still employed by the company but it is uncertain which of his nephews or their children was its founder.

D'Orsay, Comte Alfred: (1801-1852): Notorious dandy, subject of various biographies (see Appendix B). No clear link has been discovered between his family and that of Charles Boucher D'Orsay (1641-1714), provost of the Merchants of Paris who gives his name to Quai D'Orsay, home to French Ministry of Foreign Affairs and the Musée D'Orsay. D'Orsay's dandyism sadly overshadows his reputation as an artist. Over two-hundred-and fifty of his works are held by the National Portrait Gallery alone.

Dwyer, Miss Anne: Lady Blessington's childhood teacher evidently also tutored other wives of distinguished Irish figures but little else has been discovered of her history. She was not related to Thomas Jenkins.

Farmer, Captain Maurice St Leger: No record has been found of the family or background of Lady Blessington's first husband other than the letter referred to from his brother Walter. Sir Fystite is of course a fictitious figure.

Gamba, Count Pietro: remained Lord Byron's secretary until his death (19th April 1824) and thereafter wrote *A Narrative of Lord Byron's Last Journey to Greece*.

Hunt & O'Brien: Edmond Power invested in a firm of corn and butter merchants of this name on moving to Clonmel. The characters of Mr Hunt and Mr O'Brien are fictitious, as is Margaret Power's association with the firm. No reliable record of this period of her life has been found (she possibly was employed at the Cashel post office). Articles by Professor Ann R Hawkins of Texas Tech University indicate that she demonstrated an astute business sense in her literary career, which as suggested here might have been developed as a girl in Clonmel.

Jenkins, Captain Thomas: (c1775-1837) No reliable information about the parentage and family of Lady Blessington's sometime guardian and alleged lover, has been found. He was not related to Miss Dwyer. References have been found to an aunt and one or two sisters (omitted), but Jenkins clearly had a brother - here fictitiously called Stadfast. Mrs Jenkins and Lenshark Jenkins: are entirely fictitious.

Jenkins's Hampshire Estate: A number of references to Captain Jenkins's family house, where Lady Blessington lived for five or six years (c1808-1814) imply similarities to Sydmonton Court (home of composer Andrew Lloyd Webber). However, this house and estate are recorded as being owned and occupied by the family of Sir Robert Kingsmill until at least 1823.

Jephson, Lorenzo Hickey: Edmond Power's contemporary magistrate was possibly the son or nephew of the distinguished Irish playwright Robert Jephson, a sponsor of London's Drury Lane Theatre together with Lord Blessington's father.

MacCarthy v Watson: See Appendix B below. This lengthy trial was every bit as complex, intriguing and mystifying as indicated by the brief summary in this novel. The transcript of Edmond Power's performance in court implies that he was more intelligent and better educated than portrayed here or in other biographical works and historical sources.

Madden, Richard Robert (R R): (1798-1886): in addition to *The Literary Life of the Countess of Blessington* (1855) Madden wrote numerous lengthy (and similarly unreadable) historical works. He was also a surgeon of some promise, a lawyer, diplomat, civil servant, traveller, journalist and slave trade abolitionist, who wrote prolifically in all these capacities with little recognition.

Mathews, Charles James: (1803-1878) – As stated Mathews abandoned architecture after leaving the Blessingtons in Italy and spent the rest of his career as a comedy actor-playwright, enjoying considerable success in the West End and on the Continent. Quotations from his correspondence and anecdotes etc. are from *The Life of Charles J Mathews: Chiefly Autobiographical with Selections from his Correspondence and Speeches*, edited by Charles Dickens (1879).

Mills, Frank: Madden implies that this wealthy scholar was the historian Charles Mills who died without issue on 9th October 1826 (Oxford DNB). Lady Blessington's Idler in Italy, however, records visits to Mr Mills' villa in 1827 and 1828 and refers to a Charles Mills/Mr C Mills. It has been suggested that her host was a member of the Glyn Mills banking dynasty but again no contemporary of similar name has been traced.

Molloy, Joseph Fitzgerald: (1858-1908) Prolific Irish novelist and historian; his *The Most Gorgeous Lady Blessington* (1896) is arguably the most succinct summary of the known facts related to the countess's life.

Normanby, Constantine Henry Phipps, Viscount 'Mantalini': (1797-1863) held a number of public offices, including succeeding Lord Russell for two years as Home Secretary. He ended his undistinguished career again as British minister to the Florentine Court.

Parr, Dr Samuel: (1747-1825): intellectual, schoolmaster, political writer and habitué of Lady Blessington's salons. Though Parr was much older than the countess, they evidently enjoyed great mutual respect.

Patmore, P G (Peter George): (1786-1855) Journalist and author who knew both Sir Thomas Lawrence and the Countess of Blessington well. His works include *Sir Thomas Lawrence's Cabinet of Gems* (1837).

Power, Edmond - children: (1767-1837) Nothing other than the names of Power's first two children (Edmond and Anne) is known except that they died in childhood, probably much younger than suggested here. Michael, Margaret, Ellen and Robert were evidently born in quick succession. Mary Anne (Marianne) however was about 10-12 years younger than Margaret.

Power, Mrs Ellen (Nell): (c1767- ?) The date of Lady Blessington's mother's death is obscure. Edmond Power's first wife had died before he married Mrs Hymes in 1818. Since no reference has been found to Nell living beyond 1814, this is taken as a convenient date of death.

Power, Margaret, Countess of Blessington – Name/s: From anecdotal evidence (re Margaret and Ellen in Clonmel) the future Countess of Blessington probably did not at first use her married name after separating from Captain Farmer. (Her aborted pregnancy is fictitious). She appears to have lived as Mrs Margaret Jenkins while with Thomas Jenkins but reverted to Mrs Farmer after leaving him. Madden claims she changed her first name to Marguerite on marriage to Lord Blessington in 1818, though in 1815 Robert Power had named his first daughter Marguerite after her aunt.

Power, (Captain) Robert: (c1792 - ?) Numerous, often contradictory snippets of historical information about Robert's life and military service have been found. It is known that at some time he was employed by Lord Blessington as an estate manager and later emigrated to Canada (c1836) leaving his two daughters to live with Lady Blessington until her death. There is no record of Robert Power's wife's name or her date of death. Willard Connely *(Count D'Orsay)* states that Robert Power had five children but this is not supported by any other source.

Sadleir, Michael Sadleir: (1888-1957) Historian, biographer and novelist is best remembered for *Fanny by Gaslight* (novel and film), and less so for his *The Strange Life of Lady Blessington* and *Blessington D'Orsay: A Masquerade* (both 1934).

Stewart, Colonel William MP: (1781-1850) employed Nash to rebuild Killymoon Castle, in its 585-acre estate, after the original house was destroyed by fire in 1802. His relationship with Ellen Power is well-documented. It is mooted that Stewart paid Hume Purves to marry her and acknowledge his children. Stewart's estate was left to an unmarried sister who in 1852 sold the castle, which remains a private family home. Stewart was probably also related to Lord Blessington, whose ancestor Murrough Boyle, first Viscount Blessington (1645-1718) married an Anne Stewart and acquired Mountjoy Forest with her fortune.

Westmacott, Charles Molloy: (1788 -1868) Journalist, author and satirist, editor of The Age: *'The principal blackmailing editor of his day'*, convicted and imprisoned several times, retired to Paris for the latter part of his life.

Worthington, Alexander: No other mention of Lord Blessington's executor (together with Luke Norman and D'Orsay) has been found but it is reasonable to suggest that he was a lawyer. Similarly, little else is known about **Luke Norman**, whose character here is entirely fictitious.

--

Beauregard, Chateau de: at La Celle St Cloud on the outskirts of Paris was bombed to destruction during World War II.

10 Henrietta St, Dublin: A later poem in praise of Henrietta St commences; *Before the gorgeous Blessington was seen / Or dandy D'Orsay graced the splendid scene….* There is no record of D'Orsay visiting Dublin or being there with Lady Blessington.

Manchester Square: The number of Lord Blessington's house is unknown and is probably demolished. Richard Hely-Hutchinson, First Lord Donoughmore's nearby London home was at 4 Bulstrode St, where he died in 1825.

10 St James's Square, London: Now Chatham House, was leased to the Earl and subsequently to the Countess of Blessington from c1820 to 1836. Other occupants include prime ministers William Pitt (Earl of Chatham), Lord Derby and William Gladstone.

Seamore Place, London: (later Curzon Place) should not be confused with Seymour Place, Marylebone. This Mayfair crescent, once adjacent to Park Lane, no longer exists. Its nine terraced mansions in a variety of architectural styles – notably No 1, home of Baron Alfred de Rothschild – had all been demolished by 1936 when Curzon St was extended to Park Lane. Lady Blessington lived and held salons at no 8 between 1830 and 1836, but it is unclear if this was the same house acquired by Lord Blessington c1812.

Windham Club: After vacating 10 St James's Square the club moved to no 13 (adjacent to the London Library) until 1945 when it amalgamated with the Marlborough Club and finally closed in 1953. It has no connection with Wyndham's Theatre, Charing Cross Rd, built by Charles Wyndham c1898.

Worthing: The Gardiner Family owned Warwick House, now a residential home.

Appendix B

Selected Sources

Clay, Edith, *Lady Blessington at Naples*, (1979)

Connely, Willard, *Count D'Orsay: The Dandy of Dandies*, (1952)

Foulkes, Nick, *Last of the Dandies: The Scandalous Life and Escapades of Count D'Orsay*, (2003)

Gardner, Brian, *The East India Company*, (1971)

Hawkins, Ann R ,"Formed with Curious Skill": Blessington's Negotiation of the "Poetess" in *Flowers of Loveliness'*, (*The Transatlantic Poetess*, no 29-30, Feb-May 2003).

Hawkins, Ann R 'Marketing Gender and Nationalism: Blessington's *Gems of Beauty/L'Écrin* and the Mid-century Book Trade' (*Women's Writing*, Volume 12, No 2, 2005).

Hurd, Douglas & Young, Edward, *Disraeli or The Two Lives*, (2013)

Leslie, Doris, *Notorious Lady: The Life and Times of the Countess of Blessington*, (1976)

Lovell, Ernest J, Jr, *Lady Blessington's Conversations of Lord Byron*, (1969)

Madden, Richard Robert, *The Literary Life of the Countess of Blessington*, (1855)

Mallet, Donald, *The Greatest Collector, Lord Hertford and the Founding of the Wallace Collection*, (1979)

Malloy, James Fitzgerald, *The Most Gorgeous Lady Blessington*, (1896)

Matoff, Susan, *Marguerite Countess of Blessington: The Turbulent Life of a Salonnière and Author*, (2016)

Morrison, Alfred, *The Blessington Papers* (1895)

Munby, A N L, *Sale Catalogues of Eminent Persons*, (1971)

O'Connell Bianconi, Mary & Watson, Sydney John, *Charles Bianconi: King of the Irish Roads* (1962)

Sadleir, Michael, *Bulwer: A Panorama – Edward and Rosina 1803-1836*, (1931)

Sadleir, Michael, *The Strange Life of Lady Blessington*, (1934)

Sadleir, Michael, *Blessington-D'Orsay: A Masquerade*, (1933)

Snyder, Charles W, *Liberty and Morality: A Political Biography of Edward Bulwer-Lytton*, (1995)

Teignmouth Shore, W, *D'Orsay or the Complete Dandy*, (1912)

Terhune, Albert Payson, *Superwomen*, (1916)

An Accurate and Faithful Report of a Trial of Bagwell held before The Rt Hon Lord Norbury and a Special Jury, at Clonmel in the County of Tipperary, Summer Assizes 1804 – wherein John Bagwell, Esq, was Plaintiff and Edmond Power, Esq, Defendant for a LIBEL. (Clonmel: Printed by Edmond Power)

Report of the Trial which took place at the Clonmel Assizes for the County of Tipperary, on the 4th August 1806, wherein Charles MacCarthy Esq was Plaintiff, and Solomon Watson, Banker, in Clonmel was Defendant. (Dublin, 1807)

Acknowledgements

No words are sufficient to thank my wife Diana for her unceasing help, encouragement and impatience throughout the overextended gestation of this book. While she is unquestionably the most beautiful and best-read woman in the land, I wish to make it clear that she has nothing else in common with the Countess of Blessington - or so she tells me.

Among the underlying themes in this novel is the invaluable importance of vocational teachers. I must therefore acknowledge, albeit too long overdue, having been the beneficiary of the very best of that rare breed: Mr Hinchcliffe (St John's Green School, Colchester) and Mrs Locke and Dr Sewell (Endsleigh School, Colchester) whose wisdom has been with me for six decades and inspired the characters of Miss Dwyer and Mrs Jenkins.

Jonathon Barnes of City Lit proved another inspiring teacher without whose help and encouragement this novel could not have been completed.

I would also like to thank Professor Peter Catterall (University of Westminster) for firing my interest in history over the last twelve years - and for giving me the opening line.

My editor, Leila Dewji, deserves similar acclaim for meticulously ploughing through my manuscript and spotting so many of my errors, typos and inaccuracies – and for giving me the closing line.

Though I have not had the pleasure of meeting her, I am honour bound not only to thank, but also apologise to Professor Ann R Hawkins of Texas Tech University for my (intentional) misinterpretation and exaggeration of her brilliant scholarly analysis of the commercial motivations behind Countess of Blessington's literary work.

I must also thank Susan Matoff for her encouragement, and yield to her superiority. She has completed an excellent authentic biography of *Marguerite, Countess of Blessington* whereas I failed miserably.

Finally, I wish to acknowledge of the invaluable assistance of the staff of The Bodleian Library, Oxford, The British (Newspaper) Library, The London Library, The Clonmel Public Library, The New York Public Library, Royal Academy of Arts Archives and Library and the National Portrait Gallery. I am especially grateful to the National Library of Ireland for providing very rare copies of the Bagwell v Power and MacCarthy v Watson trial transcripts.

Last and by no means least I must offer my sincerest thanks to the staff at the Wallace Collection, in particular to archivist Andrea Gilbert and picture librarian Grace Allwood, for their incredible patience and invaluable assistance.

MC

Printed in Great Britain
by Amazon